Praise for *Gate of Darkness, Circle of Light*

"Contemporary urban fantasy at its best."   —*Locus*

"An enlightened, compassionate view of the forgotten heroes of urban society."   —*Library Journal*

"A tale with sweep and scope, interesting characters, and some impressively nasty menaces."   —*Booklist*

"Huff's sense of fun as she plays with the traditional elements should please even the most jaded of readers."
          —Charles de Lint

Praise for *The Fire's Stone*

"The delightful camarderie of three unlikely heroes and well controlled fantasy elements make Huff's adventure great fun to read."   —*Publishers Weekly*

"Huff arranges the ordinary elements of fantasy into an extraordinary tale of adventure and transformation."
          —*Library Journal*

"An exciting adventure . . . they face pirates, storms, traitors . . . each has unique talents that can bring their mission to a successful conclusion, each has weakness that could destroy themselves and a city of people."   —*Voya*

Also by
TANYA HUFF

BLOOD PRICE
BLOOD TRAIL
BLOOD LINES
BLOOD PACT
BLOOD DEBT

****

SING THE FOUR QUARTERS
FIFTH QUARTER
NO QUARTER
THE QUARTERED SEA

****

SUMMON THE KEEPER
THE SECOND SUMMONING

****

WIZARD OF THE GROVE

****

OF DARKNESS, LIGHT AND FIRE

****

VALOR'S CHOICE
THE BETTER PART OF VALOR*

*coming soon from DAW Books

OF DARKNESS, LIGHT, AND FIRE

GATE OF DARKNESS, CIRCLE OF LIGHT

THE FIRE'S STONE

TANYA HUFF

DAW BOOKS, INC.
DONALD A. WOLLHEIM, FOUNDER
375 Hudson Street, New York, NY 10014
ELIZABETH R. WOLLHEIM
SHEILA E. GILBERT
PUBLISHERS
www.dawbooks.com

DAW TRADEMARK REGISTERED
U.S. PAT OFF AND FOREIGN COUNTRIES
—MARCA REGISTRADA.
HECHO EN USA

PRINTED IN THE U.S.A.

GATE OF DARKNESS, CIRCLE OF LIGHT

For Kate.
For the future.

THE FIRE'S STONE

For Uncle Albert, who knows what family means.

ACKNOWLEDGEMENTS

I'd like to thank Hania Wojtowicz, the Metropolitan
Toronto Police Department, the University of Toronto
Archives, and Dr. Douglas Richardson at University
College for their help and patience.

I'd also like to thank Mercedes Lackey for generously
allowing me to use both *The Bait* and *The Wind's
Four Quarters*.

Gate Of Darkness, Circle Of Light and *The Fire's Stone* are, respectively, the third and fourth books I wrote. Seventeen books later, they're still two of my favorites. Why? Well, to begin with they're both totally self-contained. You don't have to read books before or after either or them in order to get the entire story. (In spite of a loyal *Fire's Stone* readership that continues to plead for a sequel.) Secondly, these were the books where I actually started feeling like I knew what I was doing; that as well as being able to tell a story (which I never doubted) I could construct characters and build plot and bring both to a logical and stirring conclusion. Finally, they're both good stories.

Even though I wasn't entirely certain these two books belonged together—one is contemporary fantasy, the other a more traditional quest fantasy—I am glad that DAW believed in them enough to give them a second life, a second chance to reach the shelves of the world's bookstores.

I guess you can tell that I'm not one of those writers who can't bear to read her early work. I like my early work. I hope you do too.

—Tanya Huff
    July 2001

GATE OF DARKNESS, CIRCLE OF LIGHT

Chapter One

"Rebecca!"

Rebecca paused, one hand on the kitchen door.

"Did you put your tins away neatly?"

"Yes, Lena."

"Have you got your uniform to wash?"

Rebecca smiled but otherwise remained frozen in the motion of leaving. Her food services uniform was folded neatly in the bottom of her bright red tote bag. "Yes, Lena."

"Do you have your muffins for the weekend?"

"Yes, Lena." The muffins, carefully wrapped, were packed safely on top of her soiled uniform. She waited for the next line of the litany.

"Now, don't forget to eat while you're home."

Rebecca nodded so vigorously her brown curls danced. "I'll remember, Lena." One more.

"I'll see you Monday, puss."

"See you Monday, Lena." Freed by the speaking of the last words, Rebecca pushed open the door and bounded out and up the stairs.

Lena watched her go, then turned and went back into her office.

"And you go through this every Friday, Mrs. Pementel?"

"Every Friday," Lena agreed, settling down into her chair with a sigh. "For almost a year now."

Her visitor shook his head. "I'm surprised she's allowed to wander around unsupervised."

Lena snorted and dug around in her desk for her cigarettes. "Oh, she's safe enough. The Lord protects his own. Damn lighter." She shook it, slammed it against the desk, and was rewarded by a feeble flame. "I know what you're thinking," she said, as she sucked in smoke. "But she does her job better than some with a lot more on the ball. You're not going to save any of the taxpayers' money by getting rid of her."

The man from accounting frowned. "Actually, I was wondering how anyone could continue smoking given the evidence. Those things'll kill you, you know."

"Well that's my choice, isn't it? Come on," she rested her elbows on the desk and exhaled slowly through her nose, waving the glowing end of the cigarette at his closed briefcase. "Let's get on with it . . ."

"They cut emeralds from the heart of summer."

The grubby young man, who'd been approaching with the intention of begging a couple of bucks, hesitated.

"And sapphires drop out of the sky, just before it gets dark." Rebecca lifted her forehead from the pawnshop window and turned to smile at him. "I know the names of all the jewels," she said proudly. "And I make my own diamonds in the refrigerator at home."

Ducking his head away from her smile, the young man decided he had enough on his plate, he didn't need a crazy, too. He kept moving, both hands shoved deep in the torn pockets of his jean jacket.

Rebecca shrugged, and went back to studying the trays of rings. She loved pretty things and every afternoon on the way home from the government building where she worked, she lingered in front of the window displays.

Behind her, the bells of Saint James Cathedral began to call the hour.

"Time to go," she told her reflection in the glass and smiled when it nodded in agreement. As she walked north, Saint James handed her over to Saint Michael's. The bells, like the cathedrals, had frightened her when she'd first heard them, but now they were old friends. The bells, that is, not the cathedrals. Such huge imposing buildings, so solemn and so brooding, she felt couldn't be friends with anyone. Mostly, they made her sad.

Rebecca hurried along the east side of Church Street, carefully not seeing or hearing the crowds and the traffic. Mrs. Ruth had taught her that, how to go inside herself where it was quiet, so all the bits and pieces swirling around didn't make her into bits and pieces, too. She wished she could feel something besides side-walk through the rubber soles of her thongs.

At Dundas Street, while waiting for the light, a bit of black, fluttering along a windowsill on the third floor of the Sears building, caught her eye.

"No, careful wait!" she yelled, scrambling the sentence in her excitement.

Most of the other people at the intersection ignored her. A few looked up, following her gaze, but seeing only what appeared to be a piece of carbon paper blowing in the wind, they lost interest. One or two tapped their heads knowingly.

When the light changed, Rebecca bounded forward, ignoring the horn of a low-slung, red car that was running the end of the yellow light.

"Don't!"

Too late. The black bit dove off the window ledge, twisted once in the air, became a very small squirrel, and just managed to get its legs under it before it hit the ground. It remained still for only a second, then darted to the curb. A truck roared by. It flipped over and started back to the building, was almost stepped on and turned again to the curb, blind panic obvious in every motion. It tried to climb a hydro pole, but its claws could get no purchase on the smooth cement.

"Hey." Rebecca knelt and held out her hand.

The squirrel, cowering up against the base of the pole, sniffed the offered fingers.

"It's okay." She winced as the tiny animal swarmed up her bare arm, scrambled through her hair, and perched trembling on the top of her head. Gently she scooped it off. "Silly baby," she said, stroking one finger down its back. The trembling stopped, but she could still feel its heart beating against her palm. Continuing to soothe it, Rebecca stood and moved slowly back to the intersection. As the squirrel was too young to find its way home, she'd have to find a home for it, and the Ryerson Quad was the closest sanctuary.

The Quad was one of Rebecca's favorite places. Completely enclosed by Kerr Hall, it was quiet and green; a private little park in the midst of the city. Very few people outside the Ryerson student body knew it existed, which, Rebecca felt, was for the best. She knew where all the green growing places hid. This afternoon, with classes finished for the summer, the Quad was deserted.

She reached up and gently placed the squirrel on the lowest branch of a maple. It paused, one tiny front paw lifted, then it whisked out of sight.

"You're welcome," she told it, gave the maple a friendly pat, and continued home.

A huge chestnut tree dominated the small patch of ground between the sidewalk and Rebecca's building, towering over the three stories of red brick. Rebecca often wondered if the front apartments got any light at all but supposed the illusion of living in a tree would make up for it if they didn't. Stepping onto the path, she tipped back her head and peered into the leaves for a glimpse of the tree's one permanent inhabitant.

She spotted him at last, tucked up high on a sturdy branch, legs swinging and head bent over the work in his hands; which, as usual, she couldn't identify. All she could see of his face were his eyebrows which stuck out a full, bushy, red inch under the front edge of his bright red cap.

"Good evening, Orten."

"'Tain't evening yet, still afternoon. And my name ain't Orten, neither."

Rebecca sighed and crossed another name off her mental list. Rumplestiltskin had been the first name she'd tried, but the little man had merely laughed so hard he'd had to grab onto a branch.

"Well, hello, Becca." The large-blonde-lady-from-down-the-hall stepped through the front door, thighs rubbing in polyester pants.

Rebecca sighed. Nobody called her Becca, but she couldn't get the large-blonde-lady-from-down-the-hall to stop. "My name is Rebecca."

"That's right, dear, and you live here at 55 Carlton Street." Her voice was loud and she pronounced each word deliberately, a verbal pat on the head. "Who were you talking to?"

"Norman," Rebecca ventured, pointing up into the tree.

"Not likely," snorted the little man.

The large-blonde-lady-from-down-the-hall pursed fuchsia lips. "How sweet, you've named the birds. I don't know how you can tell them apart."

"I don't talk to birds," Rebecca protested. "Birds never listen." Neither did the large-blonde-lady-from-down-the-hall.

"I'm going out now, Becca, but if you need anything later don't you hesitate to come and get me. She brushed past the girl, beaming at this opportunity to show herself a good neighbor. *That Becca may not be right in the head,* she'd often told her sister, *but she's so much better mannered than most young people. Why, she never takes her eyes off me when I speak.*

For almost a year now, Rebecca had been trying to decide if the white slabs of teeth between heavily painted lips were real. She still couldn't make up her mind, the volume of the words kept distracting her.

"Maybe she thinks I can't hear?" she'd asked the little man once.

His answer had been typical.

"Maybe she doesn't think."

She fished her keys out of her pocket—her keys always went in the right front pocket of her jeans, so she always knew where they were—and put them in the lock. Then she thought of a new name and, leaving the keys dangling, went back to the tree.

"Percy?" she asked.

"You wish," came the response.

She shrugged philosophically and went inside.

Friday night she did-the-laundry and had beef-vegetable-soup-for-supper, just as she was supposed to according to the list Daru, her social worker, had drawn up. Saturday, she spent at Allen Gardens helping her friend George transplant ferns. That took all day because the ferns didn't want to be transplanted. Saturday night, Rebecca went to make tea and found she was out of milk. Milk was one of the things Daru called odds and ends groceries and she was allowed to buy it herself. Taking a dollar and a quarter out of the handleless space shuttle mug, she let herself out of the apartment and walked down Mutual Street to the corner store. She didn't stop to talk to the little man, nor to even look up into the tree. Daru had said over and over she had to be careful with money and she didn't want to hold on to it any longer than she had to.

Hurrying back, she wondered why the evening had grown so quiet and why the poorly lit street suddenly seemed so filled with shadows she didn't recognize.

"Mortimer?" she called when she reached the tree, knowing he would answer whether she guessed his name or not.

A drop of rain hit her cheek.

Warm rain.

She put up her hand and it came away red.

Another drop crinkled the paper bag around the milk.

Blood.

Rebecca recognized blood. She had bleeding once a month. And Daru had said that any other time but then blood meant something was wrong and she was to call her no matter when, but Daru wouldn't see the little man and he was the one bleeding, Rebecca knew it, but she didn't know what to do. Daru had said she must never climb trees in the city.

But her friend was bleeding and bleeding was wrong.

Rules, Mrs. Ruth had often said, exist to be broken.

Putting down the milk, she jumped for the bottom branch of the chestnut. Bark pulled off under her hands, but she tightened her grip—people were always surprised at how strong she was— and swung herself up, kicking off her thongs. Men in orange vests had tried to take that branch off earlier in the spring, but she'd talked to them until they forgot why they were there and they'd never come back. Rebecca didn't approve of cutting at trees with noisy machines.

She climbed higher, heading for the little man's favorite perch. The dusk and the shifting leaves made it hard to see, throwing unexpected patterns of shadow in her way. When her hand closed over a wet and sticky spot, she knew she was close. Then she saw a pair of dangling boots, the upturned toes no longer cocky as blood dripped off first one and then the other.

He had been wedged into the angle formed by two branches and the main trunk. His eyes were closed, his hat was askew, and a black knife protruded from his chest.

Carefully, Rebecca lifted him and cradled him against her. He murmured something in a language she didn't understand but otherwise lay completely motionless. He weighed next to nothing and she could carry him easily in one arm as she descended, his legs kicking limply against her hips, his head lolling in the crook of her neck.

When she reached the bottom branch, she sat, wrapped her other arm about her wounded friend, and pushed off. The landing knocked her to her knees. She whimpered, then got up and staggered for the safety of her apartment.

Once inside, she went straight to the bed alcove and laid the little man upon the double bed. Around the knife his small chest still rose and fell so she knew he lived, but she didn't know what she should do now. Should she call Daru? No. Daru wouldn't See so Daru couldn't help.

"She'll think I'm slipping again," Rebecca confided to the unconscious little man. "Like she did when I told her about you at first." She paced up and down, chewing the nails of her left hand. She needed someone who was clever, but who wouldn't refuse to See. Someone who would know what-to-do.

Roland.

He hadn't ever actually said he could See. He'd hardly ever said anything to her at all, but he spoke with his music and the music said he'd help. And he was clever. Roland would know what-to-do.

She sat down on the edge of the bed and pulled on her running shoes, then turned and patted the little man on the knee.

"Don't worry," she told him. "I'm going for help."

Grabbing up her sweater, she stepped out into the hallway and paused. Would he be safe in there all alone?

"Tom?"

The large gray tabby, moving with stately dignity down the hall, stopped and turned to face her.

"The little man from the tree has been hurt."

Tom licked at the spotless white of his ruff, waiting to be told something he didn't know.

"Can you stay with him? I'm going for help."

He considered it while inspecting one forepaw. Rebecca bounced as she waited, but she knew there was no use in trying to hurry a cat. Finally he stood and came forward to brush against her legs, his head bumping into the hollows of her knees.

"Thank you." She reached behind her and pushed open the door. Tom went in, snapping his tail out of the way as she closed it behind him.

Heading for the stairs, she broke into a run.

Roland scowled at the scattering of money in his open guitar case. It hadn't been a good evening. In fact, for a Saturday at Yonge and Queen, it had been pitiful. A breeze lifted one of the few bills and he grabbed for it. His uncle was pretty understanding about waiting for the rent on his basement room but point-blank refused to feed him. *A twenty-eight year old man,* his uncle often said, *should have a real job.*

A teen-age girl, almost wearing a pair of pale blue shorts, came up from the subway and Roland watched appreciatively as she passed by him and stood waiting for the light.

He'd had real jobs, off and on, but he always came back to music and music always brought him back to the street where he could play what he liked when he liked. Occasionally, he filled in when local groups needed a guitarist at the last minute. He was supposed to be filling in tonight, but this afternoon held gotten a call saying both the drummer and the keyboard player had picked up the same bug as the man he was to replace and the gig had been called off. He checked his watch. Eight forty-five. Both Simpsons and the Eaton Centre would be closing in fifteen minutes and business might pick up on the street.

Drifting up from the passage that ran under Queen Street, connecting Simpsons to both the Centre and the subway, came something Roland thought he recognized as a Beatles song. The Beatles probably wouldn't have recognized it, but in the six days this guy had been down there Roland had gotten used to his peculiar interpretations. The guys who sang in the subway made more money, but they had to pay a hundred bucks a year to the Toronto Transit Commission for a licensing fee and move from station to station according to a schedule that came down from the head office. Roland refused to even consider it; licensing busking was an obscenity as far as he was concerned.

He checked his watch again. Eight forty-seven. Time flies. He scanned the few people on the street and from slogans on T-shirts—*the right to arm bears?*—assumed they were American tourists. Probably from Buffalo or Rochester. Sometimes it seemed like half of upper New York State came into Toronto on the weekends. He sighed and flipped a mental coin. John Denver came up and he launched into "Rocky Mountain High." So much for artistic integrity.

By the second verse, the satisfyingly solid thunk of the new dollar coins hitting his case had put him in a better frame of mind and he was able to smile at Rebecca when he noticed her standing in front of him. The part of his mind not occupied with going home to a place he'd never been before wondered what she was doing out so late. He usually saw her in the early afternoon when she spent her lunch break sitting listening to him play and he never saw her on the weekends. He suspected she wasn't allowed out at this hour but didn't take it for granted; he'd learned not to take much about Rebecca for granted.

"I'm not retarded," she'd told him that first afternoon, prompted by his condescending voice and manner. "I'm mentally disadvantaged." Her pronunciation of the long words was slow, but perfect.

"Oh?" he'd said. "Who told you that?"

"Daru, my social worker. But I like what Mrs. Ruth says I am better."

"And what's that?"

"Simple."

"Uh, do you know what that means?"

"Yes. It means I have less pieces than most people."

"Oh." There wasn't much else he could think of to reply.

She'd grinned at him. *"And that means I'm solider than most people."*

And the funny thing, Roland mused, was that while undeniably retarded, in a number of ways Rebecca was solider than most people. She knew who and what she was. *Which puts her two up on me,* he added with a mental snort. And sometimes she'd say the damnedest things, right out of the blue, that made perfect sense. With some surprise, he realized he actually enjoyed talking to her and looked forward to spotting her smile amidst the harried lunch hour scowls.

As Roland moved into the last chorus, he saw she was bouncing, rising up on her toes and back, up on her toes and back, the way she did when she had something important to tell him. The last something important had been the hideous orange sweater she now had tied around her waist. (*"I bought it myself at Goodwill for only two dollars."*) He thought she'd been overcharged but she'd been so proud of her purchase he couldn't say anything. It looked worse than usual tonight against her purple tank top and her jeans.

He finished the song, smiled his thanks as a fortyish man in a loud Hawaiian shirt dropped a handful of loose change into the case, and turned to Rebecca.

"Hey, kiddo, what's up?"

Rebecca stopped bouncing and stepped toward him. "You have to help, Roland. I got him in my bed, but I don't know what to do now. Or how to make the bleeding stop."

"WHAT!"

She took a startled step back. There were too many built things around, too many cars, too many people; she could feel all the pieces pushing in at her. She could feel the outside nibbling at her edges but she knew she couldn't go to the quiet inside place if she wanted to save her friend. Moving forward she clutched at Roland's arm. "Help. Please," she pleaded.

Roland considered himself a good judge of emotions—a necessary skill for survival on the street—and Rebecca was definitely frightened. Awkwardly, he patted her hand. "Yeah, don't worry. I'll come. Just let me pack up."

Rebecca nodded, a jerky motion which Roland knew meant she wasn't far from panic for her movements were normally slow and deliberate. *Where the hell is her social worker?* he asked himself, scooping change into a small leather bag. *She's supposed to be riding to the rescue, not me.* He laid the guitar down, tucked the bag along the neck, and closed the lid. *And what the hell happened? Can't stop what bleeding? Oh, Jesus, just what I need; Simple Simon stabs a pieman, film at eleven.*

He straightened up, shrugged into his corduroy jacket—wearing it was easier than carrying it, even if it was still hotter than blazes out—picked up the guitar case, and held out his hand.

"Okay," he said in what he hoped was a reassuring tone, "let's go."

She grabbed the offered hand and pulled him forward, across Yonge and east along Queen.

The light was green; fortunately, because Rebecca didn't look and Roland didn't think he could stop her. He suspected that if he tried to pull his hand free she'd crush his fingers without even noticing it. He hadn't realized she was so strong.

Wait a minute! She got him in her bed?

"Rebecca, did a man attack you?"

"Not me." She continued to pull.

He had a feeling she didn't understand the question and with no idea whether she knew what rape meant, he didn't know how to rephrase it. Trouble was, while her mind might be no more than twelve at best, her body was that of a young woman; a well padded young woman, pretty in a comfortable sort of a way. Roland could remember being disappointed himself when he caught sight of the expression that went with the curves but he knew that wouldn't discourage a lot of men and would, in fact, encourage a few. *The world,* he sighed silently, *has a fuck of a lot of shitheads in it and a distressingly large number of them are men.* It wasn't that Rebecca was innocent, she had too much unconscious sensuality for the word to apply, it was more that she *had* an innocence—though, if pressed, Roland knew he couldn't define the difference. He twisted away from the subject. The whole concept made him sweat.

One thing Roland had come to know about Rebecca: she never told lies. Occasionally her version of the truth was a little skewed, but if she said that someone was bleeding in her bed, she truly believed someone was. *Of course,* he watched the curls bob on the back of her neck, *she also believes that a troll lives under the Bloor Viaduct.* He couldn't decide whether he should get upset or wait until he was sure that there was something to get upset about.

At Church Street, Rebecca began to calm down. She walked this route every day and the familiarity of it soothed her.

It's nine o'clock, Saint Michael's told her as they passed. *Nine, nine, nine. Hurry, hurry, hurry. Late, late, late.*

She let go of Roland's hand and ran a little ahead, unable to keep herself to his pace any longer.

Roland flexed his fingers, feeling circulation return. He couldn't help but smile as he watched her run forward, then back to make sure he still followed, then forward again. It reminded him of an old Lassie movie. He hoped he'd have nothing more complicated to deal with than little Timmy trapped in a flooding river. He hoped. But he doubted it.

When they reached her apartment building, Rebecca darted up the path and snatched up a brown paper bag leaning up against the foot of the tree. She looked inside, nodded in satisfaction, and held it out for Roland's inspection.

"My milk. I left it here earlier."

"It'll be warm, kiddo."

Touching the side of the cardboard carton, she shook her head. "No. It's still cool." Then she turned the bag and pointed at a reddish-brown stain. "See."

Roland leaned forward. It looked like . . . "Oh my god, that's blood!" Someone was bleeding in her bed . . . Jesus! And here he was, dashing to the rescue. He should've called a cop the moment she showed up.

Handing him the milk—he held it gingerly, hardly able to take his eyes off the stain—Rebecca unlocked the entrance and led the way upstairs.

"I left Tom with him," she explained, pausing in front of her apartment. She gave the door a push and it swung silently open.

Roland stared into a scene of utter chaos and felt his jaw drop.
One piece of curtain hung crazily askew, swinging in the breeze
from the open window. The other appeared to have been shredded
and flung about the room. A kitchen chair lay on its back, dripping
with water and garlanded with cut flowers, the broken vase on the
floor beside it. Plants and dirt were everywhere.

In the center of the mess, sat a large tabby cat, placidly groom-
ing the white tip of his tail. An ugly scratch showed red against
the pink of his nose and one ear had acquired a fresh notch.

"Tom!" Rebecca stepped over a pile of green fur Roland assumed had been a rug before puss and his playmate had gotten to
it. "Are you all right?"

Tom curled his tail around his toes and stared up at her with
gold, unblinking eyes; then he noticed Roland and hissed.

"It's okay," Rebecca explained. "I brought him to see. He'll
know what to do."

Tom looked Roland up and down, then twisted around to wash
the base of his spine, a gesture of obvious disbelief.

"Yeah? Well, same to you, buddy," Roland growled as they
headed past him into the bed alcove. He hated cats, the sanctimo-
nious little hairballs. "Okay, Rebecca, where's this . . ."

The question remained unfinished. Rebecca sat on the edge of
her bed holding the hand of a little man, no more than a foot high.
Although he wore trousers of green and an almost fluorescent yellow shirt, the color red dominated the scene. His hair, eyebrows,
and beard looked almost orange beneath the bright red cap which
matched the scarlet bubbles appearing between his lips with every
breath. But it was the crimson stain beneath the handle of the
black knife in his chest that drew the eye.

His eyes opened, focused on Rebecca, and the ghost of a smile
drifted over his face. His hand tightening on hers, he tried to
speak.

She leaned closer.

"Alex . . . ander," he gasped.

"Alexander? But I guessed that months ago!"

"I know." He fought for one last breath. "I lied." The ghost of
the smile returned and the little man died. Slowly, the body faded
away until only the black knife and the red stains remained.

Chapter Two

Without the little man's body wrapped about it, the black knife looked smaller but no less deadly. The triangular blade, no more than three inches long, tapered down to a wicked point and the edges were honed to razor sharpness. The grip had been wrapped in black leather that now glistened with blood.

"I don't believe it," Roland muttered. "This isn't happening."

Rebecca looked up from the knife, her head cocked to one side. "But you Saw," she pointed out.

"Yeah, I know I saw. But that doesn't mean anything. I've seen a lot of things I didn't believe in."

"Like what?"

"Well, like . . . like . . ." He threw his hands up in the air and backed out of the bed alcove. "Well, things. Get out of my way, cat!"

Tom moved free of Roland's legs, his expression clearly stating that even such as Roland should know cats had the right of way. Jumping up on the bed, he circled the knife, his bristling fur making him appear at least twice his normal size. He growled and slapped at Rebecca's hand as it reached into the perimeter of his pacing.

"I wasn't going to touch it," she protested.

He sat, tail wrapped around toes, just at the edge of the blood, and stared at the dagger.

Rebecca watched him for a moment, but he neither moved nor blinked so she went into the other room to see what Roland was doing.

Roland was cleaning up. Torn curtains, spilled plants, and scattered cushions, he could deal with. Murdered figments of Rebecca's imagination were giving him just a little more trouble. Had the dagger and the blood disappeared with the body he could've convinced himself, with very little effort, that nothing had happened. But it hadn't. And he couldn't. And he didn't know what, if anything, he should do about it.

He scooped dirt back into an empty margarine container, re-settled the geranium—one of two indoor plants he could recognize and he hoped Rebecca wasn't growing the other—and put the whole thing back on the wide shelf that ran under the window. Brushing them clean, he settled the sofa cushions where they belonged and reached for a large pad of poster paper that lay crumpled in a corner.

Crumpled. Like the little man had been against the pillows.

He'd *have* to think about it sometime. Later.

The poster paper had two holes punched into its narrower edge and was obviously meant to hang on the wall opposite the window. He heaved it onto the hooks—the two-foot by three-foot pad was heavy—and smoothed down the top sheet.

Friday, it said, and the date. Then, *supper: beef vegetable soup and crackers.* And, *Do laundry: cold water, one cup of detergent, warm dry with softener sheet.* The words had been printed in block letters and stirred vague memories in Roland of primary school activity lists. He peered at the next sheet down.

Saturday, it said, and the date. *Don't forget to eat. Wear shoes.*

"Rebecca," he asked as he read the instructions for Sunday and Monday—*Be in bed by ten. Take your clean uniforms to work.* "What is this?"

"My lists. Daru and I write them on Monday after we go and get groceries." She crawled out from under the tiny kitchen table, a plastic saltshaker clutched in one hand, "And I do what they say. They remember things for me so I can think of other stuff. Except I forgot to take Friday's list down. You can if you want to."

Do laundry. Don't forget to eat. Wear shoes.

Roland wasn't sure why the lists bothered him, but they did. They seemed so horribly binding; which was ridiculous for his mother had often left *much* more explicit lists for his father. "What would happen if you didn't follow them?"

"They said I'd go back to the group home." She pulled on her lower lip. "And I don't want to go back."

"Why?" he asked gently. "Were they mean to you?"

"No." Rebecca sighed, more in weariness it seemed to Roland than anything else and just for an instant she wore an expression he couldn't recognize. "They just never let me be alone." She set the saltshaker down on the table. "Now what do we do, Roland?"

"Well, we . . . uh . . ." He waved a vague hand around at the mess. "I, uh, guess we report this."

Rebecca looked worried. "Report what?"

"That someone broke into your apartment."

"Oh. That." She smiled indulgently and shook her head. "That was just someone trying to get to Alexander, 'cause they knew he wasn't dead yet. Tom took care of it."

"Rebecca, Tom is a cat."

"Yes." She waited for a moment and when Roland seemed to have nothing more to offer repeated, "Now what do we do, Roland?"

He took a deep breath and let it out slowly. He didn't have the faintest idea.

"Daru would believe me if you told her, too."

Briefly, Roland considered telling Daru that he'd seen nothing at all. If the woman had worked with Rebecca for any length of time, she'd know the girl told the most fantastic fables believing them to be the truth—although, given what had happened tonight, perhaps the world held too narrow a view of just what truth was. That aside, Daru would thank him for supporting Rebecca in her panic and his involvement in all this dangerous weirdness would end.

Then he looked into Rebecca's eyes and discovered that, amidst all the strange and magical things she believed in, she, also believed in him.

"Call Daru," he said, surrendering to the moment and surprised at how good it felt. "I'll back up anything you tell her." He couldn't remember if anyone had ever believed in him before.

Rebecca nodded, pulled an old phone out from under the sofa, and plugged it into the jack. "I don't like the noise when it rings," she explained to Roland's raised eyebrows. "I unplug it and it doesn't."

He could see a strip of white adhesive tape along the back of the receiver, the numbers printed on it visible from across the room. Daru's number, he assumed and Rebecca did seem to be dialing it. Hooking a chair with one foot, he pulled it under himself, sat, and reached for the clasps on his guitar case. He always thought better when he was playing. Without his willing it, his fingers slipped into "Red River Valley," the first recognizable piece of music he'd ever learned. *From this valley they say you are going* . . . He watched Rebecca on the phone and wondered why that was the only line he could remember.

Rebecca frowned, took a deep breath, and began speaking in a high, tight voice. "My name is Rebecca Partridge and it's Saturday night and his name was Alexander and he lied to me, but then he died. We still have the knife, but we don't know what to do, so please tell us." She paused, wet her lips, and added, "Thank you." Then she hung up.

"Answering machine?" Roland guessed.

"Un-huh." She unplugged the phone and shoved it back under the couch.

"What if Daru calls?"

"She won't be back all weekend. The machine said so. What do we do *now*, Roland?"

A very good question, Roland thought, picking out a minor scale. They couldn't exactly report the death to the police, not without a body. Come to think of it, reporting this death, even *with* a body might not be such a good idea. He marveled at how calmly he was taking this—"this" including having his entire world view overtuned—and decided a major case of hysteria was on the shelf until the time was right. "I guess we wait for Daru to call."

"But I want to do something now," Rebecca protested. "Alexander was my friend and someone killed him."

. . . and someone killed him . . .

Roland's brain made the final connection; the little man didn't just die, he'd been killed, murdered, offed, terminated with extreme prejudice. With an effort, Roland got a grip on his thought processes. "I guess we should find out who did it." But how?

As if she'd been following his line of reasoning, Rebecca stood and said, "We'll go see Mrs. Ruth. She'll know. She knows everything."

"Then why didn't you go to her first?" Roland asked, putting his guitar away.

" 'Cause she wouldn't have come back with me and Alexander wasn't dead then."

"Well," Roland stood and stretched the kinks out of his back, "if Mrs. Ruth knows everything, by all means, let us go to Mrs. Ruth. We'd better take the knife. It's our only clue." Even playing private investigator beat staying here with that accusatory stain on the bed. If Mrs. Ruth had answers, he was all for her. So far the night had been made up too entirely of questions. He checked his watch. It wasn't quite ten o'clock.

Rebecca got a flowered towel from her tiny bathroom and managed to wrap the knife without touching it. "Are you taking your guitar?" she asked, dropping the bundle into her red bag.

"Where I go, it goes. Can your cat go out?"

"He's not my cat," Rebecca told him, getting a bowl of red pistachio nuts out of the cupboard and putting it on the table. "He's his own cat."

Tom ignored them both and sat staring at the door. When it was opened, he squeezed out and padded away on business of his own.

"Good-bye to bad news," Roland muttered after him and stepped aside to let Rebecca lock up.

The walk to Bloor Street and Mrs. Ruth was an eye-opener for Roland in more ways than one. Rebecca led him through quiet residential neighborhoods that he'd never suspected existed so close to the noisy heart of the city. And Rebecca spoke to creatures he'd never suspected existed—period. The trees and shrubs along the way were home to more than squirrels and the red and golden eyes peering up through sewer grates did not belong to rats and cockroaches.

He ducked the clutching hands of something vaguely human perched on the lowest branch of a crab apple tree overhanging the sidewalk. "Where did all these things come from?" he wondered, staring at the creatures who were not moths fluttering around a streetlight.

"The littles? They've always been here."

"Oh, yeah? Then why haven't I ever seen them?"

Rebecca considered it for a moment. "Have you ever looked?" she asked.

"Looked?" He waved a hand at the shadows. "Why would I look for things I don't believe in."

"Then that's why you never saw them."

"But I see them now."

She smiled. "Now you're looking."

"No I'm not, I . . ." After the undeniable reality of the dead little man, how could he help but look? How could he help but believe? "I . . . What the hell is causing that?" He pointed to where a larger than average front lawn undulated up and down, up and down, like some sort of turf-covered waterbed.

Rebecca stopped and studied it, head to one side, squinting a little in the uncertain light. "I don't know," she said at last. "Should we find out?"

"No!" Grabbing her arm, he pulled her quickly along. "I don't think we should find out. I don't think we should have anything to do with it." He hung on until the disturbance was two blocks and a corner behind them, and then he let her go. She had a funny expression on her face and Roland hoped she wasn't angry.

"Penny for your thoughts?" he asked gently.

"Okay."

He waited.

"You offered me a penny," she pointed out.

"That's just a . . . oh, never mind." He pulled a handful of change out of his pants' pocket, separated a penny, and placed it in her hand. It seemed easier than explaining.

"I was just thinking that we haven't seen a little since that lawn moved."

Roland took her arm again. "Is that bad?"

"I don't know."

"Right." He picked up their pace. "How much farther to this Mrs. Ruth?"

"Not far. We're almost at Spadina. See?"

She pointed and Roland could, indeed, see the busy thoroughfare at the end of the quiet little street they traveled and he got the impression as they moved out into the light and the noise that they were stepping out into another world.

At least these dangers I understand. He herded Rebecca out to the road, then had to pull her from the path of a speeding truck.

"Rebecca? Oh, damn . . ." The girl's eyes were wide, whites showing all around the irises, and her head whipped back and forth so quickly he was afraid she'd dislocate it. A car, swerved to miss them and she froze, her hand closing about his arm.

"Jesus!" His arm felt like it had been caught in a vise. "Rebecca, let go!" He couldn't shake free of her. The Spadina bus went by and she wailed, a high-pitched keen that made the hair on the back of his neck stand up. "Rebecca! I won't let anything happen to you, but we've got to get across the street." He began to drag her forward; if he couldn't get her to let go, he might as well get some use out of that deadly grip.

Spadina would have to be four fucking lanes wide, he thought when they at last reached the opposite curb. His arm, below the tourniquet of her hand, was starting to go numb.

She didn't begin to calm until he got her a little way down the dark side street. Sagging against a tree, she released his arm and the wild look went out of her eyes.

"What do you do when you're alone?" he asked, watching the marks left by her fingers turn from white to red. If she went that crazy crossing a street, how could this Daru person let her wander about?

"I go down to the stop lights . . ."

Roland dimly remembered a set of lights a block south of where they'd crossed.

". . . and I cross on the green. I never try to race the yellow. Then I walk back to this street on the sidewalk." She stared at him gravely, still breathing a little quickly. "You're not supposed to cross without the green light."

Her panic, he realized suddenly, had been partially about the speeding cars and partially about breaking what she perceived as the rules. This bothered him the same way the lists back in the apartment had. Rebecca lived a very fettered life although, he had to admit, probably a safe one if she always crossed on the green. Safer than his own, anyway.

"Are you ready to go on?"

Rebecca nodded. "We're really close," she said as she straightened. "Just down here and then turn and go to Bloor."

"Can't we stay out where it's light?" Spadina would get them to Bloor just as easily.

Out on Spadina, two Jeeps and a BMW roared by and Rebecca winced, her expression speaking her preference very strongly.

"It's okay," Roland patted her shoulder, "we'll go your way."

Her smile made it worth the risk. He looked down the street to where the great bulks of chestnut trees seemed to soak up the streetlights. Almost.

The traffic sounds faded quickly as they walked and the silence grew. Roland began to get a very good idea of why the phrase, "It's too quiet," had become a cliché of old horror movies. Even the noise of his guitar case brushing against his jeans was curiously muted. The lit windows of the houses they passed seemed farther from the sidewalk than he knew they could possibly be. They saw no littles and, by now, Roland was definitely looking. He could feel sweat soaking into his T-shirt and it had nothing to do with the heat.

Rebecca pressed up against his side, her expression more wary than frightened.

"Don't worry, kiddo," he said in what he hoped was a reassuring tone, "it's only . . ."

And then the lawn they were passing attacked them.

Except it wasn't a lawn anymore. Roughly humanoid, it swatted Roland aside with one massive arm and lunged for Rebecca.

She stood her ground, the red bag holding the dagger clutched tightly under her elbow.

The thing touched her, jerked back, and crumbled formless to the ground; a harmless pile of man-shaped earth.

Roland scrubbed dirt out of his eyes and stood. He'd scraped an elbow raw hitting the pavement, but other than that and a bruise or two he wasn't hurt.

"What the hell was that?" he demanded, his voice rising in a nervous shriek.

"A nasty thought," Rebecca said seriously. She looked him over, nodded, knelt, and began to shovel handfuls of dirt off the sidewalk and back where it belonged.

"Say what?" He detected a distinct note of panic and forced himself to calm down. After all, no one had been hurt. By a lawn. Attacking. "I don't think I want any more to do with all this," he murmured, though he suspected it was far too late—that it had been too late when he'd let Rebecca drag him off.

"A nasty thought," Rebecca repeated, continuing to lift double handfuls of dirt off the concrete.

"Right." He checked his guitar case, thankful now that he'd spent the extra money on a good one. "What was it doing?"

Rebecca frowned. "I don't know. But Mrs. Ruth will."

"Then let's go see her, shall we?" His voice still sounded strained. He marveled that someone who couldn't cross a street without falling into little pieces could take something like this so completely in her stride.

"In a minute." She brushed the remaining soil into a pile and placed it carefully back on the ruin of the lawn. The little space for growing things left in the city needed to be taken care of. Frowning, she righted a small piece of sod. Only a very nasty thought would rip grass out of its home. "Maybe we should tell the person who lives here about this. So he can replant things."

"Uh, no."

"No?" She stood, wiping her hands on her jeans.

"No. He wouldn't believe us. He'd think we did it."

"But I'd never do something like that."

Even in the darkness, Roland could see how hurt she looked. "I know, kiddo." He patted her awkwardly on the shoulder. "How about we keep going? It's getting late and we don't want to catch Mrs. Ruth in bed."

"We won't." Rebecca sighed and began walking again. "He really wouldn't believe me?"

"No." Roland rubbed his chest where he suspected bruises were rising to join the mark of Rebecca's hand on his arm. Believing in something, he was forced to conclude, had nothing to do with its reality.

It turned out Rebecca had good reason to be so certain they wouldn't catch Mrs. Ruth in bed; she didn't have a bed. Mrs. Ruth lived under the lilacs at Trinity United Church.

What now? Roland wondered, as Rebecca beckoned him into a leafy tunnel. Then he shrugged and dropped to his knees, crawling past two heavily laden bundle buggies, sliding his guitar case along the grass. *Well, it isn't Delphi, but it is centrally located.*

One of the exterior church lights shone directly above the small triangular area between the lilacs and the building, making it the best lit place Roland had been in since they'd left Rebecca's apartment. That was about all it had going for it as it stank of urine and unwashed bodies. Roland breathed shallowly through his mouth, and got only as close as necessity dictated to Mrs. Ruth, who sat with her back against the limestone of the church.

A bag lady oracle. Why not? He hoped his expression remained noncommittal. *It's no weirder than anything else that's happened tonight. In fact, it's considerably less weird than being attacked by a lawn.*

Mrs. Ruth appeared to be in her late forties or early fifties although Roland knew she could be younger; life on the streets tended to strip youth away in record time. The stringy hair that escaped from under her red kerchief was about fifty/fifty brown and gray and her eyes were a washed out hazel between pink lids. Rolls of fat kept her face from wrinkles and she had almost no eyebrows. In spite of the heat, her round little body hid beneath layers and layers of grimy clothing.

"So? So?" Her accent hovered somewhere in Eastern Europe.

"What is it this time that you bother an old lady, bringing strangers to her home?"

"This isn't strangers, Mrs. Ruth," Rebecca told her earnestly. "This is Roland."

"Roland?" Her brow furrowed and she dropped the accent. "Oh, yeah, the Bard."

"Musician," Roland corrected.

"Look, bubba," her washed out old eyes focused on him and he had the strangest impression of being transparent, "you want my advice or not?"

"Well, yeah, I guess . . ."

"Then you can stop contradicting everything I say." She pointed a grimy finger at him. "I say you're a Bard, you're a Bard. I say you're a wienie, you're a wienie. And," she added, "I strongly suspect you're a wienie."

"Oh, no, Mrs. Ruth, he isn't. He Sees."

Mrs. Ruth sighed, her breath smelling of mint gum. "You're not listening again, Rebecca. I just said he was a Bard and *all* Bards have the Sight, so he must. Q.E.D., whatever that means. Now then, get to the point, why are you here? Not that I don't enjoy your company, but I have things to do."

Probably missing the midnight madness sale at the local dumpster, Roland speculated as Rebecca opened her bag and dumped the rolled towel out on the grass. Carefully she flipped back the ends, shaking her head sadly at the bloodstains on the cloth.

Mrs. Ruth sucked breath through yellow teeth. "Where did you find that?"

"In Alexander."

"Who is?"

"Was. He was the little man in the tree outside my apartment building. Someone killed him."

"And you think I know who did it?"

"Do you?" asked Roland.

"Sort of. It's a long story." She reached out, snapped off a dead branch, and poked at the dagger with it. "This weapon belongs to an Adept of the Dark Court." Her mouth twisted into something close to a smile. "Should I start at the beginning?"

"Please," Rebecca said. And Roland found himself nodding.

"Our world is a neutral area, a sort of buffer zone, between the Dark Court and the Light. Back in the bright beginning, creatures from both Courts wandered freely through it, fighting when they met. When life indigenous to the area developed, barriers were raised around it in order to give that life a chance to grow without interference." Mrs. Ruth snorted. "Both Dark and Light, by their nature, love to interfere. Only the gray folk, the creatures with no alliance to either court were permitted to pass back and forth through the barriers at will.

"Unfortunately, both the Dark and Light still want in, seeking to use our world to strengthen themselves. The Dark chips away at the barriers and slips nasty bits through . . ."

"A nasty thought attacked us," Rebecca interrupted, "on our way here."

Mrs. Ruth tapped the knife. "This attracts them. How did it attack?"

"It made a body out of dirt."

"Dirt?" She, snorted again. "Stupid."

"Wait a minute," Roland protested. "Do you mean to tell me we were actually attacked by *a nasty thought wrapped in dirt?*"

Mrs. Ruth shrugged. "You tell me. You were there."

"Well, it . . . I mean, I . . ."

"Look, bubba, let's just say you were attacked by a bit of unformed Darkness and leave it at that. Okay? Now," she looked pointedly at him, "if there are no further stupid questions, I'll go on. The Dark slithers in when and where it can, but the Light waits to be invited. Actually," her expression softened, "you'd be surprised by the number of people who ask for a little bit of Light to enter their lives. The balance stays pretty even. The Light gains strength by conversion, free choice being part of its nature. The Dark couldn't care less how it builds followers and finds terror the easiest tool.

"A dagger of this kind," Mrs. Ruth glared down at it, "can only be wielded by an Adept of the Dark Court. Obviously, an Adept of the Dark Court has come through."

"Can they do that?" Roland asked.

"Listen up, bubba," Mrs. Ruth advised, "I just said they did." She rubbed her chin, leaving a smear of dirt on the sweaty skin, and frowned. "Of course, it takes a lot of power and the Dark isn't known for doing things without a reason, so it's my guess that something big is coming down."

"Something big?"

"Something that'll let them recoup the power they lost and

then some. Something that the death of your little friend was just the barest beginning of. Or to put it bluntly, you've got a whole heap of shit to deal with."

"Deal with?" Roland groaned.

"Deal with . . . Ignore . . ." Mrs. Ruth shrugged. "Your choice. You can always let the world and every living soul on it plummet down into eternal Darkness. Let anger and fear and uncaring rule. Don't get involved."

Rebecca turned to him, eyes wide, and he saw again the little man bleeding out the last of his life on her bed. Saw the headlines in the newspapers he'd stopped reading because war and pain and hunger held no thrills for him. Sighed. "Why me?"

"Beats me, bubba. You wouldn't be my first choice."

"What do we do?" Rebecca wanted to know, leaning forward eagerly.

"You start by asking for help. This whole mess has knocked the balance of Dark and Light enough out of kilter that an equivalent Adept of the Light should be able to get through the barriers if invited."

An Adept of the Light? Roland repeated to himself. *Oh, wonderful, more weirdness.* "Why do we need help?"

A cracked, yellow nail tapped on the towel just beside the dagger's blade. "You know how to deal with this?

"No," he admitted.

"Then call someone who can."

"Call someone? Right. I suppose they're in the book?"

"Yes," Mrs. Ruth told him, "they're in The Book." The capital letters were very apparent in her voice. "But you'll never get your hands on a copy. Use the gray folk. Have them carry a message."

"But Alexander was the only little I actually spent time with," Rebecca protested. She paused. "Except the troll, but he never travels. And you know how long it takes before a little trusts you."

Mrs. Ruth sighed and patted Rebecca's knee. "No, I don't. I've never heard of a gray one trusting anyone but you. As you've no time now to make new friends, I suggest you send a message with the dead."

To Roland's surprise, Rebecca nodded thoughtfully and said, "I could do that."

He poked her shoulder. "With the dead?"

"Uh-huh." She smiled. "I know a ghost."

"Great." He began to back out of the bushes. "I guess that's it, then." Trouble was, he had no trouble at all believing Rebecca did, indeed, know a ghost.

"I wouldn't worry about ghosts, bubba," Mrs. Ruth chuckled, correctly interpreting the expression on his face. "If they're the worst you have to deal with before this is over, you're luckier than you deserve to be."

"Oh, that's really bloody encouraging," Roland muttered, not caring if the old lady heard.

Rebecca scooped up the dagger with the towel and stuffed it back in her bag. "We'd better keep this. We can give it to the Light when he comes."

"Couldn't we . . ." Roland began.

"A very good idea," Mrs. Ruth interrupted him sternly.

Rebecca beamed and began to follow Roland out. "Sometimes I have one."

Free of the bushes, Roland straightened and took a deep breath. Even the car fumes that lay over Bloor Street like a blanket were an improvement. He figured he'd carry Mrs. Ruth's distinctive perfume with him for the rest of the night.

"Hey, Bard!" Her red kerchief was a splash of contrast amidst the dark green leaves. "Two things!"

He turned.

"First, don't get cocky. You've barely finished your first fourteen years. You're still in training."

He waited and wondered if the second thing would make as little sense.

"Second, you got a buck for a cup of coffee?"

Chapter Three

Walking back the way they'd come, down dark, tree-lined residential streets which now seemed threatening rather than quiet, Roland considered the nature of good and evil. He'd never really thought much about the subject before but then he'd never had a night like this before. Somehow, the mythic tale of Light and Dark made sense coming from Mrs. Ruth. The bag lady—like Rebecca, he realized—was just too real to doubt. And about Light and Dark once roaming the world? Well, it made as much sense as any other creation myth. Mrs. Ruth hadn't said at what speed indigenous life developed, so that took care of Darwin and—Rebecca's bag bumped against his thigh and he could feel the weight of the black dagger—some pretty solid evidence seemed to be piling up on her side.

Spotting the dark on dark shadows of the destroyed lawn, he took hold of Rebecca's arm and tried to steer her out onto the empty road.

"But, Roland," she twisted free, "walking on the road is dangerous!"

"So is being attacked by landscaping," he pointed out.

"But the nasty thought has left." Rebecca turned slowly about, scanning the neighborhood. "I think."

"Let's not take any chances, okay?" She looked unconvinced, so he added, "Too much depends on us."

"Oh." She thought about it for a moment. "We could go back to the corner and cross?"

"Yeah, fine." They could go back to Bloor Street and take the subway for all he cared, he just had no intention of passing that lawn. "You lead, I'll follow."

And that, he added to himself, *about sums it up.* He didn't really need to believe any of this. He'd deal with it the way he'd dealt with almost everything else life had thrown at him over the years—by not dealing with it at all, letting it carry him willy-nilly where it would. He doubted he'd even get around to having the hysterics any normal person would feel entitled to. *Someday,* he thought as Rebecca turned them south, *I've got to develop a backbone.*

A wild and overgrown rosebush reached past the fence intended to confine it, hooked into the shoulder of Roland's T-shirt, and hung on. He tugged, it stuck.

"Wait a sec, Rebecca, I don't want to tear . . ." He turned his head and came face to face with a tiny little person, sexless as far as he could tell, clinging to his T-shirt with both miniature hands, its green-brown legs wrapped around the branch of the bush. It grinned maliciously at him as he tried to twitch free. The rose bush whipped back and forth, but the creature lost neither hold.

Rebecca peered up at it. "You let go right now," she commanded.

It stuck out a surprisingly pink tongue.

"This man is a Bard," she warned, "and if you don't let go, he'll write a song about what you do with bugs."

The creature looked indignant and let go. Its fingers, Roland saw, ended in claws almost as long again as the fingers themselves. One of those fingers snapped up in a rude gesture, then it scampered down the branch and out of sight.

"What does it do with bugs?" Roland asked as they walked on.

"I don't know." Rebecca shrugged, then stared at him very seriously. "You mustn't let the littles get away with things, 'cause the more things they get away with, the more things they do. Pretty soon you wouldn't have any quiet. None at all."

Roland had a sudden vision of his apartment crawling with tiny little men and women, each with tiny little brains, and tiny little opposable thumbs. *And I thought roaches were a problem. . . .*

They came out on Harbord Street, a block from Spadina, and headed for the lights.

"Rebecca, where are we going?"

"To see the ghost."

"No, I mean where in the city."

"Oh." She took a deep breath and pronounced each syllable carefully, her usual habit with words of more than two, "To the university."

The University of Toronto took up a large area in the center of the city, its old, ivy covered buildings an interesting contrast to its young, denim covered students. They'd cut across a corner of it on their way to see Mrs. Ruth. Now, they headed into its heart.

"I didn't know there was a ghost at the university."

"You didn't?"

The streetlight illuminated her expression of disbelief very clearly and Roland felt like he'd just admitted he didn't know in what direction the sun rose in the morning.

"But he's famous. He's been on television."

"The ghost was on television?"

She thought about that while they waited for the light to change. "No," she admitted. "But they told his story." She thought a moment longer. "But they didn't tell it very well. They got lots of stuff wrong. I don't think they talked to Ivan at all."

"Ivan? That's his name?"

"Uh-huh." The light changed and she took his hand. "Come on."

This crossing of Spadina differed drastically from their first. Rebecca walked quickly, but she stayed calm and Roland marveled at the difference.

"Rebecca?"

"Yes?" She kept her eyes on the walk sign they were approaching.

"What do you do if there aren't any lights. At all."

"Then I cross at the corner and I look both ways and I don't run 'cause then I could fall. 'Cept I wouldn't, but Daru says I might. Or I use a magic crossing."

"A magic crossing?"

"You know." They stepped up on the curb and she turned to smile at him. "With the big yellow lights and the lines on the road where you stick out your finger and the cars stop."

Crosswalks, Roland realized she meant, although magic crossings were as good a name for them. Personally, he was afraid every time he stuck his finger out he was going to lose it; that some jerk in a Firebird would roar by and take it off.

"Uh, Rebecca, this ghost of yours . . ."

"He's not my ghost. He's the university's ghost."

"Whatever . . . he's not, uh . . ." Roland searched for the word. A number of movie ghosts, with gaping wounds and grayish-yellow skulls visible beneath decaying flesh paraded across his mind. Finally he pulled the word from Rebecca's vocabulary. ". . . icky?"

Rebecca understood and shook her head. "Oh, no. He's a little misty sometimes, but he's not icky. It's a really sad story."

"If I'm going to meet him . . ." And Roland was not thrilled about that, he had problems with dead people that didn't stay decently dead in fiction. He didn't know how he was going to react in real life. ". . . perhaps you'd better tell me."

"I'll remember better if I sit down, 'cause then I won't have to think about walking, too."

They were on the campus now and Roland graciously waved her to the grass surrounding the university library. Between the streetlights and the floodlights on the building, shadows didn't stand a chance and the brittle brown lawn looked about as threatening as a bowl of shredded wheat. With most students home for the summer, the area was deserted.

Rebecca sat down, putting the bag with the knife on the ground beside her. She waited patiently until Roland got settled, and then she began.

"His name is Ivan Reznikoff and he's a stonemason. That means he makes buildings and stuff out of stone. Well, he doesn't anymore, but he used to." She paused, Roland nodded, and she went on. "He was born in Russia, but he's been in Canada so long that he's a Canadian now. He's been a ghost for over a hundred years."

"But how did he become a ghost?" Roland prompted.

"He died."

She isn't doing it on purpose, Roland reminded himself and he kept his voice calm as he asked, "How did he die?"

"His friend stabbed him and threw him down the stairs and his body fell into an air shaft and no one knew it was there and no one looked 'cause he was just some poor dumb Russian and no one cared."

Roland heard the stonemason's voice in the last few words.

"See, his friend made a gargoyle thing that looked like him and Ivan got mad and started to make one like his friend. Actually," she confided, "it doesn't look at all like him so I guess he had a reason to get mad. Anyway, he saw his friend, 'cept they weren't real friends now, with his girlfriend—her name was Susie and he talks about her a lot—and he ground his teeth and she said, *What's that sound?* and the friend said, *It's only the wind* just like in the story with Sister Anne."

She'd lost Roland at that point, but he nodded anyway.

"And then he attacked his friend with an ax. He says he was drinking or he wouldn't have done it and he's pretty sorry about it now. His friend ran inside and the ax hit the door—I can show you the door—and then they chased each other up to the top of the tower and Ivan got stabbed and pushed down the stairs and he died. And now he's a ghost."

"What happened to Ivan's ex-friend?" Roland asked, fascinated in spite of himself.

"Nothing. See, they didn't find the body for years and years, not until after the big fire. The tower wasn't finished and Ivan's friend . . ." She frowned. "I wish I could remember his name 'cause he wasn't Ivan's friend anymore. Anyway, this person put the body deep in an unfinished part, then I guess he finished it and no one found it, then they had this big fire and they found him. Maybe the person and Susie got married and lived happily ever after." Sweeping her fingers lightly over the grass, she added, "I don't think we should say that to Ivan."

"Uh, right. No point in hurting his feelings," Roland agreed. Putting aside for the moment the question, "Do ghosts have feelings and if so, can they be hurt?" he stared at Rebecca. There had been, for an instant, another Rebecca superimposed over the one he knew. It had looked, Roland thought, both more and less like the Rebecca he knew. Had looked like the Rebecca that should have been. . . .

"What are you staring at, Roland?"

He started and forced a nervous smile. "Nothing." For nothing remained but the memory. *A trick of the light,* he decided, although given the night he'd had he wouldn't be at all surprised to find he was seeing things. Things that weren't there as opposed to things that were there but he didn't believe in even though he could See them. *Life was a lot less complicated yesterday.*

"Can I keep going, Roland?"

"Yeah, please, keep going."

"Okay. Anyway, when they found Ivan they buried him in the square place, 'cept back then it wasn't square because the new part made it square and that's where we're going to find him now."

"At his grave?"

"Uh-huh."

"On the university campus?"

"Uh-huh."

"Rebecca, I don't think that's legal." The story had sounded pretty plausible until she'd gotten to the burial. Now Roland was beginning to think the whole thing existed only in Rebecca's head. "You can't just bury people in the closest bit of unoccupied dirt."

"He wasn't people by then. Just bones."

"Still . . . Who told you all this?"

"Ivan."

Roland sighed. Ivan was an authority hard to argue with. He got to his feet and held out a hand to Rebecca. "Let's go, then." His watch said it was twenty to eleven and a lifetime of horror books and movies told him he didn't want to meet this guy— giving the story the benefit of the doubt—at midnight.

Rebecca slung her bag over her shoulder and stood. Where the bag had rested, the grass appeared scorched. Rebecca looked down at it and shook her head sadly.

"Grass doesn't have a lot of protection," she sighed.

"Yeah, right. Are you sure you should be carrying that thing?" He shifted to put a little more space between himself and the bag.

"You mean the dagger?" She patted his arm comfortingly. "It's okay. I'm stronger than grass."

Roland allowed himself to be hustled along, glancing back only when they got to the corner and had to wait for a green light. The scorch was a clearly visible puddle of darkness against the dull yellow grass. He blinked and looked again. Beside it, arcing out in a gentle curve about six inches wide and four feet long, grew a swath of new green grass. In his memory's eye, Roland saw Rebecca absently stroking the lawn in front of her as she talked.

I'm stronger than grass.

Does she even know she did it? he wondered, staring down at the top of her head and remembering the other face that had briefly masked hers.

The light changed and they stepped off the curb. Roland, his eyes still on Rebecca, tripped over his guitar case.

Rebecca caught him, steadied him until he found his feet, and then propelled him across the intersection. "You have to be more careful crossing the street," she chastised.

Roland twisted around and took one last look at the two marks on the lawn. "Yeah, right," was all he could find to say.

They turned south, down behind a block of residences, onto

one of the many footpaths that crossed the campus. Every twenty feet or so, an old-fashioned lamppost stood in a circle of light and Roland got the impression that they hurried from one island of safety to another with the darkness between wrapping about them, trying to get to the dagger. He peered down at Rebecca, but she seemed unconcerned so he tried to take his cue from her. It didn't quite work.

"So Ivan hangs around the university, eh?

"Uh-huh. When people who don't See see him, the university is in danger."

"Does he ever haunt the place where he died?"

"No. He didn't die until he got to the bottom of the stairs, and it's in a cupboard in the principal's bathroom now. If he haunted that, no one would ever see him."

"How do you know all that?"

"Ivan told me, He watches them fix things up, do reni . . . reni . . ."

"Renovations?"

She beamed, becoming for a moment one more circle of light. "That's it. He likes to keep an eye on things."

They reached a small open area and Rebecca pointed down a fire access to a wrought iron gate set in the space between two buildings, one of new yellow brick, the other old and gray.

"We'll go in through there."

"Isn't that a private section?" In his experience, gates meant keep out.

"No, it's a green part," Rebecca explained, "and green parts belong to everyone."

Roland hoped campus security felt the same way. He didn't really feel up to explaining this evening to anyone else, particularly to someone in a uniform, trying to charge them with trespassing.

A closer inspection showed that half the gate was angled slightly open and they both squeezed through.

Ghost or no ghost, Roland decided, as they walked into the court, *this is spooky.* He clutched the handle of his guitar case tighter, taking reassurance from the sweaty plastic.

The court wasn't large, but trees broke the light from the buildings into patches of flickering shadow, now concealing, now revealing at the whim of the wind. With his back to the new addition, Roland had no trouble believing himself in the cloisters of a medieval monastery. Across the central bit of open grass—

which he would not cross for love or money; he couldn't imagine being more exposed—he could see the rear of what had to be a chapel, the stained glass windows cut into eerie patterns by the trees. The only sounds were the whisper of leaves and the soft pad of Rebecca's running shoes as she walked along the raised flagstone path to the northeast corner.

Shadow patterns, dark and light,
Keep the secrets of the night.
Silence shrouds the empty . . .

"Roland! Come on!"

Jerking himself out of the song lyrics, shoving them away where he could work on them later, Roland hurried to where Rebecca waited at the edge of the grass. Her voice sounded unnaturally loud, as if it had bounced back off the old stones. The skin along his spine crawled as he realized that even the leaves had ceased to rustle and the whole place had taken on an air of expectant listening.

"What now?" he asked in a nervous whisper.

"Now we talk to Ivan." She stepped down onto the grass and walked a little way out from the buildings.

"Uh, Rebecca, Ivan can't be buried where you're standing."

Rebecca looked down at her feet and then up at Roland. "Why not?"

He pointed. "Because you're right beside a sewer grate. If he was ever there, they'd have dug him up when they put it in."

"It's okay." She dismissed the sewer grate with a wave of one hand. "He's still here."

Roland sighed. Then he blinked. Then he felt his eyes widen and his jaw drop and his heart start thudding like a jackhammer.

Something drifted up from the ground about a foot from Rebecca. It looked like a wisp of smoke, or a weirdly contained patch of fog, but as it swirled and grew, Roland caught glimpses of deep-set eyes, tendrils that could be long curly hair, and a pair of large, workman's hands.

Suddenly, he knew what it meant to gibber in terror because he desperately wanted to do it, and he was barely able to wrestle down the urge to run screaming all the way home. The eyes were the worst; they didn't just exist, they stared.

The final form was a column of mist, vaguely man shaped, a

little over six feet high. It was so thin in places that Roland could see Rebecca through it. His heart began to slow to a more normal speed as he realized he had no really good reason to be frightened.

Rebecca put her hands on her hips and glowered. "How can I talk to you if you keep shifting around. You get solid, Ivan!"

"No. I don't want to." The voice, thickly accented, sounded as wispy as the form appeared and sulky at the same time.

"Why not?" She crossed her fingers and hoped he wasn't in one of his moods.

He was.

"Because. Go away. I don't want to talk to you. Nobody cares about me. Everyone ignores me." A deep sigh came from the center of the mist. "Go away," he repeated. "I want to rest in peace. Not that anyone cares."

He began to sink downward, back into the earth, but Rebecca lunged forward.

"Ivan, don't!"

He stopped sinking and twisted to avoid her grasp. "You don't care. No one cares."

This guy sounds more like the ghost of a little old lady than a Russian stonemason, Roland thought as the mist rose a little in the air and sped toward the west wall.

"Come on," Rebecca called and dashed off in pursuit.

Roland hesitated. He really didn't want to step away from the shelter of the buildings and cross that open area.

"Come *on!*" Rebecca called again.

He shrugged and started after her. It wasn't as bad as he'd feared, but he still had the impression of watching eyes. *I wonder what Ivan shares his last resting place with?* Shadows shifted by the chapel wall. *On second thought, I don't want to know.* He put on a burst of speed and caught up to Rebecca.

Together they pounded back up onto the flagstone path and down the arched passage that led through the west wall. The column of mist floated before them, almost disappearing as it passed under one of the old-fashioned lamps. It paused, streaked upward, and vanished behind the ivy that wrapped around the circular extension on the southwest corner of the building. The gargoyle that was peering out over the ivy came suddenly to life.

"Holy shit," Roland rocked to a halt, staring.

The first gargoyle settled back into stone and the second snarled down at him.

"Come on." Rebecca tugged on his arm. "I know where Ivan's going."

She headed around to the front of the building with Roland close behind, his running hampered by his total oblivion to where he put his feet. He couldn't take his eyes off the gargoyles animating one after the other, paralleling their course. He let Rebecca guide him around a small flower bed and up onto the lawn and he narrowly avoided slamming into her as she stopped.

Directly in front of them were two gargoyles, close together and tucked low in a corner. The one on the left slowly came to life.

"Okay, Ivan," Rebecca had reached the end of her patience, "stop playing games. We chased you so you know it's important. Now, listen."

"I'm listening," the gargoyle sighed.

The bits of broken carving that filled the gargoyle's mouth in combination with the Russian accent made its speech practically incomprehensible. Yet Rebecca seemed to understand.

"Mrs. Ruth says there's an Adept of the Dark here and we need you to take our . . ." She turned to Roland, looking for the word.

"Invitation?" Roland suggested.

"Yes, that's it. We need you to take our invitation to the Light so an Adept of the Light can come through and fight him."

"No."

"But Alexander died!"

"So." The gargoyle shrugged stone shoulders. "Death isn't so bad. You get used to it. Why should I travel far from my home, such as it is."

"But . . . you . . . oh!" Rebecca stamped her foot and the gargoyle smiled.

Roland noticed that some of the pieces of broken carving had once been teeth, teeth that had probably protruded a fair amount. "Look," he said, stepping forward and thereby surprising himself almost as much as Ivan, who hadn't appeared to notice him before, "you're supposed to appear when the university is in danger, right?"

"Right," the gargoyle agreed suspiciously.

"Well, if the Adept of the Dark gains the upper hand, the university, along with everything else, will be in a lot of danger. Shouldn't you do something about that?"

Ivan thought for a moment and Rebecca bestowed a smile of

such benediction on Roland that he suddenly, inexplicably, wished he could do more for her; climb mountains, fight dragons, drive away the Darkness with his own two hands . . . *Uh, never mind.* He stomped hard on the last thought.

"No," the gargoyle said at last, "I just appear. I don't do things." It pointed one skinny, deformed arm at the guitar case. "You got something to drink in that?"

"No. Just a guitar."

"A guitar?" The gargoyle sighed. "I haven't heard music in so long . . . Play me a song."

Roland opened his mouth to tell the ghost just what he could do with that request, then closed it again. If music indeed had charms . . . He laid the case on the lawn and took out his old Yamaha. When he'd bought her, more than a dozen years ago, she'd been the best he could afford, but still a long way from a top of the line guitar. Through seasons on the street, folk festivals small and large, and smoke-filled rooms beyond counting, she'd never let him down, her voice as sweet and clear as the day he'd bought her. When he talked to her, he called her Patience, although he never let anyone know he did either.

He slipped the strap over his head and sat on the lowest step of a small, stone flight of stairs. Beneath his butt, as he tuned, he could feel the dip worn in the rock by thousands of climbing feet.

Both Rebecca and the gargoyle that was Ivan waited expectantly.

"*Across the steppes the wind is blowing*
Bringing songs and scents of home
Can you feel it? Do you know it?
How far, how far, how far it blows.

The music he had for the old Russian folk song had actually been written for the bandura so Roland had to adapt it as he played, leaving him little leisure to observe his audience. Fortunately, melody and lyrics were simple and Roland soon lost himself in the song.

"*Now your travels have all ended*
Lay your head upon her breast,
Let the wind blow on without you.
It blows, it blows, but you may rest."

The last notes drifted away and Roland rode them out of the music.

Slowly, mist seeped out of the gargoyle and spun itself into a tall, broad featured man dressed all in black with long curly hair topped by a conical hat. Around his waist he wore a stonemason's apron. A single tear trickled down his cheek, catching the light of a nearby lamp.

He spread large hands, scarred with the marks of stone and tools. "I would embrace you if I could. You took me back to my mother Russia as I have not been in over a hundred years. Ask, and I will do your bidding."

"We need you to take our invitation to the Light. That's all."

Ivan nodded. "This I will do. You have wakened such feeling in my heart."

"Was that you playing?"

Rebecca gave a little shriek and Roland whipped around. An officer of the Campus Security Police stood at the edge of the lawn. Roland suddenly noticed how exposed they were, sitting on the front steps of the oldest building in the university with nothing between them and anyone passing on the sidewalk, the road, or crossing the grassy common. And he'd been playing old Russian ballads to a ghost.

"Is there some kind of problem, officer?"

"Hell, no." The security officer smiled broadly. "I was just doing my rounds and I heard you and I thought I'd come over and say how pretty it sounded. It's nice to hear a song that isn't all random noise."

"Uh, thanks."

"This time of night you're not going to be disturbing anyone, residences are at the back of the college—not that there's many in them at this time of the year. No, you guys can—" he broke off, squinted, and shook his head. "That's funny, I could've sworn I saw three of you as I came across here. Great big fellow with a funny hat . . . "

"That was Ivan," Rebecca told him seriously.

"Reznikoff? The ghost?" He chuckled. "Sure it was. Maybe you'd better be moving along after all if you're seeing ghosts."

Roland leaned over and set the guitar in its case. "We were just going anyway."

"I will not fail you, singer. Your message will go to the Light." Ivan tipped his hat to Rebecca and faded away.

The security officer was not so easily gotten rid of. He walked them around King's College Circle, proving to Roland that he knew the title and first four lines of every Beatles song ever written.

"I like the yeah, yeah, yeah one best," Rebecca put in as they passed Convocation Hall.

"Why?" Roland asked.

"Because I can remember almost all the words."

Over her head, the security officer tapped a finger against his temple. Roland shot him a vicious look in response which he missed, caught up in professional concern about a group of shadows crossing the common, the bright ends of lit cigarettes red punctuations amid the black.

"I gotta go; those kids could burn this whole place down; that grass is too dry to smoke on it. Specially if what they're smoking is grass if you know what I mean. Been nice talking to you." And he bounded away.

"Roland?"

"Yeah?"

"You did a really good thing with Ivan."

"Thanks, kiddo." It took him a little by surprise that her words meant so much. They walked in quiet companionship down to the corner.

At College Street, a well lit artery that would take them straight to Rebecca's apartment, Roland looked back the way they'd come; up the short straight bit of King's College Road, across the Circle and the dark common to where a chipped and crumbling gargoyle hung in the night. He'd just spent time talking to a stonemason who'd been dead for over a hundred years. He'd received mystical advice from a bag lady. He'd seen an imaginary little man die. It had been quite a night. Now they'd asked for help and their job was over. He hoped that all the wonder so suddenly visible in the world would not disappear with equal suddenness.

Headlights on the far side of the Circle caught his eye and despite the distance he could hear the roar of an engine. Sports car, he decided and, along with Rebecca, carefully looked both ways before they crossed the street.

The roar grew louder as the headlights raced around the Circle and sped straight for them.

Roland dove forward but Rebecca froze, pinned in the glare.

The world slowed as he turned and knew he couldn't reach her in time.

. . . and then she was thrown into his arms and they were both rolling on the pavement as the brilliant red fender brushed ever so lightly against the bottom of her shoe.

Tires squealing, the car turned onto College Street, fishtailed slightly and accelerated away. Something squat and faintly luminescent clinging to the rear bumper, flashed them a cheery salute and began to rip its way into the trunk, stuffing great handfuls of metal into its mouth.

Roland helped Rebecca to her feet and pulled her the rest of the way across the road. She didn't seem panicky, merely shaken. He supposed it was because this time she'd followed the rules and so wasn't at fault.

"Are you okay?" he asked, looking her over critically.

"Yes," she nodded. "Are you?"

"I think so." He popped open the guitar case to see how Patience had survived. "Yeah, I'm fine."

Rebecca pointed to a manhole cover lying slightly ajar in the middle of the street. "The little came up out of that and pushed me out of the way."

Roland noticed that the pointing finger was unmoving in the air. *His* hands were shaking like leaves in a high wind.

She turned to face him. "Did you notice, the car had no driver?"

He swallowed. "No. I didn't."

"Should we tell the police? Daru says bad drivers should be taken off the road."

Roland could just imagine explaining this to the police. "No. No, police. If it didn't have a driver, who could they take off the road?"

"Oh." She sighed. "Roland, let's go home."

"Good idea, kiddo."

They started walking east, just as the clocks in the city's towers started to ring midnight. When the bells quieted, Rebecca touched Roland gently on the arm.

"You have lines on your forehead. What are you thinking about?" she asked.

He laughed, but the sound had little humor in it. "That it isn't over until the fat lady sings."

Rebecca considered that for a moment.

"Roland?"

"Yeah, kiddo?

"Sometimes you don't make any sense."

Chapter Four

Roland stopped just inside the door to Rebecca's apartment and stared. The minor bit of tidying they'd done before going to consult Mrs. Ruth had left the apartment only marginally less chaotic than it had been when they'd first arrived. Now, it was spotless. All the dirt had been swept off the floor and the floor had been not only scrubbed but waxed and buffed to a warm glow. The plants stood in a neat and leafy row on their shelf in front of the window. The tattered shreds of the curtains had been . . . He leaned his guitar case against the wall, crossed the room, and peered more closely at the fabric. Tiny stitches joined each piece in nearly invisible seams.

"That's impossible," he murmured, more for form's sake than anything; if nothing else, this night had proven to him that impossible was a word that seldom applied. He turned, watched Rebecca scoop up the bowl of empty pistachio shells from the table, and followed her into the tiny kitchen. It gleamed.

"What happened here?" he asked, backing out again. The room was too small for two people and a conversation.

"The apartment got cleaned," Rebecca told him, dumping the shells in the garbage.

"Yeah, I noticed that." He took a deep breath. It even smelled clean. Not like cleansers or detergents, just clean. "But who or what did it?"

"I don't know." Her voice came muffled from behind the refrigerator door. "Does it matter?"

He looked round the spotless room, sighed, and shrugged. "I guess not," he admitted. The way things had been going tonight a magical maid service seemed comparatively normal. He gave himself a mental pat on the back for taking one more bit of strangeness in stride. And then he remembered the bloodstain on the bed.

The double doors that separated the bed alcove and the bathroom from the rest of the apartment were almost closed. The left, Roland noticed, had been dogged down. The right, he tentatively pulled open.

All he could be sure of in the spill of light from the living room was that Rebecca's double bed remained in place. He moved carefully down the narrow space between it and the wall, groping for the half remembered chain of an old-fashioned wall light. It took him a moment, running his hand up and down the wall in near darkness, but his fingers finally closed on the chain and he pulled.

The pale green blanket—the same pale green blanket he was sure—looked new. Nothing marked it to show that a little man named Alexander had died on it earlier in the evening and Roland was willing to bet the sheets below it were similarly unmarked.

Tom lifted his head from his paws and glared at the light.

"I thought you'd gone out," Roland muttered.

Tom yawned, pink tongue curling up delicately, clearly not giving a damn what Roland thought. He settled back into his hollow between the pillows with the air of a cat who plans to stay the night. Only by the quivering white tip to his tail did he give any indication that Roland still existed.

Quashing the urge to give the furry flag a tweak, Roland made a quick trip to the bathroom—immaculate as expected—and headed back out to the main room.

"If you want the light off," he said to the cat as he passed, "you get up and turn it off."

Rebecca was leaning halfway out the window.

"What are you doing?"

She straightened and tossed her curls back off her face. "Putting out a bowl of milk for the littles."

"What?"

Patiently, she repeated herself.

"Okay. Why?"

"Because they like it."

He took a deep breath. Why not? He was just going to have to get used to an absence of explanation in his life from now on.

"You're sure that the Adept of the Light will come here?" he asked.

"Yes. Even if Ivan doesn't say who sent him and give my

address—which I don't think he knows so he can't—we have the
dagger and that should attract him."

That made sense. In fact, upon reflection, it made a great deal
of sense and up until tonight Roland had thought sense and Rebecca were mutually exclusive. Either she was smarter than previous observation indicated or he wasn't handling things as well
as he thought.

Or a bit of both, fairness forced him to admit.

The bag, still zippered shut, lay in the middle of the floor,
Roland pushed it under the table with the toe of one desert boot.
No sense leaving it lying out in the open where it might attract
more than the Light. He shot a suspicious glance at the dirt in the
flowerpots.

Rebecca yawned and Roland suddenly felt exhausted.

"I'm going to bed now," she told him. "The Light can wake me
up when it gets here."

They both seemed to take it for granted that Roland was spending the night.

"Do you want to sleep with me?"

Roland closed his mouth, took a deep breath, and told himself
sternly to clean up his gutter mind. Her face was as innocent and
guileless as a child's, open and trusting, the faint sprinkling of
freckles across her nose and cheeks adding a wholesomeness that
was almost cliché. But her body . . . Her breasts were heavy, the
nipples denting through both bra and tank top, with more freckles
scattered lightly across their upper curves. Below a remarkably
tiny waist, her hips flared then tucked down into muscular thighs.
A little plump in this age of anorexia, but the flesh was firm and
the form most definitely woman. *When the kid says sleep, she
means sleep, you pervert. Nothing more.*

"No. Thanks. I'll sleep on the couch."

"Okay." Rebecca yawned again and headed for her bed. "Good
night, Roland."

"Good night, kiddo, pleasant dreams."

"I always have pleasant dreams."

Roland grinned. In that calm assurance, he found the Rebecca
he knew again and could banish the ripe form of the other from
his mind. He checked that the door was locked, lifted Patience
from her case, and flicked off the light. Settling down on the
couch, a huge old piece of furniture at least as long as his six feet,

he began to pick out a quiet melody. He hadn't needed light to play for years.

He heard the mattress creak as Rebecca got into bed and then he heard her murmur peevishly; "Move over, Tom, you're hogging all the space."

Good thing I didn't take her up on her offer. All I need to finish off the evening is a cat fight.

His hands continued making music without him and after a few moments he realized he was playing an old Irish Rovers' hit.

Oh, no, he chided himself, moving his fingers away from that, particular tune, *that's just a little too close.*

"It's dark down here tonight."

Police Constable Patton peered through the open window of the patrol car and frowned. "It's always dark down here," she pointed out acerbically. "Too god-damned many trees."

It was, in fact, easy to forget they were driving through the heart of a major city. Rosedale Valley Road followed the bottom of one of Toronto's many ravines and on either side huge trees crowded the pavement, looming out over this slash through their domain, intimidating the infrequent streetlights, and generally making Man aware in no uncertain terms that, down here at least, he was an intruder.

"Rally lights," PC Patton muttered. "That's what we need, rally lights."

"You worry too much."

"You don't worry enough." She turned from the window to face her partner. The litany was a familiar one, guaranteed to take place once a shift. Maybe she did worry too much, but surely that was better for a cop than never worrying at all. "Don't forget to slow down right before we get to the bridge."

PC Jack Brooks smiled, the expression hidden in his heavy moustache. "You figure they'll come back?"

The young woman shrugged. "Beats me. Who can tell with transients? All I know is it's too damn dry for them to be lighting any fires down here."

"Can't argue with that, Mary Margaret."

She rolled her eyes at her given names. The son of a bitch insisted on using them together, refusing to call her Marge like everyone else did. "And why can't you argue with it?" she asked. "You argue with everything else I sa . . . Holy shit!" She grabbed at the dashboard as Brooks swerved to avoid the glowing white shape that darted out from among the trees. But it was too close. And they'd been moving too fast.

There was a jar as the fender hit it, then a double bump as it went under front and back wheels.

Brooks fought the car to a stop, his curses accompanying the scream of rubber on asphalt. Both officers grabbed for hats and sticks and scrambled out onto the road. They could see what they'd hit about fifteen feet away, the night making it no more than a pale, crumpled shape against the pavement. They paused for an instant, knowing there was no way it could still be alive.

"Someone's big white dog?" Brooks offered.

"Maybe." She took a deep breath; dead people had always been easier for her to deal with than dead animals. "Come on."

Brooks reached it first, knelt down, and froze. Away from the car, his vision had adjusted quickly to the lack of light and he could clearly see what they'd hit. It couldn't have been more than three feet high at the shoulder, each slender leg ending in a tiny, cloven hoof. Its head was as delicate as a flower and from its brow grew a spiraled crystal horn. An onyx eye gazed up at him, bright with pain, and he realized that, it still lived, although as he watched the brightness began to dim.

"Jack, what is . . . Mary, Mother of God . . ."

This isn't possible. This can't be possible. She knelt as well and, while her right hand sketched the sign of the cross, her left reached out and gently stroked the long white hair. It flowed soft and warm under her trembling fingers, as real and as insubstantial as a summer breeze.

The unicorn sighed, one long drawn out breath that carried the scent of moonlit pastures, shuddered, and died.

The road was empty between them.

Tears running down his cheeks, Brooks reached out and touched the spot where it had lain. "I'm sorry," he whispered. "I'm so sorry."

"Jack!"

His head snapped up at the urgency, at the fear, in his partner's voice. She was on her feet, her nightstick angled across her body, the knuckles of both hands white. A rustling in the underbrush drew his gaze to the side of the road.

Black on black. And a fetid smell that made him choke.

Slowly, he rose from his knees, fighting against a fear that threatened to paralyze him. An ancient fear, of the dark and of the unknown things that dwell in it. *Run,* screamed a voice in his head, *RUN!* But training held, and carefully, they backed up to the car. Where they sat, hearts pounding, palms damp with sweat, although no threat had followed them.

"That thing . . ." The words cracked into a myriad of pieces so she tried again. "That thing," marginally better, "drove it out onto the road."

"Yeah." He didn't trust his voice for more.

They sat a while longer until the headlights of an oncoming car snapped them back into the real world.

In the harsh glare of the passing vehicle, which had slowed considerably upon spotting the patrol car, PC Patton shot an anxious glance at her partner. His face looked drawn and tired, but he seemed okay. She gave thanks to all the saints that she hadn't been driving.

"We didn't see anything," she said at last.

"No," he sighed, the sound a faint echo of the unicorn's dying breath, "we didn't."

He started the engine and they continued their patrol.

A single white hair blew off the car fender and was lost in the night.

Roland, always a light sleeper, came fully awake at the first knock. He shook his head to clear the last remnants of a dream— Mrs. Ruth dancing naked in the moonlight was a dream bordering on nightmare—and tried to swing his legs off the couch.

A warm and furry weight held them right where they were.

In the dim light, for no city apartment is ever completely dark, Roland could see the faint golden gleam of eyes. He kicked.

"Ouch! Damn it, cat . . ."

The second knock got lost in the brief scuffle that followed.

"Roland, what's wrong?"

He squinted against the sudden glare. Rebecca stood by the light switch, a fuzzy blue dressing gown belted around her, her hair an even more unruly mass of curls than usual. He pointed at Tom who sat washing one shoulder with sublime indifference.

"That cat bit me!"

"Why?"

"Well . . ." He had the grace to look sheepish. "I, I kicked him."

"Why?"

"Because he was sleeping on my feet."

The third knock diverted Rebecca's attention. "There's someone at the door," she said with a happy smile. "It must be the Light."

"Yeah, maybe." Roland's bare feet made no sound on the smooth wooden boards as he padded around the end of the couch. "But the odds are just as good it's the Dark."

Rebecca looked thoughtful. "I don't think the Dark would knock."

The fourth knock sounded a bit impatient.

"Okay, okay, we're coming." The chain lock clattered against the wall. "Stay behind me, kiddo."

"Why?"

"For protection."

"Against the Light?"

Roland sighed as he worked the deadbolt. "We don't know that it's the . . ."

A young man in his late teens or early twenties stood framed in the open door. His eyes were a stormy mix of blue and gray and Roland's gaze dropped before them, seeking stability in the speckled brown pattern of the hall carpet. When the world had stopped spinning and he thought he had his pulse under control again, he took a deep breath and began working his way back up, taking inventory as his vision climbed: black boots; tight and faded jeans; a red bandanna knotted just above one knee; three belts, thick with studs surrounding slim waist and hips; one arm circled halfway from wrist to elbow with a jangle of silver bracelets in all sizes; a blinding white T-shirt with the sleeves ripped out sporting a single, tiny button . . . a happy face, white on black.

Roland paused for a moment at the long, golden line of the throat, then snapped his eyes up before he chickened out. The point of the young man's chin just missed being delicate and his face missed being pretty by the same small margin. A large silver hoop pierced one ear and his heavy sweep of hair darkened gradually from white blond at the tips to golden blond at the roots. Roland didn't think it was dyed.

Then he smiled and Roland forgot everything he'd just seen in the sweet sensuality of the expression.

"Jesus Christ."

The smile quirked into an equally fascinating grin.

"Not quite." His voice caressed the words like verbal velvet. "Can I come in?"

"Uh, yeah." Forcing his gaze to one side, Roland stepped back. He felt dizzy. He felt other things as well, but he refused to acknowledge them, pushing them down with panicked force. *Forget that, I'm too old for a major lifestyle change. I don't care how pretty he is.* When he turned, the young man was bending over Rebecca's hand.

It should've looked ludicrous—a heavy metal wet dream genuflecting before a tousle-haired, vacant-eyed young woman in a fuzzy blue bathrobe—but it didn't. It looked right. It looked more right than anything that had happened to Roland since his mother had died four years ago. He could see the song in it, hear the music, feel the power.

"You have called, the Light has come. Lady, my name is Evantarin."

His silver bracelets chimed as he lifted her hand to his lips.

Rebecca looked momentarily puzzled until she figured out what he was doing, and then she grinned. "Hello Evantarin, my name is Rebecca."

"Perhaps," he said, and Roland added the twinkle in those stormy eyes to the music he heard, "but I will call you Lady, and you will call me Evan. Evantarin is for those who do not know me well."

"Okay." She nodded, satisfied with his explanation although it made no sense to Roland at all. In trying to work it out, he lost the threads of his song.

"No." The word came out almost as a moan. It had been the most perfect song. . . .

"Don't worry," Evan reached back and touched Roland's arm. "There will be many more songs before this is over. And you will find that one again, I promise."

Roland's eyes widened.

"What else could have caused you such pain?" Evan answered the unasked question. "You are a Bard; or will be." He spread his hands in a fluid gesture that spoke eloquently of understanding. "Such pain could only be the loss of a song." Then he started and the stormy eyes snapped down. "Small furred one, you surprised me."

Tom sniffed the offered fingers, then butted his head against Evan's hand, a deep rumble beginning in his throat.

"I'm going to make tea," Rebecca told them, including Tom in the declaration. "Everyone sit down."

I don't believe this, Roland thought a few moments later. *It's ten after three in the morning and I'm sitting drinking herbal tea with an Adept of the Light.* At the other end of the couch, the Adept yelped as Tom's kneading claws dug through his jeans. *I don't even like herbal tea.* Every time he looked at Evan he could hear the broken pieces of the music, but they came and went as they would; he could no longer hold them.

He cleared his throat and Rebecca looked expectantly up at him from where she sat cross-legged on the floor.

"The first thing we have to determine,"—*Good lord, I sound like Uncle Tony at his most pompous*—"is just who exactly you are." The expression on Rebecca's face stopped him for a second, but he took a deep breath and continued. These were words that had to he said, even if Rebecca thought he'd lost his mind. "I mean, we've been assuming you're from the Light and for all we know you could be a trick of the Dark."

"Oh, Roland." Rebecca frowned. "Can't you See?"

Roland opened his mouth to defend himself, but Evan broke in.

"He does not See as well as you, Lady, and the Dark can appear to be very fair. Our foe is strong, and will use any tool he can to achieve his ends." Rebecca nodded thoughtfully and Evan turned to meet Roland's eyes. "But if you do not See, surely you Hear."

And the song burst forth again, whole for an instant.

"Yeah, okay," Roland muttered, his tone brusque to distract the others from the tears in his eyes, "but I had to ask. I mean, you look like . . ." Words failed him.

Evan looked worried. He glanced down at himself then up at Roland. "Is it not suitable? As I crossed the barrier, I let the power form me as it would." He tossed his hair back off his face and frowned. "I like it, but maybe . . ."

"No, no!" Roland broke in, stifling the ridiculous urge to reach out and brush the frown away. "You look great."

"Do you really think so?" Evan ducked his head a little sheepishly. "It's foolish, I know, but I have always been vain. If my appearance . . ."

"Your appearance is fine, I really think so. In fact, I think . . ."

I think I'm in over my head. I mean he's . . . And I . . . Oh, shit.
Roland could tell by Evan's expression that the Adept knew ex-
actly what thoughts were chasing themselves around in his head.
He felt his face grow hot.

"Roland, all good people wish to become closer to the Light.
When the Light has physical form," Evan shrugged, a graceful
movement that involved his whole body, "that desire is physical,
as well." Then the grin returned and one silken eyebrow rose. "I
don't mind."

His tone hovered between acceptance and invitation.

Roland forced himself to hear it as the former.

Rebecca poked at the toe of Evan's boot. "I like the way you
look."

The grin softened. "And I like the way you look, Lady."

"Becca!" BANG. BANG. BANG.

Rebecca's fingers tightened around her mug. "It's the large-
blonde-lady-from-down-the-hall."

"Becca, I know you've got a man in there!" BANG. BANG.
BANG.

"Old news," Roland muttered, irrationally peeved that Evan
got this reaction and he didn't seem to count.

"I'm not going away until you open this door!"

"Does that mean she'll go away when I open it?" Rebecca
sounded completely confused. "Why does she want me to open
the door if she'll just go away?"

"Never mind, kiddo." Roland began preparing his best
scathing glare. "I'll get it."

"No." Evan lifted Tom, who had gone boneless in contentment, off his lap. "Let me."

"Be my guest." Roland waved a gracious hand but got to his
feet anyway. He wanted to be in a position to see the reaction
when Evan opened the door. He'd feel a lot better if he knew that
the Light Adept carbonated hormones as a matter of course.

"Becca! Don't make me call your social wo . . . Oh." The
large-blonde-lady-from-down-the-hall froze, one dimpled set of
knuckles raised. "Oh," she said again, and the hand came down to
stroke her peach muu-muu smooth over her hips.

"Is there a problem?" Evan asked.

"Becca," she wet her lips and appeared to be struggling for
breath, "has a man in her apartment."

"Yes." From her new expression, eyes half closed and cheeks

bright pink, Roland assumed Evan had smiled. "Is there a problem with that?"

"Oh, no."

She swayed and Roland hoped she wasn't going to faint, overcome with desire. He didn't think the three of them could lift her.

"There's no problem with . . ." Her sway moved her line of sight past Evan and onto Roland. "Two men. Two men! Oh. Oh. Oh . . ." Her mouth worked soundlessly for a moment before she could get the words out. "How dare you take advantage of that poor helpless child." She tried to push by Evan but he was a rock. "Becca! Becca, you come here."

"Why?" Rebecca asked calmly.

"They can't hurt you when I'm here. You come to me and we'll call the police!"

She glared up at Evan and Roland suddenly realized the emotion behind the new outburst. One man; Rebecca had obviously been misbehaving. Two men; they had to be forcing themselves on a helpless simpleton. After all, how could Rebecca have two men while she had none.

Evan sighed, "We haven't got time to unravel this."

Where Evan had stood rose a column of light wrapped about a figure of blinding beauty.

"Go back to your bed," said the figure.

The large-blonde-lady-from-down-the-hall pressed one hand to her mouth, the other to her chest.

"Things will be better in the morning." The figure raised a hand in benediction and petulant lines relaxed into an expression of peace.

She nodded, half smiled, and left.

Just for an instant, through eyes squinted almost shut, Roland thought he saw great white wings arching up to brush the ceiling. All his senses gave a sudden jump as he tried to understand; then Evan stepped back and closed the door. He glanced over at Rebecca, but she merely appeared satisfied the disturbance had ended. Great white wings. The heat Evan generated by his looks, by his presence, began to warm him in a different way—for which he gave thanks as desiring an attractive young man made him acutely uncomfortable. Desiring an angel could be considered a mystical experience, he supposed.

An angel . . . An Adept of the Light . . . It made a certain amount of sense and he marveled at how calmly he was taking it.

His sense of wonder must have shut down for a time, fearing overload.

"There now," Evan sat back down on the couch and picked up his mug, "where were we?"

"I said I liked the way you looked then you said you liked the way I looked," Rebecca told him. "Do you want more tea?"

"Yes, please."

She took the empty mug and padded over to the table where a teapot sat under a hand-crocheted cozy. "Do you want more tea, Roland?"

"Got coffee?"

"No, just tea."

Roland glanced at the inch of greenish-yellow liquid remaining in his mug. "No thanks." Carefully avoiding claws and teeth, he slid Tom back toward Evan and sat down. The cat shot him a scathing look, uncurled, and leaped off the couch. "I think the time has come for explanations."

"Yes," Evan accepted his tea with a nod of thanks, "you're right, it has."

"You can start with what you did to Mrs. Grundy."

"That's not her name," Rebecca pointed out, refilling her own mug and returning to her place on the floor.

"It's just a nickname," Roland explained. "It's what you call a nosy neighbor." Rebecca repeated the name silently to herself, filing it away for future reference. Roland turned to Evan who gave another of his whole body shrugs.

"I merely let more of the Light show through. Fortunately, she had enough goodness in her to respond."

"She'll probably be back in the morning, making trouble. You should've made her forget she ever saw us."

"I couldn't. Neither the Light nor Dark can do other than work with what is already present." Evan took a long swallow and continued. "When I told her things would be better in the morning, I gave her a chance to build her own explanations. She'll probably decide that the entire incident was a dream."

And she'll probably spend the rest of the night dreaming about you, Roland added to himself, With the image of great white wings at the front of his mind, he said, "Are we in the middle of a battle between heaven and hell?"

"Heaven, hell; good, evil; Light, Dark. Names mean very little."

"Is that a yes?"

Evan nodded. "Essentially."

"Oh, great, oh, that's just great." Roland buried his face in his hands, ignoring the little voice in the back of his head that kept crowing, *What a song! What a song!* Mrs. Ruth had told him pretty much the same thing, but it sounded more definite coming from Evan. *This is what comes from being a nice guy. Do a friend a favor and what do you get; front row seats at the Apocalypse.* He didn't hear Rebecca ask him if he was all right. He didn't hear anything but the roaring in his head as all the strange events of the night caught up with him and hit at once. Fear and confusion, but mostly fear, raced around and around and around, chasing a tail of panic. Under it all, he felt vaguely reassured that he was finally having the kind of reaction this stuff called for.

The soft tick tick of claws on vinyl yanked him out of the maelstrom and he whirled to snarl over the couch back; "Touch that case again, cat, and you're potholders."

Tom removed his paws from the guitar case with one last tick and stretched out on the floor looking bored.

"Roland," Evan's touch was warm and comforting on his bare arm, "you needn't be involved any further. I will understand if you choose to walk away."

And he would understand, Roland knew that, but Rebecca wouldn't and without him being aware of how it had happened, the girl's opinion had become important to him. She stared up at him now, sure of his answer. He couldn't betray her trust. He just couldn't.

"Hey, it's my world. I'll do what I can to protect it." Acceptance, commitment, and peace. He felt good. *Still scared shitless, but good.*

"What do we have to do, Evan?" Rebecca stirred her cooling tea with a forefinger, then popped the finger in her mouth.

"You know that an Adept of the Dark walks in your world, more powerful than any who have come through in many centuries but he is only a gatekeeper. On Midsummer Night . . ."

"Next Friday," Rebecca added.

Now how does she know that? Roland wondered. *I wouldn't know when Midsummer Night was if it bit me on the ass.*

"Next Friday," Evan agreed, acknowledging Rebecca with a small bow, "the barriers that keep this world from interference thin. The Dark One will open a gate on that night, allowing his kind to enter as they will. He must be stopped."

"Well, if we've got a week . . ." Roland began.

A raised hand and a jangle of silver cut him off.

"A week is no time to find a mortal man in a city this size, let alone one with the powers of Darkness at his command and already he begins to tip the balance, killing or driving out the Light and the Gray."

"He killed Alexander!" Rebecca snagged her bag and dumped it on Evan's lap.

His lip curling in disgust, Evan pulled out the rolled towel and carefully unwrapped the dagger. "Yes." He hissed the word out between clenched teeth. "He killed your friend, Lady, and others; there are many lives bound up in this evil tool."

"Don't touch it!" Rebecca cautioned.

Evan smiled, a strange, fierce expression. "I can't." He brought his hand to within an inch of the black metal, but not even Rebecca's two hands pressing on top of his could cause it to go closer. "Blood and lives guard this obscenity against my kind and it would take blood and lives to lift that guard." Flipping his hand over, he clasped Rebecca's for a moment. "Too great a price to gain control of a dagger."

Rebecca nodded, face serious, as she asked, "What should we do with it?"

"Keep it. Guard it. Do not touch it."

"I can do that."

His smile was a caress. "I know."

The look they exchanged made Roland very uncomfortable—he had no wish to discover why—so he cleared his throat and they both swiveled to face him. "Well, how do we go about finding this guy?"

"I don't know." Evan sighed. "I am not even certain where he will attempt to open his gate. If I knew . . ."

"You could meet him there and send him back where he came from!" Rebecca caroled bouncing a little.

"No, Lady, it will not be that easy. The Dark Adept and I are evenly matched for the balance must be kept."

"Why don't you open your own gate?" Roland asked. "Then the Dark and the Light'll still be evenly matched."

"And they will fight a terrible war across your world and your world will be laid waste regardless of the winner." He shook his head, his multishaded hair drifting about his shoulders. "No, our only chance is to find him and stop him ourselves. My only fear is that he will find us first . . ."

"Rebecca!"

Only Tom managed to regard the door with his usual élan.

Tap. Tap. Tap. "Rebecca, are you okay? Open up!" Tap. Tap. Bang. "I know you're awake, I heard talking."

"It's Daru!" Rebecca scrambled to her feet, and headed for the door.

Roland checked his watch. "It's four-thirty in the morning," he muttered.

Rebecca flung open the door and Daru strode into the room, her sari an exotic contrast to her expression; worry and exasperation about equally mixed. Roland felt his jaw drop for what seemed the hundredth time that evening and wondered how a woman could look so concerned and so intimidating at the same time.

"What is going on, Rebecca?" Daru took the younger woman by the shoulders and examined her quickly. "I just got back from a family party and found the damnedest message on my answering machine. Have you killed . . . Who is he?"

Daru's expression, Roland realized, was not one of adoring fascination, an expression he'd almost come to believe was Evan's due. She was curious only, and, he noticed, completely ignoring him.

Evan rose and bowed, a gesture that, considering his appearance, should've looked theatrical and false but didn't.

"I am Evantarin, Adept of the Light."

Daru inclined her head graciously. "And I am Daru Sastri, Metro Social Services." Something that was almost recognition surfaced for a moment in her eyes, then it faded; she sighed and turned back to Rebecca. "Rebecca, stop bouncing, close the door, and tell me what's happening."

With a visible effort, Rebecca brought her feet back to the ground, pushed the door closed and chained it.

"We're going to save the world from Darkness," she declared, beaming.

Daru sighed. "Honey, I've had a long day, so why don't you make me some tea and start at the beginning, okay?"

"Okay. The beginning is when Alexander got stabbed."

Rebecca headed for the kitchen and Daru glided over to the couch.

Which came first, Roland wondered, *the woman or the sari?* He'd never seen a sari worn where the woman didn't move with regal grace.

Evan waved Daru into the seat he'd just vacated and she sank down looking grateful.

"You're taking this very calmly," Roland said to her.

An ebony eyebrow rose.

"Oh." He flushed. "My name's Roland. Roland Chapman. I'm a friend of Rebecca's."

"Well, Roland," she slid her sandals off and tucked one small foot up underneath her, "I just spent over twenty-four hours with my very extended family. For the moment, I have lost my ability to be surprised by anything."

"That," Evan said thoughtfully, settling himself on the floor, "may make explanations easier."

Chapter Five

In the master bedroom of the Imperial Suite at the King George Hotel, the sleeper stirred. He savored for a moment the feel of the sheets brushing against his skin, the pressure of the mattress firm beneath his shoulder blades, the softness of the pillows, and the texture of the shadows upon his closed eyes. The full lips curved up into a smile of complete contentment and the eyes opened.

As clear and brilliant a blue as a summer's sky, they focused on the patterned ceiling, followed the pattern's loops and swirls to a wall, and slid down it. Light, made rosy by the curtains, spilled into the room.

The young man on the bed stretched, bringing to the action the single-minded determination of a particularly self-satisfied cat, then swung bare feet to the plushly carpeted floor and padded naked to the window. Throwing aside the masking fabric, he gazed out at the heart of the city.

"Another beautiful day," he murmured, brushing thick black hair off his face. "Sunny and hot." He pronounced the word "hot" almost like a command.

Resting on the skyline of the city, the sun blazed and, although the day had barely begun, the air wavered with heat distortion.

He placed his hand against the glass, long fingers spread, and a wheeling pigeon plummeted down seven stories to the pavement. It narrowly missed an elderly couple out for a stroll, crashing practically at their feet and spraying them both with feathers and blood.

The shrill shriek of the old woman brought back his contented smile.

In the shower, he gloried in the sensation of the water, changing the shower-head from needle to massage and back again. He towel-dried briskly, rubbing the creamy ivory of his skin to a warm pink glow, then stood for a time posing before the full-length mirror, admiring the smooth ripple of muscles. His body, he knew, was a work of art, each piece in perfect proportion to the rest, just as he had designed it.

But such a body needed something to sustain it.

With the receiver tucked beneath his chin, he dressed as he ordered breakfast.

". . . and the coffee is not to be made until seconds before the pot leaves the kitchen." He pulled a light blue Oxford cloth shirt out of the closet and shrugged into it, tucking it down into his jeans and buttoning the fly. "Yes that's correct, Mr. Aphotic." Hanging up, he grinned in appreciation of his own cleverness. Aphotic meant dark, and Dark was all the designation he had, for the Darkness kept its bits and pieces too close to allow them the individuality of names. Reaching for a pair of deck shoes, he checked the loafers he'd worn the night before.

The blood had not, as it turned out, stained the leather. A bit of a surprise really, as there'd been rather a lot of it. In a city of this size it hadn't taken him long to find a young woman who would allow him to "cut" her for a ridiculous sum and once her permission had been given and the money had changed hands not all the screamed, moaned, or whispered "no's" could invalidate the contract. And as he'd worked with her agreement, the balance of Light and Dark had not been unduly disturbed. And as the balance had not been disturbed, he had attracted no attention that might make his purpose here more difficult to carry out. Freed from the constraints of ritual, for last night had been solely for his own enjoyment, he'd allowed his imagination full reign and had taken his time.

Breakfast, when it arrived a few moments later, was superb. He rolled the flavors of eggs, and sausages, and mushrooms fried with garlic and ginger around on his tongue and washed them down with juice so fresh it had still been in the orange when it left the kitchen.

"Master!"

A shadow, six inches high and occasionally humanoid, swarmed up the walnut legs of the table and paused by the coffee-pot.

"Master! An Adept of the Light has passed the barriers!

"Yes, I know." He sucked at his fingertips, getting the last of the butter and croissant crumbs. "Did you think I wouldn't notice such a shift in the balance?"

"No, Master, but . . ." It rose up and created arms in order to wave them about.

"But?" His tone made the word a threat.

"But I function to give you information, Master. I am your eyes and ears."

"Then see, hear, do something useful, and find out how this Adept came through." He poured himself coffee, added liberal helpings of cream and sugar, and drank half of it before he spoke again. The shadow wavered and fidgeted. He put down his cup with a satisfied sigh, then his expression hardened. "Tonight, find out who provided passage for this Adept, how much they know, and whether they can be used in the ritual."

"Yes, Master, but . . ."

"Again but?"

The shadow writhed and keened, a high-pitched, drawn out sound like nails on a blackboard. "No, Master. No but."

He sighed and stretched as it fled. These smaller pieces of Darkness were almost useless and he wondered if breaking it off had been worth it. His glance fell on the morning paper and the headline caught his eye. *Jays and Tigers Neck and Neck as All-Star Break Approaches.*

"A ballgame," he mused, scanning the article. "Just what I need, a sunny Sunday afternoon at the ballpark. Crowds of people, the competitive spirit . . ." Just for a moment, he wished he could postpone the opening of the gate for a few days; next weekend the Yankees would be in town. "Ah, well," he tossed the paper onto the floor, "you can't have everything."

He shoved his room key into the pocket that held his wallet and headed for the door. Throwing it open, he almost collided with a chambermaid carrying a load of towels.

"Houseke . . ." She lowered the hand raised to knock and stared at him, her eyes wide with need. She was very young and very pretty and he'd taken her brutally the first two mornings he'd stayed in the suite, twisting her responses until pain and pleasure became indistinguishable.

This morning, he merely looked at her with disgust and pushed past.

He could hear her tears and feel the heat of her shame on his back. His step became jaunty. It was going to be a great day.

*   *   *

"What've you got, Steve?" PC Patton got out of the squad car and slammed the door. Behind her, she could hear Jack doing the same. They'd been off duty, heading back to the station, when the call had come in and as it was on the way they'd pulled into the supermarket parking lot to see if they could help. She noticed that Police Constable Steve Stirling, a veteran who in his years on the force had acquired a reputation for being completely unshakable, looked decidedly pale. His partner, a rookie policewoman mere weeks out of the academy, had obviously thrown up and was just as obviously considering doing it again.

"It's in the dumpster," Steve said shortly, glaring at the gathering crowd.

Frowning, she swung herself up on the dumpster's side and took a deep breath before peering in; the stink alone could've caused Steve's partner to puke. Spread out on top of the usual, rotting, grocery store garbage was what looked like the entire contents of the meat department, chops, sideribs, roasts, all covered in a moving carpet of flies. And then she noticed that one of the roasts had a face.

Teeth clenched, she dropped back down to the pavement and thanked God and all the saints it had been hours since she'd eaten. As Jack stepped by her, she grabbed his arm.

"Don't." It wasn't their call. He didn't have to look.

He looked at her instead, reading the horror of what she'd seen in her eyes, nodded, and moved away.

"What a fun start to the day." Steve had come to stand beside her and together they watched another three cars arrive, one carrying the police photographer. "You could be sitting down at the station with a cup of coffee about now. Don't you wish you'd kept going?"

"Yes." She didn't have to add anything else; "yes" said it all.

"All right, let me see if I've got this straight." Daru rubbed her eyes and accepted a fresh cup of tea with a nod of thanks. "This coming Friday, Midsummer Night, an Adept of the Dark is going to open a gateway between this world and the Darkness. You," she inclined her head toward Evan, "have been brought from the Light to stop him. You two," she nodded at Roland and Rebecca, "are going to help."

"That's it in a nutshell," Roland agreed.

"Fine. Count me in."

"What?"

She swallowed her mouthful of tea, sighed, and said slowly and distinctly, "I'm going to help, too."

"You mean you believe us?" Roland stared at her in astonishment. The tale had taken the rest of the night in the telling and now, in the bright light of Sunday morning, he wasn't sure he believed it himself.

"I believe the evidence of my eyes," Daru said testily, the sweep of her hand covering both the black dagger and Evan. "Haven't you ever read Sherlock Holmes?"

"Huh?" The lack of sleep, combined with the roller coaster ride he went on every time Evan looked at him—*Just keep telling yourself it's a religious experience.*—had put Roland on less than firm mental footing.

"When you have eliminated the impossible, that which remains, however improbable, must be the answer. If Evan exists, and he does . . ." Evan flashed a smile at her over his shoulder, then went back to enjoying the different textures of light as it poured through the curtains. ". . . and if I believe what he is, and I do . . ." A moment staring into the Adept's eyes had been almost enough without the more blatant show of glory. ". . . then the rest of it must be true as well. And if our world is about to be overcome by Darkness," her mouth thinned into a hard line, "then I don't intend to sit by and let it happen."

No, Roland thought, *I bet you never have.* As a caseworker at Metro Social Services, Daru fought in the front line against Darkness every day.

"Rebecca, honey," Daru swiveled around and tried to see into the kitchen, "what are you doing?"

Rebecca popped her head back out into the living room. "Making breakfast." With full light she'd pulled on an old pair of turquoise track pants and a yellow sweatshirt with the sleeves ripped out. "There's scrambled eggs made with milk, 'cause I got some last night, and sausages done under the broiler. I unfroze the whole package instead of just three for me. I'm making toast, too."

"All that at once?" Daru sounded doubtful.

"The stove does most of the work," Rebecca explained seriously. "And the toaster."

"Do you have any jam?" Roland asked, wandering over and sticking his head in the fridge.

"The jam is behind the catsup. It's peach." She leaned farther out of the kitchen and handed him a small can and the can opener. "You can feed Tom."

He juggled the can on his palm, sighed, and glared at the cat.

Tom, who knew very well what a can of that size and a can opener meant, leaped off the couch and wove a pattern around Roland's feet; a dignified pattern, of course, expressing anticipation and only the smallest amount of hunger.

"Oh, all right." Roland moved forward and set the cat food down on the table, Tom modifying his dance to accommodate the steps. "But I want to make it perfectly clear," he called to the kitchen, "I'm doing this for you, not for him."

"Tom doesn't care, as long as you open the can."

Cramming the blade of the can opener down, Roland glared at Daru. "Why do you let her waste her money on this stuff?"

Daru raised an eyebrow. "You prefer another brand?" she asked, pitching her voice just to one side of sarcasm.

"Skip it." He wrestled the top off, his nose wrinkling at the smell, then he placed the open can on the floor. Tom sniffed it, gave it cautious approval, and began to eat, Daru flashed him what Roland interpreted as a superior smile and headed for the bathroom. Feeling outnumbered, Roland reached for his guitar and soothed his spirit by putting music to the pattern of sunlight and leaf shadow that played across Evan where he stood in the window.

"So much pain," the Adept murmured, watching an ant traveling the length of the window ledge, a smaller insect held in its jaws. He filled his lungs, tasting the concrete and steel and asphalt, tasting the sorrow and hatred and pain, and sighed. The Dark had so much to work with. But the sunlight warmed him and breezes brought the sound of children's laughter and he had neither the ability nor the desire to deny hope.

Roland saw Evan's shoulders sag and added a minor scale, then he saw them lift again and picked up both tempo and tone. He felt an audience and with a skill honed by years on the street, where a direct glance could scare away a paying customer, he slid a peek out of the corner of one eye.

Daru stood beside the couch, her gaze flicking from him to Evan and back.

Under the weight of her regard, he stopped playing and turned to face her.

"I could see your music," she said, wonder in her voice. "Like a mirror made of sound . . . I could see . . ."

Roland felt his face go hot and he dropped his eyes, fumbling with his pick.

"Breakfast." Rebecca poked a filled plate out of the kitchen and Roland scrambled to get it, the action covering his embarrassment. He could only handle praise when it came as cash. Praise from Rebecca, for reasons he'd never quite been able to fathom, was the only exception.

Watching Evan eat kept distracting Daru and Roland from their own food, for he took delight in not only the taste but the textures and the smells, making scrambled eggs and sausages a sensual experience.

"Don't they have food where you come from?" Rebecca asked as Evan drew his fingers down a piece of toast, examined the gleam of margarine, then licked his finger tips.

"Of course," he bit off the end of a sausage and his eyes widened with pleasure as he separated all the many tastes it contained, "but, this is new. And every facet of newness should be discovered and enjoyed."

Rebecca nodded. "That's what I think, too."

Daru hid a smile, remembering the first time she'd taken Rebecca out for pizza and the girl had poked her fingers into the melted cheese, then spent close to five minutes experimenting with the stretch factor of mozzarella.

Her face softens when she smiles, Roland thought, having placed himself where he could see Daru as well as Evan. *Makes her look less like a hawk.* After years of protesting that it didn't mean anything, Roland had decided, looking at Daru, he knew exactly what striking meant when used as a physical description. Not pretty, not beautiful, but, well, striking—dark gold skin, eyes so black the pupils and irises were one, a high forehead, a proud arch of a nose, a pointed yet still determined chin, and the whole thing surrounded by a thick fall of ebony hair. Not exactly cold, but stern. He made plans to pick up his flute if he ever got home, for her song flew too high for his guitar.

"You got something to say to me?" Daru snapped, suddenly aware of his regard.

And bitchy, Roland added to his mental list, dropping his gaze.

Stern and bitchy. Behind the pale curtain of hair, Roland could see the Adept grinning and wondered, not for the first time, just how much of his thoughts Evan could hear.

"So, uh," he got up and began stacking empty plates, "feels like its going to be a hot one again today."

"Yes," Evan sighed, the grin banished. He rose lithely and returned to his place by the window. "And when it's hot like this, with blinding glare and the air heavy and still like a sheet of heated glass, tempers fray and good people can be pushed to the edge and over."

"You mean *he's* causing this?" Roland asked over the sound of the sink filling.

"Yes," Evan said without turning.

"But it's summer," Roland protested. "I know Canada gets called the Great White North, but it does get hot here in the summer."

"Not like this," Daru put in thoughtfully. "Not this hot, for this long, in June. A week or two in August maybe . . ."

"What are you going to do about it?" Rebecca asked, getting right to the point.

"I'm doing it, Lady."

Daru's brow quirked for that was the first time she'd heard Evan title Rebecca.

"There are rain clouds to the south and west and I'm encouraging them in this direction. In two days, the city will have relief."

"Why not sooner," Roland wanted to know, handing the pile of clean plates to Rebecca to put away.

Evan spread his hands, his bracelets chiming softly. "Rain travels at its own speed. Move it too quickly, it dissipates. Move it too slowly, it gets bored and falls."

"Rain gets bored?"

"A simple word to cover a complicated . . ." He tugged on a strand of pale hair, searching for the word.

"Thing?" Rebecca offered.

"A complicated thing, yes." They shared pleased smiles and again Roland sensed another level in the exchange.

"There's something I've been wondering about." Daru paced the length of the small apartment while she spoke.

Join the club, Roland thought, settling Patience on his lap. The last time he'd been sure of anything had been just before Rebecca showed up on his street corner.

"You came here because Rebecca invited you, right?"

"Roland had a voice in the invitation," Evan pointed out, "but that's essentially correct."

"Well, how did *he* get in?"

In the silence that fell while they waited for Evan's answer, the only sound was the scrape of Tom's tongue smoothing the black stripes of his tail.

"There are two possibilities," Evan said at last. "That a man or woman in this world did a deed of evil and called to the Darkness while doing it . . ."

"Black candles, and pentagrams, and human sacrifice," Roland murmured, and Patience wailed a discordant accompaniment to his words.

"Yes," Evan sighed, "the Darkness has been called that way. But this time, this time I think it moved on its own to take advantage of the weakened barriers of Midsummer Night. Although, in a way, *he* was invited, too. . . .

"This world has much darkness in it and it calls always to the Darkness outside the barriers. After a time, the barrier weakens enough for a bit of Darkness to slip through. Usually a bit so small it comes with no real body of its own and either dissipates, leaving a general feeling of bad humor in its wake, or it finds a host and does what it can to create a permanent residence. These bits of Darkness can't survive long where even a little Light stands against them."

He filled his cupped palm with sunlight, then scattered it off his fingertips in lines of delicate filigree. "Of course, the Light in your world calls in like kind. Sometimes, a deed of such Dark or Light is done that larger creatures can answer; goblins and boggins, unicorns and fauns. To pass an Adept, the Darkness waited until the call became almost unbearable, saving up the wearing at the barrier, directing all its resources to a single goal." He sighed again. "Which, thankfully, it seldom manages, self-discipline not being one of its stronger characteristics. When the time was right, it moved, forcing through a bit of itself large enough and strong enough to open the gate for the rest. I don't imagine the passage through the barrier was a pleasant one.

"You sound almost sorry for *him*," Daru said, frowning.

"I regret anyone's pain," Evan told her, no trace of apology in his voice. "Even his. But that will not stop me from destroying him."

"I don't understand what you mean, 'forced through a bit of itself'?" Roland had turned and twisted the statement but still could make no sense of it.

"There is only one Darkness as there is only one Light. As he is a piece of the Darkness, so I am a piece of the Light. The Darkness holds its pieces close, not trusting in them to stay, but the Light wants nothing to be a part of it that doesn't choose to be there."

"If you love something, let it go. If it comes back to you, it's yours. If it doesn't, it never was." Rebecca blushed as they all turned to stare at her. "I read it on a T-shirt," she explained, chewing her lower lip, afraid from the reaction she'd said something wrong.

Evan tossed his hair back off his face and his eyes sparkled. "But that's it exactly.

"It is?"

"Exactly," he repeated.

Rebecca nodded, content. "I thought so."

Daru reached over and gave her hand a squeeze then turned again to Evan. "Are you strong enough to defeat him?"

"One on one, just him and me?" Evan shrugged, the sparkle gone. "To keep the balance we are of equal power, but the Dark is often self-indulgent, bleeding power away to keep itself amused."

Daru sighed. "That was a straight yes or no question and your answer was neither."

"All right, then," he smiled, "probably. But first I have to find him."

"Can't you just, oh, I don't know," Roland plucked a scale up his G-string, "cast a spell and know where he is?"

"No. Unless he actually tips the balance, I must find him the same way you would find any mortal man."

"In less than a week?"

"Yes."

"Do you know what he looks like?"

"I'd recognize him if I saw him."

It was Roland's turn to sigh. "Do you know just how big this city is? With how many people?"

"Yes," Evan said again, "but I have help."

Roland and Daru exchanged looks that placed them in complete agreement for the first time since being introduced.

"And as well," Evan continued, ignoring the expressions of

disbelief on the faces of two members of his audience, "we should find where he plans to open the gate . . ."

"Can you put any parameters on *that?*" Daru interrupted.

"Oh, yes . . ."

She relaxed a little.

". . . the area must be fairly large, open, and the earth must not be bound by concrete and steel."

"A park," Rebecca suggested, bouncing.

"Do you know how many *parks* there are in this city?" Roland protested.

"Yes." Rebecca's tone was so perfectly serious that Roland could only conclude she did, indeed, know how many parks there were in the city.

"We need a map." Daru stood and adjusted the folds of her sari. "I have one in my car. I'll be right back."

Hoping no one noticed, Roland watched her leave. He felt like a shit, but the sway of her hips beneath the draped silk was worth it.

When she returned, she held a folded map of Toronto, what appeared to be clothing draped over one arm, and a yellow rectangle of paper about eight inches long.

"I don't suppose you fix parking tickets?" she asked Evan, tossing both the ticket and the map on Rebecca's table.

"Sorry, not my department. Give unto Caesar and all that."

Daru nodded, unsurprised. "You've read the Bible."

"I've read all your great works of literature, the Bible, the Koran, Shakespeare, Wells, Harold Robbins . . ."

"What!"

He winked, taking five years off his apparent age. "Kidding."

Daru rolled her eyes at him and headed for the bathroom to change.

"Have you read Winnie the Pooh?" Rebecca asked. "He's my favorite."

"Of course I have," Evan told her, perching carefully on the windowsill between two plants, stretching out his legs, and crossing his booted feet, "there's great wisdom in Pooh."

"For a bear of very little brain," Rebecca agreed.

This was another side of Rebecca Roland had not been aware of. "Do you read it by yourself?" he wanted to know.

"Yes." Rebecca's brow furrowed in indignation. "I can read

harder books than Pooh." She paused, thought for a moment, and added, "But not much harder."

"Rebecca," Daru said, returning to the living room in white cotton shorts and a matching shirt, "has a complete set of Paddington Bear books."

"I like bears," Rebecca told the company proudly. "I have a bunch of the Berenstain Bears books, too."

Rebecca, Roland realized, probably read for pleasure more often than the majority of college graduates.

Daru spread the map out on the table and Rebecca bent over it.

"Are the parks the green bits?" she asked.

"Yes, that's right."

"Sometimes," Rebecca sighed contentedly, "things make sense. Parks are green bits," she explained to Evan as he joined them.

The table was small, the apartment was warm, and Roland, who'd never had much interest in parks anyway, soon decided he'd rather watch from a distance than be part of the crowd. From the sound of it, Rebecca did, indeed, know every park in the city, how many trees each contained, and who—or what—lived in each tree.

Tom leaped up on the sill, balanced for a moment in the open window, then disappeared. Roland assumed he wouldn't have jumped if he hadn't thought he could make it safely to the ground, so he continued strumming and didn't mention the cat's departure.

Probably has to take a leak. In fact, that's not a bad idea.

He wandered into the bathroom, did what he had to, and returned to find the other three still poring over the map.

". . . no, that's all up and down and there's too many trees . . ."

"Parks," he muttered. And, "Parks!" he said louder. There was one park he knew about . . . "Rebecca, does this tv work?"

"What?" she looked around the apartment, as if unsure who'd spoken.

Roland repeated the question.

"Oh, yes, it works. But it only works on channel five and channel nine."

"That's great, just great. I need channel nine. Can I turn it on?"

"Sure." She bent back over the map. "No, that one's too long and skinny."

Like everything else in the apartment, the small portable television on the shelf over the radiator was spotless. Roland unwound the cord from the hooks on the back—Rebecca, apparently, was not a big tv fan—found the nearest outlet, and plugged it in. If he remembered the starting time correctly, he shouldn't have missed much more than the opening pitch.

As the picture faded in, black and white and a little fuzzy, he saw he'd judged it just about right; top of the first with one out and a runner on second. With the volume turned low, he settled down to watch something he understood.

In the bottom of the third, he felt the couch shift and heard the soft chime of Evan's bracelets as the Adept settled down next to him.

"Who's winning?"

"Detroit—one, nothing."

"The Jays' prima donna still benched?"

"Yeah," Roland sighed, "he . . . Wait a minute!" He spun to face the Adept, found him almost unbearably close, and successfully fought the urge to discover whether his hair was as silky as it looked. "What do you know about baseball?"

Evan waited until the Bluejay at bat popped out before answering. "Television signals pass easily through the barrier."

"You mean you watch tv in heaven or elfland or whatever you call the place you come from?"

"I call it home. And yes."

"What on," Roland asked facetiously, unable to help himself, "crystal balls?"

"Of course not, balls roll all over the place. Any good sized piece of crystal with a reasonably flat surface will do."

"You're not serious." He took a closer look at Evan's face. "You are serious. Well, I'll be damned."

Evan grinned and stretched. "Not likely," he said.

Roland found himself mesmerized by the pulse that beat at the base of Evan's throat. He heard the crack of a bat and the crowd at the stadium yelling but couldn't seem to tear his gaze away. He noticed Evan had the same clean smell as Rebecca's apartment. He sighed and closed his eyes, seeing again the vision of great white wings.

"Daru and the Lady have gone to the store. I hope you didn't want anything. You seemed pretty involved in the game."

Opening his eyes, Roland glanced around the apartment. He and Evan were alone. "No, nothing." He watched the sunlight glint on the golden tips of Evan's lashes. They were sitting very close. Desperately, he searched for something to say as the silence was beginning to say too much. "Why do you call her that . . . Lady?"

"It's a term of respect."

"Not of endearment?" Roland asked suspiciously.

"Aren't they often the same thing?"

"You know, it's next to impossible to get a straight answer from you."

"The Light has never provided easy answers."

Roland snorted, "That's exactly what I mean." *What's wrong with this picture,* he thought as with an effort he turned his attention back to the broadcast. *The women folk go shopping while the men folk watch the game. Except that one of the women folk is a few pickles short of a barrel, the other keeps wondering what rock I've crawled out from under, and one of the men folk is an angel. Of sorts.*

"Daru, why don't you like Roland?"

Daru picked up a third can of lemonade concentrate, studied it for a moment, and dropped it in the basket. "What do you mean, Rebecca?"

"Well," Rebecca squeezed the rye bread gently while she spoke, "you show him your government face all the time."

"I don't dislike Roland. Have you got mustard at the apartment?"

"Yes."

"I just don't know him very well."

"Then you should get to know him better. Roland is nice."

Daru sighed; three years as Rebecca's case worker and almost that long as her friend enabled her to leap ahead to what Rebecca actually meant. "I'm not going to sleep with him," she said quietly. "Get a head of lettuce please."

Rebecca obediently picked a head out of the pile, weighing it in her palm before passing it over, "Why not?"

"Because I don't want to."

"Why not?"

"Because I don't know him."

"But you would get to know him if you slept with him."

The woman at the cash register looked up, interested. Daru felt herself flush, glad her complexion was too dark for it to be easily seen. The most obvious, and annoying, manifestation of Rebecca's disability was her lack of a volume control. Everything she said, she said in her normal speaking voice. Her normal, fairly loud, speaking voice.

"He wouldn't sleep with me."

"Rebecca, hush." Daru's opinion of Roland rose upon hearing he'd refused Rebecca's offer—the odds were better than good that Rebecca had been the one who'd offered—and simultaneously fell for she felt she knew why. Rebecca might appear to be a precocious ten-year-old, but she was an adult woman for all that and Roland had no right to think of her as a child. Of course, she was amazingly childlike and Roland deserved credit for not taking advantage of that. Except she wasn't a child and . . . Tangled up as usual in Rebecca's sexuality, Daru sighed and paid for their groceries.

But after they'd left the store, while she was still thinking about it, she asked, "Are you remembering to take a pill every day?" God knew she'd had enough trouble getting the pills approved; considering mentally disadvantaged adults as sexually active gave most of the department spasms.

"Don't worry, Daru," Rebecca shifted the grocery bag and smiled reassuringly, "there won't be any babies." It wasn't exactly a lie. She didn't exactly say she took the pills. Daru just wouldn't understand that babies came when babies came and little pills wouldn't make any difference. Rebecca wished she could explain it, then everyone could stop taking the little pills.

"He's there. He's at the ball park."

"What?" Roland whirled to stare at Evan. "Look, just because the outfield misses an easy catch doesn't mean *he* had anything to do with it. The Jays have been known to snatch defeat from the jaws of victory before."

"And have balls changed direction as they fell before?

"Sure. The stadium's right on the lake. It's one of the windiest in the league."

"Look at the flags, Roland." Evan pointed at the screen and Roland had a sudden vision of the ghost of Christmas yet to come at Scrooge's grave. "There's no wind."

"Yeah, but . . ."

"And that earlier decision . . ."

"He could've been out; after all, the second base ump was right there."

"But he looked safe, didn't he?"

"Yeah." Roland had to admit it.

"And what of that error that the umpire just didn't see?"

"It happens." But even to his own ears he didn't sound so sure.

"It's him." Evan rose, lips set in a thin line. "He's there. I don't know what he thinks he's doing, but he's there. I have to try to find him. We may never get this kind of a chance again."

"I hope he arrives a little more conventionally than he left," Roland muttered, suddenly alone in the apartment. He reached out and with a trembling hand touched the empty indentation smoothing out of the couch. "Gone. Just like that." He laughed nervously and went back to watching the game. It was the only thing he could think of to do.

"Well, hello, Becca." The large-blonde-lady-from-down-the-hall beamed as Rebecca and Daru came into the small lobby of the apartment building. "Have we been grocery shopping, then?" she asked brightly, wiping at her face with a large square of pink cloth. Not waiting for an answer, she turned to Daru and added in the same artificial tones, "It's just so sweet of you to come here on your day off and help our Becca out."

Daru smiled tightly.

"You're probably wondering why I'm waiting down here. Well, my sister's boy is coming to pick me up and take me out to their lovely house in Don Mills. They have central air conditioning."

"He must be very strong," Rebecca said, intrigued.

"Who must, Becca dear?"

"Your sister's boy who's coming to pick you up."

"Isn't she just precious?" the large-blonde-lady-from-down-the-hall asked Daru in a stage whisper. A horn honked at the curb and she lumbered to her feet. "You be a good girl now, Becca. And you," she waved a pudgy finger at Daru, "you let me know if I can do anything to help."

Rebecca watched as she made her way out to the street and sighed. She'd been looking forward to seeing someone pick up the large-blonde-lady-from-down-the-hall, but the sister's boy had come in a car instead.

"I guess Evan made her a dream that worked," she said as they climbed the stairs.

"I guess," Daru agreed. "Rebecca, do you want me to talk to her again?"

"You can talk again, but she won't listen again."

Daru had to admit that she wouldn't.

"I don't mind," Rebecca continued, " 'cause mostly I feel sorry for her."

"Sorry for her? Why?"

" 'Cause she always has to be her and that mustn't be very nice most of the time."

Daru was still mulling that over as they entered the apartment which felt almost cool after the baking heat of outside.

"Where did Evan go?" Rebecca asked, setting the bag of groceries on the table and pulling out the package of ham.

"To the ball game," Roland said shortly, not taking his eyes off the television.

"Why on earth . . ." Daru began.

"Because *he's* at the ball game."

"Oh." She sat down beside Roland and peered at the screen.

The crowd roared as a pitch swerved and the umpires inspected both the ball and the Tigers' pitcher. The crowd roared louder when both passed the inspection.

In the bottom of the sixth, a Jays' runner slammed into the Tigers' second baseman and in the screaming match that followed both managers were tossed from the game.

As Rebecca handed out ham sandwiches— "People still have to eat."—a ground ball leaped out of the shortstop's glove, rolled between his legs, and away. The roar of the crowd had become a constant and ugly background noise.

During the seventh inning stretch, BJ Bird stepped backward and fell off the dugout roof. The announcer said he thought the mascot had been trying to avoid a bottle thrown by a Detroit fan when it happened.

"I didn't see a bottle, did you?" Daru asked.

"No," Roland told her. "I didn't."

Several fights broke out between fans wearing headphones, the radio announcer having said the exact same thing.

In the eighth inning, two obvious errors went uncalled and a star player, a favorite with the fans, put up an argument over his third strike and got thrown out of the game. The roar became a snarl.

The Tigers hit the only home run of the game in the ninth but the Bluejays couldn't seem to find the ball.

The final score: three to two, Tigers.

From the general admission seats came screams of "Cheat! CHEAT!" and the stands erupted.

"This is so fucking un-Canadian," Roland muttered. "A riot? I don't believe it."

They watched in silence as the camera zoomed in on the seething mass of people, some screaming in anger, some screaming in panic. The play by play announcer did his best to report what he saw;

"The exits appear blocked with bodies . . . I can see parents trying to lift their children up out of danger . . . The police are trying to regain control . . . My god, that man has a bat . . ."

The color commentator kept repeating, "Oh shit, oh shit, oh shit . . ." until someone turned his microphone off.

As the camera swept the stadium, it found one tiny island of calm. Up behind home plate, a double row of empty seats, between him and the riot, a dark haired man watched and waited and, as he felt the camera focus on him, he looked up and smiled.

"That's *him!*" Roland and Rebecca yelled together.

Daru felt her heart thud as the bright blue eyes on the screen met hers.

Then suddenly, a blaze of white light burned out the image and the television went dark.

Chapter Six

". . . And to recap our top news story of the day, a riot at Exhibition Stadium results in four dead and seventeen injured. No charges have been filed yet in the incident. Police are withholding the names of the dead until next of kin can be notified. I'm Heather Chan and this has been the news at six."

The constable who had the desk turned the radio down as the news ended, and shook his head. It all sounded so tidy once it hit the news; four dead and seventeen injured, no muss, no fuss, no mention of the noise, or the stink, or the hopeless feeling you got facing a riot involving almost forty thousand. Of course, that was from a cop's point of view and no one ever seemed much interested in that.

He pulled a stack of arrest reports over to his terminal and began inputting the information they contained. The thing that really pissed him off about what had gone down at the stadium was the paperwork. With all divisions undermanned—the flu bug sweeping the city seemed to have a preference for the police—the last thing they needed was a doubling of the workload. He squinted at a colleague's scrawl, decided the name had to be O'Conner, and hoped Fourteen Division appreciated what the other stations in the city were doing for them.

"Hey, Harper." An auxiliary dropped another pile of paper on the desk.

"Hey, yourself," he grunted. "There'd better be a stack of those for you, Wojtowicz, or you're toast."

She patted the pile beside her own terminal and for a few minutes the only sound was the faint click click of the keyboards. "So, have they figured out what caused the riot?"

He glanced over, envying the effortless way her fingers moved over the keys compared to his own hunt and correct method. "Didn't you hear the news? The Jays lost."

Wojtowicz snorted. "That's not news. And no cause for a riot."

"Not all by itself maybe." Harper ticked the points off on his fingers. "One, the Jays lost to the Tigers. That upset a lot of people. Two, the umpires called a bad game. It happens. It upset a lot more people. Three, which may also be the reason for two, it's hot out there; you could fry an egg on a batting helmet if you wanted to. In hot weather people get irritated faster and are more likely to do something about it." He grinned at her skeptical expression. "They teach us that psych stuff at the academy. A hot, angry crowd like that and I'd have been more surprised if there hadn't been a riot."

"But what about all the tv cameras burning out?"

"What cameras? I didn't hear about that."

"There was a flash of bright light, and all the tv cameras burned out. I was watching the game at home before I came in."

"Aliens," Harper said dramatically.

Wojtowicz rolled her eyes, "Right. Little green Bluejays fans."

"Okay, terrorists."

"Up from Buffalo for the game? Get real."

He spread his hands in surrender. "Okay, I give up. I don't know why the tv cameras burned out. Nor do I particularly care."

"What about the way the riot stopped, as suddenly as it began?"

"Who can tell what a mob will do?"

"No," she shook her head, remembering her reaction while watching the game. "Something about the whole thing felt wrong."

"It was a riot," Harper pointed out. "It's not supposed to feel right."

"You know what I mean."

He thought about it for a moment, but finally shrugged. "Hot weather makes people do strange things."

"But it's only June!" she protested.

"Yeah, I know." He looked out the glass doors and watched the heat shimmer up off the road. "God help us in July and August."

Daru turned off the television. The news had told them nothing they didn't already know and Evan still hadn't returned. "Well . . ." she said, with a helpless shrug at the other two.

"Deep subject," Roland murmured, reaching for his guitar, "turn it sideways and you've got a tunnel."

"Oh, that's a lot of help!" Daru snapped at him.

"Turn what sideways?" Rebecca wondered.

They ignored her.

"What do you want me to say?" Roland sneered. "Let's put the wagon train in a circle? Form up an intrepid band of rescuers and go after him? We don't know where he is. We don't know *if* he is. He might have lost already and we're fucked. Have you thought of that?" He slashed his hand down on the strings, then sighed and leaned his forehead against the smooth wood.

Daru opened her mouth to tell him just what she thought of his defeatist attitude, but Rebecca tapped her lightly on the shoulder and shook her head.

"Don't be mad at him, Daru. He's worried about Evan and being worried makes him cranky."

Roland looked up, his expression unreadable, met Daru's eyes, and shrugged. "I'm sorry. She's right."

The phone rang. Daru and Roland jumped, but Rebecca, almost as though she'd expected it, dropped to her knees and dug it out from under the couch. It rang again.

"It's Evan," she said, holding the phone out.

"How do you know?" Roland asked as Daru took it and lifted the receiver to her ear.

Rebecca held up the end of the cord, the plastic jack between thumb and forefinger. "It's not plugged in."

"Yes, yes, I understand. I'll be right there. Fifty-two Division? Why all the way up . . . Overcrowding? Oh. Yes, I know where it is. No more than fifteen minutes. You, too." She hung up, took a deep breath, and said, "It was Evan. I have to go and bail him out."

"Bail him out?"

"Well, vouch for him." She paused and her lips twitched just a little. "He doesn't have any ID."

Roland chuckled. Daru chuckled. Then the two of them roared with laughter while Rebecca watched, completely confused.

Still laughing, Daru stood, scooped up her purse, and headed for the door. "We'll be back as soon as possible," she said, and left.

Roland wiped his streaming eyes. "No ID," he repeated, setting himself off again. "No ID."

Rebecca shook her head. Sometimes so-called normal people made no sense.

*　　*　　*

She crossed the cobbles in front of Fifty-two Division with short, jerky steps, her mind paying no attention to her feet. How dared they give her a parking ticket when she was only in the spot for a minute or two. Okay, maybe ten, but where else was she supposed to park? Getting a spot downtown was like pulling teeth, no, harder than pulling teeth, and she'd give the cops an opinion or two along with her twenty bucks. She felt the impact of a shoulder, began to fall, then a strong hand pulled her straight and steadied her.

"Thanks," she snarled at her rescuer. As she pushed past, she glanced up at his face. Her frown curved up into a smile, and she got lost in the smile he flashed in return. Not caring how it looked, she stood and stared after him until he and his companion got into a beat up old Honda hatchback and drove away. He wasn't even her type, too young, too flash, way too pretty—she made it a point never to get interested in men significantly prettier than she was—and completely irresistible.

"Now that," she sighed to the evening air, "is a man worth making a fool of yourself over." With a final melting glance in the direction he'd disappeared, she pulled open the door and stepped inside the station, her earlier pique forgotten.

"Play the one about the unicorn again." Rebecca bounced where she sat. "The one your friend wrote."

"I played it already, kiddo. Two songs ago."

"I know," she told him, rolling her eyes, "I said play it *again*." Roland smiled. "Oh, *again*. Pardon me."

Rebecca thought about it, brows drawn down, teeth working on the edge of her left thumbnail. "Okay," she said, after a minute. "You can play what you want to, but you've got to play the unicorn song first."

"You win," Roland surrendered, still smiling. He didn't mind playing for Rebecca—even though she usually wanted the same I songs sung over and over—because she listened so intently, becoming completely involved in the music. Audiences like that were few and far between.

He plunges through the forest night,
his eyes are wide with fear.
Behind him, he can hear the sounds
that say the hunt is near.

Out of his whole repertoire, Rebecca's favorites were the simple tunes with the fantastical lyrics that one of his oldest friends had been sending to him in every letter she'd written over the last five or six years. He'd tried to fool her a couple of times with songs that were alike in theme and structure, but Rebecca always knew. Once, he'd played her one of his own pieces of music. She'd listened as intently, head cocked to one side, and when he'd finished said, "It's very good, Roland, but it isn't quite." And then had not been able to tell him *what* it wasn't quite. He never played her one of his pieces again. Mostly because, deep down, he agreed with her.

As he finished, they heard voices in the hall and the door opened.

"Evan!" Rebecca flung herself to her feet and across the room, rocking to a halt inches from the Adept. "Are you okay?"

"I'm fine, Lady." He smiled; a little wearily, Roland thought. "Thank you for your concern."

"You got arrested!"

"Yes." He stroked a curl back off her face. "I did."

Rebecca turned to Daru and her eyes widened. "You got chicken!"

"Yes." Daru handed her the red and white striped bag. "I did."

Rebecca buried her face in the bag, took a long appreciative sniff, then turned and showed it to Roland. "Roland! They got chicken."

"I can see that, kiddo." He stood, holding Patience against him, scanning Evan for any signs of . . . of . . . anything. In his experience, cops weren't kind to young men with no ID they pulled in out of a . . . situation. "Are you all right?"

Evan spread his arms. "As you see, I'm fine."

Roland continued to look. *Taking advantage of the excuse to look your fill and hide the feeling under concern,* said a small voice in the back of his head which he ignored. Rebecca put a plate heaped with chicken and french fries and coleslaw in one hand, lifted his guitar out of the other, and replaced it with a fork.

"Eat," she said, so he did.

Later, when the bones had been picked clean and he'd recovered his equilibrium—a process he hoped he wasn't going to have to go through every time he saw Evan though he rather suspected he would—he asked, "What happened?"

Evan fed Tom a piece of skin. The cat had arrived just as they were sitting down to eat. "I stopped the riot," he said simply. "I couldn't stand the hurting, the fear. He got away. I think he knew it would happen like that. I think he's somewhere laughing at me, right now." His fine features looked pinched and drawn. "Stopping the riot took all the power I had."

Daru almost didn't recognize her own voice as she said, "By saving those people, by letting *him* go, you may have doomed the rest of the world to Darkness."

"I know."

And there was nothing more to say, because he did know, better than they ever could, and the pain in his voice, in those two words, was enough to bring tears to a heart of stone.

PC Harper pushed his keyboard to one side, laced his fingers together, and stretched. His shift was almost over and he could practically taste that icy cold beer waiting for him at home. He could coast through the next hour and a half, What was going to happen at nine-thirty on a Sunday night in Toronto the Good?

He heard the door open but before he could turn to look, he had a pretty good idea of what he'd see. The air conditioning, already straining to defeat the heat, simply couldn't cope with this new assault as well; old dirt, old sweat, unwashed clothes, and over it all the pervasive stink of stale urine.

"Hey, bubba, you gotta minute?"

Breathing shallowly through his mouth, Harper stood and walked slowly over to the counter. This was the worst part of being so shorthanded, he had no choice but to deal with this old lady, no chance to suddenly have to go to the washroom, leaving her to the other guy on the desk. Damn. "And what can I do for you?" he asked, keeping his tone neutral with an effort.

"You know the girl what got killed last night? I think I seen who did it. You interested?"

"Wha . . ."

Mrs. Ruth sighed and shook her head. "The girl what got killed last night," she repeated slowly. "I think I seen who did it." He still appeared a little shell-shocked, so she added, "I was on my way to the dumpster and I seen this guy leaving the parking lot. I didn't think nothing of it at the time, but he smelled a little funny. Then I heard about what happened through the grapevine, so I come in to tell the cops."

"Smelled funny?" He wondered how she could possibly tell.

"Yeah. Not like expensive perfume or hair junk. Like blood." Her voice took on a grimmer tone. "And I know what blood smells like."

"But if you went to the dumpster, you must have found the body." *It always happened,* Harper sighed to himself. *Any kind of sensational crime brings out the nut cases.*

Mrs. Ruth's eyes narrowed. "I didn't say I went to the dumpster," she snapped. "I said I was on my way. I got distracted and never made it. Now, are you going to call someone out here who can take my statement and a description of this guy or am I going to have to get angry?"

Her voice so reminded him of a teacher he'd lived in terror of all through third grade that his finger hit the intercom button before he even knew he'd moved it.

Mrs. Ruth smiled.

". . . I mean, why should I let him push me around?"

"Why, indeed."

"He thinks he's hot shit just because he drives a BMW and has some hot shit computer job, but I'm just as good as he is."

"Better."

"Damn right!"

The Dark Adept leaned forward, placing his forearms carefully between the beer rings on the table. "After all, where would his type be if not for you. One of the men who actually makes what they consume."

"Yeah. That, too!" He tossed back the beer in his glass and held it out for a refill, long past the point of wondering why the pitcher never seemed to empty. "And you know what else? That son of a bitch has the nerve to tell me I can't put my garbage at the edge of the driveway. We share the fuckin' driveway, you know, and he thinks he can tell me not to put my fuckin' garbage there."

"Perhaps it's time to do something about him."

"Yeah." He scowled. "P'raps it is." Abruptly he pushed back his chair and stood, swaying slightly. "Do something about him right now."

"Do you still keep your shotgun in the back of the hall cupboard?"

"Yeah." His eyes narrowed. "Yeah. That'll show the son of a bitch." He staggered off through the crowd, bouncing off chairs and tables and people, letting neither curses nor spilled beer distract him from his course home. And his hall cupboard. And the lesson he was going to teach that fancy-ass that lived next door.

"That," the Adept sighed, "was almost too easy." He caught the attention of one of the waitresses and beckoned her over with a toss of his head.

"Oh, he's a cool one," she murmured to her companion, tucking her tray under one arm and twitching her short skirt into place.

The other girl peered in his direction. "He looks dangerous."

"You think anyone with a gleam in his eye looks dangerous."

She shook her head, teased hair bobbing with the motion. "Yeah, but he looks really dangerous. Like, like a sharp knife."

"Poetic." Moistening bright red lips, the summoned girl sashayed off, with one last comment, "Don't worry, honey, I can handle him."

"That's settled it, then." Daru slipped her pen back into her purse and tore the top sheet of paper off the pad in her lap. "I'll go in tomorrow, do everything that absolutely has to be done and book the rest of the week off. Roland and Evan will start showing Evan's drawing around the hotels." She glanced at the sketches, Evan had done of the Dark Adept based on the glimpse he'd gotten of him at the ballpark. The sketches were good; detailed down to the collar buttons and the faintly contemptuous expression. "Are we sure he's going to keep looking like this?" she asked.

"Oh, yes," Evan told her. "Until he goes through the barrier again, he's as tied to that body as I am to this one."

Daru nodded, satisfied, and Roland shoved an image of being tied to Evan's body out of his mind.

"And tomorrow after I get off work," Rebecca announced, "Evan and me . . ."

"I," Daru corrected automatically.

"Yeah. Evan and I will go and ask the littles to help look." She sighed. "I wish I could take the rest of the week off."

"As much as we need you, Lady, you are needed there more."

"Yeah, but . . ."

"Did you not say there are three of your co-workers off sick already?"

Rebecca sighed again. "Yes, three. It wouldn't be fair to Lena for me to go away, too. Then she'd have to make all the muffins herself."

"Don't look so sad." Evan pulled his happy-face button free, leaned forward, and pinned it to Rebecca's shirt. "You see many people in your job; hear a lot of conversations. If anything strange is going on, people will talk about it and you can pass it on. Someone listening to people carrying on their ordinary lives may give us the clue we need. It's the ordinary lives he'll disrupt the most."

"Okay." Rebecca nodded reluctantly, raised her hand and trapped his. She ran a finger down the line of bracelets, causing them to ring together, smiled at the sound, and did it again. "But why can't we start tonight? It isn't too late."

"It is much too late," Daru declared, standing. "None of us got much sleep last night, and you and I," she said pointedly to Rebecca, "have to be up early in the morning." She turned to Roland. "We are leaving. And you," she turned back to Rebecca, "are going to bed."

"Maybe I should stay?" Roland offered.

"Maybe you should go home and get some clean clothes," Daru replied.

"But . . ." He looked from Evan to Rebecca and then up at Daru. Their expressions were merely curious. Hers was almost challenging. "Yeah, I guess you're right."

"Daru is almost always right," Rebecca told him.

"Really." He stretched over the back of the couch, looking for his guitar case. "Doesn't that get tiring?" The case had slipped down and was lying flat on the floor, just out of reach.

Daru smiled. "No. It doesn't."

"Mrs. Ruth is *always* right," Rebecca added to the room at large.

Daru rolled her eyes. "Mrs. Ruth is a bag lady, Rebecca. That in itself is not very right."

"Have you met Mrs. Ruth?" Roland asked, coming around the couch to stand by his case.

"I haven't had the pleasure."

"You're missing a treat." He bent over and flipped open the unsecured lid. "You've . . . Get out of there, cat!"

Tom glanced up, blinking a little in the light, and yawned. His back followed perfectly along the curve of the case and all four paws lay flat, claws securely anchored in the felt lining.

"Go on! Scram!"

"I guess he thought it was a cat bed," Rebecca offered as Tom stood, stretched, and poured himself out over the side.

"I don't care what he thought," Roland snarled, kneeling and brushing off the covering of cat hair. He grunted as Tom butted against his ribs with almost enough force to knock him over, and pushed the cat away. Tom looked pleased with himself, came back, and did it again.

Daru stifled a laugh. "I think he's trying to piss you off. Cats always know."

"Know what?" He eased Patience gently down, snapped the lid shut, and straightened. "Come on, let's go."

"You'll meet me here tomorrow morning?" Evan asked.

Roland's expression softened as he turned to the Adept. "Yeah. Eight-thirty, like we agreed." He waggled a finger at Rebecca. "Take care of him until then, kiddo."

Rebecca nodded matter-of-factly. "Oh, I will." She smiled at Evan and he mirrored her expression.

Roland could no longer deny what was right in front of his eyes.

"Hey, if you think . . ."

Daru's hand closed like a steel band just above his elbow and she had him hustled out the door and it shut behind them before he had any idea of what she was doing. When she released him, he rubbed his arm and glared at her.

"Do you know what's going to happen in there tonight?" he sputtered.

"I know." Her voice was ice. "Do you?"

"Yes, I do. They're going to . . . uh . . ."

Daru sighed and her voice grew a little kinder. "Think about it for a moment, Roland. Think about what Evan is. He certainly isn't going to take advantage of a poor little retarded girl." Unexpectedly, she smiled. "And I don't think Rebecca will be taking advantage of him. Come on." She started toward the stairs. "I'll drive you home."

Thinking about it as commanded, Roland scrambled to catch up. "Doesn't it bother you?" he prodded as they crossed the small lobby.

"Why should it? Evan, by his nature, is incapable of doing evil and Rebecca, for all her disability, is a physically mature woman with all the—" she considered her next word as she pushed open the door—"urges that entails."

"You mean when she asked me to sleep with her . . ."

"She meant it euphemistically? Yes, probably." Daru glanced

both ways and started across College Street, Roland trailing in her wake. "Look, you can't keep the mentally disadvantaged so protected from the world that they never get a chance to learn from it. Rebecca has a job and an apartment, why shouldn't she have lovers, too?"

"Because she could get hurt!"

"Emotionally? So can we all. And actually, her simplicity protects her from creating a lot of the emotional torments we lay on ourselves. Physically? There isn't a woman in the world safe from that. It stinks, but there it is. You think she lacks the judgment to avoid the men who'd take advantage of her? Well, you're wrong. Rebecca has a childlike ability to see right to the heart and the fakes, the phonies, and the psychos can't touch her. Now that's not some kind of special power that applies to all the mentally disadvantaged, but it certainly applies to Rebecca." She stopped by her battered green hatchback and fished in her purse for the keys.

Roland lifted his head and watched something that was definitely not a squirrel scamper along the hydro wires.

"She sees little people in bushes," he muttered.

Daru followed his gaze and snorted. "So do you."

In answer to Roland's unspoken question, she shrugged and said, "So do I. After looking into Evan's eyes, I'd be more surprised if I didn't see them." She tugged open her door, slid in, and leaned across to pop the lock on the passenger side.

"Doesn't *that* bother you?" Roland asked, stowing his guitar in the back seat.

"Why should it?" Daru put the car in gear and pulled carefully out of the parking space. "They'll live their lives and I'll live mine. Poverty, hunger, and discrimination bother me a lot more. Where to?"

"Neal, just east of Pape, north of the Danforth."

"I know it."

They drove in silence for a while; Roland's mind turning over the way he saw Rebecca, Daru's on the traffic.

"Until she was twelve," Daru said suddenly, braking for a light, "Rebecca was a normal little girl. Then one Sunday, on a drive out into the country, a truck broadsided the family car. The impact threw Rebecca clear and when the emergency vehicles arrived the truck and the car were burning and she was the only survivor. They found her lying in a ditch by the side of the road, covered in mud and blood. According to the medical report, she began to menstruate that day, probably during or just after the accident."

Roland squirmed, made more uncomfortable by the reference to menstruation than by the deaths of three people. *It's not my fault,* he excused himself, *that's woman stuff.*

"Her most serious injury was a skull fracture; a large piece of bone pressing down on her brain. She'd lost so much blood that the doctors were afraid she wasn't going to make it, but she sailed through the surgery to a quick and complete recovery. Well, physically complete. It didn't take long for the brain damage to become apparent. In less than a year, her reading skills deteriorated down to a very basic level, she lost all her math, and most of her ability to deal with abstracts."

"With what?"

"Abstracts. All the things that people have created to clutter up their lives. A hundred years ago, maybe even fifty in parts of the world, she would have been fine. She'd have gotten married, raised children, cared for living things, spending her whole life within established parameters dealing with things she is quite capable of dealing with. But life today," her hands left the steering wheel for a second and spread helplessly, "it just doesn't give her that option. Doctors and social workers soon found that since she couldn't deal with abstracts, she couldn't take shortcuts. Everything, thoughts and actions, had to be done one well-defined step at a time. Still, it wasn't bad enough to institutionalize her, so she stayed in a series of foster homes."

"What about relatives?"

"She hasn't any." Daru slammed the car into third, the motion violent and barely under control. "When she was fifteen, her foster father came to Children's Aid and confessed to a long string of sexual attacks on children supposedly in his care."

Roland had a sudden vision of the man drawn and quartered. Prompted, he had no doubt, by the grinding anger in Daru's voice.

"He'd tried the same thing on Rebecca. He said he didn't remember what happened, that the next thing he knew he was on his way to confess. I read the report. He kept repeating, 'I didn't realize,' and bursting into tears. All Rebecca ever said about it, both in the report and later when I asked her, was, 'I showed him what he'd done.'" She paused as she maneuvered the car around a bus and onto Neal Street. "No, I don't think you have to worry about Rebecca. Besides, I've never seen her as stable as she was today."

"Evan?"

"Well, it's hardly the situation." Her smile flashed white in the darkness, a gleaming counterpoint to the heavy sarcasm in her voice. "It would make sense. He is the Light, after all, and one would think he's supposed to bring out the best in people. Say when."

Roland pointed at his uncle's house and Daru pulled over. He got out, fished his guitar from the back, closed the door, then leaned back in the open window. "Thanks for the lift. And for the information. You've . . ." he sighed. Evan and Rebecca. Right. "You've given me something to think about."

"Here's something else." She met his eyes and he almost flinched, so uncompromising was her expression. "You were upset because of Rebecca, granted, but I don't think her disability had anything to do with it. I think you're more upset because she gets to sleep with Evan, and you don't."

He watched the car's taillights until they disappeared around the corner and, with Daru no longer there to argue the point, he said, "That's ridiculous." Then he turned and went into the house, ignoring whatever it was that snickered at him from the peonies.

Evan rested his cheek against Rebecca's hair, his eyes half-closed, his breathing shallow. She snuggled hard against his chest and he smiled sleepily, stroking one hand lightly down her damp back. An hour in her arms had done much to replace the power he'd expended quelling the riot. By morning . . .

The balance shifted, suddenly, painfully, and he barely managed to stop himself from crying out.

Here I am, said the Darkness. *Come and get me if you dare.*

He knew it was a challenge intended to take him when he was weak and unprepared, still drained from the afternoon's effort. Knew the Dark would not have issued it if it thought he could win. Knew, and knew that the Darkness knew, that he couldn't refuse.

Gently, he lifted Rebecca to one side of the bed and slid out from under her outstretched arm. She stirred, and half woke, calling his name. He leaned forward and lightly kissed her brow.

"Sleep, Lady," he said, tasting the salt tang of her on his lips. Tonight he would keep her safe, and tomorrow, and for all time if he could. She had enchanted him with her clarity from the moment he first saw her and what Darkness would do to such sweet simplicity . . .

Rebecca sighed and settled back against the pillows. Seen through Evan's eyes, she glowed with a warm and golden light.

Tom stepped into the alcove and leaped up on the bed, heading for his regular, now vacated, place.

"Watch her, little one," Evan murmured. "Stay with her while I am gone."

Tom spread one paw in the air and began to wash between his toes. He didn't need Evan to tell him what to do.

Evan straightened, fully clothed in the instant between one heartbeat and the next, touched the flaring curve of Rebecca's hip one last time to keep the memory fresh, and then moved toward the Darkness.

. . . an alley, shadowed by more than the night. He heard voices, laughter, and walked cautiously forward.

"No . . . Please. . . ."

He stumbled as a wave of Darkness roared down on him, and then he broke into a run.

At the end of the alley, under the weak red light of a flickering fire exit sign:

A boy, mid-teens, up against a wall, both hands to his face and blood seeping through his fingers.

At his feet, another. Facedown in a spreading puddle.

In front of him, five laughing shadows with knives.

Beyond, a well-dressed man who spread his arms and smiled a welcome. A smile only Evan could see.

"Not so pretty now, are you, shithead?" One of the shadows strutted forward and prodded at the boy's shoulder with the butt of his knife. The red light reflected off his shaved head and turned the tattoos covering it to purple. "We're gonna have us some fun with you."

"Here I am," purred the Darkness. "Your chance to take me out."

Behind his hands the boy whimpered, and his pale pants suddenly darkened at the crotch.

"Hey! He pissed himself!" One of the shadows found this hysterically funny.

"Bad boy," sneered another. "And bad boys have to be punished."

"Shall we cut his prick off?" asked the first, dropping his knife point to the top of the stain.

"Cut his prick off!" screamed the shadows in enthusiastic agreement.

"Or maybe there's something you should take care of first," the Darkness suggested. He glanced at his watch. "Do hurry. I haven't all night."

Evan moved forward, into the shadow's circle, conscious of a cold fury that lives would be so blithely spent to trap him. He couldn't not save the boy.

"Well, what have we here?" The leader of the gang, sensing new prey, turned and sneered. "Some sort of fucking white knight riding to the rescue?"

The others laughed and the circle closed about Evan. The pleasure they took in causing pain lapped at him, surrounded him, isolated him, and would weaken him in time.

"Please," he said softly, his hands open, his arms spread, "let the boy go. Put down your knives. Release the Darkness." All beings capable of choosing had to be given the choice.

"Turn from darkness?" The leader advanced, knife cradled loosely in his right hand. "We got us a fucking preacher here, gentlemen."

"Looks like a fag," observed a gang member with swastikas tattooed on both cheeks.

"Let's cut *his* prick off!" The third voice rose and almost cracked with excitement.

That afternoon, Evan had given himself to a stadium full of rioters, reminded them of the Light and helped them push away the Darkness. The five he now faced only narrowed their eyes against the glare and gripped their weapons tighter. They had no Light left in them for him to reach.

He saw the blade out of the corner of one eye and ducked. The steel slid through his hair and he slammed an elbow into the wielder's stomach. A boot heel, sticky with blood, just missed his knee and he kicked out in return, sending the gang leader to the ground.

"Bastard!" the leader shrieked, scrambling back to his feet. "Take him OUT!"

Leaning against the alley wall, Darkness laughed.

It was the wounded boy, who could've run to safety but instead grabbed a dangling scalp lock and yanked a knife away from Evan's ribs, that gave Evan the strength to do what he had to.

A great blaze of light flared up from his clenched hands.

The fight ended very quickly after that.

"So He drove out the man," the Dark Adept said, straightening, "and He placed at the east of the garden of Eden cherubims, and a flaming sword which turned every way, to keep the way of the tree of life."

Evan sighed and drew the bar of light back into himself. "If you want a quote," he said wearily, scrubbing his hand across his face. "Think not that I am come to send peace on earth: I came not to send peace but a sword."

"For behold, the darkness shall cover the earth, and gross darkness the people."

"That's only half the verse," Evan pointed out.

The Dark Adept shrugged. "I forget the rest." He moved gracefully out into the alley, confident that the Light had so depleted its power it was not, at present, a threat. That it retained enough power to deal as it had with the gang of toughs had surprised him a little, for he knew that calming the multitudes at the stadium had left it virtually helpless. He could have taken it then, wiped the Light from this world for a time, but it wouldn't have known what hit it and where would be the fun in that? Fortunately, the Light, so predictable, was easy to trap. And, also fortunately, his shock troops had worn the enemy down further. Although he wouldn't have minded if they'd finished the job, it was perhaps better this way. He raised his hand and snapped it forward.

Evan grinned and threw up his arm, his exhausted stance vanishing with the motion. His silver bracelets caught the whip of Dark power and broke it into a thousand harmless splinters. He didn't know why so much of his strength had returned so quickly—perhaps this world had more good in it than he thought—but he rejoiced in the surge of power. The Darkness was in for a nasty shock. Quickly he threw a dozen shining disks and his grin grew wolfish as one got through a hastily erected defense, and the Dark Adept cried out in pain. His eyes began to glow and he advanced palms up . . .

. . . on nothing.

He stood alone in the alley with the wounded boy and the corpse of the boy's friend.

He extended his senses as far as he dared, but the Dark Adept had left no trail to mark its retreat.

Sobs tearing at an innocent's throat drew him back to himself.

Gently, he reached down and touched the boy's shoulder, giving comfort and easing pain.

"Richard's dead," he heard whispered from between bloody fingers.

"Yes."

Hazel eyes peered up at him, lashes matted together into points. "Can you bring him back?"

"No."

"But you made those others," his voice broke, "disappear."

"I did," Evan admitted. "But I cannot defeat death."

The barricade of hands dropped, one falling to rest lightly on Richard's stiffening back. The boy was no more than fifteen, if that. Blood continued to seep slowly from the gash across his cheek. "What are you?" he asked.

"I am a warrior against the Darkness, Matthew." The boy's head jerked up at the sound of his name. "As you have become this night. Your scar will be a warrior's mark. Wear it proudly."

And Matthew knelt alone.

"Wear it proudly, indeed," Mrs. Ruth snorted, stomping out of the shadows. "What bloody help is that? Men!"

Matthew started and spun around. When he saw the short, round shape of the bag lady trudging forward, dragging an overloaded bundle buggy behind her, the terror on his face slid into confusion. "Who . . ."

"Just someone picking up the pieces, bubba. Let me see that face," She pinched his chin and he tried to flinch away, although not from pain; the breath washing down over him was redolent with onions and garlic. "Prompt medical attention to this and it may not scar at all. Warrior's mark. Humph."

"Wha . . ." Matthew tried to look away and found he couldn't. All of a sudden he just didn't have the energy to turn his head. The old woman's eyes were black and deep and he had the strangest sensation of falling.

"We will go out and call the police now. You will tell them how those wicked boys cornered you and your friend and how when I came up the alley they ran away. Maybe they thought I was the Mounties, I don't know."

Matthew let her help him up and, leaning heavily on her shoulder, they made their way toward the street. He saw, he heard: the punks, the knives, Richard falling, the sudden noise of the bag lady's approach, the sneering faces vanishing into the darkness. "Why . . ." He looked down at his hands. They were covered with blood. "Why don't I feel anything?"

"Shock." Mrs. Ruth tightened her arm about his waist. "Don't fall down on me, bubba. I'm too old to pick you up again."

They got to the phone and Matthew somehow managed to dial the emergency number. In a shaking voice he told the story Mrs. Ruth had given him while the bag lady nodded in approval.

Let the policemen look for a gang of no-goods matching those descriptions, she thought, catching Matthew as he slid down the glass of the phone booth. The two of them sagged to the sidewalk together and waited there, listening to the sirens coming closer. *And if they never find them, which they won't, so what. It'll keep them from having to deal with other things. From trying to deal with other things.*

She remembered the laughter of the Darkness and knew he was spreading a shroud over the city. *For a while.*

Chapter Seven

The alarm clock had barely begun to chime when Rebecca stretched out an arm and switched it off. Knowing full well that lingering meant being late for work, and being late for work was very bad, she sighed and swung her legs out of bed. Then she paused, reached back, and stroked a finger gently down the soft skin over Evan's spine.

He stirred but didn't wake.

Rebecca checked the clock and sighed again. Four minutes after five, no time to cuddle. Daru said she had to be in the shower by five after five and as she watched, the four shivered and changed.

The shower washed away the last bits of sleep and she sang quietly to herself as she scrubbed her hair, toweled dry, and reached into the medicine cabinet for the little pink package of pills. Monday morning's pill dropped into the toilet.

She placed one hand just below her navel and with the other reached out and shoved the plastic handle down. "No babies," she murmured quietly to the sound of the water swirling away. And beneath her hand she felt her body agree.

When she returned to the alcove, Evan was watching her through half-closed eyes.

"Wind and rain, Lady," he murmured. " 'Tis but the middle of the night and yet you have risen."

Rebecca giggled. He'd talked that way during lovemaking. She liked it. It sounded like a fairy tale. She didn't always understand it, but she liked it.

"I'm going to work," she explained, pulling on clothes. "The first batch of muffins has to be ready by seven o'clock."

"My life shall be bleak without you."

Even Rebecca's literal mind recognized this as blatant flattery. "Silly." She grinned, drew a fingernail down the exposed sole of his foot, and laughed as he whipped it away. Slipping her own feet into thongs, she gathered up her fresh uniforms and went into the other room. Her red bag was under the kitchen table, the black dagger still inside it. Carefully, she reached in, grabbed the rolled towel, and lifted it out. She could feel the edges of the weapon even through the layers of terry cloth.

Now what? Her eyes lit on the shelf over the television. it would be safe there because nobody could touch it accidentally; they'd have to make an effort.

Pleased with herself for thinking of it, she pushed her plush dragon to one side and put the towel on the shelf. Then she packed her uniforms, took her keys off the hook by the door, and went to say good-bye to Evan.

He roused enough to twine his fingers in her damp hair and pull her face down to his. "Be careful, Lady," he whispered, "for Darkness waits."

"I'll be careful," she agreed against his mouth, took another kiss for the road, and left. *He tastes different in the morning,* she thought, *more like apricots and less like apples.*

Outside, the air was clear and still. The early morning light had a fragile feeling to it. Rebecca paused beneath the chestnut tree, looked up, and remembered.

"Oh, Alexander." She sagged against the trunk and her eyes filled with tears. She'd just realized, really realized, she'd never see her friend again.

Five thirty, called the cathedral bells, still blocks away. Five thirty.

Rebecca straightened. "I know," she sniffed. "I'm coming."

At ten minutes to six, slightly out of breath, she ran down the stairs and into the cafeteria kitchen. Waving at the elderly woman already at work wrapping danishes, she crossed into the locker room, dressed, and went to find Lena.

As expected, the supervisor was in her office and Rebecca began the morning ritual.

"Good morning, Lena."

"Morning, puss." Lena looked up from her coffee and smiled.

"Would you fix my hair, please?"

"Don't I always? C'mere."

Rebecca perched on the indicated corner of the desk, handing Lena a brush and an elastic.

Balancing her cigarette on the edge of the chipped saucer she used for an ashtray, the older woman shook her head at the state of Rebecca's curls. "You forgot to brush this morning."

"Never mind. Did you have a good weekend?"

Rebecca's memory traveled from Alexander to Evan. "Not exactly," she admitted. "But it got better at the end."

"Want to tell me about it? Tilt your head, puss."

Rebecca tilted obediently. "Well," she said at last, "the little man who lived in the tree outside the building where I live got killed, then Roland and me got attacked by a lawn, then Ivan the ghost went for help, then Evantarin came through from the Light and he stayed with me."

"Evantarin stayed with you? Who is Evantarin?" Lena snapped the elastic around Rebecca's newly tamed hair with unnecessary force. She worried about the girl spending her weekends with no supervision and wondered why Social Services didn't have her safely in a Home somewhere.

"He said to call him Evan and he's sort of an angel, I guess. He glows and he came to fight Darkness." She reached up and touched her netted ponytail, hoping, as she always did, that her hair could breathe while it was bound so tightly. "Am I done?"

"You're done," Lena told her, relieved Rebecca's visitor had turned out to be just another figment of an uncontrolled imagination. "And you'd better get started. Those muffins won't bake themselves."

"'Cause if they did I'd be out of a job," Rebecca replied seriously. She liked it when she knew the proper thing to say. Gathering up her brush, she headed out into the kitchen.

"What are you grinning about?" asked the last woman of the shift to arrive, sticking her head in the office as Rebecca skipped away.

Lena took a long pull on her cigarette. "Rebecca has an angel visiting her." The smoke trickled back out through her nose. "His name is Evantarin and he's come to fight Darkness."

"Yeah?" The other woman's gaze dropped to the newspaper she held and the headline, *Man Shoots Neighbor; Claims "The Yuppie Son-of-a-Bitch Deserved to Die."* "Well, I wish him luck, he's gonna need it."

*   *   *

"And what are you doing up so early in the morning?"

Roland turned from the bookcase and shrugged. "I couldn't sleep, Uncle Tony, so I thought I'd look something up. Do you mind?"

"Mind? Hell, no." He peered at the book in his nephew's hands. "An encyclopedia eh? I don't suppose you're looking up something pertaining to gainful employment?"

"Not exactly." Roland closed the book and slid it back on the shelf. "I got called a bard this weekend, I just wanted to see what it meant. This wasn't very helpful."

"What do you expect?" Tony asked, doing up the last few buttons on his work shirt. "We got that set at the grocery store, $1.99 with every five dollar purchase. Siddown and have a cup of coffee with me and I'll tell you all I know about bards before I leave for the shop."

Roland followed his uncle into the kitchen and watched him fill two mugs from the automatic coffee machine on the counter. "How do *you* know about bards?" he asked, fishing the cream out of the fridge.

"Books," Tony told him, handing him a mug and waving him into a seat. "I read the right kind of books. That's the problem with you kids today, you don't read the right books. You need more history and less of this Hollywood adultery crap. Now, for starters, a bard was more than just a musician." He studied the cream swirling into his coffee and added two heaping spoonfuls of sugar. "Where was I? Oh, yeah . . . A bard used music the way a wizard would use magical spells, using his music to influence reality . . ."

Spellbound, Roland listened, the events of the weekend having banished disbelief.

". . . course not every musician was a bard. It took a special talent and years of study. Seven years studying, seven years practicing, and seven years playing is how I think it went." Tony snorted. "Twenty-one years. And I thought a five-year electrical apprenticeship went on forever. So anyway," he stood and put his empty mug in the sink, "you're what . . . twenty-eight? You started with this nonsense at about fourteen; hell, you've barely done your second seven years."

Don't get cocky . . . Mrs. Ruth's words came back to him and finally made sense.

"And even if I believed all that stuff—which I'm not saying I do or I don't—if you're a bard, things have gone downhill since the old days. Johnny Cash, now that was a bard. You, you'd be better off if you got a job."

Roland started, his thoughts had wandered miles away. "Uh, I think I've got one."

"Good." Tony paused at the door. "Try to see this one through to the end for a change."

As the door closed, Roland studied the guitar calluses on his fingertips and wondered whose voice kept muttering sepulchrally in his head that the end was near.

"It's not like Michelle to be late."

"Everyone's late sooner or later," her companion pointed out philosophically.

"Yeah, but Michelle's gone gaga over one of the guests, taking a little extra time to clean his room if you know what I mean. You'd think she'd be here early with bells on."

"Come off it. Sweet, little, innocent Michelle?"

"Well, sweet, little, innocent Michelle could hop into every bed she makes for all I care." The key jammed in the lock and it took vigorous jiggling to free it. "Just as long as she's on time for work. I don't want to get stuck doing her half of the shift as well as my own. That's weird, it's unlocked already." The door swung open and she groped around the corner for the light. "Smells like a toilet in here. And there's something all over the floor."

"Oh, no! Look at this mess."

Brushes, cleansers, shampoo, and soap fanned out from an overturned cleaning cart.

And then they looked up.

Dangling above the cart, her tongue black and protruding, was Michelle, a curtain sash tight around her neck and great scratches down her throat where she'd tried to tear it away.

Hands behind his head, the Dark Adept listened to the distant sounds of screaming.

"I might as well stay in bed," he mused. "Breakfast is likely to be delayed."

"Master?"

His gaze flickered off the ceiling and down to the shadow squatting like a stain against the blue sheets. "Get off the bed," he commanded coldly. "If I have to tell you again . . ."

"Not again, Master." The shadow moved from the bed to the small table beside it. "Master, the Adept of the Light . . . I saw, I heard."

He frowned, remembering the pain the Light had caused him. He had expected to win and the pain had been greater for that. "What did you see?" he asked, his voice cold. "What did you hear?"

The shadow quivered at its master's tone, but it knew better than to hesitate. "There are three, Master. A man and two women. They help and they know they help the Light. They hunt you, Master."

"Fools." He stretched and then worked the fingers of his left hand into the muscles of his right shoulder. A white pucker marked the perfect flesh and the wound, although it had healed in the hours since their confrontation, still throbbed. Four nights and five days until he could open the gate and this world had suddenly ceased to be amusing. Not for the first time, he wished his original passage through the barrier had been made closer to Midsummer Night, but the barrier had to be passed when the opportunity arose and Midsummer Night could not be moved. His entire body convulsed with the memory of the crossing.

"How did you get so strong, my shining brother?" he wondered aloud when his breathing had steadied and the sweat that beaded his skin had dried. "After all you'd been through, you should have fallen into my hands." The Light, like the Darkness, could draw strength from many things, and the Light had found friends. "Give me their essences!" he demanded suddenly.

"Yes, Master." The shadow flattened to paper thinness against the polished oak. "But I hold only two, the man and one woman. The other was . . . was . . . was too . . ."

"You failed." The Dark Adept waved away the shadow's excuses.

"But, Master, she was . . ." The shadow's protest became a howl and it snapped through several shapes until it lay pulsating weakly and wearing no shape at all.

"I said, you failed."

"Yes, Master." It barely had a voice remaining.

"Give me the two you took." He showed his teeth as the shadow slid over to his outstretched hand. "And we will see, my pretty adversary, what we can do about removing you from your strength without leading you straight to me."

*   *   *

Daru threaded her way through the rabbit warren of overflowing cubicles that made up the Department of Social Services, a computer printout in one hand and a bagel balanced precariously on a cup of coffee in the other. She sidestepped a sullen teenager without looking up, muttered a greeting of sorts to a colleague, and scowled at the list of names and numbers she held. Things couldn't possibly have gotten this bad over the weekend. Could they?

She turned into her own tiny square of office space, scooped a stack of file folders off her chair, and searched, without much hope of success, for a place to put them. Sighing, she piled them with others on the floor, grabbed at the falling bagel she'd forgotten she still held, and splashed coffee across an overdue report.

"Ms. Sastri?"

"What?"

The young woman backed up a step at the expression on Daru's face. "Uh, Mr. Graham just went home sick with that flu bug—he threw up in the elevator, said he felt fine until the fifth floor then, blammo—and Ms. Freedman and Mr. Wu both called and won't be in." She offered the armload of files she carried. "The director says you're to deal with these." Backing up another step would take her out of the cubicle, so she settled for leaning away and smiling nervously. "Don't shoot me, Ms. Sastri, I'm only the piano player."

Muttering under her breath, Daru took the papers and set them with exaggerated care on the desk. "Is that all?" she growled.

"Uh, no. I'm supposed to remind you, you're due in court in twenty minutes. But you probably knew that . . ." she added, exiting a lot more quickly than she'd entered.

Daru sank into her chair and buried her face in her hands. In less than thirty seconds, her case load had tripled.

"I'll just finish up what has to be done and take the rest of the week off." She mocked herself and her blithe promise of the night before. She should've known it wasn't going to be that easy.

"Uh, Ms. Sastri, police on line one. Apparently they picked up a derelict with your name and this number on a card in his pocket."

It was never that easy.

"I thought you said you'd be early?"

"Yeah, well I got delayed." Roland pushed past the Adept and into Rebecca's apartment, Tom following close on his heels. He leaned Patience gently against the wall, the motion obviously carefully controlled as he practically quivered with suppressed energy. "First, the subway took forever to arrive." Unable to remain still, he began to pace, arms waving for emphasis. "Six—not one, not two, but six—trains went by going the other way. The platform got packed. Some turkey dropped a lit cigarette on my case. I barely avoided going up in smoke, and then I got yelled at for flicking the damned thing to the floor. Okay." He spread his hands and took a deep breath. "I can deal with that. So the train finally comes and we're crammed in like sardines, then, between stations, in the middle of nowhere, we stop and the lights go out. A kid starts to scream and the fat, smelly lady behind me grabs onto my ass. I try to get out of her reach, step on a foot not my own, and a riot nearly breaks out. Are you smiling?"

Evan brushed his hair back off his face and schooled his expression. "I wouldn't do that." It hadn't exactly been a smile.

Roland scowled, stomped along another two lengths of the room, and aimed a kick at the cat. He missed by a considerable margin, but Tom hissed and dove under the couch. Irrationally, Roland felt better.

"The cat had no part in your troubles," Evan pointed out gently.

"You don't know that," Roland snarled. "He was waiting for me at the corner."

"I sent him to watch for you."

"Oh."

"I think you owe him an apology."

"Forget it." Roland stopped pacing and glared. "I am not apologizing to a cat."

Evan merely looked at him.

After a moment, Roland's gaze fell.

"Oh, all right," he muttered and turned his head vaguely in Tom's direction. "I'm sorry I kicked at you."

Safe under the couch, Tom growled.

Only Evan's presence kept Roland from growling back. He straightened out the fingers that had turned to fists and made a conscious effort to calm down. So he'd had an irritating morning. That didn't give him the right to make everyone else's day miserable. He could feel the weight of Evan's regard and he let it sink down over him, smoothing out jagged edges and filling in gouged nerves.

"I guess I'll laugh about this later," he sighed.

Evan grinned.

"I said *later.*" The grin remained and Roland found himself returning it. He couldn't help it; a morning's worth of petty annoyances just couldn't stand before the strength of Evantarin, Adept of the Light, which, when he came to think about it, was a damned good thing considering what they'd be facing later on.

Evan's gaze grew speculative as the silence stretched between them and Roland felt himself begin to flush, suddenly very aware that Evan wore only his jeans. The skin of the Adept's chest and stomach stretched smooth and golden over lean lines of muscle, and Roland's hand slowly rose toward it.

Oh, no! Not that, too. Not this morning. Calling up the last of his earlier irritation, Roland forced his hand back down, wet his lips, and asked curtly, "Have you had breakfast?"

In the moment Evan took before answering, Roland realized that should the Adept force the issue he'd be unable to resist and his entire sexual orientation would crumble. He wasn't sure how he felt when Evan merely turned to the table and pointed proudly at the toaster.

"I made toast."

He sounded so much like Rebecca that Roland allowed himself to relax. "Well, put some clothes on and we'll grab coffee before we start."

"Sounds good." Evan nodded and went into the bed alcove.

Roland followed Evan's progress by the soft music of his silver bracelets. He wondered if he took them off to sleep. Which led him to wonder if he took them off to . . . *Stop that!* he railed at himself. *You are developing the worst case of gutter mind.*

Evan dressed was a lot easier to deal with and the two of them gathered up the sketches and left the apartment, with Tom slipping out just as they were about to close the door.

"So where do we start?" Roland asked as the three of them moved down the hall.

"At the top," Evan told him. "The Darkness is every bit as predictable as it accuses the Light of being. And besides, would you stay in anything less than the best if you didn't have to?"

"You aren't," Roland pointed out, nearly tripping over Tom who darted suddenly ahead and down the stairs.

"Haven't you heard that friendship buys a better bed than money?"

Roland snorted. "That sounds like it came out of a fortune cookie."

"Ever wonder where fortune cookie fortunes come from?"

"Give me a break."

"No, really, they're our second biggest export."

"I know I'm going to regret this . . ." They stepped into the sunshine and Roland squinted up at his companion. "What's your first?"

"Light beer."

Roland rolled his eyes.

"Get it, Light beer. Light . . ." Evan sighed. "I'll work on it."

"You're sure you haven't see him?"

The woman on the desk at the King George Hotel shook her head. "No, I . . ."

"Think carefully, Sheila," Evan broke in, his voice pitched to elicit confidences. "This is more important than you can know."

Roland spent an instant wondering how Evan had known the woman's name, then he saw the brass name tag pinned to her uniform blazer. *Score one for the real world,* he thought.

She studied the sketch again, chewing the pale gloss from her bottom lip. "No, I'm sure I'd remember if I'd seen him."

"Damn," Roland cursed under his breath. "Strike seven." They hadn't quite started at the top—the King George most definitely—for there were a number of lesser hotels between it and Rebecca's apartment. It had occurred to Roland when they were starting out that they might have a little trouble getting hotel employees to cooperate, given that they had no official reason for their request, but Evan's presence seemed to inspire everyone from the manager to the cleaning staff to help. And in every hotel so far someone—male, female, young, old; it didn't seem to matter—had slipped the Adept a private phone number and the whispered confidence that perhaps later they might remember more.

"But you see," Sheila continued, handing the piece of paper back to Evan and smiling shyly, "I've been on vacation for the last two weeks. Let me just get one of the others."

"Thank you."

Her eyes went dewy at Evan's gratitude and Roland had to bite down on his tongue to keep from saying something cutting as she went into the office. He sincerely hoped he didn't look quite so soppy when Evan smiled at him. That he rather suspected he did, did nothing to improve his mood.

Unnoticed, a bellhop moved from the end of the marble counter and headed toward the elevators. Mr. Aphotic would want to know there were people looking for him. He'd probably be grateful enough to hand over another packet. *And another packet,* the bellhop's pale eyes gleamed, *would get me through the next few days on top of the world.*

"Jack," PC Patton nudged her partner. "The two at the desk."

"That's them," he agreed. "Fits the description to a T."

They started across the lobby.

"Uh, Evan."

Evan looked up. He'd been following the pattern of the marble, fingertips stroking the cool stone.

"I think we've got a problem." Roland had been approached by too many cops during too many years on the street not to know when the minions of the law were bearing down with him in mind. The man and the woman advancing toward them didn't look angry but neither did they look pleased.

"Can we have a word with you, gentlemen?" It wasn't quite a question. It wasn't quite a command.

Evan inclined his head graciously. "Certainly, officers."

Somehow feeling as if she'd just been granted a boon, PC Patton led the way to a quiet corner. They'd been off shift for barely eight hours, were beginning a double thanks to that damned flu bug, and she had no wish to be patronized by some long-haired juvenile delinquent no matter how pretty he was. That she recognized how pretty he was, and that a direct look from his stormy gray eyes caused her heart to dance, pissed her off further. "They told us at the Ramada you two were showing around a picture. Let's see it."

Roland considered the reaction he'd likely invoke by asking for a warrant, decided against it, and watched silently as Evan handed over the sketch.

PC Brooks opened the file folder he carried and the two constables compared the identikit picture to this new one.

"Accurate to about ninety percent," he murmured.

"Where did you get this?" PC Patton demanded, waving the sketch.

"I drew it," Evan told her mildly.

"Don't get smart with me, punk," she snapped. "This man's a suspect in a murder and if you're withholding information I'll have your ass behind bars so fast your hair will curl."

Roland didn't know whether Evan was capable of lying but he didn't think this was exactly a good time to find out. "We got it from the same place you got yours," he said quickly. To his relief, Evan kept silent.

Both of PC Brooks' eyebrows rose. "The old lady . . ." he began but broke off as his partner glared at him.

The old lady? Roland repeated to himself. *The old . . .* "Mrs. Ruth." The expressions on both faces told him he'd guessed correctly. He could almost feel the tension ease, so he assumed they had no idea that it was a guess. They still weren't happy, but they no longer fingered handcuffs.

"I don't know why she came to you two," PC Patton growled. "Whether you think you're some kind of vigilantes or what." She crumbled the drawing of the Dark Adept into a tight ball in one fist. "But stay out of this. Do you hear me?"

"We hear you," Evan said softly.

She jerked her head toward the exit. "Now get!"

They got.

After the air conditioning in the lobby, the heat outside hit them like a solid wall, pulling sweat out on their skins in seconds. The trapped exhaust from thousands of cars filled the air with a grayish-yellow haze bitter to breathe. Although two blocks away on Yonge Street brightly colored summer crowds surged back and forth, here the sidewalks were blessedly empty.

"I don't believe we got out of that," Roland marveled as they walked down the three shallow steps and away from the hotel.

Evan shrugged and shoved his hands. behind one studded leather belt. "We were a complication, with paperwork they'd rather avoid, so I pushed on that. It wouldn't benefit the Light if we spent the next few hours at a police station making statements none of them would believe."

Roland shook his head; if only it were always so easy. "Let me guess. You don't ask the cops for help because none of them have the ability to See?"

"That's right. And the ones who do, get blinded or ground up and spit out by the system pretty fast, the system being interested in Justice not Truth."

Heavy philosophy for a man who just learned to make toast, Roland thought, leaning on a newspaper box, carefully keeping bare skin off the hot metal. "Now what?"

"We wait. The police will leave, the Darkness can easily shield itself from them, and then we . . ." He trailed off, his eyes focusing on the newspaper.

"We go in and talk to the other clerks?"

"No. There's no need."

Roland turned and squinted at the paper, trying to find what had brought that note into Evan's voice. *Police Hunt for Murder Suspect Intensifies* read the largest headline. *But we knew that.* He wondered how Mrs. Ruth had been able to give the police a description of the Dark Adept and then he saw the smaller type, almost hidden by the glare of sunlight on the box.

Chambermaid Suicides at King George and it drove the question from his mind.

"He's here," Evan said, his expression now stern and cold. "Come on. There has to be another door, one the police can't see from the desk."

"It's a big hotel, Evan. How will you know what floor he's on? What room?"

"Now that I know he's here," his lips pulled back to show his teeth, "I can find his room."

They found a side door, marginally smaller than the ornate brass and glass monstrosity leading into the lobby, and slipped through it, managing to reach the fire stairs undetected.

"He'll have shielded himself in the lobby," Evan explained as they climbed, "but I doubt he bothered on his own floor. He'll have left a residue."

As they peered out through every door, Roland had visions of sticky tarlike trails of Darkness ground into the plush cream colored carpets but when Evan pulled him out onto the sixth floor and said, "This is it," he didn't see a thing; the carpet, and the salmon pink walls were unmarked. Then Evan reached back and brushed a hand across his eyes and he almost lost his lunch.

The Adept moved without hesitation down the corridor, Roland following behind, his gaze not dropping from the small of Evan's back. The glimpses he got with his peripheral vision were bad enough. When Evan stopped, Roland looked up. The brass number on the door read, "666."

"Well, at least the Dark has a sense of history," he murmured under his breath, wondering if the number was an accident, a joke, or a warning. If he were watching this in a movie, he'd be screaming, *No! Don't open that door!* about now. A sense of, well, evil, for lack of a better word, seeped through the wood and paint. He swallowed and wet his lips, nervous but not afraid; the whole thing seemed too unreal to be frightening.

Evan laid his palm just above the lock and the door swung silently open.

Darkness lay everywhere in the suite. It hung in ebony spider webs from the ceiling and pooled in viscous puddles on the floor. Great moldy patches grew from the walls and in some of them Roland thought he saw faces. He could hear the hum of the air conditioner, but the room still stank of stagnant water and things less savory.

"Gone," Evan growled, turning around slowly in the center of the suite.

Roland threw up an arm to cover his eyes as Evan flared and the Light burned all traces of Darkness from the room. As much as he wanted the whole thing to be over, relief over the postponement of Armageddon made his knees weak. And then he heard the elevator open and a familiar voice echo down the hall.

"For chrisakes, Jack, we don't need backup to question a suspect. Besides, if he tries anything, I'll *gladly* shoot him."

Now he was frightened. Cops, he understood.

He grabbed Evan by the back of the T-shirt and yanked him close, filling him in on their situation with a few choice words. Evan ignored him and Roland thought of a few other choice words he wanted to deliver even though he didn't have the time.

Evan appeared disoriented and the voices were getting closer. The hall, Roland remembered, stretched straight and wide from the room to the elevator. No possibility of slipping out without being noticed. Desperately, he scanned the suite. The bedroom or the bathroom? No, they'd be trapped. Behind furniture? Nothing big enough that wasn't right up against a wall.

Maybe they should just try to brazen it out.

"The door's open."

In the following silence, the sound of holsters opening was unnaturally loud and completely unmistakable.

Maybe not.

Roland shoved an unresisting Evan into the only hiding place they had time to reach; the coat closet near the door. During the next few seconds of noise and confusion, he closed his eyes and prayed.

It might not have helped, but it certainly didn't hurt. When things calmed down, the police stood in the center of the sitting room with their backs to the closet.

"I think he's flown," PC Brooks said softly, his head cocked to catch the smallest sound.

Roland tried to get his heart to beat a little less loudly. Any minute now, any second, he knew those blue clad backs would turn and it would all be over; they'd be up as accessories to murder and the Darkness would move on unopposed. A small voice in his head cried "Shame!" that he cared more for the former, but Roland ignored it. He dug his elbow into Evan's ribs and again got no response.

"I think you're right," PC Patton agreed. "But let's make real sure. Come on."

The bedroom. I don't believe it, they're going into the bedroom! Roland got a tight grip on Evan's arm and laid his other hand against the inside of the closet door. The tiny opening he'd left limited his line of sight and although he saw the police starting toward the bedroom, he had no way of knowing if they'd actually entered. He forced himself to wait, watching his watch count off fifteen seconds—the longest fifteen seconds of his life—and then he moved, dragging Evan out of the closet, out of the suite, and out of the hallway, not stopping until the two of them stood, reasonably safe, back in the stairwell.

No shots. No shouts. No sounds of pursuit.

Relief hit so hard his knees almost buckled and he sagged against the bannister, eyes closed, waiting for his entire body to stop trembling with adrenaline reaction.

"Roland? Are you all right?"

"Am I . . ." His eyes snapped open and he slammed Evan up against the wall, his fingers digging into the Adept's shoulders. "Where the fuck were you? I needed you and you buzzed out!"

"I was searching for our enemy," Evan explained calmly, acknowledging but not reacting to Roland's anger. "I thought I had a trail. I was wrong. How did you need me?"

"While you were gone, the cops showed up! I thought you said the Darkness could shield himself from them?"

Evan managed to shrug, despite Roland's hold on him. "He

must have let the shields drop when he left." Then his expression softened. "How did you need me?" he repeated quietly.

Roland's voice grew shrill and it bounced around the stairwell like a swarm of angry bees. "I needed you to get us out!"

"But *you* got us out." Evan reached up and covered Roland's hands with his own. "Thank you." He smiled.

Roland tried to snatch his hands away, but his arms refused to cooperate. He could feel the warmth of Evan's skin through the thin cotton T-shirt and that warmth began to spread, drying his mouth and snatching his breath away before it did him any good. It moved lower, igniting an answering warmth in him.

"Evan, I . . ." He didn't know what he wanted to say and could only stare helplessly at a pulse in the golden throat, afraid to meet Evan's eyes.

"There is never shame in loving, or in wanting to love," Evan said softly, lifting his hands and freeing Roland's. "Nor is there harm in wanting without having if you are not so inclined." One eyebrow arched. "Although your body may try to convince you otherwise."

Roland felt his ears turn red, his body's reaction all too evident, against the crotch of his jeans. *The flesh is willing, but the spirit is freaked.*

"Being wanted does not hurt my feelings or insult me." Evan smiled again but much more gently, without the blazing heat of before. "Rather the opposite, actually."

Wetting his lips, Roland managed a smile of sorts in return, his arms falling slowly to his sides. "All I want to do is beat your head against a wall." His voice was a little shaky, but not so much it couldn't be ignored. "You left me to save our asses."

Evan brushed a shock of hair back out of his eyes. "And you justified my faith in you," he pointed out, respecting Roland's need to pretend, at least externally, that nothing had just happened.

"Well," Roland lifted his chin and squared his shoulders, "let's get out of here before the cops decide to search the stairwell." Evan nodded and Roland started down the first of the six flights. He wondered if Evan knew how close he'd come that time to tossing aside twenty-eight years of social and sexual conditioning. What had Evan said: *there is no harm in wanting without having.* He hoped the Adept was right; he might be able to come to terms with the wanting but the having would be more than he could handle. On the other hand, less than twenty-four hours ago, he'd denied the wanting, too. Did that mean that twenty-four hours from now . . .

A middle-aged man in a maintenance uniform came through the fourth floor fire door and plodded upward past Roland, past Evan. Just within earshot, obviously intending to be heard, he muttered, "Damn queers in the stairwell."

If he had anything more to add, it drowned in Roland's laughter.

Chapter Eight

"But where's he gone?" Rebecca asked, handing out tall glasses filled with an equal amount of pale green liquid and ice cubes.

Roland took a cautious sip and grimaced; iced herbal tea. Wonderful. He'd meant to pick up a couple of cans of pop on the way back to the apartment and now he was paying for his memory lapse.

"Has he gone to another hotel?" Rebecca settled to the floor, her back up against the couch, her eyes on Evan who sat perched on the window ledge.

"It's unlikely," Evan told her, taking a long drink with, Roland noticed, every evidence of enjoyment. "He's probably gone to a private house."

Her eyes widened. "But who would want to have him?"

Evan sighed. "You'd be surprised at how many people would love to have him, Lady. He can make himself very agreeable."

"Let me use your guest room and I'll cut you in for shares when my side rules the world?" Roland guessed.

Evan nodded. "Something like that." He turned and looked out the window, murmuring softly to the night, "And the devil took him up onto an exceeding high mountain, and sheweth him all the kingdoms of the world, and the glory of them; and said, All these things I will give thee, if thou wilt fall down and worship me." He sighed and faced into the room again, his eyes shadowed. "He won't, of course, give up anything, but mortals never seem to realize it. And what can I offer to fight that?"

"Your sparkling personality?" Roland suggested. Both Evan's brows rose and he stared at Roland, who only shrugged. "I hate to see an Adept of the Light feeling sorry for himself," he explained. He wondered for an instant if he'd gone too far, if he'd misjudged

Evan's mood. He didn't think so, he'd seen that expression in his mirror often enough to recognize it when he saw it again.

Evan frowned, opened his mouth to speak, seemed to reconsider, and suddenly smiled.

Roland relaxed muscles he hadn't consciously tensed.

Rebecca tilted her head and chewed on a bit of hair, not entirely certain she understood what had just passed between the two men. "I believe in you, Evan," she offered, reaching out to touch him gently on the knee.

He covered her hand with his. "That gives me both strength and joy, Lady."

Roland looked at their two hands lying against the faded denim of Evan's jeans, fingers intertwined, and reached for his guitar. He had to give a voice to the music that he heard.

The phone rang.

"Damnitalltofuckingshit!"

Rebecca jumped and sat blinking at Roland in astonishment. *She* disliked the jangling bell that broke the peace into pieces. She hadn't realized others felt the same.

The phone rang again.

"It's probably Daru," she pointed out, dragging the phone from under the couch. "She always calls on Monday nights. I always plug the phone in the wall on Monday afternoons when I get home from work. Hello?" She dropped the receiver away from her mouth. "It's Daru."

Roland buried his head in his hands, as the music danced tantalizingly out of reach. "Of course it is," he muttered. "Who else?"

"She can't come tonight."

"What?" He lifted his head. "Give me the phone." Almost snatching it from Rebecca's hand he barked, "What do you mean you can't come tonight? We're trying to save the world here, not fucking get together for bridge!"

"Fine." Daru's voice worked like sharpened steel on the words. "You do that. You go save the world. I'm trying to save the people on it!"

Roland barely got the receiver away from his ear in time as Daru slammed down her end so hard it could be clearly heard throughout the room. Even Tom looked up from his meal. "She, uh, can't come tonight," he said, hanging up.

"But I already told you that."

"Yeah." He pushed the phone back under the couch. "I know."

Rebecca swiveled around to face Evan again. "What will we do without Daru?" she asked anxiously. All their plans had been made for four people.

"Roland will have to come with us."

"To see the littles?"

"Yes."

"No." Roland raised his hands as Evan's gray eyes and Rebecca's brown ones fixed on him. *They've the same kind of single-minded intensity*, he realized. *Once you've got their attention it's a little overwhelming.* Until Evan arrived, he'd never understood how Rebecca's simplicity could be strength. Now he wondered how he could have missed it. "I'm not spending the evening talking to things in bushes and down sewers. I'll stick to the original plan and see what I can hear on the street."

"I don't like you being alone," Evan said, making one of his disconcerting shifts into Evantarin, Adept of the Light.

"Daru's alone," Roland reminded him.

"So why put two of you in danger."

"Is Daru in danger?" Rebecca demanded.

"Alone, we are all easier prey for the Darkness."

"Fortune cookie platitudes again," Roland scoffed.

Evan's eyes narrowed. "But truth nevertheless."

"Look, if I'm alone, too, Daru's chances are fifty percent better because he might just come after me."

They were both on their feet now, bodies leaning forward, chins up, and teeth showing.

"And if he does?"

"You can fight him for my body."

"That's not funny, Roland!"

"It wasn't meant to be."

"You're not supposed to be fighting each other." Rebecca pushed between them. "Stop it. Now." She glared from one to the other, her expression daring them to continue.

Evan spoke first. "I'm sorry," he said softly. "I don't want you hurt."

Roland drew a long shuddering breath. "I don't want me hurt either. But I've been with you all day. I need some time to myself." His voice begged Evan to understand.

Understanding, unexpectedly, came from Rebecca. "Caring for

someone makes more bits and pieces than you can deal with sometimes. Doesn't it?"

Caring? Was that it? Is there more here than just sexual attraction? He might be able to handle caring. He managed a grin, a nod, and a shaky, "Yes."

Evan sighed but all he said was, "Be careful."

The heat of the day seeped back out of concrete and asphalt, keeping the temperature high even though night had fallen. A hundred heads bobbed up and down as the current on the sidewalk swept them from one patch of bright light to the next, and a dozen different stations blared from car radios as drivers cruised up and down the strip. Sweat and perfume mingled with car exhaust into the distinctive smell of a summer night in the city.

The streets feel different. As Roland joined the surging crowds heading south on Yonge, he could feel the difference against his skin. Others felt it, too, for the laughter had a brittle edge and the crowds surged back and forth with a kind of jerky desperation.

You don't want to know, he told them silently. *You really don't want to know what it is.* Trouble was, *he* knew. Knew that somewhere in the city Darkness moved. And should it move on him tonight, he'd be facing it alone. He searched the faces that swept past, in and out of his vision in a kaleidoscope of eyes and mouths and noses, cheeks and chins, smiles and frowns, brown, black, white, yellow in a thousand combinations.

Fuck it! He dropped his gaze to the ground, his stomach tying itself in knots. *I wouldn't know him if I saw him.*

Rebecca was with Evan. Daru was nice and safe in her office. He was all alone.

"I must be out of my fucking mind," he muttered.

A pair of teenage girls stared and swung wide around him.

He considered stopping and busking for a while at Gerrard but the smell from the pizza place combined with his case of nerves had him swallowing convulsively, so he kept moving south. At Edward, an old man sat playing the accordion, badly, and at Dundas, at the north end of the Eaton Centre, an entire four-piece band, complete with amplifiers, raised the ambient noise at the corner by about a hundred decibels. The lyrics they screamed tied sex to pain and Roland tried not to listen as he pushed his way through the gathered crowd. He passed junkies and rummies, runaways and hookers, heading for the relative security of his usual spot at Queen.

Across the street, he saw two kids, no more than fifteen, buy a small package from an older man in a black leather jacket. They did it openly, knowing no one would bother interfering. Roland gritted his teeth and walked on. *And I'm one of the good guys.* He tightened his grip until the plastic handle of the case cut into his palm. *And we wonder who asked the Darkness in. Every fucking one of us.* Anger, even anger at himself, made him feel stronger, so he held onto it.

A man stood on Roland's corner. Long dirty hair hung lank and greasy down his back, bare feet stuck out from under stained and filthy jeans, and a dark red cross, recently painted, gleamed damply on his soiled T-shirt. "The end," he cried, his voice surprisingly deep and resonant, "is near!"

"I don't need this," Roland groaned. "I really don't need this. Not tonight." Eyes forward, refusing to see the crazy, he stepped over a puddle of vomit—the smell lost in a hundred others—and headed for the other spot he frequented.

The large open area at the Bay Street end of the Simpson's Building held a dispirited looking flower seller, a hotdog vendor, and a steady stream of tourists heading for both old and new City Hall. Roland set his guitar case carefully on the pavement, lifted out Patience, and left the case lying open. He checked the tuning, watched a young woman walk by, her breasts moving almost languidly under her loose tank top, and, suddenly melancholy, began softly playing "If."

While he sang, voice and fingers on automatic, passing conversations flowed over and through him.

". . . doesn't start until nine-forty, I checked the paper."

"Of course, he says it was just a business lunch."

"Look Marge, I'll make a deal with you. You let me keep the beard and you can get your ears pierced."

". . . coming on top of that chambermaid's suicide this morning, too."

The two men were walking slowly and Roland strained his ears to catch the rest.

"Well this wasn't a suicide. Just some junkie who scored big."

"A bellboy shoots most of a gram of heroin into his arm and it's an accident? *I* think there's something going on at the King George."

"Yeah? But who can tell with junkies?"

Who indeed? Roland mused, letting the song trail off. Had they seen the bellboy that afternoon? Talked to him perhaps? Could they have saved him? He pushed those thoughts away and tried to bury his feelings in sarcasm. *At least he's marking his trail.* It didn't work. Sarcasm was too frail a crutch to support the load he carried now. *And we're always one body behind.*

"And just what do you think you're doing?"

Roland turned and came guitar to belly with one of the fattest cops he'd ever seen. The guy looked like he'd stepped out of a bad Burt Reynolds comedy right down to the little piggy eyes gleaming out from within folds of fat.

"I asked you a question, boy."

He even sounded like he came out of a bad Burt Reynolds comedy, but Roland felt no urge to laugh. Give these types a nightstick and the right to use it, and they did.

"Is there a problem, officer?" He kept his voice level, calm, empty of any possibility of insult. If Darkness had sent this man, it had barely taken a touch.

"If there wasn't a problem, would I be wasting my time talking to you? You're blocking the sidewalk. Move on." And under the first layer of words, ran the second. *Go on, you no-good hippy, argue. You aren't worth shit and we both know it.*

Years ago, Roland might have protested. Pedestrian traffic moved easily around him and no one had complained. Years ago, Roland had ended up spending the night in jail with three busted ribs. He squatted, laid Patience away, and snapped the guitar case closed.

The cop stood, watching him, until the curve of Bay Street hid his bulk.

With the roar of the subway vibrating the entire western slope of the Don Valley, Evan and Rebecca crawled through a hole clipped in the fence and scrambled up under the massive cement support of the Bloor Viaduct.

"Look at the plants!" Rebecca yelled over the shriek of the rails.

The plant life covered the ground with luxuriant greens in spite of the almost constant noise and vibration from the Viaduct above and the exhaust fumes wafting up from Bayview Avenue below.

Even the recent scorching temperatures seemed to have had no effect on it.

"The troll takes care of it. It's what he does." The subway passed and her last word rang out into relative silence. She giggled and added in a lower voice, "He takes care of the bridge, too."

Evan glanced up the length of the huge pillar to where steel girders angled away into the night then he dropped his gaze back to the ground. The troll was their last hope for information. None of the gray folk they'd met and warned had been able to offer anything in return. Many had simply shrugged the warnings off. Most of the gray folk in this city were young, with scant concern for anything outside their immediate sphere. The older, more traditional creatures, were few and growing fewer.

A tree, standing where no tree should be, caught and held his gaze. He cleared his mind and the troll graciously inclined his head.

The troll's manner gave the impression of height—although he wasn't really very tall—and bulk—although he wasn't very large.

Rebecca smiled and stepped forward. "Lan," she laid her hand on his arm and the moss he wore bent under her touch, "this is Evantarin. He's my friend."

The troll thought about that for a moment, while another subway train screamed by up above. His whiteless eyes studied the Adept, then he nodded again.

"There is a Darkness in the land," Evan began, but the troll held up a gnarled hand. "If you know," Evan asked, "why haven't you gone to safety? Trolls are enough in the Light that destroying you would add to its power."

The troll smiled. "I am safe," he said, his voice rolling out as slow and sure as a river moving to the sea. "This small Darkness will not try to destroy me. It knows I am too strong. It will not waste strength it needs to deal with you. And if the barriers break and the large Darkness comes, I will not leave my garden."

"We're trying to stop the Darkness, Lan," Rebecca told him earnestly, pleased he wanted to talk. Sometimes when she visited, they just sat quietly for hours. "Evan says trolls are wise. Do you know anything that will help?"

"I know how to help things grow. I know bridges." He bent and straightened a tiny seedling twisted by the wind. "I have not thought of other things in many years."

"Perhaps it's time," Evan said softly.

The troll raised his head and looked down the length of the viaduct, across the two huge arches and the smaller supporting ones at each end, then he dropped his gaze back to Evan.

Under the troll's steady regard, Evan's chin went up and he tossed his hair back off his face.

The troll held up a cautioning hand. "You need not show me your glory, Adept. I have walked in the Light. Lady . . ." Evan started, hearing his name for Rebecca from the troll. "There is a small bird tucked up in the ivy. It has fallen from its nest and I am too heavy to climb up and put it back."

"Would you like me to, Lan?" Rebecca gave a little bounce.

"If you would."

"I'll be right back, Evan." She scrambled farther up the slope and disappeared around the base of a bridge support, obviously familiar with the ivy the troll spoke of.

They waited while another train passed, cocooned by the noise, then the troll said, "If you win, take her with you."

"What?"

"In another time, where she could grow roots, her innocence would not matter, but this time uproots her constantly. It is cruel to her and I wish her to be at peace. Do this and I will be in your debt."

Completely taken aback, Evan turned and walked a few steps away. Men and women had gone through the barriers in the past, although none in recent memory. He held Rebecca up against the world he came from and she slipped into place, barely rippling the image. *Perhaps she draws me so because she reminds me of home.* He shuddered as he thought of how he would feel, trapped in *this* world, and he marveled that her clarity had stayed unblemished for so long.

"It must be her choice," he said softly. "But if we win, I will ask her to come with me."

"If you lose, Adept, it will no longer be a problem."

The World's Biggest Bookstore stayed open late and drew a steady stream of customers, although nothing like the crowds that still jostled together a block away on Yonge. Roland pulled Patience up to his chest and just let his fingers run over the strings for a moment, soothing his jangled nerves with her familiarity. His wariness of police could tip easily over into an irrational fear if he let it and he had no intention of allowing it.

Unfortunately, suspecting that Darkness sat just out of sight playing on his insecurities made it worse.

"I said get in the car!"

Roland opened his mouth to explain that his jacket had snagged and he couldn't free it with his hands cuffed behind him when the nightstick came down on his shoulders. He tried to twist away and fell back against the cop, knocking him to the ground. Back, ribs, legs, head; he lost track of the blows . . .

Resisting arrest, they'd said in court. Attacking a police officer. And the cop's partner, who'd done nothing except watch, did nothing again. Because of his youth, he was given a suspended sentence. He'd just turned fifteen.

"You got a reason to be blocking the sidewalk?"

Guitar strings cut into Roland's fingers as his hands clenched and he turned. A trickle of sweat, that had nothing to do with the heat, rolled down his side. There were two of them, standing close enough that he could smell soap and aftershave.

The larger, red-haired cop pulled out his occurrence book. He knew fear when he saw it and in his business, fear meant guilt.

Daru sighed and pushed the file across the desk. She'd finished off what paperwork she could, but a stack, at least as large, still waited on court dates and personal visits. Her week was already full, but that wouldn't stop new problems from occurring, new people from needing help, new battles from having to be fought.

Switching off her desk lamp, she was suddenly aware that only the emergency lights remained on.

"Ten-forty?" she snapped at her watch, as though it were somehow at fault. Her voice echoed in the silence and when it died away, she realized the only sound she could hear was the beating of her own heart.

"Sounds like I'm the last one off the floor again." She stood, scooped up her purse and headed out of her cubicle for the elevators, threading her way carefully through cluttered narrow corridors which seemed even more cluttered and narrow in the dim light. The quiet was so complete that she wondered if she might not be the very last person in the entire building.

She pushed the elevator button and waited. And waited. Occasionally they turned the elevators off at night, leaving her with a long walk down seven flights of badly lit stairs. She hated those stairs; the lines of sight extended only half a flight up and half a flight down and the tiniest noise echoed and reechoed off the cement walls, creating imaginary dangers and masking any real ones. The chime of the arriving elevator made her jump and, stepping inside, she chided herself for being startled by a sound she heard a hundred times a day.

The underground garage was brightly, almost garishly, lit, angles standing out in sharp relief. Daru squinted and, ignoring the signs that instructed pedestrians to keep to the walkways, strode diagonally across the empty lot to the section where she had parked her car. She rounded a corner, stopped and swore. The lights were out.

She leaned back around the corner. Through the open door of the elevator, a patch of cooler yellow spilled out into the white glare of the fluorescents. *I should go up to the lobby and tell security.* But as she watched, the doors closed, and she could hear the machinery hum as the elevator began to climb. Behind her, the darkness waited.

No more than thirty feet away, her beat up hatchback sat, a shadow in the dark. By the time the elevator returned, she could be in the car and on her way home. She took a step, and then another, surprised at how quickly she moved into a complete absence of light. Surely the brightness from the rest of the garage should spill over.

She found the car with her shins. "Damnit!"

The word dropped into the darkness and disappeared.

With one hand on the car, and the other fumbling in her purse for her keys, Daru moved around to the driver's door and searched for the handle. *I've opened the stupid thing a thousand times . . . ah, there.* Keeping her thumb against the edge of the lock, she brought the keys forward and stabbed them into the hole. They jammed halfway and her violent tug to free them flung them to the ground.

Biting back profanity, Daru dropped to her knees and began to pat the concrete.

Then she froze, arms extended, fingers spread, suddenly aware she was no longer alone. She felt the hair on the back of her neck lift, and she held her breath, senses straining. And heard a soft, almost silken sound. And then again, closer.

And she remembered that Darkness walked the city.

Her search became a frantic scramble, masking all further sounds. She didn't need to hear it. She knew it was still out there.

The tip of one finger touched metal. Her knuckles left skin on the concrete as she snatched up the keys and scrambled to her feet.

Then she couldn't find the handle. . . .

Then she couldn't find the lock. . . .

Then the damned key wouldn't fit. . . .

Then something touched her back.

She shrieked and spun around, arm raised.

"Here now, Miss, be careful. I just thought you could use a little light on that." The security guard lifted his flashlight and shone it against the car's door.

Daru took a deep breath and forced herself to stop trembling. The old man smiled kindly, neither surprised nor upset by her reaction.

"It's a pretty spooky place down here when the lights are out," he added, glancing around.

She followed his gaze, noting that the darkness had become more gray than black. She could see her car, not clearly, but she could see it. Wetting dry lips, she murmured, "Thanks," unlocked the door and climbed in. As she drove away, she thought she saw, just for a second, a shadow in her headlights where no shadow should be.

With no reason to hold him—no outstanding warrants, no previous record, not so much as an unpaid parking ticket—the police had no choice but to let Roland go. He'd spent a bad twenty minutes, stammering over his name, forgetting his address. Every time he'd opened his mouth, they became more convinced he had to be guilty of something. They'd asked him to put the guitar down, so he didn't even have the comforting weight of Patience in his hands.

Finally they waved him off, sending him on his way with a stern, "We'll be watching you."

It struck him, about a block later, that one, and possibly both of the cops were younger than he was. He had a feeling it wouldn't have helped if he'd realized that earlier. Shaken, his balance eroded, he headed for Yonge Street and the anonymity of the crowds. At the moment, Darkness seemed preferable to another run-in with the Metropolitan Toronto Police.

The four-piece band still blasted out its version of rock at the north end of the Centre, but its audience had thinned. As he watched, another group of teenagers wandered away, joining the steady stream of people moving south. No one was coming north.

Puzzled, he followed the crowd.

The open area, just down from the big central doors, was packed with bodies, some swaying, some nodding in time, all standing quietly listening to a single voice and an acoustic guitar.

Roland pushed his way forward, using his case as a battering ram where necessary, until he stood just one row back from the singer. He couldn't see the big attraction. A dark haired man, about his own age, stood strumming a shining new, black Ovation, his voice pleasant enough but not really great. Certainly not up to the quality of the guitar. And then, his curiosity satisfied, he listened, really listened, to the song.

He couldn't understand the words, if it had words, but had picked up the feeling easily enough. Despair. Disillusionment. Hopelessness. He found himself swaying in time, agreeing with the sentiment. What was the point of it all anyway. No one else cared, why should he?

Evan cares, chided a small voice in his head.

It's Evan's job to care, he told it, wishing it would shut up so he could hear the music.

What about Daru? it asked.

Her job, too, he pointed out gleefully, getting the better of that small voice for the first time in his life.

And Rebecca?

He didn't have an answer for that. Rebecca cared because Rebecca cared, no other reason. Suddenly the music didn't make as much sense and he jerked his head to clear it.

The singer looked up and smiled right at him.

Roland backed up fast, ignoring cries of outrage as he banged into people, disregarding the muttered curses he left marking his path. He didn't stop until his back pressed up against an ad pillar and a mass of bodies were between him and the Darkness. His heart pounded so hard that he couldn't hear the music, but he knew it went on.

And he knew he had to do something about it.

I can't. The police will come again and this time they won't just talk.

He was panting as if he'd just run a race.

I can't. I can't fight Darkness alone. Evan is supposed to be here!

All around him, men and women of all ages swayed and nodded, their faces growing bleaker.

I can't.

But he fumbled for the clasps of the guitar case and pulled Patience free, holding her before him like a shield.

He had to, for the Darkness was taking something he loved, warping it and making it ugly. He couldn't let that continue.

There wasn't anyone else.

But what would be strong enough to lift the disillusionment that lay like black syrup over the crowd? What was strong enough to span the generations listening spellbound to Darkness? He chose and discarded and chose and discarded again. Then he realized if he had only one chance, he had only one song. His fingers strummed the opening chord and he prayed that John Lennon, wherever he was, would lend a hand.

By the fourth line, the heads closest to him began turning.

By the sixth, they'd shaken off the Darkness and the effect was spreading.

Roland let the song sing itself, giving himself to the lyrics and the music and blocking everything else from his mind. The song had to be all there was, leaving no room for Darkness to get in.

As he finished "Imagine" and moved without pausing into "Let It Be," he saw tears glimmering on more than one cheek and suspected his own were wet. He felt the power of his singing, of his playing, move out from his voice and fingers and find a place to grow. *This* is worth believing in, said the power. Hope. Life. Joy.

He slid into "Can't Buy Me Love" and saw toes beginning to tap. And then he saw the smiles and knew he was winning.

He stopped singing when his voice had died to a croak and saw without any real sense of surprise that he'd been at it for a little over two hours. The crowd, laughing and talking, began to break up. The occasional frown or mutter remained, but the overpowering sense of despair had vanished.

Roland stretched cramped fingers and grinned. *Beatles, one. Darkness, zero.*

"I think," said a quiet voice at his shoulder, "we should talk."

Roland's grin widened. After this, he could deal with the cops. He turned, and froze.

Darkness smiled.

Chapter Nine

"You play very well," the Dark Adept nodded at Patience still cradled in Roland's arms. "You'd be superb with a better instrument."

Roland's hands tightened against the polished wood. "I'm happy with what I have," he said, indignation breaking through his fear.

"Of course, you are." Standing his own guitar case on end, the Dark Adept leaned companionably against the top of it. "If you weren't happy, you wouldn't be so good. But surely you must have wondered what it would be like to play on a really top of the line guitar. One with a decent resonance and strings that don't go sharp when you least expect it."

Of their own volition, Roland's fingers found the A-string. It did tend to go sharp, regardless of how many times he changed the string or how carefully he tuned it. And Patience, for all she'd been the best he could afford at the time, had always had a slightly shallow sound. *I must have been crazy to go up against him with just . . . Hold on!* He forced his gaze away from the Darkness and out over the last of the dispersing crowd. *I won.* His sense of accomplishment came flooding back and with it his self-confidence.

"I'm happy with what I have," he repeated, his tone refusing all further discussion. He laid Patience carefully in her case, caressing her gently as he settled her against the felt. When he straightened, the plastic handle secure and familiar in his hand, the Dark Adept had moved around in front of him, blocking his path.

"Walk with me."

"Do what?"

"Walk. You have nothing to fear from me now. You defeated me. You can afford to be magnanimous."

Talk about taking a walk on the wild side. Roland stared fixedly at a point beyond the cotton clad shoulder and tried to get his thoughts in order. He was not going to go for a stroll with this deceptively friendly young man and that was final. But Evan needed information—where the Darkness hid, where the gate would be—and this might be the best, probably the only, chance to get it. Sure, there'd be risks, but wouldn't it be worth it? He could still feel the residue of the power he'd put into the music warming him. Besides, up close, the Darkness didn't seem that frightening. He had defeated him and he could do it again.

Two large, blue clad figures coming into his line of sight from the south made up his mind.

"Walk where?" he asked, moving away to the north.

The Dark Adept fell into step beside him. "Oh, just around."

They walked in silence until they turned left onto Dundas and then the Adept said, "I'd like to make a deal with you."

Roland's head snapped around in astonishment. "A deal? What kind of a deal?"

"In return for what you most desire, you will cease to help the Light."

The tone was so matter-of-fact, Roland could only say, "You're tempting me?"

The Adept smiled a little sheepishly. "Well, it is what I, uh, do."

In spite of everything, Roland couldn't help but laugh. They turned left again, into the small park behind the Centre, moving across the grass toward the looming spires of Trinity United Church. "So tempt, but I'm warning you, I don't want anything you can give me."

"But you have been wanting different things of late."

The curve of Evan's cheek, the long line of thigh, the heat in his hands . . .

"No," Roland shook his head violently. "No. No, I haven't."

The Dark Adept looked surprised. "You deny your desire for the Light?"

His mouth opened to say, "Yes," because he couldn't admit to Darkness something he wasn't ready to admit to himself. Then he stopped, suddenly aware of the danger in giving Darkness a lie. The lie, he realized, would deny the Light, the words that made it up were unimportant.

"No," he said again, slowly and carefully. "I don't deny my desire."

"But you said . . ."

"I denied that I've been wanting *different* things of late." That wasn't exactly true, but Roland thought he could get away with it. "I've wanted love before. What difference does plumbing make?" *What indeed?* he asked himself, turning the idea over and feeling like he'd just been hit with a brick. *Holy shit, Evan was right. There* is *no evil in loving. Wait until I see him again, I'll* . . . He stopped the thought, unsure of just what he would do but sure, at least, that he'd stopped running. The light by the church door illuminated the face of Darkness and Roland realized he'd won again.

"That wasn't my offer," the Adept snapped as they headed back toward the Centre. "That isn't what you most desire."

"Well?" Roland prodded, willing to be, as Darkness had suggested, magnanimous in winning.

The Adept took a deep breath and placed his hand against one of the glass doors leading into the mall. It swung open.

"Hey, it's after midnight. That shouldn't be unlocked."

"It wasn't." The Adept grinned back over his shoulder, his blue eyes almost black in the dim light. "Coming?"

Roland shrugged—*In for a sheep, in for a lamb* . . . —and followed.

The inside of the Eaton Centre looked like a different place at night, like a set waiting for actors. Their soft soled shoes made no sound against the tiles as they crossed the wide concourse and paused just inside the glass doors leading out onto Yonge. On the other side of the glass, the area they'd played in was now empty of everything but trash.

The Darkness waved a long-fingered hand. "I offer you what you had out there tonight . . ."

"That's already mine," Roland scoffed, touching the last warmth of the power. "That came from within me, not from something outside. You can't give it, and you can't take it away."

"You didn't let me finish," the Dark, Adept sighed. "I give you what you had tonight, with your own songs."

"With my own . . ."

"Yes. Your words, your music will have the power to move people. Not just you singing and playing the words and music of others."

"Mine . . ."

"Now," Darkness smiled, "is that not what you desire above all else?"

"Yes." Roland barely got the word out. To have the piece that was somehow missing from his songs. to finally have a voice of his own. To have music he'd created mean something to others; to move them to tears, or laughter, or anger; to last and have the same effect long after he was gone. He'd often thought he'd sell his soul for that. Now he was being given the chance.

"Well, do we have a deal?"

Evan didn't really need him. Besides, tonight he'd done his bit to defeat the Darkness. He'd beaten it not once but twice. Wasn't that enough?

"Roland?"

His songs. His music.

"Do we have a deal?"

A red and white fried chicken wrapper blew up against the doors.

Roland they've got chicken.

I can see that, kiddo.

Would Rebecca want to listen to his songs if he gave in? Somehow he didn't think so. But weighed against the rest of the world, did it matter what one simpleminded girl thought?

He could feel himself trembling and he couldn't raise his head. His voice was scarcely audible. "No."

It mattered.

"No?"

He knew he should feel exalted that he'd proven strong enough yet again, but he only felt an aching sense of loss.

"You're making a mistake, Roland." The Dark Adept shrugged. "But it's your mistake to make."

"You're taking this very calmly," Roland said with some surprise, not entirely sure he liked this nonchalant attitude toward his sacrifice.

The Adept placed his hand against the door and the lock snapped back. "You win some, you lose some. Oops," he paused, "looks like your friends in blue are still out there. I don't think they'd be very happy to see you coming out of a locked and closed building."

Roland looked from the two cops to the Dark Adept and knew he was saying quite possibly the most stupid thing he'd ever said, but his fear of the police was immediate and his fear of the Darkness was, well, confused. "What should we do?"

"We go out the back, of course."

They made their way back across the concourse to a door that would bring them out on the other side of the church.

"We've circled right around Trinity," Roland said as they paused under the same exterior church light.

"Yes," said the Dark Adept, "I know."

Roland leaned back against the stone and took a deep breath of humid air. "I can't figure you out. You're not at all what I expected. You're so, well, up close, you're not very frightening."

"Oh?" said the Dark Adept. And suddenly he was very frightening.

Roland's legs gave out and his knees slammed down on the concrete. His mind, trying to deal with the immensity of the evil it faced, could deal with nothing else. He tried to look away and couldn't. He tried to scream and couldn't. He fought his mouth around one word and it came out as a whimper. "Evan . . ."

Darkness smiled. "Too late."

"Hey Marge!"

PC Patton paused, one hand on the station house door, and waited for the auxiliary who, having gotten her attention, ran up waving a piece of paper.

"I found that guy you were looking for!"

"That was fast." She let the door close and held out her hand.

The auxiliary relinquished the paper, grinning widely. "It wasn't hard. I mean, he's a little distinctive. I'm not surprised you remembered seeing him."

Scanning the printout, PC Patton nodded thoughtfully. "No, neither am I." The picture didn't do him justice; it couldn't capture the moving highlights in his hair or the incandescence of his smile. She'd known when she saw him at the hotel that she'd seen him before. "So, we scooped him up at the riot . . . Evan Tarin eh? Well," she shoved the paper in her pocket, "thanks, Hania, you never cease to amaze me with what you can pull out of that computer."

Hania shrugged and smiled. "It's what I do. *That* was an easy one."

A few minutes later, sliding into her seat in the patrol car, PC Patton tossed the printout on her partner's lap.

"Told you so," she said as he picked it up.

PC Brooks merely grunted as he read the information.

Her expression smug, PC Patton drummed her fingers on the dashboard. "I knew there couldn't be *two* men that good looking in the city."

"Well, thank you very much, Mary Margaret." He handed back the paper and started the car. "What do we do now?"

"He was released to a Daru Sastri from Metro Social Services."

"Yeah. So?"

"So we finish this shift, and maybe tomorrow we check her out. This Mister Tarin has some connection to our murderer and I want a few words with him and his friend."

"Should've had them this afternoon."

PC Patton frowned. "Yeah, I know." She still didn't understand why she'd let those two walk out the way she had; no names, no nothing. It wasn't the sort of thing she normally did. She shot a glance at Jack from the corner of her eye. It wasn't the sort of thing *they* normally did. "I guess the heat got to us."

"You really believe that?"

She laughed humorlessly. "Since that night in the Valley, I don't know what I believe."

"Personally, I believe what I always did."

"You always believed in unicorns?"

"Yep."

"Elves and pixies, too, no doubt."

"Uh-huh."

"Ghoulies and ghosties and things that go bump in the night?"

He didn't answer for a moment and all kidding had left his voice when he said, "That goes without saying."

And then they sat quietly, watching the night go by.

"But where is he, Evan?"

"I don't know, Lady. I can't find him."

"Is he dead?"

"No. I'd know if he were dead . . ."

The world felt wrong. Roland forced his eyes open and instantly closed them again as even that little bit of light drove spikes into his brain. He had the worst hangover he could ever remember having; his mind had been put through a blender, an iron bar cinched his stomach toward his spine, and his entire body wanted to puke. Again. The smell made it pretty evident that he already had. If his head would just quit flopping around," maybe he could . . .

He remembered the Darkness, the terror, the pain, and he began to keen, arms and legs thrashing feebly.

"Told you it lived."

A tightening of the vise around Roland's middle squeezed him out of his hysterics, leaving nothing in his world but a fight for breath. When he no longer seemed to be in immediate danger of passing out, he opened his eyes again.

The ground bobbed by about four feet from his head, just beyond the reach of his flopping fingertips. A blurred brown blob came into and out of his line of sight and he wondered muzzily what it was. By focusing everything he had, which at the moment wasn't much, he managed to gain enough control of his arms to push against whatever held him. It didn't budge although it felt warm and vaguely resilient under his hands.

It tightened again and his arms dropped, his vision went yellow, then orange, then . . .

"Killing it now!" boomed a second voice followed by a sound like a clap of thunder, then, blessedly, the pressure eased and Roland sucked in great lungfuls of foul smelling air.

When his vision cleared, it cleared completely and he suddenly recognized the blurred brown blob as a bare and dirty foot.

About a size thirty, triple E, he thought dreamily, swinging back and forth. Then the implications hit him. "Jesus!" Panic gave him the strength to twist his head and look up.

The giant that carried him tucked beneath one massive arm had to be fifteen feet high. His buddy, walking alongside, was a little shorter. Each wore a number of foul and rotting hides, roughly shaped into a sleeveless shift.

He punched and kicked and when that had no effect, he tried to squirm free. He disturbed large numbers of flies which lifted from the hides, circled and settled again. But the giants ignored him. His strength gave out and his head fell, reality condensing to the patch of ground that swayed below him. Watching the dirt path turn to rock, he muttered, "I don't think I'm in Kansas anymore." It wasn't original, but it was the best he could do under the circumstances. He didn't seem to have any fear left—it had seeped out with his strength and now he just felt numb—but he supposed that would change as soon as more information gave him a better idea of what to be afraid of.

The giants waded through a pile of rotting garbage and the stench wafting up from it sent Roland's stomach into spasms. He began to retch again. This proved too much for his oxygen-starved body and he slid back into unconsciousness.

He came to, minutes later, when he landed to sprawl across a soft, yielding mound laced with rigid chunks that dug into his bruised ribs. It was the best resting place he'd ever had. Not even the smell bothered him as he lay there and gloried in his ability to breathe freely. He couldn't see a thing and his ears buzzed loudly, but he felt better than he had in—his mind skirted around the memory of the Darkness—hours. Suddenly, there was light and, without moving, Roland could see one of the giants standing about ten feet away, his shadow dancing over a stack of oddly angled objects that sparkled in the firelight. In his hands, looking like a toy when measured against his size, he held Roland's guitar case.

Roland started and tried to push himself up. His hand sank through its support with a wet, tearing sound and into a cavity filled with what felt like rice pudding. But the grains of rice were moving. Scrambling back until his knees touched rock, he stared in horror at what he'd been lying on. Most of the bodies had decayed past recognition, the buzzing had come from a billion flies, and the chest cavity he'd broken into writhed. Given the flies, it didn't take a genius to figure out why, even in the bad light.

Only his reaction to the bodies kept Roland from reacting to the maggots. Although a good part of him wanted to run about screaming "Get them off me! Get them off me!" he only gave his arm a shake and knelt, eyes wide with shock.

Like most of his generation in his part of the world, the only body Roland had ever seen had been laid out like a wax doll, looking as if it had never been alive. These bodies were both more and less real and the only reference Roland had for dealing with them came from movies he'd much rather have forgotten. No chance of mistaking this for a movie though, or even a nightmare. Neither movies nor nightmares had this kind of immediacy. His knee began to ache as something dug into it and he shifted to one side, glancing down. Three quarters of a finger had been crushed under his weight, the joint glistening and exposed. He began to tremble uncontrollably and felt a scream welling up from his gut.

"I wouldn't scream if I were you." The jaw of one of the corpses was moving and its voice was the voice of Darkness. "Remind those two that you're here and they may decide to have an early lunch."

Roland whimpered, but that was the only sound he made. He peered back over his shoulder. One giant still tended the fire, the other dug through the rubbish against the far wall of the cave.

"There is a way out," the Darkness continued. "All you have to do is call on me. Ask my help and I'll take you home." The lips of the borrowed mouth were incapable of it, but Roland could hear the smile in the Dark Adept's voice as he added, "Don't wait too long."

"Wait too long," Roland repeated weakly as the corpse fell still. His mind tottered on the edge of insanity and he stared into the black depths with something close to anticipation.

That's it, quit, sneered the little voice in his head. *Take the easy road, just like Uncle Tony always says.*

Escape beckoned. Roland stepped back. *The hell I will.* He forced his body to stillness. *These guys are dead. They can't hurt me. And if they tried, one good shove would break them apart.* Brave words even if he didn't entirely believe them. His overactive imagination kept animating the grisly remains. *He wants me too terrified to think, so my only option is to call on him. Well, he can just* . . . He pushed his thoughts away from the Darkness—that way would only lead back to the edge—and turned them to the immediate task of getting away from the giants. The Dark Adept had, in a way, done him a favor for his terror at the Darkness so overwhelmed him it didn't leave much room for more mundane fears and, by concentrating on survival, Roland found he could cope.

"Drink now. Eat it later."

That sounded encouraging.

"Eat it now. Before it dies."

That didn't.

Roland turned cautiously. The larger giant sprawled on the floor by the fire, his back propped against a heap of debris, a wooden keg cradled on his lap. The smaller sat chewing on the end of a femur.

"Eat it now," he repeated sulkily as the bone splintered with a loud crack. Roland winced. "Not as good dead."

"Won't die," insisted the other, taking a long pull from his keg. "Nothing broken."

"Always die," muttered the first.

It would, Roland realized, be very easy to fall into the trap of considering the giants foul-smelling buffoons. They might not be very intelligent, but the pile of bodies behind him testified to their effectiveness. As he'd been unconscious when they picked him up, he was, he suspected, probably the first meal they'd ever dumped in their larder that hadn't been beaten almost to death. And if no one had ever tried to escape before, his odds of success improved immeasurably. All he had to do was move silently through the shadows by the wall, slip unseen out of the cave, and run like hell.

Trouble was, the smaller giant was sitting between him and Patience and he wasn't leaving without her.

He watched the larger giant pour a seemingly endless stream of liquid into his mouth, while the smaller sucked the marrow from the bone he chewed like it was some kind of yellow-gray peppermint stick. Surely they would have to piss, or something. Sometime. Hopefully they'd leave the cave to do it. To occupy his mind, he picked maggots off the hand and arm he had inadvertently plunged into the corpse. In a way, that was the most horrible thing that had happened so far for in it he had been an active participant, not just an observer. The temptation to shriek, "Get me out of here!" and to pay any price for that deliverance grew with every moment he waited, with every larva, with every fly, with every glimpse or half glimpse of the rotting bodies around him until his nerves were stretched tighter than his guitar strings.

Finally, the smaller giant stood and kicked his companion, who only snorted and closed his hands more firmly about his keg.

"Going out," he declared. "Don't eat!"

That sounded fine to Roland. He froze as his captor stomped by, then scrambled across the bone-strewn cave until the giant's bulk cleared the cave entrance. *Get Patience and get out. Get Patience and get out* was the litany Roland moved to. *Get Patience.* His hands clutched at the guitar case. *And get . . . holy shit.* Although Roland didn't play the harp, he had friends who did and he'd spent enough time with them to recognize that the instrument so carelessly tossed on the pile of rusting armor—all rosewood, tarnished silver, and twisted gold—had at one time belonged to a master. His fingers itched to run over the remaining strings or to stroke the smooth curve, but he held back. He knew if he touched it, he'd take it, and that was theft. Even from this pair of steroid cases, theft was wrong. And a man walking in Darkness had better be damned careful about abusing the Light.

He leaned away, paused, and suddenly decided; leaving the harp on this pile of garbage, leaving it to be shattered or, worse yet, fall slowly to pieces from neglect would be a greater abuse of the Light than stealing it. As he lifted it, careful not to sound the few strings still intact, he hoped the Light would see it that way. Tucking it up under his arm, he again reached for his guitar case.

With the plastic handle back in his hand where it belonged and Patience's familiar weight hanging at his side, Roland turned and discovered that the larger giant was not, as he'd thought, asleep.

Surprisingly pale eyes peered out at him from under bushy brows and an incredibly vapid smile stretched the thin lipped mouth.

Great. He's pissed. Maybe he'll think I'm a hallucination.

"Meat?"

And then again, maybe he's got the munchies. Shit! Roland ducked a wild grab and raced for the entrance of the cave, abandoning stealth for speed. *Maybe I should stop and try a lullaby.* The giant roared and lurched to his feet. *Maybe not.* He exploded out into early morning sunlight, swerved around the very startled smaller giant who made a half-aware attempt to scoop him up, and took off down the rock strewn slope. If he could get to the forest, a mere hundred yards or less away, he would easily outdistance his larger and clumsier pursuers among the trees.

He hoped.

"Are you sure I should go to work, Evan?" Rebecca stood in the doorway anxiously watching the Adept pace the length of her small apartment. "I could stay home and help you look."

"And I would love to have your help, Lady." Evan added two steps to his pacing and caught up her hand. "But you know that every disruption further weakens the barriers between your world and the Dark. And if you don't go to work . . ." He rested his cheek against her palm.

"If I don't go to work, it would disrupt a lot of people." Rebecca nodded solemnly. "But Roland is one of my specialest friends. I wish I could help find him."

"We each have our part to play, Lady." The storm had died in his gray eyes and he appeared unnaturally still.

"I understand." She sighed. "But I would rather be with you."

"And I would rather you were with me, Lady." And he would, for he felt stronger when she was with him, more confident, better able to reach the Light although he didn't understand why. But he suspected Roland had been taken to trap him and he didn't want Rebecca around when the trap was sprung. He couldn't risk that. He couldn't risk her. At her job, she'd be safe. And the rest of it, as far as it went, was true.

Branches slapped at his hair, caught and tore at his T-shirt, and raised painful welts on the unprotected skin of his arms. Roland ducked his head to keep a particularly aggressive evergreen out of his eyes and swore as his toe caught under a protruding root and he nearly pitched onto his face. He could move faster and more easily if he dumped the harp, leaving one hand free to force a path through the brush, but the same streak of stubbornness that kept him out on the street in all kinds of weather kept the instrument under his arm. He barked his shins on a log, swore again, and stopped running.

At first, he could hear only the sound of his own breathing. After a time, he stopped puffing like an entire aerobics class and the other sounds of the forest began to filter through.

Bird song.

Leaves rustling in the wind.

Two branches rubbing together with a soft shirk, shirk.

More importantly, he didn't hear the crashing of underbrush or the bellowing of giants. It had been touch and go for a while, but not even the smaller giant could get up any kind of speed among the trees and Roland, with an agility born of desperation, had soon pulled ahead. From the sound of things, he was now safe.

He set the harp gently against the log and leaned Patience out of harm's way behind the bole of a huge tree. Then he indulged in a well-deserved fit of hysterics.

When it was over, he felt much calmer. Tired, and still afraid, but no longer stretched almost to the breaking point. He sat down on the log, wiped his damp cheeks with the back of one hand, and sighed.

"Now what?" he asked the harp.

One of the broken strings stirred in the breeze and chimed softly against the whole string next to it.

Roland smiled, for the first time in quite a while. "You're welcome," he said, then reached back a long arm and drew Patience from her refuge.

The case had picked up a few more dents and abrasions but the guitar seemed fine when he took her out to examine.

"This is my lady," he told the harp, unsnapping the guitar strap and setting Patience back gently against the foam and felt. "I imagine you were someone's lady once." Cradling the harp in his lap he managed to attach the strip of embroidered canvas to the curling end pieces. "And a lady deserves a better resting place. There." He slung the strap over his shoulder and stood.

"A little low, perhaps, but it does leave me a hand free for defense." *Or de-giants*, he added silently, his inner voice sounding very who-are-you-trying-to-kid.

He shifted Patience slightly, settling her securely—more for the feel of her in his hands than any other reason—and firmly closed the lid. By his hip, a soft tone sounded. From inside the case came a muffled but firm response.

He opened the lid.

Patience looked no different. He ran a finger over her strings. She sounded no different. Except that she never used to sound without him playing her. Finally, as minutes passed and both harp and guitar remained silent, he shrugged and closed the case again. Considering everything else that had been happening to him, this rated about a three out of ten and no more than the amount of worry it had already evoked.

"Okay," he straightened. "My loins are girded. How do we get out of here?"

He seemed to remember having read something, sometime, about moss growing on the north side of trees. The moss around him grew where it liked and in a couple of places that meant all over the tree. The forest stopped him from getting a fix on the sun and no helpful boy scout eager to earn a woodsman's badge appeared to direct him.

"And I don't know where I'm going anyway."

Finally, he decided to keep heading the way his wild flight had been taking him—vaguely downhill—holding tight to the thought that eventually he had to meet someone who could show him the way home. Turning to the Darkness *couldn't* be the only answer.

And that damned little voice asked, *But what if it is?*

"Excuse me, don't I know you from somewhere?"

Evan turned and glanced at the young woman. She was just as she seemed and not a construct of the Dark, so he smiled and said, "No, I don't think so."

She reached out and gently touched his arm above the bracelets. "Are you sure?" Her fingertip drew tiny circles on his skin.

"Yes."

Moving slowly, she ran her hand up his arm until it kneaded his shoulder. She swayed closer until her breasts pressed up against his chest. "It doesn't matter," she sighed, "we're together now."

For a moment, Evan stood stunned by the burning desire in her eyes, then with a shake of his head he gently pulled himself free. *Light is attracted to Light,* he thought walking on with a smile as the young woman continued on her way with only a vague memory of the entire incident, *but it's never worked quite that way before.*

By the time he'd walked the two blocks between Rebecca's apartment and Yonge Street, it had worked "that way" with another three women, one old enough to be a great-grandmother, two men, a thirteen-year old boy, and an embarrassingly amorous dog. He stopped at the corner to think about it, aware that at least two pairs of eyes were gazing at him in open need.

He can do nothing to me directly, lest I find him, so he thinks to slow my search for both him and Roland by throwing these people in my way. As he'd put no one at risk, Evan had to admire the deft touch the Darkness had shown. It would be impossible to do any searching if he had to stop every two feet and disentangle himself from another admirer; the cost in both time and power would be enormous if these first two blocks were any indication. And then he thought it through to another level and went cold with rage.

He is manipulating the Light in these people; not the Darkness, but the Light!

As Evan's power flared with his anger, the three people closest to him, their desire for the Light already forced open by the Dark Adept, fell to their knees, their expressions rapt and beatific. Evan felt himself responding to their need, felt his power manifesting, and knew that each could see a private vision of the Light. The urge to continue, to pull at least these three over fully into the Light, was strong and perhaps the greatest temptation his kind faced in this world.

For Light could destroy the balance as easily as the Darkness.

And any destruction of the balance weakened the barriers and aided the Dark.

He forced his power down and moved to repair the damage. The Light had been too strong for him to erase the memory of it completely, but he did what he could to lessen the impact. Then he retreated to the safety of Rebecca's apartment and brooded over what to do next.

Roland's stomach growled and his mouth flooded with saliva, as he fought to free the harp.

"Oh, you picked a perfect time to get intimate with a bush," he muttered, trying to untangle the mess of leaves and twigs and harp strings. His fingers seemed unusually clumsy, probably because his entire mind was on the enticing smell of roasting meat. If he turned, he could see the outline of a building in a clearing just visible between the trees, a building he'd be at right now if the harp hadn't jerked him off his feet when it tied itself to the bush.

He frowned as he carefully unwound one of the broken strings from about a sturdy branch. Granted he'd been charging forward pretty fast, his feet propelled by his hunger, but he thought he'd secured the string to the harp better than that; it shouldn't have come loose. His stomach growled again. It had been over twelve hours since he'd last eaten and he was starved.

"There." He got the harp free at last and swung the strap over his shoulder. "Now if you don't mind, I'm going to see about getting some food." With Patience back in his hand, he headed for the clearing. "Maybe I can sing for my supper. Breakfast. Whatever."

The harp chimed softly. Patience answered.

Roland sighed. "All right, I'll be careful. After all," he reached back and patted the carved wood, "I don't suppose you enjoyed that any more than the bush did. But you," he added, giving Patience a gentle shake, "you're in a case. What have you got to complain about?"

Muffled by felt and vinyl came the unmistakable sound of a G-string, violently plucked.

"Women." Roland rolled his eyes. It didn't really bother him that his guitar now made noise independently of his touch. He'd always thought of her as having a personality of her own and this just seemed an extension of that. *Besides*, he thought, pushing his way slowly through the underbrush, *when you've almost been eaten by giants at dawn, nothing that happens during the rest of the day can surprise you much.*

He paused at the edge of the clearing and stared in astonishment. *Except this.*

The walls of the small gabled cottage were squares of gingerbread, stacked one on the other and mortared with a hard white icing. The round shingles on the roof were cookies—chocolate chip by the look of it—and the door and the window shutters appeared made of peanut brittle. In the yard beyond, Roland could see several round pens he assumed were for livestock as these were made of wood. A small brick oven smoked by the side of the cottage and from it came the delicious odors that Roland had been following.

He drew in an appreciative noseful and raised his foot to step forward into the clearing. Then he put it down again, an elusive memory nagging at him. This all seemed so familiar. . . .

The door to the cottage opened and he froze as a little, old, white-haired lady bustled out. She carried a large wooden paddle and Roland realized she was on her way to remove whatever roasted in the oven. He'd never seen a paddle of that type used outside a pizza parlor before, but then he'd never seen an outdoor oven or a house made of gingerbread before either, so he shrugged it off. He wouldn't bother her now, she could burn herself. He'd wait until she'd moved a safe distance from the heat and then he'd see about getting some breakfast.

Her hand wrapped in her snowy white apron, she pulled open the oven door and the smell from inside intensified.

Roland swallowed rapidly as his mouth flooded. *I'm so hungry I could eat a . . .*

. . . child.

A boy about seven years old lay curled in a fetal position on the end of the paddle. His hair had been reduced to frizzy stubble by the heat. His skin, except where the fat had broken through and still sizzled and popped, was a well-done golden brown.

Roland's stomach heaved, the world twisted, and his last hysterical thought before he turned and fled was, *In the story, she never undressed them first.*

Had it been capable of it, Evan's astral form would have sighed as it moved in ever widening circles out from the Eaton Centre. Although without a body he could take no action, Evan had spotted the residue of power easily enough—the Dark Adept had made no attempt to hide it—and he now knew what had happened to Roland although he still didn't know exactly where the musician was. He could find him, in time, but time was what he didn't have, not if he hoped to stop the Darkness by Midsummer Night.

With Roland's life balanced against all the others in this world, Evan could make only one decision; the Darkness had to be stopped. If he failed, then Roland was no worse off than the rest of his people. If he succeeded, and Roland still lived, he would find him then. He only hoped by then Roland would still want to live.

Back in Rebecca's apartment, Tom jumped up on the Adept's lap and butted his head into the crease between jeans and T-shirt. The lack of response seemed to annoy him and he sat back, tail lashing. Anchored by claws sunk deep into denim, he leaned forward, sniffed delicately, and snorted. Ears back, he dropped to the floor and stalked toward the window, pausing on the ledge to express his opinion with an eloquent howl. Then he snorted again and leaped down out of sight.

Except when the cramps dropped him to his knees to spew bitter tasting bile on the forest floor, Roland continued to run, getting as far as he could from that horror in the clearing. He didn't see what he stumbled over or slammed into or plunged through, his mind reeling with images of giants and corpses and children baked a toasty brown.

When at last he fell, without the energy to rise again, the images danced round and round and round, leaving him with a single thought.

I want to go home.

I don't care what it costs. I want to go home.

I can't take it anymore.

Nothing happened. Apparently, the Darkness wanted him to surrender out loud.

He sobbed, a tortured, choking sound that ripped at the lining of his throat, then he managed a breath deep enough for words.

"I want," he cried . . .

"Well, what have we here?"

The voice was a warm, deep, and friendly drawl and so far removed from everything that had been happening to him that Roland grabbed onto it with everything he had left.

"Are ya'll hurt, young man?"

"I . . ." He managed to get up on an elbow and turn until he was looking up into the concerned features of a large brown bear. A large brown bear wearing a pair of overalls and with a spotted kerchief knotted around his neck.

"I . . ." Roland repeated weakly. And fainted.

Chapter Ten

"Now just as soon as ya'll finish eating, Papa'll guide you to the edge of the forest."

"Me, too! Me, too!" Baby Bear banged his spoon against his wooden porridge bowl and nearly spilled his milk.

Roland grabbed the mug and moved it to a safer spot, receiving a smile of thanks from Mama Bear that he tried to accept in the spirit in which it was offered, ignoring the mouthful of sharp teeth now revealed. Not that he appeared to be in any danger from these bears; from the moment Papa Bear had carried him into the cottage, they'd shown him nothing but kindness.

"Uh, no thanks." He waved away another helping of porridge. The bowls, even Baby Bear's, held an obscene amount of food and Roland, afraid of offending the cook, had eaten all he'd been given.

Mama Bear shook her head. "Ya'll don't eat enough to keep a squirrel alive," she scolded, clicking her claws against the scarred tabletop. "Why, you'll fall ovah from hungah before you've been on the trail ten minutes."

"Now leave the Bard alone, Mama," Papa Bear growled, picking up his bowl and licking it clean. "He knows when he's had enough. And if you're not goin' to finish that honeycomb . . ."

"Please, go ahead." Roland pushed the piece of comb across the table and watched as Papa Bear ate approximately a pound of honey in two bites. *It's amazing what you can get used to,* he marveled. When he'd come to, tucked snugly into Baby Bear's bed with Mama Bear draping a cool cloth across his brow, he'd whimpered and shrunk away from what looked like a new installment in the day's nightmares. Mama had merely continued to wipe his face and murmur comforting words in her gravelly voice. Finally, convinced he was safe, he'd started to cry and she'd held him, stroking his back, careful of her strength and his relative frailty. Worn out by terror, he'd eventually drifted off to sleep.

Baby Bear's cold nose investigating his right ear had jerked him awake a short time later. His startled yell had started Baby Bear squalling, brought Mama Bear running, and resulted in such a normal domestic scene that there was no room for fear.

"Nothin' like a little snack between breakfast and lunch." Papa Bear pushed back from the table with a satisfied belch. "You've got a long way to travel, Master Bard, so we'd bettah get goin'."

"I don't know how to thank you," Roland began, as the whole family moved to the door with him. He slung the harp over his shoulder and picked up the guitar case. "You saved my life." His throat closed up and he felt perilously close to tears. "I've no way to repay that."

"Nonsense." Mama Bear patted him on the back and almost knocked him to his knees. "Bards are special and we'd do the same for any of them." She handed Papa Bear his hat, beaming benevolently. "Still and all, it's a good thing Papa heard youah instruments calling or he'd have just thought you were some po animal blundering by and, well, it's unlikely you'd have survived till noon."

"Yes." Roland's free hand dropped back to stroke the smooth wood of the harp. "I know." He had no memory of anything save horror during his wild run through the bush—Patience and the harp could have been playing "The Battle Hymn of the Republic" for all he knew—but he had a very clear memory of what had caused his panicked flight and knew he'd carry it to his dying day.

Papa Bear unwound Baby Bear from about his leg, handed him, wailing, to his mother, and pushed Roland out the door.

"Ah hate to see the little guy cry," he confided as they crossed the clearing surrounding the cottage. "But it's just too dangerous foah him in the forest. And you," he straightened to his full height and looked down at Roland, "you're lucky you've got me with you. Yup," he dropped back down to his usual hulking slouch as they stepped under the first of the trees and he bent a small sapling out of his path. "There's things in this forest with teeth that bite and claws that catch."

"Jabberwocks," Roland murmured.

"Why, that's it exactly. Mama tell ya'll about them?"

"No." Roland tightened his grip on Patience's case and carefully kept his gaze away from the deep shadows that pooled under certain trees. "I think I'm beginning to get the hang of this place."

Mrs. Ruth banged the newspaper against the edge of the garbage can, dislodging a half-eaten cherry danish and an apple core.

"People," she snorted, glaring at the damp, sticky splotch, "should have more consideration." Usually, she picked up her paper first thing in the morning and avoided the day's trash, but this was an early afternoon edition and if the glimpse she'd already managed was any indication, she needed to see it. "Hrmph. Dumping their leftovers on my paper!" She transferred her glare to a young woman hurrying past. "I ask you, why don't people take the time to eat properly? Bowel problems. Mark my words, they'll all end up with bowel problems."

The young woman averted her eyes and hurried a little faster. She just didn't have the time to deal with crazy old bag ladies.

Mrs. Ruth spread the paper across the top of her overflowing bundle buggy and squinted at the headline. *Modern Miracle; Angel Appears at Yonge and Carlton*. The story below it reported that a number of independent witnesses had spotted a glowing man with wings standing on the corner during the morning rush hour and that reactions from the various churches were still forthcoming. Mrs. Ruth snorted. "I'll give you a reaction. Someone got a little too big for his britches." Shoving the paper down behind a perfectly good hockey stick found in a pile of otherwise disappointing garbage, she began to drag the squealing and protesting buggy down the street.

"If you want anything done right," she informed two businessmen as she pushed between them, "you've got to do it yourself."

"Go on! Scram!" Papa Bear bent, picked up a chunk of stone, and heaved it at the pair of red shoes. They skipped back out of the way and danced off through the underbrush.

Roland swallowed heavily and managed to keep his gag reflex under control. There'd been feet in the shoes, wrinkled and mummified but quite definitely feet, the ankle bones gleaming dully where the dried flesh had pulled away.

"Damn nuisance, those things," Papa Bear growled, stomping forward. "Not dangerous, though."

"Great." Roland tried not to sound sarcastic. *Lions and tigers*

and bears, he thought, *would be a nice change.* Then he glanced
at Papa Bear and added, *Okay, cancel the bears.*

"Ms. Sastri?"

Daru grunted an affirmative without looking up. The bureaucracy had just spit out a new pile of forms needing immediate attention and she was already three days behind on her fieldwork;
she had no time to spend on idle chatter.

"Ms. Sastri, if you could just spare me a few moments of your
time."

The voice was warmly persuasive; a voice that accepted service as its right. It made the hair on the back of Daru's neck rise,
this voice that sounded vaguely familiar even though she knew
without a doubt it belonged to none of the men in the office.

The sooner I deal with him, the sooner I can get rid of him. She
sighed, initialed the top two papers on the pile, pushed the whole
stack to one side and swiveled her chair around in the same motion. "I can give you one mo . . ." she began and trailed off as she
realized who stood just inside her cubicle.

His dark hair was cut fashionably short, a thick lock falling
gracefully forward over his brow. His eyes were very blue, surrounded by a fringe of indecently long lashes. Teeth showed brilliant white against ivory skin. He wore a pale gray, raw silk suit,
not an Oxford cloth shirt, but Daru recognized him immediately.
She wondered if Evan knew how accurate his sketch had been.
He'd even captured the contempt that lurked below the surface
charm.

"Yes?" Her voice, she was pleased to note, quavered only a little and she quickly gained control of that. An enemy seen and
available to be grappled with was less frightening than one skulk-
ing in shadows. "How can I help you, Mr. . . . ?"

He spread long fingered hands. "My name is unimportant. And
I rather think that I can help you. May I sit?"

"Can I stop you?" Daru smiled tightly and waved in the direction of her second chair which was almost buried under case his-
tories. She didn't see how he did it, but the bulging files were
suddenly stacked neatly on the floor and he was crossing one leg
over the other, twitching the trouser crease back into place.

"I have come to make you an offer," he said.

"If you're going to take me up on a mountaintop," Daru

snapped, wondering if anyone would hear her if she screamed, "make it fast. I have work to do."

"A mountaintop. Yes." He drawled the words as though they left a bad taste in his mouth. "As you have no time for pleasantries, I will dispense with them myself. I offer you the power to deal with all of this." The sweep of his arm encompassed the entire department. "No paperwork. No government red tape. No being forced to stand by as situations go from bad to worse. I can give you the power to deal with problems, to solve them as they happen."

No more children destroyed in front of her eyes. No more men and women swept away as she watched helplessly, resources stretched too thin to save them. "And as my part of the deal?"

"You will cease to fight me."

"Well, that makes your whole deal kind of worthless, doesn't it, because that's what all this is." The sweep of her arm mirrored his. "Fighting you." Her eyes narrowed. "You see, I know you and you're not some pretty young man in an expensive suit. You're the landlord who rents a shithole basement apartment with no heat and a toilet that doesn't work to an immigrant family for nine hundred and fifty dollars a month because you know they're desperate for a place to live. You're the punk who beats his pregnant girlfriend almost to death because she forgot to buy beer. You're the father who rapes his ten-year-old daughter, then blames what he did on her. And you're every judge, and every jury, and every lawyer who lets those bastards get away with it." Her eyes blazed and her fingers curled into fists. "And I will never stop fighting you."

For a moment, Daru held him pinned with her gaze, then he stood and smoothed a nonexistent wrinkle from his jacket. "You know, Ms. Sastri," his voice picked up an edge, "you are beginning to annoy me."

"Well, good," Daru snarled, "because you've *always* annoyed me. Now get the fuck out of my office!"

The Dark Adept shook his head. "Such language," he chided, but he left.

Daru straightened her hands, laid them flat on the desk to stop their shaking, and tried to remember how to breathe.

*   *   *

"Say, Jack, doesn't he look familiar?" Standing just outside the elevators, PC Patton pointed with her chin at the man walking out of Social Services.

PC Brooks frowned. "Isn't he . . ."

And then a pair of bright blue eyes swept the thought, and all thoughts connected to it, away.

"You look lost, officers," he said, stopping before them. "Can I help?"

Lost was the word for it all right; once past the public sections, Toronto City Hall became a hopeless rabbit warren. "We're looking for a Daru Sastri."

"Oh, I'm terribly sorry." And he looked most terribly sorry. "She's out of the office now and there's no way of knowing when she'll be back."

"Do you know where she's gone?"

"Out in the city somewhere, that's all I know." He smiled. "Would you like to speak to someone else?"

"No." PC Patton sighed. *Out in the city somewhere. Great.* "It had to be her."

The Dark Adept Watched them get back into the elevator and enjoyed their disappointment. He hoped whatever they'd wanted Ms. Sastri for had been important.

The forest ended suddenly. One moment they were pushing past—or in Papa Bear's case, plowing through—the underbrush and the next moment they were looking out at a prairie that stretched to the horizon.

"Well, son, this is as fah as Ah go." Papa Bear absently scratched himself behind one ear, claws digging deep into the thick pelt and coming up with something many-legged and squirming which he absently flicked away. "Too much sky out theah foah me, but if ya'll follow the sun, things should come out all right."

"Follow the sun," Roland repeated, peering up into the vaulting dome of blue that was the sky. His eyes, grown used to the shadowed light of the forest, watered and he blinked rapidly to clear them. The sun, almost directly overhead, burned hotter and higher than the sun at home.

"Good luck to ya, Master Bard." Papa Bear clapped him carefully on the back.

By clutching at the nearest tree, Roland managed to keep his feet. "I can't thank you enough for all you've done . . ."

"Heck, 'twern't nothin'." The huge bear looked embarrassed. "Ya'll just put us in a song someday."

"I will," Roland nodded. "You can count on that." He stood for a time, watching Papa Bear stomp back to the cottage—and to Mama Bear, Baby Bear, and a yellow-haired kid who hadn't shown up yet—then he stepped out onto the grassland.

Walking was easy and he thankfully lengthened his stride. The grass grew to about ankle height, one blade pretty much like the next, stretching as far as he could see in any direction but back. The weight of the forest slipped off his shoulders like a discarded cloak and he left it lying where it fell, letting the sun wrap the memories in a cushioning layer of light. Heat seeped into the tattered places in his mind, warming and soothing, and as he walked he thought about nothing at all.

When a roll of the land dropped the forest out of sight, Roland sat and ate the lunch Mama Bear had packed for him. Then, still in a haze of heat and light, he stood and walked on, his shadow streaming out behind him.

Pain across the bridge of his nose brought him back to awareness. He reached up, touched his face gently, and swore. The skin, he knew, would be a bright, tight red. He squinted down at his forearms, just beginning to burn.

"I might have known," he muttered. "Nothing around here comes without a price." Now firmly back in the world, he sighed and did the only thing he could; he kept walking. A very short distance later he realized the price was higher than he'd thought. He'd seen no sign of water and he was suddenly very thirsty.

"Follow the sun and things should come out all right," he mocked, licking dry lips. "All right for who?" With every step, he could feel the sun sucking moisture out of him. The honey and biscuits lay like a lump in his stomach and the sweet aftertaste only intensified his need for a drink.

He stood equidistant from the two cathedrals, enjoying the way his presence washed out whatever influence for good they might have. They were symbols of the Light, but he was a piece of living Darkness and against him they didn't stand a chance. Leaning against a storefront, he waited for the enemy's third companion. Although his servant had been unable to take an impression, it turned out not to matter for the impressions of the other two were filled with her image.

"Rebecca," he murmured the name and considered what he knew. Were she merely an innocent he would take great delight in her destruction, but she was a simpleton as well and that saved her. What pleasure could there be when the victim remained unaware? No, he would disrupt the careful structure of her world, upset the balance she needed to deal with life, and send her weeping and wailing back into the arms of the Light as a further burden and distraction.

A slow smile spread across his face as he thought of the Light Adept so cruelly caught on the horns of a most exquisite dilemma. If he went out, the people he claimed to care so much about got hurt, used, twisted by their desire for the Light, their desire for him. Yet if he stayed in, his search was curtailed, not stopped but certainly not as effective.

"I am a genius," he murmured, and straightened as he saw his prey approaching.

Because it was what she did, Rebecca looked in all the pawn-shop windows, but she hardly saw the jewelry although it sparkled gaily in the afternoon sun trying to attract her attention. The Darkness had sent Roland away and she didn't have the heart for pretties. She reached the last of the windows and frowned. Something was missing. A watch with two huge emeralds caught her eye. Two minutes past three it told her.

Past three.

What had happened to the bells?

Rebecca's heart began to beat hard, the way it did when things went wrong.

What had happened to the bells?

Three minutes past three, said the watch.

Four minutes past.

Five minutes past.

What had happened to the bells?

Unable to stand it any longer, she whirled about and stared from one tower to the next, panic rising.

"Ring," she pleaded. "Ring."

And the Dark Adept felt the bells move within his hold. He tightened his grip. They trembled and moved again.

"That's impossible," he snarled.

Slowly, bit by bit, the bells pulled free. He fought them, but he couldn't stop them and when at last they rang they rang him as well, pealing inside his head, clanging and clamoring until he cried out and clapped his hands futilely over his ears. He felt his weapon against the enemy fall, knew the enemy felt it, too, and all but shrieking in frustration, he fled.

Rebecca sighed in relief as the pattern of her world continued unchanged. The watch in the pawnshop window must have been wrong.

As the sun began to go down, the air grew chill, the heat of the day quickly dissipating. Roland shivered, his thin T-shirt now much the worse for wear, and, swaying slightly, he stood glaring into the setting sun. He didn't know how long he'd been heading toward the gray bulge in the distance, but it didn't seem to be getting any closer. Suddenly his legs gave way and he sat, heavily, on the grass.

This is ridiculous, he thought, swallowing blood. The fall had driven his teeth through his tongue and he was crazily thankful for even that much moisture. *It's only seven. I left the bears' cottage at about eleven. Only eight hours. I can't be this thirsty.* But he was, thirsty and tired and sunburned and cold.

The sun dropped below the horizon and the temperature plunged another few degrees. Hunched in on himself, Roland wondered what pleasures the night would bring. *Werewolves. Vampires. Ghouls. A herd of stampeding dragons.* Just because he hadn't seen any wildlife didn't mean it didn't exist. *And in this place it would likely come out after dark. Of course, I'd have to survive the exposure long enough for it to get to me.*

He looked up at the sky and shivered again, but not from the cold this time. All around him, the sky came down to meet the earth in an unrelieved curtain of black. Sitting there, alone in the darkness, he felt he was the only living thing left in existence, that existence itself ended just beyond his fingertips. Only the comforting weight of the guitar case against his leg, and of the harp tucked up under his arm, kept him from wailing. Had the sun left enough moisture for tears, he would've cried.

Eventually, his head fell forward and, exhausted by despair, he slept.

The harp woke him, sending a note singing into the night. Roland jerked his head up and wondered for a moment where he was. Then he remembered, and moaned. The whole wretched experience hadn't been a dream.

The moon had risen while he slept and rode high and full in the starless sky. Each blade of grass on that seemingly endless prairie stood out, silver edged against a tiny, perfect shadow. If he strained, he thought he could make out the darker shadow of whatever it was he'd been using for a landmark.

In the distance, he heard the rumble of thunder. It drew closer, growing in volume and intensity.

"Wait a minute," he lurched to his feet, eyes wide and breathing quickened, "that's not thunder, that's . . ."

A double line of horsemen pounded out of the darkness, the moonlight setting the silver inlaid in their armor and their tack on fire. Roland stood paralyzed while they raced closer and closer until, at the very last second, when the beasts and the riders filled all sight and sound and smell, the lines split and swerved off to either side to continue their gallop in a mad circle about him.

As far as the city-bred Roland could tell, the animals were normal horses and therefore only normally terrifying with their wild eyes and flashing hooves and great slabs of teeth, but the riders were clad in fantastical armor and he had no idea what rode beneath it. Two arms, two legs, and a head were all that could be taken for granted.

He was almost ready for it when the first spear thudded into the earth at his feet. Then the second grazed his shoulder, drawing a thin line of blood, and he flinched aside, a whimper rising from deep in his throat. When the third took a small piece from his thigh, the pain became a part of the terror and he lost his grip on where one ended and the other began. They were all around him; he couldn't run, he couldn't hide so he shuddered and closed his eyes, clamping his teeth shut on the scream that fought to get free. *I'll die quietly at least,* he swore bleakly. *And Darkness can stuff it up his ass.*

The harp began to play; an eerie and peculiar tune, for few strings remained intact.

The thundering hooves quieted and then ceased to thunder entirely.

Roland dared to open his eyes and as he did, the harp fell silent. He felt rather than heard something approaching behind him and, not entirely certain it was a good idea, he turned slowly to face it.

The horse stopped less than a body length away and the rider hung the reins over the elaborately chased saddlebow. Silver and black gloves were removed to expose literally lily-white hands. Slender fingers moved to lift the bird's head helm. Roland had no clue what kind of a bird it represented, he only knew pigeons and it wasn't one of them. Masses of ebony hair cascaded down over shoulders and breasts and jade green eyes stared at him curiously from under slanted brows.

Roland swallowed. Excluding Evan, she was the most beautiful creature he'd ever seen, from the tip of her delicately pointed ears to the sweeping curve of her cheek to the moist gleam of narrowed lips.

"The harp you carry," her voice, although hard and suspicious, was as beautiful as her face, "how didst thou come by it?"

"I, uh, rescued it." He couldn't seem to straighten his thoughts.

"From where?"

Roland shifted the weight of the harp on his hip, dimly aware of the wound on his thigh protesting the movement and of fresh blood soaking into his jeans. "From, uh, a giants' cave." And then, because an honorific seemed needed, he added, "Ma'am."

"The harp belonged to my brother."

He wondered which hunk of rotting meat the brother had been but he said, "I'm sorry."

"Thou art human."

It didn't seem to be a question so he kept silent, content for the moment merely to watch her.

"And yet the harp accepts thee." She frowned, changing her beauty but not lessening it. "Art thou a Bard perchance?"

"Uh, yes." He remembered what Uncle Tony had told him about Bards. "That is, I am but I've, uh, still got seven years to go."

She shrugged the remaining seven years aside and repeated, "A Bard."

"Your Highness . . ."

Roland jerked as one of the other riders spoke. Staring into the depths of the lady's eyes, he'd forgotten anyone else was there.

". . . what shall we do with him?"

"We shall take him with us." She smiled and Roland felt his heart do back flips. "The hill has been long without music."

*   *   *

Bouncing painfully on the back of a saddle, Roland tried to keep one eye on Patience and the other on the harp and both of them on the rider in the bird's head helm, giving himself a headache to go with the ache in his other end. As far as he could see, what with the darkness and the movement and his fear of sliding off and being trampled by those galloping along behind, the instruments were doing better than he was. The rider before him wore a cat's head helm but not even his most desperate attempts to hang on to the armored torso could tell Roland whether he was clinging to a man or woman.

The hill turned out to be the bulge in the landscape Roland had been trudging toward for most of the afternoon; he was certain of it the moment it loomed out of the darkness. He saw the princess wave a hand and a large section of the hill misted away. Pale gray light spilled out of the opening. Horses and riders surged forward and Roland, still struggling to stay seated, was swept underground.

Some moments later, holding Patience protectively, his mind buzzing with images of color and light, he limped after the princess as she led the way through a set of great carved doors. He had a jumbled impression of an immense vaulted room filled with people and a murmur of surprise that tracked them as they walked the length of it. Roland kept his eyes on the princess, his head filled with paeans to her beauty that drowned out the pain and fear.

Across one end of the room was a dais and as Roland and the princess approached it, men and women moved aside to reveal a man seated on a great black throne.

Good lord, but they look alike, was Roland's first thought. His second was, *Am I out of my mind?* for the man on the throne had dark red hair and pale gray eyes.

"Thou hast returned early to my sight, Lady Daughter." He didn't sound pleased. "What hast thou brought to me?"

"Two things, Lord Father." She held up the harp. "My brother's harp is found and he who carries it is himself a Bard." She paused briefly then added without expression. "A human Bard. The harp accepts him."

Roland felt every eye in the place on him. Pinned by the king's level stare, he realized why he thought the two looked so much alike despite their radically different coloring; their expressions and their mannerisms were identical.

"I can assume," the king said dryly, "that thou didst not best my son in battle and wrest the harp from his stiffening hands?"

"Uh, no, sir." How did he get the harp? His memory seemed to go back only as far as his first sight of the princess. With an effort, he reached further and pulled out the answer. "I, uh, rescued it from a giants' cave."

"Pity. But the giant would have silenced him, so the result is the same."

Roland got the impression that the late prince had not been very well liked.

The king continued. "Thou hast returned to me one of the treasures of my kingdom. Ask and it shall be thine."

He must know the way home. Home. Roland fought to hold onto the word but the princess was here and infinitely more real and her presence kept pushing everything else away. "I . . ." His throat closed up and his tongue stuck to the roof of his mouth as he suddenly realized how very thirsty he was. "I, I'd like a glass of water, if I could."

The king frowned.

Roland felt the people surrounding him draw back and he heard the clank of metal plates as the princess and her riders turned to stare.

"A glass of water," the king repeated.

The silence lengthened and stretched. Roland desperately wanted to scratch his nose but was afraid to move.

Slowly, the king smiled and the court began to breathe again. "Water for the Bard," he commanded. "And when thou hast been refreshed and reclothed, Sir Bard," the smile broadened, "we will feast!"

Roland found himself surrounded by a swirling crowd of brightly clothed men and women, all laughing and talking and fussing over him. He lost sight of the princess and his leg began to hurt. The snatches of conversation he heard made little sense, so he stopped trying to listen; not difficult as no one actually spoke to him. A silver goblet was placed in his hand and he thankfully drank. Now he only felt tired, confused . . .

And short, he added silently as he came face to chest with yet another swelling bosom. Even the women stood well over Roland's almost six feet.

He was pushed and pulled and chivied along until he ended up in a small, steamy room with two young women and a deep tub of hot water.

". . . clothes."

"What?" That last statement had obviously been addressed to him. "I'm sorry, I didn't hear."

The young woman giggled and pushed a short chestnut curl up behind the point of her ear. "I said, thou hast to remove thy clothes. Unless thou wishes to bathe in them?"

"Uh, no." He leaned the guitar case carefully against a stone bench and stared stupidly at the silver goblet in his hand.

The second woman, whose black hair hugged her head in a sleek cap, sighed and stepped forward. "I have no wish to be at this all night. If thou wilt but stand still, Sir Bard, we shall manage. Moth, if thou wilt stop giggling and help . . ."

Roland meant to protest when two sets of surprisingly strong hands began dragging down his jeans, but he just didn't have the energy. Before he had time to be embarrassed, he was in the tub and the hot water started to soak away his aches and pains. The water turned pink as dried blood washed away and he shrieked as it hit the now open cut on his leg.

"Just wait." Moth pushed him down and held him.

"There's that in the bath to help thy wounds if thou wilt give it a chance."

He didn't have much choice so he sat, teeth gritted, until the pain faded. Slowly, he began to feel better than he had in—he thought back—one day. It had all happened in just one day!

It's amazing how soon you can get used to things. He'd thought it first watching Papa Bear eat. He thought it now as two beautiful young women bathed him. And then he realized his body wasn't nearly as blasé about the situation as his overloaded mind.

"Best not waste that, Sir Bard," Moth giggled, digging soapy fingers into knotted shoulder muscles, "or her Highness will in fury rage."

Roland blushed, squirmed, and discovered there was no way to hide. His brain reluctantly shifted out of neutral. "Her Highness?" he managed.

"Thou hast impressed her mightily." Moth lathered his hair and scrubbed vigorously. When she finished pouring a pitcher of warm water over his head, she added, "First thou wilt feast and then thou wilt frolic."

Roland knew what frolic meant where he came from, so he tackled the first bit of information. "I impressed her?"

"Most surely. With your request of his Majesty her father."

"My request?"

"Thou wast expected," the other woman said dryly, holding out a large towel for him to step into, "to beg for thy life."

That took care of the small physical problem.

He allowed himself to be dressed in borrowed finery and led to the feasting hall, all the while hoping that if begging was necessary he'd be given another chance. That thought vanished at the first sight of the princess who nodded approvingly and drew him to her side. He sat where she indicated, mesmerized by the startling contrast between her pale skin and the black satin of her gown.

"Alabaster and ebony," he murmured, and flushed as she smiled.

The feast passed in a kaleidoscope of sights: Although the short haired servers dressed in a bright array of colors, those being served wore only combinations of black and red and silver. Roland had never realized that red and black and silver could come in so many shades, could sparkle and shine and burn with such intensity.

And sound: Laughter rose frequently over the noise of eating and drinking, but it had a brittle edge as though the ones who laughed knew secrets their listeners did not.

And taste: Roland ate everything that appeared before him, reveling in foods that had the texture of silk and the flavor of sunshine, the sharp tang of a winter's day, the thick richness of midnight.

And smell: The scent wafting out from the heavy mass of Her Highness' hair wrapped around him, capturing and intoxicating him, leaving no room for other scents and very little room for thought.

He couldn't hold onto fear or even wariness. Everyone he saw was young and beautiful and, after the king and the princess, they deferred to him. If he was to be killed in the morning, he'd worry about it then and probably go smiling to the firing squad. Or the local equivalent.

When the last of the food had been cleared away, the huge room fell silent.

"And now, Master Bard," the king announced, "mayhap thou wouldst honor our company with a song."

A server approached carrying the harp, cleaned, restrung and as beautiful as Roland knew she would be. He ran a gentle finger down the sweet curve of her, and smiled.

"I beg your pardon, sir," he said, "but I'll stick with the lady I know."

The feel of the silence changed, but the king merely waved a graceful hand and replied, "Thy choice, Sir Bard."

Moving slowly, for he suspected he'd had just a little too much of the deep red wine, Roland opened the case and pulled Patience free. "It's called a guitar," he answered the king's raised eyebrow. Running up a scale, he felt in control of events and when he started to play he gave himself over to the music.

They kept him playing until his hands were cramped and his voice had faded to a husky whisper. Then, amid cries of praise and adulation, the princess took his arm and led him from the room.

If she'd asked him, he would have pleaded exhaustion, but she didn't ask—only stripped them both, mounted, and rode him to climax after shuddering climax. Roland had no idea where he found the energy, but his body kept responding to her demands so he gave in and enjoyed it.

He woke amid pitch blackness, completely disoriented. Panicked, he thrashed about, then jerked up into a sitting position. Gradually, soft gray light filled the room. He saw the glimmering silver and red tapestries, the huge oval mirror, and the discarded clothes strewn about. Turning slightly, he saw a tangled mass of blue-black hair spilling over an ivory breast. He remembered and lay back smiling.

The light faded until the room was once again in total darkness.

He sat up.

The light returned.

He lay down.

The light faded.

Not bad, he thought. *I could grow to like this place. Good food, great clothes, a beautiful woman. And they appreciate music.* He dozed a little, images of life as a court favorite dancing through his head, and then he sat up again.

"Bathroom," he sighed. He considered waking the princess for directions but decided against it. Following his nose, he found the little room off the hall that served the purpose. When he returned, bright gold eyes peered up at him from the end of the bed.

"Where the hell did you come from?" he murmured, frowning.

Tom meowed imperiously, working his claws in and out of the mattress.

"Shhh!" Roland put his finger to his lips. "You'll wake her." He dropped the robe he'd found and looked thoughtful. "In fact, that might not be such a bad idea. Now that I'm rested I'm sure we can find something to do." Sliding back onto the bed, he bent his head over ruby lips.

"JESUS CHRIST!" He whirled around and glared at the cat. "You scratched me, you little shit!" He grabbed at his right cheek and his hand came away streaked with blood. "I'm going to skin you for a . . . a . . . Jesus Christ," he repeated, only this time it was more like a prayer. For the first time since he'd gazed at the princess, all jade and ebony and silver in the moonlight, he was thinking clearly.

A quick glance at said princess showed she still slept soundly. A quick glance around the room and he spotted his watch.

"Two forty-three," he muttered, strapping it on. It had to have been close to dawn when last night's party had finally broken up. That made it two forty-three in the afternoon. He looked at the princess again. The middle of the day. And she was sleeping *very* soundly. Gently at first, and then more violently, Roland shook her shoulder. Her chest still rose and fell, but that remained the only sign of life.

His heart beating painfully hard, he raced to the mirror and studied his neck. There were no puncture wounds.

Tom snorted.

"Well, she could've been," he hissed, feeling like a fool. "Where the hell *did* you come from?" he demanded again, bending down and staring at the cat. "Did Evan send you to find me?"

Tom twisted, and began washing the base of his tail.

"Oh, that's very helpful." His tone was sarcastic, but it *was* helpful. Despair just couldn't be maintained in the face of such sublime indifference. He straightened and dragged both hands through his hair. *I've got to get away before she wakes up.* Because if he didn't, Roland knew, if she smiled at him again, he'd be unable to leave. So far, things had been pretty terrific, but he strongly suspected when Royal Interest in their new toy waned, the situation would be very different.

He dressed quickly in the black silk and velvet he'd worn to the feast—he had no idea where his jeans were—picked up Patience, and started for the door. Tom padded out ahead of him.

The cat certainly looked like he knew where he was going and as Roland certainly did not, he followed the cat. The hallways glowed, then faded as they passed.

Even if I'd been in my right mind on the way up last night, I'd never have remembered this. The maze of corridors twisted and turned and doubled back on themselves with joyous abandon. *Fortunately, I'm too lost to be scared.* That didn't quite make sense but neither had life lately, so Roland let it stand. Nor was it entirely accurate. It sounded as if he and Tom were the last two creatures alive and that silence weighed on him. In spite of his best efforts to banish it, the phrase "the silence of the tomb" insisted on sitting in the forefront of his mind. He'd never understood it before; he did now.

Tom padded on, oblivious.

They passed a large open archway that Roland was sure he'd never seen before. Although Tom kept walking, Roland, for curiosity's sake, stuck his head into the room. In the dim light he could just barely make out a black rectangle flanked by two white triangles about five feet high. He took a step farther in and the two white triangles became two pyramids of skulls that stared back at him out of empty sockets.

All at once, the statement *"He expected thee to beg for thy life."* made sense.

Roland hurried to catch up with Tom.

As his footsteps faded away, the blackness above the altar began to thicken into more than just an absence of light.

"So you think it will be that easy, do you?" The Dark Adept smiled. "While your hosts sleep, you will slip back out into the light without even thanking them for their hospitality." The smile hardened and the ebony brows drew down. "I think not."

The small park was empty. He took steps to keep it that way. Leaning back on the bench, he stretched out long legs and lifted his face to the sun while his mind made a visit to the shadow realms.

When they reached the great feasting hall, Roland almost didn't recognize it. Empty of the court, it looked bleak and cold, the silvers dulled to gray and the blacks only to a reminder of who ruled in this realm. Roland shivered and moved closer to Tom as they began picking their way across to the door on the far side. They'd covered half the distance when a questioning note rang out. Roland paused, sighed, and turned. As he expected, the harp was leaning up against the great black throne.

"A fine way to treat a treasure," he said softly, squatting and stroking its graceful curve one last time, hating to leave an instrument he'd become so absurdly fond of. Sneaking out while everyone slept was one thing—with luck he'd be forgotten before breakfast ended—sneaking out with a national treasure was something else again. Regretfully, he stood and spread his hands. "I guess this is good-bye." The harp sounded again. "I wish I *could* take you with me." Very conscious of Tom's impatient stare, he turned to go. This time the note fairly vibrated throughout the room.

Roland winced and glanced around. "You're going to wake everyone up," he warned. He could feel the harp gathering itself together for another note and because it was what he wanted to do anyway, he scooped it up in his free hand.

"It was her idea," he explained sheepishly to Tom, who sat by the door, tail lashing the air. From within the case, Patience chimed an agreement.

Tom snorted, walked out the door and straight into what looked like a solid wall. There was a faint but audible thunk as his skull came in contact with something marginally harder than it was. Tom blinked, sat down, and began vigorously washing a front paw.

Nervously, Roland shifted his grip on the harp. "Yeah, okay. I believe you. You meant to do that." He glanced over his left shoulder, the hairs on his neck rising—he'd heard, or thought he'd heard a sound, metallic and recurrent, just beyond the point where the soft gray light dimmed and died. Forcing his gaze back down to the cat, he hissed, "If you know the way out, I suggest you take me to it."

Refusing to be hurried, Tom gave his paw a final polish, then used it to pat at the wall. His tail lashed. He dropped into a crouch, his head snaked from side to side, and he hissed.

The sound grew louder; identifiable. Metallic, yes. Footsteps. More than one set.

"Tom!"

The cat's ears flattened and he growled low in his throat, his attention still fixed on the wall.

"Yeah, okay. You're working on it." *I don't believe I'm depending on a cat.* Roland's armpits were wet, the black silk sticking to his skin. He could smell his own fear. Almost without willing it, he turned to face down the corridor.

"Oh, shit!"

A figure in a suit of black armor, similar to that worn by the riders but with more metal and less leather, stalked out of the shadows. A second followed a pace behind.

"I thought this lot slept all day," Roland protested to the universe at large. *It isn't fair! Maybe if I give back the harp* . . . Then he smelled the slightly sweet odor of rotting meat and knew these guardians were beyond reasoning with.

"No, not again." He backed up a step. The grinning decaying faces in the giants' larder jostled for position in his memory. "I can't . . ." He swallowed and backed up another step. "I can't deal with that again." Another step and a half turn; turning to run. Something soft gave way under his foot.

He screamed, both in pain and terror as Tom yowled and dug sharp claws into the delicate skin behind his ankle. "I'm not a fighter!" he shrieked at the disinterested cat.

And then he didn't have a choice.

He dropped flat under the first swing, throwing Patience and the harp into what he hoped was safety at the base of the wall. The end of Patience's case dragged across the harp strings and they sang out, a discordant counterpoint to the clash of metal. Roland watched the great black sword arcing down toward him suddenly change direction and go skittering off point first against the stone floor.

The harp. The harp controlled the guardians. Or discouraged them. Or something. He scrambled out of the way of another blow, then felt himself slammed sideways as the second guardian brought a mace into play. *My shoulder! It broke my fucking shoulder!* But it hadn't, not quite, for fingers wiggled in a hurried experiment still worked. It hurt like hell, but he could use the arm. *The harp! I've got to get the harp.* He ducked a whistling blow that sprayed chips from the wall when it landed and in panicked desperation fell to the floor and rolled.

His knee crashed into the harp and the sword point descending toward his eye wavered, lightly kissed his cheek—leaving a searing line of pain behind—and vanished from sight. He pushed himself up with his good arm and collapsed against the polished wood as something pounded into his kidneys. Retching and blind with pain, he clawed at the silver strings.

The Dark Adept shifted slightly so that the sun fell directly on his face. The harp was barely more than an annoyance. Without the skill to play it, it would do this so-called Bard little good. He would finish this quickly. He was growing bored.

Breathing heavily, Roland forced his eyes back into focus. The random noise he was pulling from the harp appeared to be holding the guardians where they were. They stood swaying slightly, black armor creaking, arms moving in directionless jerks. As he watched, they turned and began making their way slowly toward him. He raked his fingers back and forth, filling the corridor with sound. They fought it and continued to advance.

"Hey, bubba, spare a buck?"
Jerked out of the shadow realm, the Dark Adept snarled and reached for power—and barely stopped himself in time. It would do his plans no good if he set a beacon for the Light. He spat a curse at the ragged old woman standing before him. He would remember her and deal with her later.
She clicked her tongue at him. "If you ain't got it, bubba, just say so. Ain't no call to be rude." Shaking her head and muttering about the ways of the young, she waddled away, dragging a protesting bundle buggy after her.
The Dark Adept ground his teeth. He did not rule in the shadow realm, though much of it called him Lord, and it would take time and effort he could not spare to reestablish contact. The guardians would have to finish alone.
"I should have flayed that old woman alive," he growled. It still wasn't too late. He sprang to his feet, whirled about, and . . .
There was no old woman in the park.

Tom howled suddenly and Roland's heart slammed up into his throat. "What!" he screamed spinning about. His jaw dropped as the cat disappeared into what seemed to be a solid wall. "Right. Sure."

Tom howled again, sounding barely farther away than he had an instant earlier.

One of the guardians jerked back and forth until it looked as if it had to fall and the other dragged along on a twitching leg but both kept coming.

"Right," Roland repeated. He only had seconds to decide. *Well it can't be worse.* Snatching up Patience, he flung himself at the wall, closing his eyes at the last instant.

A metal hand closed about his ankle.

A jumbled impression of dark, then gray, then light, and the horrendous sound of something tearing that was never meant to tear.

He landed on grass, warm and dry and smelling slightly dusty in the warmth of the sun. For a moment, he did nothing but breathe and then, because it felt so good, he flopped over onto his back and did it some more. With one arm thrown up against the sun's glare, he took inventory.

His cheek. His shoulder. His back. His thigh. His ankle. His ankle?

"Oh, shit!" Metal fingers still dug into the bone.

He had to look, he knew it, but it took him a few minutes to gather the nerve. Finally, he sighed and sat up. The black gauntlet gleamed dully in the sunlight, the jagged edge where it had been torn from the rest of the armor a brighter black. Roland kicked his leg experimentally. The gauntlet hung on.

"GET IT OFF ME!"

During the wild thrashing that followed, the gauntlet brushed against the harp and fell free.

Roland took several deep breaths. "Nobody asked your opinion," he snarled at Tom, who'd sat quietly, tail curled around toes, watching the whole thing. Somehow, Roland managed to get to his feet. He glared down at the gauntlet. "Empty. The smell was a put-on. He was using my own fear against me. That lousy son of a . . ." He drew back his foot, thought better of it, and kicked viciously at a tuft of grass instead.

Tom stood, stretched, and slowly began pacing away.

"Yeah, all right. I'm coming." Carefully, Roland bent and picked up the two instruments. He hadn't felt this bad since peewee hockey, but he'd be damned if he'd fall over in front of a cat.

An hour and seven minutes later, they came to a path. Fifty-six minutes after that, the path split, one route heading down into a pleasant valley and the other snaking up a rocky, barren mountain that had somehow managed to remain unseen until they actually got to the fork.

"Yeah, well, I've read *this* book," Roland sighed and collapsed on a convenient boulder. "And if you think I'm going to climb that mountain, you're out of your furry little mind." He shifted gingerly to ease the bruising across his back. "I'm going to be pissing blood as it is."

Tom yawned, pink tongue delicately curled.

"Same to you, hairball." Wincing, Roland stood. "So let's get going already . . ." He turned on to the treacherous path, made doubly so for him because he had no hands free to help him climb and he would not abandon the harp. Not now. Not after all they'd been through together.

Tom bounded ahead, pausing to wait for Roland at each new obstacle with a superior look on his face.

As darkness fell, the faint call of hunting horns sounded in the distance.

Roland tried to climb faster.

The horns grew louder.

Eventually, the path ended. So did the mountain.

Gasping for breath, Roland staggered to the edge of the cliff and looked off. All he could see, far below, were fuzzy white specks that had to be clouds.

Down at the base of the mountain, armored figures brushed with moon-silver highlights rose in their stirrups and shrieked their challenges.

"Now what?" Roland asked the night.

Purring loudly, Tom brushed against his legs, then leaped from the edge, his tail streaming behind him like a pennant.

"Oh, no," Roland took a step back, "I am not jumping off a cliff after a *cat*. Forget it. No way." He considered the alternatives. "I'll take my chances with the princess before I do something so damned stupid." And in his mind's eye he saw the jaw of the corpse move as the Darkness told him there was no way out save through him. He squared his shoulders. "Oh, hell, might as well make it *my* choice . . ." Like a swimmer entering cold water, he limped forward and threw himself into the air.

Patience and the harp played a harmony to his scream.

Chapter Eleven

"Please, let me help you with that."

The large-blonde-lady-from-down-the-hall positively preened as she allowed the handsome young man to haul her shopping cart up the stairs.

"A woman like you," he purred, "should be carrying urns, like a Cretan goddess, or flowers like a nymph of the spring. Not groceries."

She simpered as she dragged herself up the stairs behind him and, although she didn't usually have breath enough to talk and climb, managed to pant, "My brother-in-law says I've got the best bone structure of anyone he's ever seen."

The Dark Adept smiled. "Your brother-in-law is very perceptive. He waited patiently on the second floor for her to catch up. "But what could your husband be thinking of to allow you to walk about unescorted." His voice dropped. "There's a lot of strange people in this city, dangerous people. Especially for a lovely woman alone."

"Don't I know it." She rested a moment, one hand fluttering over her heart, like a pudgy. hummingbird amid the purple flowers of her shirt. She lowered heavily mascaraed lashes. "Unfortunately, I don't have a husband."

"A wise decision not to limit yourself to just one man. A woman like you needs to be free."

She agreed with him all the way down the hall.

Selfish, vain, and stupid, he thought as they reached her door. *Mine for the taking.*

"Would you like to come in for a while? We could have tea. Or wine, maybe. I think I have a bottle of very nice wine." She smiled in the way she thought a woman of the world would smile.

"I'd love to come in. I have plans for you."

"Oh. My." She fumbled with her key in the lock, the almost forgotten sensation of being wanted making her clumsy.

By the time the glasses had been dug out of the clutter, he was no longer bothering to hide his aspect. She was his.

"Come on, bubba, open your eyes. I got better things to do than sit in an alley with you all night."

"Mrs. Ruth?" Roland tried to focus on the bag lady, but her face kept slipping sideways and going misty around the edges. It didn't seem worth the effort to keep them open, so he let his eyes close. *I don't feel very good. In fact, I feel like shit.* His entire body ached, but pain seemed localized in his right shoulder, his left leg, across the small of his back, and his face. First the right cheek. Then the left. Then the right again. It took him a moment—his brain ached as much as everything else—but he finally figured out what was happening.

"Mrs. Ruth . . ." He wet his lips and tried again. "Mrs. Ruth, please stop hitting me."

"Not until you open your eyes, bubba."

Roland sighed. Why bother. Left cheek. Right cheek. Left . . . "Ow!" His eyes snapped open. "That hurt!"

Mrs. Ruth sat back on her heels and looked pleased with herself. "It was supposed to. Now get your ass in gear. You've got work to do tonight."

"Where am I?" He winced as she frowned. "Uh, never mind. I'll look." Teeth clenched, he heaved himself up on his elbows. Mrs. Ruth blocked the view to the front, so he carefully turned his head from side to side. In one direction, a rusty blue dumpster rose up out of the evening gloom and the smell of rotting foodstuffs suggested he was in back of a restaurant. In the other direction, much farther away, traffic rolled past the alley's mouth, the sound of engines muted by distance. He could just barely see the edge of a sign: Peking Gar . . .

"Chinatown." And then it sank in. "Chinatown. I'm home." He looked at Mrs. Ruth, who nodded. "Home," he repeated, struggling to sit up. He still wore the black silk and velvet and just beyond his reach the harp gleamed in the uncertain light. Images flooded back; the giants, the child, the forest, the bears, the sun, the prairie, the spears, the princess, the black armor, and the final terrifying plunge off the cliff. . . .

"Shhh, bubba, shhh." Mrs. Ruth shoved a handkerchief into Roland's hands and patted him comfortingly on a shaking shoulder.

Roland swallowed a sob, fought for control, and got a fingernail's grip on it. He sucked in deep, shuddering breaths and scrubbed at his face with the square of cloth—which, surprisingly, smelled of fabric softener. The memory of fear mixed with the mind-numbing relief at being home, brought him as close to total loss of self as anything that had happened in the shadow realm.

"I know, bubba, I know." Not just meaningless sounds of sympathy, she sounded as if she did know, which steadied Roland further. "You've been through horrors few men can imagine, but as bad as it seems now, it'll make a better Bard of you in the end." The sympathy left her voice and she returned to a brisk no-nonsense tone, "You can have a wallow in it later. At present there are those who need you."

"What happened to Tom? Did he get back?"

"Of course, he did. He's a cat, isn't he?"

Roland had no idea what being a cat had to do with things, but he nodded anyway and began convincing his battered, body that it had to stand.

Two nights to Midsummer. Two nights. Only two. The words ran through Evan's thoughts, a litany that looped around and around. He sighed, wishing he could take the time to enjoy this world. In so many ways, it was so much closer to the Light than to the Dark; both in its people and in the lives they had made for themselves.

The day's rain had washed the sticky heat from the air and the evening breezes were delicately scented with the presence of green and growing life. Evan didn't care for cities; they barricaded their inhabitants away from the things that mattered. But as cities went, this one wasn't bad; there were trees and open spaces and evidence that it hadn't become more important than the people who lived in it.

A group of children swirled around his legs and ran off down the street, their laughter filling the evening with Light. Evan smiled after them, a gentle benediction. One small girl stopped, turned, and stared back at him, her expression puzzled, wondering why she was drawn. Evan sketched a sign in the air between them and the girl smiled as well, one hand reaching out to touch the delicate lines of Light.

"Marian, come on!"

Their eyes met and Marian nodded solemnly, then whirled and, whooping, ran off to join her friends.

This is why the Darkness must be stopped, Evan thought, and bent his mind once more to the task at hand.

He didn't exactly understand what had happened yesterday between Rebecca and the Dark Adept. When he'd arrived, freed from the glamour his enemy had thrown about him, the struggle was over. Only the power signatures and Rebecca remained.

"The watch in the pawnshop window was slow, Evan," Rebecca had said, wide-eyed at his sudden appearance. But the power signatures told him that the Darkness had attacked and something had stopped it, something huge that had barely stirred and yet had still slapped the Darkness down.

Today, he'd walked Rebecca to work and back, spending the time between finding the faint path the Dark Adept had left when he'd fled, too rattled to mask properly. Tonight, he traced it, hopefully tracking the Darkness to its lair.

Two nights to Midsummer. Two nights. Only two.

"Where the hell have you been?"

Roland sighed and sagged against the wall of Daru's cubicle. "It's a long story," he said, shifting the weight of the harp on his shoulder.

"It had better be a good one. Rebecca's been worried sick." She looked him up and down and snorted. "You look like you've been to a costume party."

A shadow passed across his face. "No. It wasn't quite a party."

Daru's expression softened slightly. It looked to her like Roland had done a little growing up in the forty-eight hours he'd been away. He had a depth now that she hadn't seen before. "What happened to your face?"

"It's nothing." He touched his cheek where the point of the black sword had drawn a delicate line and ran his finger along the crimson beads of dried blood. "I don't want to talk about it."

"You tangled with the Dark Adept." She wasn't asking, but Roland nodded anyway. "You okay?"

Roland drew in a deep breath and exhaled slowly. Things

seemed to stay together. "There was a time," he said, "when sanity hung by a hair. It's not a lot more secure now, but in comparison, yeah, I'm okay." He made the effort and straightened, ignoring the screaming pain in his kidneys. "Mrs. Ruth says we, you and me, have to get to Rebecca's right away."

"Mrs. Ruth says?"

"That's right."

"Rebecca's friend, the crazy old bag lady?"

"Right again."

Daru frowned and waved a hand at her buried desk. "I've still got stacks of paperwork to get done if I want to get out into the field tomorrow and you're telling me to just leave it because some crazy old bag lady says I should?"

Roland shrugged. His shoulders felt like they weighed a hundred pounds. Each. "Look, I only know what Mrs. Ruth told me. She says Rebecca needs us, both of us, and that's good enough for me."

"You believe her?"

"Yes."

"Why?"

Roland's eyes narrowed. He didn't need this. "Because once you've become intimately acquainted with Darkness," he snarled, "it gets real easy to distinguish the Light."

Meeting his gaze, Daru had to believe him. She stood and snatched up her purse. "Let's go," she said, and led the way to the elevators.

Rebecca stared at the orange juice in the pitcher. There'd been more the last time, she was sure of it. She picked up the empty can and frowned at the label. Most of the big words made no sense but she could read, "Fill with three cans cold water." She looked into the pitcher again. Maybe they meant another, bigger can? Maybe the can was bigger last time. She thought she'd gotten the same kind. The picture was the same.

The sudden loud banging on the door startled her and she narrowly missed dumping the entire problem in the sink.

Maybe it's Roland, she thought, hurrying across the apartment. *Maybe he's come back!* She fumbled with the chain, twisted the lock off—Evan had insisted she use both anytime he wasn't with her—and threw open the door.

"Oh," she said.

The large-blonde-lady-from-down-the-hall filled the open doorway. Her hair, usually lacquered to a bouffant neatness, was in wild disarray. Her face, beneath the streaked remnants of thick makeup, was puffy and pale. Under the lilac muu-muu, her body shivered and shook, free of the restraint of girdle and bra, and, with a kind of horrified fascination, Rebecca watched the tips of her massive breasts swaying back and forth.

"It's all your fault!" she shrieked, lurching forward.

Rebecca tried to close the door, but the large-blonde-lady-from-down-the-hall had her weight against it and it wouldn't budge. She stumbled back as the woman staggered another step or two into the room. "What's all my fault?" she pleaded, growing more frightened by the second. "I didn't do anything."

Heavy arms spread and in one hand a carving knife gleamed dully in a white-knuckled grip. "This used to be a decent building until you moved in!" She lunged, the knife swooping down through the air in a murderous arc.

Rebecca stumbled away, whimpering. The blow missed, but she felt the cold air of its passage. "I don't understand!" she wailed. She wanted to run, but the large-blonde-lady-from-down-the-hall was between her and the open door.

Stagger. Slash. "You should all be locked up!" Stagger. Slash. "Away from normal people!" Stagger. Slash. "Why should we have to look at you?" Stagger. "DISEASED!" Slash. "CRAZY!"

The knife missed, but a flailing hand slammed Rebecca up against the wall. Her fingers touched the edge of something hard and metal. The empty orange juice can. Snatching it up, she threw it as hard as she could. It clanged off the far wall, distracting the large-blonde-lady-from-down-the-hall just long enough for Rebecca to grab the pitcher of orange juice and throw it in her face.

She screamed and clawed at her eyes, dropping the knife.

In her corner, Rebecca trembled. She couldn't go past to get to the door. She just couldn't.

Eyes streaming, the woman stared at Rebecca and smiled. "It doesn't really count, killing you," she said with terrible clarity, "because you're different." Leaving the knife where it had fallen, she advanced.

Rebecca scuttled along the wall, throwing everything she touched. The toaster from the top of her tiny refrigerator. Plants

from the windowsill. Her plush dragon from the shelf over the tv.
The rolled up towel . . .

The towel smacked the large-blonde-lady-from-down-the-hall
on the chin and unrolled. The black dagger fell out at her feet.
Swollen lips drew back off the great white slabs of her teeth and
she bent to pick it up.

It looked absurdly tiny in her huge hand and not at all dangerous.

And then Darkness began to spill out of the blade.

A strange silence fell as the two women watched the shadow
cloud spin once around the hand that held the dagger. Then it settled and began to grow.

When it reached the dimpled flesh of her elbow, the large-
blonde-lady-from-down-the-hall began to shriek. "Get it off me!
GET IT OFF ME!" She tried to drop the dagger, but her fingers
wouldn't respond. The shadow slid across her shoulder and
began to cover her chest, gaining speed. The shrieks became a
wordless wail and then cut off as the shadow surged up and over
her face. Hazel eyes stared for an instant out of the Darkness,
their expression a mixture of pain and puzzlement.

As the body hit the floor, the shadow and the dagger disappeared.

From the back seat of the hatchback came a chord so doom in-
voking that Daru, listening to it, almost ran the car off the road.

"What was that?" she demanded, narrowly missing a cursing
cyclist.

Roland swiveled around in his seat. "The harp," he said
shortly.

"Why . . ."

"I didn't."

"Then wha . . ."

His lips thinned. "I think we'd better hurry."

Tires squealing, Daru pulled up under the no parking sign in
front of Rebecca's building and she and Roland tumbled out.
They could hear the screams from where they stood.

With Patience slamming against his legs and the harp tucked
under his arm, Roland dashed up the path after Daru.

"The door," she cried, pounding on the glass. "It's locked!"

"What?" Roland skidded to a halt. "Don't you have a key?"

"Why would I have a key?" Daru protested. "I don't live here!"

"Oh, fucking great! There has to be a back . . ." From the guitar case came the muffled sound of a piercingly high note. The harp twisted in his grip and echoed it. Loudly.

But not quite loudly enough. A couple of cracks appeared, but the door held.

"Oh, yeah?" Roland set Patience carefully to one side and rested the harp on his hip. "Plug your ears," he told Daru, took a deep breath, and plucked the thinnest string, throwing himself into the single note as he'd thrown himself into the music.

The glass door trembled and shattered.

The sound still cutting through his head, Roland scooped up Patience and followed Daru into the building. He slipped on the broken glass and slammed his injured shoulder painfully into the wall. The world went away for a second and when it returned, the hall seemed to be heaving up and down and he couldn't hear a thing over the echoes ricocheting about the inside of his skull. *I should've known I'd pay for that*, he thought, somehow managing to get to the stairs and up them.

Daru pushed through the crowd of tenants gathered in front of Rebecca's door and stepped into the room.

"Oh dear god."

The apartment looked as if a major battle had taken place. Broken plants and shattered pots were scattered about and a fine layer of dirt covered everything. The couch had been shoved almost to the opposite wall and a large, bloated body in a purple gown lay beside it, the position too boneless for anything living. Rebecca crouched in the corner by the radiator, knees drawn up to her chin, eyes squeezed tightly shut, rocking back and forth.

Daru stepped over a toaster, and knelt by the body on the floor. Her fingers sinking deep into the rolls of fat, she probed the neck for a pulse. Nothing. Daru noted it without surprise. Over the years she'd seen a number of corpses, but none had looked as *dead* as this woman. She wiped her hand on her thigh, for the skin had been both cold and clammy, then reached out and tugged the purple fabric down over dimpled legs. *Death has little enough dignity,* she thought, knowing full well what the police opinion of her action would be. Tampering with the evidence was not highly thought of.

Then she went to Rebecca.

"Ah. Ah. Ah." With every panted breath, Rebecca gave a little cry; a confused, wounded sort of sound.

"Rebecca? Rebecca, it's me, Daru. Open your eyes, honey.
Everything's okay now, I'm here."

Rebecca gave no indication that she'd heard. Her cries began
to grow louder and her rocking more violent. Suddenly, she
threw herself sideways and Daru barely caught her before she
slammed her head into the radiator.

"Hey, kiddo, relax, it's over now. It's all over."

Roland reinforced Daru's grip and between them they held
Rebecca immobile.

She fought to get away and her cries changed to shrieks of,
"No! No! No! No!"

"What about slapping her?" Roland suggested, shouting to
make himself heard.

"Too risky. It might frighten her more. We've got to calm her
down. Reach her somehow."

Roland frowned and tried to remember why this all seemed so
familiar. A long, long time ago—*No,* he corrected, *less than a
week. It just felt like forever.*—Rebecca had panicked. He stood,
dragging Rebecca and Daru with him. "We've got to get her outside."

"What?"

"Outside. Look, don't argue, trust me. This has happened before."

Daru shot a horrified glance at the body.

"Not that!" Roland snapped, giving Rebecca a little shake.
"This!"

With no better ideas, Daru helped Roland maneuver Rebecca's almost dead weight out of the apartment, through the
crowd of open-mouthed onlookers, and down the stairs. By the
time they reached the first floor, they could hear sirens approaching.

"At least one of those lamebrains had the sense to call the police," Daru grunted as they struggled to get Rebecca past the
shards of glass. "Now what?"

"Here." Roland moved off the concrete path and onto the
grass. He turned and shoved Rebecca up against the trunk of the
tree.

Her cry cut off in mid-wail. She took one great shuddering

breath, collapsed against the rough bark, and started to sob, sinking slowly to the ground.

Roland knelt and gathered her up in his arms, murmuring all the comforting nonsense he could think of.

The first of the police cars pulled up. And then the second.

Daru went to meet them. *This* she would handle.

"Sastri? Daru Sastri? Of Social Services?" PC Patton couldn't believe her luck. Of all the people to be at the scene. "I'd like to have a few words with you about a friend of yours. A Mr. Evan Tarin."

"Now?" Rumor around the Department had it that Daru's eyebrows could slay with a movement. She used that movement now.

PC Patton felt herself flush. Beside her, she heard Jack fidgeting. "No, not *now,*" she muttered.

By the time Daru allowed them to bother Rebecca, the body had been taken away, witnesses' statements had been recorded, and the carving knife had been removed as evidence.

"Rebecca," PC Patton kept her voice pitched low, the voice she used for small children. "Rebecca, I need to ask you some questions." Sastri had told her something of Rebecca's background and she'd promised to go carefully. "I'm not an ogre!" she'd snarled. Sastri had apologized.

Rebecca lifted her head from Roland's chest and scrubbed at her face with the palm of her hand. "You're the police," she said, sniffing. "The police are our friends."

"That's right. The police *are* your friends." *So-called normal people should be this cooperative.* "And I need to ask you, what happened in your apartment tonight?"

Rebecca's mouth twisted and her eyes filled again but she answered the question reasonably calmly although all in one breath. "She knocked on the door and I answered and she said I should be locked up and she had a knife so I threw the juice at her and now I don't have any and she dropped the knife but she still tried to hurt me then the Darkness ate her."

"The Darkness ate her?"

"Uh-huh." She buried her face again.

PC Patton stood. "You heard?" she asked her partner.

PC Brooks nodded. "It matches what the witnesses said pretty exactly. Except that last bit. Darkness ate her. I wonder what that means."

"Beats me." PC Patton turned to Daru. "You know?"

"I have no idea," Daru told her truthfully. She didn't add that she intended to find out.

"Well Homicide says it looks like a massive coronary." PC Patton nodded her head in the direction of the three shirt-sleeved men standing on the sidewalk. Without a murder to attend to, they were catching up on personal business. "So I guess we don't need to worry about it. Are you going to stay with her tonight?"

"If she doesn't, I will," Roland spoke up.

PC Patton nodded down at him. *You can trust a man with eyes like that*, she thought as they walked back to the patrol car. *He looks like he's been through hell and survived. Dresses strangely, though.*

"She didn't recognize me," Roland said, wonder in his voice.

Daru snorted. "You don't look the same."

Roland shrugged and lifted Rebecca to her feet. "Come on, kiddo. Let's go inside."

Rebecca hiccuped. "Darkness ate her, Roland."

"I wonder what she means," Daru murmured.

Over Rebecca's head, Roland's eyes met hers.

"*I* wonder where Evan is," he said.

"We still didn't talk to her."

PC Patton yanked the steering wheel around and the patrol car squealed onto Dundas Street. "I know."

"I think we should tell the sergeant."

"Tell the sergeant what? We don't have anything to tell him."

"Yeah, but . . ."

"We'll talk to him after we talk to her."

"I don't know, Mary Margaret."

"I do." She outmaneuvered a streetcar, the sudden acceleration pushing them both back in their seats. "Just leave it, Jack."

This was the place. Anyone who could See could have spotted it, for a pall hung over the three-story Victorian house. Evan had been very careful in following the Dark Adept's trail to this lair, using only a tiny fraction of his power, barely enough to do the job, not quite enough to give him away. Therefore, it had taken many hours to do a job he could've done in seconds, but he

hoped that meant the Darkness remained unaware that it was discovered.

He sent a probe into the house and found only one life—dark
but human—and ample evidence that he had come to the end of
the trail. Pushing his hair back off his face, he strode up the walk
and rang the bell. He heard it echo throughout the house, then
heard footsteps approaching.

"Yes, can I help you?" Gray hair, pale blue eyes, and star-
tlingly black brows. An assured voice, carefully modulated but
devoid of emotion, even of curiosity.

It took all of Evan's control to not flare up and turn this man
as far to the Light as he now was to the Dark. Instead, although
his hand trembled with the need to hold himself in check, he
reached out, touched the man on the chest and returned him to
what he had been before the Dark Adept had begun to warp and
destroy. He left him, however, the memories of the Darkness and
of what he had nearly become.

Eyes wide, the man gagged and ran from the door.

Evan entered and closed it quietly behind him. Silently, he
followed the path of Darkness up the stairs and into what had
once been a large and attractive bedroom. It wasn't quite as bad
as the hotel, but then the Darkness had been here a shorter time.

Suddenly the balance shifted and he nearly cried out, so intense was the shock. He did cry out a moment later when, pro-
jected from her now distant apartment, Rebecca's terror hit him.
Tears streaming down his face, he stood rooted to the spot while
his heart tore slowly in two.

*I am sorry, my Lady, but if I must sacrifice you to destroy the
Darkness, I will.*

The Dark Adept whistled as he turned up the path to the
house, the very picture of a successful young executive. He'd enjoyed himself this evening; as he saw it, he couldn't lose.
Whether Rebecca lived or died, the Light would be more than occupied with the need to stop his tool. And what a tool, a lifetime
of delusions and imagined slights honed into a weapon. Her vir-
ginity was an added bonus, taken only because she treasured it.

He pushed open the door and started up the stairs.

"Master, above you!"

The warning came barely in time. The Dark Adept threw himself below the blaze of glory, the very proximity twisting him in pain. He snarled up into the face of the Light, and vanished.

Evan came slowly down the stairs, his aspect shining out around him.

"Twice now," he said to the man who trembled and whimpered and hid his eyes, "you have freely chosen the Darkness. A second chance is not given to many. You will not get another." He clasped his hands together and the sword of Light rose up from their joining.

The only illumination in Rebecca's apartment spilled in through the windows, the ambient glow of a city night. Rebecca had been given a mug of warm milk and put to bed. Daru lay stretched out on the couch, her braid trailing on the floor. Roland sat in one of the kitchen chairs, picking out a lullaby on Patience. When Evan appeared he stood up slowly, and more slowly still put down the guitar.

"Welcome back," he said.

Evan's face lit up. He'd truly thought he'd never see Roland again. "You also," he said, joy wound about the words.

Roland refused to return the smile. "Where the hell were you?" he demanded. "Rebecca needed you."

"I know." The joy was gone. "I felt her fear."

"And you didn't care?"

"I couldn't come."

"I suppose you couldn't come when I needed you either?" Roland pushed past him and flipped on the light. Evan glowed too much in the darkness, became too unreal, too hard to accuse.

Daru muttered a complaint and sat up, rubbing her eyes. She saw Evan, saw the expression on Roland's face, and decided greetings could wait.

"Well?" Roland grabbed Evan's shoulder and yanked him around. "Where were you when I was . . . I was . . ." His voice broke and he dashed away a tear. "When I needed you . . ."

Evan spread his hands, the silver bracelets chiming softly. "Not even to save you could I leave my fight against the Darkness. I'm sorry."

"Sorry doesn't cut it!"

"The strongest steel," Daru said quietly, "goes through the hottest fire."

"Yeah?" Roland whirled on her. "Well, no one ever asks the

steel how it fucking feels about it, do they?" He snapped his head back to face Evan, knowing that Evan was right, knowing he couldn't expect to count for more than every other life threatened by Darkness, but also knowing it hurt anyway. "Then what about Rebecca?" he asked.

"I understand, Roland." Rebecca's voice came tentatively from the door to the bed alcove.

Roland's anger deflated. "So do I, kiddo," he sighed. He met Evan's eyes. "Really." But he didn't try to hide the hurt.

Evan nodded, acknowledging the pain for that was all he could do, and turned to face Rebecca. "I would have come to you if I was able," he told her.

She smiled. "I know."

"Well," Daru tucked her legs up, making room on the couch, "you'd better sit down, Evan, and we'll fill you in on what you missed. Unless you already know the details.

"No, I don't." He came and sat down, pulling Rebecca with him and tucking her in the circle of his arm close against his heart. One by one, beginning with Roland waking up in the alley—by unspoken agreement, no one asked him what had gone before—they told him about the events of the night.

"And then when the police people left," Rebecca finished, "we came upstairs and Daru made me wa . . ." She frowned in puzzlement toward the window. The others turned.

Tom sat on the window sill looking inordinately pleased with himself, a squirming piece of Darkness in his mouth. He leaped down, padded across the silent room, and dropped his burden at Evan's feet.

A cage of light appeared around it.

"Thank you," Evan said gravely to the cat.

Tom yawned.

"What is it?" Daru asked, peering down at the shifting black blob.

"Just what it looks like. A piece of Darkness broken off and given a limited life."

"It's alive?"

"Oh, yes. And there's no more of it here than in the hearts of many people, an amount easily overlooked. I imagine the Dark Adept used it as his eyes and ears."

"What are we supposed to do with it?" Roland wanted to know, amazed that his voice remained so calm. He couldn't decide whether he wanted to stomp the disgusting little thing into the floor or run screaming from the room.

The Light Adept stretched out his hand, the cage became a sphere and rose about four and a half feet from the floor. "We are going to question it."

The blob contracted in on itself with a terrified squeak. "Don't know anything!" it shrieked.

Evan continued as though the interruption hadn't occurred. "And it is going to tell us of its master's plans." The cage glowed brighter.

It would be easy to feel sorry for it, Daru thought, squinting, *if it wasn't so symbolic of the whole problem. Darkness takes over a little piece at a time and we all shrug it off until it's too late.*

The Dark Adept's messenger twisted and writhed in the cage, staying as far from the sides as it could.

Evan waited and the others waited with him.

"He opens the gate on Midsummer Night," it whined at last.

"We know that. Where?"

Roland strongly suspected that Evan could get a concrete sidewalk to confess using that tone.

"He didn't speak of it. Truly. Truly. Truly. The sacrifice must set the gate!"

"Sacrifice?"

The piece of Darkness shifted as far away as it could get from the menace in Evan's voice. "Blood prepares the way," it whimpered.

The cage contracted and the Darkness keened as it came in contact with the Light. In a few seconds, only a dazzling mote of glory remained, then it, too, disappeared.

"Is it dead?" Rebecca asked.

Evan shook his head. "You can't kill Darkness," he told her, "merely banish it for a while."

Behind Evan's back, Roland rolled his eyes at Daru. She shrugged. In her experience, when the world occasionally reduced itself to platitudes, the only response was to go on. "What sacrifice?" she asked.

"The gate must have an anchor in this reality," Evan explained bleakly. "Tomorrow night an innocent will die to provide it." His fingers curled into fists. He spun about and slammed them against the wall. "And I can't stop him until I know where!"

Rebecca reached up and caught his hands in hers. "You'll find him," she said with absolute certainty. Daru and Roland nodded in agreement, less in absolute certainty than in hope.

Evan pulled Rebecca into his arms and rested his cheek on the top of her head. "I pray you are right, Lady," he answered wearily.

"Is there anything more we can do tonight?" Daru asked.

Evan shook his head without lifting it.

"Well, then," she stood, hanging her purse strap over her shoulder, "I think we'd better pack it in. You want a ride home, Roland?"

"I thought I'd stay. If nobody minds."

Rebecca turned in Evan's embrace and smiled brightly. "I don't mind, Roland. You've already slept on the couch."

"Evan?"

He looked up. "It's good to have friends around you."

Daru headed for the door, rummaging for her car keys. "Rebecca, you have my home number. If anything, and I mean anything, else unusual happens tonight I want you to call me."

"Okay, Daru."

The door closed behind her and Evan pushed Rebecca toward the bed alcove. "Return to sleep, Lady," he told her. "I will join you in a moment."

Rebecca nodded and stifled a yawn. "Should I make Tom get off the bed?"

"No. He has earned his place tonight."

"Okay. Night, Roland."

"Good night, kiddo."

Alone with Evan, Roland didn't know what to say, where to start.

The Adept spoke first. "Are you all right? I mean, physically? The shadow realms are . . ."

"Yeah, they are." Roland couldn't keep the anger out of his voice. *And I think I've earned the right to be royally pissed off.* He could hear a song in the anger, but Evan was waiting patiently for an answer so he took a quick inventory, opened his mouth to list damages, and stopped dead. Nothing hurt. Frowning, he thought back; he could remember pain as he knelt beside Daru in Rebecca's apartment and the effort of getting the nearly hysterical girl down the stairs and over to the tree had almost had him in tears but after that . . . He could remember no pain after Rebecca had calmed, accepting the sanctuary of his arms. "I'm fine," he said at last, because he was, even if he didn't understand why.

Evan nodded. "Daru is right, you have strengthened."

Roland spread his hands. "I survived."

"You came to terms with yourself." The blue-gray eyes pleaded for understanding as he added, "I would have come for you if I could." His voice had roughened and Roland suddenly realized that the decision had hurt Evan almost as much as it had hurt him. Maybe more; Evan was supposed to be the white knight, riding to the rescue was his job.

"Hey, don't worry. I do understand." And he did. Finally. He clasped Evan's shoulder lightly and the Adept looked at him in surprise, sensing the new lack of restraint.

"You've come to terms with that as well?" he asked, a small smile beginning to form.

Roland returned it. "Yes," he said. "I have." He spun Evan lightly about and pushed him toward the bed alcove. "We'll talk in the morning."

"Good night, Roland."

"Good night, Evan."

"That piece goes there."

"This piece goes here."

"Is that the last of the dirt?"

"I think so."

"Bread cooker goes back on the cold box."

"Plant is busted."

"So fix."

"Can't fix plant."

Roland wasn't entirely certain he was awake. He could feel the couch beneath him and the sheet draped across his legs, but the high-pitched voices drifting in and out of his head seemed more like a dream. He supposed he could open his eyes and find out one way or another, but it just didn't seem worth the bother.

"Brush floor."

"Polish bread cooker."

"Polish everything."

"Sparkly clean now."

He had a vision of a horde of tiny people all dressed like Errol

Flynn in *Robin Hood*. ". . . but the shoemaker and his wife never saw the little folk again," he muttered.

"What is Bard muttering about?"

"Bard stuff. Get back to work."

Chapter Twelve

"Roland? That you?"

"Yeah, it's me, Uncle Tony." Roland went up the four stairs from the door to the landing and rounded the corner into the kitchen. "What are you doing home? Shop closed today?"

"Nah. Your aunt's back went out again last night and I'm driving her to the doctor's at eleven. You got yourself a new girlfriend? I notice you haven't been home for a couple of nights."

Green eyes and ebony hair and a lithely muscled body wrapped in satin. "No. It's just that job I told you about."

Tony frowned and closed the paperback he'd been reading, tapping the ends of blunt fingers on the cover. "You aren't mixed up in anything illegal, are you?"

"Nothing illegal, Uncle Tony." Roland felt his lips curl up into something that was not quite a grin as, unable to resist, he added, "You can definitely say I'm on the side of the Light with this one."

"Side of the light," Tony snorted. He peered at his nephew through narrowed eyes. "Still, it seems to be doing you good, settling you down some."

Roland sighed. He couldn't see it. The tiny mirror in his bathroom had shown him the same face it always had, albeit with a new nick from paying more attention to his profile than to his shaving. He was also getting a little tired of people telling him how much he'd matured, not having considered himself particularly childish before. "I'd better be going. I just dropped by to change clothes."

"Wait a minute." Tony tilted his chair back and plucked an envelope off the counter. "This came for you yesterday. Looks like it's from that singer friend of yours." He held it out.

"Looks like," Roland agreed, glancing at the Tulsa, Oklahoma postmark as he shoved the narrow envelope in the back pocket of his jeans. "Tell Aunt Sylvia I hope her back feels better."

"You coming home tonight?"

"I don't know."

"Well, try to get some sleep. You look like hell."

Roland paused halfway down the stairs and leaned back around the corner. "I thought you said it looked like this job was doing me some good?"

"What's inside a man has nothing to do with the amount of sleep he's getting."

A platitude worthy of Evan, Roland thought, and said, "You sound like you've been talking to a friend of mine." He waved and headed for the door.

"Sounds like you're getting smarter friends," Tony called after him.

Roland laughed and was still smiling as he got on the subway and headed back downtown.

"Daru must be still out in the city somewhere." Roland hung up the phone and shook his head. "I talked to her answering machine this time instead of her secretary, but the message was the same. She'll call when she gets in. It's nine seventeen. I'm beginning to think that woman does nothing but work."

"Her work is important," Evan pointed out. "She fights the Darkness constantly, and today she can only be more successful than we were."

The day had brought them no closer to finding out where the Dark Adept intended to open the gate. It had been long and frustrating and they'd accomplished absolutely nothing.

"Well, maybe we can guard the sacrifice." Roland picked up one of the pineapple muffins Rebecca had brought home from work and then put it back down. He didn't really feel hungry and his mind kept playing word association games. Sacrifice. Victim. Corpse.

"How?" Evan demanded, both hands working through his hair because they wouldn't lie idle at his sides. "He can choose from a city full of people. His only criteria is innocence." Both men turned to look at Rebecca, who puttered around the tiny kitchen making tea. "She is the only one I *know* I can protect," he added in a softer voice.

"So all we can do is wait?"

"Wait until he begins and hope I can stop him before he finishes. Yes."

"Will you be able to save . . ." Roland's voice trailed off at the look of pain in Evan's eyes.

"I will do all I can, but . . ." Evan's voice trailed off in turn.

"There must be something else we can do!" Roland smashed his fist down into the couch. Under the window, the harp buzzed faintly, an echo of his emotion.

Rebecca set the teapot down on the table. "We could ask Mrs. Ruth if there was something else we could do. Mrs. Ruth knows everything."

Somehow, Roland thought, remembering the bag lady bending over him when he woke in the alley, *I don't doubt that in the least.* He threw up his hands. "I'm willing to give her a shot at it. It beats sitting around here waiting."

"Very well," Evan agreed, forcing his hands to still with a visible effort. "You will go and speak to Mrs. Ruth, a wisewoman at the very least, it seems, and I will remain here in case the Darkness moves before you receive an answer. *For here, in this security, I can best guard my Lady. He will not have her even if I succeed at nothing else.* "Will you stay with me, Lady?"

Rebecca looked from Roland to Evan and frowned. She feared that Mrs. Ruth might not talk to Roland if he came alone. Mrs. Ruth could be very rude. But Evan wanted her to stay, needed her to stay even though she didn't quite understand why. "If Roland remembers the way," she decided at last.

"I remember, kiddo." He picked up Patience, told the harp he'd be back—it replied with a mournful sort of a chirp but seemed willing to let him go—and headed for the door.

"Wait!" Rebecca grabbed up a muffin, ran across the room, and pushed it into his hands. "Sometimes Mrs. Ruth is nicer if you bring her things."

"Thanks, kiddo." He winked at her, nodded at Evan, and left. There was no need for either of them to tell him to be careful.

Roland took the streetcar to Spadina and the Spadina bus north to Bloor. Three young women got on, laughing and talking, brightening the bus with their presence, and a chubby baby in a carrier smiled beatifically at him. He watched a teenager with a green mohawk give his seat to an old Oriental lady buried under packages and decided the world might be worth saving after all.

Humming a quiet tune to the motion of the swaying bus, even the knowledge that tonight Darkness might take another life couldn't completely destroy his mood. He'd been in enough Darkness lately. He was going to enjoy this little bit of Light.

What with traffic tie-ups, he enjoyed it for longer than he'd intended. He could've walked the distance just about as fast. *Well, now we know why heroes never take public transit,* he thought as he joined the surging crowd at the back door. The day had been hot, the people reflected this, and one of the anonymous bodies had a parcel of fresh fish. *Next time, I walk.* The exhaust fumes on Bloor Street seemed like country breezes by comparison.

Only one bundle buggy stood guard by the lilacs and Roland began to get a bad feeling when he dropped to his knees and stuck his head into the leafy tunnel. It smelled too good under there for Mrs. Ruth to be home.

She wasn't.

But in the middle of the cleared area where the bag lady usually sat, a peeled stick had been stabbed into the ground and skewered on the tip of it was a trailing gray banner. Roland reached out and plucked it free.

"A Dominion receipt?" he wondered. Then he turned it over.

Written on the back, the pale pencil marks barely visible against the limp and grimy paper, were the words: "Who raised the barriers?"

Who indeed? Roland thought, frowning. He wondered if Mrs. Ruth always left cryptic messages when she went out or if she meant this specifically as an answer to the question he'd come to ask.

What do we do now?

Who raised the barriers?

Not that it was much of an answer, he concluded.

Shoving the paper in his pocket, he crawled out from under the lilacs and stood, ignoring the curious stares from passersby. The traffic crept by on Bloor Street in a steady stream, giving him no reason to assume Spadina had miraculously cleared up since he'd gotten off the bus. He checked his watch and sighed. Ten thirty-three. Why weren't all these people at home with their families?

I'll do a quick search through the neighborhood. She can't have gone far, she left half her worldly possessions behind.

*   *   *

Daru kept up appearances until the elevator door closed behind her, then she sagged against the graffiti covered wall. She couldn't remember the last time she'd looked forward to a hot shower with such desperation. Tossing back her braid, she checked the time. Eleven seventeen. Well, that explained it. She shouldn't have let Mrs. Singh talk her into that third cup of coffee.

As the elevator ground its weary way down the remaining nine floors, she worked out the time it would take to get from where she was in the Jane/Finch corridor to Rebecca's apartment in the heart of the city. There, at least, the hour would work for her; at this time on a Thursday the parkway should be empty. *Though I'll probably arrive too late to be of any help.* Sometimes it seemed like that was her entire life, following behind the Darkness, picking up the pieces, and trying to patch them together again.

She didn't regret her decision though, continuing with her job rather than throwing all her time in with Evan. People depended on her. Not faceless masses of humanity, but individual people. They needed her and she had no intention of letting them down. The little battles often win the war, as her Uncle Devadas always said.

The elevator wheezed to a stop in the lobby and the door slid open in a series of quivering jerks, burying the legend, "Tony loves Shelley, and Anna, and Rajete, and Grace."

"Busy boy, that Tony"; Daru noted as she strode across the dimly lit lobby. Half the lights had been smashed again and she made a mental note to call the building manager first thing in the morning. She picked the electrical tape off the lock, restoring its function, and it closed behind her with a satisfying click. All unarrived "boyfriends" could now sleep in the dumpster.

She'd parked her car under the one remaining streetlight in the visitor's parking, half expecting, as she always did, never to see it again. The underground garage was moderately more secure—provided the door worked at all—but Daru had been staying out of underground garages lately.

After pumping the gas a few times, just to let the ancient car know she meant business, Daru turned the key in the ignition. Nothing happened.

"Don't be, ridiculous," she snapped, trying it again with identical results. "The battery can't be dead," She popped the hood and got out to investigate, more because she hated inaction than because she knew what she was looking for.

The battery wasn't dead. It was missing.

Daru's father, who clung as tightly as he could to a traditional Hindu lifestyle, had always worried that the manners and morals of the people she worked with would rub off on his daughter. The manners and morals hadn't, but over the years she'd picked up an extensive vocabulary he would not have approved of. She worked through it now, beginning in English and continuing into French, Hindu, Portuguese, Korean, and the three words she knew in Vietnamese—which were biologically inappropriate to an automobile but made her feel a lot better.

She checked her watch again. Eleven twenty-seven. Transit ran until midnight. Throwing her purse over her shoulder, she locked the car and headed for the bus stop. Just before she reached it, a bus roared by.

She remembered a few words she'd forgotten back by the car and also repeated a few of her favorites under her breath. Then, with ill-grace, she settled down to wait the scheduled twenty minutes between buses.

The night seemed to grow darker.

A week ago Daru would have blamed it on her imagination. Now, she knew better. A warm breeze rubbed against her. Riding on it came a sweet familiar smell. She scanned the area and spotted the red glow at the edge of the shadow cast by the apartment building. The darkness was too deep to penetrate, but as she watched the glow moved two feet to the right, intensified briefly, then moved two feet again.

Three of them.

She could remain perfectly still and assume they hadn't seen her. But that would be a fool's assumption for the skin on the back of her neck crawled in response to the menace in their stares.

She could try to make it back to her car, locking the doors and hoping the light in the parking lot would make them wary. Hoping futilely.

If she hadn't fixed the lobby lock, she could've gone back to Mrs. Singh and called for help. But she didn't regret it for if the lock kept her out, it also kept out the three who watched.

Remaining in the bus shelter only meant she would be easily cornered.

Her back straight, she started down the sidewalk toward the

distant lights of a major intersection. She supposed she was
frightened, deep down, but anger was the only emotion she was
really aware of. Anger that this was even happening. Anger that
she couldn't stand and fight.

"Hey, pretty momma."

The voice came from just behind her left shoulder. How had
they gotten so close? She didn't waste time wondering. She began
to run.

The glow of the streetlights didn't seem to reach the ground
and Daru ran in a kind of twilight zone, the slapping of her leather
soles against the concrete almost, but not quite, drowning out the
sounds of pursuit. She used all her breath for running; in this
neighborhood a scream would bring no response.

Suddenly, almost directly in front of her, a young man held out
both hands, his smile a humorless flash of white. "Let's party," he
purred.

Too close to swerve, she dropped her shoulder, slammed him
out of the way, then saw another two approaching out of the darkness. "More?" she panted and risked a quick glance back along
her path. The original three seemed to be gaining. Daru knew she
should stay on the main road, but she didn't see how she could.
Taking in great lungfuls of the humid air, she put on a fresh burst
of speed and darted up the dark alley between two buildings.
Maybe she could lose them in the maze of high rises.

Behind her, she heard nasty laughter. "Why run, baby? You
know you'll enjoy it."

She followed twists and turns and did everything she could,
but the pack stayed on her. And grew larger. Echoes bounced
about between the buildings and she knew that sooner or later,
tired and confused, she'd take a wrong alley and end up . . .

Chest heaving, she leaned against a concrete wall and tried to
catch her breath, ears straining to pick immediate danger out of
the sounds of pursuit. That way; coming up the alley from her
right. And . . .

Oh, blessed god, from the left as well!

She straightened and prepared to take a few down with her.

"Yo. Bubba."

Savagely, she bit back the scream and whirled around. Behind
her, a pudgy little bag lady pointed at a bulging bundle buggy.

"Get in."

"What?"

"In. To the buggy."

"Mrs. Ruth?"

"Unless you'd like to be on the wrong end of a gangbang?"

Daru got into the buggy. Somehow. The rags and bits of odds and ends that strained at the wire sides were only a thin layer of camouflage, the center was empty. Knees up by her cheeks, arms tight about her shins, Daru peered up at the bag lady's scowl.

"Why . . ." she began.

"Quiet, bubba," Mrs. Ruth said conversationally and piled an armload of rags on Daru's head.

Footsteps ran by going left.

Footsteps ran by going right.

Protesting shrilly, the bundle buggy began to move.

"Where . . ." Daru called.

Mrs. Ruth patted the top of the rags firmly. "Quiet, bubba," she said again.

Rebecca yawned and buried her face in the crook of her arm, squirming into a more comfortable position on the couch.

"Lady." Evan's voice seemed to come from very far away. "Why don't you go to bed."

"'Cause I'm going to help you," Rebecca explained, yawning again. She pushed herself up into a sitting position and turned to face Evan who stood at the window. "We're going to fight the Darkness together."

He smiled at her and crossed the room to smooth tangled curls away from her face. "When the Darkness," he began, but Rebecca's fingers closing tightly around his wrist cut off the words.

"Look!" She pointed with her free hand at the white mist seeping in through the open window.

Evan frowned but held his power in check. Whatever else it was, this was not a thing of the Darkness.

The mist swirled into a column and took on the vague shape of a tall man with long curly hair and a workman's large hands.

"Ivan?" Rebecca's eyes widened. "What are you doing here?"

Evan recognized him now. This was the spirit that had guided him from the Light.

"Ivan? Why won't you talk to me?"

"I don't think he can, Lady. He has wandered far from the place he is tied to and has no strength for speech."

"But why? He never leaves the campus. Never. I didn't think he could."

"Lady, is there a large open area near where this spirit makes his home?" He knew he was right before Rebecca answered for Ivan lost all definition and the column of mist began to spin.

"Uh-huh. There's a big round field right in . . . Is that the place, Evan? Is Darkness *there?*"

"Yes, Lady, I think so," He bent and kissed her quickly, his eyes alight with the anticipation of battle. He would arrive before the sacrifice began, before the balance shifted. This time, Darkness would not escape!

"Evan, I want to go, too!"

"I'm sorry, Lady, the way I must travel, you couldn't keep up."

"I could," Rebecca protested scrambling off the couch. "I've got running shoes!" she wailed to the suddenly empty apartment.

The small body lay half its length above the grass, held in the air by bands of Darkness. Behind it stood a man who smiled as he raised his left hand above his head. From that hand arced the curved blade of a black dagger.

Evan wasted no time on subtlety. He gathered his power and shot a mighty bolt of pure white Light directly at the chest of the standing man, using over half of the strength he had available in a desperate attempt to stop the knife from falling.

The concussion knocked him backward and slammed him to the ground, leaving him momentarily blinded by the sudden explosion of energy that followed his blow.

The Dark Adept began to laugh. "Pretty fool," he said.

His voice, Evan realized, came from about twenty feet left of . . . "Illusion," he cried bitterly and struggled to clear his sight.

"No. A mirror. It showed you what you wanted to see and reflected your power back at you. Most of *my* power went into it and, were you able, you would find me an easy target now. But the Light is *so* predictable. You reacted exactly as I had anticipated, although I'd hoped you might throw everything and destroy yourself. It would have saved me the bother of dealing with you when I finish here."

Evan gained his feet and took two swaying steps toward the voice, barely able to see a shadowy outline through the starbursts of light that still blurred his vision.

The bells of the city began to ring midnight.

"Too late," the Dark Adept mocked.

At that instant, Evan's sight cleared.

He saw a curly, haired child of no more than four stretched out in the exact center of the King's College Circle common. He saw the black knife touch her throat. He saw the blood on the grass.

And the balance shifted.

Evan cried out in pain and dropped to his knees, clutching at himself in a desperate attempt to hold together. He felt the Darkness approach and forced himself back on his feet to face it.

"Pretty fool," the Dark Adept repeated, his features sharply delineated by the amount of power he now carried.

The black whip sliced skin off the arm Evan threw up to shield his face. And then from his side. It cut lines of pain into his legs and slashed his defenses into pieces.

"I have won," the Darkness purred.

The black bolt hit Evan squarely in the chest and would have thrown him entirely off the common and onto the pavement of the Circle had he not slammed into the trunk of a young oak and slid down it to the ground. He lay limply for as long as he dared, calling up what little power remained to him. He was so tired and it hurt so much. When he thought he could do it without screaming, he took hold of the tree and, using it as a staff, struggled to his feet. Beneath his hand he felt the strength of the living wood rising from its roots deep in the earth, then, to his astonishment, he felt that strength flow through the contact and into him. Although no breeze moved them, above his head and down the whole line of oaks edging that arc of the Circle, leaves rustled as the trees entered the battle on the side of the Light.

Compared to what the Darkness could call on, now that the sacrifice had so drastically shifted the balance, it wasn't much, but Evan welcomed it with his whole heart. He lifted his head, brought his hands together and from them blazed the Light.

"You really haven't got the sense to know when you're beaten, have you?" asked the Dark Adept, sauntering closer. "If you give up now, you'll still exist tomorrow and can watch this world fa . . . Damn you!" For an instant, but only an instant, he stared, face twisted with pain, at the stump of his arm. Then it was whole again and he was raising it to point at Evan.

Evan parried the first blow. And the second. The third snapped his head around and the bar of Light flickered. The fourth lifted him off his feet and the bar of Light died.

*   *   *

"We've got *what* going on at King's College Circle?" PC Patton asked, making a puzzled face at her partner.

"Fireworks," the dispatcher replied, the weariness in her voice clearly audible over the radio. The flu bug had put the whole force on extended shifts. "Two reports of fireworks and one of some nut-case with a light-saber."

PC Brooks mouthed, *Luke Skywalker?* and PC, Patton shrugged.

"We're on it," she sighed.

The Dark Adept spread his fingers and looked down through the spaces at Evan, curled up and panting on the grass. "You should have run when you had the chance," he said, and flew backward as something hard rammed into his stomach, knocking him flat on his back and leaving him gasping for breath.

"Don't you hurt him anymore!" Rebecca screamed, standing over Evan, chin thrust forward and hands balled into fists. When she'd reached the Circle and found that Evan had fallen, she'd moved without thinking, lowering her head and launching herself at the Dark Adept.

A physical attack was the last thing he'd expected and so it had worked. "Oh, I'll hurt him," he gasped, sitting up and drawing his fury around him like a cloak, "but first, first, I'll hurt you."

He raised his hand to strike and suddenly found himself wrapped in mist. Mist that thickened and thinned, inexplicably blocking his sight and therefore his blow. Snarling with rage, he struck at it instead.

"You can't hurt me," the mist whispered, and two pale eyes met his. "I'm already dead."

"Oh, you're wrong," the Darkness warned. "You're very wrong. But destruction now is too good for the lot of you." Brushing a bit of grass off his jeans, he smiled. "Live. Live and know you failed when tomorrow I open the gate and the barrier falls. Why should I give you an easy out when you'll torture yourselves more exquisitely than I ever could for the next twenty-four hours." He vanished, his laughter merging with the sound of distant sirens.

Rebecca dropped to her knees and lightly touched the tip of one finger to the purpling curve of Evan's cheek. "Evan," she sobbed, "he's gone. What do I do now?"

Evan heard her as though from a very long way away. He couldn't find the strength to reply. And he couldn't face her with his failure.

"Evan?" She plucked at the torn sleeve of his T-shirt. There were wounds and massive bruising all over his body, but instead of blood each cut seeped Light. "Evan? You've got to get up!"

"He can't, Lady."

At the sound of the deep, slow voice, Rebecca whirled around and flung herself up and into the arms of the troll. "Oh, Lan, I don't know what to do," she cried.

Lan merely held her and silently stroked her back.

"He's hurt. Bad."

"I know, Lady. I felt his pain."

She sniffed and wiped her eyes on the hem of her tank top. "The police are coming," she said, turning her head to better hear the sirens.

"They will take him from you."

"They will?"

"He is not of this world. Let me take him to safety, Lady, for I owe him a debt."

"Yes. Yes." Rebecca pushed herself away and stared up at the troll, tears still spilling down over her cheeks. "You take him 'cause I can't carry him and I'll tell the police what happened. Daru says if I'm in trouble I'm to go to the police." As the patrol car roared up in a blaze of sound and light she whirled and started across the common to meet it.

Lan has Evan. Don't tell them about Evan. Rebecca tried to keep that separate from all the other bits and pieces, but car doors slammed and people started shouting and she felt everything beginning to get all mixed up. She stumbled over a tiny body, nearly invisible in the night, and the Darkness that rose up around it almost knocked her to her knees. The sacrifice. A number of the bits and pieces got away and she cried out.

PC Patton strained to see what was going on in the dark center of the common. "These things look pretty," she muttered, jerking her head at one of the old-fashioned street lamps, "but they give bugger all in the way of light."

PC Brooks shifted his grip on his nightstick. "Someone's coming. Sounds . . ." He paused. It sounded like a wild animal in pain, but the moving shadow looked like a person. "It's a girl," he added a few seconds later as the runner came closer to the light.

"Not just any girl." PC Patton stepped forward and Rebecca ran right into her arms, forcing her back a step to keep them both from going down.

"He killed her. He killed her," she sobbed, clutching at the policewoman with a desperate grip. "She was just a little girl and he killed her. It's too late now and he got away!" The last word rose to a wail.

By the second sentence, PC Brooks had radioed for backup. By the third, he'd snapped the searchlight on and flooded the Circle and the common it contained with light. By the fourth he was halfway to the small, pale shape lying crumpled on the grass.

PC Patton forced Rebecca's fingers to loose their grip on her shoulders, a little surprised that it took all her strength to do it, and she cradled the distraught girl in her arms. "Who killed her?" she demanded, shouting over the sirens of two arriving cars. "Who."

Rebecca buried her head away from the noise and the confusion and whimpered. She wanted to go home.

"Rebecca? Rebecca!"

"Roland?" Rebecca's head snapped up and she wrenched free of PC Patton's hold, throwing herself across the space between them and into Roland's arms in the same desperate motion.

Somehow, Roland managed to keep his feet. "Shh, kiddo, shh. I'm here." He shuffled them both sideways until they stood on the grass, his hands running in soothing patterns up and down Rebecca's back. There were a million questions he wanted to ask, but he only whispered comforting words into her curls and provided an anchor for her to catch hold of. Soon they were the only island of quiet amidst the lights and the sirens and the men and women who had no idea of the real horror they'd stumbled upon.

No one noticed that the common had acquired another oak tree. Or that when the confusion died down the tree was no longer there.

Later, at the station:

"I've been staying with her, because of," Roland waved a hand, "last night." *Believe me,* said his voice, truth and sincerity behind every word. He hoped he wasn't laying it on too thick. He wasn't sure what he could do without Patience or the harp.

Heads nodded.

"I thought she was safe at the apartment." Which he had. "She suggested I go to Bloor to get some things." Which was true. "The Dominion there is open twenty-four hours," Which it was. Although he wasn't at it. "I was on my way back when I heard the sirens and saw the lights, so I went to investigate." And considering the scenarios he'd dreamed up on that wild run, seeing the "fireworks" for what they were and knowing what the Darkness was capable of, what he'd found had been almost a relief. "I have no idea what she was doing there."

"I followed him," Rebecca whispered, the first coherent words she'd spoken since Roland had appeared back at the Circle. "I have running shoes and I followed him."

"Followed who?" asked a homicide detective gently.

Rebecca butted her head into Roland's side and stared at the detective with wide, uncomprehending eyes.

"Did you follow your friend?"

She reached for Roland's hand. Evan was hurt. "Yes."

But because they didn't know about Evan, the detectives asked the wrong questions. And because Rebecca answered only what they actually asked and they heard her answers through the label they'd placed on her, they never found out what really happened.

"Did you see who killed the little girl?"

"Yes."

"Did you see him actually do it?"

"No."

"But you did see him?"

"Yes."

"What did he look like?"

When she described the suspect they were already looking for, they were happy and they believed and they stopped asking questions.

"You'll remain available," they said as Rebecca carefully printed her name at the bottom of her statement.

Roland said they would.

Not until they were in the cab on the way back to Rebecca's apartment, did he get a chance to ask about Evan and even then he could barely force the question past the sudden fear in his throat. *He couldn't be . . .*

"He got hurt, Roland," Rebecca sniffed. "And Lan the troll took him away."

"Took him where, kiddo?

"Somewhere safe."

Where would a troll think was safe, Roland wondered. And then the cab pulled up in front of Rebecca's building and he knew.

"Roland, look!" Rebecca sprang out of the cab.

"I'm looking, kiddo." He paid the cabbie and exited only slightly more slowly. It was something to look at. Strange and wonderful creatures perched in every available nook and cranny. The old chestnut sagged under the weight of the littles in its branches.

Every eye was on Rebecca as she ran through the still broken door and pounded up the stairs.

By the time Roland reached the apartment she was kneeling by the bed, her hands running lightly up the length of Evan's naked body.

"I don't remember," she lamented in a voice so lost it pulled tears from Roland's eyes. "I don't remember what to do."

He touched her gently on the shoulder, not understanding but offering what support he could. He forced himself not to look away from the bruising and the half healed wounds. *If he can stand the pain of bearing them, I'll just have to stand knowing that he does.*

Tom stared up at them both from his position on the other pillow, his expression, Roland thought, vaguely accusatory. *You let this happen,* said the set of his whiskers.

"Lady?"

"I'm here, Evan." Rebecca pressed her face against his shoulder.

The Adept sighed and seemed to relax into her touch. When she moved away, he opened his eyes. The stormy gray had become bleak and leaden.

"Roland," he acknowledged the other man weakly. "I failed."

Roland licked away a tear that had reached his mouth. "There's still tomorrow," he said, fighting to keep his voice steady.

Evan let his eyes fall closed. "There may *only* be tomorrow."

Chapter Thirteen

"Roland?"

"Mmmph." He dragged himself up through flannel layers of sleep and managed to focus on Rebecca's face. "Wazzup, kiddo?"

"I'm going to work now."

"Work?" Twisting his brain into some semblance of rationality, Roland tried to sit up with a distinct lack of success. A large, furry cement block lay squarely in the middle of his chest. "Are you quite comfortable?" he demanded.

Tom yawned.

"Wonderful." Roland gagged. "Cat food breath. Just what I need first thing in the morning." The light that spilled through the curtains had an unused look. He checked his watch. Five thirteen. "Or last thing at night," he added. It had been barely four hours since they'd left the police station.

Rebecca lifted Tom to the floor.

He stalked off, pointedly ignoring them both.

"Now then." Roland got himself up onto his elbows. "Why are you going to work?"

"Because." Rebecca looked confused. "It's what I do."

She wore jeans and an old turquoise bowling shirt. Her hair clustered in damp tangles around her face. She'd obviously been up for a while and she certainly looked wide awake, but Roland noticed the dark circles under her eyes and the way she was worrying at her full lower lip.

"You're tired, kiddo," he said, swinging his legs off the couch and sitting up. "You didn't get much sleep last night. Why don't you take the day off."

"No," She shook her head, her hair fanning out with the motion. A drop of water hit Roland on the chin. "I'm not sick. Daru says you never take the day off unless you're sick."

Roland knew better than to argue against a "Daru says" so he tried a different tack. "But Evan . . ."

Rebecca's face softened. "Evan is mostly okay now, but he isn't finished yet. When he wakes up, he'll be better."

"And he'll want you here."

"Yes." Her expression became serious again. "But he said before I have to keep doing what I do so the Darkness doesn't," she hesitated over the word but got it out, "disrupt ordinary things." She sighed. "I think this is how *I* fight the Darkness. Don't you see, Roland? It isn't big or important, but it's what I do."

"I do see, kiddo." He reached out and took one of her hands, squeezing it gently. "And you're right. It's the ordinary things that are important. That's what we're all trying to save in our way."

Rebecca smiled and Roland felt the warmth of it wrap around him like two strong arms. "I knew you'd understand," she said. She freed her hand and headed for the door. As she slid the chain lock open, she paused and glanced back.

"It's Friday," she told him, as though she'd just realized a happy coincidence. "On Friday, I make blueberry muffins." And then she was gone.

Roland shook his head, slid the chain back on, and padded to the bathroom. When he came out, he paused beside the bed and stared down at Evan. In the dim light of the bed alcove, the Adept's skin seemed to glow faintly. His head was tossed back, multihued hair spread over the pillows, and the long delicate line of his throat exposed. Most of the bruising had faded to ugly gray smudges and the wounds were fine white scars. One long-fingered hand lay curled on his stomach. The other had been flung out, as though even in his sleep he'd tried to hold Rebecca as she left, and now it dangled off the bed. Roland eased it up and carefully laid it on the sheet.

He looks more fragile now, almost healed, than he did last night so badly hurt. Strong emotions surged through him and Roland tried to put a name to what he felt. It wasn't desire, although he could—would—no longer deny that warmth was there. It wasn't pity, although he felt that, too. A week ago, he would've seen where this was leading and gone no further. A week ago, he'd been a different man. He moved quietly out of the bed alcove.

It must be love.

Not for Evan, not really. But for what Evan was. For what Evan had agreed to do. To suffer and perhaps be destroyed so that a world not his own would not fall to the Darkness.

Suddenly too restless to sleep, he lifted Patience from her case, sat down on a kitchen chair, and began to play, letting his emotions form the music. He sang the words as they came to him, allowing them to choose their own patterns. When he finished, the pale light of dawn had long since been replaced by the strong sunlight of a summer's day and he'd found a song that would be a part of every piece of music he'd ever play from now on.

> *"And I never can again be free*
> *For you are in my music*
> *And the music's all of me."*

It was the tag from one of his old songs, one of the ones that Rebecca had said, "wasn't quite." It suddenly had a new relevance.

He stood, stretched, and realized he'd had an audience, for the movement sent them scurrying for cover. They moved too fast for him to really See, but hovering just on the edge of his awareness was the sense they approved. He checked his watch. Nine forty-five? He'd been playing for four hours?

Christ. Time sure flies when you're having . . . having . . . whatever it was I was having.

Four hour's without changing position should have left him all but crippled. He seemed fine. Except that his mouth was so dry it stuck to itself. Fortunately, because he just wasn't up to making tea, herbal or otherwise, he remembered he'd shoved half a package of sugarless gum in his pocket yesterday. But which pocket? Two guitar picks, a crumpled Dominion receipt, sixty-two cents in change, and the letter from Tulsa later, he found it and popped a piece into his mouth with a sigh of relief. It'd hold him until he could get to a cup of coffee.

He shoved the picks, the receipt, and the coins back into his jeans and took a closer look at the letter. It was unusually thin, their monthly correspondence tended more to bulk rates, and he hoped nothing had gone wrong. A quick glance into the bed alcove showed that Evan still slept, so he sat down again and tore open the envelope.

There were two sheets of paper. Scrawled across the first was a single sentence: *I don't know why, but I thought you could use this.* The second was a handwritten sheet of music with the notes sprawling sloppily up and down the staff, testimony to the speed in which they were written. Melody, harmony, chords; all there. And the lyrics . . .

Roland propped the paper up against Rebecca's teapot and again reached for Patience. Humming softly to give himself a reference, he slowly worked his way through the chording. It wasn't difficult—D, Dm, C, Dm—but it took him a while to put it together with the eerie tune. Finally he nodded and started again from the beginning, this time actually singing the words.

> *"Wind's four quarters, air and fire*
> *Earth and water, hear my desire*
> *Grant my plea who stands alone—*
> *Ma . . ."*

"Roland!"

The intensity of the cry jerked Roland to his feet and spun him around.

"Roland, Where did you get that song?" The Adept was framed in the door to the bed alcove, panting slightly, hair wild, eyes bright.

"A friend sent it," Roland offered, keeping his voice soothing, wondering if this was some sort of crazy reaction to the damages of the night before. "Why?"

"Because it's the answer! Don't you see? It's a goddess invocation!"

"A *goddess* invocation?" Roland began to protest, then paused. He didn't read much, Uncle Tony was right about that, but he seemed to remember from a comparative mythology course he'd once taken that back even before all the Olympus stuff people had worshiped a goddess of some kind. Or a couple of goddesses. "Okay, a goddess invocation." It still sounded strange, but then things hadn't been exactly normal lately anyway.

Then another memory surfaced. Mrs. Ruth's voice came out of the past. *This world is sort of a buffer zone between the Light and the Dark. When life indigenous to the world developed, barriers were raised around it.*

Roland pulled the Dominion receipt out of his pocket and turned it over.

Who raised the barriers?

Silently, he handed it to Evan, willing to bet he now knew the answer.

"I am such an idiot!" the Adept exclaimed, first reading Mrs. Ruth's message, then scanning through the lyrics of the song. He hadn't sounded happier since he'd arrived. "We can stop him! As late as it is, we can stop him!" Laughing with relief, he grabbed Roland by the shoulders and swept him up into an enthusiastic embrace.

After a few seconds of mutual back pounding, they pulled apart.

"Now," Evan punctuated the word with a wave of his arm, "we . . ."

"Uh, Evan . . ." Roland swallowed heavily. The imprint of warm flesh still clinging to him made it difficult to think. "Before we do anything, could you please put some clothes on."

Evan looked down the length of his body, then up at Roland.

"Sorry," he said, and dashed into the alcove to dress.

Not bloody likely you're sorry. Roland gave a mental snort, but he couldn't stop a stupid grin from taking up residence on his face. *First we save the world. Then we think about . . . whatever.*

When Evan came back out, the clothes that had been all but destroyed during the battle were clean and new. His bracelets and earring sparkled with light and even the happy face button was back on his T-shirt.

"Now," he began again, wrapping the third belt around his hips and buckling it, "we kick ass."

"How?" Roland asked, tucking Patience back in her case. "We use this song to call up some goddess and she sends the Darkness back where it belongs?"

Evan got an apple out of the fridge and bit into it. "Essentially," he said, wiping a dribble of juice off his chin with the back of his hand.

Roland sat back on his heels. "There's got to be more to it than that."

"There is," Evan agreed cheerfully.

"What?"

"I don't know."

"What!"

"Look, Roland, there's millions of people in this city. One of them has to be a witch."

"I think you got hit too hard on the head last night. Witches, as in ugly old ladies with warts and broomsticks, are not real." A sudden memory of a child baked crispy and brown left his lips pressed white. "At least not here."

"No, not here," Evan agreed, his voice soothing away the terror. "But witches, as in pagans, worshipers of the old ways, are real. And all we have to do is find them. They'll know how to use the song."

Roland sighed and stood. "Okay," he said and found himself, smiling. Evan's mood was catching. "How do we find them? The Yellow Pages?"

Evan spread his arms, his eyes shining. "Why not? It's a place to start."

There were no witches in the Yellow Pages. Or the white pages. Nor was there anything listed under wicca or its derivatives.

"Wicca?" Roland asked.

"Mmmm." Evan flipped to the Churches listing. "It's the old word. Unity, Wesleyan, damn. Maybe under temples." A moment later, he slammed the book shut. "I don't believe that in a city this size there's no listing for temples."

"Try occult," Roland suggested.

There was nothing listed under occult.

"Parachute," Evan murmured. "Parade supplies, Paralegal agents, Parapsychologists, see Astrologers, Psychic Consultants, Etc. Well, it'll give us a jumping off point."

"You really think this is going to work?"

"Yes. It feels right." The way Evan said *right* left no room for doubt.

There were twenty-five listings under Astrologers, Psychic Consultants, Etc., in the Toronto Yellow Pages, from simple listings of personal names, to tea rooms, to companies that sounded more like slick investment firms. Roland pulled Rebecca's phone out from under the couch and plugged it in. He listened. Unplugged it. And plugged it back in again.

"I'm not getting a dial tone." He tapped the receiver gently against the floor. "Still nothing."

Evan took the receiver and held it to his ear. After a second his lips drew back and his brows drew down.

Roland assumed the Adept heard something he hadn't. He was sure of it a moment later when Evan slammed the phone down with enough force to crack the plastic. "We're cut off?" he asked tentatively.

"Yes," Evan agreed, and the anger in the word made Roland flinch. "He dares to detail to me what the Darkness will do to this world. Beginning with those who have helped me."

Roland backed out from under the lilacs and stood, dusting his knees off. "As far as I can tell, she hasn't come back yet."

Evan drummed his fingers on his uppermost belt and looked distressed. "I hope she hasn't been taken by Darkness."

"Yeah." Roland relived a few moments of what that meant. "So do I." He took a deep breath. "Well, do we go get our future told. See if it lasts beyond tonight?"

Two of the listings in the Yellow Pages were in the Bloor/Spadina area. The first was almost directly across the street from Mrs. Ruth's cubbyhole. *Madame Alaina*, said the warped and fading sign in the second floor window, *Stars, cards, palms. No appointment necessary.*

A smaller and even more faded sign had been tacked to the door leading up and over an ancient drugstore; at least Roland thought it was a drugstore. The light was so bad and the windows so dirty he couldn't be sure. The stairwell smelled strongly of cooked cabbage.

"This is nuts," Roland whispered as they reached the first landing and Evan raised his hand to knock.

"Trust me," Evan told him.

Roland sighed.

Evan knocked.

A few minutes later the door opened and a girl of about fifteen looked them up and down. She ignored Roland, her dark eyes fastening on Evan as if he was a present she'd like to unwrap. Without adjusting the volume of the cassette player she wore on her belt, she pushed a pair of headphones down around her neck and smiled broadly. The hit song of a popular new wave band came tinnily through the tiny speakers.

"Can I do something for you?" she asked, looking hopeful.

"We need to see Madame Alaina?"

"Oh. Her opinion of them dropped a few obvious notches "You're not cops, are you?"

"No."

"Well, grandma's not seeing anyone today."

"It's important."

"Yeah, it always is." She shrugged lycra-covered shoulders. "Doesn't make any difference. She won't even get out of bed. Says it's the end of the world. Try coming back tomorrow."

"Tomorrow will be too late."

Her eyes grew shiny at the pain in Evan's voice.

Yeah, well, teenage girls are susceptible to that sort of thing, Roland thought, ignoring the moisture that had risen in his own. "Uh, wait a minute . . ." he added aloud.

She half looked at him, most of her attention still on the Adept.

He took a deep breath and continued, feeling like a fool. "You, uh, wouldn't know any, uh, witches, would you?"

This time she really looked at him and didn't like what she saw. "Witches, yeah, right." She took a fluid step back and closed the door firmly in their faces.

Roland turned to Evan and shrugged. "Guess not."

Evan sighed.

They clattered down the stairs and back out onto the street.

"I would have liked to have spoken to the grandmother," Evan said quietly as they walked west toward the neighborhood's other astrologer. "She would have had wisdom to pass on."

"What? Evan, the woman was in bed because she thinks the world is going to end."

Evan's silence spoke louder than words.

Roland felt himself flush. "Oh. Yeah."

Child Slaughtered at King's College Circle! The headline stopped them both and they stared for a moment at the paper. Smaller headlines read: *Man Deliberately Strikes Four With Car* and *Arsonist Torches Nursing Home, Seventeen Die.*

"It begins," Evan said, and walked on.

In the distance, sirens wailed.

The second address led them to a small frame house, bright blue and looking out of place among all the exposed brick and open concept renovations. Knee-high weeds filled the lawn, but upon closer inspection they turned out to be wild meadow flowers. Roland recognized the daisies and black-eyed susans although the rest still looked like weeds.

Evan rang the bell and they could faintly hear the first two bars of Beethoven's "Ninth Symphony" chime through the interior.

The woman who answered the door wore her long salt-and-pepper hair parted in the middle. Her flowered dress dropped yards of fabric from a square cut yoke to just above her ankles. On her feet, Roland noticed, were a pair of hundred dollar German sandals.

"Yes?" she said, smiling at them.

"We're looking for Sky Mackensie."

"I'm Sky. But you're looking for something else."

"That's right." Roland had always thought Astrologers, Psychic Consultants, Etc., were a group of loons and charlatans and here was the second one proving him wrong.

"You're looking for a past-life justification for why you turned your backs on society to pursue a forbidden love in this existence." Behind her, crystals strung all along the hall split the sunlight into rainbows.

"Uh, no." *Score one for the loons and charlatans.*

"No?"

"No," Evan told her firmly. "We're looking for witches. Wiccans?"

She touched one hand to her breast. "I went to university with a witch. She kept filling the bathtub with herbs and dripping candle wax all over the porcelain. We didn't stay in touch, though. I married Owen and I think she joined a lesbian terrorist group. I'm sorry. That's probably not much help."

"Not much," Roland admitted. The cuckoo clock in the entry said it was almost twelve. They had to get moving. "But thanks for your time."

"And if you ever do need to find a past life . . ."

"We'll keep you in mind."

"I take VISA and Mastercard," she said and closed the door.

On the walk to Chinatown, Roland could feel Evan's mood hardening with every step. "Penny for your thoughts?" he offered at last.

"In a city of this size, someone must be following the old ways," Evan sighed. "After last night, the balance has shifted too far for me to stop him on my own."

"You're not on your own," Roland reminded him.

"Yes. I know." He tossed his hair back off his face and two middle-aged women dressed all in black fell silent to watch him pass. "But we have so little time."

The Chinese astrologer was, like Madame Alaina, up a flight of stairs and over a shop. But where Madame Alaina had worked from a crowded apartment—the glimpse they'd had of it through the open door had shown that it overflowed with embroidered pillows, beaded curtains, and fringe—this looked more like a small doctor's office, white and clean. Two padded chairs faced a large desk, the walls were hung with calligraphy, and interesting smells came from the large jars that filled a floor to ceiling wall unit.

"Can I help you?" A young Oriental man came through an interior doorway which led to a small kitchen.

"We're looking for," Roland pulled the piece of paper out of his pocket and ran down the list, "John Chin."

"I am he."

"Oh."

The young man smiled. "I know," he said, "you thought I'd be older."

"Well . . ."

"It's all right. I'm used to it. I . . ." His voice trailed off and he stared past Roland.

Roland turned. Evan was just Evan as far as he could see, all traces of aspect tidily tucked away, but the astrologer looked as if he were having a vision.

John took a step forward and bowed. "How may I help you, Holy One?"

Maybe he is having a vision. Vision or no, John Chin was undeniably aware of what Evan was. Roland tried not to feel jealous and for the most part succeeded.

Evan took the question at face value. "We need to find those who know the old rituals of the goddess."

"The Wiccans?" John asked, never taking his eyes off Evan. "They run a store called Arcane Knowledge up on Dupont. I can get you the exact address."

"Please."

He went to his desk and pulled out a brown leather address book. "Fourteen forty-six Dupont," he said after a moment.

"Fourteen forty-six," Evan repeated. "Thank you."

They were at the door when John's call stopped them.

"Holy one. The signs . . ."

Evan sounded weary as he answered. "Are all true."

"How can I help?"

Roland shielded his eyes as Light filled the small room, bouncing back off the white walls, and illuminating the astrologer.

"You help by being what you are." Evan spoke from the center of the glory. "The Light gains its strength from such as you."

Out on the sidewalk, swept along by the crowd, Roland rubbed his watering eyes and asked, "How did he know what you are, I mean before your little display of pyrotechnics? And you know," he frowned, "I don't think he even squinted when you lit up."

"In a simpler age, he would have been a saint."

"A saint? Oh." Roland tried for a nonchalance he didn't feel. "Oh, is that all."

"That attitude," Evan said, the weariness back in his voice, "is what allowed the Darkness to enter in such strength."

"I'm . . . I'm sorry."

"No, I am." Evan reached out as though to wipe the stricken look from Roland's face. "I'm tired, and I spoke without thinking. Please, forgive me."

Roland shrugged. "You're tired," he agreed, flagging down a cab. "Come on, let's go save the world."

Arcane Knowledge was a small store tucked between a Bank of Nova Scotia and a fish and chip shop. The display window, no more than two feet wide, held maybe a dozen pieces of silver jewelry scattered across a square of black velvet. Roland braced himself for major weirdness, but the bats and black cats motif he half expected turned out to be a number of normal looking displays of books, crystals, candles, and jewelry. Behind the counter were bags of dried plants and the whole place smelled much like John Chin's office with a faint overlay of hot oil and halibut.

He followed Evan to the counter and rolled his eyes as the young woman behind it began to hyperventilate. He might not recognize a saint when he saw one, but he sure as hell recognized hormones.

"We're looking for the Wiccan Church," Evan told her. "Can you help us?"

"Help you?" she repeated. "Oh, yes."

Evan waited for a moment and Roland hid a smile.

"The Wiccan Church?" Evan prodded at last.

"Oh." She straightened and attempted to pull herself together. "Yes. They, uh, own this store. I mean the church part doesn't, but the same people do."

Bingo! Roland thought. *We've got you now, you son of a bitch.* He saw the tension go out of Evan's shoulders and knew the Adept had feared this would be another dead end.

And then the clerk continued, "But they've all gone out of

town for some sort of," her hands windmilled, "thing. That's why I'm here all alone."

"They've gone out of town," Evan repeated slowly.

"Yes. They've got property in the country and they're there for the weekend."

"I have to speak to their Priestess." He leaned forward and she gulped as his face stopped inches from hers. "It's vitally important."

"There's no way to contact them. They don't even have a phone."

"No . . ."

"They'll be back on Monday." Her voice came out in an overwhelmed squeak.

"There may not be a world for them to come back to on Monday!" His voice had risen and the young woman cringed, her hands over her ears, her eyes squeezed shut against the vision he presented.

Although his own heart had turned to lead in his chest—there would be no help from the Goddess, any goddess, once again they faced the Darkness alone—Roland touched Evan lightly on the back. The muscles felt as if they'd been sculpted of stone.

"Hey," he said softly. "You're scaring her."

And then he was glad his heart was lead, for the look on Evan's face would have broken it.

"Roland, I . . ."

"I know." Not caring who saw, his fingers traced the curve of Evan's cheek. "I was counting on it, too. Come on." He jerked his head toward the door. "Let's go home and see if we can find another way."

Bit by bit the bleakness faded. Evan nodded. "Yes. There's always another way." His chin came up. "Thank you."

"Hey, things are never as black and white as you think they are." Evan's lips twitched and Roland felt himself flush." Uh, forget I said that."

"No." Evan caught up the hand that still rested on his shoulder. "I will remember it for it is true and it is something that both the Dark and the Light too often forget." He leaned back over the counter and turned the brilliance of his smile on the cowering clerk. "Forgive me, I didn't mean to frighten you."

She rose hesitantly and tried a nervous smile of her own. "It's okay." And she really thought it was until she noticed, a few moments after the door closed behind the two young men, that every crystal in the store was glowing with a soft white light.

"All right, let's see what we've got." They walked up the path to Rebecca's building, having ridden the bus back in silence. It was past two. In less than ten hours, the world would end. Roland flicked the fingers of his free hand up to mark points. "We've got an Adept of the Light . . ."

"A slightly battered Adept of the Light," Evan corrected as they stepped through the still empty doorframe.

"If you like," Roland agreed. "A street musician everyone keeps calling a Bard although," his tone stopped Evan's protest, "I have it on good authority I'm not there yet. A magical harp said Bard can't play." In her case, Patience sounded a C, high and sharp. "A guitar that he can. A goddess invocation we don't know how to use. A social worker we can't find, and Rebecca. Hell," he stood aside while Evan dealt with the lock on Rebecca's apartment door, "with all that arrayed against him, the Darkness should be shaking in his shoes."

A small coffee colored shape scurried down the curtains and out the window as they entered.

Roland froze, but Evan didn't appear disturbed so he relaxed. On the other hand, Evan did appear to be communing with something Roland couldn't see. "Are you all right?" he asked nervously, wondering if he had time to get Patience free and if it would do him any good if he did.

"I'm an idiot!" Evan exclaimed for the second time that day. "I am an idiot."

Roland closed the door and slipped the chain on. "Why?" he asked.

"We know how to call the Goddess."

"We do?"

"Yes!" Evan threw out his arms and his bracelets emphasized the word like a silver percussion section. "The *song* is the invocation."

"Yeah. You said that this morning." Roland set Patience down and sat gingerly on the edge of the couch, keeping half his attention on the Adept and the other half on the window; just in case their visitor came back. "You also said this morning that we needed a witch. What's changed?"

"We needed the Wiccans as a focus, needed their rituals as a focus to guide the invocation to the goddess."

"I repeat. What's changed?"

"Roland," Evan threw himself down on his knees and caught up both the other man's hands in his, "you will sing the song. Rebecca will focus it."

"Rebecca." Roland was very proud of the way his mind kept working. Given the circumstances.

"Rebecca. The gray folk watch over her. She has a simplicity, a clarity that is rare even amongst the Light. In the arms of the earth, she calms. Think of it, Roland, how it all fits together."

Roland thought of it. "They used to say that the simple people, people like Rebecca, had been touched by God, that they were his special children."

Evan's eyes were almost as silver as his jewelry. "Who raised the barriers?" he asked. "She watches over the world and She watches over Rebecca."

"Are you sure this will work?"

"No." Evan shook his head, his hair hissing across his shoulders like silk. "I'm not sure. But I have hope again and that *is* one of the biggest differences between the Dark and Light."

"Just hope?"

"Wars have been won and lost on it."

Twisting one arm in Evan's grasp, Roland looked at his watch. "Two forty-eight. She'll be starting home soon." Evan's fingers lit fires where they rested along his wrists. "What, uh, what shall we do in the meantime?"

Evan's grin was pure mischief as he answered. "I think you'd better rehearse your part a time or two."

Roland sighed, freed one hand and pulled the now much folded piece of music from his back pocket. "You know," he said, "you don't make it easy for people?"

"Rebecca!"

Rebecca paused, her hand on the kitchen door fairly trembling with her need to get home.

"Did you put your tins away neatly?"

"Yes, Lena."

"Have you got your uniform to wash?"

Rebecca chewed on her lip but otherwise remained frozen in the motion of leaving. Her food services uniform was folded, not as neatly as on other Fridays, in the bottom of her red bag. "Yes, Lena."

"Do you have your muffins for the weekend?"

"Yes, Lena." The muffins had been shoved on top of her soiled uniform. She waited impatiently for the next line of the litany.

"Now don't forget to eat while you're home."

Rebecca nodded for the motion was a part of it, too. "I'll remember, Lena." One more.

It never came.

Rebecca waited, unable to move until the last words were spoken. Unable to turn around to see what had stopped them. She could hear a strange gasping sound, a scuffling against the linoleum, and then a voice she knew, although she couldn't remember from where.

"You had been warned, Mrs. Pementel, that the smoking would probably kill you." The Dark Adept looked down at the cafeteria supervisor who writhed at his feet, one hand clutching at her chest, the other scrabbling against the floor. "A proportionately high number of women over fifty who smoke are taken by heart disease. What's that?" He bent slightly forward as the purpling lips formed silent words. "Help you? Oh, but I have helped you. Without my assistance you would surely have lived for another twenty-four hours." He smiled pleasantly. "And you wouldn't like the world in another twenty-four hours."

He watched the last moments of pain and he captured the last breath, drawing it into himself with deep enjoyment. Only then did he turn to study Rebecca.

He still hunted the other woman. She would fall in time, for there were a great many men who ran as hounds in this hunt. When he felt her taken, he would be there to observe the end. As for the other who assisted the Light, the so-called Bard had experienced the shadow lands and the Dark Adept anticipated showing him true Darkness. But this one . . .

"I don't know what came to your aid the last time," he said to Rebecca's back, noting with pleasure how the muscles twitched visibly in their desire to move, "but it can't help you now. You built this trap yourself. I merely used it." Stepping forward, he cupped the curve of her waist in both hands.

Rebecca trembled but could no more twist out of his grasp than she could continue out the door. The last words had to be spoken.

"And the beauty of it is," he murmured into her hair, his breath very hot on her scalp, "this afternoon's work has not affected the balance in any way. I simply helped your late friend down a path she was already well along and your problem is a natural consequence of that. But perhaps you still don't understand." His hands glided upward, briefly caressed the heavy swell of breasts, and came to rest about her throat, the thumbs pressing painfully into the soft flesh under her jaw.

"The Light will not be able to save you," he purred. "For he will not know you are caught until it is too late and by then he will be dealing with me. And he will lose. And when I am finished destroying him, I will come and claim you. I will enjoy that. You won't."

And very suddenly she was alone with the pain his hands and his words had left. Desperately, she grabbed onto the quiet place the way Mrs. Ruth had taught her to and while silent tears streamed down her face, she fought the bindings that held her with a single-minded determination. Evan needed her help. She had to get to Evan.

At Evan's touch, Roland stopped muttering lyrics and frowned up at the Adept. "I haven't much time to learn this," he began and shut up as he caught sight of Evan's face. "What is it?" he whispered, glancing around nervously.

"Listen."

So he listened. Within the apartment: the rhythmic rasp of Tom's tongue across a paw, the hum of the refrigerator, the steady dripping of the bathtub tap. Outside the apartment: traffic, voices, and bells.

Bells? At least two sets of bells seemed to be clanging wildly, pealing out a discordant clamor. Roland looked at his watch. Three twenty-one.

"Rebecca's in danger," Evan said. And vanished.

"Mrs. Pementel? Mrs. Pementel!" The cafeteria door swung open and the accountant came face to face with Rebecca who was still standing with one arm outstretched to push open the door. "Oh," he said with a forced and uncomfortable smile, "it's you." When it became obvious she wasn't going to move, he inched around her, wondering nervously what all the eye rolling was about. He didn't care how good a worker she was, the girl should

be in a home. "Have you seen Mrs. Pemen . . ." The question suddenly became redundant.

"Oh, my God!"

Dropping to his knees beside the body, he groped frantically
for a pulse. There didn't seem to be one although he wasn't entirely certain he was prodding the right places. *What if she's dead?
Ohmygod! I've touched her!* He scrambled to his feet, took two
steps away, then scurried back. *Help. I should go for help. But if
she isn't dead, I should do something. Do what? Seconds count.*
He cried out as a flash of brilliant light threatened to blind him.

"Rebecca? Lady? Are you all right?"

Rebecca? That was the retarded girl's name. The accountant
scrubbed at his eyes until he could see a tall young man with a
mane of strangely colored hair bending over the girl by the door.
"Here now," he sputtered. "What? How?"

Evan ignored him. He could See the binding that held Rebecca
in place, but he had no idea how to break it and Rebecca's voice
was as bound as her body. He could feel the foul taint that said his
enemy had been here, but Darkness hadn't set these bounds.

"You, there. I need help!"

Reluctantly, Evan responded. He couldn't not respond, not and
remain as he was. He turned. He Saw Rebecca's bindings stretching back to the body on the floor.

"Who was this woman?" he asked, pushing past the flabber-
gasted accountant who sputtered in indignation. The bindings
looped around her, yes, but they originated with Rebecca. *Oh,
Lady, what have you done to yourself?*

"I said, I need help!" The accountant waved an ink-stained
hand toward the floor, not knowing why he expected this punky
young man to be able to do anything but sure that if he only ex-
erted himself everything would be all right again. "She needs
help!"

Evan had no time for finesse and it was Evantarin, Adept of the
Light, who raised his head and allowed the mortal to meet his
eyes. "She is beyond my help," he said.

Ohmygod! A corpse. I'm in the room with a corpse! I'm . . .
The thought became lost in shifting storms of blue-gray and in a
voice the seemed to echo inside his head.

"I must help the living now. Who was this woman?"

"Pementel. Lena Pementel, the cafeteria supervisor." Incipient panic had been calmed; or delayed, for he could still feel it, buried deep and straining to get free.

"Did you know her well?"

"No. Yes. I don't know. We saw each other every Friday to do the budget for the next week."

"Every Friday?" Evan stepped forward.

The accountant watched his reflection grow in the strange gray eyes and squeaked, "Yes. She came up to my office . . ."

"Your office? You never saw the ritual?"

"What ritual?"

Evan took a deep breath and forced his voice away from Command. For the first time in his existence he envied the Darkness' ability to cut to the heart and not worry about the damage done. "The ritual that frees my Lady," he said under tight control. Rebecca was helpless, the Darkness could return at any time, and he wasn't strong enough to protect her.

"Well, uh, last week I was ready early and I, I came down here."

"And?"

"And they, uh, talked to each other."

"What did they say?"

"I don't remember." He spit the words out in a rush and ducked. When nothing happened he dared to glance up. What he saw made him squeeze his eyes shut again.

"Then you must relive the time . . ."

He sat in the office and waited while the cafeteria workers filed out calling their good-byes and exchanging sly looks about Lena's visitor. The retarded girl, Rebecca, was the last to leave. She'd barely reached the door when Lena called out to her.

"Rebecca!"

The girl paused, one hand on the door, and he wondered how long this was going to take. He'd figured coming down to the cafeteria would speed things up and he could get home early for a change.

"Did you put your tins away neatly?"

"Yes, Lena."

A pity she was retarded, he thought, she was actually kind of attractive in a lush sort of way.

"Have you got your uniform to wash?"

"Yes, Lena."

*In fact, that combination of lushness and innocence was pretty
erotic.*

"*Do you have your muffins for the weekend?*"

"*Yes, Lena.*"

*Good god, it went on forever. No wonder it took Mrs. Pementel
so long to reach his office every Friday.*

"*Don't forget to eat while you're home.*"

*The girl nodded, her head bobbing up and down like one of
those dogs you saw on dashboards of sixties cars. He snorted quietly to himself. The dogs probably had more in the way of brains.*

"*I'll remember, Lena.*"

"*I'll see you Monday, puss.*"

"*See you Monday, Lena.*"

The accountant started. He'd heard a voice. He knew he had.
And the cafeteria door swung back and forth on its hinges. But
there was no one down here. He'd come down to get Mrs. Pementel because it was after three and she still hadn't shown up in
his office. And the cafeteria was empty. Of course, it was empty.
There were no retarded muffin makers stuck in the doorway. No
eyes that looked into his soul and found it wanting. That would be
ridiculous. He was working too hard.

He took a step forward and the toe of his recently polished
brown oxfords kicked into a yielding obstacle. He looked down.

"Mrs. Pementel? Mrs. Pementel!" Dropping to his knees beside the body, he groped for a pulse. "Oh, my God! She's dead!"

Chapter Fourteen

The patrol car moved slowly around King's College Circle, its searchlight sweeping across the common. The police barricades had been taken down late in the afternoon, but the cars had been instructed to swing around the site when they could.

"You think he'll return to the scene of the crime?" PC Brooks asked as his partner stared fixedly out the window along the beam of the searchlight. He could see only grass and trees and maybe a faint chalk mark gleaming white in the sudden glare. He wondered what she saw.

"I hope he does." PC Patton ground the words out, her gaze locked on the center of the common. "I hope he comes back. I hope we're here. And I hope the son-of-a-bitch gives me the chance to blow him off the face of the earth." She saw a child's body lying discarded on the grass, although she knew the actual body had long since been taken away, and she knew she'd continue to see it until the child's murder was avenged.

They completed the circuit and PC Brooks switched off the light. On cue, the radio hissed and the dispatcher's emotionless tones called out: "Officer needs assistance, Bloor and Yonge, northeast corner. Repeat, officer needs assistance, Bloor and Yonge, northeast corner."

PC Patton thumbed the switch. "5234 responding." She settled back as Jack hit the siren and the gas simultaneously, one hand on her nightstick, her mouth a thin line. Right now, busting a few heads seemed a fine idea.

Behind them, Darkness thickened in the Circle.

Rebecca pulled her big orange sweater out of the closet and put it on. She wasn't cold and didn't expect to be cold. She wanted it for comfort. She'd bought it herself, no one had helped her and, although she couldn't have explained what she meant, it stood for independence. Strength. Besides, it was bright and Daru always said to wear bright colors at night so the cars could see you—the first Rebecca had heard that cars *could* see.

"Are you all right, Lady?"

She leaned back against Evan's chest, rubbing her head against his shoulder. "I'm a little bit scared, Evan. I still don't think I understand what you want me to do."

"I want you to listen to Roland sing. Really listen. And I want you to just be yourself."

"Is that all?"

"Yes. That's all."

"I think I can do that." She sighed. "I'm still a little bit scared, Evan."

"So am I, Lady." He laid his cheek against her curls and his arms tightened protectively around her. "So am I." He remembered the promise he'd made the troll and was ashamed he'd had to be asked. If they won, if they both still lived, and if she agreed, he would take her with him when he returned to the Light. There, her innocence would be protected, her clarity would remain undimmed. He had realized, when he'd seen her trapped and touched by Darkness, just how much this meant to him. Such a life should be cherished and this world would not do it.

But first they had to win. And they both had to survive.

"It's past eleven," Roland called from the main room. "We'd better get moving."

Rebecca twisted in Evan's arms and hugged him hard, then took his hand and led him out of the alcove. "Did you call Daru while I was asleep, Roland?"

"I called, kiddo." He wouldn't meet her eyes. "She wasn't at the office all day. I left a message there and on her machine at home."

Rebecca frowned. "I wonder where she is."

Roland looked down at his guitar case, up at the ceiling, out the window, and over at Evan. Evan nodded.

"We fear the Darkness has taken her, Lady."

"Taken Daru?"

"Yes."

"Did *you* look?" she asked Evan.

He shook his head. "I don't have the power to spare," he explained sadly.

"Then you don't know the Darkness has her."

"She hasn't called, kiddo. Not us and not her office."

"That's okay." Rebecca pulled the sweater tighter around her shoulders. "Daru works very hard and is very busy. She can't always phone for every little thing."

Roland wasn't going to be the one to try to convince her. Although he personally believed that they'd never see Daru again, what would it hurt if Rebecca believed differently? *And after tonight it may be a moot point.*

From its place beneath the window, the harp sighed, rather as if a breeze had touched each string in sequence.

"I think it wants to go with us," Rebecca said.

"Not an it, kiddo, a she," Roland corrected, stroking a polished wooden curve. "And when this is over, I promise I'll learn to play her." *Provided I have fingers left to play with.*

The harp sighed again.

Rebecca echoed it. "I wish I'd heard your song," she sighed.

"You needed to sleep, Lady."

"I know."

"And you will hear the song in time."

"I know." They left the apartment and she carefully locked the door. "It gave me the neatest dreams though."

Behind her back Roland and Evan exchanged a speaking glance.

"What kind of dreams?" Roland asked.

"Like someone was telling me all kinds of things that I'd forgot. And it wasn't Roland telling me either, it was someone else though even in the dreams I knew it was Roland singing."

"What kinds of things did they tell you?"

"I don't know." She shook her head, "When I woke up, I forgot again. Maybe when I really hear you sing . . ."

"Maybe," Roland agreed.

A half a block from the apartment building they noticed they'd picked up a fourth companion.

"Rebecca. That damned cat is following us."

"No, he isn't."

Roland looked down at Tom and up at Rebecca. "Yes, he is. He's right here!"

"But he isn't following us," Rebecca pointed out. "He's walking beside us."

"I don't care where he's walking, tell him to go home."

"Cats go where they want to, Roland," Rebecca said. She thought everyone knew that.

Evan squatted down and Tom butted up against his legs. "It is a great battle we go to, small furred one, and while we do not doubt your courage, neither do we wish you to be hurt."

Tom placed one paw on the Adept's knee, his claws fully extended and just barely pricking into the denim.

Evan smiled. "You are a mighty warrior," he agreed, long fingers digging into the cat's thick ruff. "If you truly wish to join us, you may."

"I'll carry him across busy intersections," Rebecca offered.

Just great, Roland thought, as they continued walking. *As if we didn't have enough on our plate.* Although well aware that Tom had led him back to the real world, Roland's opinion of the cat, of cats in general, had not significantly changed. And as far as he could tell, Tom's opinion of him had not changed significantly either. The parallel scratches he'd acquired on his wrist that afternoon testified to that. He caught sight of their reflections in the glass doors of Maple Leaf Gardens and shook his head. *I wonder what the rest of the world thinks of this.*

The rest of the world didn't seem to notice. For eleven thirty on a Friday night in a major city, there was nothing strange enough about them to attract attention.

. . . except for one little boy, up long past his bedtime, who watched them go by with his mouth open and continued to stare after them until his mother shook him and told him to behave.

By the time they reached Yonge Street, with its traffic and its crowds, Roland felt as if they were walking through a movie. Everything seemed unreal, removed just a little bit from where they were; lights were too bright, shadows too sharp, sound too brittle, and the warm air slid over his skin without making contact. He had the impression that nothing existed until he looked at it, and it stopped existing when he turned his eyes away. The others felt it, too, for Evan held his hands away from his sides and he continuously swept the area around them with his gaze. Rebecca chewed on a lock of hair and watched only Evan, leaving her feet to find their own way without guidance. Even Tom lay quietly in Rebecca's arms, ears down, the tip of his tail snapping back and forth against her hip.

The light at the corner was red, and it stayed red for what seemed like a very long time. The crowd that stood with them shifted restlessly, constantly in motion, and it suddenly struck Roland just what kind of movie they were in. *It's a western. Just before the stampede, and when it starts you know the hero's best friend is going to get knocked off his horse and killed.*

"There's a storm coming," Rebecca said with absolute certainty.

"Yes," Evan agreed, "there is."

Roland wondered briefly if they were talking about the same thing and then decided it didn't matter. Sweat dribbled down his sides and his T-shirt stuck to the center of his back. He shifted his damp grip on the plastic handle of the guitar case and began reviewing the words to the invocation. It beat thinking.

The light changed. Finally. The traffic on College surged forward. A black Corvette speeding south on Yonge tried to beat the odds.

With a scream of tires and a slam of metal meeting metal, a brown Mazda plowed into the Corvette's side, throwing it into the path of an orange taxi. For the first few seconds, only the cars screamed. Then they came to rest in a twisted smoking heap and the people began to yell.

Evan threw himself forward and Roland yanked him back.

"It's eleven thirty-eight, Evan! We haven't got time to help!"

The taxi driver sprawled half out of the window. The blood dripping from his mouth pooled on the road below.

"Let me go!" Evan twisted free. "You don't understand. I *have* to help them!"

"I do understand." Roland tried not to see. Tried not to hear. Tried not to feel. "But you can help them best by defeating the Darkness!"

Evan took a step toward the wreck.

"Evan," Rebecca's quiet voice cut through the noise, through the hysteria. Both men turned to look at her. If he'd thought about it at all, Roland would have assumed she'd be panicking, but to his surprise she looked almost serene, an island of calm in the midst of chaos. "If you stop here, Roland and I will go on without you."

Evan jerked as though she'd hit him. He gave one anguished

cry and plunged through the gathering mob, running toward the Circle.

Tom flowed out of Rebecca's arms and followed, quickly disappearing amid the forest of legs and feet.

"Tom!" Roland called. "You stupid . . ."

Rebecca took his hand. Hers was cool and dry. His was trembling.

"Tom can take care of himself," she said. "Come on."

They began to run, pushing past the ghouls that always gathered to warm themselves around disaster and pounding down College Street in pursuit of the Adept.

Not until King's College Road did they catch up with Evan. He stood, staring up into the Circle, face bleak, hands shoved into the pockets of his jeans.

He looks so absurdly young, Roland thought as he let go of Rebecca's hand and stood gasping for breath. The air didn't seem to have any substance in it and running had burned a copper taste into the back of his throat. He couldn't see Tom anywhere although a rustling in the bushes up ahead could've been the cat.

Slowly, Evan turned to face them, his eyelashes clumped together in damp spikes, and his cheeks wet. Rebecca moaned a quiet protest and threw herself into his arms. Roland, jealous of the comfort being given, being received, and hating himself for it, concentrated on breathing. Then a strong arm pulled him into the embrace and, for the moment it lasted, everything was all right.

When they pulled apart, hands lingering for a final touch, they *all* stood and stared up into the Circle. The streetlights grew more sallow, more wan, the closer they came to the Darkness until eventually the Darkness devoured their light entirely. The great turreted silhouette of University College that normally rose beyond the common was not black enough on this night to show against the starless sky.

Roland looked at his watch. Eleven forty-six. Fourteen minutes.

"Why," he'd asked Evan that afternoon, *"can't we go there early, like maybe before the sun sets, call up this goddess, explain the whole thing, go home, and let her handle it?"*

Evan's answer, as it often was, had been another question. "And will we ask a goddess to wait on our convenience?" This question he'd answered himself. "No. We will call her when we need her." He'd smiled at Roland's disgusted expression. "There is a maxim from the old ways that has carried over into the new; the gods help those who help themselves."

"Fortune cookie platitudes again," Roland had snorted.

Tipping his chair back, Evan had swung one booted foot up onto the kitchen table. "Some of those fortune cookies are pretty smart."

They walked toward the Circle; Rebecca holding Evan's hand, Roland holding Rebecca's. The contact helped, made it possible to keep putting one foot in front of the other, even knowing what waited at the end of the road. As they moved closer to the Darkness, the sounds of a busy city at night began to fade until they traveled in a silence unbroken except for the soft silver chime of Evan's bracelets. They didn't speak. It had all been said.

"So, uh, Evan, what's the Dark One going to be doing while I'm singing?"

"Trying to stop you."

Roland had suspected he knew the answer before he'd asked. He'd been right. "And you'll be?

"Protecting you."

"I'm not doubting you or anything, but can you?"

Evan had smiled sadly. "I cannot defeat him, the balance has shifted too far for that, but I should be able to distract him long enough for you to finish the song. And then it will be out of our hands."

They walked around the Circle for a short distance, avoiding the actual area of the Dark Gate, and stepped onto the grass under the bordering arc of oaks.

Something rustled softly and Roland felt a gentle touch against his hair. He looked up. The tree branch above him was empty of littles and there wasn't a breath of air to move it. He shot a glance at his companions, but they seemed unaffected so he shrugged and let it be. Now didn't seem to be the time to start worrying about trees.

As they moved closer to the center of the common, the Darkness became almost a physical presence, oozing out from the place where blood had been spilled and swirling about their ankles, reaching misty tendrils toward their knees, climbing a little higher with every pass.

"Back," Evan growled. "This world is not yet yours." He

spread his arms and except for the seething mass which marked the sacrifice, the common cleared.

"That's better," Roland said approvingly. Then he noticed that the rest of the world, the world outside the Circle, seemed separated from them by a barrier of smoked glass. He could see through it, but not well, and buildings were hazy and unreal.

Eleven fifty-seven.

"Uh, Evan," Roland put the guitar case on the grass and unsnapped the clasps, "as I never saw this song before this morning, what if I screw up?"

Evan clasped him lightly on the shoulder, his grip a reassurance, but all he said was, "Don't."

"Don't," Roland repeated. "Right." He lifted Patience out of the case and swung the strap around his shoulders as he stood. *Four verses, two choruses, and a Dm to a F change. Why me?*

Because you're all they have, said the little voice in his head.

Evan took Rebecca's face between his hands and looked deep into her eyes. "Thou hast my heart, Lady. Keep it safe."

Rebecca sighed, bit her lower lip to stop its quivering, and placed her hands over his. "I love you, too, Evan."

Roland waited for the clinch, but it never came, only a soft kiss and a parting. Moisture rose in his eyes and he blinked furiously to clear them. When he could see again, the Adept stood before him. Everything he wanted to say—good luck, be careful, kick ass—seemed too trite, so he only nodded once and hoped Evan would understand.

Evan nodded once in return.

"You have come to meet your destruction. How . . . noble."

He wore a black velvet robe that absorbed what little light remained. Behind him, the gate continued to grow.

As Evan turned to face the Dark Adept, his expression changed and he looked, just for that instant of turning, heartbreakingly sad. In the few seconds it took for Roland to understand, Evan had moved too far away for the Bard to stop him.

"He thinks he's going to die out there!" Roland whirled to face Rebecca who watched Evan with a kind of yearning desperation.

She sniffed. "I know."

"We can't just let him . . ."

"We have to let him."

"But there must be something we can do!"

"There is." She wiped her nose on her sleeve, never taking her eyes from Evan. "Sing."

The gate was taller than both the Adepts who stood before it, ten or twelve feet wide, and still growing.

His heart in his throat, Roland strummed the first chord, knowing as he did, he condemned Evan. The Dark Adept had no need to fight until the music gave him reason. Weighing Evan against the world, the world almost lost, but he forced his fingers to play on. Behind him, he could feel Rebecca listening with the single-minded intensity she brought to everything she did.

Then, the Dark Adept looked past Evan, met Roland's eyes, and smiled. *You are mine,* said the smile. *You know it, and I know it. And when this is all over, I will claim you.*

Roland's fingers faltered. He forgot the chords. He forgot the music. He forget everything but the Darkness. He began to tremble uncontrollably.

"Roland." Rebecca grabbed his shoulder, her fingers digging deep into the muscles, forcing his awareness away from the Dark Adept although he still heard her words down the length of a long tunnel. "Evan won't let him hurt you."

Evan.

If he's willing to die for my world, I can damn well sing for it.

His fingers found the chords again. He began the first chorus.

By the end of the second line, the Dark Adept's complacent smile had slipped.

At the end of the third, he snarled and attacked.

The Light rose up to block him.

"Fireworks reported in the vicinity of King's College Circle. 5234, can you respond?"

PC Patton glared at the radio. "The streets have gone crazy and they want us to check on fireworks?" They'd spent the last hour clearing up a near riot at Yonge and Bloor.

PC Brooks shrugged and reached for the microphone. "Remember what happened the last time someone reported fireworks in the Circle." He flipped the switch. "5234 responding. We going in alone?"

"All other units are currently occupied, but backup will be available if requested."

"Good. We're going in alone." PC Patton forced the car, steering mechanism protesting, around a tight U-turn and pushed the gas to the floor. "We've got first shot at that bastard if he's back."

"And we'll deal with him by the book, Mary Margaret," her partner said mildly.

She bared her teeth in what might have been a smile. "I'll make him eat the fucking book."

Evan staggered backward under a vicious strike but stopped the blow before it could get through to Roland. Roland did the only thing he could; he trusted in Evan's strength and kept singing. He didn't know if the Goddess was listening but he could feel the power building and every hair on his body stood on end. As Evan blocked another arc of black energy that left his right arm hanging useless at his side, Roland began the first verse.

> *"Eastern wind blow clear, blow clean,*
> *Cleanse my body of its pain,*
> *Cleanse my mind of what I've seen,*
> *Cleanse my honor of its stain."*

Although he'd been expecting something to happen, the touch of the wind on his left cheek almost made him miss a chord change. He turned slightly into it so he could match what the last two lines would bring. Out of the corner of his eye, he saw the Dark Adept snarl, but neither the snarl nor the attack that followed could distract him now that the east wind had swept the tangles from his mind. He was still terrified but that didn't seem to matter anymore.

> *"Maid whose love has never ceased*
> *Bring me healing from the East."*

The Dark Adept howled.

Roland ignored him. For the east wind now brought an answer. Her hair streaming out about her, clad in a short white tunic, Daru stood just in front of Roland and slightly to the right. She faced the Darkness, her hands curled into fists at her sides. Even from the back, she didn't look like the Daru he'd known, for the power in the song was a pale copy of the power in her.

"Southern wind blow hot, blow hard,
Fan my courage to a flame,
Southern wind be guide and guard,
Add your bravery to my name.
Let my will and yours be twinned,
Warrior of the Southern wind."

And the wind that came out of the south, smelling of steel and blood, dressed Daru in golden armor and hung a mighty sword at her side.

Evan collapsed to one knee, but just in time threw his good arm up to tangle the black whip in his bracelets. Very faintly over the music came his cry of pain.

"Western wind blow stark, blow strong,
Grant me arm and mind of steel
On a road both hard and long.
Mother, hear me where I kneel.
Let no weakness on my quest
Hinder me, wind of the West."

The wind now blew against his right cheek and Rebecca lifted her hand from his shoulder. As she walked past him to stand beside Daru, Roland's mind worked furiously, but no coherent thought managed to make its way out of the shock.

Rebecca?

And the weirdest thing about it was that while Daru had obviously taken on aspects of the Goddess, Rebecca looked just the same. Tangled curls, freckles, big orange sweater.

So maybe the Goddess has been with her all along, the small voice in Roland's head suggested.

Roland refused to deal with that.

Evan's head snapped back and his mouth hung open as he fought for breath, but somehow he kept the Darkness in its place. Light drained from a dozen wounds.

Even before he began the last verse a chill traveled the length of Roland's spine. Internal or external, he wasn't sure. His back was to the north.

"Northern wind blow cruel, blow cold,
Sheathe my aching heart in ice,

Armor round my soul enfold.
Crone, I need not call you twice.
To my foes bring cold of death!
Chill me, North wind's frozen breath."

Her black robes whipping about her in the freezing wind, Mrs. Ruth suddenly stood next to Rebecca. She no longer looked like a fat old lady, although she was still that. She no longer looked harmless.

The force of the blow lifted Evan into the air, where he writhed for an instant before falling to the ground.

And Darkness lost sight of the larger battle in its need to destroy what remained of this bit of Light.

Roland's chin came up and his eyes blazed as he gave the last chorus everything he had, throwing the song as a shield over Evan.

"Wind's four quarters, air and fire
Earth and water, hear my desire
Grant my plea who stands alone—
Maiden-warrior, Mother, and Crone."

As the last note died away into silence, the Goddess spoke; one voice through the three mouths of her trinity.

"It is done."

The Dark Adept, his hand still raised to deliver the final blow to the Light, laughed for the clocks had begun to ring midnight.

"Too late," he said.

And the Gate opened.

"Holy Mary Mother of God, Blessed Jesus, and all the saints, what the fuck is that?" PC Patton slammed her foot down on the brake and the patrol car screamed sideways across King's College Circle until the tires of the passenger side snugged up against the curb.

She let the engine die and sat staring out the window, her knuckles white on the steering wheel.

The siren wailed for a second after the engine had quieted. PC Brooks leaned forward and switched it off. It was unlikely that anyone on the common heard.

A slab of Darkness twenty feet square stood in the center of

the common, a slab so impermeable the mind insisted it was solid
even when confronted with the evidence that it was not. From out
of it, formed of Darkness and shaped by it, came a creature out
of an addict's nightmare. As it stepped free, it rose up on powerful hind legs, its scaled body gleaming dully black, and raked the
air with massive furred paws. Great curved talons shredded the
night and each of its seven heads opened a fanged mouth and
roared.

"They're shooting a movie here tonight, right?"

"I don't think so, Mary Margaret."

Beside it stood a man in black; at his feet lay a crumpled figure.

"That's him! The guy in the sketch! The bastard who's been
carving up the city!"

"Are you sure?"

"Of course, I'm sure!"

Facing it were three women; one in golden armor, one in long
black robes, and one in a big orange sweater. They looked familiar, although the eye refused to See them as individuals. They
also looked at least as dangerous as the creature they faced. Behind them stood a man with a guitar.

More afraid than she'd ever been in her life, PC Patton
stepped out of the car and walked around it to stand by her partner's door. Slowly he got out to join her.

"Do we call for backup?" he asked, his hand plucking at his
holster.

"No."

"Then what do we do?"

She looked from the beast to the man to the women and
frowned. Something big was going down, something . . . She
looked at the women again and chewed her lip. "We wait," she
said at last.

"Oh, shit!" Roland took an involuntary step back as the seven
heads shrieked.

Mrs. Ruth muttered speculatively, Rebecca sighed, and Daru
loosened her sword in its sheath.

The Dark Adept shook his head, stroking the beast lightly on
one obsidian flank. "Kill it," he taunted the Maiden. "Destroy it.
But the Darkness will continue to come and sooner or later you
will fall and the body you wear will be killed. Without you, the
rest of the One in Three is nothing." His smile was satiated as he

rubbed himself up against an enormous haunch. "And you cannot close the gate, for blood was spilled to open it."

"What?" Roland so far forgot himself that he stepped forward again. "What does he mean, you can't close the gate? That's what you're here for!"

The three bodies of the Goddess turned and again three spoke as one.

"Blood is needed to cancel blood."

The Crone continued alone. "An unwilling sacrifice opened this gate, Bard. It will take a willing one to close it."

The seven heads of the beast roared again.

And Roland understood.

He was all they had.

I don't want to die.

He wet his lips and very, very carefully laid Patience on the grass.

I don't want to die.

The first step was the hardest thing he'd ever done in his life. The second and third were no easier.

You'll probably never know this, Uncle Tony, but I'm seeing a job through to the end.

He moved between Rebecca and Mrs. Ruth. Between the Mother and the Crone.

Please, don't let it hurt too much.

Then something small and heavy darted through his legs. He staggered, recovered, and saw Tom launch himself into the air, hissing and spitting.

The great front paws of the beast dragged Tom off a head that now glared from only one eye and with a single, easy motion ripped the cat in two. As the blood splashed on the ground, the Goddess cried, "Done!"

And the Dark Gate disappeared.

"No!" screamed the Dark Adept. "It was just a cat!"

The Goddess smiled and the Dark Adept quailed before her. "There's no such thing," she said, "as just a cat."

In one fluid motion, Daru unsheathed her sword and charged, the great golden blade whistling around her head in a glittering arc.

The battle happened too quickly for Roland to follow and very little of the noise and confusion of actual blows struck by either side penetrated past the knowledge that he still lived. He

picked up Patience and held her tightly, as if the familiar feel of
the guitar could convince him of his continuing reality.

The beast had only two heads remaining when it finally fell.
It thrashed once and faded from sight, leaving behind a stain on
the grass and a stench that lingered until the east wind blew it
away. The Maiden stood in the center of the stain, leaning on her
sword, the golden armor dripping with dark fluids. Her teeth
were bared and her eyes blazed. She threw back her head and
laughed.

The Dark Adept began to back away, his entire body twisted
with panic. With his eyes locked on the Goddess, he couldn't
watch the ground and when his heels slammed into Evan's side,
he fell. For an instant they lay face to face, the Dark Adept and
the Light, then Evan, who had lain there conserving the very little strength he had left, drove a small dagger of Light into the
heart of Darkness.

The Dark Adept wailed, and died.

Roland never saw Rebecca move. One moment she stood by
the Crone, the next she knelt by Evan, his broken body gathered
up in her arms.

His head lolled against her shoulder and although he tried, he
couldn't raise his hand to touch her cheek. "Forgive me, Lady."
His velvet voice had been broken as well. "I was blind."

She stroked his hair. "There is nothing to forgive."

He sighed, fighting the pain for a few seconds more of life.
"I'm glad," his eyes found hers, "you're here at the end."

"What end?" She leaned forward and kissed a pain line from
his brow. "There are no ends, only beginnings. The Circle always
comes around."

He managed a weak grin. "Fortune cookie platitudes," he
whispered.

The Mother smiled and the world sang in response.

"Perhaps," she said.

Tears streaming unheeded down his cheeks, Roland felt his
heart start beating again. *I should have known she wouldn't let
him die.* And when a moment later Evan stood before him, holding open his arms, Roland went to him and held him with everything he had left.

"I thought you were dead," he sobbed into the warmth of
Evan's shoulder.

"I thought I was, too," Evan answered into his hair. "And then I thought you were."

"He didn't even like me."

Evan understood. "Who can say with cats? We will honor his memory, for he was a mighty warrior against the Darkness. But it's over now. We won."

"Over?" Roland pulled back a little to look into Evan's eyes. "Over?"

The Adept nodded.

"Over," Roland said yet again. Then reaction set in and his knees gave out.

Evan held him until he steadied.

"We won."

Smiling, Evan nodded.

"Then the world is balanced again?"

"No." The Crone stood before them. "The world will not be balanced until the Light returns to his place."

Evan gave Roland's shoulders one last squeeze then released him and moved to Rebecca where he dropped to one knee and bowed his head. "I would not presume to ask this, Lady, save that I gave my word to another. Would you come with me when I go?"

Roland felt as flummoxed as Evan looked when the Goddess answered, the mouths of all three women moving with the words.

"Yes. For it will right a grievous wrong."

The Crone actually laughed at their expressions and, as Rebecca pulled Evan to his feet, said, "I suppose you want an explanation."

Evan seemed incapable of speech, so Roland forced out a single word. "Please." And, with a shudder, he hoped that it would not draw the Goddess' attention to him.

To his relief, the Crone alone began to speak. Bad enough in itself but the parts were not nearly as overwhelming as the whole.

"Only the Goddess is eternal. These bodies we wear are as mortal as any born of woman. When they die, the aspect they contain moves on. When the body of the Mother dies, the aspect moves instantly to a vessel that has just begun to menstruate. The last time this happened, it coincided with the accident that killed Rebecca's parents. The trauma brought on Rebecca's blood, the Mother needed a vessel . . . At the instant of possession the aspect is operant and the Mother is a healer. So she healed.

"Had the accident happened a week earlier, Rebecca would have died, never knowing the touch of the Goddess. Had the accident happened a week later, Rebecca would have died and the Mother would have moved to the next vessel in line. Because the accident happened at the exact moment it did," the Crone spread her arms and the sleeves of her robe flapped in the sudden chill wind like the wings of a great black crow, "Rebecca lived and the Mother was trapped in a flawed vessel, one that could neither properly contain her nor release her."

"We were drawn to her," the Maiden spoke for the first time, "to protect her."

Again the three gave voice as one.

"I am the fulcrum on which the balance depends."

Roland made a triangle with his hands, then crumpled one corner.

"That's it exactly," agreed the Crone. She turned to Evan. "If you take the vessel with you, the Mother will be free to move on and it will not be so easy for the balance to be disturbed again."

And if the Mother moves on, Roland thought, *how much of Rebecca will be left?*

Evan didn't seem to have any doubts. "Will you come, Lady?" he asked again, but this time for himself, not for a promise.

Rebecca nodded, eyes shining. "Yes."

"Done!" said the Goddess and a shimmering curtain appeared in the air. "Return to the Light with our blessing."

"Wait!" Rebecca pulled out of Evan's grasp and spread her arms. The mangled bits that were Tom came together until a pale gray tabby with a proud white tip to his tail lay on the grass. She knelt by his side and stroked the length of his body. "Good-bye, dear friend, I'll never forget you." A silver tear splashed against the soft fur, then she held out her hands and the cat sank into the earth. "Journey safely until you find fat mice and thick cream and a loving hand always willing to scratch behind your ears."

Roland wiped his eyes and sniffed. *You don't even like cats,* he reminded himself, but the old argument had lost its force.

Rebecca took his head between her hands and pulled it down to kiss his brow. "My mark is on you," she said, "my protection and my love."

This is a Goddess, said the small voice in Roland's head.

This is Rebecca, Roland told it.

He hugged her tightly. "Be happy, kiddo."

"You, too, Roland. I think you've found your music now."

"I think so, too, kiddo."

She pulled the key to her apartment out of the front pocket of her jeans and handed it to him. "Will you take care of my plants?"

"Sure thing."

"And see the littles get their milk?"

"A bowl every night," he swore.

She smiled at him then and the whole wretched week was suddenly worth every bit of pain and terror.

She moved away and Evan took her place, gently adding his blessing to hers.

Roland took a long look—it would have to last him—and said, "I'm sorry we didn't . . ."

The silence grew as the Adept took a long look in return. Then he winked. "Maybe next time."

Next time! screamed the little voice in Roland's head. *Next time!*

Shut up, Roland told it.

Arms about each other, Evan and Rebecca stepped into the Gate and for a moment Roland thought he saw a warrior in blue and silver with a jeweled sword at his hip, a being of glory whose great white wings brushed the top of the Gate, and the Evan he had come to know, all three together in one. Then the glowing images formed over Rebecca, too, although instead of a sword she cradled a bound sheaf of wheat.

Then, just for a second, the shimmer cleared and he could see past them into the Light. He took a step and then another and then the Gate faded and Mrs. Ruth stopped him with a hand on his chest.

"Bards can See, but they can't ever go through," she explained though not unkindly. "It's one of the things that makes them Bards."

"But . . ."

"Forget it, bubba."

He looked at her, really looked at her, and saw just a fat old bag lady bulging out of an old black dress. Daru wore white shorts and a shirt, the only sign of the Maiden-warrior the cast mark on her forehead.

"It's really over," he sighed.

Mrs. Ruth snorted. "Don't you ever listen, bubba? Nothing

ends, The Circle always comes around." She reached up and slapped him lightly on the cheek with one pudgy hand. "Go home. Get some sleep. Learn to play that fancy harp you've acquired. Stay out of trouble. Don't be a stranger. And you," she waved the hand at Daru, "eat more. You're too skinny."

Then she turned and waddled away.

Roland knelt to put Patience in the case and looked up to see Daru staring down at him.

"What are you going to do now?" she asked.

Roland shrugged and stood, "What she told me to do, I guess."

Daru nodded. "That's always wisest."

"So are you . . ."

"I'm just myself. By tomorrow I won't remember that I was ever anything else."

"But her?" Roland jerked his head in the direction Mrs. Ruth had taken.

"The Crone Remembers. It's part of her job." Daru sighed and stretched. "I don't know about you, but I could use some coffee."

Roland thought about it for a minute. "Yeah," he said, "me, too."

They walked across the common toward the lights of College Street and the normal sorts of strangeness found in twenty-four hour doughnut shops.

"So this, uh, Maiden thing, you don't . . ."

"No."

"Oh."

On the other side of the common, Police Constables Patton and Brooks shook themselves free of the stupor they'd been wrapped in and got back into their car. The person—or thing, they were no longer sure—responsible for at least two deaths would never be brought to trial, but Justice of a sort had been done and they were satisfied.

"We, uh, going to report this?" PC Brooks asked, tapping his fingers against the dash. His partner raised a sarcastic eyebrow and he flushed.

PC Patton thumbed the microphone switch.

"Go ahead, 5234."

"We're just leaving the Circle."

"And the fireworks?"

"The situation took care of itself. 5234, out."

She put the car into gear, and they drove away into the darkness that was nothing more than the darkness of a summer's night.

Overhead, a creature that was not quite a squirrel ran along the hydro wires on its way to spread the news.

THE FIRE'S STONE

Chapter One

When the procession reached the edge of the volcano, the thief abandoned all dignity and began to scream. The priests ignored her, allowing her terror to bury the droning of prayers. The crowd, packed onto the platforms that hung over the crater, murmured in satisfaction; it was, after all, her terror they had come to hear.

"They say she actually got her hands on The Stone." The pudgy merchant dabbed at his ruddy forehead with a scented cloth. The heat of the sun above, combined with the rising waves of heat from the molten rock below, had driven the temperature in the viewing areas distressingly high. "They say she came closer than anyone has in the last twenty years."

"They say," repeated the young man, forced into proximity, and thus conversation, by the press of the crowd. His voice hovered between scorn and indifference. His gaze stayed on the stone. Red-gold, as large as a child's head, it sat enthroned on a golden spire that rose up out of the seething lava some thirty feet beneath the platforms. A captured fire burned in its heart, the dancing light promising mystery and power. The Stone kept Ischia, the royal city of Cisali, from vanishing under a flood of fire and ash, from choking in the sulfuric breath of a live volcano. *And they say the thief actually got her hands on it.* He applauded her skill if not her good sense.

The prayers ended.

The priests of the Fourth, their dull red robes like bloodstains against the rock, stepped back and two massive acolytes lifted the bound and writhing body into the cage.

A collective almost-moan rose from many of the spectators on the public platforms and the young man wondered if this execution was intended to be a religious occasion. The religion of the region, not only of Cisali but of the surrounding countries, operated on a number of complex levels involving both priests and wizards, secular and nonsecular rituals. The One Below—a type of mother goddess as near as the young man could determine—had borne nine sons, the Nine Above, and the Fourth—none of them had names—was the god of justice.

The screams took on a new intensity.

The young man's gaze flickered to the royal platform. Only the twins were present. The descent would be feet first, then, and slow. It was said in the city that the twins were also bound to the Fourth although they had never entered the priesthood and were certainly not wizards.

Justice. His lips twisted up off his teeth.

"You're, uh, not from the city." The merchant was definitely more interested in his neighbor now than in the day's event.

Ginger hair, cropped shorter than was currently fashionable, pale skin, sharp features, and a slight build marked said neighbor as an outlander. Amid the placid and pleasure loving city dwellers, his scowl and brittle intensity marked him just as surely. There were few outlanders in Ischia, certain policies of the king had been set up to discourage them from staying.

"Is this your first time watching The Lady?"

The young man merely grunted. He thought the local name for the volcano—or more specifically for the crater—ridiculous.

"Perhaps," the merchant wet his lips and reached out a tentative hand, "you would let me buy you a drink?"

"No." The hand was avoided; the young man radiating disgust.

The merchant shrugged, disappointed but philosophical—outlanders, who could fathom them—and again turned his attention to the crater.

Smoke rose from the thief's soft leather shoes.

Making his way down the terraces, slipping deftly between merrymakers, the young man considered the fate of thieves in the royal city. He hefted the weight of the merchant's purse, lifted almost without thinking as he'd left, and the corners of his narrow mouth quirked upward in what served him for a smile. Well, the man *had* offered to buy him a drink.

"Aaron!"

The outlander looked up. Pale fingers stopped playing in the contents of the merchant's purse. Brows, a lighter ginger than his hair, tufting thickly over the center of silver-gray eyes, rose.

"Don't waggle those demon wings at me, boy. That was the third time I called you. What keeps you so enthralled you ignore me in my own house?"

"I went up the mountain today. To see the drop."

The old woman on the couch snorted. "Disappointed you, did it?"

Aaron scowled, animation returning to his sharp features. "You don't know what you're talking about, Faharra." He shoved the purse deep in the pocket of his loose trousers.

"Oh, don't I?" Clawlike fingers plucked peevishly at the fringes of her silk shawl. "I still have my wits about me, boy. More wits than even you give me credit for." She tried a knowing laugh, but it turned to a fit of coughing that left her gasping for breath and glaring fiercely. "I see more than you suspect. Get me some wine." As Aaron moved to the small table by her couch, she snared the edge of his tunic. "Not that crap. My granddaughter has it so watered, I could wash with it. There's a flask of the good stuff in the trunk."

The trunk, a massive ebony box entirely too covered in ivory inlay, was locked. It took Aaron less than five heartbeats to deal with it.

"You'll kill yourself with this stuff one day," he remarked conversationally, handing her a full goblet.

"And who has more right?" Faharra drank deeply and licked withered lips. Although her hands shook with the tremors of age, she didn't spill a single drop of the wine. "For sixty-two years I was the best gem cutter in Ischia." She took another swallow. "I cut the emerald that sits atop the royal staff. One huge stone it is and emeralds aren't easy to cut, let me tell you."

"You've told me," Aaron broke in, bored. He refilled her goblet until the deep red wine trembled just below the metal edge.

"And if you behave yourself, I'll tell you again."

She drank in silence for a moment while Aaron replaced the now empty flask and relocked the trunk. Let the granddaughter wonder. He wiped away the barely perceptible smudges his fingers had left on the ebony, then went and sat on the wide marble window ledge, gazing out over the tiny garden at the city beyond.

"You got sunburned," Faharra said at last. "Good thing you usually work at night."

Pale fingers touched a high cheekbone. He winced and his

eyes rose to the red-gold light just barely visible over the rooftops of the upper city.

"Don't worry, lad." The old woman's voice was almost kind. "You'll get your flogging. They only drop those who try for The Stone."

Aaron's gaze snapped down from the mountain. Although his night vision was very good, the shifting shadows of dusk defeated him and he could barely see the ruin of the gem cutter amidst her shawls and blankets and pillows. His voice when it came was hardly his own. "What?"

"You think I don't know why you settled here, boy, after all your years of wandering?" Faharra rolled the rich summer taste of the wine around her mouth and decided. She was too old to continue dancing around Aaron's pain; her time was fast running out and unless he listened to her, she feared Aaron's was as well. She could see him very clearly, outlined against the evening sky. But then, she had always been able to see him clearly. "We flog our thieves to death. Flog them to death in the market square." Her mind wandered briefly back to the days in the market when her hands had been steady, her eye true, and her skill sought by kings. "Flog our thieves to death," she repeated, sliding back to the present. "But we have to catch them first."

The thief at the window might have been carved in stone, so still he sat.

"You're too good a thief, Aaron my lad. If you truly want your cousin's death, you're not going about it very well."

Faharra watched his face tighten and his jaw set and knew what ran through his mind. Only the memory of his cousin's death closed him up that tightly, shut him even further within himself than he usually was—and that was far indeed. She wanted . . . oh, she wanted many things: her youth, her skill, her patience, time. She saw Aaron as the last jewel she would ever cut. No, recut, for he was already a diamond, hard and brilliant but with a flaw deep in the many faceted heart of him.

Soon, someone or something would strike that flaw and the young thief would shatter into a million tiny shards. Faharra intended to prevent that and she thanked the Nine Above and the One Below every day for the accident that had brought Aaron into her life; had brought meaning into her life just when she thought meaning had degenerated to bowel movements and watered wine.

The thief, who had slipped shadow silent over her window

ledge, had no way of knowing she had fallen from her couch and rather than call her granddaughter—the patronizing bitch—had decided to spend the night on the floor. As comfortable a place as any, old bones ached on down as much as on tile.

Sidling along the couch, reaching for the tiny gold hourglass that stood on the table beside it, the thief had stepped on her.

"Watch where you step, you clumsy ox," she'd snapped. *"I didn't live this long to be a carpet for such as you."* Remembering, she smiled. Aaron's jaw had dropped and those wondrous eyebrows had risen, the perfect picture of surprise. And when she had refused to call the watch, surprise became, just for an instant, something else entirely—another emotion that passed too quickly for Faharra to define.

"I get few enough visitors as it is, boy. I'm not of a mind to have those I do get arrested."

He had lifted her back into bed, then sat on the window ledge while she talked at him—she in the darkness, he silhouetted against the night sky.

That first night, she recalled suddenly, was the first of the many times she had told him of the emerald. Well, nothing wrong with pride in a job well done.

As he finally readied to leave, she'd tossed him the hourglass.

"Take it, boy. I've no need to watch the sands of time run out."

He'd smiled then—a real smile, not the twisted expression that usually served—and as he disappeared she'd called out, "Come back!" She'd just realized the emotion that had followed surprise. Disappointment.

A thief disappointed that she hadn't called the watch?

That was the first question.

He came back. Not that night, but a week later she had roused in the darkness to find him sitting on the window ledge.

Why had he returned?

That was the second question.

Faharra had soon found that her midnight visitor was more questions than answers. He clung to their developing friendship with an intensity that astonished her. He was young. He was passably attractive, in a sharp, outland sort of way. Why was he so desperate for companionship? Even thieves had friends. What made her safe when the rest of the world was kept at a distance.

Aaron had saved her from boredom, from loneliness, from lying alone and forgotten in the darkness. She would save him from himself. She chipped away at his shell of stone and night by night uncovered bits and pieces of his past, enough so she could ask further questions.

He had left home at barely fourteen. Why? He had chosen to become a thief, a profession he excelled at, true, but not one destined to provide a steady income, peace of mind, or a ripe old age. Why? She might be safe, but young women terrified him and young men were fiercely taboo. Why?

Actually, it took little digging to find that the taboo against young men was strictly cultural. In Aaron's homeland the soil was poor, the growing season short, and the neighbors likely to torch the crops at any real or imagined slight. Every child was another pair of hands and every pair of hands was desperately needed. Same sex pairs produced no children and same sex love went from being impractical, to being a crime, to blasphemy against god—a god Faharra felt held asinine ideas of what constituted blasphemy, and who in their right mind could believe there was only one god anyway?

Blasphemy was punished by fire.

Unfortunately, Aaron's religious instruction had been intense.

"I was Clan Heir," Aaron had explained with a shrug, *"and Clan Chief rules both people and priests."*

Perhaps. But Faharra watched him watching the crowds that passed outside her garden and wondered if, maybe, the priests thought they were saving him from the fire.

From Clan Heir to thief. Quite the fall. And more than just a thief. . . . Where others plodded, Aaron danced. Where others fell, he soared. How better to deny a father whose word was absolute law. Faharra had been pleased to run into that answer at last. Her own father had been the worst kind of horse's ass and she had been overjoyed when her strong-minded mother had finally divorced him. Her personal theory said that one father could do more to mess up a child's life than every mother in existence put together. She realized she was not entirely without bias on this matter, but that was all right; she blamed it on her father. What had Aaron's father done to turn his son so far from him and what he stood for?

Aaron's mother had died in childbirth.

Aaron felt—had been made to feel—responsible for her death. Was that what made Faharra safe as a friend? That she was too old to bear children? And Faharra added a hearty thank the Nine and One for that.

It took her ten months of poking and prodding and sifting tales to get to the one question that led to all the rest.

"Aaron, what happened to your cousin? What happened to Ruth?"

Aaron grew so still Faharra could almost see the stone she had spent long months chipping away reforming around him. He grew so still he might have become stone himself. When he finally spoke, his voice, in painful contrast, was almost matter-of-fact.

"My father had her flogged to death."

And then he disappeared; slid off the window ledge and into the night, carrying his own darkness with him.

In the tedious hours between Aaron's visits, Faharra had held his past up to the light, turned it, studied it, and knew she had all the answers but one. What had happened up in the northlands so many years ago that the pain still ruled Aaron's life?

"My father had her flogged to death."

That was the easy answer. It explained nothing more than why he'd finally settled in Ischia where thieves died under the lash. Looking for his cousin's death, he'd someday make the mistake that would guarantee it.

When he came back, the walls were thicker than ever.

Faharra knew the weak spot now, knew where to place her chisel and strike the blow, but she was afraid. *I'm all he has,* she told herself. *Can I destroy the walls without destroying him, too?* And in back of that . . . *He's all I have. I can't risk driving him away.*

"Selfish, selfish, old woman!"

"Crazy old woman," Aaron muttered.

Faharra started and realized she had spoke aloud. While she had lain, wrapped in memories, Aaron hadn't moved. It was full dark now, with no moon or stars to break the blackness, but she could still see him on the window ledge, a shadow against the shadow of the night. He swung his leg over the sill, balanced half in and half out of the room.

"Aaron." She grubbed among the things she had to say to him but couldn't hold one long enough to bring it clear. "Come to-morrow," she managed at last.

She felt his eyes on her; studying, weighing, knowing, she was

sure, what she wanted to say. It was, after all, the only thing un-
said between them.

"All right." A long pause, as though he were examining his
words. "Tomorrow." Then he was gone.

Faharra drank the last dregs of wine in the goblet and sighed.
If he returned tomorrow then maybe, just maybe, he was ready to
admit to the pain that made his choices for him. And maybe, just
maybe, she would have time to cut this last gem, her greatest
work, before she died.

Aaron moved across the rooftops of Ischia, almost happy although he wasn't sure why. He leapt lightly from a marble corner,
clung for an instant around the scaled neck of a gargoyle, and
dropped to a balcony railing ten feet below. His soft leather shoes
whispered along the ornate iron, then he launched himself across
an alley to land cat-quiet on the flat roof of the building one story
down. He paused, checked that he remained unobserved, sped
across the width of the roof, and swarmed up the intricate carv-
ings on the adjoining building until he was once again three stories above the street.

Let other thieves slink in alleys, he would take the high roads
of the city.

Two buildings and a heart-stopping swing from a flagpole
later, he dropped onto the wall around Faharra's garden. He patted his pocket; the gaudy cluster of gems had survived the trip. He
looked forward to hearing Faharra heap abuse on the jeweler who
had created the ugly brooch.

*"More good stones are ruined by the setting some asshole jew-
eler puts them into than by a hundred gem cutters with bad eyes
and drinking problems."*

She'd said it before.

He paused and remembered what else she was likely to say
tonight. His stomach twisted. He stared ahead at the black rectangle of her window. His brows lowered until they met in a deep vee
above his nose, looking more like demon wings than ever. Then
he shook his head and went on. His teeth were clenched and his
shoulders had knotted with tension, but he went on.

I'll humor the old lady. She deserves that much at least. More,
he could not admit to, not yet, although the thought—the hope—
of putting his burden down had become almost too strong to ignore.

He stepped gingerly onto the branches of a slender fig tree, then swung one leg over the wide marble sill of Faharra's room.

The room was very quiet.

Aaron's stomach twisted tighter.

The couch was a shadow against the far wall. Even with eyes adapted to the night, Aaron could not pierce the smaller shadows piled on it.

He slid into the room and padded silently across the tile floor. The old woman slept so seldom now, he didn't want to wake her. He'd just make sure she was comfortable and leave.

By the end of the couch his foot touched something. Something that rocked and sang metal against stone. He bent. Faharra's goblet. Not quite dry so someone, probably a servant, had poured her a drink before she slept.

He could see the wasted body of the gem cutter now, lying amidst the pillows and shawls and blankets. Another step and he could see her face.

She looked very annoyed.

Her eyes were open.

He touched her hand. The fingers were just beginning to stiffen.

"How did you know," he asked the god of his father, in a language he had not spoken for five years, "that I loved her?"

Chapter Two

Scented smoke curled about the mausoleum and the finger bells of the mourners broke the evening into a thousand tiny pieces of sound. Perched high on one of the more ornate tombs, safely out of sight, Aaron blocked his ears against the noise which threatened to shatter him as well.

Faharra's granddaughter had spared no expense and the procession from the house to the temple crematorium and then out into the necropolis had been a spectacle worthy of the best gem cutter Ischia had known.

"And yet while she lived," Aaron growled softly from his vantage point, "you couldn't spare an hour to sit with her, nor any kindness to lighten her day."

Her thickening figure nearly hidden beneath her funeral draperies, the granddaughter appeared the picture of bereavement as hired dancers carried the brass urn into the squat marble building that held fifteen generations of her family's remains. When they emerged, when the wailers had sent a last chorus to the gods, she turned and, tenderly supported by two of her closest friends, led the procession back to the city.

Aaron watched the tottering figure leave and his lip curled. If that fat sow felt anything at all, it was pleasure at being the center of attention. Not for a moment did he believe that the red and yellow veils hid sorrow.

When he could no longer hear the maddening chimes of the finger bells and the heavy scent of sandalwood had been swept clean by the evening breeze, he dropped silently to the ground.

The door to the mausoleum was locked and the lock wound tightly about with red and yellow ribbons.

A violent twist tore the ribbons loose and a heartbeat later

Aaron dropped the lock on the ground beside them. The door, well oiled, swung silently open. He stepped inside.

He worked and lived in shadow, but this darkness felt different, a part of the mausoleum like the brass fittings or the carved friezes. It etched a boundary about the light spilling in through the open door, cutting it into a rectangle of gray on the floor and barely allowing it to spread beyond. At the edge of the dim illumination, almost in the center of the tomb, stood an altar; the Nine Above grouped about the One Below who cradled a brass urn in marble arms. Faharra. She would stay in the deity's embrace until another of her family died and then her urn would be moved back to the shelves that lined the walls.

Aaron couldn't see the shelves—behind the altar the darkness thickened into a solid black wall—but he could feel the weight of the dead and was thankful he had no need to pierce their sanctuary. He had come for what lay with the One Below. The gods of Ischia held no terror far him, for without belief a god is nothing and Aaron believed only in death.

At the edge of the rectangle of light, he paused and stretched an arm out into shadow. *No, not quite.* His hand groped at air. He would have to take one, maybe two steps past the boundary.

He suppressed a shudder. Crossing into the darkness, even the less well defined darkness by the altar, felt like crossing into the realm of the dead, into their world not just their resting place, and the demons of his childhood flickered for an instant around the perimeter of his sight. Then his hands lay on the urn and he could ignore the darkness and the dead now that he held what he wanted.

Quickly working the stopper free, he dipped a tiny gold vial into the coarse ash. Until this morning it had held Faharra's favorite perfume and the smell of jasmine still lingered. He'd stolen it while the funeral director worked not twenty feet away. Once filled and sealed with a bit of wax, he hung the vial about his neck on a piece of silk cord, tucking it safely under his shirt. As he pushed the stopper back into place, he frowned. The granddaughter had been true to the end; the urn was plain brass, embossed but not jeweled. An insult to the greatest gem cutter Ischia had known.

The greatest gem cutter Ischia had known . . .

An idea crept into the back of his mind.

He straightened and raised one foot to turn and leave. Without really knowing why, he put it down again. Just barely visible, the face of the One Below gazed out at him with serene compassion.

"She hated to be left alone in the dark," he whispered, the voice barely recognized as his own. He pressed the vial against his chest. "Now she won't be. Not entirely." He tried to stop the cry of anguish that was rising up from the place where it had lain hidden for the last two days, but it proved too strong. It rose and built and when it crested it caught him up and dashed him down and he was lost within it.

A shriek of horror brought Aaron back to himself and he gazed stupidly about, wondering where he was. The white blob of the fleeing, and still shrieking, acolyte told him only that he remained on temple grounds. Vague memories of a run through darkness, slamming into stone, falling and rising and running again, were of little help. The fig tree beside him said more for the number of tombs had long since crowded any trees out of the necropolis. He looked up to see a hawk-nosed woman glaring down at him and after a moment of terror realized she was stone.

The Nobles' Garden.

The bodies of the nobility were given to the volcano, their likenesses then carved in anything from granite to obsidian and placed in the section of the temple grounds reserved for such monuments.

The acolyte, walking alone among life-sized statues of the dead, had seen coming at him out of the darkness a face apparently unsupported, for Aaron's clothes were dark. Assuming the obvious, he screamed and ran.

With a brief bow to the lady's memorial, Aaron headed for the temple wall at a quick trot. He strongly suspected the acolyte's report would be investigated by a less impressionable mind and he had no wish to tangle with the temple guards.

A broad scrape across the back of one hand oozed blood, but his wild flight seemed to have done no more damage than that. Although his throat was dry and sore, he felt calm, almost serene. During the remaining hours of the night he would repay the friendship of the best gem cutter Ischia had known.

Her final resting place deserved to hold a sample of her art.

He would return to her the emerald from the top of the royal staff.

*   *   *

"Although I hesitate to ask and you may tell me it's none of my business . . ." The fat man ran stained fingers lightly down the heavy gold chain until they rested on the medallion that hung from it. ". . . how did you come to acquire this?"

"You're right, Herrak. It's none of your business." Aaron stood motionless in the shadow of a heavily overladen bookcase, blending with the clutter of the room, his eyes never leaving the enormous man behind the desk. "Will it pay for what I need?"

"A man in your line of work should learn more patience," Herrak chided, the smoke-stick bobbing on his lower lip. He hefted the chain in his left hand and with the right dusted ash from the protruding shelf of his stomach. Almost nonexistent brows drew down in concentration and a slow chuckle escaped with the next lungful of smoke. "However you managed it," he said at last, "His Grace is not going to be pleased to find it missing."

"Forget His Grace," Aaron growled. "Get on with it." He'd stolen the chain just after leaving the Nobles' Garden; to get to the royal staff he would have to get onto the palace grounds, but only Herrak had the means for that and Herrak's price was high. The fat man had no need for further wealth, he desired the different, the dangerous, the unique to shuffle into the rat's nest of his townhouse never to be seen again by any eyes but his. Aaron had not dealt with Herrak before but knew he was the only man in Ischia who had what he needed tonight.

And if the chain and its medallion were too little? Aaron beat the thought back. They couldn't be. Not enough night remained for him to find something else and get the emerald as well. His Grace's security system had already cost him too much valuable time.

"The charm you need, my friend, is costly," the fat man murmured more to himself than to the young thief. He hefted the chain once more and smiled, his eyes almost lost behind the bulges of his cheeks. "But I think this will meet my price. The irritation its loss will cause His Grace is almost worth the price alone. Almost," he repeated hurriedly in case Aaron should get ideas. "Yes, this will get you your charm."

"And a grappling iron."

Herrak's nearly buried eyes beamed with anticipation. Almost as much as the treasures it brought, he loved the bargaining, the give and take, the jockeying for position, the power of words. He spoke the first phrase of the ritual; "Do you haggle with me, then?"

Aaron's lips thinned and the demon wings of his brows drew down over his eyes. "No. The charm is useless alone. I get both, or no deal. I can put the chain back as easily as I took it."

For a moment there was no sound except the soft beat of a moth's wings against the glass chimney of the lamp. Herrak couldn't believe his ears. An ultimatum? Had this, this thief just given *him* an ultimatum?

"Make your choice," the thief continued. "I haven't much time."

It could be a bluff, but Herrak didn't like the young man's tone. He fingered the medallion, and chose. "And a grappling iron," he agreed. Stretching out an arm, he snagged a small wooden box off a pile of precariously balanced bric-a-brac, opened it and plucked out a tiny twist of silver. "This will not stop magical attacks, but it will get you through the wards."

Leaning out of the shadows, Aaron snatched it from him. "And the iron."

A pudgy finger pointed.

Both the charm and the folded hooks disappeared within one voluminous trouser leg, and the young thief jerked his head once in Herrak's direction.

"You're welcome," Herrak said dryly to the space where Aaron had been. He stroked the chain and imagined His Grace's expression when he awoke and found it missing. Rumor had it that the chief magistrate slept with his chain of office draped over his bedpost; the only time he took it off. A pretty bit of thievery that.

Spitting the wet end of the smoke-stick from his mouth, Herrak settled the chain about his neck. Definitely worth what he'd paid for it. He almost wished he could see the young thief's face as the weakened hook broke free and he plummeted to the ground. "Never mind," he comforted himself for missing the treat, "if he survives the fall, I shall enjoy hearing about his execution."

The stone of the gargoyle he clung to began to warm under Aaron's body heat and of the two, the gargoyle looked more likely to move. Behind him, Ischia lay as quiet as it ever got. Before him, the palace sprawled to the very lip of the volcano, a counter-balance to the massive bulk of the temple that loomed out of the darkness on the far side, the reflected fire from the crater staining its walls. The wall around the palace rose no more than seven feet high, a symbol rather than an active deterrent. Stretching above it, invisible and easily forgotten, were twined the wards of the court wizards.

Aaron had studied the stories of those thieves who had attempted the palace as an artisan would study his craft. One of two things always happened. Either the charm they had purchased failed, in which case the wards destroyed them, or the beasts that watched the grounds at night tore them apart. There were legends, of course, of thieves who had blithely walked in and blithely walked out with treasure enough to build palaces of their own, but the truth lay with the broken bodies hanging lifeless on the gate at dawn, a grisly reminder to others who might try their luck.

For the wards, Aaron had to rely on the charm Herrak had sold him. He didn't like it, it gave the control to another, but he had no choice. If he was to get Faharra's emerald, he had to go over the wall. As for the beasts, Aaron preferred to take his chances with the two-legged kind, for their senses were easier to manipulate.

An errant breeze wandered up from the town, bringing a scent of baked fish and apricots. Aaron's stomach tightened. He couldn't remember the last time he'd eaten. Time enough for food when he had the emerald.

"You don't take care of yourself, boy. You're too skinny by far."
Too well trained to start, his hands tightened involuntarily around the stone throat of the gargoyle. The voice of memory had been growing louder since he'd left the fat man's.

"Be quiet, old woman," he told it. *"I'm doing this for you."*
He dropped his gaze to the sentry post almost directly across from his perch on the top of the single storied addition to the Duce of Lourence's townhouse. By royal decree no residence might look out upon the palace, but the Duce who had built the addition had been an ambitious man and attempted to bend the rule by cutting no windows in the wall on the palace side while leaving the flat roof as a terraced patio with a direct line of sight. The Duce had not survived his first garden party. His successors were less ambitious and longer lived. Aaron was the first creature larger than a gull to walk the terrace in three generations.

As Aaron watched, the sentry's jaw tensed, stifling a yawn, and she shifted the crossbow slightly in the crook of her arm.

Soon.

He began to work his muscles, readying himself for the run on the palace wall.

The heavy slap of leather-soled sandals against the cobble-stones jerked him to full awareness and he leaned slightly forward, the pale gray of his eyes gleaming between narrowed lids.

Now.

As the sentry stepped out to greet her relief, Aaron moved. Shadow silent, he swarmed down the ornate stonework of the Duce's Folly, sped across the cobblestones and leapt for the top of the palace wall. The soft toes of his boots found an easy purchase against the rough stone and he propelled himself up and over, dropping lightly on the balls of his feet into a small courtyard. The whole thing had taken under a minute, just less than the time it took for the sentry to be relieved, the only time when all attention was not on the wall.

He listened for the alarm, but all he could hear was the sound of his own blood pounding in his ears.

Crouched in shadow, he stripped the leather bindings from below his knees and replaced his boots with sandals. He re-arranged his small pack so that the straps were hidden and made his way cautiously along the courtyard wall to the covered walk running the length of one side. Following the faint indentation worn in the marble by other, more legitimate feet, he came to an open arch that led to the main courtyard just inside the palace gates, checked the position of the inner sentry, then stepped boldly out into the light.

"Half the trick of thieving," he'd told Faharra, *"is to behave as though you have every right to do what you're doing."*

"And the other half," Faharra had snorted, *"is having more balls than the Nine Above."*

The demon wings had flown in broad astonishment. "All Nine?" he'd asked and been rewarded by the old woman's laughter.

He wore the dark green livery of the chief magistrate, liberated earlier in the evening when he'd taken the chain. It would blend with the shadows as well as the black he normally wore but better still, it would hide him in the light. Even at this time of night, it would not be unusual for messages to move between the chief magistrate and the palace.

The sentry at the inner arch watched Aaron approach with a minimum of interest. Anyone who came by him had already passed the gate, had already been recognized, had already been declared safe. His time could be better spent burying his face between the soft mountains of his Lia's breasts. As Aaron came closer, into the light of the torches that flanked the sentry post, he did wonder briefly why the chief magistrate had taken an outlander into his employ but it was none of his concern after all . . .

"State your business," he droned, dropping the point of his pike.

"Package for their Royal Highnesses."

The twins were always referred to thus, as a single unit. Aaron had no idea why he had chosen them as his silent accomplices, but he remembered the thief inching feet first into the volcano. . . .

The pike snapped up, the guard's fingers moving restlessly along the haft, itching to make the sign of the Nine and One. To come between the twins and their toys was never healthy. "Straight ahead to the first cross corridor, make a left, pass four corridors, make a right, give it to the guard at the end of the long gallery."

A nod, the barest bending of his neck, and Aaron passed into the palace.

The sentry shivered as the outlander went by. The eyes in the pale-skinned face had been flat and dead and empty of all emotion, like chips of silver-gray stone. He'd seen corpses with more life in their eyes.

May he and their Royal Highnesses have the joy of each other, he thought and tried to lose the chill in the memory of Lia's flesh.

The corridors, built wide and high to catch the breezes, were, for the most part, empty. The few who moved about at this hour— servants tending the lamps that broke the palace into bars of light and shadow, a drunken noble on her way to the Nobles' Quarters, a pair of yawning ink-stained clerks scurrying home to bed—paid him no mind for the livery of the chief magistrate was well known and if he walked in the palace, he'd passed the gate.

The dim and the quiet settled over Aaron like a cloak, wrapping him in a feeling of safety both false and dangerous. Aaron recognized it, but didn't seem to have the energy to deal with it. He felt as though he were dreaming and the further he walked, the stronger the feeling grew. At the end of the long gallery, he almost trusted the dream enough to let it carry him forward into the sight of the guards.

And then he remembered that trust meant betrayal.

He faded into the darkness caught in the deep bay of a shuttered window and froze. The louvers had been left open to allow
the air to circulate, but fortunately they had been angled in such a
way he would not be seen from the gardens. The livery would not
carry him past the two guards at the door leading to the royal
apartments and that one small door was the only exit deeper into
the palace.

"He keeps it in an anteroom off his bedchamber."

Aaron rested his forehead against the polished wood and
waited for Faharra to finish. He couldn't work when she was so
close.

*"Perhaps he fondles it before he sleeps. There's more life in a
well cut gem than in many a well born woman."*

His eyes on the distant guards and his other senses spread
about the gallery, he slipped the latch from the shutters and
opened one just enough to ease through. The hinges sighed
faintly. He froze and listened to the silence, then risked an alarm
once more as he pushed the shutter closed and secured it with a
bit of wax.

"You're too good a thief, Aaron my lad."

"Yes," he agreed silently, watching his hands as though they
belonged to someone else. *"I am."*

Moving quickly, for the air smelled of dawn and the servants
would be stirring soon, he changed back to his boots and rescued
the baggy bottoms of his trousers, working by touch while his
eyes grew reaccustomed to the dark and his ears sifted the night
for any sound of an alarm.

If the dogs were close. . . .

Halfway down the length of the gallery there was a wall; the
barrier to the private gardens of the royal family.

Aaron had no idea if it was warded.

If it was, he didn't know if Herrak's charm would work again.

"It isn't easy to cut an emerald that big, let me tell you."

"You've told me, Faharra," he responded softly, and leapt for
the top of the wall.

He crouched there for a heartbeat, balanced against the night,
weighing his next move, then he flung himself through the air a
body length and more and into the arms of a honey locust. He'd
take the high road when he could.

The snap of a broken branch.

A low grunt of pain.

The royal garden stirred as the hunters came to see what had made the sound.

Aaron, his back tight against the slender trunk of the tree, pressed his hand against his hip and breathed shallowly through his nose. The smell of jasmine was almost overpowering, but keeping his teeth clenched prevented the pain from escaping. The branch he'd snagged had not been able to bear his weight and as he'd fallen the broken end of another had slammed into his hip. His fingers were sticky.

He shifted, precariously balanced on a branch not much larger than the one that had broken, and shrugged out of his pack. He didn't have time to give in to pain. The blood would bring the hunters and he had to be ready.

"The Clan Heir fights through pain!"

"Shut up, Father," he spat. "I'm not doing this for you."

From around the dark bulk of a hedge, belly low to the ground and tail lashing, came the first of the hunters. The other two quickly followed, drawn by the blood scent. They were larger than the mountain cats of Aaron's childhood, bulkier, less sleekly muscled. They grouped around his tree and one reared, claws spread wider than Aaron's hand, ripping deep gouges in the bark.

While other thieves had made the sign of the Nine and avoided their comrades hung on the palace gates in fear that the luck of the dead would rub off on them, Aaron had learned the lessons they offered. The great cats had declared their presence on more than one of the bodies. He broke the seal on the package he carried, careful not to touch any of the pungent herb with his hands.

The blood scent became suddenly of secondary importance. Rounded ears snapped forward and slitted eyes opened wide. Curiosity joined forces with this new and enticing smell and together they won. When the herb package crashed down behind a hedge, the hunters followed.

Aaron slid to the ground, keeping his weight on his arms as long as possible, then he hurried along the garden paths toward the bulk of the palace. He didn't know how long the herb would hold the hunters so he moved as quickly as he could, ignoring the pain because he had to, ignoring the warm wetness that slowly molded the thin cotton trousers to his leg. For the same reason he had gone over the wall at the sentry post, he now headed toward the one rectangle of light looking down onto the garden; an enemy seen could be avoided. Bypassing the windows on the lower floor—they would lead only to confrontations with guards patrolling the corridors—he pulled free the grappling iron and a soft length of silk rope.

In all of Ischia, only the temple and the palace were free of the ornate stonework that provided ladders for the city's thieves.

The thin metal hooks of the grapple were padded, but when it struck the tiled edge of the roof it rang dangerously loud. Aaron paused, sagging against the cool stone, but no new lamps were lit and no one appeared against the light on the balcony his rope ran so close beside. Stretching until his hip blossomed freshly with blood and pain, he grabbed the rope, braced his feet, and forced his body up the wall.

Just past the balcony, where he carefully kept his eyes from the spill of light lest he lose the dark, Aaron felt the rope tremble in his hands. Then it jerked. Then he slid sideways a few feet. Then he fell.

If the slide had moved him another hand's span . . .

If his injured leg had obeyed his will for a few heartbeats more. . . .

The edge of the balcony railing caught the back of his calves. It spun him round, clipping his forehead against the stone, and slammed him down on his back on the balcony tiles.

He thought for a moment that the green lights exploding in his head were the emerald he sought, shattered now beyond retrieval, shattered beyond even Faharra's ability to repair.

The emerald. . . .

He had to get the emerald for Faharra.

He tried to rise.

The face bending over him drew back, and tossed an obstructing shock of deep black hair away from pale blue eyes.

Aaron forgot how to breathe, forgot how to move . . .

Ruth. His cousin had tossed her black hair so and often teased him to cut it for her, short like a man's, so it would no longer fall in front of her eyes. Her pale, winter blue eyes.

. . . forgot the pain of the present as the pain of the past tightened its grip. And, lost in the past, he didn't see the sword descending.

Chapter Three

The forged steel struck the balcony railing with enough force to mark the softer iron, the noise of the blow echoing through the garden and frightening a pair of night roosting birds up into the air with a wild flurry of wings. His Royal Highness Prince Darvish Shayrif Hakem, third son of the king, slid his gaze along his scimitar's blade to where it rested some four feet above the pale throat it had been intended to hit.

He frowned and drank deeply from the large gold goblet in his right hand.

"I miss'd. I nev'r miss." Something had distracted him. He peered down at the sharp featured face. Something. . . . Recognition danced just beyond his grasp although he *knew* he'd held it an instant before.

"Bugger the Nine!"

Frustration turned to anger and the anger, riding the crest of the night's wine, poured down on the body at his feet.

Eyes narrowed in concentration, he pulled the weapon back, ignoring the shriek of protest as the tip hit the marble of the balcony floor and dragged across it. The creature—The boy? The man? The thief?—had not moved since he had fallen so unexpectedly out of the night.

"Just hold still for a little . . . bit . . . longer. . . ." His sword seemed to have gotten heavier, but he managed to heave it up into the air where it dipped through dangerous figure eights a hand's span above his bare shoulder. The thief merely continued to stare, although Darvish, drunk as he was, would have willingly bet the contents of the treasury that those strange silver eyes were not focused on what was in front of them.

Which is me. Darvish took another drink, the muscles of his sword arm bunching as he kept the weapon precariously aloft. *The rude little prick; staring at me without even seeing me.* The sword swung down again.

The song of steel striking stone a finger's span from his ear snapped Aaron up out of the past. He jerked, and blinked, shattering the memory that held him immobile, and the blue and black spun about until they returned to the face of the young man standing splay-legged above him. It wasn't his cousin. His cousin was dead.

"Shit!" Darvish tossed back half the remaining wine.

"Miss'd ag'in! I cannot poss'bly be *that* drunk." At least the thief now looked aware, an improvement of sorts even if it would make him harder to hit. Scrubbing his forearm across the dribbles of ruby liquid running down his chest, Darvish yawned, swayed, and lost his grip on his anger. He waited to see what would happen next. It was only fair, after all, to offer his visitor a move.

The emerald. Through the pounding in his head, Aaron remembered. He had to get to the royal staff and steal the emerald that crowned it. He'd failed Ruth and she'd died. He wouldn't fail Faharra even though she was already dead. He would get her the emerald, her finest work, to adorn her tomb. He had to get her the emerald. Fear and pain and hunger and grief lashed his thoughts into chaos, but through it all the great green stone shone like a beacon. He clutched desperately at its light, using it as an anchor and a lifeline, allowing the darkness to take the rest. Nothing else mattered.

Rolling to his knees, away from the distorted image of his face on the curved blade of the sword, he swayed and retched, his empty stomach clenching and unclenching like an angry fist. The pattern in the marble blurred and ran an inch from his nose and he fought the seductive urge to lay his head on the cool stone and surrender. But no. Not this time. He wouldn't surrender and he wouldn't run away. Gasping for air, barely clinging to sanity, he forced himself to his feet.

"Mov'ng," Darvish observed appreciatively, draining the goblet and tossing it with drunken aplomb over the balcony railing.

The muted sound of metal bouncing on grass was lost in Aaron's labored breathing. One step, two, moving blindly, his eyes fixed on Faharra's emerald, he put out a hand to brush a barely perceived obstacle out of his way.

The icy fingers of the intruder, splayed against the prince's chest penetrated even through seven hours of steady drinking. This was *not* the way a thief caught by an armed man should act. Indifference caught Darvish's wandering attention the way fight or flight would not have. He was so taken by surprise that the blow, weak as it was, pushed him to one side.

"Hey!" He lunged forward, his sword clattering forgotten to the floor. The sudden movement shifted the load of wine he carried and twisted the room on its axis.

With one of the prince's arms about the younger man's waist and the other flailing for balance, the two staggered forward together in a caricature of friendship until the edge of the bed caught them just under the knees and they fell. The warm flesh struggling under him decided Darvish on a new course of action and he fumbled for the ties to his captive's trousers.

Vaguely aware of silk and softness below him, Aaron began to fight against the unseen force holding him from above. Nothing would—nothing could—stop him from getting to the emerald and placing it in Faharra's tomb where it belonged. And then the weight lay still against his back. With a desperate squirm, he was free.

As he careened off the wall, groping for the door, the body on the bed began to snore.

Light first, hot and bright; lying across him like a blanket of molten rock drawn up boiling from the volcano. Then sound, a scream that drove barbed points into his ears again and again, pieces breaking off to work their way in deeper still. Gradually, he became aware of self. His skull felt too small for what it had to contain and arms and legs refused to respond. There were lead weights on his lids and a fire had lodged below his breastbone and was eating its way out.

Darvish moaned.

The sound, quiet as it was, brought bare feet padding toward the bed.

He wet his lips with a tongue barely less dry and croaked, "Close. The. Shutters." On the second attempt, he made himself understood and seconds later sighed in relief as the burning bands across his chest and face faded away.

He wanted nothing more than to lie there forever, unmoving, but his bladder insisted otherwise. Slowly, carefully, eyes still closed, he sat up, took two shaky breaths, and spewed the contents of his stomach all over the bed. Gentle hands eased him back against the pillows and a cool cloth wiped his face clean. He felt the soiled, stinking bedding stripped away and knew what he had to do. Teeth clenched, he raised a trembling hand into the air. Those same gentle hands spread his fingers and placed a clay cup within their curve. With help, he got the cup to his lips where it clattered against his teeth, but he managed to swallow the entire contents.

As always, it tasted worse than he remembered and for a moment he was sure he was going to die. Fires ran up and down the length of his body. He arched, spasmed, and collapsed covered in sweat. He'd complained once to a Wizard of the Third that the cure was almost worse than the affliction it cured. The wizard hadn't smiled as he'd replied, "It's supposed to be."

Feeling almost human, Darvish opened his eyes.

Oham, whose large, almost painfully ugly presence had been a solid constant in the prince's life for nearly ten years, slipped the now empty cup from lax fingers and said, face and voice carefully expressionless, "Highness, your bath is prepared."

"Of course it is." Darvish held out his arms and the dresser pulled him carefully to his feet, stripping off the red silk trousers he'd slept in the moment he was standing. "But first I have to . . ."

The youngest dresser approached with the waste pot, his knuckles white around the curve of pale green ceramic.

Darvish smiled and with much of his weight resting on Oham's thick shoulder, thankfully relieved himself.

"You're new," he said when he finished, reaching out and lightly pinching the boy's chin.

"Yes, Highness." The boy blushed and backed respectfully away with the brimming pot.

"Have you a name?"

Thick lashes lowered over velvet brown eyes. "Fadi, if it please, your Highness."

"Whether it pleases me or not . . ." And it did please him. Darvish ran an appreciative look down the slim figure and sighed; it would please him more in a couple of years when the boy was bedable. Except by then he'd be gone. They always were.

"And now, Oham, the bath."

"Yes, Highness."

It amused Darvish how carefully the large dresser walked as together they made their way to the small tiled room off his bedchamber. The wizard's potion had overcome much of the damage done by too much wine, but his head still felt precariously balanced on his neck as if the slightest jar would topple it off. Oham knew that, of course, this was not the first such walk they had taken.

The water in the deep copper tub steamed invitingly, scenting the room with a faint odor of sandalwood. Darvish slid into it with a satisfied sigh and lay back, eyes half closed with pleasure.

He moved obediently to the pressure of Oham's hands, giving himself over to both their gentleness and their strength. Not until he was being dried did he remember and stiffen.

"Bugger the Nine!"

"Highness?" Oham stopped moving the combed cotton towel over the broad muscles of the prince's back and stepped away, unsure of how he had erred.

"No, not you!" An imperious hand indicated the dresser should continue. "My most exalted father has informed me I am to be married."

"I had heard, Highness." Oham offered nothing more.

"To a chit of a girl, barely sixteen, who I've never met, for the sole purpose of tying this country to hers."

"Your pardon, Highness, but is that not the reason that all princes marry?" He knelt to dry the prince's legs, his gaze fixed on the blue-green tiles in the floor.

"Yes," Darvish spat out the word and closed his teeth on the ones that tried to follow; the real reason he'd drunk himself into unconsciousness after the interview with his most exalted father.

The third dresser, who stood by the door waiting to serve, the perfect ubiquitous servant, reported to the lord chancellor, who reported to the king. He was a nondescript man of indeterminate age fitting neatly between Oham and the boy, and only the latest in a series sent to keep an eye on the third son, who, having no real power of his own, might be tempted to try for someone else's. Darvish made certain they had plenty to report as he filled his life with wine and his bed with every willing body he stumbled across and he had the lord chancellor's spies beaten as often as they gave him any kind of an excuse.

With a vicious mental shove, he pushed back the words and the feelings that went with them. For the first time in twenty-three years his father had had a use for him. Except he hadn't been asked, hadn't even been allowed to regard it as a service to the

country. It had been a command; with no room in it for the one
commanded. *You will marry this girl. Consider yourself betrothed
and act accordingly.* Although Darvish had no wish to be married,
that hadn't driven him to the night's excesses.

"I need a drink."

"Highness." The lord chancellor's eyes and ears presented a
goblet, filled and waiting.

And that was the other thing; they made sure, these dressers
who owed their loyalty to another, that he stayed on the path he'd
chosen when he'd been old enough to understand—had been
made to understand—his position at court.

Bugger them all. He drained the goblet, his throat working
against the barely watered wine, two streams of red running down
from the corners of his mouth. When he finished, he belched,
yawned, and smiled. *Could be worse, I suppose. They could've
slapped me into the priesthood.*

He stretched, working the kinks out, then obediently followed
Oham back to the bedroom and stepped into the blue and silver
trousers held out for him. He shifted his shoulders as a white silk
shirt settled over them, enjoying the touch of the smooth fabric
against his skin. Then he shifted them again, and had to admit he
was, as he'd suspected, losing muscle tone. While Oham wound a
silver sash about his waist, he tried to work out how long it had
been since he'd gone to the training yard. One week at least,
maybe as much as two; it was hard to say, the days all blurred
with a wine-sodden sameness. He accepted his refilled goblet,
then tipped back his head to drink as the chancellor's man began
to pull an ivory comb through the wet mass of his hair. The tines
caught against the movement and the comb dug sharply into his
skull.

Darvish jerked, swore, smiled, and said, "Ten lashes."

"I will see to it, Highness." Oham's voice almost showed satisfaction.

Still smiling, Darvish stepped into his sandals and ran his fingers absently through Fadi's hair as the boy knelt to lace them.

Out in the garden, the scream that had wakened him sounded
once more.

"What the One was that?"

"Peacocks, Highness," Oham told him placidly, deftly re-
placing the goblet with a piece of bread. "The Most Blessed

Yasimina received them as a gift and loosed them in the gardens this morning.

"Pea what?"

"Cocks, Highness."

"That's what I thought you said." He took a bite of the bread, thickly spread with chopped dates in honey, and headed for the balcony. "What the One is a peacock?"

"A bird, Highness."

"Right." Throwing back the shutters, Darvish stepped outside and squinted down into the garden just in time to see a large blue bird trailing a tail even larger disappear behind a bush. Of all the changes that had occurred since his eldest brother had married the Princess Yasimina, this looked to be the noisiest.

"Peacocks," Darvish repeated to himself. "I suppose she *always* had peacocks back home in Ytaili. I suppose her-brother-the-king had a hundred or so roaming about *his* garden." He rubbed at his temples as a high-pitched shriek bounced jagged edges off the inside of his skull. "I *suppose* I'm not permitted to shoot them," he sighed.

"No, Highness."

"Perhaps the city won't agree with them and we can ship them off to Ramdan. . . ." No fair that his second brother should miss all the fun just because he'd run from court to raise his family.

"They were sent to lift the Most Blessed Yasimina's home-sickness, Highness."

"Well," Darvish aimed an imaginary crossbow at a scuttling bird, "if they get her to stop wailing they can scream under my window all they like." Her homesickness had driven half the court to distraction, none more so than her husband. It amazed Darvish that the crown prince had developed such strong feelings for a bride he'd known barely a year and had wed only to prevent a war. Strong enough feelings to allow this intrusion into the previously restful gardens.

I'll bet you asked Shahin, *Father. Didn't just tell him he was to be married. I'd have wed gladly if you'd only asked.* Not that his wedding would carry the weight that Shahin's had. His brother had married a Princess of Ytaili, wiping out centuries of conflict between the two countries. He would marry a child with no political importance at all.

He squinted up at the sun burning yellow-white in a cloudless sky, mid-afternoon by the angle. More or less his usual time for rising. Leaning on the balcony railing, his eyes half closed against the light, he finished the bread.

"I had the strangest dream last night, Oham. I dreamed a thief fell into my room. A quite attractive . . ." His palm, caressing the iron rail, found a mark that shouldn't exist, cutting off both the motion and the words.

"It was no dream, Highness. The guards found this thief you speak of staggering about the halls near dawn."

"So he's real." The prince ran a finger up and down the scar his sword had left and grinned, remembering how his dream had almost ended. "Where is he now?"

"Their Royal Highnesses have him in the Chamber of the Fourth, Highness." Oham's hand rose in the sign of the Nine and One.

"What!" Darvish whirled about to face the dresser who regarded him placidly.

"It is, Highness, where thieves and such are taken."

"Not this thief, by the Nine." In memory, pale eyes devoured his face once more. His heart began to pound painfully in his chest and fury burned the morning's wine away. "This thief's mine! Not theirs, mine!" He had always found the twins' diversions repellent, but the thought of them taking pleasure from the pain of something he considered his own drew his lips back off his teeth and curved his hands into fists.

Fadi scrambled out of the way as Darvish stormed by and then looked wide-eyed to the older dresser for guidance. Oham merely shrugged. What happened outside the prince's suite was not his concern. Inside, he did what he could.

Somewhere out of sight, the peacock screamed again.

As the guards snapped to attention and the heavy door swung open, a ripple of anticipation moved through the crowd of courtiers waiting in the long gallery outside the royal apartments. Fans were set aside, silks were patted smooth, and expressions ranging from polite interest to rapt adoration were fixed firmly in place. When they saw which royal emerged, the languid posturing, suitable for the heat of the afternoon, resumed. His Royal Highness Prince Darvish, while undeniably the life of any party, was useless as a purveyor of royal favor. Either he forgot the request entirely, the wine driving it from his mind, or he did something which so enraged his most exalted father that he was not permitted to approach the throne for an indefinite period of time.

Those closest bowed as he passed and wondered where he could be off to in such a scowling hurry. Neither the hurrying nor the scowl was like the prince.

"Well, I hope he's not going all dark and brooding," sighed one elderly noble to no one in particular. "We've quite enough of that going on now."

Out in the corridors of the palace, Darvish picked up his pace. If the thief had been with the twins since early morning there might not be much left to save. He fought to keep the full extent of his fury from showing; the last thing he needed was an interrogation from one of the lord chancellor's . . .

"Good afternoon, Highness."

. . . agents. Or worse yet, the lord chancellor himself. As a member of the royal family, Darvish held the higher rank but the lord chancellor held the trust of the king. The prince would be expected to pause, to converse, to place his concerns in a position of secondary importance, to recognize the lord chancellor's power. Darvish came to a decision between one step and the next.

"Give it to the Lady," he said pleasantly, without breaking stride.

"Highness!"

The prince quickly left the plump and elderly lord chancellor behind, blowing protests into an empty corridor. Later, when his thief was safe, he'd take the time to enjoy the shocked disbelief in the old man's voice. And he'd pay for it, later, when his father heard, but that didn't matter now.

The Chamber of the Fourth was deep in the oldest section of the palace, carved out of volcanic rock and close enough to the crater so the heat of the lava and the smell of the sulfur permeated the entire area. As Darvish crossed from frescoed walls and tiled floors to chiseled stone, the marks of the tools still raw generations after they'd been made, he began to seethe, dwelling on the injustice that brought *his* thief down to *this* place. By the time he reached the chamber, he'd worked his rage up to a fever pitch and had half convinced himself that the twins had stolen a prized possession.

As his palm touched the door, someone screamed behind it. A hoarse hopeless scream, from a throat that had almost no screaming left.

It rooted Darvish to the spot as it climbed and peaked and died.

Not until silence ruled again did it release him. He kicked open the door, sending it slamming back against the wall.

The room was not large and the stench from a dozen kinds of smoke and as many kinds of pain was almost overpowering. He gagged, recovered, and sucked his next breath through his teeth. Two slim figures in unrelieved black, bracketing a table like pillars of night, looked up at the sound. Identical hair and clothing, chosen to minimize sexual characteristics, made it nearly impossible to tell them apart even in the bright light of the half dozen hanging lamps that illuminated their work. Heavy kohl, outlining eyes almost amber, distracted from minor facial differences. But Darvish had known them all their lives and knew without question who held the red coal poised at the end of long pincers and who only watched.

"Shakana!" he bellowed at his younger sister. "Drop it!"

She smiled, graciously inclined her head, and let the smoking coal fall to rest on the blistered chest bound before her on the table.

The scream pulled Darvish the length of the room and he used the momentum to throw his brother aside. With the calluses of his sword hand, he swept the coal onto the floor.

Shakana danced back, flicking the skirts of her robe away from the sparks, her sandals making sucking noises as they left the floor.

"You have no right," she began, but at Darvish's wordless growl, reconsidered and held her tongue. Eyes locked on her brother, she rounded the table to help her twin rise.

The thief's arms and legs had been manacled to lengths of chain, then pulled tight; not yet to dislocate only to hold immobile at the extreme limit of their stretch. His head had been enclosed in a steel vise, the band across his eyes grooved to hold heated iron pellets. Thankfully it was still cold and empty. Three deep gouges ran the width of each thigh; wizard marks, for flesh and blood were necessary to trace the thief's trail through the palace. His genitals were swollen but intact. On his chest . . .

. . . obscenely red against skin almost white, blisters bubbling up from the most recent burn even as Darvish watched, the marks of four live coals dropped and allowed to cool while the flesh below cooked. The two oldest had broken and split, blood and other fluids still oozing from their angry centers.

The twins had barely gotten started.

With hands that wanted to tremble, Darvish fought the bolts out of the head vise and as gently as possible eased it free. The thief began to toss his head back and forth, whimpering softly.

"Don't!" Darvish snapped, reaching for the manacles. "Stay still."

The tossing stopped. The whimpering continued.

His twin still gripping his elbow, Kasil stepped forward, hands stained from contact with the floor. "You can't do this, Darvish," he whined as the iron bands fell clear, exposing torn and abraded wrists. "He's ours."

"The One he is," the older prince snarled, struggling with the last fastener. "He came into the palace through my room, that makes him mine."

"But he's in *our* room now," Shakana pointed out coldly.

"Your room?" Blood had dried around the bolt, nearly welding it to the band. "I thought this was the Chamber of the Fourth. . . ."

She glared. "We serve the Fourth."

"You serve your own perverted appetites." He twisted viciously and inch by inch forced the bolt clear. With the thief lying unbound on the table he turned and faced the twins, a crazy light having nothing to do with the lamps burning in the depths of his eyes. "I'll fight you for him," he offered.

"Don't be . . ." Kasil tried to take another step forward but Shakana stopped him.

"He means it, Kasil."

Darvish smiled, grimly, the thief momentarily forgotten in the anticipation of beating both pointy little faces into an unrecognizable pulp. It was his turn to step forward. The twins stepped back.

"Highnesses?" Two guards stood in the doorway, a third hanging limply between them. He was conscious, but terror had quite obviously sapped the strength from his legs and made it impossible for him to stand.

The guard on the left bowed as well as he was able. "Highnesses, this is the man who let the thief past the inner gate."

Shakana's face wore the expression a farmer's might while examining a bullock in the market. "He looks strong."

"Strong," Kasil agreed.

Darvish's bark of laughter brought a moan from the new prisoner and worried frowns from the twins. He ignored both—he had the thief, but the guard would die; nothing he did changed anything, he found it bitterly amusing. Carefully, he lifted the thief from the table. "You've got something new to play with," he said as he settled the suddenly dead weight. The barely visible rise and fall of the tortured chest became the only indication he carried a living man. "I'll take what's mine and go." The copper head lolled against his shoulder and fell back, exposing the long pale line of throat.

"Darvish . . ."

He had to pause anyway, so the guards could move clear of the door, their burden beginning to babble incoherent prayers as they moved further into the room.

". . . what are *you* going to do with him?"

Darvish threw a dangerous smile back at the twins, careful not to let the strain of carrying what was after all a full grown man, show. "Whatever I please," he said.

Chapter Four

Pain. Old pain, constant pain, and for that Aaron was grateful. The body could get used to anything in time, even, given a chance, the searing agony that existed where he thought his chest should be. It hurt to breathe. It hurt to think about breathing. Blind instinct tried to move him out from under the hurting. Training told him to be still. It was always better to be still, until you knew.

"He's conscious, I'm sure of that."

"He looks the same to me."

"You're not a healer, Highness." The middle-aged woman sat back on her heels beside the pallet and stretched. Formidable brows drawn down, she studied the work already done, then reached into the wicker basket resting on the floor by her right knee.

The prince peered over her shoulder. The thief had been under the healer's care for almost an hour but, Darvish had to admit, he still looked like shit. Between the twins and the wizards and the guards who had found him originally, there was hardly an inch of his pale body that wasn't coming up in purple and green bruises. His wrists and ankles wore bracelets of raw meat where he'd tried to twist free of the manacles and his chest was a bubbling mass of blisters and destroyed flesh.

"Can you fix him, Karida?" he asked.

The healer snorted as she eased the cork out of a squat clay pot. "He's not a toy, Highness, that careless playing has broken and a glue brush and a steady hand can fix. He's a man. A young one, but a man. I wonder if you realize that."

"Of course I do," Darvish replied, mildly indignant.

"Then what do you plan on doing with him?" Karida set the

cork to one side and dipped the first three fingers of her right hand into the pot.

"You mean after you've finished gluing him back together?"

The tone was so guileless, she had to sternly suppress a smile. "Yes."

"I'm not entirely certain."

She glanced up, although her hand continued to gently spread the salve over the thief's burned chest. "You're not?"

Darvish smiled his fecklessly charming smile. "Why worry about it now."

The pain was cooling. Dulling. Drawing back its edges until it no longer was all that Aaron was. Groping like a blind man in new territory, he tried to find the rest of himself. Something firm but yielding cradled his back and head. A bed? Perhaps. It didn't fit where he felt he should be, but it seemed most likely. He began to distinguish separate pains in his arms and legs, but next to the great pain, they were nothing, so he ignored them.

Then he remembered.

He had failed. Again. And he hadn't died. Again.

And now it seemed he wasn't likely to.

The physical pain no longer seemed so great.

The moan escaped before he could stop it.

"He moaned!"

"You sound, Highness, as if you've taught him a new trick." Karida restoppered the jug and replaced it in the basket, then rose lithely to her feet in a single, fluid motion. "He is very ill. I will be staying."

"You don't have to," Darvish began, but she cut him off.

"I know I don't." The healers enjoyed relative autonomy within the palace hierarchy.

His smile softened for a second into an expression few were permitted to see. "Thank you for coming."

"You're welcome." She looked him up and down with a critical eye and added, her tone dry, "Besides, it makes a nice change from the lover's complaints you usually call me to take care of. How is that by the way?"

"All better." Darvish spread his arms as if inviting her to see for herself.

She declined the invitation. "And if you'd keep away from

those cheap whores, you'd stay better. If you must visit the market-place, why can't you stick to the expensive establishments? The One knows you can afford it."

"Because high-class whores," Darvish told her with a wink, "are too little different from the ladies of the court. I'm looking for a change of pace after all."

"Highness." Oham bowed when the prince acknowledged him and continued, holding out an armload of red silk. "It is time to dress for evening court."

"And for my most exalted father. . . ." An eyebrow quirked at the healer. "Maybe it's a good thing you're staying."

"Darvish."

"Shahin. What a pleasant surprise." Darvish smiled at his eldest brother and extended the smile to include the guard that followed the heir even into the royal wing. The guard returned the smile. The heir did not. The heir merely looked down his hawk-like nose with the expression of disgust he always wore in Darvish's presence.

"Are you drunk yet?"

"Please, at this hour? Give me credit for an ability to pace myself, at least."

"I heard about what you did today."

"Of course you did." Darvish kept the bright smile pasted in place, but behind it he tried frantically to figure out his brother's interest. Years ago, before the wine, they had been friends—as much friends as the difference in age and the heir's position had allowed. Was there enough of that friendship left for Darvish to appeal to it? For him to ask Shahin to intercede with their father for his thief's life?

He forced his eyes to meet Shahin's for a heartbeat and then he allowed his gaze to drop. The older prince's face showed no indication he remembered anything but the wine.

"Why did you do it?"

The tone and the expression reminded Darvish so much of their father that his palms grew damp. "Save a man's life?" The laugh sounded false, but it was the best he could do at the moment. "Oh, I don't know. You've got Yasimina, she's got her peacocks, maybe I wanted a pet of my own."

Shahin's lip curled up, teeth very white against the black of his beard. "You're a disgusting . . ." Words failed him and with a final withering glare, he strode into his own apartments.

Darvish shrugged as the door slammed shut and the guard took up position outside it. "Nobody understands me," he sighed melodramatically, and, with his heart curiously heavy, continued down the corridor. He needed a drink.

From his position at the far end of the long audience hall, Darvish could barely see the great black throne let alone the man sitting upon it, but even through the milling crowds of courtiers he could feel the king's presence. He snagged a drink off a passing tray and let the familiar taste of the wine soothe him while he contemplated strategy. Sooner or later, one of his most exalted father's pages would find him and request that he approach the throne. Darvish harbored no illusions that the king remained long ignorant of anything that happened within the palace and his actions of the afternoon had probably been reported by several different people, those watching him, those watching the twins, the lord chancellor himself. Given that Shahin knew, the king certainly did. The question became, did he stay as far from the throne as possible, assuming out of sight out of mind, thus putting off the confrontation? Or did he begin now to work his way through the crowds so that when the summons came he had less far to walk under the eyes of the court.

He exchanged his empty goblet for a full one and decided on the latter; he had no objection to being talked about but he preferred to have more choice over the subject.

"Highness."

The low, throaty voice drew his head around in an almost involuntary action.

"Lady Harithah." He caught up the dimpled hand she held out and brushed his lips across its back. She tasted of some rare spice that set his pulses racing.

Eyes that sparkled like amethyst in sunlight looked up into his for an instant with unmistakable desire, then curved lids stained violet were quickly, and demurely, lowered. "I trust this evening finds you well, Highness."

"It does now," Darvish murmured, watching the almost sheer silk rise and fall across her breasts. He'd been admiring the lady from afar since she'd arrived at court, her much older and very protective husband in tow. Up close, she was unbelievable, with deep curves a lover could get lost in. He had smiled at her but nothing more, for even a royal prince does not cuckold one of the First Lords of the Navy. Except that now the lady seemed to be offering.

"I have heard your Highness has an interest in antique weapons. I have a sword of my husband's in my suite, if you would care to see it after court."

It still wasn't a good idea. "And your husband?"

The tip of her tongue lightly touched the full center of one moist lip. "My husband is at sea, Highness."

And when the Nine drop paradise in your lap it is not a mere mortal's place to say it's a bad idea. "I would be honored, Lady Harithah. Your room," he kissed the back of her hand again and turned it over and laid his lips gently against the palm, "after court."

As she walked away, each rounded buttock imprinted the silk of her full trousers for one warm second. Downing the wine remaining in the second goblet, Darvish reached for a third. And then he remembered.

The thief. When court ended, he should return to his injured thief. *Why?* He tapped the nails of his free hand against the embossed bowl of the goblet. *He's unconscious, he won't even know you're there. And Lady Harithah most certainly will.* His stomach growled and he headed for the nearest of the small circular tables piled high with delicacies. *Besides, Karida's with him.* Picking up a pastry, he shrugged off the memory of silver-gray eyes. *He doesn't need me.*

The evening had advanced well into night by the time Darvish felt the light touch on his elbow and the murmured "Highness" that meant a summons from the throne. He finished reciting the bawdy verse he had just composed for a limpid-eyed young lady, who blushed at the attention while her friends shrieked with laughter. He bowed theatrically at their applause, red silk sleeves billowing with the motion, and, when he straightened, took a kiss in payment. Then he turned—calmly, as if his heart had not begun to pound painfully behind his ribs—and acknowledged the page.

She inclined her head, fingers properly laced against the pale gray tunic, body positioned the requisite two paces away—close enough for privacy, far enough for movement. "My lord would see you now, Highness."

He bowed again, a gesture just on the verge of mocking.

Composure unruffled, she turned and walked away, knowing that whatever he felt, however he acted, the prince would follow.

The throne had been carved many, many years before from a single block of obsidian and as he approached, Darvish kept his gaze on the gleaming black stone rather than the man sitting upon it. It was supposed to be a symbol of how the king controlled the volcano, and it impressed most people as it had been designed to. Darvish, however, had sat upon it. He had been very young and had been beaten for it afterward, but he remembered how cold and hard it had been and at that moment he gave up any desire to ever sit upon it again.

Of course, I'll never convince our most cautious lord chancellor of that. . . .

The lord chancellor stood to the left of the throne, his plump hands tucked into the full green sleeves of his robe, his round face serene. The serene face, Darvish well knew, was the most dangerous. The serene face meant his mind was already made up and only an act of the One Below could change it.

To the right of the throne, one hand resting lightly upon the stone, the other folded behind his back, stood Shahin, Crown Prince and Heir, Light of his Father. His expression had not changed since their earlier meeting.

I have not had enough to drink. I thought I had, but I was wrong. Too close to the throne for serving tables or servants, Darvish slipped a nearly full goblet of wine from the surprised fingers of an elderly lord and tossed it back. It was sweet and cloying, not the light mountain wine he preferred. *Still, princes can't be choosers. And anything's better than no wine at all.* He winked at the lord as he returned the goblet.

Then nothing stood between him and the throne. Even the page had faded away.

Heart beginning to pound, he continued forward, eyes on the tiles in the floor. When he caught the gleam of gold, the outermost edge of the royal crest that marked the actual boundary of the throne, he dropped to one knee and rested his head for an instant on the other. As a member of the royal family, he did not have to wait on the king's grace to rise, but the timing was delicate—too short a time and he was accused of being disrespectful, too long and they accused him of sarcasm. Either charge was usually true. Often, both were. Tonight though, for some reason, he felt tired—

nothing more, nothing less—so he stayed down a little longer and figured they could make of it what they would.

He lurched slightly as he rose, the most recent wine shifting queasily in his stomach, but his voice was steady as he spoke the ritual words.

"You requested my presence, Most Exalted?"

Darvish couldn't remember the last time he'd called the man father to his face. Tradition called for him to keep his eyes lowered until the king spoke. He didn't. He never did.

The king's eyes were as obsidian black as the throne he sat on and showed as much warmth as he looked down at his third son. "You took something from the Chamber of the Fourth this afternoon," he said without preamble and without emotion. "Why?"

"Not something, Most Exalted. Some*one.*"

Long fingers stirred on the broad arm of the throne. "Do not make me repeat my question."

As if I could, Darvish thought and barely stopped the wine from voicing the thought aloud. He drew breath to tell the story he had concocted over the course of the evening's drinking and dallying, paused, and said instead, "I didn't like what was being done to him."

"It was no more, Most Exalted, than what is done in the Chamber of the Fourth," the lord chancellor interjected smoothly.

"I didn't like what was being done to *him,*" Darvish insisted.

"Is he your lover?" The question was asked without curiosity or caring; only because it was inevitable the question be asked.

"No, Most Exalted, just a thief who fell from the night onto my balcony."

"Why, then, did you take him from the Chamber of the Fourth? Merely because you could?" The lord chancellor leaned a little forward, his position challenging.

He wants me to say yes, Darvish realized, *so that they can come and take the thief away. Merely because they can.* And out of the blurry memories of the night before came the sight of the thief's face, just after he'd opened those amazing silver-gray eyes. Something . . . Darvish raised his head and looked the king full in the face, speaking slowly as he sorted his feelings into words.

"There was already so much pain, I couldn't let them add any more. . . ."

"So you took it upon yourself," and the tone asked, *who are you,* "to stop it."

"Yes, Most Exalted." It was the only honest conversation he'd had with his father in years, and Darvish could see the man was not impressed. *What do you want from me?* he wanted to ask. But he didn't. He knew the answer. Nothing.

"Let him keep the thief, Father."

"What?" The king echoed Darvish's thought. He turned to stare in puzzlement at his eldest son.

Just for an instant, Darvish saw a speculative look in Shahin's eyes he'd never seen before, then it passed, replaced by the scorn he recognized only too well.

"If nothing else, it will teach him he must accept responsibility for his actions."

"But my prince," the lord chancellor protested. "A thief. Loose in the palace. An *outland* thief."

The emphasis drew the king's brows down, as it had been intended to, Darvish was sure.

"What of it?" Shahin's hawk gaze crossed the throne and pinned the older man. "It is not as if he will ever be unobserved."

Darvish wondered if he heard another meaning beneath his brother's words, if the "he" Shahin referred to was not the thief but Darvish himself. He turned the words over, but the wine frustrated his search.

"I have thought on this matter."

The ritual words jerked Darvish back to the question at hand.

"The thief should have died had you not saved him. He therefore has no life save what you give him. If . . ."

The tone said, *When.*

". . . you tire of him, he dies."

"As easy as that to dispose of a life, Most Exalted?"

Even the background babble of the court seemed to fade as Darvish watched his father's brows draw in. He wanted to say something to cancel the comment, but anything he could think of would only make matters worse.

The crown prince gave a snort of disgust before the king could speak. "You should know," and his voice cut like a scimitar's edge, "you've disposed of your own."

The danger passed and the king nodded slowly, acknowledging the wisdom of his heir's remark. This third son was not worth wasting anger upon. "I have finished with you," was all he said and he would have said the same to anyone as he dismissed them from his presence.

Darvish dropped to his knee again, then stood and backed the nine and one paces away. With the suggestion of a nonchalant smile carefully pasted on his face, he turned and plunged into the crowd of courtiers.

Frowning thoughtfully, Shahin watched him go. For years he had been convinced that Darvish was nothing more than he seemed; a wastrel, a buffoon, an embarrassment. Tonight—earlier in the corridor, and here—he thought he saw something more, that perhaps there was still a prince left inside the fool.

"You look worried, Highness."

"Do I?" While Shahin recognized that the man excelled at his job, that he had guided the king and therefore the kingdom on a prosperous course for years, he couldn't warm to him. Back when Darvish had first begun to drink, Shahin had asked the lord chancellor if something worthwhile could not be found for the younger prince to do.

"You'd trust something worthwhile to that?" the chancellor had replied as they watched a giggling Darvish being hoisted out of a fountain.

"No," Shahin had answered, and turned his back.

But now he wondered if perhaps he should have said yes.

"You're worried about something, Highness."

"Nothing," the heir lied and, warned by his tone, the lord chancellor backed away. Shahin watched his brother accept a goblet of wine and drain it. Was it too late?

Once they knew he was not likely to bring down the king's wrath upon them, Darvish was quickly surrounded by laughing young men and women who pressed food, drink, and themselves into his hands. He lost himself in their circle for a time and then danced his way to the Nobles' Quarters where the Lady Harithah kept the promises of her smile.

Darvish responded with enthusiasm—a dead man would've responded with enthusiasm—but somehow, his heart wasn't in it.

"Highness, the thief is awake."

Darvish stretched his toes out over the edge of the bath and regarded them sleepily. "Thank you, Fadi," he said when Oham had moved the razor far enough from his throat for speech. "I'll see him when I'm bathed. Has he spoken?"

"No, Highness. He just lies and stares at the ceiling."

"Go back to watching him," Darvish yawned. "Tell me if there's any change."

"Yes, Highness." The boy bowed, his gaze dropping from the rim of the tub where he'd anchored it to the prince's body shimmering under the water. He flushed, turned quickly, and began to hurry out of the room.

"Fadi."

He turned back slightly more slowly than he'd turned away.

Darvish grinned. He wished he had the energy to tease the boy, who was curious, obviously, but who was still considerably too young. *And I am too exhausted to live up to the expectations of a thirteen-year-old.* He'd gotten even less sleep than usual the night before. *Nine Above, it's no wonder her husband spends so much time at sea.* "Is Karida still with him?"

"No, Highness. She left this morning. Just after you . . ." Fadi paused, unsure of how to describe his prince being all but carried in by two grinning guards wearing only his shirt and his sandals. Squirming a little under Oham's gaze, he settled finally on, ". . . returned."

"And I'll bet she had a few things to say about my return, too."

The young dresser opened and closed his mouth. He couldn't repeat what the healer had said. Not to his prince. He squirmed a little more.

"Go." Darvish took pity on the boy and, with a wave of his hand that arced a spray of scented water through the air, dismissed him. "I can pretty much guess what she said anyway. Watch my thief for me."

Thankfully, Fadi sped out of the bathing room.

The ceiling was stucco. Aaron knew stucco. It crumbled under probing fingers and left its mark on hands and boots and clothing. A good thief stayed away from stucco. And Aaron was a good thief.

"You're too good a thief, Aaron, my lad."

"Not too good, Faharra," he told the memory. *"Or I wouldn't be where I am."* He was in the palace although he didn't know where and he still lived although he didn't know why. The angle of the wall told him he was low, on a pallet, not a bed. The pain that rose and fell with each breath advised against movement, but he tried to rise anyway, to see more of his failure. Teeth clenched, fighting the agony, he got his head up, but it did him no good as

his vision blurred into jagged slashes of red and yellow and they became all he could see.

"Hey." A gentle hand pushed him down. "You're not supposed to do that. Karida'll have my butt if you undo all her hours of work."

Aaron struggled to focus on the speaker suddenly perched beside him. The large block of cream was a robe. The black above it, a tangle of damp hair. The blue—the winter blue—eyes. He closed his own.

"Are you in pain? I can call the healer."

It was a man's voice. Ruth was dead. He opened his eyes again.

"That's better."

The brilliant white smile that accompanied the words drove the image—no, the man—further from Aaron's memory of his cousin. She had never smiled like that in her entirely too brief life.

"Look, have you got a name? I can't go on referring to you as the-thief-that-fell-onto-my-balcony indefinitely."

He swallowed, once, twice, before he pulled a voice up out of the knife edges in his throat. "Aaron." It didn't matter what he told them. Not any more.

"You sound worse than that One abandoned peacock, Aaron. Here."

One large hand slid behind his back and the other held a metal rim against his lips. The pain of being moved was nothing against the feel of the chilled water in his mouth, cooling and soothing the abraded tissue.

"In case you're curious . . ."

He wasn't.

". . . my name is Darvish, these are my rooms, and I pulled you out of the Chamber of the Fourth. You owe me your life."

Why didn't you let me die!

Something of the the thought must have shown on his race, for the voice hardened slightly.

"If you want to die, just say so. You aren't that far from it."

One word would bring him the death he craved, but Aaron couldn't speak it. Had never been able to speak it. He'd lived with the knowledge of his cowardice eating away at him for years. Not even this close to death could he just give up and slide past the barrier. He would have to live. Again.

Darvish hadn't quite known what to expect from his thief,

gratitude maybe but certainly not such bleak and utter despair. He'd seen men and women go to the volcano with more joy. It made him profoundly uncomfortable. He stood and frowned down at the young man on the pallet. "The healer says you can have as much fluid as you can handle. . . ."

There was no response. No reaction at all, as if the inner misery left no space for anything else.

Darvish suddenly didn't want to be in the same room with all that pain. It made him feel guilty, although he didn't understand why. He had nothing to feel guilty about. He'd saved Aaron's life.

"Oham!"

"Yes, Highness."

With the robe billowing out behind him, he strode back into the bedroom, heels slamming down into the brightly patterned rugs. "Get me my leathers. I'm going to the training yard."

Three hours later, winded, bruised, and aching, he felt a little better.

Nothing like getting your ass kicked, Darvish thought as Oham spread liniment over a battered section of ribs, *to get rid of guilt. You're in pain. I'm in pain. So stop looking at me like that.*

Aaron actually seldom looked at Darvish at all. Over the next few days he lay quietly, wrapped in almost tangible despair. He remained stoic while Karida treated him. He almost never spoke. Fadi brought him the waste pot periodically and if he needed to, he used it. He never asked for it. He never asked for anything.

Standing motionless and unseen in the shadow of a building, Shahin watched the arms master criticize Darvish's last session.

". . . and much too slow," he finished as the panting prince held out his hands to help the defeated pair of guards to their feet.

It hadn't looked too slow to Shahin, he'd been impressed by his younger brother's skill. For too long, he'd lumped Darvish in with the twins as unsalvageable, cursed by the wine as the youngest members of the royal family had been cursed by their birth—his hand sketched the sign of the Nine and One—but that would have to change.

Darvish, strangely unwilling to put up with the pointed questions and snide comments of his friends, spent a lot of time at the training yard.

"Looking at the bright side," he grunted as Oham wound a

dressing about his throbbing knee, "if this keeps up I'll soon be back in shape. Or in pieces," he added, sighing, sticking a skinned knuckle in his mouth.

Even the wine held less allure than usual.

And then his most exalted father met him one afternoon in the corridor, ran cold eyes over the grimy and sweat-stained leathers and said with no discernible emotion at all, "It appears that thief will be the making of you."

Darvish made no reply, but that night he put on his gaudiest silks and he didn't sober up for three days.

"You look like shit."

Darvish belched, handed the cup now empty of wizard's brew to Oham, and squinted in the direction of the voice. For reasons he could no longer remember, although he assumed they'd made perfect sense at the time, he'd had Aaron, pallet and all, brought from the sitting room to the bedroom. It must have been a good idea, the thief was talking.

"You don't look so terrific yourself," he pointed out, balancing precariously on one leg as Oham stripped off his filthy trousers.

Aaron, reclining against a massive mound of pillows Fadi had piled at one end of his pallet, dropped a shoulder slightly, the closest he could come to a shrug. Any greater movement pulled at his healing chest and threatened to send him back into darkness. His lip curled as he watched the activity by the bed. "You're one of the royal princes," he said.

"Right first time," Darvish agreed, scraping at something he couldn't identify that was caked on the back of his left hand.

Aaron's brows drew down as he tried to remember. "Darvish. . . ."

Oham whirled about, the chains that held his sleeveless vest in place straining against his indignant breath. "You will call him Highness."

"Why?" Aaron asked dryly, lids falling to hood his eyes. "What will he do to me if I don't?"

"You can die!" Oham snapped.

"Yes. I can. *But I won't,* he thought, *my father's god isn't done with me yet.* The thought didn't bother him. Nothing bothered him any longer. He had no feelings, he had no life. He'd spent the last few days cutting all that loose. Let the hand of his father's god fall where it would. It didn't matter.

"He can call me what he wants," Darvish said, weaving his way to the bath. "Stop glaring at him, Oham, and come here. I'm likely to drown this morning without help." *And besides,* leaning heavily on the dresser the prince managed to get first one leg then the other over the edge of the tub, *I think I'd like to be called by my name for a change. And it looks like that black cloud he had himself wrapped in is finally gone, thank the One.* The cloud had been replaced by nothing at all, but Darvish was used to that.

Bath over, and feeling if not better at least as if death was no longer imminent, Darvish sat quietly watching the thief while Oham tried to work the tangles out of his hair. "So," he said at last, more because he wasn't up to silence than because he wanted to know, "what were you after that night you fell at my feet?"

Aaron dropped his gaze from the patterns of sunlight and shadow playing across the ceiling to Darvish's face. Why not tell him?

"I was after the emerald on top of the royal staff."

Oham made a choking noise and across the room, Fadi almost let a platter of bread and fruit drop to the floor. From where he was cleaning the bathing room, the lord chancellor's man strained not to miss any further confessions. Darvish only grinned.

"I figured you couldn't be after The Stone, being as how you don't strike me as a complete idiot. The emerald, huh?" He shook his head admiringly. "Why?"

Aaron's lips thinned. "Personal reasons," he grunted. Faharra was his; her memory only the second thing worth keeping in a life of failure.

"Suit yourself." Darvish took a peach from the offered platter and began to peel it fastidiously. "I'd ask you to join me," he said as Fadi gathered up the fallen peel, "but Karida says you're on fluids for a while yet. I think she's expecting you to regain your color." A drop of juice splashed against the wall over Aaron's head as Darvish gestured with the dripping fruit. "Of course, you being an outlander, this is probably as much color as you'll get."

It could have been an insult. Guided by their king, the people of Ischia tended to think outlanders were little better than barbarians and at best they treated them with patronizing tolerance. The attitude had made much of Aaron's thievery easier. "Your eyes are blue," he said mildly.

Darvish wiped his chin. "My grandmother was from the north. Fairly far north. A treaty bride."

"The king is half an outlander?"

"I suppose that is what it means, yes." The peach pit sailed over the balcony railing. "But never mention it to my most exalted father."

Aaron shrugged his minimal shrug once again. He doubted he'd be mentioning anything to the king. And if the king's third son, his blue-eyed son, failed to see that his very existence reminded the king he was only half of the land he ruled, a land he had tried to empty of other reminders, well, it wasn't Aaron's business to point it out if said third son was too blind to see it on his own. And frankly, he could care less. The insecurities of the king were not his problem.

"What are you going to do with me?" he asked instead. Not that he cared anything about that either—although his heart, apparently unaware of his feelings, beat faster while he waited for an answer.

"You mean when you get better?"

"Yes."

Darvish studied the way the sunlight turned Aaron's hair to burnished copper, the way the slightly lighter brows rose at the outer edges then tufted thickly over the center of those amazing gray eyes. It was a pity about the scarring but even so the lithely muscled body had appeal. He grinned, his meaning very evident. "I'll think of something."

Aaron's lips drew back off his teeth. "I'll see you in the Lady first."

Oh, so it's like that, is it? Pity. Darvish stretched and reached for another peach. He'd never taken an unwilling lover, and he had no intention of starting now. Enough men and women threw themselves in his path that he had no need to exhaust himself seducing one skinny thief. "Well, as long as we understand each other," he said.

Chapter Five

"Chandra? Chandra!" The piercing call echoed up the tower stairs, followed by a rustle of fabric and a heavy wheezing that suggested the person climbing could call or climb but not both.

The slim bronze figure sitting at the exact center of the tower roof gave no indication that she'd heard anything at all. Her long dark hair streaming out behind her like a pennant, she sat motionless, staring into the setting sun.

"Chandra!" The cry rose in volume; closer now, less muffled by stone and distance. "Chandra!" A head, wrapped in yards of purple veiling, popped up through the open trapdoor. The small black eyes, all that were visible of the face, widened as they saw the girl. "So there you are, Chandra. I might have known you'd be up here."

The sun having finally dropped below the horizon, Chandra turned from her contemplation of the rapidly purpling sky. "Yes, you might have," she said, "as I'm *always* up here at sunset."

"But not tonight!" Two plump hands beginning to show the marks of age, waved in the air like hysterical pigeons. "The messenger has come from King Jaffar."

"I know, Aba. I saw the arrival from my window. What with the banners and the horns and all it was hard to miss." She began to smoothly braid the heavy fall of chestnut hair. "The message has little relevance, however, as regardless of King Jaffar's answer I will continue to refuse to marry anyone."

"Oh-ho, big words." The older woman clucked her tongue at Chandra's glare. The young became outraged so easily. "You may say that now, poppet. . . ."

"I have been saying it all along, Aba, so it's hardly my fault if my father doesn't listen." Chandra's father, to her disgust, had made a long habit of only hearing what he wanted to. "And you needn't put it down to maidenly modesty," she added emphatically," for I haven't any."

"Modesty indeed!" The black currant eyes widened, suddenly aware of her poppet's state of undress. "For pity's sake, Chandra, put a robe on before someone sees you!"

"How?" Chandra waved a graceful hand around. The tower was the tallest building on their country estate and from where she sat all she could see was sky and the cradling circle of mountains that made up the horizon.

"You *know* what nasty boys are like!"

Actually, she didn't—she never associated with people her own age, they were so *young*—but as her old nurse seemed to be working herself into a foaming fit, Chandra unfolded from the full lotus she'd been in for the last two hours, touching her forehead briefly against each knee as she straightened the leg. "My robe is in my rooms," she pointed out when she was standing, her tone just bordering on smugness, "and you're blocking the stairs."

Chandra watched her father paring an apple and wondered if she should speak first. Her position was, after all, a simple one; she was not going to marry Prince Darvish. Or anyone else for that matter. Ever. But so far marriage had not been mentioned—although the weather, trade, the olive crop, and the new bay stallion had all been trivialized—and Chandra was hesitant about bringing the subject up herself. *"When battle can no longer be avoided,"* Rajeet, her teacher, had told her, *"it is always wisest to discover your enemy's strengths and weaknesses and use those against him."* Of course, her father's only strength was weakness and that made it more difficult. Rajeet, being a Wizard of the First, and the First the god of war, never seemed to take that into account.

She watched the peel spiral to the table in one long strand and remembered how much that had impressed her when she'd been small, how whenever a crate of the imported fruit had arrived she'd begged him to peel one for her immediately. Many things had impressed her about her father then; he'd been a giant among men, everything a lord should be. They'd ridden together, walked together, read together. He'd shown her how to treat the people she would one day rule with wisdom and compassion. And then her mother had died, leaving an aching void where there had once been gentle laughter and warm arms, a void made larger because something in her father had died as well. Chandra had been ten. She'd tried to comfort him, but he would not be comforted, alternately raging and weeping, calling for the One Below to take him, too. Chandra, the child, couldn't understand what she'd done wrong. Her mother's death had not been her fault, she knew that even then, but somehow she had failed her father.

Even now, six years later, Chandra could not think back on that time without shuddering. Her potential as a wizard only just recognized, she had thrown herself into her studies, hiding from what her father had become and from her inability to help, piling up texts and tracts and her new knowledge between them. If he had no room in his heart for her, then she would make no room in her heart for him. Her power replaced her father's love and all the attention she'd given to him, she now gave to it.

Eventually, her father had found enough of himself to be a competent administrator, nothing more.

He reached for the scented linen napkin by his plate and rubbed at the apple juice on his fingers. Chandra resisted the urge to drum her own fingers against the lacquer tabletop. Would he never get to the point? Finally, he set the napkin carefully aside and the server moved forward to remove the low tables and bring in the cups of sweet coffee. Chandra let the first sip roll slowly across her tongue. A passion for the thick, rich drink was the only remaining activity she shared with her father and, although she knew it was foolish—a wizard should remain aloof from such ties—she could not bring herself to break that last link.

Lord Atman Balin settled back against the cushions and gazed at his daughter over the edge of the thin porcelain cup. He watched her swallow, saw the expression of pleasure spread across her face, and wondered if it was too late to find the little girl he had lost. Things had been so simple before the One Below had taken his beloved Matrika. When the three of them had lived in that perfect world, Chandra had been a laughing, happy child, open and accepting; he didn't recognize the silent, closed young woman she had become who seemed to watch everything he did with distant disapproval. She hadn't understood how he'd felt when his Matrika had been torn from him. And when he finally was able to explain, she hadn't wanted to hear. He sighed, his breath sending mahogany ripples across the surface of the coffee. It hurt that his daughter refused to understand him.

He could only hope that she understood what was expected of her as the only daughter of the ruling house; he feared, however, she did not. Thus tonight they dined alone.

"The messenger has returned from King Jaffar."

Chandra remained silent, waiting.

"He approves of the marriage alliance between you and his third son, Darvish."

Chandra had expected as much. The island her father ruled, while not large, was in a strategic trade position between the mainland and Cisali, King Jaffar's much larger island. Since her great-grandfather's time, they had been loosely allied with Cisali and it made sense that her father had sought a husband for her among Jaffar's sons, strengthening the alliance. There was only one problem.

"I am *not* going to marry this Darvish, Father. I told you that when you sent the proposal. It would have been better for all concerned had you believed me then."

"It's a good match."

"I know that, Father." Chandra had never argued that point. The facts were undeniable; the alliance held benefits for both countries and on a personal level the prince was by all reports, even allowing for the bias of marriage brokers, neither unattractive nor halfway to the One Below. "I am a Wizard of the Nine and I am not going to marry *at all.* Ever." She'd seen what marriage had done for her father: a few years of happiness, then almost total destruction. That wasn't going to happen to her.

"Then you wish your cousin Kesin to inherit. . . ."

"No, I do not wish my cousin Kesin to inherit." She hated it when her father's voice picked up that self-pitying whine. "Kesin is an ignorant lout without the brains the Nine gave pigs." *And you only bring him up to manipulate me into this marriage. Well, it's a dirty trick and it won't work!*

"Kesin inherits if my line does not continue," her father pointed out, smugly, she thought, sure he had outmaneuvered her. "As he has issue already, *you* must have a husband and an heir before I die." He spread his hands triumphantly, the red and yellow sleeves of the mourning robes he still wore fluttering ominously. "You are my only child."

"That's not *my* fault," Chandra snapped, setting her cup aside and rising to her feet. "You're not an old man. You are fully capable of siring more children."

"More children. . . ."

The pain on his face drove a knife into Chandra's heart, but she ignored it. He had to learn to face reality. He had to become strong, as she had.

"You don't understand," he said softly.

Chandra matched this man against the memories of her father and wondered how he could have become so weak. She didn't understand his pain nor why he insisted in wallowing in it. Her ears grew hot. It was embarrassing to see him like this.

"Chandra," his voice turned suddenly pleading, "you are all I have left of your mother. I want all this to be yours. You mustn't let Kesin destroy everything."

"*I* mustn't let Kesin destroy everything?" The rest of what she wanted to say caught in her throat and threatened to choke her. *I am not the one who spent years weeping and wailing! I am not the one doing just barely enough to get by!* But there was no point in saying it; her father never listened to facts, he just got emotional and started wringing his hands.

She bowed, her own emotions under rigid control, tossed her braid back over her shoulder, and left the room.

And the worst of it is, she thought as she returned to her tower, *I can't let Kesin inherit because he* will *destroy everything.* The thought of Kesin living in her house, riding her horses, attempting to rule her people made her feel almost physically ill. It wasn't that her cousin was a bad man, but he hadn't been raised to rule. Chandra knew her father had taken her final silence as assent rather than the denial of his emotions it actually was. He hadn't actually seen her for years. Ignoring her wishes, he would go ahead with the marriage plans. She would have to find another solution.

". . . always a solution, Chandra." Rajeet's image in the basin of water wavered and shook, her voice fading in and out. To actually communicate in this way took the combined concentration of both wizards involved and Rajeet's mind was obviously not on the conversation. ". . . don't wish your cousin to inherit and your father refuses to have more children . . . duty to the land, however, as . . . barely sixteen, ask your father . . . can be postponed a few years."

"Rejeet, you don't understand." Rajeet's brother had certainly picked a fine time to demand Rajeet come home and help him win a war—right when Chandra needed her most. She drew herself up as well as she was able, given her position over the bowl, and declared, "I am a Wizard of the Nine. I will never marry."

The image stopped wavering for a moment as the older woman smiled. "Never is a very long time at your age."

"You don't believe me?"

". . . believe in this instance it does not matter, Chandra. I assume . . . told your father?"

"Yes. But he doesn't listen." Chandra had long since given up believing there was a way to make him listen.

"Then . . . your intended."

"How?"

Rajeet's nostrils flared, a sure sign she had reached the end of her somewhat limited patience. ". . . a Wizard of the Nine; think of something!"

The image flickered and once again the bowl held nothing more than clear water.

"Very well," Chandra told her reflection now mirrored on the water's surface, "I shall. I don't need her any more than I need Father."

A sound in the courtyard drew her to the window and she peered down at King Jaffar's messenger, horns and banners and all, riding out. Her father had given him an answer. Well, she would give the whole lot of them another.

He can't even run his own life, she thought, pulling her head in, *I don't know what makes him think he can run mine.*

She flipped at the multifaceted crystal hanging down from the mobile in the window and, brow furrowed, watched the tiny rainbows that danced around the room. Rajeet had hung the mobile the day she'd arrived at the estate.

"Most people," she'd said, holding up a clay disk, *"are opaque to power, like this clay, but every now and then a child is born with the ability to act as a focus. Most of these children,"* here she started to hang nine curved ovals of colored glass from the disk, *"can focus only a small amount of the power available. They become Wizards of the First to Ninth, concentrating that small ability to focus on the single disciplines of the Nine Above."* She'd lifted the disk into the sunlight and each piece of dangling glass threw its signature into the room.

"Every once in a great while," she'd continued, *"a child is born who can focus more than just a part of the power."* Then

she'd hung up the crystal. It caught the sunlight and divided it and its signature held not one but all colors. "These children are very rare and they become Wizards of the Nine."

"You have the potential to be a Wizard of the Nine," she'd said. "If you study hard, there is very little you will not be able to do."

Rajeet, Chandra decided, for all she'd been only a Wizard of the First trained in the discipline of the god of the sword, had been right. She stilled the wildly swinging crystal. "I am a Wizard of the Nine and I *will not* marry Prince Darvish."

"I *know* he's supposed to be handsome and young, Aba, that's all anyone will tell me about him. There must be more."

"Well. . . ." The old nurse drew the word out as she drew the ivory comb through her charge's damp hair, pleased the girl was taking an interest at last. "He's a third son and that can't have been easy on him." A fair woman, she was willing to make excuses for some of the things she'd heard. "The heir has a place and a role to play, and a second son is always welcome in case, the Nine and One forbid, something should happen to the heir. But a third son," she sighed gustily, "a third son can never be certain of where he belongs. Don't wrinkle your forehead like that, poppet, you'll make lines. I feel quite sorry for your Prince Darvish."

"He's not *my* Prince Darvish." Chandra frowned.

Aba smiled, her eyes almost disappearing behind the curves of her cheeks. "As you wish, poppet." She continued to work the comb through the heavy mass of hair.

"What about his family? His brothers?" Rajeet had taught her an object could often be defined by its surroundings,

"Shahin, the heir, is much like his father. Kinder, they say, and less proud but as alike in appearance as if he'd been crafted out of wizardry. He made a treaty marriage last year, with a princess of Ytaili yet. Everyone hopes their marriage will stop the fighting. . . ."

"They aren't exactly fighting, Aba," Chandra protested.

"And they aren't exactly at peace either," Aba told her firmly. "Now, Ramdan, the second son, lives in the country. The heir and heir apparent are often separated thus, so that if some disaster befalls one, the other is safe. He married very young and has six, no, seven children. His marriage is his chief happiness, they say."

"You needn't keep dwelling on marriage, Aba."

"Not if you don't wish it, poppet." She paused while she worked out a tangle. "Then there's your Prince Darvish."

Chandra gritted her teeth but decided to let the possessive stand. It just wasn't worth the effort.

"They say he's an excellent swordsman." Most of the other things they said about Prince Darvish, Aba was not going to repeat. "They say his father never looked favorably on him from the moment of his birth."

"Why not?"

"He has blue eyes, poppet, and reminds King Jaffar that his own mother was not of Ischia."

"So?"

"The king is fiercely proud."

"Well, it was hardly the baby's fault he got blue eyes." For the first time Chandra felt something other than distaste for the prince.

Aba, sensing sympathy, intoned mournfully, "No, but it's been the burden he has to bear."

Chandra snorted, refusing to be manipulated by her nurse's tone. "Is he the youngest, then?"

"No. When Prince Darvish was nine, the twins were born."

Aba's voice sounded so peculiar that Chandra swiveled around to face her. "You're afraid of them? Why? You've never even met them. You've never even been to Ischia."

One plump hand made the sign of the Nine and One. "Their Royal Highnesses were cursed at birth."

"Cursed?"

Aba nodded. "Both were born with their faces covered, hiding from the gods even in the womb. The midwives wished to have them put to death immediately, bad enough to be a twin with only half a soul but to be cursed as well . . . but the king did not give his permission. They say he was too proud to acknowledge his seed could be cursed. He ignored them completely."

"Their mother . . ."

"She agreed with the midwives, and never saw them from the moment of their birth. Servants raised them as royal children are raised."

"Do they know that everyone wanted them dead?"

"They were cursed. . . ."

"Cursed?" Chandra leapt to her feet and paced an agitated

length of her room. "I am a Wizard of the Nine, I don't believe in curses. What happened to them?"

"They were given intense religious instruction in the hope that the curse could be lifted."

"And," Chandra prodded.

Aba sighed. "They found a place with one of the Nine."

"Which one?"

"The Fourth."

"Hah!" Chandra slapped her fist into her palm. "I just bet they did, it gave them a chance to get their own back. I can't *believe* their mother wanted them dead. I don't like her, I don't like King Jaffar, and I'm glad I'm not marrying their stupid son." She took a deep breath. "What happened to the queen? No one ever mentions her."

Aba's eyes filled with tears. "She died in the last wave of fevers. The fevers that killed your blessed mother."

Chandra threw herself down on a pile of cushions and began picking at a silk fringe. Aba was almost as bad as her father about it. "At least King Jaffar didn't fall to pieces."

"Chandra!"

"Well, he didn't!"

Aba drew herself up to her full height, looking like an indignant purple pigeon. "Queen Cizard was a cold woman. They say she placed her duty to the realm above all else, above her husband, above her children. They say her death caused barely a ripple in her family. Your father loved your mother. . . ."

"More than he loved anything else. I know, Aba. More than he loved himself. More than he loved his country. More than he loved me."

Tears trickling down her face, Aba took a tentative step forward, and then stopped as Chandra's gaze pinned her where she was.

"I didn't put my father up on that pedestal, Aba. He climbed up by himself. He had no right to fall." She would have helped him, but he wouldn't let her so he had only himself to blame for the distance between them. He chose to be weak. She never would.

"When you're married yourself, perhaps you'll understand," Aba offered. An unresponsive child could be held until the hurting eased. But a wizard—the old nurse sighed—she had no idea of how to deal with a wizard.

"I will never marry."

"They say Prince Darvish has an—*How to phrase it—*

independent outlook. He will surely not expect you to give up yours."

Chandra's eyes narrowed. "He won't get the chance."

Aba shook her head in surrender, veils fluttering. She didn't understand. For a short while things had been going so well. Leaving Chandra on the cushions, she went to turn down the bed.

"Aba? Who do you refer to when you say, *they* say?"

"Why the servants, of course, poppet." She turned and waggled a finger wisely. "If you wish to find out about someone, question the servants. They're always around, but people seem to forget they have eyes and ears and tongues. I've been questioning every servant that has arrived from Ischia since this marriage was first proposed. I wouldn't let my poppet marry a stranger."

Chandra nodded thoughtfully. "Thank you, Aba."

The old nurse preened.

Shoulder muscles protesting, Chandra dumped the basket of earth out onto the roof of her tower and gave thanks that the oblong pile was finally large enough. She wanted nothing more at the moment than to take a long rest—she was a wizard not a laborer—but the stars of the Nine were too far along in their dance for her to risk losing the time. Tucking her sleeveless robe up between her knees and murmuring words of power as she worked, she began to shape the damp soil, following the instructions on the ancient scroll exactly and trying not to think of all the ways it had listed that things could go wrong.

It was harder than she'd anticipated. Theoretically, it was nothing she couldn't manage, but over the last few years, as her reach had at times exceeded her grasp, she'd learned that the distance between theory and practice was often greater than it appeared. This night's work, she felt, would be worth the risk although it didn't help that she had to work by starlight alone. Expending power to create any illumination would change the configuration of what she built. It hadn't occurred to her to bring a lamp.

Finally, although the murmured words became muttered at the end, a rough but definitely female form lay staring sightlessly up at the night. Chandra sat back on her heels and studied it critically. It didn't look much like her, she had to admit. It looked, well, ominous.

Don't be ridiculous. She turned aside to retrieve the rest of her supplies. *You're a Wizard of the Nine. That's a pile of dirt. It's nothing unless you choose to make it.*

Out of the corner of one eye, she saw movement and her mouth went suddenly dry. It wasn't supposed to move. It couldn't move.

It can't be going wrong already!

How do you know? asked a little voice in the back of her mind. *You've never done this before.*

Biting her lip to contain the unwizardly whimper that tried to escape, Chandra slowly looked down at her golem, straining to see details in the darkness. Maybe this wasn't the great idea she'd originally thought it. A night wind, heavy with the scent of damp earth, crossed the tower and dislodged a small ball of dirt, rolling it down off the stubby fingers to break into nothing against the stone.

Chandra remembered how to breathe. "Idiot," she said softly.

Hurrying now, having wasted enough time on stupid fears, she pushed two oval agates into the dark on dark indentations left for eyes and, moistening the dirt with a bit of saliva, stuck nine of her own hairs to the top of the head.

Keeping a close watch on the dance of the Nine, she readied the vellum strip and her ivory dagger, checking once more the words she'd inscribed on both. As little as she looked forward to marriage, she looked forward to being ripped to pieces by her own creation even less. Drawing the cool night air slowly in through her nose and out through her mouth, she sought the calm that was going to be very necessary in a few short seconds.

She couldn't find it. Her heart began to pound painfully hard. She needed the calm to guide the power down the paths she'd chosen. It wasn't there. In its place was the knowledge of what the golem would do to her if she failed. Of what the power would do to her without the calm to guide it. She wasn't ready for this. She should never have tried it without Rajeet, who, while not a Wizard of the Nine, was still a very powerful Wizard of the First.

She should stop. Now. Before things went that one step too far. Give up. Let the ship with the first installment of her dowry sail tomorrow without her. Think of something else.

Or marry the prince. Anything was better than what could happen here if things went wrong,

No! This is ridiculous. I know what I'm doing. She grabbed at the rising panic and held it, breathing deeply.

You're acting like your father, she berated herself, beads of sweat chilling the skin between her breasts. *Emotional. Hysterical. Stupid. If something goes wrong, it's those emotions that will have destroyed you just like they destroyed him. You are not like your father!* No, she wasn't. Not any more. Familiar anger took the place of fear and as the stars wheeled into position, Chandra slid into the calm and drove the point of the knife into the heel of her thumb.

Nine drops of blood struck the hollow in the center of the sculpted breast. When the ninth drop hit the earth, glistening almost black in the starlight, Chandra placed the rolled vellum in the lipless slash that was the golem's mouth.

Then she closed her teeth on a scream as the power of the Nine—more power than she'd ever channeled before—roared through the focus she had created.

"All on board?" The second mate's cry cut easily through the noise at the docks to the sailor at the head of the gangway.

"Aye, sir. Two nobles, six servants, and a whole heap o' gee-gads finally loaded."

"Six? They told me five."

The sailor looked confused. Wasn't that what she'd said? "Aye, sir. Two nobles, five servants."

"Five?"

"Aye, sir."

The mate drew breath to bellow, then abruptly changed his mind. Five, six, what did one landsman more or less matter.?

So it went the whole three days of the voyage. Five servants. Six. And no one seemed to think it mattered.

Chandra enjoyed herself hugely. She ate with the servants— themselves unsure if they were five or six—and slept hardly at all. She had worried, at first, about the nobles her father would send to accompany the dowry—if they knew her well, she doubted she'd be able to hold the spell—but the two lords had seen her at court maybe twice in the last five years and so wouldn't be a problem. Unnoticed, or at least unremarked, she spent her days investigating this new world of wood and water and hemp and tar and her nights marking the subtle variations in the dance of the stars.

This is not an adventure, she told herself sternly as the ship plunged over a wave and the salt spray beaded her hair. *If I can get the prince to back out, then I've gained the time I need to deal with Kesin and the inheritance.* Given time, she was confident

that she'd come up with a final solution. A seabird skimmed past
the sail and Chandra grinned, feeling a momentary pang of sympathy for her poor golem stuck supposedly sulking back in her
tower; and thank the One she never went to court at this season,
for the intricacies of that would have been far beyond the golem's
limited abilities. At the thought of the golem, she sobered briefly,
rubbing her hands over the sudden gooseflesh on her arms. She
hadn't realized that focusing the necessary power to animate her
double would hurt so much. *So I might as well enjoy any new experience that comes my way.* Even now, she could feel a faint echo
of the pain sizzling through channels still raw and abraded. *I've
paid for it.*

Late the third evening, when there were only clouds to be seen
hanging dark and brooding over the ship and the waves were
nothing more than rolling black shadows, Chandra settled in a
sheltered cranny, the small silver bowl she scryed with between
her knees. From under her plain, brown servant's tunic, she
pulled out the locket that had arrived with the messenger from
King Jaffar.

"My prince begs you to accept this," had said the letter, a letter because she'd refused to see him. *"It moves directly from his
hand to yours."*

Chandra doubted that very much, but the portrait and lock of
black hair the locket contained would be enough for her needs if,
of course, the hair came from the prince. She rolled the soft strand
between her fingers. If it had come from Prince Darvish, they
were very careless about wizardry in Ischia. Perhaps she'd set
them straight on that as well, while she was there.

With the locket propped to use for reference, she cast a hair
down on the water in the bowl, drew the focus tight and fed power
through it. Tensing a little at remembered pain, she was relieved
to feel only the old familiar tingle. Rajeet disapproved of this sort
of wizardly eavesdropping, but she also said that knowledge was
strength. At this point Chandra figured forewarned was forearmed
and anything new she could learn about her unintended betrothed
could only help.

The water grew dark, then light, then a face began to form. It
seemed to be the face in the portrait, at least as far as Chandra
could tell through the contortions.

At first she thought the twists and grimaces meant torture, for her line of sight was limited to the face alone, but as she carefully pulled back, stretching the bounds of the focus, she understood.

Then the hair dissolved and the bowl was empty of vision and water both.

And for that, they want me to give up the power of the Nine? Chandra asked herself, putting the remaining hair safely back in the locket. She grabbed for her bowl as the ship rolled and it slid toward the rail. If the prince was as independent as Aba had said, it shouldn't be too hard to talk him out of the proposed marriage. Forehead creased, she reviewed what she'd been able to see of the prince's partner. It could only help her arguments that he obviously preferred his women more . . . fat.

Early the next morning, Chandra leaned her arms on the smooth wood of the railing and mourned the end of the voyage. They'd been at sea just long enough to show her a whole new world to learn, new lines of power, new focuses, new ways of thought. And now she had to leave it all to convince a prince that he didn't want to marry her. Life, she decided after a careful weighing of the facts, was on occasion most unfair.

She watched dawn brush the white terraces of Ischia with delicate highlights but was not impressed, her gaze drawn instead to the thin line of smoke rising above the top of the city. She assumed it came from the volcano, although she couldn't be certain as from her angle the crater was completely surrounded by buildings. *That* impressed her. That wizardry could protect an entire city built right to the edge of an active volcano.

The Stone of Ischia had taken nine Wizards of the Nine nine years to create. Chandra sighed. After she had dealt with Prince Darvish, she'd spend some time with it before she started for home. She focused a tendril of power toward the heights, then quickly snatched it back; something felt very wrong. Frowning, she wondered if she had breached one of the city's defenses. Surely The Stone would not repulse a Wizard of the Nine?

"Here now." The second mate dropped a weatherworn hand onto her shoulder and turned her about, pushing her gently toward the cabins where the five actual servants were readying their noble charges for disembarking. "You'd best get back with your own lot, then. We'll need the rails clear for lines."

Chandra shot one last, puzzled glance at the drifting plume of smoke, then walked slowly inside to join the others. She would have preferred to remain at the rail and watch the pilot ship guide them into Ischia's harbor, but now was not the time to toss off the carefully built layers of deception. And anyway, with the dual forts at the harbor mouth sliding by on either side, it was time she worked out her next step.

Quiet kid, thought the mate. *But I reckon that's part of being someone what serves. All six of them were quiet types.* He ran his fingers along a taut length of rope and lost the thought in the twists and turns of hemp. *Yep. Five of the quietest landsmen we ever carried. Though it beats the Eighth out of me why two fancy-asses need a half dozen people to take care of them.*

Chapter Six

Naked, his hair still damp from the bath, Darvish leaned his forearms on the balcony railing and looked out at the world. The early morning light clearly delineated buildings, gardens, even Yasimina's One abandoned peacocks. *It's like a mountain wine,* he decided, turning his arms so that the beads of moisture glowed, a scattering of tiny crystals. *A libation poured by the Nine onto their mother below.* He couldn't remember the last time he'd seen the sun before noon.

He only saw it today because Lady Harithah had remembered her husband would be arriving this morning and had canceled their assignation. Unwilling to settle for second best, he'd been in his own bed reasonably early and practically sober.

Waking with a clear head. . . . Darvish stretched and smiled. *What an interesting concept. Maybe someday I'll try it again.* Then he remembered that not only Lady Harithah's lord would be arriving today but also the first third of his bride's dowry.

His bride. The word was a bad taste in his mouth and a little of the light went out of the world. *Consider myself betrothed. Thank you very much, O Most Exalted Father.* Maybe he should tell her about the challenge he'd made to the whores of the city, male and female, last year in the middle of the market square. *And if that doesn't disrupt Father's plans,* Darvish smiled sardonically, *I'll tell her how I almost won.*

"Highness?"

He turned slowly. "Fadi."

"Highness, the healer says that she is busy this morning." The young dresser, keeping his gaze carefully level with the prince's knees, held out a squat clay pot securely stoppered with a round of cork. "She said . . ." He took a deep breath and felt his ears begin to burn. He just couldn't use the words the healer had used in front of his prince. Why did she keep doing this to him?

"She said as long as I was up I could spread that stuff myself?"

"Yes, Highness. Mostly." His prince sounded amused and for Fadi that was almost worse than anger. Except that Prince Darvish never got angry. He was difficult at times, but Fadi knew that was the wine, not his prince. *His* prince was the best master in the palace and all the things his friends had said would happen to him when he came to serve, hadn't. He was a little disappointed about some of that actually. His ears burned hotter as he felt sure the thought lay naked on his face for his prince to read.

If it did, Darvish chose to ignore it. "Thank you, Fadi."

As the pot changed hands, their fingers touched and the young dresser sighed. Managing to stifle a sigh of his own, Darvish's smile softened as he watched the boy hurry away. *I was never that young.*

Fadi's adoration depressed him at times. What remained to adore once the attraction of the flesh had been denied? And he'd made it very clear that Fadi was too young for *that*. Both to Fadi and to others. His smile iced as he remembered the expression on the Lord Rahman's face as that noble had been informed what would happen to his genitals if he ever spoke again of laying a hand on the prince's young dresser.

"And speaking of laying on hands . . ." Darvish worked the cork from the pot and sniffed at the pale green salve. It had a clean, fresh scent that cleared his head of the overpowering odor of jasmine rising up from the garden below. ". . . I suppose I'd best get this over with."

At the balcony door, the lord chancellor's man met him with a silver tray and a carafe of wine. "Highness." He bowed, his voice straddling the thin line between service and subservience. "Your wine."

Darvish watched a ruby drop trail a thin line of color down the chilled metal. It just didn't go with the morning. "No, I don't think so."

"But, Highness, you always have wine in the morning."

"Don't ever presume . . ." He clasped both hands tighter about the pot of salve in case one should play traitor and reach out, out of habit. ". . . that you know what I will always do."

"Highness." The dresser bowed again, the marks of his last

beating still visible above the neckline of his vest. He expected another, the knowledge in his voice.

This, Darvish thought with a sudden rush of sympathy, *is the one man in Ischia whose place I would not exchange for mine.* "Don't you have something to do?"

"Yes, Highness."

Darvish watched the dresser scurry thankfully away. Perhaps the lord chancellor would have the man beaten later when he made his report—a pity, still, he wasn't going to drink unwanted wine to prevent it.

The old lord would, of course, see plots and machinations in the decision, but that was hardly surprising as he saw plots and machinations in anything. In everything.

Aaron, sitting cross-legged on his pallet, set aside his empty breakfast bowl and reached for the large goblet of water that Kadira had insisted he drink with every meal. Black silk trousers set off the pallor of his skin and threw the circular pattern of scars into sharp relief. He looked up as Darvish came in, saw the prince had still not dressed, and quickly looked away. It did little good. Over the days of his healing he had seen the prince too many times for looking away to erase the sight from his memory. He felt the blood rise to his face and a pounding start between his ears. *Men were not meant to gaze upon one another,* the priests of his childhood had told him. *That is the beginning of the path to the fire.* He shifted just enough to pull at the scars, welcoming the pain as a distraction.

In the old days, he would have had anger to shield him but he had put that aside with his old life. He had nothing now unless this prince chose to give him death.

Darvish knew his nudity bothered Aaron so he went unclothed as often as he realistically could. Any reaction was better than none at all and that was the *only* reaction he'd seen evidence of. He watched the blush rise and fade, then he set his teeth and approached with the salve.

If he had known when he carried the thief from the Chamber of the Fourth that he carried a stone who, once the initial and still unexplained despair had faded, would sit staring at him from behind walls thicker than those that ringed the palace, he would have left him with the twins. No, not that perhaps, but the last thing Darvish needed was a man who acknowledged him even less than his father did. His excesses meant nothing to Aaron; at least his father felt disgust.

He meant nothing to Aaron.

I saved your life, he wanted to shout. *Don't I get anything in return?* Apparently not.

Aaron made him uncomfortable in a number of ways: Darvish had thought himself an expert at merely existing from day to day, but the outlander made him appear a rank amateur. And Aaron did it without the wine.

One word and the thief would be there to bother him no more. Darvish knew he could never speak that word. If only to prove his father wrong.

"His life is yours. When you tire of him, he dies."

"The healer's busy." Darvish squatted by the pallet and dipped two fingers into the pot.

Aaron braced himself for the prince's touch. The salve smoothed over the jagged edges between the new skin and the old, but the easing was almost lost in the feel of the strong brown fingers that stroked it on. It seemed as though his heart began to beat to their rhythm. From under lowered lids he snatched a glimpse of the prince's face and the concern there surprised him—as much as it would have surprised the prince had he been able to see it.

The surprise drove a crack into the stone surrounding him and a question wailed free.

"What do you want from me, Darvish?"

Startled blue eyes met equally startled gray eyes for an instant, the question hanging in the air between them. Then the gray eyes cooled back to ice and only the blue acknowledged the question had been asked.

"What do I want from you?" Darvish repeated softly. He had seen, in that instant, a loneliness that matched his own, recognized it from a hundred thousand reflections in a hundred thousand mirrors. It stopped the glib answer and it stopped the leer.

What do you want from me?

Like ripples in a quiet pool, other questions spread out from the first.

Why did you save my life?

Why do you care?

Something. . . .

Darvish remembered the look on Aaron's face the first night on the balcony, the pain that had nothing to do with the injuries that had brought him down. Maybe because his head was clear, without the usual insulation of wine, Darvish suddenly remembered his thoughts from that moment. *This is someone who knows. He'd understand how I feel.*

He looked at Aaron's face now and realized what he wanted. *What do you want from me?*
I want you to be my friend.

But he wasn't going to say it. Even though he'd bought and paid for that friendship with Aaron's life. He couldn't take that risk. He asked for the one thing he knew he'd get.

"Nothing." Darvish shoved the cork back into the flared neck of the pot, his voice a soft contrast to the almost violent action. "I want nothing from you."

Aaron nodded, his fingers so tightly interlaced that the knuckles stood out bone white. "I can give you that," he whispered, relieved. One corner of his mouth twisted up and without really meaning to, he smiled. The wrong answer would have shattered him into little pieces. He could feel how close he'd come, but he was still whole.

Darvish stared at Aaron's face. *He's smiling?* Slowly, his own mouth began to curve and, shared, the moment stretched.

"Highness?"

Oham's quiet voice drew Darvish around and Aaron's face became expressionless once again, but a link, tenuous and unacknowledged, remained.

"Highness, His Most Imperial Majesty commands your presence in the small audience chamber. Immediately. He requires also that you bring the thief.

"When you tire of him, he dies."

It wouldn't be the first time His Most Imperial Majesty had changed the rules.

"Well now, Aaron," Darvish said with the false sincerity usually saved for social occasions and members of the court high in the king's favor. He tossed back his hair and stood, crossing the room and lifting the carafe with both hands. Hands that trembled, just a little. "It seems we had our talk just in time." The wine ran in crimson lines down from the corners of his mouth and over his chest. Breathing heavily, he tossed the now empty container onto the bed and grinned, his eyes too bright. "I guess I'd better get dressed."

You gave me his life, Father. At Darvish's sides, his hands curled into fists. *I'll fight you if you try to take him from me.*

Tension filled the small audience chamber, tension so palpable that Aaron almost raised a hand to brush it from his face. Like sheets of lightning before a summer storm, it radiated out from the four who waited for them and lifted the fine hair on the back of his neck.

As they crossed the room, the only noise the light slap of their sandals against the tile, Aaron took stock of the doors, the windows, the guards, the habits of years reasserting themselves. It would be a difficult but not impossible job and probably worth it for the heavy gold lamp brackets alone. Lastly, he noted the people.

The throne in the small audience chamber was rosewood, intricately carved and highly polished. The king, however, was still obsidian and between the gray of hair and beard his expression was black. To his right, the crown prince also showed anger, but it was equally mixed with speculation as he watched them approach. The shaven-headed priest was simply terrified and the lord chancellor—Aaron recognized the fat man immediately, Darvish's drunken ravings were quite accurate—had set his face in no readable expression at all.

From his position a pace behind the prince, Aaron watched Darvish drop gracefully to one knee and mirrored the motion a heartbeat later. His half-healed chest allowed him little grace and his thighs trembled as he rose, but he set his jaw and pretended he hadn't spent the last three ninedays flat on his back. As he lifted his head, a glare from the lord chancellor drew his gaze.

A man's ears don't stop hearing just because he no longer wishes to live, and while Aaron healed he'd listened. He'd listened to the words and to what was behind them. He knew who paid the third dresser.

You're a fool, he thought at the broad sweep of Darvish's back, while returning the lord chancellor's glare with a cold stare of his own, *if you think this man is not dangerous just because he is fat and old.* But then, he already knew Darvish was a fool.

From the expression on the lord chancellor's face, Aaron suspected that the obeisance made to the king by a thief was supposed to differ from that made by a prince. Tough.

"You requested my presence, Most Exalted?"

Darvish had thrown back two additional goblets of wine on the way through the palace and Aaron marveled at how little the amount of alcohol he'd consumed had affected him. His voice sounded clear and his hands hung steady by his sides. Nor did he appear affected by the tensions in the room. The muscles of his back were knotted, Aaron could see that clearly through the thin white silk of his shirt, but he'd brought that tension in with him.

The silence the followed Darvish's ritual words stretched and lengthened and the air became heavier still. It seemed that the colored tiles in the mosaic behind the throne grew both muted and more distinct. Aaron's eyes narrowed. He'd assumed, like Darvish, this meeting had been commanded to tell the prince his thief must die, but now he wasn't so sure. He ignored the faint taste of relief. He wanted to die. He waited to die.

And then the king spoke, thunder to herald the storm.

"The Stone has been taken."

"Nine Above . . ." Darvish breathed and Aaron silently echoed it. The Stone held the volcano. Without it Ischia would die. "Who?"

Slowly, all eyes turned to Aaron.

"It wasn't me," Aaron said dryly, wondering how they expected him to have stolen anything when he could barely walk. "I was with him." He jerked a thumb at the prince and felt strangely pleased when, after an astounded moment, Darvish grinned and stepped back so that they stood side by side.

"That does not necessarily excuse you," the lord chancellor snapped.

"Are you accusing my Most Royal brother of taking The Stone?" Shahin's question was silk, but it was the silk of the garrote. Over the last few weeks, the heir had been discovering more and more how much he disliked his father's omnipresent councilor. That the man was devoted to the throne, he did not doubt, but some of the ways that devotion had been expressed he did not care for at all. In the opinion of the crown prince, the lord chancellor needed to be reminded of his place.

The lord chancellor recognized the tone and hurriedly bowed. "Oh, no, not at all, my prince. But he does share quarters with a known thief. . . ."

"And we all know that if said thief had stirred at any time during the night you'd have known of it a heartbeat later. So let's stop this foolishness," the word was directed equally at the lord chancellor, Darvish, and Aaron, "and get to the point." The hooded eyes pinned Aaron to the spot. He felt not unlike a rabbit must, caught in the gaze of a great hawk. "You could not have taken The Stone, but you will know who did. Tell us."

Aaron considered the other thieves of Ischia. He owed them nothing, after all.

"If The Stone is missing, what holds the Lady?" Darvish asked suddenly, a hint of fear appearing in his voice.

The priest spoke for the first time, her voice a clear, light soprano growing shrill with the strain of remaining calm. "Not even a living volcano constantly erupts. The wizards of both the temple and the palace focus power to block the smoke and smell, hiding the theft from the people. They stand ready should the worst occur."

Darvish nodded. "So the wizards know," he murmured, relieved. "Who else?"

"Only we six and a senior priest at the temple." Her fingers worked against the red and yellow tassels that hung from her belt of office, but her face remained impassive. "If the people find out . . ."

"If the people find out," Darvish repeated, "then the panic will destroy Ischia before the volcano has a chance."

"I'm glad to see the wine has not completely rotted your brain, little brother."

Under the sarcasm, Aaron was sure he heard approval in Shahin's voice, but before he had a chance to ponder it the king spoke again.

"Who has The Stone, thief?"

Aaron had weighed all the thieves of the city and found them wanting. "The thief came from outside Ischia."

The king's teeth flashed in the gray of his beard. Not for an instant did Aaron believe the expression was a smile. "You are very sure."

"I am." *He uses his power like a sword, much as my father used his like a club.* With the thought came memories—a huge red-bearded man, a dark-haired girl crouched at his feet, her blue eyes wide with terror—and with the memories came a storm of emotion—guilt, anger, terror, pain—too thick to breathe through. *NO!* He slammed both memory and emotion back down behind the walls where they belonged. *I am through with all that!* He added denial to the walls until nothing remained but the void.

"Aaron?"

The void and Darvish. But Darvish he could deal with. He should never have left the prince's rooms. He should have stayed there, waiting to die.

Aaron avoided the prince's gaze—concern could break the walls again—and spoke directly to the king. "I could not have done it and I was the best."

"The best?"

The lord chancellor's words were a verbal sneer of disbelief.

Aaron merely replied, "Yes." They could believe him or not, he didn't care.

Plump hands spread and the lord chancellor smiled. "And just look where you are."

"That is hardly his fault," Darvish snarled.

"And this is hardly to the point," the priest broke in. "Squabbling like children will not help us to recover The Stone." She suddenly recalled whom she chastised and flushed. "Begging your pardon, Most Exalted."

Aaron barely heard the argument. Hardly his fault? "What do you mean, that was hardly my fault?" He'd failed. Who else could bear the blame?

Keeping a wary eye on his father, Darvish turned and glanced down at the younger man. "Didn't I tell you? Bugger the Nine," he ignored the gasp from the priest, "I thought I had. Your grappling iron had been deliberately flawed. It couldn't have happened by accident and it couldn't have borne your weight."

Deliberately flawed. *Deliberately* flawed. Cold fury rushed in to fill the void—fill it and overflow it. Aaron didn't see Darvish step back. He didn't see king, prince, priest, and lord chancellor watching him, faces wearing nearly identical apprehension. He saw a fat face, smoke-stick bobbing on one full and greasy lip.

When he spoke his voice came out like shards of ice.

"There's only one place in Ischia The Stone can be."

Not even the strong breeze off the harbor could sweep away the mixed smells of rot and dirt and too many people in too little space. Darvish fought against the urge to breathe through the fabric of his sleeve, as many young nobles did when one thing or another brought them down to this part of town. He scowled at a whining beggar, stepped over a pile of garbage—the bloated flies nearly covering it were so well fed they ignored him—and wondered if the volcano might not be preferable.

Behind him, he could hear the three guards muttering obscenities, they liked this place even less than he did. He, at least, knew they were here for a reason. They thought only that their prince had sold something he shouldn't have, the prince's pet thief knew where it was, and they were the muscle in case he had trouble getting it back. Not exactly a shining purpose to ease a walk through the worst slum in Ischia.

"Will three be enough?" Darvish had asked.

"Do you ever travel with more than three?"

"No."

"Then more will cause suspicion. Questions will be asked and the more questions the greater the chance the people will find out and panic." The priest shook her head, dark stubble a shadow against her scalp. *"Above all else, the people must not find out that The Stone is missing."*

"How fortunate for us all, Darvish, that your reputation allows you access to such people without raising the type of comments that would lead to questions. You'll have your sword," Shahin added. *"Perhaps you'll have a chance to prove you can use it as well as a bottle."*

Aaron's eyes were too cold to be human. *"Herrak has no guards about him—he would have to share his treasures, then. He has the best wards his money can buy. But I have been through Herrak's wards before, they know me. And Herrak thinks I'm dead."*

His most exalted father wouldn't have been depending on him, Darvish knew, if he had any other choice. But he didn't, for the priest was right. Above all else, the people must not know. It was Shahin Darvish didn't understand; his words had been almost more a challenge than a dismissal.

Aaron stopped in front of a townhouse that looked as though it were about to collapse under its own weight. Each of the three stories was sinking at different angles and the stone, which might have been white once, now barely held its shape in infinite shades of gray. Only one piece of the obsidian inlay that had long ago made this building the showpiece of the neighborhood remained, tucked up under the perch of a crumbling gargoyle.

The recessed door opened directly onto the filthy street. In its shelter, Aaron spoke practically his first words since leaving the palace; "They stay out here."

As one, the three guards turned to the prince.

"You might as well," Darvish agreed. "If he wanted to kill me, he could have done it easier last night." One of the guards turned a snigger into a sneeze. Darvish ignored him. He knew what they thought. "You're not needed inside and I'd prefer not to exit into any surprises."

Body blocking the exact motions, Aaron worked his fingers against the latch, twisting them with an agility that suggested the manacle scars had not destroyed his skills. The door opened just enough to allow him to slip inside. Darvish, larger and heavier, squeezed through behind with more difficulty. The guards philosophically settled down to wait. This wasn't the first time His Royal Highness had gone into a strange house leaving them to secure the door.

"Course, they're usually not quite so . . ." The first guard let the comment trail off, moving his foot away from a small unidentifiable mound of gray.

"Yeah? Well, you weren't along when his nibs tucked inta Black Sal's." The second smiled with satisfaction as she added, "They tossed him out just before dawn. We hadta carry him home. Yep, he's bin in places worser than this and come out again. Got the Nine's own luck up his ass does our royal master." She hacked and spit, scoring a direct hit on a roach.

The third guard only watched the now closed door and hoped that her prince wouldn't need her.

"Stand still." Aaron's voice cut the small anteroom into smaller pieces still. "Don't touch anything."

"When will Herrak know we're here?"

"We crossed the first ward at the mouth of the alley. He's known for some time."

"Oh." The outside door slid silently shut and Darvish discovered that the termite ridden boards facing the street were only a thin veneer over solid oak planks. "Aaron, you can't open this door from the inside." Nor, given the lack of maneuvering room, did he think he could break it down. The trapped air was hot and heavy and Darvish had the sudden uncomfortable thought that they stood in an inescapable oven.

"I can open the outside door." Aaron lifted his hand to knock on the inner door of the anteroom. "but we're going in." As his knuckles brushed the polished wood, the heavy door swung silently open.

"Unlocked?" Darvish asked, loosening his sword in its sheath.

"Shouldn't be," Aaron grunted.

"Right." Perhaps Herrak had already run with The Stone. Perhaps they were walking into a trap. Darvish pulled the scimitar free.

Moving cautiously, they entered a corridor barely wider than the prince's shoulders. The towering walls were composed of Herrak's treasures stacked haphazardly to the ceiling. The hanging lamps, guttering as they used the last of their oil, were almost worse than no light at all. Shadows leapt and lunged and a myriad of dark nooks and crannies drew the eye. An oppressive smell of mold and decay contributed to the claustrophobic feeling and dust motes danced in a glittering fog that thickened every time they moved.

Aaron stopped suddenly, his head up, his expression demonic in the half light. "This is wrong."

Breathing shallowly through his teeth, Darvish dropped into a fighting stance. *And how can you tell what's right in a place like this?* Above his head a lamp sizzled and sighed into darkness. "What's wrong?" he asked, ears straining for a sound, any sound, they weren't making themselves.

"The lamps. He has a servant to tend them."

"Do you think he's left with The Stone?"

The thief barked with derisive laughter. "What? And leave all this?" As suddenly as he'd stopped, he sprinted forward.

Darvish scrambled to catch up.

The narrow corridors didn't change although the building materials did from time to time. Here, almost ten feet packed with bales of clothing. There, furniture jammed tight between floor and ceiling. At the top of a flight of stairs, a statue of a sad-faced man that could only have come from the Nobles' Garden. No rooms, no halls, only the never ending maze of Herrak's possessions. The lamps continued to die.

How much farther? Darvish wondered. He couldn't ask aloud, he didn't have the breath to spare. Keeping up with the thin figure of the thief took almost all he had. Worse news—over the sound of his labored breathing he could hear an inhuman wail, rising and failing, permeating the maze like smoke. *I may have to fight that.* For now, he fought the tremors that shook his body and

threatened to shake his blade like a leaf in a storm. He needed a
drink to steady his arm.

Then the walls began to change. Bookcases now, jammed with
racks of scrolls and heavy leather-bound tomes. Then the walls
stopped. The wailing grew louder.

Weapon ready, Darvish traced the sound to its source.

Tucked up against the base of a heavily laden desk was a small
man, dressed all in dark gray, staring wide eyed at the stubs of his
hands. His sleeves had fallen back and the jagged ends of his forearm bones jutted charred from flesh that eased from black to red,
angry red lines disappearing under the fabric of his shirt. Blood
dribbled from holes chewed out of his lips and his chest heaved
with the breath necessary to keep up the constant keening wail.

He shouldn't be conscious. Darvish closed his throat against
the urge to vomit and took a shaky step forward. As he drew
closer, unable to look away, a little more of the blackened flesh
dissolved. There was no smell of burning or rot, just, very faintly,
the bitter scent of the volcano. When he was close enough, he
lifted the man's chin with the flat of his sword—the eyes were
completely and totally insane.

It took two blows to get the head right off. Panting slightly,
Darvish wiped his sword on the body. *At least the wailing's
stopped.*

But the room was not quite silent and dreading what he'd see,
he turned to face the source of the moaning. Over by one of the
bookcase walls, Aaron stood staring at an immensely fat man, his
face expressionless and cold. The fat man moaned, the sound
rolling around the great echo chamber of his belly before being
released to thrum against the heavy quiet. His hands cupped the
air in front of the circle of his face, red to the wrist, the tip of each
finger crowned in black.

"Apparently," Aaron said without turning as Darvish came to
stand by his side, "there is a price for touching The Stone."

"Where is it?" Darvish slapped Herrak's hands down with the
flat of his blade. He wanted out of this place. "Where is The
Stone?"

Herrak's eyes showed yellowish white all around and his
hands rose back up as though pulled by an invisible puppeteer.

"Answer, you fat fool!" Darvish slapped the hands down again
and this time the edge of his sword drew across Herrak's palm.

The red flesh parted, but no blood welled up to fill the wound. "Tell me, where is The Stone?"

"Gone," Herrak moaned from behind his rotting fingers.

"Gone where?"

He had to repeat the question a second and a third time before Herrak responded, moaning, "The mirror took it."

"What mirror?" Darvish rubbed his face. It was very hot in Herrak's hidey-hole and the blood of the thief, soaked onto the layers of carpeting, added its signature to the dust and mold and dead air.

Aaron pointed, his long finger appearing whiter than ever.

Almost hidden by Herrak's bulk, was a three-foot oval that Darvish had taken to be a slab of framed obsidian. A closer look and he saw it was a black mirror, its surface absolutely non-reflecting.

One more step and the edge of his sword was at Herrak's throat. Close enough to smell terror, sharp and strong, he breathed the question into the fat man's face. "Where. Is. The. Stone?"

"The wizard has it."

"Wizard?" *Bugger the Nine! We've lost it!* A slight movement of the sword brought another spate of information. Darvish couldn't understand why. Given what Herrak faced alive, death had to be welcome.

"The mirror came to me from the streets. . . ."

"Who brought it?" Aaron snapped.

Herrak's eyes searched the past for a name. "Yaz," he said at last. "Yaz brought it."

"Where did she get it?"

"I don't know. It didn't seem important. I wanted it, you could see eternity in it."

Together, Aaron and Darvish looked again at the mirror. They could see exactly nothing.

"Spelled," Aaron grunted. Darvish nodded.

"You could. You could." Herrak protested. "I saw it. I saw eternity. Then he came."

"Who came?"

"The wizard."

"He came here?"

"No. To the mirror." A spasm of pain twisted Herrak's face and his fingers twitched and danced and grew a little blacker. When it passed, he needed no prodding to continue. "He said he would trade me a thousand precious things for The Stone of Ischia. A thousand for one." For a second he peered out from between rolls of fat, eyes hard, and Darvish caught a glimpse of the power that had made Herrak king of his own small part of the city. He realized that the man barely held on to a tiny fraction of his mind and would shortly be as insane as the dead thief. Suddenly Herrak twisted and fell to his knees, his whole body quivering from the impact. "He sent the thief through the mirror last night," he gasped. "I had The Stone just before dawn. Had to kill Jehara."

"His servant," Aaron supplied.

"She said we killed Ischia." The grimace almost became a smile. "A thousand precious things for one. I passed it through the mirror. I held it." His fingers were black to the second joint. "The thief had already begun to scream." The last word rose in volume until it was almost a scream itself.

The Stone, the heart of Ischia, was gone.

"The wizard," Darvish grabbed Herrak's shoulder and shook him viciously, "where is he?"

"In the mirror!"

Darvish's grip sank deep into the dimpled flesh.

"Where is the other side of the mirror?"

"I don't know!" Herrak wailed. One of the nails on his left hand curled off and drifted silently to the carpets.

Darvish let the fat man go. Ischia was doomed. He lifted his sword.

"No."

The very calm and control of Aaron's voice, so much in contrast to his own raging thoughts and Herrak's tortured whimpering, stopped the scimitar's downward swing.

"The thief is from Ytaili." He held out a small amber teardrop, the thong threaded through it sticky with blood. "This type, this color is found only in Ytaili, near Tivolic, the capital city. The royal family favors it."

"How do you know," Darvish snorted, not willing to accept a new hope quite so quickly.

"I stole one once."

Ytaili. Six days at sea with good winds. A day to find The Stone. Six days back. A nineday and a half. Surely the wizards can hold the volcano for that long. Perhaps Ischia can live. The relief that came with that conclusion left Darvish feeling physically weak. Then he remembered. *Ytaili. Where Yasimina's brother was king.* He stood for a moment, scimitar point resting against the carpets and watched three nails fall from Herrak's hands. The whimpering had become a constant background noise.

They had the answer, and yet, there was something more. He looked past Herrak to the mirror. Many wizards preferred to scry in mirrors, it wasn't a skill tied to any of the disciplines, but he had never heard of a wizard who could move things through a mirror. *A wizard who can move a solid object through a solid object. . . .* A sudden fear stroked cold fingers down the prince's spine and he allowed himself to be distracted by the fat man rather than search out its source.

We have all we'll get from him, Darvish thought, shifting to a two-handed grip and lifting his sword again.

"No." For the second time, Aaron's cold voice stopped the beheading swing before it had begun. "What has he done to deserve mercy?"

What indeed? Herrak had been responsible for the theft of The Stone. And the loss of The Stone would destroy the Ischia Darvish knew. The nobles could get clear, they had the means and estates elsewhere to retreat to. But Darvish's people, the whores, the wine merchants—he shot a quick glance at Aaron—the thieves would die, if not in the panic, then boiled alive by the rivers of molten rock that would soon follow. And Herrak would have killed them.

Darvish sheathed his sword.

Herrak had done nothing to deserve mercy.

His face blank, Aaron turned silently to lead the way back out through the maze.

They had barely started between the first of the bookcases when Darvish realized that Herrak was trapped. He was far, far too fat to make it through the narrow aisles of his own house. His treasure boxed him into that one small room and probably had for years.

"He has poison in that room," Aaron said quietly as though he'd been following the line of Darvish's thoughts. "A quick death if he has the courage to take it." His voice was bitter and the line of his back so straight and hard that Darvish felt it would ring like steel if he tapped it.

They were halfway down the first set of stairs when the screaming began.

Chapter Seven

Shifting her burden on her hip, Chandra tried to look properly subservient. It wasn't easy. Her head hurt. Fanfares had been blowing at intervals since they left the docks; the bells that dangled from the ornate palanquins set up a constant brassy jangle, the crowds cheered and yelled, and, once they realized that this was the dowry procession, shouted a number of crude comments about her future unintended that set her ears burning. Things they would certainly not have shouted had Chandra been officially present. She hoped. There were a number of things about Prince Darvish that Aba hadn't mentioned.

Remaining with the servants until they were actually in the palace had seemed like a good idea back on the ship, but now she wasn't so sure.

Still, it's not everyone that gets to carry her own dowry. And, she added philosophically, *it could be worse.* The four muscular bearers carrying Lord Assahsem had her complete sympathy as they struggled up the steep streets under the weight of the corpulent ambassador. *"Hang on,"* she thought at their glistening backs as his lordship gave a little bounce and four sets of knees almost buckled, *"we're nearly there."*

The litters themselves she found fascinating. Back home, people who didn't wish to walk rode or rented a *shau*, a two wheeled carriage pulled by the man or woman who owned it. After climbing her third, or maybe fourth, set of stairs, she realized that wheels would be completely impractical in a city built on so many levels. Her calves began to ache.

As the small procession—half a company of guard, litters for the two nobles welcoming the dowry as well as the two delivering, the six servants carrying the dowry, the other half a company of guard—crossed the last terrace before the palace gate, Chandra reached out and lightly brushed the wards surrounding the palace with power. If they were too specific. . . .

Might as well use pots and pans and a piece of string, she snorted silently. The wards were predominantly of the Fourth and served only to tell if the wall had been breached. *I could have spelled a notice-me-not against this in my first year of training. Someone in this city must be growing rich selling charms to thieves.*

The gate was not warded at all and in the wake of Lord As- sahsem's grateful bearers, Chandra passed unnoted into the palace. She placed her small chest with the rest of the dowry, bowed beside the other servants, stepped back, and then com- pletely surpassed them at fading quietly into the background. Not one of them remembered they had once been six.

A short time later, having gently persuaded a senior servant to tell her where Prince Darvish's rooms were and having discov- ered that he was not at present in the palace, Chandra headed for the nobles' viewing platforms to get a look at The Stone. Al- though she could feel great currents of power moving about the volcano, she couldn't feel The Stone and she began to grow un- easy. She was a Wizard of the Nine. Why wasn't it calling to her?

The guard at the entryway surprised her even as she passed him easily. She hoped there wasn't a ceremony of some kind going on. She wanted a chance to really study the artifact without the bother of keeping her presence masked. Moving cautiously, she peered out onto the platform.

Four wizards—one of the Second, one of the Fourth, two of the Eighth—stood at the railing, focus directed down into the crater. Chandra frowned; wizards seldom cooperated across disci- plines. Curiosity warred with common sense and curiosity won.

Dropping her minor disguise spells lest her power signature give her away, she slid along the back wall of the platform, the tile mosaic warm against her shoulder blades, heading for a position where she might safely get a glimpse of The Stone. Given time and materials, she could build a notice-me-not so strong not even another wizard could spot her, but as she had neither, she'd trust to luck.

As she moved past the barrier of silk clad backs she could see, across the crater, a small cluster of wizards on the temple platform as well, their multihued robes billowing in the hot updrafts from the molten rock below. Her frown grew more pronounced. Obviously, she'd stumbled onto some sort of ceremony; one she'd never heard of. She'd studied everything written on The Stone of Ischia and recognized none of what was going on. Something had to be very wrong.

She leaned forward slightly and, yes, there were wizards on what had to be the private royal platform. A quick glance up to the open areas of the rim showed the public platforms were empty.

She could feel the power gathered, waiting to be focused, and she could feel the power spread like a net over the crater's mouth.

Stranger and stranger.

Inch by inch she moved toward the railing.

Then the Wizard of the Second turned and looked directly at her, so close that she could see her reflection in the drops of sweat that beaded his high forehead. His fleshy lips parted and he snarled, "Have you been sent to bring us refreshment? This is hot work."

He thinks I'm a servant! Quickly, gracelessly, she bowed. "Yes, Most Wise." *If wizards are called something different here than they are at home. . . .* "Do you and your Most Wise brethren desire wine or ices or chilled fruit juices?" *Thank the One for this tunic!* She managed to move a hand's span closer to the rail.

"Wine, *and* ices, *and* chilled fruit juices," the Wizard of the Second informed her. "And be quick about it!"

"Yes, Most Wise." A step. A bow. Another inch and she'd be able to see into the seething cauldron of the volcano. Her left foot lifted to step again.

"What is going on here?"

The grip on the back of her tunic almost jerked her off her feet and Chandra found herself dangling from the fist of the Wizard of the Fourth.

"It's a servant, Amarjite," sneered the Wizard of the Second. "Release her so she can get my ices."

Chandra did her best to look obsequious, but her heart beat so loudly she was certain it could be heard over the rumble of the shifting lava. *If they find out who I am, I'll be sent home in disgrace. I'll have failed, just like Father.* Then she looked up into the completely expressionless face of the Wizard of the Fourth and her throat closed around a fear greater than failure. Wizards of the Fourth learned any number of techniques that Chandra had

never been trained to protect herself against; techniques that
would shatter crystal as easily as clay.

"A servant," said Amarjite, coldly, "has no business being out
on the platforms. Use your head, Simmel, instead of your stomach." He shook her like a mongoose would shake a snake. "What
are you doing here, girl?"

He wasn't going to believe her, no matter what she said. She
could see that in his eyes. But there must be something she could
do. She was a Wizard of the Nine! Failure became unimportant
next to what awaited her and she began opening herself to power.

The great metal door leading off the platform of executions
slammed back, the crash of iron against rock causing even Amarjite to jerk and turn. Out onto the platform, like two slender black
shadows, came the twins. Behind them, a burly guard dragged a
bleeding body.

"Nine and One, what now?" Amarjite snarled.

Would this be a chance? Chandra wondered, trembling, and
for the moment held the power back.

"They're going to want to drop the body into the Lady," Simmel observed.

"I know that, idiot."

The Wizard of the Second smiled unpleasantly at his colleague. "Then you'd better stop them, hadn't you? Before they destroy the net."

"*I* had better stop them?"

"Well, I can't." Simmel spread pudgy hands and his expression
changed to smug triumph. "I'm too fat to walk the path. Besides,
you're a Fourth, they *may* listen to you."

With an oath, Amarjite threw his captive down. "Watch her,"
he commanded, and strode off the platform.

Chandra stayed where she had fallen, peering up at Simmel
through a loosened shock of hair. She didn't have to fake the terror.

"Oh, get up and stop looking at me like that," he whined. "I
want my ices." Opposition by Amarjite had been enough to convince him, for pure obstinacy's sake, that this child was no more
than she appeared. The final command cinched the issue. Wizards
of the Fourth had no business giving commands to Wizards of the
Second.

Using the carved stone of the platform for support, Chandra
scrambled to her feet, her relief so great it made her dizzy. From
where she stood, she could see her ex-captor hurrying down a nar-

row path cut into the side of the volcano, his russet robes billowing out behind him. Turning her head only a little, she could see into the crater.

"My ices," prodded Simmel.

Her face carefully expressionless, she bowed and all but ran back into the palace. She'd seen a golden spire rising out of the molten rock, but its crown was empty.

Where was The Stone of Ischia?

Just inside the door, she forced herself to stop. There was one more thing she had to do before she was safe. With fingers that refused to quit shaking she unraveled a thread from the bottom edge of her tunic, tied a loose knot in it, and waited, peering back through the crack at the platform.

She could feel the Wizard of the Fourth's anger while he was still climbing the path. The instant he backed Simmel into her line of sight, before he had a chance to voice that anger, she shook out the knot.

"Forget."

And then she realized she'd made a major mistake. Forget was a spell of the Fourth, one of the few she knew. Amarjite turned his head and looked directly at her.

She focused more power.

"Forget!"

Simmel's face went blank.

The Wizard of the Fourth fought back, his hands clawing at the air.

"FORGET!"

Between one heartbeat and the next, Amarjite's face smoothed and he began grumbling about the twins.

Temples throbbing, Chandra reached out and gently brushed the spell across the two Wizards of the Eighth who had been silently focusing power into the crater the entire time. While she doubted they'd been aware of anything but their own actions, she was too shaken to leave loose ends behind her.

She should leave now, before someone else spotted her. She should slip unseen through the palace and confront Prince Darvish. She should. . . .

Very, very carefully, she slid a finger of power onto the focus of the Wizards of the Eighth, riding it down and through the net. Hiding her power signature within the borrowed focus, she touched the place where The Stone of Ischia should be. And frowned.

Laid over the residual power imprint of The Stone was the taint of another power; like a thin film of grease or a layer of smoke. Too ephemeral for a wizard less powerful to even notice, it told Chandra exactly nothing about who had left it. It came out of no type of power she recognized.

Where was The Stone of Ischia?

And with whom?

"Ytaili." King Jaffar rubbed the bit of amber between his fingers. "Are you sure?"

"No, Most Exalted. Not entirely."

"No?" The lord chancellor leaned slightly forward, his expression just hinting at triumph. "Then you have brought us exactly nothing. The Stone, and Ischia, are still lost."

Aaron felt Darvish stiffen beside him and heard what the words and their tone said to the king. *"Darvish has failed again."* He met the lord chancellor's eyes for a heartbeat and then deliberately turned his head away, dismissing him. He spoke directly to the king. "This color is found in small quantities in only one place, just outside Tivolic, the capital. The Royal Family of Ytaili favors it."

"We have only your word for that, *thief.*" The fury that throbbed in the veins at the lord chancellor's temples found its way into the last word.

Again Aaron met the lord chancellor's eyes. One shoulder lifted and dropped in the minimal shrug his scars had forced on him. The action said louder than words, *"I don't care what you think. You have no power over me."*

"Ytaili," the king repeated, softly.

With a visible effort, the lord chancellor forced his voice back to calm reason. "A pity His Highness killed the one man who could have told us something."

There it was again, *"Darvish has failed."* From the corner of his eye, Aaron looked up at the prince. *He uses you to consolidate his power with the king, a convenient scapegoat, and you gave him that power over you with your so obvious need to be noticed by your father.* He had walked that path himself. *Don't give him what he wants now.*

But Darvish merely tossed his hair back off his face and said, with an eloquent wave of one hand; "The thief was dying, Most Exalted. To carry a screaming man whose arms had rotted away through the streets—even," he inclined his head slightly, "if *I* were carrying him—would surely cause the questions we're trying to avoid."

The king stared at his third son for a long moment, his expression unreadable. When he finally spoke, sarcasm gave the words a cutting edge. "Then as we have lost one thief, it is fortunate we retain another." He turned his gaze on Aaron. "Give me, thief, the benefit of your experience."

Aaron let the silence stretch, his eyes locked on the king's. He had stopped responding to any power but his own five long years ago when he left his father's keep.

"The old pain rules you still, my lad."

He allowed the faint creak of leather as Darvish shifted beside him to drown out the memory of Faharra's voice. She was—had been—a crazy old woman. When he judged his point had been made, when an outburst from the lord chancellor seemed imminent, he told what he knew.

"The thief who took The Stone had the help of a wizard. That wizard now has The Stone. The thief has been recently in Ytaili, most probably Tivolic. The thief was hired by someone who paid, or was going to pay, him a great deal. . . ."

"How do you reason that?" Shahin stepped forward, away from his place by the rosewood throne and spoke for the first time since Aaron and Darvish had returned to report The Stone truly lost.

"He stole nothing for himself. Therefore, he was paid. The risks were great; he was paid well. He wore a piece of amber that could have only come from a member of the Royal Family of Ytaili. . . ."

"My wife," said Shahin, his voice dangerously quiet, "is a princess of Ytaili."

Aaron had known that, the wedding festivities had involved the entire city, the people rejoicing that the ancient antagonism between the two counties had ended at last. He bowed his head slightly, eyes carefully lowered to hide the thought they held. Powerful help from inside the palace would remove the remainder of the obstacles between a thief and The Stone.

"How dare you," the lord chancellor spat the words at Aaron, "accuse the Most Blessed Yasimina of involvement in this, this traitorous act."

"He accused no one," Shahin turned his quiet, dangerous voice on the lord chancellor.

Still scowling at the thief, the lord chancellor exclaimed, "I saw his face, my prince." Then his tone and his expression softened. "No one who knows your wife could believe such a thing." He bent slightly and spoke his next words to the king. "She writes to her brother, King Harith, Most Exalted, but surely that does not make her a traitor."

The king looked up at his eldest son, brows drawn down, "She writes to Harith?"

"She's homesick, Father." Shahin turned an expression of loathing on the lord chancellor. "I see the letters, there's no harm in them."

"Just as I said," the lord chancellor pointed out gently.

"Hypocrite!" Shahin used the word like a cudgel. "You insinuate even if you don't dare accuse."

"Would you listen if I did?"

"You've never liked her. You argued against this treaty and our marriage from the first."

"The kings of Ytaili have long desired this land." The old lord addressed the king directly. "I merely suggested it might not be wise to allow them so close, that perhaps the prince should marry within Cisali as you did, Most Exalted." He turned back to the heir. "My prince, the Most Blessed Yasimina's brother *is* an enemy of your Most Exalted father and . . ."

"*Was* an enemy of my Most Exalted father. My marriage ended that. And even if he landed an army on our shore, that would not make my wife an enemy as well."

"No, my prince, but . . ."

"Enough."

The command dropped Shahin's fists to his sides. He bowed to his father and moved back to stand at his right hand, having almost breached the barrier of the throne.

He loves her, Aaron realized. *He loves his treaty bride and he's afraid the lord chancellor might have been right all along. The prejudices against outlanders he's been raised with strengthen that fear.* That the people of Ytaili came from the same stock, with the same coloring, language, and beliefs, would help only a very little.

"This amber would be as effective and less incriminating an identification than a royal seal," Darvish offered thoughtfully into the silence.

"So you accuse my wife as well. You're saying she recognized the amber and allowed the thief into the palace?" Shahin's face held the look of a man who wrestled with inner demons.

"No." Darvish took a deep breath. He felt sorry for his brother but sorrier for the fate of Ischia without The Stone. "I'm saying it's possible that *someone* recognized the amber and allowed the thief into the palace."

Someone.

Yasimina.

"There is always the possibility," the lord chancellor pointed out, "that the thief had stolen the amber long before and wore it as a momento of his crime. That he has not been near Ytaili or Tivolic in many years."

King Jaffar's finger tightened on the amber as though he would force it to speak. "Is this possible?" he demanded of Aaron.

"Yes." It was possible and Aaron would have left it at that—he cared nothing for the city nor the people in it and had, in fact, been deriving some pleasure in imagining Faharra's granddaughter waddling desperately, futilely away from a river of molten rock—except he caught the faintest shadow of triumph crossing the lord chancellor's face. *What do you have to be triumphant about, old man?* Curious, he continued; "But it isn't likely. The amber could be recognized as stolen and this man was too good to take that kind of chance. He had to have been given it."

"And this brings suspicion back to my wife?" Shahin asked the question calmly enough, but his face betrayed his anger and fear.

"No one brings suspicion on your wife, Shahin, but you will speak with her and discover what she knows."

Although a different response could be seen in the set of his shoulders, Shahin said only, "Yes, Father."

"I have thought on this matter," the ritual words carried the clash of steel, "and I will send a force to Ytaili to recover The Stone."

The lord chancellor leaned forward, plump hand extended almost to the black silk of the king's sleeve. "Most Exalted, if I may make a suggestion, sending an army to Ytaili would cause the questions we cannot have asked and would no doubt start the war with Ytaili we are anxious to avoid. It would not get back The Stone."

"Those are criticisms, Lord Chancellor. I have yet to hear a suggestion."

"Send a small force, Most Exalted. One man perhaps. Or two."

On the other side of the throne, Shahin gripped the king's shoulder. "Send Darvish."

Darvish closed his eyes. Aaron could feel him waiting for the laughter that would surely follow.

No one laughed.

"He could travel," Shahin went on, still speaking directly to the king, "not as a prince but as a swordsman looking for hire. He could pass with ease. His habits are certainly not those of a prince and even the arms master admits he is uncommonly skilled."

"Yes," agreed the lord chancellor, his eyes alight with sudden enthusiasm, "and send the thief as well in case The Stone must be stolen back. They can be soul-linked so he cannot run."

Soul-linked, Aaron snorted silently. What a waste of wizardry. Why didn't they just ask? It wasn't as if he had anything better to do. His life before the palace was ash. His life within the palace was only marking time.

Obsidian eyes weighed Darvish silently. "*This* is the only chance for Ischia?"

Darvish winced, a motion too small for any but Aaron to see. "It is the best chance, Father."

"And if the people ask where he is?"

"We tell them, Most Exalted, he is in seclusion, preparing for his wedding."

"And they'll believe that?"

"Again, his reputation works for us, Most Exalted. Seclusion in this case would be taken to mean recovering from a lover's complaint he could not bring to a gently bred bride."

King Jaffar nodded, once. He wasn't convinced but with both his heir and his lord chancellor agreeing for the first time in weeks, he would accept their judgment. "You and your thief," he told his third son coldly, "will go to Ytaili and bring back The Stone."

Darvish bowed. "I am honored to serve, Most Exalted."

Aaron wondered if any heard, buried deep beneath Darvish's self-mockery, the ring of truth. He suspected Shahin did. The crown prince had just handed his brother a chance to save himself as well as Ischia.

Soul-linked. Darvish probed at the new and uncomfortable feelings the wizard had left. Every thought seemed to carry with it a faint echo and he felt a sudden desire to scratch he suspected wasn't his. *Soul-linked.* If Aaron moved more than ten of his own body lengths away, he would fall screaming and the pain would continue until the distance was closed.

Darvish had caught Aaron's eye during the short ritual, offering sympathy, camaraderie, he wasn't sure what. To his surprise, Aaron had not rejected him out of hand and his wry acknowledgment of what was being done to them both made the whole thing easier to bear.

Soul-linked. He snorted as he pushed open the outer door of his apartments. *And all I wanted was a friend.*

It had been an afternoon of surprises and the wine he'd drunk on the way back through the halls had not managed to dim the pounding of his heart. His most exalted father had trusted the saving of Ischia to him. To him.

To him. Nine Above!

His laugh sounded forced. "Losing The Stone must have really rattled him."

"Who?"

"My Most Exalted father, of course." The laugh no longer sounded like a laugh at all.

"Why?" Aaron asked, following the prince across the sitting room. "Because he's sending you after The Stone?" The transition from goat to champion couldn't be an easy one. He hoped Darvish could make it. Not that he cared.

"Because he's sending *us* after The Stone," Darvish corrected. "A thief and a drunk. Nine Above, he must be out of his mind."

"A thief to catch a thief. And perhaps it's time to prove you're more than a drunk."

Darvish stopped and looked back over his shoulder at the younger man. "Am I?" he asked, then sighed and turned away. "I need a drink."

Shahin thinks you are. So does the lord chancellor . . . or he wouldn't have tried so hard to make you into one. Aaron scowled at Darvish's back and thought suddenly of the brooch he'd been taking to Faharra that last night. *"More good jewels are ruined by their settings. . . ."* For a crazy old lady, she'd been pretty smart.

"I said," Darvish raised his voice above the distant cries of the peacocks, "that I need a drink." He frowned. No dresser appeared from the bedroom, filled goblet on tray, apologizing for making him wait. All was silent and still.

For a panicked instant he feared his father had taken them away, a punishment of some sort he wasn't meant to understand. Then he called himself several kinds of fool and silently pulled his sword. His most exalted father barely acknowledged *him*, his servants were less than nothing.

If they were able, they would have answered his call. Something prevented them.

He motioned for Aaron to continue moving about and, tufted brows high, the thief obeyed. Using Aaron's noise as a cover, he slid along the wall and peered through the arch into his bedroom.

A young woman sat cross-legged on the near corner of the bed, calmly braiding a luxuriant fall of chestnut hair.

The point of his weapon hit the rug with a muffled thud.

"Who the One are you?" he demanded. She looked vaguely familiar, sort of pretty in a thin, serious way. Had he asked her to meet him here and then forgotten? It wouldn't be the first time although he generally preferred his women older. He took a step into the bedroom. Behind her, stretched out side by side on his bed, were all three dressers.

The scimitar moved back up into a fighting position. "What have you done to them?"

"To who?" She finished the braid and flipped it back over her shoulder. "Oh. To them. Relax." Unfolding her legs she stood and stretched. The top of her head came no higher than the center of Darvish's chest. "I've put them to sleep. When I'm gone, they won't even remember it happening." Brown eyes flecked with gold rested for an instant on Darvish's face. "Your portrait was accurate enough, I suppose. They left out the baggy bits, but your eyes *are* very blue, aren't they? Now, what have you done with The Stone?"

". . . and so when I found no one else knew it was missing, I came back here to wait." Chandra spread both hands in a gesture that clearly said her story was finished, and waited for a response. She hadn't mentioned her capture by the Wizard of the Fourth.

That she, a Wizard of the Nine, should have been frightened so by a wizard of lesser ability was, was. . . . Well, it wasn't any of their business anyway.

Darvish took a deep breath, opened his mouth to speak, and had a swallow of wine instead. It had been a peculiar sort of a day, to say the least. "Look," he said, pacing the width of the room, "I don't want to marry you either, but at the risk of hurting your feelings, there's more important things going on right now."

"Why should that hurt my feelings?" Surely he didn't think that she'd consider a treaty marriage neither party wanted more important than The Stone of Ischia? "What *happened* to The Stone?"

"It was stolen. Just before dawn." Darvish saw no point in hiding it from her. He could see her storming into the throne room and demanding the information from his most exalted father. If the situation hadn't been so One abandoned serious he'd be tempted to let her do just that. "The thief is dead. We think The Stone is with the wizard who arranged the theft in Ytaili. . . ."

"Of course it's with the wizard, where else would it be? Ytaili's a big place." She raised both brows sarcastically. "I hope you have better directions than that."

Darvish sighed wearily. "All evidence points to Tivolic and someone in the royal family being involved. Aaron and I will start there."

"You and Aaron?" She looked from the tall prince, admittedly muscular but showing definite signs of dissipation, to the slight thief, who for all his breadth of shoulder stood barely taller than she did and who moved as if even breathing hurt. "Why?"

"Because we're the ones who tracked it to Ytaili. Because we've got the best chance to succeed. Because the fewer people who know the less chance of panic. Because. . . ." He searched for another reason. "Because we can slip away without being missed." Say something often enough, forcefully enough, and you could almost convince yourself, Darvish discovered. Almost. *Because they know it can't be done and they're setting me up to fail.*

"Oh." Chandra considered the options. It made sense. Of a sort. She turned to Aaron. "You're soul-linked to him. Why?"

"I'm a thief." He turned his head to face her but let the rest of his body remain still on the pallet. The day had left him weak as a baby. He ached, his head pounded, and they still had to catch the evening tide out of Ischia. "They think I'll run."

"Will you?"

"I doubt it."

"I've never met a thief before."

"I'm not surprised."

"I'd like to talk to you about it later."

"Later," he agreed shortly. She reminded him of Faharra, of how the gem cutter must have been when she was young. He didn't want to like her. He had nowhere to run. Even if Herrak's interference meant he, Aaron, hadn't failed Faharra it didn't, it couldn't, cancel how he'd failed Ruth. Lightly, very lightly, he touched the soul-link. It had been a confusing day.

"Well," said Chandra, in the tone that said this settled things to her satisfaction, "I'm going with you."

"Not if all the Nine showed up and demanded it." Darvish refilled his goblet and took a hasty swallow. "You're going home. Trust me, no one's thinking much about marriage plans right now and your people are going to be worried about you."

"My *people,*" she mimicked with an edge to her voice, "don't even know I'm gone and won't miss me when they find out."

Darvish considered arguing the point, but Chandra's expression told him she wouldn't listen. He decided not to bother. He was hardly the person to be counseling someone about their home life.

"And what are you and Aaron going to do when you find this unknown and, I might add just in case you haven't caught on yet, *very powerful* wizard with The Stone?"

"What do you mean?"

"I mean what are you going to do? Whack him with your sword while Aaron picks his pocket?"

"Something like that." Darvish had another drink. This kid had a vicious tongue.

"It would make sense to take a wizard along."

"We don't have a wizard."

"You have me."

"And *you* can't come."

"Why not?"

"Uh. . . ." Darvish had wanted to take a wizard along, but they were all needed in case the volcano erupted before The Stone was retrieved. The lord chancellor had been most apologetic. "You're too young."

Chandra smiled. What a jerk. "I'm old enough to get married," she pointed out.

"Look, Chandra," Darvish tried being reasonable, "*why* is it so important for you to come?"

Her nostrils flared in an unconscious imitation of Rajeet's expression. "I *told* you. The Wizards of the Nine created The Stone. I'm a Wizard of the Nine and, unless you know another one I don't, the *only* Wizard of the Nine around. That makes me historically responsible for The Stone." She tossed her braid back over her shoulder. "And besides, if I help you recover The Stone, I'll be in a better bargaining position to refuse this marriage."

"The marriage won't . . ."

"And if you don't take me with you, I'll tell the whole city The Stone is missing."

"You wouldn't!"

"Try me."

She didn't look like she was bluffing.

Darvish finished his wine and glared at her over the rim of the goblet. She met his eyes, smiling smugly. "Bugger the Nine," he sighed at last. "You win. You can come. Not," he added a little sulkily, "that I could stop you anyway."

"I was wondering when you'd figure that out."

"Figure what . . ."

"That you couldn't stop me."

"Then why . . . ?"

Chandra spread slender hands. "Because I'd prefer we have this conversation now rather than on the deck of a ship or at the palace in Tivolic where you'd give the whole mission away."

Darvish had never liked being patronized and he liked it even less when it was done by a girl half his size and seven years his junior. "They never told me you were a wizard," he growled.

Chandra shrugged. "They never told me you were a drunk. I'd say we're even."

"Yeah? Well, you're . . ." A strange, strangled noise cut him off.

Aaron, his arms wrapped tightly about his body in a futile attempt to keep his chest from moving, rocked in the grip of helpless laughter. It sounded slightly rusty, as though it had been a long time since it had been used. And it sounded just a little desperate.

Darvish and Chandra turned identical faces of aristocratic disdain on the writhing thief.

Aaron didn't know why he laughed, unless it was at the thought of the three of them—a drunken prince, a runaway child-wizard, and a failed thief—taking Ytaili by storm and returning in triumph with The Stone of Ischia. *Soul-linked. I can't get away. I'm going to have to go through with this.*

Perhaps he laughed because he'd forgotten how to cry.

Chapter Eight

"I'll meet you at the docks" had been such an easy thing to say back in the quiet of the palace. Chandra shifted her weight and wove the notice-me-not tighter around her. Her un-betrothed and his thief were leaving from the temple, from the prince's "seclusion," so she couldn't leave with them and besides, hadn't she traveled to Ischia on her own?

"I'm a wizard, remember," she'd snapped at Darvish's warnings. *"Remaining unseen is one of the most basic of disciplines."*

When the prince had looked to Aaron for support, the outlander had studied her for a long moment and said, "There's a row of seven warehouses just in front of the docks, meet us at the western end."

Darvish had protested and Aaron had replied, "She's a wizard." His tone had added, let her prove it.

She'd bridled at the prince's grin and stomped from the room. Then she'd had to return to lift the sleep off the dressers. She couldn't remember the last time she'd been so embarrassed.

"I'll get his stone back for him," she muttered, her voice lost under the screams of a thousand seagulls, "and then he'll be sorry he laughed. He'll see. *I* am a Wizard of the Nine."

The rough, undressed stone of the westernmost warehouse dug into her back and the docks of Ischia spread out before her.

Sailors swaggered everywhere, rolling their weight from one hip to another as though they still walked decks, gold gleaming in ears and noses and teeth, every second word a curse. Merchants, either comfortably fat or cadaverously thin, spoke with pursers and captains arranging cargoes and payments and bribes. Whores kept heavily kohled eyes open for opportunity and as Chandra watched, a skinny girl, younger than herself, followed a laughing sailor down between two large piles of rope. Common men and women of Ischia searched the docks for bargains—a bit of silk barely salt stained, a fish not quite freshly dead. Nobles, perfumed sleeves lifted to mask the constantly changing smells of the area and the ever present reek of the less fortunate, searched for thrills, with their guards present in case those thrills got the upper hand. Just at the edge of her hearing, a beggar whined for alms but received, from the shrieks of pain that followed, a less gentle reward.

For over five years Chandra had lived on a quiet country estate with her teacher, her servant, and her old nurse. Once a month her father traveled to her. Once or twice a year she traveled to her father's court.

The docks of Ischia swarmed—there could be no other word for it—with people. Too many people.

In the midst of the procession she had been part of a larger whole. Here, she sat alone. Not that she was frightened. She was a wizard. And a Wizard of the Nine, besides. There was a certain, raw power in it all. There were just so many people. . . .

When the prince and the thief finally arrived, she almost didn't recognize them. The movement of the crowd around them drew her attention, but it took a moment of puzzled staring before she realized who the lithe outlander and his huge hireling were.

Darvish, his hair cropped swordsman short and whiskers a dark shadow along his jaw, looked much less pretty than he had in his long hair and exaggerated court fashions and *much* larger. The heavy cotton and plain sweat-stained leathers showed well-defined muscles, and the grubby white sunrobe he wore could've been poled to make a tent. He still looked like he drank too much, but he didn't look as weak as he had surrounded by silks and softness. He looked nothing like a prince.

Aaron did. Not a single movement was wasted. He looked neither to the left nor the right, his expression hidden within the shadows cast by the stiffened edges of his sunrobe hood. Chandra knew much of his bearing came from his recent injuries—movements were restricted in many ways by burns not quite healed—but he still looked as if he owned the city. Like he stood alone at the top of a mountain and nothing could topple him from the peak. Chandra was impressed in spite of herself; her father had once been a man that strong.

*   *   *

"There's the warehouse." Darvish waved a hand in its direction, studded wrist guards flashing for a moment in the wide sleeves of the sunrobe. He knew he shouldn't be enjoying himself, that his city and its people were in great danger, but he couldn't help it. For at least a nineday, maybe longer, he was free. Free of the palace, free of the plots, free to prove himself to his father. "Where's that girl?"

"Here."

Darvish couldn't stop the jump back, so he added a glare and dropped his hand to his sword hilt. He was not going to look ridiculous in front of this girl he was not going to marry.

Chandra allowed herself a smug smile. She wasn't fooled. And up close, he still smelled of wine. "Your eyes are brown," she said peering up at his face. "A good idea although I could have cast a stronger spell. I doubt this will hold much past morning."

"It doesn't have to last beyond the docks," Darvish snarled, shifting the weight of his shield on his back. It caught on the small pack he wore and, brows down, he yanked it free. "And there won't be much left of a good idea if you tell the whole city."

"My words were pitched to carry only to you."

"Next time, O Awesome Wizard, spare me as well."

"Next time . . ." Chandra looked beyond his bulk, saw Aaron regally indifferent, blushed and fell silent.

"I'm going to find us a ship," Aaron said, his voice as expressionless as his face. "Stay here." He slipped easily into the movement of the crowds although the press of people set his teeth on edge. If they wanted to go on bickering, they could do it without him for a time. Even as a small part of him envied their ability to say what they thought, he despised the waste. Their constant sniping served no purpose, it only wasted time, wasted words.

"One Below, boy, you count out your words like a miser."

Aaron had looked down at the old gem cutter from his perch on her window ledge. "Didn't one of your own poets say that empty words show an empty mind and silence speaks most eloquently of all?"

Faharra had snorted and waved one clawlike finger at the thief. "It wasn't meant to be an excuse for never holding up your end of a conversation."

The pain of Faharra's death had burned down to a gentle ache during his anger at Herrak. His failure to gain the emerald for her tomb, although it still tormented him, no longer weighted every breath. Without it, the walls had weakened and it was getting harder to maintain the void.

"I don't want to know their thoughts," Aaron muttered, deftly sidestepping two whores and a bleeding beggar. He could see danger in that, for what if the thoughts they started speaking began to concern him. If the thoughts Darvish began speaking. . . . *I must be out of my mind; I should've told them to find their own Stone, stayed at the palace and been quietly tortured to death. Before Faharra died, I had my life under control. This is all your doing, old lady.*

From out of memory, he heard her laugh and he allowed himself a small smile in answer.

Darvish watched Aaron cut his way through the crowds like a sword through silk. He moved with an intensity that easily marked his progress in spite of his lack of height. *I could do that,* Darvish realized suddenly. *Just walk the docks like a normal man.* No one expecting a performance from the prince. No one reporting that performance back to the lord chancellor. There were no guards at his back, no spies in the shadows, just him and Aaron and . . .

Chandra. He looked down at the girl who stood arms crossed and foot jigging against the smooth stone of the paving blocks. Maybe a wizard *would* be a help. The poor kid had her own problems and Darvish had never been good at holding a grudge.

"That's the ship you came in on, over there," he told her, waving a hand at a sleek vessel moored toward the eastern end of the harbor. From her masts, she flew the royal colors.

Chandra glanced briefly at the ship and said, "I know."

So it's to be that way, is it. He grinned and added, "I'm sleeping with the captain's wife."

This time Chandra glanced briefly up at Darvish, her eyes hooded with boredom. "I know," she said again. To her surprise, after an astonished second, Darvish threw back his head and roared with laughter and just for an instant he looked like a very nice man indeed. Chandra found herself smiling in response.

At the sound of the laughter, one or two people turned but when they saw a brown-eyed swordsman, not their blue-eyed prince, they went back to their own concerns.

"Your pardon." Even behind the illusion Darvish's eyes twinkled. "That was a boorish thing to say, wasn't it?"

He was inviting her to share the joke, Chandra realized, a joke at his own expense, and the apology had actually sounded sincere. Her smile broadened, she couldn't help it, but by the Nine he confused her.

Then suddenly, the laughter vanished, and the prince's expression turned inward.

"What . . ."

He chopped off Chandra's question with the edge of his hand. Something tugged. . . . He almost had it. Something just this side of pain. Eyes narrowed against the red-gold light of the setting sun, he scanned the crowd for Aaron. There . . . then he jerked, and swore, and raced toward the slight figure who had taken one step too many and crumpled to the ground.

Darvish could feel only the echo of Aaron's agony, not the pain itself, but he knew what Aaron felt and although it eased as he drew closer, the soul-link still screamed through his head like the wrath of all Nine Above.

Scrambling to keep up, Chandra found it difficult to believe that a man of Darvish's size and habits could move so quickly. The crowd scattered, shrieking.

"I didn't touch him, I swear it on the One Below. I never laid a finger on him!" The sailor backed away, hands raised protectively.

Darvish ignored him.

Aaron knelt, forehead resting against the paving stones, body shuddering with each shallow breath. Teeth clenched, he raised his head, then carefully sat back on his heels. A circle of curious faces swam around him and he heard Darvish say, as though from a great distance, "He's not used to the heat." It was a voice only a complete idiot would argue with and no one in the crowd seemed willing.

He tried to rise and the motion sent aftershocks of pain slamming through his body. Strong hands caught him, and held him. Where they gripped, it hurt a little less and then it hurt a lot less and unbidden came the strange thought that, here, he was safe. His vision cleared. He realized he was resting in the circle of Darvish's arms. He pulled away.

"I can stand," he said, and he did.

After a moment, the world steadied. "Perhaps," he said, pulling the hood of the sunrobe back over his face, "we'd better stay together."

Darvish drew in a deep breath and slowly, very slowly, let it out. "Perhaps," he agreed.

"That's it?" Chandra asked, brows up and hands on hips.

"No, not quite." Darvish wiped damp palms on his trousers. "I need a drink."

Chandra rolled her eyes. "Of course you do," she sneered.

"And your business in Tivolic?" the purser asked, counting out the small pile of silver and copper coins into three stacks, one for each passage. When the young man made no answer, he looked up, his lips parted to repeat the question. The words stuck behind his teeth. The outlander's eyes were very pale, almost silver-gray, and nothing, absolutely nothing, of the man showed within them. He felt completely overwhelmed and it didn't make much difference that, even sitting, the purser was almost as tall.

Aaron held the purser's gaze for a moment longer and then, because the question was one he had every right to ask, he answered it. "We're looking for someone."

It was not an answer calculated to make the purser feel more secure and the outlander's clipped accent made it sound more dangerous still. But they had a cabin empty and the captain liked the *Gryphon* to travel full. . . .

His gaze flicked back to where the young outlander's companions stood by the door. "A swordsman, you say?"

"Yes."

"And a girl?"

"Yes."

"The swordsman's?"

"Her own."

More emotion in those last two words than all the others that went before it. *Which,* the purser wondered, *did this outlander lay claim to, the swordsman or the girl? Given the strange prejudice of outlanders, probably the girl.* "She's a wizard?"

"As I said."

"What discipline?"

Aaron could almost feel Chandra's eyes boring circles into his back as he answered. "She hasn't decided yet."

"You bring no trouble on board."

Aaron nodded once.

"And if we're attacked, your swordsman and possibly the wizard will fight."

"Attacked?"

"Pirates," the purser said shortly.

Aaron nodded again and this time the purser echoed it, scooping the coins off the table and into his belt pouch. "Ship's the *Green Gryphon*. We sail with the tide. If you're not on board, you get left behind. No refunds."

Aaron nodded again, flipped the hood up on his sunrobe, and silently the three left the warehouse.

The purser watched them go, whistling tunelessly through his teeth. Outlanders, who could fathom them. This one looked honed to a razor sharpness and ready to cut at the wrong word.

"Use my own name?" Darvish muttered as they headed across the docks to the *Gryphon*. "Are you crazy?"

"I know of four other Darvishes," Aaron told him, "a tavern keeper, a tailor, a gardener, and a blind beggar. They're all about your age. When a prince is named, the common folk are encouraged to use the name as well."

"Why?" Darvish asked. He'd never heard of this.

"To confuse curses. Have Chandra strengthen the illusion that keeps your eyes brown." He almost smiled. "The best lie holds a part of the truth. You'll be just one more Darvish named for the prince."

"What about me?" Chandra pulled on Aaron's sleeve.

"People usually steer clear of wizards. They'll ignore you until they want something."

"Do I use my own name?"

"Is anyone looking for you?"

Chandra thought of the golem waiting patiently for her to return. Of her father who hadn't even realized she was gone. "No."

"Then use the name you'll answer to. It's safest."

Thieves, Chandra realized, narrowly avoiding a pile of fish guts, *have a lot of specialized information.* "Why a merchant ship?" she asked a few minutes later as they neared the *Gryphon*. "Aren't we supposed to be in a hurry?"

"It's leaving tonight," Darvish snapped. He'd been thinking about the blind beggar with his name, trying to compare their lives. "What did you want me to do, commandeer a warship? We're trying not to attract attention."

"Well, maybe," Chandra sniffed, put out by his tone, "you're trying too hard."

Are we? Aaron wondered. Why hadn't they been given, not a warship, but a courier? The crew need only be told they were on a mission for the king, the small, sleek ship could get them to Tivolic in half the time of a merchanter, and it would be there, waiting for them when they needed to escape with The Stone. With a princess of Ytaili in Ischia, royal couriers would frequently go between the two countries. No questions would be asked if one went out tonight.

He supposed someone had their reasons. He would have given a great deal to know who that someone was and what the reasons were.

The salt sea air, the smell of tar and sun-warmed wood giving up its heat into the night—Chandra drew in a deep breath and let it sigh back out in pure contentment. Below her feet she could feel the gentle slap, slap of waves against the hull. Above her head, rope and canvas creaked and billowed as the great square sail trapped a bit more wind. As far from any of the ship's lights as she could get and remain on board, Chandra leaned back and watched the Nine dance across the sky. She would have preferred a faster ship, a ship that could dance across the water, but this would most certainly do.

She would return The Stone to Ischia. A Wizard of the Nine was greater than any single discipline even if she couldn't figure out what exact discipline they faced. Even if—she pushed aside a moment of doubt—the wizard who stole The Stone could do things with mirrors she'd never heard of. *That* would put an end to any stupid marriage plans and give her time to deal with the problem of her cousin and the inheritance.

For the present, she would learn what she could of her companions, their strengths and weaknesses, so she could put them to the best use when the time arrived.

Darvish leaned against the stern and looked back at the lights of Ischia, breathing in the last scents of his city as the offshore breeze pushed the *Gryphon* out to sea.

I'll make you proud of me, Father. The thought had more the tenor of a threat than a promise.

He lifted his wineskin in salute, then half drained it to drown the fear that even returning The Stone and saving the capital would not be enough.

* * *

Up in the bow, Aaron stared into darkness, remembering the way the pain had eased in the circle of Darvish's arms.

It was the soul-link, he told himself. *The soul-link made it safe. Nothing more.*

Out of the darkness came voices from his childhood, stern priests who invoked an unforgiving god. *Man and man is a sin and a blasphemy. That way lies the fire.*

What kind of god makes love a sin? Faharra had asked. *Too little of it in the world as it is.*

It was the soul-link, Aaron told them both. *The soul-link made it safe. Nothing more.*

"Not another bloody letter."

The page shrugged and handed the small leather pouch embossed with the royal seals of both Ytaili and Cisali to the courier's captain. "I don't know what it is, ma'am. I was told to emphasize," he stumbled a little on the unfamiliar word, "that it had to be in Tivolic as soon as possible. That you're supposed to catch the evening tide."

"I can see the urgent cord, boy." She tapped one callused finger on the red silk string sealed around the pouch. "And don't tell me how to sail. I've been doing it for longer than you've been alive."

"Yes ma'am. I mean, no ma'am." He skipped back as the captain barked an order, the ropes were tossed clear, and the courier slipped the dock. Shoving his hands deep in his trouser pockets, he lingered for as long as he dared. That was the life; racing across the ocean, daring wind and wave, getting the message through whatever the cost. He sighed and headed back up the innumerable terraces to the palace. Maybe he should apply to the navy. Nothing ever happened in Ischia.

Safely clear of the harbor, the captain turned the package over and frowned at the royal seals. "Well, all I can say is, if it's from Her Most Blessedness, and if she wants more bloody peacocks, she can find another ship to carry them."

"Tired of beating on the crew?"

Darvish threw himself down by Aaron in the shade and grinned at Chandra. "Nine, no," he answered; "I got tired of them beating on me." The last two mornings, Darvish had picked out the largest men in the crew and challenged them to spar. He said he did it to stay in training, but his companions suspected he did it for fun, the no-holds-barred, gouging, biting type of fighting the sailors did couldn't be called training by any stretch of the imagination. The last two nights, he'd gotten drunk with them, having passed rapidly from landsman to compatriot.

"I know he's supposed to be pretending to be a swordsman," Chandra had sniffed at Aaron, "but does he have to do it so well? He's still a prince and he should act more like one."

The demon wings had risen. "Why?" Aaron had asked. "You don't."

"I am a Wizard of the Nine," she'd replied haughtily.

Aaron had gestured at the prince, surrounded by sailors, teaching them a soldier's song with impossibly lewd lyrics. "This is what he is."

Aaron and Chandra, the crew ignored. They returned the lack of interest.

Mopping his face with a double handful of his sunrobe, Darvish shot a questioning glance at the small silver bowl tucked into the curve of Chandra's crossed legs. "Have you found The Stone yet?"

"Not exactly," Chandra frowned. "I can tell it still exists and that we're heading toward it, but any details it burns out." When she'd last tried, just before sunrise, the power surge almost destroyed her scrying bowl. But she wasn't going to tell Darvish *that*. Nor was she going to mention the touch that had stroked lightly across her focus and diverted it. This was between her and that other wizard.

"At least we know we're going in the right direction and that it hasn't been destroyed."

"I keep telling you, no wizard in his right mind would destroy The Stone of Ischia."

"What if this wizard isn't in his right mind?"

Chandra snorted. "You're just saying that to be annoying!"

"Probably," he admitted, unrepentant. He prodded Aaron gently with a bare foot. "You put that salve on yet?"

"Hmm?" Deep in the protection of his sunrobe hood, Aaron's eyes were closed. The motion of the ship and the heat of the sun had filled the void and it just wasn't worth the effort to empty it out again. He was warm, he was comfortable, nothing even hurt very much.

"The salve?" Darvish repeated.

He'd brought the small pot up on deck, but, no, he hadn't applied it. He managed a single shake of his head.

"Do you want me to do it?"

A lazy flick of a pale finger seemed to indicate that Darvish should go ahead.

Shaking his own head, Darvish knelt and pried the cork from the pot. "There isn't much left," he warned, flicking Aaron's sunrobe open. The yellow silk trousers—"If I have to look less like a prince, you have to look less like a thief."—were low on Aaron's hips and he hadn't bothered putting his shirt on at all. *And a good thing, too,* Darvish thought with a wry smile. *I don't think I'm up to undressing him. And stopping.* He watched the brown of his fingers against the white of Aaron's chest and tried not to think of anything in particular.

The salve was cool against the scars and the gentle circular motion was the final thing Aaron needed to relax him completely. He felt like he didn't have any bones.

"You know what you need, Dar?" he murmured. "You need a war."

It took Darvish a moment to get past the diminutive. No one had called him Dar since his grandmother had died. He ran a line of salve carefully down the join of new skin and old, taking enough time for the lump in his throat to dissolve. "I thought it was war, amongst other things, we were trying to prevent," he said at last.

"No, no, you *personally* need a war." Darvish got the impression Aaron was speaking almost to himself. "I had a cousin like you once, a great fighter; soldiers, common people would follow him anywhere. Father said Joshua was the best *kar kleysh* he'd ever had."

"Kar kleysh?"

Eyes still closed, Aaron frowned. "You'd call it a war chief, uh, a commander." One corner of his mouth twitched upward. "Of course, the tricky part was commanding Joshua. You're like him, Dar. You need a war to be appreciated."

"Maybe I should start one when we get to Ytaili?"

The same corner twitched upward again. "Maybe."

"Kar kleysh," Chandra repeated thoughtfully. "I've never heard that language before. Where exactly are you from?"

Aaron sighed deeply. "A very, very long way from here."

"But where exactly? And why did you leave? And why become a thief, for the Nine's sake? You're an intelligent man, well-born, I can't imagine anything so drastic that it would force you to make that kind of choice."

Between one heartbeat and the next, stone walls slammed back into place, muscles tensed, and Aaron returned to the real world. *No,* he thought, *I don't imagine you can. Ruth was three years younger than you when she died.* In one fluid motion he gained his feet and without speaking turned and walked to the bow where he could be alone with the memory of the screaming.

Darvish savagely shoved the cork back in the pot and thought about how much he'd like to wring Chandra's neck. "That was just brilliant," he snarled.

"What?" Chandra protested. "I just asked him some questions."

"Well maybe next time, O Awesome Wizard," Darvish stood and glared down at her, "you'll think about the answers you might get and then you'll think again about asking. And now, just so you have ample time to disapprove, I'm going to get drunk."

Alone, Chandra chewed her lip and picked at the tarred end of a piece of rope. The rules governing people made the most difficult wizardry with its chants and measurements and potential for disaster look both easy and safe. At least the rules of wizardry never changed. "It wasn't my fault," she told her shadow. Her shadow didn't look convinced.

"Courage, little sister." In the red-gold light of The Stone, the man's expression appeared deceptively kind. "Win through, prove yourself worthy, and you need never be alone again."

"I feel sorry for her," Darvish said, as the two men leaned on the rail and watched the sun extinguish itself beneath the horizon. "She's so busy saying, *If you don't need me, then I don't need you* to her father that she's never acknowledged how much he hurt her."

Aaron grunted and Darvish continued. "She's hiding that hurt behind anger." He grinned. "And occasionally an obnoxious personality." The light of the sun gave his skin a ruddy cast and turned the brown illusion over his blue eyes almost purple. "I wish there was something we could do to help her."

Aaron turned, looked steadily at Darvish for a moment, then

shook his head in disbelief. "The blind leading the blind," he snorted and walked away, still shaking his head.

The gentle roll of the ship sent the huge figure crashing into a wall, where it rested for a moment before going on. It squinted against the night and the fine misting of rain, spotted its destination, and lurched determinedly forward. Two tries opened the door and, ducking under the low lintel, Darvish fell into the tiny cabin.

"Get off me, you ox! You're all wet!"

Slowly and carefully, Darvish stood and then reached out and considerately stopped the wild rocking of Chandra's hammock, "Though you'd be a . . . sleep."

"I was until you landed on me!"

Darvish thought about that for a moment. Oh," he said. "You asleep . . . Aaron?" He peered into the dark shelf of the cabin's narrow bunk.

The thief's pale eyes glimmered eerily. "I was."

"Oh."

As Darvish continued to loom over him, Aaron stirred uneasily. "You stink," he said. "Go to bed."

The prince sighed and straightened. "Go to bed," he repeated morosely, somehow managing to find his hammock and get into it. "Go to bed alone. I'm in the . . . middle of th' ocean. Risking my . . . life . . . an' I'm with a virgin ana stone. Aaron doesn't like boys," he added after a second, "an' I respeck that."

You're not a boy, Aaron thought.

And the priests said, "Man loving man is foul in the sight of the Lord."

"An' Chandra's just a child. A baby. Only sixteen. S'okay to be a . . . virgin when you're still a baby. I unnerstand. Really."

"Look," Chandra said suddenly, "it's nothing personal." Maybe if she explained, he'd drop it. This might not be the best time nor place, but the darkness made it easy so she continued. "It's because I'm a Wizard of the Nine."

"Wizards," said Darvish, from the shadowed depths of his hammock, "don't have ta be . . . virgins. I know tha fer a fact. Four facts, in fact. Five if you figger . . . one of 'em was twice."

"But not all wizards are the same." It had become very important that they understand. "Wizards make themselves a focus for external power, channeling it into the forms they choose. Most wizards can focus only a small amount of the power available and the forms they can channel to are limited by the discipline that makes them Wizards of the First or the Second or the Ninth. Wizards of the *Nine* are capable of focusing *all* available power and the forms are limited only by their level of training."

"But virgins . . ."

"I'm coming to that. To focus that kind of power, the wizard must be strong. Sex weakens you. Marriage weakens you. Love weakens you most of all. I won't lose my strength, myself, in another person. I won't do it. I won't."

"Then don't." Aaron's voice was steel and stone and ice.

"We'll get The Stone," Darvish said around a yawn, "and that'll show them all." He yawned again and almost instantly after his breathing slowed.

Chandra took a deep breath of her own and shakily released it. As much as his habits disgusted her, she found herself liking Darvish much more than she'd have ever liked the pretty princeling she'd expected. We'll get The Stone, he'd said. We. Her and Darvish and Aaron. If Aaron wanted to be part of a we. . . .

Then, over the prince's gentle snores she heard him say, "Good night, Wizard."

She smiled. *We'll get The Stone.*

"Good night, Thief."

". . . but Gracious Majesty, if you want it done away from the harbor—we search for a single ship and the ocean is large."

King Harith stabbed a beefy finger down on the map, a square cut ruby flashing deep red in the lamplight. "How hard can it be?" he demanded. "The *Gryphon* sails from here," the finger moved, "to here. You tell a ship to wait here, and when *Gryphon* sails by it's ours. Simple."

"Most ships, Gracious Majesty," the Lord of the Navy tried again, "cut over to the north current somewhere along here. . . ."

"Good." The king nodded his heavy head. "The perfect place for an ambush."

"But, Gracious Majesty, we have no way of knowing where they will cross to the current."

"Of course we do," the king snorted. "Take a Wizard of the Seventh along, find out where the winds blow tonight. You can have a couple of ships in the area by tomorrow morning?"

The lord nodded. It hadn't really been a question.

"Good, anyway, have the wizard find out where the winds would put the ship onto the current and be there. Seventh is a god of storms, after all, he should be able to figure out a few One abandoned winds. I want that ship and everyone on it destroyed completely. Take a Wizard of the Fourth along as well, they're good at that sort of thing."

The Lord of the Navy took a deep breath and said in the most innocuous voice he could manage, "Could that not be interpreted as an act of war, Gracious Majesty?" Not only could Ytaili not afford a war at this time, but to break a treaty just less than a year old would panic other treaty partners and start something they couldn't hope to control.

"Of course it could be interpreted as an act of war, you One abandoned idiot," King Harith growled. "And that's why," his eyes glittered in the lamplight and he smiled, "you're leaving no witnesses." One way or another, treaty or no treaty, he would get Cisali, if not by the war his people refused to fund, then by less overt means. To that end, he had helped the wizard Palaton steal The Stone and now, he would prevent Ischia's heroes from stealing it back.

Chapter Nine

Head pounding, guts heaving, miles away from a cure, Darvish staggered to the rail to throw up.

"Now a sailor'd time it t'the swell, so it don't splash back on the ship."

"The Nine can time it," Darvish muttered, and spat. He straightened up and glared at the mate, who grinned genially back at him. "What the One were we drinking last night and may She have mercy on me for doing it?"

"Rice wine."

"What wine?"

"Rice wine." The mate's grin broadened and the early morning sunlight gleamed on a pair of gold teeth. "You bought a keg out of cargo."

"Good for me." He clenched his teeth on another spasm, and managed, barely, to keep control. "Charged me double, did you?" he asked hoarsely when he could speak again.

"You didn't *have* quite double. We cut you a deal."

"Thank you." A callused hand clapped him jovially on the shoulder and the shock of the blow echoed through his head. Only his death grip on the rail kept him standing. The mate, while not quite the prince's height, had shoulders and arms so heavily muscled that he appeared in constant danger of tipping over. Darvish had sparred with him twice and he hoped never to meet the man in a serious fight. "If you're looking for some exercise, I don't think I'm up to it."

"Nay, I wondered if you wanted somethin' to eat. We've a fine mess of roe fried up with big chunks of onion."

Darvish growled out most of a curse before he had to heave his guts over the rail again. "You have a sick sense of humor," he snarled when he could.

"You're not the first to say it," the other man admitted, laughing. He leaned his massive forearms on the rail and squinted into the distance. "Now then. What's that there?"

Suspecting that he'd already found The Stone, that someone had slipped it into his skull during the night, Darvish peered in the direction the mate seemed to be looking. "It's land," he said at last.

"Aye. It's the Ytaili coast. There's a strong current north the captain likes to ride close in. But look there," he pointed, "by that great white lump, what do you see?"

The dark bank of land merged into the sea at one edge and rose up to disappear into a gray veil of morning mist at the other. Darvish, attempting to ignore the additional pounding that focusing caused, finally found "the great white lump." It was probably a cliff, and an immense one to be visible even as a blotch of color from this far out. He could just barely see a tiny black speck, no, two specks bobbing up and down on the waves before it, silhouetted against the white at the top of each crest.

"Ships?" he guessed.

"Can't think of what else it could be. Can you? But the question is," he continued without waiting for an answer, "what're they doing just sitting out there?"

"Fishing?" Darvish asked and winced as that brief enthusiasm sent a spike through his head.

"Could be. 'Cept there ain't nothin' to catch in there; too close to the current." He scowled and pushed back off the trail. "Captain'd best be told." Another scowl into the distance and he was gone.

"What are you looking at?" Chandra had done a finding for one of the sailors who'd lost a new awl and had been paid with a bright red silk shirt. She didn't usually care much about clothes but she'd never had to wear the same plain brown tunic for almost a nineday before. Her new wide sleeves billowed in the wind as she leaned over the rail beside Darvish.

"Ships," Darvish told her shortly, his attention more on keeping his stomach quiet.

She narrowed her eyes and leaned forward to the edge of safety. "Where?"

"That way." Aaron had come up on her other side and now he pointed. "By the white cliffs."

"How can you tell it's a cliff?" Darvish wanted to know, curious if Aaron could actually see clearly that far.

"What else could it be?"

Darvish shrugged and immediately regretted it.

"That doesn't look like much fun," Chandra observed when he'd finished and was wiping his mouth.

Darvish glared at her over the back of his hand. "And you only studied for five years to figure that out?"

An errant breeze crossed the distance between them and Chandra vigorously fanned the air in front of her nose. "Why do you do it if this sort of thing happens afterward?"

"Why do I do it? You mean why drink?"

"Yes. Why?"

He smiled viciously. "Because I do it so well." Then with a mocking bow he turned and walked away.

Chandra sighed and bit her lip. "I did it again, didn't I?"

"You ask too many questions," Aaron said quietly, his eyes still apparently locked on the ships in the distance.

As the sun rose and the mists burned off the land, the *Gryphon* drew closer to the white cliffs. The strange ships, slightly larger but still not large enough to be identified, remained where they were, riding the swell and waiting.

"Can they see us?" Darvish asked, back at the rail, a ship's biscuit in one hand and a wineskin dangling from the other. At that moment he was as close to contentment as he'd been in years. The court had receded into the past and he could do nothing about The Stone until they reached Tivolic.

"Aye, they can see us but no better than we can see them." The mate refused the offered wineskin.

"Could it be pirates, waiting to draw us into a trap?"

"Aye, could be. Could be ships in trouble. Be better to stay out here and avoid them entirely, but the captain don't want to miss the current. It's a bitch of a row without if the wind drops." He hacked and spit over the side. "Can't tell from here. We have to go in."

"But if it's pirates and you go in. . . ."

"We'll be in a wind abandoned heap of shit for sure. And if it ain't pirates, if they're in trouble and we don't go in that's the same kind of help we'll get when we need it."

"So it might be ships in trouble or it might be pirates pretending to be in trouble to lure you closer?"

"Aye." His massive hands twisted around the rail and the wood creaked alarmingly. "Sailed with a captain once who had a brass tube with circles of glass set in it. Forget what she called it, but when you held it to your eye you could see for miles. Wish we had one now."

Darvish chewed thoughtfully on the biscuit. "Was it magic?"

"Nay, just something she'd picked up in the east."

"I wonder if there's something magic can do. . . ."

"Aye, mumble a deal of nonsense and charge more'n you've got for it." The mate pursed his lips and rubbed at the sweat on his chest. After a moment he sighed. "Go ahead. Ask her. Even if she doesn't do any good, I don't imagine a slip of a thing like her could do much harm."

As Darvish headed back to the stern and their cabin, he noticed that the crew worked with one eye on the job at hand and the other on the ships in the distance. No one sang, growled orders were reinforced with muttered threats, and the loudest noises came from the *Gryphon* herself; the wind straining against her sail, the sea slapping against her hull. Darvish glanced up onto the sterncastle and saw the captain standing by the great sweep oar, one hand resting lightly on its secured end. Although a braided gray beard covered most of the captain's face, what little remained visible did not look pleased.

Better you than me, Darvish thought as he ducked and went into the cabin.

The hammocks were slung against the wall and Chandra lay on the bunk, hands behind her head, getting lost in the grain of the wood above her.

"Chandra, we need you to scry those ships."

She blinked and slowly came back to herself. "What?"

Darvish hooked the cabin's one small stool out of the corner it had been shoved into, pulled it over to the bunk, and sat down. "We need you to scry those ships," he repeated earnestly.

Chandra swung her legs out and sat up carefully, the bunk left her a little headroom but not enough for enthusiasm. "The ships by the coast?" she asked.

"Yes. We need to know if they're pirates soon enough for the captain to change course if he has to. And I might add, he doesn't want to."

"Well, I'd like to help. . . ." Darvish opened his mouth. Chandra stopped him with an upraised hand. "But I can't. I'd need a piece of the ships to scry them."

"Bugger the Nine!" Darvish stood, and kicked the stool aside. "We have to know what's going on." He slammed a fist into the cabin wall. "Where's Aaron? Pirates are just thieves in a boat, maybe he'll know how to identify them."

"I don't know."

"How can you *not* know? This isn't that big a ship."

Chandra looked up from buckling her sandals and frowned. "He wanted to be alone. I'm sure *you* could find him if you looked, *you're* the one with the soul-link, but Darvish," she stood and tossed her braid behind her shoulder, "there might be something else I can do."

He paused, bent over to clear the low lintel, and half turned. "What?"

"There's a spell, a distance seeing spell." Her chin came up. "I don't see so well in the distance, so I use it a lot. I could cast it and take a look at those ships."

"And how could you tell if they were pirates?" he asked, not unkindly.

"Well, there must be some way of telling."

"There is; they swarm screaming over the side, swords drawn and start hacking the crew to bloody bits." He grinned, shrugged, and came back into the cabin. "Could you cast it on someone else?"

She never had, but . . . "Yes, of course I could."

"Could you . . ." Darvish took a long pull on the wineskin while he tried to slap an idea into shape. "Could you cast it on *something* else?"

"What?"

Quickly, Darvish explained the brass tube the mate had mentioned. "So if you could make something like that, a distance tube that anyone could look through. . . ."

"It isn't a hard spell," Chandra said thoughtfully. She'd used it often enough that she could probably cast it in her sleep. A spell she knew less thoroughly she wouldn't dare to modify. Rajeet, her teacher, had warned her time after time to follow the parameters of a spell exactly, but new spells had to come from somewhere.

And Wizards of the Nine were not meant to be tied as other wizards were. She took a deep breath. "Get me a small piece of coal and a little bit of dry sand."

"Sand? Chandra, we're at sea!"

"Ask the cook," came Aaron's quiet voice from the door. "He banks his coals with sand."

"Aaron, that's brilliant!" Darvish turned the full force of his smile on the younger man, then pushed past him and ran for the bow.

"It is very clever," Chandra agreed.

"I notice details," Aaron muttered, trying to get his traitorous heart to start beating again after being caught in the vise of Darvish's smile. When he felt the heat had faded from his face, he pushed back his sunhood and came into the cabin. "*Can* you make a distance viewer?"

"Of course I can, I'm . . ." She stopped and wilted a little under Aaron's gaze. He didn't accuse, he didn't even look like he didn't believe her; he just looked. "I think I can," she amended with a sigh. "It should work."

"Is it dangerous?"

She opened her mouth to say no, then closed it again. Magic worked through well defined rules to focus power into something entirely new which—and realistically she had to admit there was a slight chance things could go wrong—might not hold it. "There's a possibility of danger. . . ."

"Then why do it?"

This time there was only one answer. She could say "to help the ship" or "because Darvish asked me to," but she didn't think Aaron would believe either. "To prove that I can."

Aaron grinned. Chandra returned it. Just for a moment they understood each other perfectly.

"All right, I got the coal and I got the sand and the cook thinks I'm out of my mind," Darvish rushed back into the cabin and his excitement made the tiny room seem smaller still. "Anything else?"

Chandra took the dish of sand and the pieces of coal and placed them carefully in the center of the stool. "I need a tube; it has to be fairly stiff, but it can't be metal. . . ."

"Why not? The mate talked about a brass tube."

"If I mark on a brass tube with charcoal, the symbols will rub right off and as soon as they're gone, so's the spell. I need some-

thing hollow that charcoal will stick to that's about this long." She
held her hands about six inches apart.

"I had thought of the perfect item," Darvish waggled his eyebrows rakishly, "but it turned out to be too big."

"And she'd have to remove it," Aaron put in dryly from the
bunk, where he'd tucked himself to get out of the way. "You
wouldn't like that much."

"What . . . ?" Chandra looked from one to the other. "Oh." She
scowled up at the prince, who winked. "Is that all you ever think
abou . . . no, it isn't! Give me that!" She pulled the wineskin
down off his shoulder and shook it.

"Hey!"

"Never mind!" She shoved it back into his hands. "Finish it!"

A little bemused but willing to oblige, Darvish did as he was
told.

"Now cut the neck off, here," she drew a line on the leather
just below the thickened spout with her thumbnail, "and here." A
second line was drawn just above the bell.

A few moments later Chandra peered through the narrow end
of the flared tube and said, "Now get out."

"Get out?"

She put her hand in the small of Darvish's back and pushed,
waving Aaron up from the bunk and out the door in the same motion. "I need to be alone to work. You're too much of a distraction."

Darvish beamed back over his shoulder at her. "That's the
nicest thing you've ever said to me." Then he followed Aaron out
onto the deck. As she pulled the door closed, she heard him say,
"My sword, your brains, and her talent . . . that wizard with The
Stone doesn't stand a chance."

It could have been the wine talking, it *probably* was the wine
talking, but it was nice to hear anyway.

"It's a what?" The mate looked suspiciously at the piece of
wineskin dwarfed by Darvish's hand.

"A distance viewer." Darvish held it out to him again, his
thumb and forefinger carefully in the places that Chandra had indicated.

"It's a chunk of One abandoned wineskin with black marks
on it."

"Yes it is," Darvish agreed. "But it's also a distance viewer."

The mate snorted and spat, his opinion obviously clear.

"I thought you wanted a closer look at those ships?"

"Aye."

"This will give it to you. You saw me look through it, it won't hurt you."

"Ain't afraid of it."

"Then take it. I've seen the ships, but I don't know what I'm seeing." At his most charming, Darvish could persuade a frog to sing. "Just try it. What have you got to lose? Hold it here and look through the narrow end."

The mate grunted and, obviously humoring the other man, placed his fingers by Darvish's and lifted the cylindrical bit of leather, still smelling strongly of fermented grape, to his eye.

"Nine Above and One Below," he breathed. Through the flaring end of the wineskin he could see the ships they'd watched through most of the morning only now, instead of a vague silhouette impossible to identify, he saw two masts, the sails down but not secured, a hull narrower and higher than the merchant ship, an anchor rope running taut down into the sea. The second ship could have been cast from an identical mold. "Nine Above, they're navy!"

He spun away from the rail and bounded for the sterncastle, waving the distance viewer over his head like a very small and grubby flag. "Captain! Captain!"

"What's that all about?" Chandra wondered, jolted out of her fit of the sulks by the mate's strange behavior. Darvish had insisted *he* present the viewer to the mate;

"Please, let me. You're a wizard, you have other skills."

"You think if I gave it to him he wouldn't take it."

Darvish looked down at the mutilated wineskin. "Well, yes."

He hadn't exactly said she was tactless, but he'd implied it. It hadn't helped her mood to realize he was probably right.

Darvish raised a questioning brow at Aaron, but the thief only shrugged. "I have no idea," the prince admitted. "But before we go and find out, let me see your hand."

"My hand?"

"Your palm, let me see it." He smiled down at her. "Aaron isn't the only one who notices things, you know. You've been holding your left hand like it hurts you since you came out of the cabin."

"It's nothing."

"Let me see."

The tone said, *let me help,* and it was the kind of voice her father had used when she was young and had hurt herself, a voice he'd used before her mother had died and he'd. . . . But Darvish was weak, nothing like the strong man her father had been then, much more like the man he'd become.

"Hand wounds are the most difficult to tend yourself," Darvish said reasonably. "You're going to need both hands if we're to get The Stone."

He had a point. Chandra turned her palm up and held it out.

An angry red circle, both like and unlike a burn, cut across the mound of her thumb and curved around the base of her fingers.

"Aaron? Do we have any salve left?"

Aaron, who'd stood quietly in the background through the testing of the distance viewer, nodded and said, "A little." He slipped off to get it.

"What happened?" Darvish asked, gently flexing the fingers. The bones of Chandra's hands were so tiny and delicate they reminded him of bird bones and her wrist slid with room to spare through a circle of his fingers.

Chandra shrugged. "I had to block the open end to set the spell. I guess," she added ruefully, "I shouldn't have used my hand."

"I guess not," Darvish agreed solemnly, unsure of her reaction if she laughed.

They stood awkwardly for a moment almost but not quite holding hands.

His hands are warm. And rough, not like a courtier's hands at all. And they were so large, Chandra realized, that he could probably completely enclose her fist in his. *Why doesn't he say something?*

Darvish couldn't think of anything to say. All the glib and clever phrases he used at court didn't apply to someone who'd become a friend; although it was a strange and tentative sort of friendship, really more like comrades-in-arms. He'd never had one of those before either, well, not before Aaron and he wasn't likely to end up holding Aaron's hand. Not if Aaron had anything to say about it.

"Dar." They both jumped and shot Aaron looks so identically relieved that he had to hide a grin. He held out the squat clay pot. "There's a little left in the bottom."

"Right." Darvish shoved Chandra's hand in Aaron's direction. "You do it, I'm going to see what the captain has decided. We

seem to have changed course." He smiled strangely down at the
wizard, spun on his bare heel and almost trotted off.

"What was that all about?" Chandra wondered, the lines
smoothing out of her forehead as the salve soothed the pain out of
her hand.

"I think he likes you," Aaron told her, his voice expressionless,
his heart strangely heavy.

Chandra remembered a number of the things the crowd had
shouted as the dowry procession had made its way to the palace.
"I can't see why," she sniffed.

A moment later they followed Darvish to the sterncastle where
a great sweep oar had been untied and the two steersmen had
turned the *Gryphon* to the very edge of the wind. The captain still
peered through the distance viewer, his legs braced against the
roll of the deck and his gaze locked on the navy ships. When he
lowered his arm, he stood quiet for a moment longer, then nodded
once at Chandra and said, "My compliments, Most Wise." It was
the first time anyone on board had used the honorific. "You have
saved us from a great disaster."

Behind him, sunlight gleamed on gold teeth. The mate beamed
as though it were all his idea.

"You have my thanks, Most Wise," he continued. "For the
losses you have saved us, your passage price will be refunded.
Now, about this viewer. . . ." His eyes glittered. "Will it work for
anyone?"

"Yes, of course," she answered, tossing her head. "The spell is
in the tube, but it will only last as long as the symbols on the outside do, so be careful. Why?"

"If you had a brass tube and proper etching tools?"

Chandra shrugged, she was getting a little tired of explaining.
"Then it would last a lot longer. Not forever, but longer. Now,"
she crossed her arms and frowned, daring him to cut her off again,
"why are you running away from navy ships?"

The captain's expression froze and the glitter grew harder. Behind him, gold teeth disappeared. The mate flexed his massive
arms and waited for orders.

Aaron and Darvish stepped up to stand beside her and Darvish,
who had been trying to think of a tactful way to ask the same
question, muttered, "You do like to live dangerously, don't you?"

The silence grew.

The two steersmen, the captain, and the mate. Not completely impossible odds if it comes to it, Darvish thought.

There was an almost imperceptible change in the captain's expression and Aaron knew the balance had tipped. As he didn't know which way, he kicked out the fulcrum. "They're smugglers," he said. "There's four bags of ground kerric nut in with the spices."

"But kerric nut kills!" Chandra exclaimed.

"In large enough doses," Aaron agreed.

"Well, I'm glad we've got that settled." Darvish spread empty hands and grinned his patently irresistible grin. "We'd prefer to stay clear of the Ytaili navy ourselves."

The captain glared at Aaron. Aaron stared steadily back. Although it was difficult to tell for certain, down in the depths of the captain's beard, one corner of his mouth may have twitched in a rueful acknowledgment. "I bet you would," was all he said.

"Captain, Sir!"

"What is it, Ensign?"

The ensign leaned as far over the edge of the fighting top as she dared. "They've changed course, Sir."

The captain of the *Sea Hawk* turned and, shading his eyes, peered in the direction of their quarry. The ship, facing them dead on all morning, now angled about forty-five degrees to port, paralleling the coast rather than heading straight for it.

"Sink the Nine," he swore. "Most Wise!"

Both wizards looked up at the bellow.

"Is that soul-link still on board?"

The Wizard of the Fourth closed her eyes for a moment in concentration. "It is," she sighed. She had come only because the king had ordered it. Ships made her sick.

"Then the waiting is over." The captain rubbed his hands in anticipation. *Pretend you're in trouble, let them get in close, then take them.* He hated that sort of order. The *Sea Hawk* was meant to swoop down into battle, not sit like the cheese in a trap.

"So there's honor amongst thieves after all," Chandra observed, picking at a sliver of wood.

"Not at all," came the answer from the shadowed depths of Aaron's sunhood.

"Then why . . ."

"Are we alive?" Aaron finished. "The captain figures he can use us." It had been a calculated risk mentioning the smuggling. "He could have easily decided if we weren't for him we were against him," he explained. "Now he knows whose side we're on."

"They're raising their sails," Darvish called out, running up fully armed. "They're coming after us."

"We need a wind," the mate added, right behind him. "The captain wants to see you, Most Wise."

The captain wanted a wind. "One in my sails, one that they'll have to tack across to reach us. Can you give me such a wind?"

Chandra pulled at the end of her braid and thought about it. Gentle breezes to cool a garden or a sleeping room, she'd called many times. A wind was a difference in intensity not form, easier in that than the distance viewer. She tossed her braid behind her shoulder. "Of course I can."

"What do you need?"

"Another piece of coal, a dagger," she held her hands apart, "with a blade about this long, a ribbon," the distance between her hands lengthened, "about this long and," she looked down at her feet, "a circle of the deck off limits to everyone but me."

"They have a wizard." The Wizard of the Seventh held his face into the freshening wind and sniffed. "This wind is power called."

"Well, turn it," commanded the *Sea Hawk*'s captain.

"They have a wizard," Chandra gasped. "They're trying to turn the wind."

"Can they do it?" Darvish asked, taking a long pull on the wineskin that dangled from his sword hand.

"I don't know." Her brow furrowed and the ribbon, beginning to tangle, flew straight and true once more.

The *Gryphon* surged forward; the sail belled taut.

"I thought I ordered you to turn that wind."

"It isn't as easy as all that," the wizard panted. "Their wizard is *very* powerful and responds to everything I do by pulling in yet more power."

"I don't care what you have to do," the captain roared. He had never failed in a commission for his king, and he had no intention of starting now. "Stop that ship!"

*   *   *

The wind rose and above the *Gryphon* the sky grew black.

"It's too much," the captain screamed over the protests of his ship. "The mast is about to come down. Stop it!"

"I can't!" Chandra's hair, free of the braid, whipped around her. "There's too much power!"

"Why are you stopping?" The captain glared down at the Wizard of the Seventh. "I thought your god controlled the winds."

"Storms," corrected the exhausted wizard from the deck. He raised a shaky arm and pointed over the captain's shoulder. "And it's in His hands now."

Chandra's ribbon tied itself in a knot.

The storm broke.

The *Gryphon* bucked and wallowed as frantic figures crawled over her, lowering her sail, securing lines and hatches.

"Get below!" The mate dragged Chandra to her feet and thrust her at Darvish. "The last thing we need now is landers on deck!"

"I can walk!" Chandra protested with what little energy she had remaining.

Darvish ignored her and lurched toward their cabin. He grabbed at a line as the ship rolled and a wave sucked at his feet, then dove through the door that Aaron had wrestled open. Shoving Chandra onto the bunk, he lunged back at the door and, adding his strength to Aaron's, dragged it closed.

Inside the tiny room, it was like being in a drum as the wind and waves beat at the ship, trying to drive her down. Strained timbers shrieked and moaned. They couldn't talk. They could barely think.

Darvish emptied the wineskin he carried. Then he sat, wedged in a corner, and worked the leather in his hands. Pulled it. Twisted it. Waiting. He hated waiting. He didn't do it well.

Aaron, his feet braced against the bunk, his back against the wall, sat wrapped in the void and waited to die. He was good at it. He'd been doing it for the last five years.

"If you truly want your cousin's death, you're not going about it the right way."

"Any death will do now, Faharra."

He shoved the small voice that dared suggest he couldn't die while Darvish needed him back behind the walls and drowned it out with Ruth's screams.

Chandra turned her back on the two men and chewed her lip, blinking rapidly to clear the heat building behind her eyes. She'd failed. She'd never failed before. *She* was a Wizard of the Nine.

The ship dropped out from under them. Even Aaron cried out as it slammed back up to meet them as they fell.

"That is it!" Darvish pulled himself to his feet and settled his sword on his hips.

"What are you doing?" Chandra yelled. She could hardly hear herself over the howl of the storm.

The prince unhooked his shield, slipped his arm through the strapping, crashed into the wall, and said in a sudden lull, "I'm going out for a drink."

"You're what?" Chandra couldn't believe her ears, then the storm struck again and nearly threw her from the bunk.

Aaron dove for Darvish's legs, but the deck heaved and he grabbed at air.

The wind whipped the heavy wooden door out of Darvish's hands and slammed it up against the outside wall. A smaller man would have been pulled from his feet, but Darvish only laughed and staggered into the storm.

Aaron scrambled upright and, clinging to the wall, somehow made his way outside. The world had become a seething mass of gray, clouds and wind and rain and sea, impossible to tell where one ended and the other began. He squinted and could just make out a darker mass by the rail and beyond that a line of black. Darvish? And land? With arms made strong from a thousand midnight climbs, he inched his way forward, hand over hand, scarred chest muscles protesting as more than once they held his entire weight, feet having been swept or blown out from under him.

The ship rolled and he watched the rail and the prince-shaped shadow beside it, slowly, majestically, go under. Then the *Gryphon,* like a great dog, shook herself upright again. By some fluke of the storm, he could see that section of the rail clearly. It was empty.

Aaron let go of his hold and took one step, two; by three he was running. Then the storm picked him up and dashed him against the rail. He sucked in salt water, coughed, and pulled himself to his feet.

Someone grabbed at his arm.

"Are you crazy?" he screamed at Chandra.

"Are you?" she shrieked back.

Then the ocean reached up and took them both.

Barricaded into her bunk, the Wizard of the Fourth wanted to die and it didn't help that the Wizard of the Seventh kept declaring in a smug voice that no one ever died of seasickness. She could care less that the soul-link had left the *Gryphon* and not if the king himself commanded it would she leave what she *knew* was her deathbed to give the information to the captain.

Chapter Ten

The sunrobe tangled around Aaron's legs, wrapped about him like a shroud, and he struggled desperately to be free of it. The world had no up nor down, only surging gray waters that threw him end over end, a giant's plaything with no will or direction of his own. His lungs screaming for air, he fought free of the clinging fabric and, able to use his legs at last, kicked frantically for the surface. Just as he thought he must breathe or die, that even water would be better than the burning pressure behind his ribs, his head broke through into air.

Rain and spray drove into his face, alternating sweet water and salt. He gasped and coughed but managed to ride to the crest of the next two waves. To his right he thought he saw a dark circle of water; Chandra's head perhaps or even Dar's, he had no way of knowing how close or far the prince might be, only that he was not yet ten body lengths away. Then a seething white wall crashed down upon him and again he fought the ocean for his life.

"Well, if you really want to die, young Aaron my lad, why don't you just stop fighting?" The Faharra of memory spread scrawny hands. *"No, wait, pardon me, that would be giving up and One forbid you should give up."*

Another gasp for air. Another wave hurling him deep and around and over. He could no longer tell if the constant roar came from the storm or from inside his head. The pouch at his waist—their remaining money and his tools—grew heavier and heavier, dragging him down. He clawed at the water, broke free again, and slammed into a spinning body with enough force to throw stars against the water and knock him limp.

For an instant they were tangled, arms and legs moving together in a violent dance, then the storm caught them up and swirled them apart.

"Dar . . ." Aaron realized it almost too late, and just managed to hook a finger under a bit of leather harness. The larger man was limp, the weight of his sword pulling against the body's natural tendency to float, only the strength of the waves keeping him from sinking to the bottom. Aaron couldn't tell if the prince moved on his own or if his limbs thrashed about at the mercy of the storm. He could only hold on and struggle to keep them both on top of the waves that lifted them and threw them toward the shore. And he could only hope that the ocean hadn't already won, hope that he didn't drag a corpse by his side.

I don't care for him, he told the god of his father. *I don't care. There's no reason for him to die.*

Almost contemptuously, the ocean spit Chandra up on shore. She cried out as a rock gouged into her knee, grateful to have the air to cry out with. The waves still sucked and pulled at her legs and she knew she had to move, that the ocean could take her back as easily as it had let her go, but she didn't have the strength. Water ran from her nose as she coughed and choked. Her arms and legs felt as though the bones had dissolved and washed away.

A wave surged beneath her, lifted her and she clutched desperately at the rocky shore, not caring that sharp edges and broken shells cut into her fingers. Panic pushed her forward, scrambling on her hands and knees, head bent under the weight of sodden hair, eyes half closed against the sheets of rain that continued to lash her face.

When at last she thought she should be safe, when only the spray could reach her, she collapsed, cheek pressed into the rock.

That was when the terror struck, when she realized she could have died. Not all her wizardry could have saved her and even the bright and shining father of her childhood would have been helpless before the fury of the storm. She started to shake and couldn't stop, her teeth clattering in her head like loose pebbles in a bag. She couldn't catch her breath, her heart raced, and without her willing it her knees curled up to her chest.

One Below, I could have died. . . .

The warm lines of tears brought her back. She was a Wizard of the Nine, and wizards don't cry. She'd vowed that at ten and she clung to it now. Breathing deeply through her nose, she forced her body to calmness, clenched her jaw to still her traitorous teeth, straightened her legs, and sat up.

The world was gray from her feet to the horizon; rocks and water and rain and sky. She couldn't see the ship. She couldn't see much beyond the great gouts of spray that veiled the shore. She'd never felt so alone.

And then something heaved itself up out of the water.

The scream broke through before Chandra realized it was Aaron. He stood, stumbled, and fell back to his knees. One arm stretched out behind him, he crawled for land.

Afterward, Chandra couldn't remember how she'd gotten to Aaron's side, how she'd dared go back into the waves she'd so narrowly escaped. She could only remember grabbing Darvish's other arm and the two of them pulling his dead weight up onto a gravel beach. Together, they heaved him over on his stomach and Aaron began to push the water from his lungs, his lips moving in what Chandra assumed was a prayer.

An eternity later, Darvish gasped, gagged, and vomited bile.

They waited out the rest of the storm under the dubious shelter of a rock overhang. Darvish staggered to it mostly under his own power and then lapsed into semiconsciousness, moaning softly from time to time. They found out why when Chandra lifted the prince's head into her lap—he'd begun to thrash and she didn't want him spilling what little brains he might have left out on the rock—and her palms came away red with blood.

The cut wasn't large, but it crowned a nasty bit of swelling that covered almost the entire back of Darvish's head.

The storm ended about midafternoon, almost as suddenly as it had started. One moment they were pinned in their shelter by sheets of rain and driving wind, the next a broad beam of sunlight bathed the shore in golden warmth and behind the scattering clouds the sky was brightly blue.

Aaron pulled himself to his feet and staggered out onto the rapidly drying stones. His wet clothes clung to him and he shivered. "We can't stay here," he said wearily.

Chandra crawled out from under the overhang and sat back on her heels. The sky still glowered an ugly purplish gray to the north and neither the *Gryphon* nor the two ships chasing her were in sight. "Are we stranded?" she asked, her voice sounding thin and tired.

"They won't be back for us."

"Aaron, what should we do?"

She sounded young and scared. Aaron shuddered. Ruth had sounded much the same.

"Aaron, what should we do?"

That had started it all. He heard her scream. He heard the whip come down.

"Aaron?" Chandra touched him lightly on the arm and he jerked away and almost fell, his expression equally twisted with guilt and pain. She didn't understand. He was the strong one. "Are you all right?"

He managed a breath and slammed the wall back into place, ignoring the cracks and weakened areas because he had to. Later, he could strengthen them. Later. Now, Dar and Chandra needed him and that need was weakening the walls and how had it happened? He hadn't let anyone need him for so long. . . .

"Aaron?"

"We can't stay here," he said again, what remained of the walls firmly in place.

Somehow, working together, they moved Darvish back away from the sea into a small sheltered hollow crowned on two sides with spindly wind-warped trees. His head had stopped bleeding, but he was never more than half conscious and when they got him lying down again, he lost his hold on that.

"We'll need water," Aaron panted, blinking sweat from his eyes. He skinned off his wet shirt and spread it in the sun to dry. "And a fire, and food." After a moment's hesitation, he unbuckled the pouch and laid it by the shirt.

Chandra waved a hand back past the trees. "I can make a fire once the wood dries and call water, too." She sighed, and added, "If there's any so close to the sea to call." Even out of sight, the crash of the surf was a steady background noise. "I don't know what to do about food." Her eyes dropped to Darvish. "Or him."

"I'll take care of the food," Aaron said shortly. "The gods will have to take care of him." Then he climbed out of the hollow and back toward the shore, the scars on his chest standing out in angry red circles.

It hurts him to care, Chandra realized, stripping off her own wet clothes and spreading them out to dry. *I don't know why, but it hurts him to care.*

She looked down at Darvish and saw he was shivering. Squatting by his side, she began working at the straps and buckles of his harness, slipping the sword belt out from under him and laying the whole thing to one side. It surprised her a little how heavy it was; had the sea been any less violent she had no doubt it would have taken him straight to the bottom. His harness clear, she pulled off his sodden half boots and worked him carefully out of his shirt. Without even thinking of what she was doing she picked the knots out of his trouser laces, hooked her fingers in the waistband, and tugged the wet cotton down over his hips.

Oh, she thought a moment later. *So that's what it looks like. How . . . bizarre.*

When Aaron returned, he carried a dozen or so oysters and a handful of oval rocks from the beach wrapped up in the wet bundle of his sunrobe. He'd found the robe floating just off shore like a great undulating mat of cream colored seaweed and waded out to retrieve it. It was just at the edge of the soul-link. As he'd bent forward to scoop it up, the pressure had begun to build behind his eyes and he'd hurriedly retreated, dragging the robe through the water until he reached safety.

He stood at the edge of the hollow and looked down. Tented in the silken strands of her drying hair, the ends just brushing the ground all around her, Chandra sat cross-legged, staring into a hollow she'd scooped in the stony soil. Aaron could see the tension in her hands, tendons ridged and spread fingers straining, and could just barely hear—no, feel—a low murmur of sound repeated over and over. Wizardry. He shot a glance at the sky, but it remained clear. Then he realized that her hair was all she wore and he jerked his gaze away.

To Darvish. Who wore less, his hair having been cropped short back at the palace.

Aaron's knees trembled and he sat, quickly, before he fell. He'd seen the prince a hundred times since the night he'd failed to get the emerald, but that didn't seem to matter now. He couldn't go down there. His mouth grew dry and sweat prickled up and down his sides. He could feel the heat of the sun on his shoulders like warm hands and could see it touching all down the length of Darvish's body. He swallowed hard and closed his eyes.

A pair of men, bound to the same stake, writhed in the rising fire. Both had been warriors, one had a wife and six children, but they'd been caught together by the priests and condemned to the pyre. Aaron's father had made him watch until the blackened ruins had resembled nothing human. He'd been seven.

He opened his eyes again.

Suddenly, Chandra sagged forward. The bottom of the bowl-shaped depression before her darkened as water welled up from its center. The water level rose, lapped at the symbols scratched around the edge, and stopped. She smiled down on it proudly, despite the pounding behind her eyes that threatened to bounce them from her head. The water had been deep and she'd had to focus a painful amount of power to bring it up.

When she'd caught her breath, she leaned forward and scooped up a handful. It was so cold it made her teeth ache. This was what her father wanted to take from her; he wanted to force her into a marriage that would weaken her until she no longer had the strength necessary to tap the kind of power magic of this complexity needed. Perhaps—the thought pushed her heart up into her throat—perhaps with no strength of his own, he resented hers. No. She shook the water off her hand and wished she could as easily shake off the thought. Lower lip between her teeth, she caught up her nearly dry hair and began to braid it.

A twist of her head to catch a loose strand and she spotted Aaron up on the ridge. He was staring down at Darvish, hunger and horror chasing each other across his face. Chandra frowned and her fingers stopped moving as she tried to understand. As though he'd become aware of her gaze, Aaron turned, emotions shoved hastily away, and looked right at her.

The color came up on his pale skin like a sunrise, red and hot. It took Chandra a moment to realize why he blushed.

"Oh," she said and hoped her darker skin hid the answering flush as she reached for her dry clothes. Aba's warnings about "nasty boys" sounded in her ears and she hushed it sternly. She knew she was in no danger from Aaron. And Darvish, well, she'd be in no danger from Darvish either even if he were conscious. It was just that with Aaron looking at her in such a way, she wasn't . . . comfortable. And she'd always been comfortable in her skin before.

She tied her trousers, tucked the shirt in, and checked on Aaron. He didn't look ready to move. Picking up Darvish's clothes, she took a step toward the prince.

This is stupid, she decided suddenly. "Hey!" she called. "I'm going to need help getting him dressed, he's too heavy to wrestle with alone."

Aaron swallowed. *This is stupid,* he decided. *This is weak.* His head came up and his jaw set. *Nothing controls me like this, nothing.*

"The old pain still rules your life."

"SHUT UP, Faharra!"

He scooped up the sunrobe and, every muscle in his body tight, walked down into the hollow.

"Darvish? Can you drink this?"

Darvish peered suspiciously into Chandra's scrying bowl. It had been tucked into the deep pocket of the wizard's trousers and was now the only container they had. "What is it?" he croaked.

"Just water."

"I need wine."

"You need water." She balanced his head against her chest and put the bowl to his lips. "Drink."

"I need wine."

"Well, it's the middle of the night and we're in the middle of nowhere, thanks to you, so where am I supposed to get wine?"

"I don't know." His head pounded so he couldn't think. "You're a wizard. Make some."

"It doesn't work that way." She let his head fall back on the folded sunrobe, not really caring if it was thick enough to cushion the wound. This was all his fault and the first thing he did was whimper about wine. Some prince.

"Aaron?" Darvish tried to look into the flickering light by the fire, but, the small movement became a violent jerk, his head whipping about out of control. "Aaron?" Aaron would understand.

"I'm here."

"Aaron, I need a drink." *That's not my voice,* Darvish protested silently. *I don't sound like that.* But those were his words, so it had to be his voice.

"Drink water." Worry sharpened his tone more than he'd intended. Aaron had hoped the prince would sleep through until morning even though he knew the craving would be stronger then. A full night's sleep would have given Darvish additional energy to fight it with. He supposed he should be grateful that Darvish had woken up at all, given the crack he'd taken on the back of the head.

"It isn't fair," Darvish moaned into the sunrobe. He hurt all over and he needed a drink. A drink would make him feel better. "It isn't fair," he moaned again.

Chandra made a disgusted noise and joined Aaron by the fire. "It isn't the bump that's making him like this, is it?"

"No." Aaron threw another branch onto the fire. They didn't need it for warmth, the night was sultry, almost as warm as it would have been in Ischia over the heart of the volcano. The fire was a comfort, and a dubious one at that.

"It's the wine, isn't it?"

"Yes."

"When we get going in the morning . . ."

"Going?"

"To rescue The Stone."

"Oh, right." Aaron hadn't thought of The Stone in some time. He listened. Darvish's breathing had lengthened into sleep again. "We won't be going anywhere in the morning."

"Because of the bump on his head?"

"No. Because of the wine."

"Here, Wizard? This is where they went over?"

The Wizard of the Fourth peered at the map. It all looked like lines on parchment to her, but the king had listened intently to the Wizard of the Seventh's explanation of the storm, had questioned the captain of the *Sea Hawk* at length and seemed to know what he was talking about. "Yes, Gracious Majesty," she agreed, "that is where I felt the soul-link leave the boat."

"Ship," snarled the *Sea Hawk*'s captain in the background. She ignored him.

"Then why, by the Nine and One, didn't you tell the captain at the time?" King Harith slammed his fist down on the map, rocking the table and making the candle flames dance.

"The captain was endeavoring to save his boat and his crew, Gracious Majesty." She drew herself up to her not inconsiderable height. "I did not think it opportune at the time."

"I don't pay you to think! I pay you for results!"

"I am a Wizard of the Fourth," she reminded him. "I belong in His chamber, Gracious Majesty, not bobbing about the ocean in a boat."

"Then go back to your bloody chamber!"

With a slightly less than gracious bow, she swept by him and out of the room.

"Wizards," he muttered to himself. "Use them when you have to and ignore them the rest of the time. Now then," a blunt finger tapped the parchment, "if they went over here," he frowned intently, "and if they survived, they'll make for the south trade road and they'll have to go through this area," he laid his hand down flat, "here."

"No. I don't want it." Darvish tried to push the bowl away, but his hand shook so badly he couldn't even make contact.

"Drink it anyway," Aaron told him. They'd been getting as much water into him as they could; he didn't know if it was helping.

Darvish drank; he didn't have the strength to avoid it, but a good portion dribbled out the sides of his mouth. His stomach clenched around it and he hoped he wasn't going to be sick again, it hurt too much. He felt terrible. He couldn't stop shaking. He was so cold.

They used his shirt for a pillow so the sunrobe could be spread out over him. Even the slight weight of the thin cotton seemed to mute the shaking. Aaron stayed in the shade as much as he could.

Aaron threw himself over the thrashing prince, but his weight was too little to do much good and Darvish's flailing arms and legs were printing new bruises up and down the length of his body. They had no way to restrain him and he had to be restrained before he broke something.

Suddenly, Chandra dropped her knees beside them, narrowly avoided a random blow, and tossed the contents of her scrying bowl in Darvish's contorted face. When it seemed to have no effect, she slapped him as hard as she could, and screamed, "Sleep!"

Darvish bucked one final time, his back arched painfully high, then slowly he relaxed.

"It won't last long," she explained to Aaron as they caught their breath. "Four hours at most. He's not enough in his right mind for it to hold."

Aaron carefully straightened Darvish's right arm. "Then hopefully four hours will be long enough."

"I'm not eating that. It's a rat."

Aaron didn't look up from messily disemboweling the small animal with Darvish's sword. "It's a ground squirrel."

"It looks like a rat," Chandra insisted.

Aaron shrugged. "There's always more raw oysters and steamed seaweed."

"Rat. Hummph. You're lucky you're sleeping through this," she muttered in Darvish's direction.

"You can't keep me prisoner here! I want to get up!"

"So get up." Aaron moved back and watched as Darvish actually made it to his feet, where he stood and swayed like a tree in a gale.

"You see!" he panted. "There's nothing wrong with me!"

His eyes were red, even through the strengthened illusion. Huge circles beneath them were darkly purple.

"You're hiding it, aren't you?" He took two swift steps to Aaron and hauled the smaller man up by his shirt front. Aaron breathed shallowly through his mouth. Darvish had been sweating heavily and he stank. "Where is it? Where are you hiding the wine?"

"There isn't any wine."

"There's always wine!"

"Not this time," Aaron said coldly. He felt Darvish's arm tremble and he kept his balance easily as the prince thrust him away.

Darvish squeezed his eyes shut tight and wrapped his arms around his gut as sudden cramps twisted his insides into knots. When they were over, he felt Aaron's gaze and opened his eyes.

"I'm sorry," he panted. "Did I hurt you?"

"No."

"You shouldn't be out of bed. Healer'll skin me if those blisters break."

Another spasm hit and he whimpered with the pain.

"Lie back down, Dar."

Yes, that was what he needed. He needed to lie down. Lying down made it a little better. He fell to his knees and crawled back into the depression his body had made in the ground, scrabbling the sunrobe around his shoulders.

Hot tears rolled down his cheeks. "I am sorry," he said again.

Aaron nodded, once. "I know."

"Was he drunk all the time?" Chandra asked, poking the fire and watching the sparks rise into the night.

"No. Once or twice a week. I heard it used to be worse."

"Before you came?"

Aaron lifted a shoulder and dropped it again. "Maybe. He drank all the time though. From the moment he woke until he went to sleep. He drank in the bath. He drank on the way to the training yards. He drank on the way back."

"And it made you angry." In all the days since she'd met him, Aaron had never made a speech that long.

Angry. Aaron hadn't been angry, not really angry, in five years. Anger. It certainly filled the void. "Not then," he said quietly, looking across the fire to where Darvish slept fitfully, "but now."

Chandra sighed and tossed her braid back behind her shoulder. "Don't you just feel like going off and finding The Stone yourself? Just leaving him?"

"No. Not this time."

"Three times pays for all."

"You never said that, Faharra."

The memory snorted. *"I'm saying it now."*

"But, Father . . ."

"No, Shahin. I have said my final word on this. You may leave with your wife if you choose to do so. I am remaining in Ischia."

Only by a great effort of will did Shahin manage to hold his tongue and when they had bowed from the king's chamber he turned on the lord chancellor.

"You were no help at all," he growled.

The lord chancellor looked confused. "My prince?"

"No one will think you a coward if you leave the city, Most Exalted." He mimicked the older man's voice. "Of course no one will think him a coward, no one knows anything about what's going on. But you *must* have known the effect that would have on him."

"I'm—I'm sorry, my prince." The lord chancellor rubbed at his temples and took a deep breath. "I wasn't thinking. I'd just come from the viewing platforms. . . ."

"And. . . ."

"The level has risen another body length."

"Can the wizards hold it?"

"For now, my prince, but. . . ." He spread plump hands wide.

"But we haven't much time."

The lord chancellor bowed his head in agreement.

"Make them shut up!" Darvish flung himself forward, his eyes wide and panicked. "Make those One abandoned peacocks shut up!"

"I will." Aaron laid his hand on Darvish's shoulder. The skin felt like it was on fire. "Lie down."

"You make them shut up!"

"I will. Lie down."

Chewing his lip, Darvish slumped back and raised his hands up before his face. "They're rotting away," he howled. "I touched The Stone and they're rotting away! I didn't mean it, Father! Make it stop!"

"Chandra, sleep him again."

The young wizard pulled at the end of her braid. "Again? It's dangerous."

Aaron watched a pulse pound in Darvish's temple, the blood banging up into it with frightening force. "So is this," he said. "Sleep him."

Frowning, Chandra pushed the prince back into oblivion, watching the tension leave Aaron's shoulders as it left Darvish's, hearing both hearts slow to a less punishing beat.

"He's draining your strength through the soul-link to help survive this, you know."

"I know."

"I think I could block him. . . ." She let the offer trail into silence, reading her answer in the silver-stone of Aaron's eyes. *Fine,* she thought. *But if you both die and leave me here alone, I'll never forgive either of you.*

"What is it? I don't want it!"

"It's an egg. Eat it."

"I don't want it. The sun's too hot."

"Eat it anyway."

"It's raw!" Darvish protested. "How can you force me to eat a raw egg?"

"So drink it." Aaron tipped the bowl between Darvish's lips.

Darvish choked, swallowed, and seconds later brought it back up again.

For the first time in four days, Chandra felt some sympathy for him. She'd have done much the same thing. Raw gull eggs were beyond what anyone should be expected to stomach.

He drank as much water as they could get to him and just before sunset, he managed to keep an egg down. A little while later he managed another.

*   *   *

"Darvish?" Chandra raised her head and peered sleepily out through the veil of her hair. Darvish, hollow cheeked and gray, squatted by the ruins of last night's fire, tearing at the charred remains of a gull. "Darvish?" She pushed her hair back and sat up. "Are you all right?"

He smiled sheepishly, swallowed, and said, "Yes, I think so." He waved the piece of meat still in his hand. "Uh, this is really good."

"Thanks, Aaron brought down two with his sling. We stuffed the body cavity with wild plums. Are you sure you're all right?"

Darvish flushed and lowered his eyes. "Yeah. I'm sure."

"Does Aaron know."

"No, he was gone when I woke up."

"He won't be far."

"No." Darvish touched the edge of the soul-link. "I guess not." He wanted to apologize, or explain, or say thank you, or something. All the things he'd done before—the drinking, the whoring—seemed to culminate in what had happened here and all the shame he'd ever felt—all the shame he'd ever denied while searching for a life that his father would notice—made its presence felt. This morning, with only vague memories of the last few days, he felt more ashamed than he would have believed was possible. It tied his tongue in knots.

Chandra watched him, her head to one side, with a speculative, almost neutral, expression. This man's weakness had been responsible for her near drowning and had kept him flat on his back and raving for three days. Because of him, she'd been battered, cast adrift, and forced to fend for herself. She'd been furious with him, disgusted that he could do such a thing to himself and, worse still, involve her, had once or twice felt sorry for him. Now she didn't have the words to describe how she felt; although hungry and tired of the whole mess formed the basis.

Darvish wondered why Chandra remained silent. He writhed internally at what he imagined must be her thoughts. *If only she'd scream at me, it wouldn't be so bad.* The silence grew and he struggled to carry it. Finally, because he could think of nothing else to do, he devoured the gull meat he still held. Although his stomach gave out mixed signals, he was ravenously hungry.

After he finished and drank three handfuls of water from the spring, he stood and stretched. He felt as weak as a kitten, a strong breeze could toss him on his butt, and his head throbbed a quiet background to every movement. A quick touch discovered the bump and healing gash and for a moment he allowed himself to believe that the wound and not the wine had been responsible for the humiliating bits and pieces he could remember. He didn't allow the delusion to last long; for all his other faults Darvish seldom bothered to lie to himself about himself. He was an irresponsible drunken buffoon. He'd heard his father and his father's lord chancellor say it often enough.

"So."

Aaron's voice added a new edge to the shame and drove it into Darvish's heart. *I was the prince, the rescuer, the provider; if only in my mind not in his. What am I now?* Would the nothingness Aaron had shown in the palace be back? The "I care too little for you to even feel disgust." Or would the disgust be there at last, wiping out even the prickly relationship that had begun to grow? Not knowing was the worst. Darvish turned around.

In his bright yellow trousers, cream shirt, and copper hair, Aaron was a blaze of light on the hillside. Darvish squinted and remembered the stories his old nurse had told him of the Fire Lords who came to burn up bad little boys. They were easy to believe in just now.

Aaron's expression was unreadable but it wasn't nothingness at least. "Are you all right?" he asked.

Darvish thought of several clever comments. "Yes," he said quietly.

As Aaron came closer, Darvish saw that the younger man's eyes were circled with purple shadow and that the flesh he had gained during his long convalescence had been pared back to bone. His face and hands were red with sunburn. Darvish flushed and looked down at the sunrobe that would have at least prevented the latter.

"Would it help if I said I was sorry?"

Aaron's brows rose and he looked openly skeptical. "Would you mean it?"

"Yes."

"Then it would help if you proved it." Aaron pushed past him, scooped up the soiled sunrobe, shook it out and put it on. It had a ragged edge along the hem where Aaron had torn off fabric to make his sling. He nodded at Chandra, who tied off her braid and picked up her scrying bowl, tucking the small silver vessel back deep in her trouser pocket.

They've come to an understanding, Darvish realized. Their

silent companionship shut him out and that hurt, but he knew it was his own fault. The knife twisted.

"Well?" Aaron looked pointedly at Darvish's shirt and sword belt.

Darvish scrambled to dress, ignoring as best he could both the weakness and the pain in his head, suddenly reminded of why they'd left Cisali and how much time had passed. As he fought with water stiffened leather, he had a vision of Ischia drowning in molten rock while he lay delirious and sick by his own hand. He could feel their eyes on him and he waited for the accusations that had to come.

"Take a good long drink before we go," Aaron instructed, fitting action to the words. "We may not have water again until we stop and Chandra can call another spring." He stood and wiped his mouth.

Chandra knelt and drank, willing to follow Aaron's lead, just as anxious to get this over with.

Darvish dropped clumsily down, sucked up as much water as he could hold, and rose awkwardly again. *Would you please scream at me,* he wanted to plead. Righteous anger would help to lance the shame.

"If you can't keep up, say so." Aaron stood and looked at the prince for a moment, throwing all his strength into the walls that kept him from alternately shrieking and sobbing in both anger and relief. Then he turned and started up the slope, needing to get away from this place that would always be haunted with images of Darvish twisting in pain.

Chandra followed him, wondering if Aaron knew why he was running away or what he was running away from. *More of those questions I'm not supposed to ask.*

And Darvish followed her.

Would it help if I said I was sorry?

It would help if you proved it.

It looked like that was all the relief, the release, he was going to get, and for the first time in his adult life it became important to prove himself to someone besides his father.

He had to rest often and although he was desperately thirsty most of the time, he never once mentioned that he needed a drink.

Chapter Eleven

"I don't think those navy ships were after the *Gryphon*. I think they were after us."

"Us?" Carefully pushing her hair away from her face with the back of her hand, keeping greasy fingers well out of it, Chandra looked up from her haunch of ground squirrel.

"Not you," Aaron corrected. "Dar and I. The man who stole The Stone couldn't have gotten through the palace carrying the equipment he'd need in the crater without inside help. And he certainly couldn't get back out carrying The Stone. That help sent a message to Tivolic, told them what ship we'd be on." He tossed Darvish a baked root that Chandra swore was nonpoisonous.

"How?" Darvish asked, juggling the root. "We didn't know what ship we'd be on."

"Easy enough to have us followed."

"No." He shook his head. "Then they'd have known about Chandra."

"So? To a palace spy, what's unusual about Prince Darvish joining an attractive young lady? Nothing. They wouldn't recognize her as your betrothed. I saw her miniature and I wouldn't know her from that. Even now."

"He made me look simpering," Chandra broke in, seething. "I hated that picture. Stupid artist."

"They won't know she's a wizard, either," Darvish said thoughtfully. "And if they ever caught up with the *Gryphon* and found we went overboard they'll think we're dead. That puts us two up."

"But they'll know you're traveling with a wizard now, the sailors on the *Gryphon* will tell them."

"I doubt it. The *Gryphon* will tell that lot exactly as much as they have to, no more, and even if they do mention you, with the storm you called up they'll think you're a Wizard of the Seventh."

"But the distance viewer isn't a Seventh, it's more First or Ninth."

"They won't mention the distance viewer to the navy," Aaron said with his twisted grin.

"Did you know they were smugglers when you bought us passage?" Chandra asked him, suddenly suspicious.

Aaron shrugged. "I suspected. Smugglers don't ask questions. We didn't need questions."

Chandra took a bite of squirrel and looked almost cheerful. She'd been useful lately in a way she'd never been before. She liked it. A lot. "Look at the bright side. We're alive and we've got resources they don't suspect. Even if there is a traitor back in Ischia, we're doing all right."

"We're also half starved, barely equipped, and walking to the capital," Aaron reminded her.

And that's all my fault, Darvish added silently, gouging at the ground with a stick. He had to add it. The others wouldn't. He'd tried to apologize for that specifically, for being so stupid as to walk out on deck during the storm; Aaron had said nothing, Chandra had rolled her eyes and said, "Don't do it again, okay?" One Below, he was going to do his best, but he still wished they'd scream at him.

"Could be worse." Chandra threw the bone into the fire.

"If you say it could be raining, I'm going to throttle you with your own hair," Aaron said mildly. It was safer to talk than to think. His thoughts kept chipping holes in the wall.

Darvish couldn't join in the banter. He felt like he had to prove he belonged again. So he turned the subject back to Ischia. "Who do you think the traitor is?" Aaron's demon wings took off and Darvish nodded. "Yasimina," he said with a heavy sigh.

"Most likely," Aaron agreed, although he'd respected what he'd seen of Shahin enough to hope he was wrong.

"Who's Yasimina?" Chandra asked, wishing for the first time she'd paid more attention to talk of King Jaffar's court.

"My eldest brother's wife," Darvish told her. "It was a treaty marriage a little over a year ago. She's the second youngest sister of the King of Ytaili." He paused and smiled a bit sadly. "Shahin loves her. She likes peacocks."

*   *   *

The soft shush, shush, of leaves stroked together by the afternoon breeze surrounded them. Up ahead, a dead branch tapped and creaked, hanging at a crazy angle from the tree. Boots and sandals crunched through last year's growth making the three of them sound like an army on the march. Even Aaron was unable to move with his customary quiet.

The dry, dusty smell of dead leaves that rose up with each step and then lodged in the back of the nose became mixed with the more potent scent of cedars off to the right. Insects danced in each slanting greenish-gold ray of sunlight, humming their own accompaniment.

Sweat dribbled down Darvish's back and he loosened his sword in its sheath. Something was wrong. Something was missing. He lengthened his stride, moving quickly past the other two and waving Chandra's question quiet. To his surprise, she cut it off. He'd expected an argument, having abdicated any right to command when he fell from the *Gryphon*.

Chandra was a little surprised herself, her mouth having obeyed before her mind had a chance to ask why.

Darvish could smell something now, something that didn't belong. Char. Men. And animals. Very close. The trees stopped suddenly, a cluster of fresh cut stumps marking the edge of the clearing. Darvish dropped behind cover and peered out.

Directly in front of him, he could see where the wood had been dragged into the camp, could see that the grass had been cropped short, could see—and smell—the pungent signature of draft animals, could see that the camp was deserted. Carefully, his hand by his sword, he moved out into the open.

The clearing was larger than he'd initially thought, but the camp seemed to have filled all available space. Evidence remained of at least five wagons, each with an indeterminate number of people. A huge fire pit had been dug in roughly the center of the clearing and Darvish made his way across the trampled ground toward it.

"Whoever they were," he called as Aaron and Chandra came out of the trees, "they were here until at least this morning. They drowned their fire, but there's a coal still hot."

"Shoi," Aaron said, pushing the hood of his sunrobe back. His face was peeling, the proud hook of his nose especially badly, "Wanderers."

"I've never heard of them." Chandra bent and picked up a scrap of bright green cloth ground into the bottom of a wheel rut.

"Neither have I." Darvish began to move toward the far side of the clearing where he could see a well defined track heading off to the northeast.

Aaron snorted. "You live on islands. Wagons make lousy boats."

"They *live* in wagons?" Chandra asked.

"Yes."

"Does Shoi mean anything?" She threw the bit of cloth back on the ground.

"It means People. Others, non-Shoi, call them Wanderers."

"What do they do?"

Aaron turned to look at her and both tufted ginger brows rose. "They wander. Wha . . . ?"

A brilliant blue bird swooped across the clearing screaming insults.

"No birds. . . ." No birds. No birdsong. For the last little while, things had been entirely too quiet. Darvish drew his sword clear seconds before the first man charged into the clearing, blade whistling down in what he obviously hoped would be the killing stroke.

Silently, teeth clenched, Darvish attacked, There were two, three, no, five of them and only one of him. For any chance at all, he had to keep them off balance.

Steel sang against steel and as the swords hissed apart, Darvish kicked the man in the knee as hard as he could. Inhaling, he ducked a wild swing. Exhaling, he cut through to guts with a backhanded slash. This was his one chance to redeem himself; he put everything he had into the fight. A left-handed swordsman had the advantage and he stretched it to the limit and beyond.

A point dragged down the length of his right arm, deep enough to hurt but no deeper.

One Below, I want my shield! He dropped, rolled, and from the ground, using both hands, cut a man off at the knees. Bouncing up inside another's guard, he slammed his weighted pommel into a temple and shoved the body away. When he turned, the man first into the clearing waited, favoring one leg. A parry, a dodge, Darvish forced him around to his bad side, swung and hacked through neck, collarbone, and into ribs.

He yanked his blade free, spun about, and there was no one left to fight.

Three men were dead, two were down and dying. As Darvish watched, Aaron gave the grace blow to one, using the man's own dagger, and moved toward the other. Two of the three dead, Darvish had killed, the third had been flung onto his back, his face a bloody ruin. A stone from Aaron's sling, Darvish guessed.

He ripped free the torn shirtsleeve and used it to wipe most of the gore from his sword before sliding the smeared blade back into the scabbard.

Then he started to shake. His legs threatened to buckle and he sucked in great lungfuls of air.

I need a drink. Oh, One Below and Nine Above, I need a drink.

At nineteen, he'd killed three men in battle while in nominal command of a squad sent to clean out a pirates' nest on Cisali's south shore. In not much more than a dozen heartbeats, he'd just doubled that.

Chandra kept her mouth covered with both hands and tried very hard not to be sick. There was so much blood, black where it had soaked into the ground and red, bright red, dark red, every kind of red, where it clung to the bodies. And those men were so very dead. Not quietly dead, like her mother, welcoming the release from pain, but brutally dead and hating every second of it.

She didn't realize the first whimper had escaped until she heard it. She couldn't stop the second nor the third. She wanted to wail or cry or keen or something.

Then warm arms enfolded her and a large hand stroked her back.

"Look away," Darvish murmured softly into her hair. "Look away, gain some distance. The less immediate it is, the less horrible it is. I know."

"So much blood," Chandra said dully, neither fighting against his arms nor relaxing into them. They were a comfort that she couldn't quite seem to find how to accept.

Slowly, Darvish turned her, pulling her gaze away from the bodies. When she faced him rather than the battlefield, she gave a strange little sigh and collapsed against his chest, dry eyed and shuddering.

"I never saw anyone die like that before," she said.

Neither have I. Darvish felt the memory of each blow in his hands, the meaty resistance of flesh, each jar as steel hit bone.

Aaron moved carefully among the bodies, fighting against the memories that threatened to overwhelm him; memories of a life he'd left behind, released as he'd released the stone from the sling. He'd killed his first man at eleven in a raid on a neighboring keep. One of the defenders had stumbled and fallen and Aaron had slammed a hand ax into his throat. After the battle, his father had lifted the head on a spear point and proudly proclaimed the Clan Heir a man. There had been a lot of blood on his father's hands, and a good bit on him as well.

He'd killed this morning for the first time since he'd left his father's keep. He'd killed without thinking, protecting Darvish's back.

"A fine shot, my son!"

"I am not your son any longer."

"I couldn't have done it better myself."

"Shut up, Father!"

But denial wouldn't take back the stone nor the sudden falling into violence that was his father's way. He had allowed himself to relax and his past had tried to reclaim him. He would have to be stronger until the past could be destroyed.

For now, however, denial was all he had.

"They're dressed like outlaws." He flopped one over on its back with a well placed foot. "Ragged, dirty. Too well fed, though." He squatted and rubbed the base of a sword blade clean, frowned, reached for another, and drummed his fingers against the steel. "They all carry swords and daggers marked with the insignia of the King's Guard."

"What?" Darvish's head snapped up.

"They were sent by the King of Ytaili."

"Now that puts a different shine on things," exclaimed a voice from the clearing's edge. "Any enemy of imperial guards is a friend of ours."

The speaker was a short, heavyset man, dressed all in greens and browns. Beside him stood a young woman, a little taller, dressed much the same. They both carried long knives and the man held a thick staff bound at both ends with brass. Their skin was darker than Aaron's but lighter than both Darvish's and Chandra's.

Aaron stood slowly, hands out from his sides. "They have an archer in the trees," he said over his shoulder. "The Shoi never travel in less than threes."

Chandra pulled out of Darvish's arms. She was a Wizard of the Nine and wasn't going to have these Shoi think she needed comforting. Darvish, like Aaron, stood with his hands out from his sides. An indifferent archer at best, even *he* could hit them shooting from cover and at that range.

While the woman scowled, her visible companion leaned forward on his staff and studied Aaron. "You're a long way from your rocks and winds and cold, Kebric," he said at last.

"I am," Aaron admitted.

"Now I've never been that far north myself," his accent lengthened the words, emphasizing their musical lilt, in direct contrast to Aaron's which clipped them off, "but I have heard that a clansman who leaves his keep, let alone one who leaves his bleak and inhospitable land is a rare bird indeed."

"I left." Aaron's hands spread wider and his tone left no room for further discussion.

"So you did," agreed the older Shoi. "So you did." He nodded genially at Darvish. "Fine sword work, young man. Can't remember when I've seen better."

Darvish flushed. His sword masters had always said he was good. He'd never quite known whether he should believe them, but this man had no reason to lie.

"The proof is in the pudding as they say," he continued. "Here you stand, barely scratched—although you should have that arm seen to. I wouldn't trust any kind of imperial lackey to keep his sword clean."

The shallow cut down the length of Darvish's right arm, now brought suddenly to mind, began to throb and burn. He'd forgotten it was there.

"And there they lie, dead." He spit in the general direction of the bodies, his head darting forward then back, the movement precise, the rest of him remaining completely still.

They hadn't moved since they'd entered the clearing, Darvish realized, not even making gestures when speaking. Even Aaron moved more, but where Aaron looked controlled, the Shoi merely looked . . . still.

"And Most Wise." A gracious nod at Chandra. "What is a gently-bred lady wizard doing out in the woods with these ruffians?"

Chandra's brows drew down. "Don't patronize me," she snapped.

Both Shoi smiled broadly and the young woman spoke for the

first time. "My uncle begs your pardon," she said, her accent, although similar, much less florid.

Not quite mollified, Chandra nodded a prickly acceptance.

"You must be very powerful," she continued, her tone not quite neutral, not quite friendly. "Your power shines like a beacon."

"I *am* very powerful." Still frowning, she asked, suspiciously, "What do you mean shines like a beacon?"

"The Shoi," Aaron explained without taking his eyes off the two at the tree line, "are power sensitive. Some say they're a race of wizards."

The older man sighed. "And some say the Kebric are a brutally violent, not overly intelligent, race of inbred maniacs. But you don't hear us spreading *that* around."

Although Aaron's lips thinned to a white-edged line, he kept silent. His father would have roared in anger and charged to the attack at the insult, at the string of insults. Aaron was not his father. He had remade himself in his own image. He held tight to that image now.

"Uncle. . . ."

"Yes, you're completely right, Fiona, that was completely, well—almost completely uncalled for. Now, if you would be so good as to retrieve Grandmother's knitting."

She nodded and moved quickly across the clearing. At the far side, by one of the wagon marks, she swung herself up into a tree and dropped back down seconds later with a handful of green wool.

"One of the children hid it," Fiona's uncle explained as she returned and handed it back to him. "Grandmother'll be glad to get it back." He smiled genially and slid the wool into his belt pouch. "And now, chance met by the trail, you may call me Edan. And this, my sister's daughter, you may call Fiona." He made no mention of the third Shoi, the archer Aaron had said remained in the trees. "You three will, of course, accompany us to our new camp. We're always eager to entertain the enemies of our enemies."

Not even Chandra needed Aaron to tell her this was not an invitation they could refuse.

The walk to the Shoi's new camp took two days, although the Shoi could have done it in one. Any energy Darvish had managed to regain had been used in the fight and to his intense embarrassment he had to rest often or fall over.

The first time this happened, Fiona had squatted beside him, pushed up his chin with one strong finger, sniffed, and said, *"Topasent."* Then she frowned and looked up at her uncle.

Edan pursed his lips and thought a moment. "Wine-chains," he translated at last. "About as close as it comes."

She nodded and, releasing Darvish's chin, asked, "How long have you been free?"

Free? What was she . . . then suddenly Darvish understood. How long since his last drink. How long since the wine-chains had come undone. He had no idea. He remembered emptying the wineskin while the storm raged and tried to breach their tiny cabin, but he didn't know how long ago it had been. Nine Above, it seemed like an eternity.

"Six days," said Aaron softly behind him.

Fiona pulled a drinking skin off her shoulder and tossed it in Darvish's lap. He jerked back and his breath caught in his throat. "Relax, it's water. Drink as much as you can and piss away the poisons." She stood and shook her head. "Six days . . . and you fought five men and won. You must have the strength of an ox. Just fighting free of *topasent* has killed others." She drew in breath as though to continue, then shook her head, turned on her heel and strode off into the trees beside the trail. They almost seemed to open and close around her so silently did she move.

"It killed her father," Edan told them, his cheek resting against the smooth wood of his staff. "He got free twice, but the third time stopped his heart."

Chandra moved to stand by Aaron so that the two of them were a shield against Darvish's back. "Well, it isn't going to kill Dar," she declared.

Darvish, lifting the waterskin to his mouth in trembling hands, wasn't so sure.

That afternoon they reached a road of sorts that followed the banks of a good sized stream. That night they camped by its side and the third Shoi came out of the trees. Once he'd set his short curved bow carefully down and had tossed two rabbits to Edan, it was next to impossible to tell him apart from Fiona in the uncertain light of the fire.

"Twins," their uncle said proudly, "very lucky. Fion and Fiona, a blessing to the family."

The younger man laughed, his teeth gleaming white in the shadow of his face. "That's not what you said when we were children, Uncle." He threw himself down on the grass with the grace of a giant cat. "He said we were demon spawn and kept threatening to abandon us by the side of the road."

Edan grinned as he gutted the rabbits. "Yes, but your poor misguided mother would never let me."

He reminds me a bit of Darvish, Chandra realized as she watched Fion help his sister string the rabbits over the fire. Although he shared the economy of movement that seemed a Shoi trait, he somehow made it seem flamboyant. *Darvish at his best, as he should have been without the wine.* She shook her head. Twins as a blessing? The Shoi were strange indeed; everyone knew twins shared only one soul between them and so had to be carefully watched.

While the rabbits roasted and sparks and fireflies danced short-lived duets, the three Shoi heard the story of the shipwreck and what happened after. It was almost impossible not to respond to a direct question from one of them. Chandra scanned for power but found nothing. Whether it was because there was nothing there or because she had no idea of what to look for, she didn't know.

"So the two of you and a sick man survived with nothing, no supplies, not even a waterskin for six days." Edan chewed thoughtfully on a piece of meat. "Difficult to believe."

"We had a sling and a wizard," Aaron said dryly. "What more did we need?"

Fion laughed, Fiona smiled, and Edan threw up his hands in defeat.

The next morning, Fiona picked up the bow and slipped away into the trees.

As they walked, Darvish leaned closer to Aaron and said quietly, "Did you notice, they never once asked us why we were heading for Tivolic in the first place."

Aaron nodded. "That usually means they already know."

They reached the camp just before sunset and the twilight followed them in, giving everything a softer and faintly unreal appearance. The circle of wagons seemed larger than it could possibly be and more children than those wagons could hold swarmed about their legs, shouting questions in the language of the Shoi and the common language of the area. The food smells from the communal fire reminded them of how long it had been since they'd eaten a real meal and Aaron and Chandra both had to

swallow sudden mouthfuls of saliva. Darvish caught the scent of
something else and clenched his fists.

"About time you got here!" An elderly woman, not quite fat,
stomped down out of one of the wagons and waved a dimpled
hand imperiously at Edan. "Come on, then. Grandmother wants to
see you." She paused then added. *"And* them."

Fion slipped away, to Edan's muttered "Coward," and the four
of them walked across to the central area. Except for the children,
no one paid them much attention.

Darvish had to both duck and turn sideways to make it through
the wagon door, but once inside there was a lot more room than
he'd expected. It was stuffy though, and the air smelled stale as if
it had been in the wagon for a very long time. A combination of
the lamp's position and the lines of the wagon drew the eye instantly to an incredibly old woman wrapped in a pile of shawls
and blankets. The remains of her hair were pulled back into a tight
steel-gray knot emphasizing the skull-like delineation of her face.
Her eyes, sunk deep into the bone on either side of a pinched
nose, were barely open. Her skin, dry and crossed and recrossed
with a multitude of fine lines, reminded Darvish of a lizard's.
He'd never seen anyone that old before. Out of the corner of an
eye, he checked Chandra and Aaron for their reactions.

Chandra merely looked intrigued. Aaron had gone completely
blank.

The old woman's voice, in direct contrast to her frail appearance, was surprisingly strong. "Have you got my knitting, then?"

Edan laid the bundle of green wool on her lap. "Yes, Grandmother. Here it is."

She sighed and it sounded like more air than that wasted
body could possibly hold. "I can see where it is, Edan, you
kokta. Get out."

"Very well, Grandmother." He didn't exactly scurry for the
door, but it was close.

"Now then." She pointed a twisted finger at Aaron and paused
for a moment for her breath to whistle in and out. "You. Relax.
I'm not going to die on you."

Aaron started but showed no visible signs of relaxing. The
Shoi—not this family but their northern cousins— had traveled
every year to the great fair that marked a moon's truce between
the warring clans. He *knew* that many of their seemingly magical

pronouncements were based on no more than observation and a deep understanding of human nature. It didn't help.

She stared from one to the other, her gaze still sharp enough to cut despite her age, then clicked her tongue. "So," she said, after rocking a moment in thought. "The Stone of Ischia has been stolen and you three have been sent to get it back. Don't you think an army would be more practical, Your Royal Highness?"

"A race of wizards," Darvish said softly. He couldn't decide if meeting the Shoi was the best or worst thing that could have happened.

Aaron's eyes narrowed. "Common sense," he corrected harshly. "They felt power move from Ischia to Tivolic. The only relic with that kind of power in Ischia is The Stone. They heard no rumor of war and then a warrior, a thief, and a wizard show up on their way to Tivolic from Ischia. They know the King of Ischia has a blue-eyed son. Here we have a blue-eyed warrior."

"But my illusion," Chandra interrupted. "His eyes look brown."

"Illusions seldom work on the Shoi."

The smug expression on the old woman's face had turned to one of deep annoyance. She spat a question at Aaron in a language that seemed mostly made of consonants.

"No," he answered.

She scowled, openly disbelieving.

"There was a wizard involved," Chandra attempted to change the subject. Making the matriarch angry didn't strike her as a particularly good idea, not when they needed so many things.

"Of course there was." Gnarled fingers picked peevishly at the knitting still on her lap. "There always is."

"And whoever took The Stone seems to know we're coming."

"Whoever indeed." A cackle of ancient laughter threatened to turn to coughing, but with a visible effort the old woman regained control of her body. "With imperial guards rotting out there you needn't blather about whoevers. If His Most Gracious Majesty doesn't have The Stone now, he most certainly knows who does." She turned to Darvish. "Didn't one of your brothers just marry a princess of Ytaili?"

"Yes."

"Well, there you have it."

Darvish shook his head. He hadn't wanted to believe it was Yasimina. Would have it rather that it was anyone else.

"You don't know that," Aaron said suddenly, his voice stone.

"So you defend the little princess, do you, Kebric?" Lips pulled back off nearly perfect teeth, intensifying the skull-like resemblance. "It won't do either of you any good. The only way to defeat a traitor is to keep him or her in the dark. You will therefore be traveling with the family to Tivolic."

Darvish pushed the thought of Shahin aside for a time. "What?" he asked, a little lost.

"Are you deaf, boy? I said you're traveling with the family to Tivolic."

"Oh." It would take a braver man than he to argue with that pronouncement. "Why are you helping us?" he asked.

"Because we want to." Her tone stated there need be no better reason than that.

"Then we thank you." Ignoring the pounding behind his temples, he bowed his most gracious bow and pressed the back of her hand to his lips. It felt a bit like kissing a lizard, dry and leathery.

"Flatterer." She looked pleased. "Now get out. I'm tired."

As they reached the door, she called out, "Prince!"

Darvish turned.

"You touch one drop of wine in my camp and I'll have your fingers broken."

"What a lovely old lady," he muttered to Aaron outside.

The demon wings flew, a silent comment weighted in sarcasm.

"What did she ask you?" Chandra wanted to know.

"She asked if any of my ancestors were Shoi."

"You made her angry."

Aaron shrugged. The old woman's first words had cut too close. He'd slashed at her pride. They were even.

That night when the fire blazed high, Chandra stood in the shadow of a wagon and watched as Darvish divided his attentions between Fion and a girl with close cropped curls who laughed low in her throat. She'd seen him overcome his need and recognized the strength it had taken to drink water instead of wine and she couldn't argue with his right to take other pleasures when they were offered, but. . . .

But what? She didn't know exactly, so she stood and watched and chewed on the end of her braid. And wondered.

"He's such a *haus.*" Fiona's low voice barely carried over the sound of a Shoi and the fire.

Chandra spit out the wet end of her braid. "A *haus?*"

"A slut."

Darvish slipped a hand behind the girl and lifted his mouth to Fion.

"Yes. He is."

"I meant my brother." Chandra could hear the smile in the other woman's voice. "If you care about him, you could be there. They would both give way."

"No." Chandra sighed. "I don't care about him like that."

"Oh."

"I don't care about anyone like that. I'm a Wizard of the Nine." Fiona shook her head. "Power is a cold companion in the night," she said and left as silently as she had arrived.

"Well, maybe it is," Chandra muttered, shoving her hand deep into the pocket of her trousers to wrap around the comforting shape of the scrying bowl. "But it's a lot more interesting in the daytime."

From the other side of the fire pit, where the flames danced strange shadows in the darkness, came the eerie wail of a reed pipe. Chandra recognized the instrument but not the tune. The shepherds who surrounded her father's country estate had never played anything so wild. A drum joined in and then another deeper pitched and then something she didn't know at all that surged through the rest, caught them up and carried them crazily along.

The music sizzled along her skin and Chandra had the ridiculous thought she must move or burn. Others had the same idea and in the light of the fire she saw the young men and women of the Shoi answer the wild call. One, two, then a surging mass of bodies circled the flames. They stamped and spun, holding her motionless watching. The music grew more frenzied and so did the dance. She knew what the call was now and with gritted teeth refused it.

I am a wizard of the Nine, she told it. *This want is not mine!*

And then a slim white shape leapt and whirled before the fire.

"Aaron?" She took a step forward, squinting.

His hair blazed red and gold like a cap of flame as he whirled and leapt impossibly high. The fire danced in reflection on skin wet with sweat. Even the scars on his chest seemed some bizarre barbaric decoration. His eyes were closed, or almost closed, and he gave himself over totally to the music. Bare feet slammed down into the dirt, the walls tumbled, and all the passion behind the walls blazed out.

The beat came faster, harder, and he followed it.

Chandra searched for Darvish and spotted him at last moving with the two Shoi into the greater privacy behind the wagons.

Turn around, she pleaded silently. *Look to the fire!* If Darvish looked, she knew he'd understand who Aaron danced for.

But he didn't turn and he didn't look.

When the music ended, chest heaving, hands fisted at his sides, Aaron disappeared into the darkness alone.

Chapter Twelve

"Have you heard, Aisha? Have you heard?"

The sandal maker continued to placidly stitch, not even glancing up as old Cemal tottered in through the open front of her shop. Two or three times a nineday he picked up a hot rumor from his cronies and gleefully spread it about the marketplace. Aisha had long ago ceased to get excited. "Have I heard what?" she asked, eyeing her work critically.

"Well...." Cemal carefully lowered his brittle bones to the rug, then took another moment to rearrange his robe over his skinny legs. These trousers that the younger people were wearing; he just couldn't see the point. "Well, Barika—you know her, the sausage maker's youngest daughter—has a friend, Habibah, who has a little brother who is a page to His Excellency the Lord Chancellor at the palace."

He paused and Aisha grunted, measuring out a length of leather strapping.

"Well, Habibah's little brother, the page at the palace, told Habibah, who told Barika, who told her father, who told me."

"Told you what, Cemal?" Aisha asked, because she knew it was expected of her, not because she wanted to know. It was possible she had enough of the tooled leather left for one more pair.

"Told me that The Stone is missing."

Her reaction was all that Cemal could have wished. She actually stopped working and looked at him, her eyes wide and her mouth open.

"Missing," he reiterated with a cackle of humorless laughter. "We're all going to die."

Aisha closed her mouth. The Stone missing? "Nonsense," she snapped.

"Not nonsense." Cemal shook his head, his few remaining strands of hair flapping emphatically. "And they sent Prince Darvish out to get it back."

"Darvish?" The sandal maker smiled. "That proves it's nonsense, old man. No one in their right mind would send Prince Darvish to the well for water."

"He hasn't been seen in the usual places for over a nineday," Cemal muttered peevishly.

"No mystery there, he's in seclusion in the temple. Something about his upcoming marriage and a case of crotch."

"But Habibah's brother. . . ."

"Is a kid. Besides," she reached over and patted his knee, "the King, and the Heir, and even His Excellency the Lord Chancellor are still at the palace. You think they'd still be there if there was any danger of the Lady blowing?"

Cemal sighed. "You're right," he admitted, heaving himself to his feet. "The Stone missing and Prince Darvish gone after it. I must be getting old to believe that." And shaking his head, he tottered out of the shop, an occasional muttered, "Old," drifting back over the noise of the market.

Aisha finished attaching a buckle with tiny meticulous stitches, then set the strap down beside the almost completed sandal. Drumming her fingers against her thighs for a moment, she frowned. From where she sat, she couldn't see beyond the stonework edging the building across the way and it had suddenly become important to see farther. Still frowning, she rose and stepped out into the street, waving an absent greeting to the basket maker in the shop next to hers.

She couldn't see the palace, the street angled too steeply for that, but she could see the spreading edge of smoke that had been hanging over the city for days. It was a very little smoke, but, born and raised in Ischia, the sandal maker could not remember smoke like it before. There could be no truth in old Cemal's words, but she felt a strange sense of disquiet touch her nevertheless. She had seen an execution at the volcano, seen what the molten rock would do to flesh if it ever broke the bonds that held it captive in the crater.

Her brother, long moved to a village on the south shore, had always said she would be welcome. Perhaps now would be a good time to visit.

*   *   *

"My prince."

"Lord Chancellor."

"The lava has risen another body length. The wizards say it will soon be up over the cup and when that happens," the lord chancellor spread plump hands, "they may not be able to hold it further."

Shahin scowled. He knew the wizards had been using the golden cup The Stone had rested in as a focus point for their power. He hadn't realized they were so dependent on it. The cup was a good distance away from the rim of the crater and if they could hold the molten rock only that far, it drastically cut the time they had remaining. And when the captive volcano finally broke free, the wizards would be the first to die. "Will they stay? If any one of them breaks and weakens the block. . . ."

"The wizards will live or die as one, my prince." The lord chancellor's bearing was smug. "Their powers are now woven too tightly together for any single strand to break free. They may give in to terror as they wish, but they cannot withdraw their power."

"You knew that would happen?"

He bowed his head, the expression on his round face unreadable. "I have always excelled at planning ahead, my prince."

So the wizards were trapped. Shahin tapped his thumb against his lip and came to a decision. "We must begin evacuating the city. Immediately."

"My prince! And cause the very panic we have been trying to prevent?"

"Better a panic now than a thousand deaths later," Shahin snapped, rising and striding to the windows.

"You would sacrifice your people now for a later that may never come?" the lord chancellor asked quietly.

The prince turned and, just barely visible beneath his beard, a muscle jumped in his jaw. His voice had the brittle edge of a man holding onto calm by strength of will alone. "You seem to have great faith in my brother considering you have never had much use for him before."

"Your royal brother, my prince, is not meant for court life. He is not now at court."

It sounded reasonable, it was the truth after all so it should, but. . . .

"We begin evacuation. Now. The guards will do what can be done to prevent panic."

"I am sorry, my prince," and he both looked and sounded sorry, "but that is your most exalted father's command to give. Not yours."

Shahin drew in a deep breath and let it out slowly. It would do him no good, it would do Ischia no good, if he antagonized this man who held the king's trust. It was a lesson Darvish had never learned. "Then I will go to my father."

"I am sorry, my prince," the lord chancellor said again. "But he will not see you."

Out in the gardens, the peacocks screamed.

"He will not see me?" Shahin repeated.

The lord chancellor stepped back, away from the expression on the heir's face, suddenly reminded of how much like the king this eldest son was. "He feels, my prince, that until the crisis is over, given the suspicions against your lady wife. . . ."

Shahin's eyes narrowed and one fist came up. With an effort so great it left him trembling, he managed to hold his reaction to that. "You will never speak to me of my wife again." His voice cut off each word and threw it at the lord chancellor. "Now, you and I together will go and see my most exalted father."

The small room in the king's apartments did not contain a throne, but it held a high-backed chair that served. The king sat, fingers steepled, his brows drawn down so that his eyes were hidden deep within their shadows.

His own eyes blazing, Shahin touched his knee to the carpet, then hurriedly stood. "Most Exalted," he began but the king raised an imperious hand and cut him off.

"Do you realize how close to treason you come?" he asked.

Shahin jerked back, blinking as though he'd been hit. His chest felt as though a block of marble had been dropped on it from a great height. He fought against the weight for the breath to speak but only managed a single word. "Treason?"

"Or were you not told that I would not see you?"

"Yes sir, by the lord chancellor, but. . . ."

The lord chancellor came forward, knelt, then rose and moved to stand behind King Jaffar's chair.

"He speaks with my voice in this."

"But why, Father?" Shahin spread his hands, anger overcoming shock. "We must work together if Cisali is to survive."

"Do not tell me what we must do!" The king rose a little out of his chair, then settled again, his face the expressionless mask he ruled behind. "I can no longer trust you. Your wife. . . ."

"I sent Yasimina to the country a nineday ago and even were she here, I do not make her privy to state secrets."

"Did you not allow her to write to her brother, King Harith, before she left?"

Shahin felt a coldness growing in his gut. Until this moment, he had heard that tone only when the king spoke with Darvish. It was all king and no father and in all ways denied any blood tie. "She wrote only to tell him she was going to the country. I read the letter, Most Exalted, there was nothing treasonous in it! He is her brother. She was homesick."

"To write to such a man at such a time is treason; the contents of the letter do not matter. To allow her to write the letter is treason. To come here to me when I have ordered that you will not is treason. Thrice you stand accused."

When Shahin had given in to his pleading bride, he had known trouble would come of it. But this, this he had not, could not have, foreseen.

Behind the throne, the lord chancellor bowed his head, his expression unreadable.

"I will be merciful. This time. You will remain in the palace and you will continue to perform those duties that do not include the throne. You will not speak with me nor in any way contact me until this crisis is over and the traitor has been found."

Shahin dropped again to his knee, but his chin came up as though he answered a challenge. "Am I suspected of being the traitor, Most Exalted?"

The two men locked eyes and after a long moment, King Jaffar looked away. "No," he said. "But you have been tainted by your outland bride. I can no longer trust you."

"Ytaili is hardly outland, Most Exalted!" Shahin protested, even though he knew it would have been wiser to keep silent.

"Ytaili tries to destroy us!" the king roared, rising to his feet. "What I do, I do for the good of the realm!"

Knowing he must choose his next words with care, lest his father reject them out of hand, Shahin laid his forehead on his upturned knee, the position of the penitent. "Then for the good of the realm I ask a boon before I am denied your presence."

Still breathing heavily, the king lowered himself back into the chair. "Ask."

"For the good of the realm, Most Exalted, order the evacuation of Ischia."

"Do not tell *me* what is for the good of the realm."

Shahin's head snapped up. "Then the people of Ischia will die!"

"If the gods will it. But they will not die by my order nor will we show Ytaili weakness to be used to their advantage." Within the depths of his beard, the king's lips thinned to a hard line. "And that is our final word."

His face a mirror of his father's, Shahin rose, bowed, and, moving with careful control, left the room.

"His Royal Highness is very angry, Most Exalted." The lord chancellor came forward into the king's line of sight.

"If you have counsel, speak. I do not need to hear you state the obvious."

Sighing deeply, the lord chancellor laced his fingers together across the curve of his stomach. "You taught him to rule, Most Exalted."

The king snorted. "He's my heir, of course I taught him to rule."

The lord chancellor bowed. "Now he wishes to."

"Do you suggest Prince Shahin plots against the throne?" The question had an edge as sharp as the knives of the Fourth.

"No, Most Exalted. I only warn that history is full of angry young princes deciding to inherit before the gods determine it is time."

Knuckles whitened as royal fingers tightened on the arms of the chair. "I have heard your warning."

Anger sustained him until he reached his own apartments and then reaction set in.

Although he had never been a good father—and Shahin as heir had seen more of him than any of his siblings—King Jaffar had always been a good king. Every word he had said had made sense.

What if the king was right? What if he had been tainted by his Ytaili bride?

He had read the letter. It had been harmless.

Shahin rested his head against the window's edge as out in the garden the peacocks screamed. His heart felt like a rock in his chest. He ached for Yasimina's touch. He hadn't believed he could ever love someone so much. Or so foolishly.

For the first time, he thought he understood why Darvish drank.

"Gracious Majesty, a runner has come in from the South Road."

"And?" The King of Ytaili leaned back against the brass and lacquer peacock tail—an inexpensive copy of the jewel-encrusted gold tail that backed his throne—and glared at the man standing before him.

"They have not been found, Gracious Majesty, and five of your guards have been killed in the search."

"Then it seems to me they *were* found, if only temporarily."

Lord Rahman, who had acted as intermediary between the King and the Captain of the Guards—through two kings and six captains—hastily rejected several entirely inappropriate reactions. "Do you wish more men sent, Gracious Majesty?" he asked just before the pause grew dangerously long.

"No." King Harith scowled, dark brows drawing down to meet at the bridge of his nose. His perfect plan . . .

Remove The Stone, wait for Ischia to be destroyed, and, with the royal family dead—or in hiding, having run like frightened children to the countryside and unable to mount a resistance—move a few shiploads of troops in and take over. A pity about his sister, her marriage to the crown prince had been very helpful to him, but he had six others and, frankly, wouldn't miss one. His people might not want to pay for a war, or so the old men on the council kept telling him, but they'd support an easy victory. Cisali would be his.

. . . seemed to be unraveling.

A perfect plan, except they traced The Stone. Traced The Stone and instead of declaring war, which would have served his plan as well—given new taxes to raise more troops he could defeat Cisali without having to resort to subversion—they sent two men to steal it back. Two men, a drunkard and a thief, and neither the navy nor the guard seemed able to stop them.

He drummed blunt fingers on the padded chair arms. The thief seemed to be the greater danger, although with five guards dead young Darvish was not the lightweight appearances had indicated. He'd have never suspected it at the wedding, never suspected Darvish consisted of anything behind the drinking and the sex, but this seemed to prove that not only could his young relative by marriage wield a sword, he could wield it to his advantage. He could do no more to stop the prince, but, he smiled, there was more than one way to skin a thief.

"Get me a scribe," he barked. "And have someone inform the Most Wise Palaton that he might better place a guard of some kind on The Stone."

King Harith had little use for wizards and less for their artifacts. Removing The Stone had been a way to conquer Cisali under the strictures his council had placed around him, nothing more. As he'd needed a wizard to do it, he'd used one, paying him with The Stone itself. He no longer cared about the wizard, or what the wizard did, but as Ischia retrieving their safeguard would ruin his plans, he would warn the Most Wise Palaton.

"Let them come, I do not care."

Lord Rahman, who had decided for security's sake to take the warning to the wizard himself, steepled his fingers and sighed. "Most Wise, The Stone has been stolen once already."

"I know." The hint of a smile added a curve to the wizard's thin lips.

"When a thing has been stolen once, Most Wise, it can be stolen again."

The wizard spread his hands, the deep blue cuffs of his robe falling back to expose thin wrists. "It was not stolen originally from me," he pointed out.

"The prince does not travel alone," Lord Rahman told him a little sharply. "He has a thief with him. . . ."

"I know who travels with Prince Darvish, I have been watching them, off and on, since just after they left Ischia." Palaton's smile broadened. He had been watching them, off and on, since that child-wizard had drawn attention to herself by trying to trace The Stone. That King Harith remained ignorant of the girl did not surprise him, the man remained ignorant of a great many things. He was politically astute, Palaton would grant him that. He knew better than to start a war his people—or more specifically, his wealthy merchants—would not support and his plan for the conquering of Cisali was well considered. It was not his fault, and surely he could not have foreseen, that the third prince would have a thief leashed at court.

Palaton considered Ytaili's king a fool because he treated the most powerful relic in existence as merely a means to an end.

"They say you're the most powerful wizard in my kingdom," King Harith had said bluntly when Palaton obeyed the imperial summons and appeared before him.

"Who says, Gracious Majesty?"

"Other wizards," the king told him sardonically. *"I assume they should know."*

"And if I am, Gracious Majesty?" He saw no reason to either confirm or deny it and while he resented being pulled away from his studies, he'd lived too long to show it. Much.

"If you are, I require your services." The king drummed on his chair arms, the sound strangely loud in the small room. *"I want Cisali. The reasons need not concern you."*

Palaton had not even wondered. The reasoning of princes never concerned him.

"I have access to the palace at Ischia. I need a wizard to help me steal The Stone." He'd paused then, in a voice that said he was through with explanations, continued, *"If you're as powerful as they say, you will steal it for me."*

At the mention of The Stone, Palaton's heart began to throb harder and faster although he carefully kept the reaction hidden. Even here in Tivolic, the power of The Stone called to him. He had never been to Ischia to see it for fear of what he might do. *"I am a Wizard of the Nine, Gracious Majesty, not a thief."*

King Harith shrugged burly shoulders. *"I'm told it needs a wizard and a thief. Thieves are easy to find. I have two in the Chamber of the Fourth right now."*

Palaton ignored the hint of threat. *"And if I assist you in this, Gracious Majesty, my reward . . . ?"*

"Reward?" The king snorted. *"I should've known it would come to that. What do you request, Most Wise?"* He mocked with the honorific, but the wizard didn't care.

Only long years of practice kept the desire from Palaton's voice as he answered. *"The Stone. If I take it and give you Cisali, you will give The Stone to me in payment."*

"Oh, I will, will I?" The answer hung between them for a moment and then the king laughed. *"Take the wizard's bauble, I've no use for it. And here I feared you'd ask for gold or jewels or land or something else my council would bitch about."* He looked the other man up and down. *"If it's useless things you're interested in, you can have one of my sisters as well, I've still four left to get rid of."*

"*No, thank you, Gracious Majesty.*" Palaton had bowed, his face impassive. "*Only The Stone.*"

Only The Stone. . . .

"You may tell your king that I will guard The Stone and keep it safe." He moved to stand by the study door, one hand holding it open in invitation, and Lord Rahman had little choice but to take his leave.

"If Ischia recovers The Stone. . . ." he began, but the wizard smoothly cut him off.

"Ischia's prince will not recover The Stone. If and when he and whoever travels with him arrive, they will be dealt with, never fear. His Gracious Majesty's plans for conquest will not be over-turned." To a servant hovering in the hall, he added, "See his lord-ship out." Then he firmly closed the door.

His Gracious Majesty's plans for conquest interested him not at all. Two of the three on their way to wrest The Stone from him interested him even less, although he would take steps to strengthen the safeguards already on his house. The third, the child-wizard, had a potential he wished to investigate but for all her power, if she would not listen to reason, she was too young to be a danger.

Knowledge was the ultimate weapon, for power without it was hollow and strength without it was brute and blind. Nine Wizards of the Nine had taken nine years to create The Stone; Palaton could access only a small fraction of it so far, but that tiny portion showed him an infinite number of doors that awaited his opening.

Kings and princes and wizards and thieves; he no longer had any interest in dealing with anything but The Stone.

"Now I don't want any argument from you, young lady." Aba grasped Chandra firmly by the arm and hoisted her to her feet. "You are going to sit in the garden whether you like it or not." She pulled the girl out of the room and began chivvying her down the stairs. "Two full ninedays is long enough for anyone to sit and sulk. I know you don't want to marry this Darvish, but he's a prince and handsome and a lot of girls have to settle for less. Your own second cousin married a man she'd met but twice and he was fat besides. Mind you, they get along as though the Nine them-selves had picked the match and your cousin, One forgive me for saying it, is now well on her way to topping her husband's girth."

Aba guided her unenthusiastic charge outside, noting as she

did that footsteps once light now plodded and even Chandra's hair seemed heavy and dull; a physical match for the newly sullen disposition. "You sit right there and get some sun. A bit of sun'll give you a different outlook on things and maybe I'll get the Chandra back I nursed."

The golem, having a rudimentary intelligence at best, quietly did as it was told and sat down on the stone bench, tucking its legs between the carved trolls that crouched beneath each end.

"Humph, yes, well . . ." Catching up the edge of her veil which threatened to take off in the freshening breeze like a great purple bird, Aba gave the still figure a baleful glare and stomped off toward the main house. She'd done what she could. She was not going to sit there and hold the girl's hand while she sulked. Chandra could without a doubt be the stubbornest . . . it was all that wizard Rajeet's fault, filling the child's head with nonsense no young lady should be expected to learn. Although Aba wished no harm on any living man, she rather hoped this war Rajeet had been called home to would go on for a good long time. Or at least until Chandra was safely married.

The golem sat. It didn't so much think as it existed, but it noted a difference between this place and the place it had sat in for so long and as much as it was capable of it, it liked this place better. This place felt right.

It continued to sit while the breezes grew and brought clouds to cover the sun. It made no move toward shelter when the first tentative drops of rain speckled the stone bench with darker gray. It stayed where it was as the clouds let go their burden and the garden hid itself behind sheets of rain.

"Oh, Nine Above and One Below!" Aba clicked her tongue and peered out at her nursling who was no doubt wet through. "Sulking is one thing, but you'd think she'd retain enough sense to come in out of the rain. She'll catch her death out there!" Stepping so close to the edge of the porch that stray gusts spattered water against her layers of veiling, she shrieked at her charge to come inside immediately.

There appeared to be no response.

"Ignoring me, is she?" Black eyes snapped and wrapping her yards of fabric close she stepped out into the rain. "You'll feel the side of my tongue for this, my girl," she muttered as a puddle proved deeper than the sole of her sandal.

"Chandra!"

Still no response.

Stretching out an arm, Aba grabbed a shoulder with one plump hand and shook it hard.

Her shrill screams brought guards and servants running, but it took some time before they understood that the pile of dirt, rapidly turning to mud and washing away, was all that remained of their lady.

Lord Balin was waiting outside the stables for his mount when the guardsman arrived on a horse white with sweat and almost floundering.

He's in my colors. Lord Balin frowned at the wet uniform, steaming slightly in the heat of the late afternoon sun, as the man threw himself out of the saddle and, in an extension of the movement, onto his knees at his lord's feet.

"My lord . . ." The words were almost unintelligible, strangled in the guard's labored breathing. "The Lady Chandra. . . ."

Strong fingers tangled in the uniform tunic and hauled the guard to his feet. All hints of vagueness were gone from Lord Balin's eyes and his voice held an edge it had not held for five long years.

"What of my daughter?"

"Struck down by wizardry, my lord. You must come at. . . ." Suddenly released, he let the last word trail off into silence as his lord raced for the stable, snatched the reins of his bay stallion from an astonished groom, flung himself into the saddle, and thundered out of the stableyard, guards scrambling to mount and catch up.

One Below, not my daughter, too, pounded through Lord Balin's head in cadence with the pounding of the hooves. Images of the bright and laughing child she had been and the silent young woman she had become chased each other around the memory of his lost Marika and for the first time in five years the living became more important than the dead. *One Below, not my daughter, too.*

He rode onto the grounds of his country estate just as the setting sun bathed the sky in red.

"In the garden, my lord!" called a guard at the gate.

He forced the exhausted horse a little farther, over lawns and through flower beds to the tiny figure huddled in purple veiling at the base of Chandra's tower. One moment he was in the saddle, the next he had the wailing woman by the shoulders and was shaking her as he cried, "Where is my daughter?"

Aba's wails grew louder as she tried to point a flailing arm at the pile of muddy clothing lying on the path.

Lord Balin felt his heart stop. Almost gently, he set the old nurse aside. Dropping to his knees, he lifted the russet tunic. A curled and filthy strip of vellum dropped from it to the path, the script covering it barely visible in the fading sunlight. It took a moment for recognition to penetrate the pain, then his heart started beating again.

"This wasn't Chandra," he said, holding the tunic tight against his chest. "She made a golem. This wasn't my daughter."

"A golem?" Aba crept forward, and peered down at the smear of mud.

"Yes." Lord Balin stood, then immediately sat again on the stone bench as his legs threatened to give way beneath him. He beckoned a groom out of the knot of watching servants and almost smiled as she waited for no further orders but raced to the stallion and led it carefully away. "A golem," he explained to the puzzled old woman, "is a creature made of earth. Chandra created one in her own image so we would think her safely here."

"While she is *where?*" Aba demanded.

He did smile this time, at the indignation in the question. Chandra alive had no business being where her nurse could not get to her. For his part, Lord Balin felt almost supernaturally calm as his memories of Marika finally settled into the past where they belonged. "My guess is that Chandra is in Ischia, trying to talk Prince Darvish out of marrying her."

The black currant eyes above the veil narrowed. "That would be just like her," Aba agreed. Then her eyes widened again. "My poor baby, alone in that great big city. What are you going to do, my lord?"

He stood. "I'm going after her."

"Well, you'd better hurry." Plump hands pushed at his arm as though to prod him into instant action. "She has two full nine-days' head start."

"She has five years' head start," Lord Balin corrected quietly. "But I'm going to get my daughter back."

Chapter Thirteen

Blinking rapidly to shake the rain from her lashes, Chandra studied Tivolic. *Not a very attractive city,* she decided. Most of the buildings, at least those she could see above the city wall and the less desirable structures outside it, were dirty yellow brick or wood or a combination of both. Only the palace appeared to be made of stone and at this distance and in this weather she couldn't tell if it was Cisali marble or the soft gray stone of her own homeland. Nor, she had to admit, did she much care.

If it would only stop raining. She tossed her sodden braid back behind her shoulder. Adventure was one thing, but she was tired and wet, her clothes clung to her, her hair weighed a ton, Aaron hardly spoke, and Dar, while he hadn't had anything to drink, was certainly indulging in other vices. And it didn't make her any happier that the Shoi had stopped her when she'd tried to push the rain away.

"The rain will stop when the Lord and Lady choose," they'd told her.

It wasn't fair.

"Feeling sorry for yourself?" Fiona asked, falling into step beside her.

"I am a Wizard of the Nine," Chandra replied haughtily. How often did she have to *tell* people that. "I am *not* feeling sorry for myself."

"Good." Fiona nodded curtly, but her eyes twinkled. They walked in silence for a moment, then she asked, "What will you do after you have returned The Stone to Ischia?"

"Not marry Darvish," Chandra said emphatically stepping over a puddle. She'd spent the day before choking on dust; at least the rain had taken care of that.

"And after?"

"Go back to my tower!" Where she'd been comfortable. And dry.

"And?"

"And what?"

"And what will you do in your tower?"

"Well," Chandra spread her hands and frowned. "I'll be a wizard."

"Aren't you a wizard now?" Fiona asked mildly.

"Yes, of course I am!"

"Then why do you have to lock yourself in a tower?"

"I am not locked in the tower," Chandra told her angrily. "Nobody bothers me there and I can search for knowledge without distractions!" The words sounded pompous in a way they never had when she'd declaimed them to Aba.

"Oh. So you have learned nothing since you left your tower?"

"Of course I have! I didn't say I hadn't! I . . . I just. . . . Oh, never mind. You're not a wizard, you wouldn't understand." No one understood her. Her father certainly didn't. Not even Rajeet did, really. Rajeet might be a wizard, but she *wasn't* a Wizard of the Nine. She just wanted to get back to her tower where people would leave her alone. Except that in her mind's eye view of her tower, Darvish stretched indolently in the chair by the fireplace and Aaron perched on the window ledge. Startled, she banished them from the vision and refused to acknowledge how empty it now looked.

"I am not feeling sorry for myself," she repeated, but Fiona had slipped away in the irritatingly silent fashion of the Shoi and only the rain remained to hear her protest.

Darvish watched Tivolic growing nearer and wondered how much longer he'd be able to use the Shoi as a distraction. The training Edan had bullied him into at dawn and dusk—added to the willing bodies that filled his nights, added to the day's walk strung out alongside the carvans—kept him too tired to do more than long for a drink. And when the longing grew particularly intense he could throw his strength behind a jammed wagon, lift a child to his shoulders, and spend the next few miles answering impossible questions—he discovered, to his surprise, that he liked children and, to his pleasure, that they liked him—or toss the ever-willing Fion behind a bush.

Many eyes and many hands kept him from self-destruction.

He'd spent the three days with the Shoi doing nothing and thinking of nothing but surviving for those three days—one day at a time. Soon he'd have to face the real world again, face it without a curtain of wine around him, and he wasn't sure he could. Find The Stone and save Ischia; didn't a burden like that deserve a drink?

When they reached the city, only Chandra and Aaron would stand between him and the wine. He couldn't use them like that. He'd failed them once already. He had to be strong for them. Chandra was so young in so many ways and Aaron. . . .

Darvish looked ahead to where Aaron's bright hair, even darkened as it was by rain, stood out amidst the blacks and browns of the Shoi. It had grown longer and now curled against the sunburned nape of the younger man's neck. Darvish suddenly longed to run his fingers along that edge and rub some of the tension out of the shoulders below. He took a deep breath and let it out slowly; he would keep that thought very definitely to himself. He'd strained the fragile relationship he had with the outland thief enough already. The comfortable camaraderie they'd shared on the ship had disappeared when he'd so stupidly fallen in the sea.

Aaron wrapped himself in silence and glared when any of the Shoi approached. As they had for the last three days, they left him alone. Except he wasn't alone. The soul-link meant that Darvish was always present and so the memory of the fire, of the dance, of the burning that had nothing to do with the flames could not be completely suppressed.

His walls were so desperately fragile now, they took all his strength to maintain. Older memories slipped out through the cracks; the way Ruth's hair had shone almost blue-black in the sunlight, her screams echoing and reechoing within the stone walls of the keep, the taste of blood on his lips. . . .

I feel nothing, he reminded himself. *I am a dead man waiting to die.*

But as fast as he emptied the void, it filled again.

Just at the place where farmland became the outskirts of the city, the Shoi turned east onto a track so faint it no longer held the mark of wheels, only the memory of their passing. The rain had turned to mist and westward, the sea lay like a sheet of silver in a gray world. The three non-Shoi stood together at the turn and watched the wagons go by; their way led into the city, to The Stone, and whatever came after their finding of it. The children waved and shouted farewells, some of the younger adults blew indiscriminate kisses which Darvish chose to catch, but only Edan stopped to talk, flanked, as usual, by the twins.

"Come to offer sage words of advice?" Darvish asked, twisting the damp leather of his sword belt. He needed a drink. But then, he always needed a drink these days.

"No, no." Edan grinned and shook his head. "No one ever listened, so we stopped giving sage advice some time ago. We just wanted to tell you that the family will be back in this part of the world in about six years. If you survive this little adventure you're on, perhaps you can travel with us again."

Behind his uncle's back, Fion seconded the invitation with a decidedly lascivious wink.

"Are we likely to not survive?" Chandra asked, her voice rising shrilly for all she tried to keep it even. She'd almost died in the sea, but that had been by chance alone. At no time since she had decided to rescue The Stone had it occurred to her that she could be walking blithely toward death. She was going to prove to her father that she was a Wizard of the Nine and a force to be respected. She wasn't going to *die*.

"You're planning on taking a powerful artifact away from a powerful wizard who has the backing of a powerful king." Edan spread his hands expressively. "May the Lord and Lady watch over you."

"I think I'll stay with the Nine and One," Darvish said sardonically. "From the sound of it, we'll need the eight extra gods."

"Hold it." Aaron's voice cut through the sound of the city and his tone rooted both Darvish and Chandra to the spot. "Where are you going?"

"To the palace?" Darvish offered, both eyebrows rising.

"It is," Chandra added, "where The Stone is."

"Is it?"

"Well . . . uh . . ." When she'd tried to reach The Stone from just outside the city, all she'd touched was POWER. It had raced along her nerves, vibrated through her bones and, even now, still pulsed redly behind her temples in such a way she remained constantly aware of it. "I don't know," she admitted, almost shrugging. "It's so close I can't find anything beyond the power signature that's hanging over the entire city."

"This citywide power signature belongs to The Stone, right?" Darvish asked. "It isn't the power signature of the wizard we're after."

"Actually," Chandra tried an unsuccessful smile, "they seem to have become the same thing."

"Wonderful. Look . . ." Darvish sighed and moved out of the way as a pastry vendor pushed past, the last of his soggy wares having been given to half a dozen skinny children and a dog. "We know," he stepped closer and dropped his voice, "the palace is involved. It's the logical place to start."

"Granted." A part of Aaron wanted nothing more than to follow blindly along with what the others decided until he got some distance back, but the greater part could not sit by and watch while the two of them stumbled around in the dark. Not when he knew how to light the lamp. Time was running out, for Ischia and for Darvish. If Darvish failed, it would destroy him as surely as it would destroy the royal city. Aaron didn't care about Ischia. He didn't care, he reminded himself, about anything, but as long as he was here. . . . "If you go to the palace looking like that," a terse nod managed to take in all three of them, damp and travel-stained and woefully ill-equipped, "the guards will move you on, or worse, find you a place to stay. Unless you plan on declaring yourselves. Which would be worse still."

"All right, then." Darvish swept off an imaginary hat and bowed. "What do you suggest?"

"An inn, a bath, and a change of clothes. Then we go out with a plan. No aimless wandering."

"But aimless wandering's what I do best."

"Dar . . ." Aaron raised his head and locked eyes with the taller man. *No bullshit,* he suddenly wanted to say, *or I walk to the edge of the soul-link and throw myself off. I don't like it when you dig at yourself.* He didn't say it. The thought alone sent him scrambling to raise defenses, something very much like terror lending him strength.

Darvish scratched at his almost double nineday's worth of beard and the self-mocking smile slid into an honest grin, teeth gleaming white against the black. "You're right," he said. "I'm wrong. I'm sorry."

"But the sooner we find The Stone . . ." Chandra began to protest.

Darvish, having made up his mind, raised a weary hand. "You're going to walk up to the first wizard you see and ask him if he has The Stone of Ischia?"

"Well, no." She glanced over at Aaron, who, fighting desperately to regain control over himself, didn't notice.

"If they suspect we're looking for it," Darvish explained, "they'll move it. Then we'll have to follow it, and then this whole mess starts all over, taking up a lot more time than an inn, a bath, and a change of clothes." He spread his hands. "We'll have to be subtle, so we'll have to listen to Aaron." He reached over and tugged gently on the end of Chandra's braid. "Neither you nor I are particularly skilled at subtle."

Chandra bridled, opened her mouth, then closed it and caught what she had been about to say behind her teeth. Honesty forced her to admit he had a point. She sighed. "I could use a bath."

Darvish stepped back and motioned for Aaron to precede him. "Lead on, then, we're in your hands."

Aaron nodded. The walls, fragile and tottering though they were, were back in place.

"Beg pardon, gracious Lords, gentle Lady." The boy was small and undernourished and when they turned in response to his call, he cringed as though he expected to be struck. "P-pardon, Lords and Lady, but you looks like you just come in to the city."

"Good guess," Darvish said, sarcastic but not unkind, "as we're standing in the middle of the street arguing not five body lengths from the South Gate."

The boy looked unsure if he should smile at this and compromised by twitching his entire face through a change of expressions too rapid to identify. "It's just that if you're lookin' for an inn, Lords and Lady," his shoulders hunched and his bare feet shuffled against the wet cobbles, "I know this place. The old lady what runs it lets me sleep by her fire if I brings in people to stay. . . ." His voice trailed off and he managed to look both hopeful and completely without hope at the same time.

"Well," Darvish's voice had picked up a gentling tone, falling on Chandra's ear much the way her father's had when he tried to calm a highstrung colt or a nervous hawk, "I can't see why not."

"No."

"But Aaron. . . ."

"We're on our way to The Gallows."

The boy snorted. "Powerful expensive at The Gallows."

"We're willing to pay the price," Aaron told him.

With a shrug that involved his entire body, the boy suddenly seemed less small and less undernourished. "Can't blame a guy for tryin'," he told them cheerfully, spun on a callused heel and trotted away. There were very few people on the street, but he vanished from sight almost between one heartbeat and the next.

Chandra and Darvish exchanged puzzled looks.

"Can I safely assume we missed something there?" Darvish asked.

Aaron got them moving with a jerk of his head. "*If* there's an inn," he told them leading the way down a narrow street where the windows almost met just over Darvish's head, "it isn't one you'd want to use. Likely, he'd take us to an alley and several of his larger friends."

"But we don't have anything to steal," Chandra protested as they flattened against a building to allow a wooden cart of glistening fish to rumble by. She tried not to gag. The smell of the street was bad enough.

"Your hair, Dar's sword, my pouch." Aaron listed their salable assets as they began walking again. "If we were very unlucky, there'd be a Wizard of the Fourth looking for semiconscious bodies to practice on."

"And if we were lucky?"

"They'd kill us."

Chandra shuddered.

"Hey, don't worry," Darvish laid a huge and comforting hand on her shoulder. "If some kid tries to kill you, I'll protect you."

"If some kid tries to kill me," Chandra snapped, twisting out from under his hand, "I'll turn what tiny brain he has to pudding."

"Can you do that?" Darvish asked, trying to keep the amusement out of his voice. The rejection hurt a little. His sword was, after all, the only skill he really had to offer in the saving of his city, but he knew bravado when he heard it.

She hesitated. If truth be told—unbidden, a memory surfaced of the five dead guards covered in their own blood and discarded like meat on the grass—she didn't think she could kill anyone, not by magical or other means. There was, however, no point in letting Aaron and Dar know that. Her chin went up. "I can take care of myself," she declared, every inch a Wizard of the Nine.

"Never doubted it," Aaron said quietly.

Chandra turned to look at him in grateful surprise and he raised one demon wing to half flight in acknowledgment.

The rapport between his companions no longer cut at Darvish as deeply—his defeat of the guards had given him back his place—but he felt a faint stirring of jealousy at Aaron's easy acceptance of the girl. *He never lowers his guard that much with me.* He was beginning to wonder why, when, from an overhanging window, came the unmistakable smell of strong wine. *How much could it matter,* he wondered instead, *if I only had one drink?*

A dozen narrow doorways later, the street dumped them out into a market square. In spite of the rain that continued to fall intermittently, a brisk business went on at wagons and packs and neat little booths that leaned together for support. The square obviously didn't belong to the rundown neighborhood they'd just passed through but to the wider streets and cleaner buildings that fronted the other sides.

Aaron led them straight across the market although there were paths around the edges that looked clearer. They had to push their way through a wildly gesticulating crowd attempting to buy live lobsters pulled that morning from the sea, and at one point they were stopped completely by three very fat women who blocked the entire aisle while they screamed in unison at a spice merchant.

Chandra tried to act as if she'd seen it all before, but the markets her father had taken her to as a child were nothing like this. Few people shouted and no one threw overripe tomatoes when their lord and his heir walked among them. She almost resented this market for dulling a cherished memory of her father.

Taller than most of the crowd, Darvish scanned the stalls for the familiar racks of clay bottles. *No wine merchants.* He tried unsuccessfully to work up enough moisture to spit. *My mouth tastes like an ash pit. Just one drink so I can peel my lips off my teeth. That's all I need. Just one.*

The Gallows stood in the middle of a row of slightly seedy, middle-class, three-story, yellow brick buildings, its name the only disreputable thing about it. The louvered shutters that covered the front wall of windows were latched closed and the entire facade had a kind of "don't bother me" air about it.

The door opened directly into the common room, cool and dim and empty but for two men pushing ivory game pieces about on a corner table. Wooden-paddled ceiling fans hung motionless in the damp air.

"What?"

The question originated from behind the bar. Chandra and Darvish exchanged unsure glances—the voice hadn't sounded friendly—but they followed Aaron toward the huge ebony-skinned woman who loomed over the counter. She didn't *look* friendly either.

Two kegs of ale and a barrel of wine lay against the back wall on a deep shelf. Rough clay mugs and goblets lined the narrower shelf above. Darvish tried not to stare.

"We need rooms," Aaron told her, both hands out in plain sight. "Two of them. The back rooms on the third floor if they're empty."

She smiled. And still didn't look friendly. "You've been here before."

"I have."

"Then you know those rooms don't come cheap."

"We're willing to pay the price."

"Humph." She grunted, relaxed slightly, and named an amount.

Aaron reached into his pouch and pulled out a handful of silver coins. "Three days," he said handing them over.

"You want the boy to stoke up the boiler?"

"Yes." He added a copper coin to the pile.

"You know where the rooms are," she waved a hand, nails gnawed to the quick, at the stairs. "And, Wizard!"

Chandra started at the sudden shout.

"Fires get lit with a tinder in here."

With effort, Chandra managed to hold onto her aplomb. "Of course," she said, pulling the end of the braid from her mouth and tossing it behind her.

"How did she know?" she hissed at Aaron as they walked to the stairs.

"The door's glyphed. She knew the moment you walked through it. Some inns won't serve wizards."

Chandra bridled. "Why not?"

"Do too much damage when they're drunk."

They were on the first step when Aaron realized Darvish hadn't followed. He knew what he'd see, but he turned back anyway.

Darvish set the empty goblet carefully down on the bar and wiped his mouth defiantly. "My throat was dry," he threw the words out like a challenge. "I just needed to wet it."

There was a number of things that could be said. From the look on Darvish's face, they'd all occurred to him so Aaron forced his lips together and said nothing. Head high, Darvish strode across the room, heels ringing against the floorboards. He kept his eyes fixed on the middle distance as he pushed past his silent companions, but his hands were fists and his jaw was tight.

"Dar. . . ." At Aaron's touch, Chandra quieted and the three of them climbed in heavy silence up the two flights of stairs.

The back rooms on the third floor were connected. One held a single bed, a few hooks for clothes and a three legged stool. The other held two beds—one large and piled high with embroidered pillows, the second narrow and plain—an armor stand and a number of low, serving tables as well as the wall hooks. The smaller room had a single window, long and narrow with louvered shutters now latched against the rain. The larger had three, the center one opening onto a tiny balcony.

Chandra went into the single room, threw the latch, then came and stood in the adjoining doorway, arms crossed and fingers tight against the damp fabric of her sleeves. Aaron sat on the edge of the narrow bed and Darvish walked across the room to stare out the window.

"Well, why don't you say it?" he growled.

"Say what?" Chandra prodded. *I hate weakness. My father is weak. Why can't I hate Dar?* Because she'd seen Darvish fighting his weakness, even if he lost occasionally, and that was more than she could say for her father.

"Say what a weakling I am, what a stupid fool. Say how I could be destroying any chance I may have to save my people. Say you don't need a drunken sot traveling with you, messing things up, getting you killed. Nine Above, say something!"

"We don't have to," Aaron told him. "You've said it all."

"Is that supposed to be helpful?" Darvish asked without turning.

Aaron's voice was almost neutral as he replied. "No."

The prince threw open the shutters and drew in a deep breath of rain-laden air. It washed over the taste of wine still in his mouth and he tightened his fingers on the wood to keep them from trembling. "It's worse now. I've reminded my hands and my mouth and my throat of the motions and I'm afraid they'll go on without me. I remember how much easier life was with the edges washed away."

There didn't seem to be anything to say after that. The silence stretched and hardened around them.

"That boy," Chandra said at last, and her voice broke the silence into pieces small enough to ignore. "He called us Lords and Lady. How did he know?" She plucked at the stained fabric of her trousers. "We look like beggars."

"Beggars." Aaron almost smiled. "You look dirty and badly clothed, but neither of you," his voice softened, "can look like any less than what you are. You don't know how."

Darvish turned to face back into the room. The rain had divided his eyelashes into damp spikes. At least they all agreed to believe it was the rain. "The boy said Lords. Plural," he pointed out.

Aaron snorted and the demon wings rose. "I'm a thief," he said, getting to his feet. His tone closed the conversation, but just in case Chandra refused to drop it, he moved to distance it further still. Onto the bed, from various places in his clothing, he dumped six fat purses, a beautifully crafted silver belt buckle and an ugly gold chain.

"We need new clothes." Apparently oblivious to the stunned reactions of the prince and the wizard, he hefted a purse, dumped the contents in his belt pouch and tossed the now empty silk bag back to the bed. "While you're bathing, I'll send the innkeeper's boy." He'd prefer to go himself, but the soul-link made that impossible. "The bathing room is beside the kitchen. She only has one tub so we'll have to take turns. If there's no hot water, complain. We paid extra for it." His tone was so matter-of-fact that it carried him out the door and almost to the stairs before either Darvish or Chandra could react.

While Chandra bathed, Darvish sat on a bench in the hall and stared at his hands twisted in his lap. He could hear her muttering and splashing and imploring the Nine for assistance through the thin wall. From the kitchen came the controlled cadences of Aaron's instructions to the innkeeper's son, a stocky lad of about ten whose complete vocabulary seemed to consist of "Yup," "Nope," and "I gotta ask my ma." He could smell something cooking although he had no idea what it was. An uneven tile caught his attention and he rubbed the sole of his boot along the raised join.

Singly and collectively, none of it was enough to keep him from thinking of the wine. He couldn't smell it, he couldn't see it, but he knew it was there. It was close. So close.

Chandra wouldn't know, and Aaron. . . .

Darvish sighed. It always seemed to come back to Aaron. How many thoughts had he had recently that ended with, *and Aaron?*

The Nine take him anyway! I haven't even slept with him and he's running my life.

He stood up. He sat down again. The bench was too hard. The air was too close. He couldn't breathe in this soup! His fingers twitched against his thighs. There would be men and women in that tavern soon, having as much to drink as they wanted. It wasn't fair.

He wanted a drink.

He needed a drink.

He drew his legs under him to stand again and Aaron came out of the kitchen.

Their gazes locked and just for a second the heat in Aaron's eyes burned away all thoughts of wine. Then they were cold again and Darvish was left trying to catch his breath and wondering if he'd imagined the fire.

With his face resembling more carved marble than flesh, Aaron settled himself beside Darvish on the bench.

He despises me now. Darvish rubbed sweaty palms against his thighs. *I can't say as I blame him. He looks like he did back at the beginning, before The Stone was stolen—stone himself. I've destroyed everything between us. Bugger the Nine, I am such an ass!*

I want to help him. Aaron clenched his teeth so tightly the pressure pushed against his temples and he couldn't understand why they didn't shatter. *It's been too long. I don't know how.* The knowledge was behind the wall. *Faharra, help me. I'm afraid.* But no comfortingly caustic voice came out of memory, only the faint sound of screams.

The tension grew until it could almost be seen, wrapping around the two of them like spiderwebs.

"Dar. . . ."

The prince jumped, landing on his feet out in the passageway, facing the bench, fists up.

The tableau froze that way for a moment, then Aaron started breathing again and, speaking loud enough to be heard over the wild pounding of his heart, said, "You hungry?"

Darvish's mouth twitched, then he snickered.

Aaron began to sputter and bit his lip to hold it back.

Then they were both holding their sides and roaring with laughter.

Sometime later, when they were burning their fingers on skewers of spiced lamb, Chandra opened the bathing room door a crack and stuck her head out. "I am *not* putting those clothes back on!" she announced, snatching up Aaron's last piece of meat and popping it in her mouth.

The demon wings rose to their full extension. "Would the Most Wise like me to find her a robe until the new clothes arrive?"

"Yes. The Most Wise would." She chewed and watched him leave, then looked down at Darvish, one bare shoulder extending into the passageway. "Are you all right?"

"I've been better," Darvish said honestly.

Chandra nodded in understanding. "Hey, me too. I've never had to wash my own hair before."

Darvish grinned. "Neither have I."

"Yours," Chandra snorted, "is short." Then she retreated to wait for the robe.

It was five sizes too big when it came, but she wrapped it around her and managed to sweep regally to the stairs without tripping. Three steps up, she paused and looked back. Darvish was laughing at Aaron's description of how to refill the tub, every inch the useless princeling. Maybe Aaron was right. Maybe screaming at him wasn't the answer. Would've made her feel better though.

Darvish was in the bath when the new clothes came. Aaron, tied by the soul-link, sat on the bench fighting to keep the finger exercises he was doing the only thing in his mind. It wasn't easy. The sound of a large body moving in water kept intruding. He sent the boy upstairs with Chandra's packages and, when he came down, into the bathing room with Dar's. He had, for a moment, thought he might deliver the second set himself, but his courage failed him.

When Aaron's turn came, he stayed in the water until his hands and feet were pink and wrinkled and the scars on his chest puckered purple. It was a breathing spell of sorts. Away from Darvish, he didn't have to fight so hard to maintain his walls.

The water was nearly cold when he finally pulled himself out, dried, and dressed. He twitched the dark green vest into place, raised his chin, and stepped into the hall.

Darvish, dressed as a private bodyguard, sat on the stairs, one leg braced against the other, stropping his sword. He smiled a welcome which turned to a laugh when he saw what Aaron wore.

"So I'm to be your hireling, am I?" he asked.

Aaron nodded. "As an outland merchant and his guard, we can go almost anywhere in the city."

"And what part does Chandra play?"

"Consulting wizard maybe. If she's willing to be less than a Wizard of the *Nine*."

Darvish laughed again and sheathed his sword, shoving the palm-sized whetstone into a trouser pocket. "I want to be there when you ask her *that*."

They were at the connecting door when Chandra began to scream.

Chapter Fourteen

The world was red slashed through with brilliant yellow and it burned. One Below, how it burned. . . .

She couldn't fight. She couldn't twist free. She could scream, but that was all and it didn't help.

The power surged through her, etching its path with fire. Caught by a nearly perfect focus, but focused on nothing, it rebounded and retracted the course, searing deeper still. Then around once more. And once more, in widening circles of diminishing intensity.

An awareness of self began to edge through the red and, as the pain relaxed its grip on her muscles, she felt her body spasm.

"Get her on her side, quickly! Before she chokes on it!"

The voice slammed into her, hammering at senses already raw. Darvish. Why was Darvish yelling? She wanted to scream at him to be quiet, but she couldn't catch her breath. She gagged and choked, her stomach heaved, and she slid back down into the red and the black.

Eventually, the black became gray and the red a throbbing that could be endured.

"I think she's coming back."

Coming back? Had she been gone somewhere? Gathering her strength, she managed to open her eyes. Only to close them instantly as the lamplight drove golden spikes into her aching head.

"Here, try again." A cool cloth stroked her brow. "I've moved the lamp."

She didn't want to try again. Didn't he understand? It hurt!

"Please, Chandra. I know it hurts, but we're worried about you."

"Go away," she muttered weakly.

"No."

She had to open her eyes in order to glare at that blunt response. The light, dim enough to bear, threw Darvish's face into deep shadow but he did, indeed, look worried.

"I'm okay," she protested as he leaned forward and stroked the cloth across her brow again. She took a deep breath and weakly tried to bat his hand away. The attempt had about as much chance of succeeding as a kitten did in dislodging a lion from a favored perch, but Darvish sat back, dropping the cloth in a basin by the bed.

"You gave us quite a scare," he said. "What happened?"

What happened? Pain happened. She had a vague memory of hitting the floor and. . . . "Was I . . . sick?"

"Yes. But don't worry, we cleaned it, and you, up."

"Wizards of the Nine don't vomit," she muttered petulantly. Her throat hurt.

"I'm sure they don't," Darvish agreed. "Except under extraordinary circumstances." He clasped her arm lightly with one large, warm hand. "Why don't you tell us what they were."

Chandra turned her head and searched for Aaron. He was leaning against the wall at the foot of the bed, arms crossed and brows drawn down. He looked even more expressionless than usual. Chandra hadn't thought that possible. *He* must *be upset.*

She turned back to Darvish and took as deep a breath as she was capable of. Might as well get it over with. "I tried to find the exact location of The Stone. He, the wizard, knew I was there and. . . ."

"He attacked you?" Darvish growled.

"Not exactly." She paused and tried to swallow with a mouth gone suddenly dry. "I need a drink." She didn't see Darvish wince, only drank gratefully from the mug he placed at her lips. The water was slightly tepid, but it helped. "He threw power at me. From The Stone. A lot of power." Her fingers plucked at the edge of the light blanket that covered her. "I had no spells set up. There was no place for the power to go. It poured in and. . . ." She bit her lip and her eyes filled with tears. Embarrassed, she blinked them rapidly away. Wizards of the Nine did not cry.

Darvish shot Aaron a concerned look and the thief moved away from the wall. Behind him, a scar three hands' spans long and one wide marked where the plaster had been blasted off the brick.

Chandra's eyes widened. "Did I do that?"

Aaron nodded. "And four more like it," he told her dryly. "Not to mention a gouge out of the floor and," a corner of his mouth twitched up, "we owe the innkeeper a new three legged stool. When Darvish kicked open the door, you were reducing it to three legged kindling."

Chandra swiped at damp cheeks with the palm of her hand. "You kicked down the door?" she asked Darvish incredulously. By leaning a little, very carefully, she could see the ruin dangling from a single twisted hinge. "The door was open."

Looking a little sheepish, Darvish shrugged. "You were screaming. I didn't want to waste any time."

"So we'll buy a new door." She reached over and poked him in the thigh. "Thanks."

"You're welcome." And then, because he *had* bit back the self-mocking words that first occurred to him as a response, he scooped up her hand and kissed it.

Something he's probably done a hundred, a thousand times, she thought, snatching her hand away. *There probably isn't a hand in Ischia he hasn't kissed. Wizards of the Nine* don't *blush.* "We still don't know where The Stone is," she snapped and instantly regretted it as her voice slapped against the inside of her skull.

"No, we don't," Darvish admitted, serious again. He stood and settled his sword back into place. "But if you're all right, Aaron and I are going out to see what we can discover."

"I'm going with you!" She tried to rise and the room whirled, patterns of black and red chasing each other behind her eyes. She couldn't stop the whimper that escaped as she lay back down. "Don't," she protested as Darvish bent over her, his face twisted with concern. Aaron had moved closer as well. She felt like a fool.

"You're right," she said after a moment chiefly concerned with riding through the pain. "You two go. I'm okay if I lie still."

They hesitated.

"Go," she insisted. "And when you find that wizard, I'm going to take The Stone and stuff it up his . . ."

"Chandra!" Darvish exclaimed, shocked. "Is that any way for a gently bred young woman to talk?"

". . . nose, Dar, I'm going to stuff it up his nose. Nine Above, you have a filthy mind."

He bowed and Aaron rolled his eyes, putting more into that brief expression than most men could get into an hour of monologue.

She tried not to laugh—it hurt—but a strained giggle escaped anyway. "Get out," she said, waving them to the door. "And for the One's sake, be careful."

The common room of The Gallows was about half full, but Aaron and Darvish attracted no attention as they crossed toward the door.

The kind of place, Darvish thought, *where the clientele minded its own business.* He had a good idea of just what kind of place it was and appreciated the sense of humor that had named a safe haven for thieves and their associates, The Gallows. Remembering what Aaron had said to both the boy and the innkeeper, he shook his head. *"We're willing to pay the price . . ."* Nine Above, how macabre.

"Remember," Aaron murmured to him, his hand on the outer door, "you're a bodyguard. Stay a sword's length behind me."

The rain had stopped and the air was cool and sweet, the stench of the city washed into the gutters and out to sea. In the quiet middle-class neighborhood of The Gallows, the streets were deserted. They stood for a moment against the inn, the prince and the thief, giving their eyes a chance to acclimatize to the night.

"The direct route will take us through an area bordering on dangerous," Aaron said quietly, his gaze sweeping up and down the street. A merchant, still wearing a sunrobe although the sun had long set, was a fluttering shadow against the darkness as he hurried home. "Hopefully your presence will be enough to discourage any interest."

"No honor amongst thieves?" Darvish quipped.

Aaron's pale eyes gleamed eerily in the light that spilled through the louvered shutters of the inn. "None," he said.

Darvish loosened his sword, squared his shoulders, and practiced a menacing scowl. Perhaps if he appeared intimidating enough he wouldn't have to kill anyone. Suddenly, he noticed that Aaron was unarmed but for a tiny, useless dagger hanging from his tooled leather belt. "You should have bought yourself a weapon."

"I don't carry weapons." Aaron's lips had thinned to a nearly invisible line.

"A man is never without his weapons."

"Shut up, Father."

"Strong and fast and completely merciless. We're drawn from the same sheath, Aaron, my son."

"Shut up, Father!"

He pushed his father's voice back behind the wall.

Darvish didn't understand why Aaron had gone so still and he only saw the flash of pain because he had his gaze locked on the younger man's face. "Hey," he said gently. "Don't worry about it. I can fight for both of us."

After a second, Aaron nodded, spun on one heel, and they moved off.

If this area borders on dangerous, Darvish thought a short while later, his gaze sweeping from shadow to shadow, sure that a multitude of eyes watched and weighed their passing, *then I don't want to see what dangerous means around here.* He knew the places in Ischia where a person dared not venture alone, but they were home and perhaps that was why this place seemed so much more threatening. *Perhaps not,* he admitted, growling a wordless warning as a figure lounging in the mouth of an alley moved marginally in their direction.

Aaron walked quickly, purposefully, like a man who knew where he was going and intended to arrive there no matter what. The weak and the stupid were usually the prey of the streets and he had no intention of appearing to be either. He wouldn't normally have taken the route they traveled, but he doubted Darvish could have kept up on the paths he preferred—his glance flickered for an instant to the rooftops—and it was undeniably the fastest *if* trouble could be avoided.

Whether trouble decided that the swordsman was just too big to risk, or it was busy elsewhere, they got through safely to a neighborhood where wealth bought security and frequent patrols by the city guard. Up ahead, they could see a blaze of light and color.

"The Avenue of the Palace," Aaron said quietly, allowing Darvish to catch up.

Darvish frowned and shook his head. Even at this distance the glow from the lamps and wizard-lights illuminated the street. They stood by a small enclosed garden, a large cat regarding them warily from the top of the wall.

"He holds an Open Court," Aaron explained as they made their way toward the lights. "Most of the participants are merchants with invitations from the Council. But if you can get past the guards at the gate. . . ." He placed a hand on the new belt pouch that bulged suggestively.

"The king's insane," Darvish muttered. "How does he keep control of the crowds."

"The open area is limited and heavily warded. The crowd itself is on its best behavior." Aaron snorted. "At least half of them are trying for titles."

"Does he do this often?"

"Five or six times a year." They had reached the entrance to the avenue and had to pause while a litter bobbed by in a flutter of scarlet ribbons. "We were lucky."

"Lucky?" Darvish glanced up the broad street toward the palace. Even from a distance, it was obvious that the men and women making their way along it were either eminently respectable or foolishly pretentious; both types Darvish normally went out of his way to avoid. "Aaron, this lot won't know anything about The Stone," he protested.

"Probably not," Aaron agreed, but they'll get us into the palace and someone there *will.*" He twitched the heavy silk folds of his long dark green vest into place and joined the parade. Grumbling under his breath, Darvish fell into step behind him.

The guard was bribed as easily as Aaron had predicted and they joined the flood streaming through the gate and into the palace.

"You've done this before," Darvish murmured against the top of Aaron's head when the crush of bodies moving through the narrow arch pressed them momentarily together. Aaron merely looked haughty and Darvish suppressed a grin.

The area of the palace available to the Open Court consisted of three large rooms leading into each other with the massive, gold embossed doors of the throne room at the far end. These doors, as well as the smaller ones accessing other parts of the palace, were closed and guarded. Three great crystal clusters hung from the ceiling in each room, all nine ablaze with wizard-light. Along the right, where huge arched windows did not begin until the wall had risen unbroken higher than a tall man's head, were tables piled with food and drink. Along the left, windows that stretched from the floor up almost the entire two stories had shutters folded back and were open to the night. Through them came the scents of lily and jasmine and in each stood a member of the palace guard. The royal gardens were off-limits.

Out in the darkness, a peacock shrieked.

Darvish set his jaw. Not even Yasimina's One abandoned peacocks deserved to die under a burning river of ash and molten rock. They *would* find The Stone in time. Unable to keep his face expressionless, he stayed close to Aaron's back and glowered.

As Aaron wandered through the crowd, brushing in and out of clusters of conversation, Darvish noticed that the honest citizens of Tivolic deferred to the young outlander. They seemed pleased to answer his questions and honored by his notice. At first, Darvish thought the reason might be tied to his proximity, but there were other private guards in the rooms—some his size, two actually larger—and the merchants they followed didn't command the same respect. He fell back a little and studied his companion.

Although shorter than most of the men and women present, Aaron somehow gave the impression of imposing height. His posture held the arrogance of complete self-assurance and his thin features were set in a mask perfectly combining polite interest and world-weary disdain. Surrounded by bright silks and ribbons and gauzes, his dark green and cream stood out as simple elegance and he carried his head as though the brilliant copper hair were a crown.

Nine Above and One Below. Darvish caught his breath in admiration. *My little thief plays a better prince than I ever could.*

Respectfully acknowledging a cluster of shaven-headed priests, Aaron strolled into the third of the rooms. During his last time in Tivolic, he had darkened his hair and skin and used the Open Court to make a survey of possible prey. A young woman back in the middle room used it for the same purpose tonight. They had saluted each other warily and continued their separate ways; after a certain level of skill, the profession held no strangers. Tonight he needed information so he became, for the men and women attending, a part of the experience of the Open Court. It didn't matter that they'd remember him, he wouldn't be working in Tivolic again.

Ignoring the guard, Aaron drifted to a window and looked up at the night sky. He took a deep breath and marked where the black edges of buildings blocked the stars. As he exhaled, he turned and continued his slow circuit, a possible route to the heart of the palace carefully filed away.

He skirted a pair of wizards, bowed to a shriveled old woman, who gazed after him in surprise, and tried to ignore his buzzing nerves. *I didn't used to have nerves.* He could feel Darvish following respectfully behind him. Nerves used to be buried with everything else, behind the wall. He hadn't realized things had gotten so bad. *I used to work alone.*

So far, no one had mentioned The Stone or Ischia although rumors of a war were rife and the merchants were grumbling of revolt should the king increase taxes to pay for it.

"The rooms are well filled tonight, Gracious Majesty."

"The rooms are always well filled for these One abandoned things," King Harith grunted, squinting through the spy hole. "I see Lord Fath is down there."

Lord Rahman bowed, in case the king could see him from the corner of an eye. "As you commanded, Sire."

"Well, he'd better be telling stirring tales of victory and honor, by the Nine, if he wants those land grants." He scowled at the distant figure of the young lord who appeared to be holding half the room enthralled. There was no way of knowing exactly what he was talking about, but it seemed to involve a great deal of arm waving, that the king supposed could represent sword thrusts. Lord Fath had been instructed to work on building popular sentiment for a war. The more volunteers he had from the merchant class, the more sons and daughters willing to put on a uniform for the glory of it, the more the parents would be willing to pay. His council would be ecstatic if he could take Cisali without the need to pay for mercenaries.

Grumbling under his breath, the king scanned the rest of the crowd. He was *not* looking forward to walking the length of the rooms and back. The Open Courts were a success. There'd been much less squawking about taxes since they'd begun, but he hated them with a passion. He never knew what to say.

Fortunately, I'm too good a king to allow my personal preference to outweigh the chance of getting this lot to cheerfully pay for a . . . "Nine Above!"

"Gracious Majesty?"

"I wasn't calling *you,* Rahman. You always did think highly of yourself." He stepped away from the spy hole. "But as long as you're here, have a look at the young man standing under the wizard-lights."

Lord Rahman peered through the tiny aperture and clicked his tongue. "Very striking, Gracious Majesty," he agreed. "Hair that brilliant a color is rare."

"It's not just the color, Rahman." King Harith waved the elderly lord back to his place. "Look at how he holds himself." The king took his own advice. "Nine Above, but I'd be happy if my son had half that much presence."

"Your eldest son, Gracious Majesty, is but seven years old. And although the outlander does indeed have presence, he looks to me, Sire, as if a sharp blow could shatter him completely."

"Nonsense. He looks strong, in control . . . familiar." The king straightened up and frowned. "An outlander with hair like beaten copper. Why do I feel I should know him?"

Lord Rahman pulled reflectively on the pointed end of his short white beard. "An outlander," he murmured. "Hair like. . . ." He released his beard and bowed. "The thief that travels with Prince Darvish is an outlander with red hair, Gracious Majesty."

"Thief?" The king studied the outlander again." He does fit the description at that. Nine Above, but the boy has balls, standing there as arrogant as you please. If this is the lad, I don't see Prince Darvish."

"No, Gracious Majesty, nor did I. And he would be very evident if he were here." Lord Rahman had met Cisali's third prince at the treaty wedding the year before. He had not been impressed by the drunken fop.

"Have the guards pick up this bold young thief, Rahman. Carefully though, we don't want to have to chase him through half the merchants in Tivolic. Oh, and Rahman." The old lord stopped, one hand on the door. "Have him brought to me here. I like his looks and I want to speak with him before he's executed."

Darvish was finding the evening easier than he'd expected. He had, after all, been playing a role at his father's court for years and hovering protectively was certainly less wearing than the contortions he went through in Ischia. Although he desperately desired a drink, he forced himself to approach that desire from the point of view of a private guard. *I am on duty. I cannot drink.* It helped. It made him feel like he had his life under control. *Maybe I should keep the job.* He hooked his thumbs in his sword belt. *I seem to be better at it than the one I was born to.*

He studied his reflection in an ornately framed wall mirror just as Aaron looked up and met his eyes in the glass. Darvish's heart lurched and he took an involuntary step forward.

Aaron felt caught, trapped; he couldn't look away. Nor was he sure he wanted to. Then his jaw dropped and whatever stretched between was shattered by the sudden realization that they were in serious trouble.

He spun on a heel and, with a jerk of his head indicating Darvish should follow, strode quickly for the exit, the length of three rooms away. *It may already be too late . . .*

"What's his hurry?" asked a young matron, watching the outlander and his guard leave with some interest.

"Probably heading for a dark corner," her husband said suggestively, piling three oysters on a biscuit.

"But he's by himself," she protested.

Her husband, who had been close enough to see what had passed in the mirror, only grinned and reached for a pomegranate.

"Why are we leaving?" Darvish demanded in an undertone as they reached the first room and were slowed by the crowd still arriving. "We haven't learned anything yet."

"The king is about to walk the rooms," Aaron muttered, glaring down an elderly man who looked too curious. "He mustn't see you."

"He won't recognize me, Aaron." Darvish grabbed the smaller man by the shoulder and spun him around, not caring how it looked. They were walking away from their best chance to find The Stone. "Look at me, I still have Chandra's illusion on my eyes and I've grown a beard!"

"Look at yourself," Aaron snarled. "With brown eyes and a beard you're a slightly larger image of the crown prince. I think he'll notice that!"

Darvish almost threw Aaron to one side, grabbed a silver tray from an astounded servant and held it up to his face. "Bugger the Nine," he said softly. *After all those years of trying to belong, was this all it took; an illusion and a beard?* "I didn't realize." He lowered the tray and shook his head. "I never looked like any of them before." Breathing deeply, he managed a wry smile. "As usual, my timing is impeccable. Let's get out of here."

They were at the gate, a single guard between them and freedom, when a shout from the room behind told them that their leaving had not gone unnoticed.

"I don't care what warned them! Go after them!"

The gate guard turned at the shout, saw two men approaching, and lowered his pike to block their way.

Aaron broke into a run, twisted at the last second, and slithered eel-like between the pike and the wall. Darvish didn't bother trying to go around. He grabbed the haft of the weapon, yanked it from the guard's grip, and smacked him hard in the chest with the butt end. The guard slammed up against the wall and slid to the flagstones, gasping for breath.

Suddenly, every hair on Darvish's body rose and his skin crawled.

"The wards!" Aaron shouted.

Cursing, Darvish dove forward just as the gate wards snapped into effect. He hit the ground, rolled, got to his feet, stumbled, and cursed again. His right foot had gone completely numb. Gritting his teeth, he broke into a staggering run. Fortunately, some feeling remained in his ankle; mostly pain, but that was better than no feeling at all. At least he retained some control.

"I wasn't quite fast enough," he grunted as Aaron dragged him off the brightly lit Avenue of the Palace and into the deep shadow of an ornate wall. He pounded his boot, trying to beat sensation back into the flesh it covered, and prayed for feeling to return. The pain spread down from his ankle. "One Below," he grunted, biting his lip at this answer to his prayer, "you deal in mixed blessings at best."

Aaron frowned as guards spilled out of the palace. Were they going to course blindly through the streets with no idea of the direction their quarry had taken? Then he growled wordlessly as the guards were joined by a robed Wizard of the Fourth. The ward. They could track Darvish by the ward.

Tersely, he explained the situation to the prince.

"So until the ward wears off. . . . It will wear off?" Aaron nodded and Darvish continued, "They know where we are?"

"Yes."

The wizard's hand was up and sweeping the avenue. At most, they had minutes remaining.

Darvish stood and deliberately put pressure on the foot. He couldn't feel the pavement under it. "What do we do?"

"We walk a path they can't follow. Can you climb?"

Darvish set his jaw. "I can do anything I have to."

He wasn't so sure of that two gardens and a rooftop later as he followed Aaron along an uneven ledge half a brick wide. It wasn't so much the width of the ledge, it was the two-story drop should his scraped fingers lose their grip. He reached for a new hold and lifted himself forward in an awkward hop, dragging his numb foot along the wall. Another two hops and he ran out of brick.

"Aaron?"

"Shh!"

The admonishment came from below. Darvish squinted under the curve of his shoulder and saw Aaron standing on a balcony one story down and five feet across open air, gesturing at him to jump. "Forget it," he muttered, searching for an alternative. There didn't appear to be one.

Two gardens, a rooftop, and the One abandoned ledge away, he could hear a woman's voice—the wizard?—yelling, "Go up, I said! Then go around, but don't let them get away!"

"I definitely need a drink." He dangled for a moment on one arm and then with a combination of brute strength and luck, managed to turn so that his back pressed against the wall. *It's not far,* he thought, looking down at Aaron and blinking sweat from his eyes. *I could just fall forward and not miss it.*

Muttering a brief prayer to the Nine and One, he jumped.

He hit the balcony standing, then dropped to his hands and knees, biting back a cry as the warded foot shot daggers of fire all the way up to his hip. Aaron pulled him erect and he leaned on the thief's shoulder for a heartbeat, catching his breath. As the pain faded, he realized he could feel the brick through both soles.

"Good," Aaron whispered when told. "The ward is fading. Stay close." And he sped, a silent shadow, down the length of the balcony.

Stay close. Darvish shuffled after him as quietly as he was able. *And all this time I thought he didn't have a sense of humor.*

One of the louvered doors swung slowly open and he froze.

Rubbing her eyes, a little girl of no more than five wandered out onto the balcony. She saw him and stopped. "I heard noises," she told him sleepily.

"Everything's under control, little Mistress." Darvish forced his voice to remain low and soothing. "Go back to bed."

Her lower lip went out. "Will you tell me what happened in the morning?"

He smiled. "If you go back to bed now."

"Promise?"

He hated to make a promise he couldn't keep. "I promise."

She nodded, satisfied, and padded back inside.

Darvish gently pushed the door shut and hurried to catch up with Aaron, his heart pounding so loudly he was sure it must wake the rest of the household. He leaned forward and placed his mouth close to the other man's ear. "She must have thought I was one of her father's guards."

Aaron, all too aware of warm breath against the side of his head, pulled a little away. "If her father has guards," he said quietly, "I suggest we leave."

Darvish looked at the iron pipe running to the roof. "Up that?"

Aaron nodded.

"Will it hold my weight?"

Teeth glimmered briefly in the darkness as Aaron smiled. "It should."

It did, but only just.

Darvish's foot had regained almost all feeling when Aaron suddenly dropped flat on the narrow top of a crumbling wall. Darvish dropped as well and then inched forward until he could grasp Aaron's ankle. "What's wrong?" he hissed. They were in a poorer neighborhood now, looking down into a narrow yard that stretched behind a row of tenements.

"They've cut down the tree that used to be here," Aaron said tightly. "We need it to get up there, to that row of balconies."

Darvish tightened his grip on Aaron's ankle until the thief turned to glare at him. He let go and smiled. "I don't think I'm up to scrambling through a tree anyway. Why don't we take our chances on the ground?"

Aaron studied the yard. It was completely enclosed, and the buildings facing it were quiet. It might be safe. He nodded, slid over to hang his full length, and dropped noiselessly to a clear patch of packed dirt.

Breathing a prayer of relief, Darvish followed. He'd had quite enough of the high roads of the city. Straightening, he unstrapped his sword from his back and buckled the belt about his waist where it belonged. The familiar weight reassured him as he crept after Aaron through piles of debris. They'd gone half the length of the yard when he noticed he was walking normally. His foot tingled faintly and then that, too, was gone.

"Aaron," he called softly.

A low growl answered and from out of the darkness stalked the biggest dog he'd ever seen.

"Aaron?" Darvish backed away slowly.

Stiff-legged, the dog followed.

"I see it," Aaron said quietly from behind him. "Keep coming, there's a gate in the far wall."

Darvish risked a glance back over his shoulder. The far wall was a considerable distance away. His hand dropped to his sword hilt. He didn't want to kill the dog and he wouldn't if he could avoid it. They were the intruders, after all. "Aaron, give me your vest." Slowly, very slowly, he reached back. There was a rustle of silk and then the fabric touched his hand. He got a good grip and just as slowly brought his arm forward again.

The dog growled louder and charged.

As the dog's feet left the ground, Darvish flung the full folds of the vest in its face. Even braced, he staggered as the massive front paws hit his chest, scrabbling through the silk. Wrapping the fabric around forelegs and head, he heaved the dog as far as he was able. It wasn't far.

Wondering how one dog could make so much noise, he turned and ran.

Aaron reached the gate and yanked back the latch, diving through into a pungent alleyway. Darvish charged through seconds later and together they pushed the heavy wooden barricade closed and held it as it trembled and shook under the big dog's charges. The gate bowed and jerked about like a live thing, but they finally managed to slam the latch down again.

"Not much point in being quiet," Darvish shouted above the frenzied barking. The neighborhood was coming awake around them. "The ward has worn off."

"Then let's head home," Aaron panted, wiping a smear of dirt off his jaw.

"There they are, by the dog!" The mouth of the alley filled with guards.

As one, they spun and took off in the other direction. Down the alley, across the street, and, out of sight for the moment, down another alley so tiny it barely deserved the name. It ended in a blank wall.

"Bugger the Nine! Trapped!" Darvish spun around and drew his sword. They could only come at him one at a time. There were worse places to make a stand.

"Dar! Through here!"

What he had taken to be shadow was a narrow passageway between the wall and the building it joined, where the soft bricks had rotted and crumbled away.

"The guards are in heavy leather," Aaron explained as he slid into the darkness. "They can't follow."

"Aaron," Darvish assumed it was exhaustion. Things weren't funny enough to merit the laugh he couldn't contain, "*I* can't follow. Even without heavy leathers."

They could hear the guards on the street, coming closer.

Darvish turned again to face them, then half turned back, his eye caught by a glimmer of light. A door, set flush with the alley wall, almost invisible.

"Aaron, what's through there?"

Aaron frowned. "The tavern we passed. But there's people . . ."

Darvish grinned. "Oh, I know there's people." He sheathed his sword and pulled the thief forward. "Now it's your turn to follow me."

The cook almost killed them when they burst into the kitchen, but Darvish wrapped an arm around her ample waist, whispered something in her ear, and moments later they were slipping out into the common room, two handfuls of ash having dimmed the brilliance of Aaron's hair.

"Can you get your hands on a sword and two sunrobes? One for each of us?" Darvish murmured scanning the noisy crowd; laborers for the most part, a few outlanders, and one or two off duty sword-for-hires, all well primed. From where they stood, he could see at least three arguments tottering on the brink.

Completely out of his depth, Aaron nodded. "What will you be doing?" he asked.

Darvish rubbed his hands together and looked positively gleeful. "Keeping the guard busy," he said. Then he walked across to the biggest, loudest man in the place, tapped him on the shoulder, and, when he turned, punched him in the stomach.

A few moments later he pulled himself out of the melee and met Aaron by the door. Aaron ducked a flying stool and handed over the larger of the two sunrobes.

"Put the sword on," Darvish told him, shrugging into the filthy garment.

"Guard!" bellowed the tavern keeper. "Guard!"

Beginning to understand, Aaron obeyed, covering his own clothes with the other stained robe.

"Now, then. . . ." Setting his teeth, Darvish picked up two

mugs of wine that had miraculously remained unspilled. He looked down at them for a heartbeat, then squared his shoulders and threw the contents of one in Aaron's face and the other in his own.

"Shall we?" he bellowed, over the sound of a table splintering into kindling.

Aaron nodded. He could hardly believe Darvish had done what he'd just done. Given the cravings he knew the wine fumes must be prodding awake, he'd never seen anything braver.

Arm in arm, they staggered into the street.

They were two buildings away, helping each other stumble home, when the guard ran past them without a second look.

With the door barely closed behind them, the lamp flame still flickering in the draft, Darvish began stripping off his clothes. He couldn't endure the wine smell a moment longer. They'd tossed the sunrobes over a convenient wall on the way back to The Gallows, but his shirt, and even his pants, still reeked and every breath reminded him of how long it had been since he'd had a drink. Naked, he walked to the window and threw the bundle out. They could get him new clothes in the morning; he couldn't stand to have those in the room.

His hands were scraped raw, his right ankle throbbed with every movement, he ached in muscles he didn't know he had, they were no closer to finding The Stone . . . *and all I can think of is how much I want a drink.* He braced his arm against the window frame and let his head fall forward. *One Below, but I am a disgusting excuse for a man.*

He heard the connecting door open and straightened up. The last thing Aaron needed to see was him feeling sorry for himself.

"Well," he said, turning, "you certainly know how to show a fellow a good. . . ." Then he caught sight of the look on Aaron's face. "What is it? Is something wrong with Chandra?"

"No." Aaron's voice was as emotionless as Darvish had ever heard it. "She's sleeping."

"Then what? What's wrong?" He watched as Aaron crossed stiffly to the smaller bed and sat down, then he walked over to stand beside him. "What is it?"

"It's nothing. I'm just tired." Aaron grabbed at the end of his shirt and went to pull it over his head, but the thin silk stuck against his chest.

Darvish squatted to get a better look and sucked his breath in through his teeth. The red-brown patterns he had thought embroidery were actually blood. "You've reopened your scars," he said softly. The fabric had dried into the wounds.

"It's nothing," Aaron repeated, yanked the shirt up over his head, and threw it across the room. A muscle jumped in his jaw, but that was his only reaction as the dried blood tore free and fresh began to run red against the pallor of his chest. The scars were an ugly inflamed purple. The skin had cracked in four places.

"Nine Above, are you out of your mind?" Still crouched at Aaron's feet, Darvish twisted and stretched a long arm back for the pitcher of water. Dragging Aaron's old sunrobe off the end of the bed, he tore off a strip, moistened it, and reached for Aaron's chest.

"No." Aaron struck his hand away.

"Don't be stupid, Aaron, you're covered in blood."

"It doesn't matter."

"It matters to me." Darvish reached out again and when Aaron lifted his hand to push him back, he grabbed it. They grappled for a moment, and then Aaron yanked his wrist free and tried to rise. Darvish pushed him back.

"What's wrong with you?"

Aaron grimaced. "You could have died out there and it would have been my fault!"

Darvish sat back on his heels. "What are you talking about?"

"In the alley. The crack. I should have known you wouldn't fit."

Darvish reached out and shook the younger man gently by one thin shoulder. "Aaron, you are not responsible for my size. Now, please, sit still and let me take care of this." When Aaron made no protest, he began to wipe away the streaks of red. "You don't *have* to live in pain," he murmured lightly, then froze as something warm and wet dripped onto the back of his hand.

Aaron began to tremble as another tear fell. And then another. He couldn't stop them.

"Aaron, what is it?"

Aaron fought for control and lost. "I always fail the ones I. . . ." Desperately, he caught the last word.

"You let the old pain rule your life, Aaron, my lad."

"Faharra?" He could see the old lady as she lay dead on her couch, her eyes staring forever into darkness.

"You let the old pain rule your life."

"No. . . ."

"Aaron, please, tell me what's wrong."

The pain in Darvish's voice drove through the last of the walls and they came crashing down.

"Ruth!" Aaron slid forward onto his knees and cried as he had not been able to cry for five long years.

Tears streaming down his own face, although he had no idea why, Darvish gathered the slim body close and held it safe. Slowly, a word at a time, the story came out.

Aaron had fought all his life to live up to his father, Clan Chief, warrior, a man whose strength of body and will was legend. Then, at thirteen, he fell in love with his cousin, Ruth, and fighting and mayhem didn't seem as important any more. His father, disapproving, promised Ruth to a Clan Chief three times her age who had used up and buried two wives already. She ran to Aaron for comfort. He gave it. His father caught them together.

Damaged goods could not be given to a fellow Clan Chief. As a warning to the other women of the keep, Aaron's father beat her to death in the courtyard. Aaron, on his knees, his uncle's hand in his hair, was forced to watch the entire thing.

"She screamed my name until the screaming stopped. . . ."

Then his father had presented the bloody whip and demanded Aaron kiss it and reswear his allegiance.

"I couldn't. I vomited. He pushed me down in it and called me no son of his. I left the keep that night and have been no son of his ever since."

Darvish tightened his grip and Chandra, who had been standing silently in the connecting doorway, stepped back at the look on his face.

"It wasn't your fault," he whispered, his voice a soft contrast to the expression of murderous rage that twisted his features. "It wasn't your fault."

"I failed her. I failed Faharra. I failed you." *If I am not my father's son, what am I? What is left?*

"What could you have done for her? Died with her? Wouldn't she rather know you lived? And as to Faharra, you were betrayed. You didn't fail her. And believe me, Aaron, you *did not* fail me."

Wrapped in the warm haven of Darvish's arms, he had to believe the last. And if that was true, perhaps the rest of what Darvish said was true as well. Perhaps. He shuddered and sighed.

Darvish felt him relax and, greatly daring, brought one hand up to stroke the copper hair.

Chandra propped the damaged door closed and, wiping her cheeks dry, climbed thoughtfully back into bed. In her opinion, the best thing for both of them now would be to admit how each felt about the other and go on together from there.

They wouldn't.

Men.

She threw herself back on the pillow, heard again the raw pain spilling out in Aaron's voice, and had a quiet cry.

Chapter Fifteen

"It's an ugly city up close, too." Chandra leaned against her window frame and frowned out at the morning. She could hear the rumble of wooden wheels against cobblestones and the musical call of the water seller as he made his rounds through the streets below. Breezes were heavy with the scent of fresh baked bread and her stomach grumbled in response. The sky was a brilliant azure blue and the light had the kind of clarity that comes only early in the day.

But the buildings were still a muddy yellow brick and besides, she wanted to be home. She missed her tower. She missed her studies. She missed her garden. She even missed Aba and being taken care of so thoroughly that she never had to consider the day to day business of living.

And she missed her father. She had realized it lying sleeplessly in the dark, wanting him to come and make everything all right.

Except he couldn't. She realized that in the cold light of day. He was only her father, and a man, and nothing he could do would make the situation they were in any better.

But, oh, it hurt to let go of the idea that he could.

She combed through her hair with her fingers and brought it forward to braid. *He was only her father, and a man.*

"Good, you're up." Darvish stood in the doorway to his and Aaron's chamber, one hand preventing the abused door from crashing back against the wall, the other clutching the folds of Aaron's old sunrobe where it was wrapped around his waist. "I wonder if you could do me a favor?"

Chandra, her hands still busy with the pattern of her braid, lifted her eyebrows in silent inquiry.

"The new clothes. . . ." Darvish felt his face flush under her regard. He hadn't thought himself still capable of blushing. "I, uh, threw them out the window last night and I, uh, was wondering if you'd go talk to the tavern boy about getting more."

"You threw them out the window?" Obviously interesting things had been going on before Aaron's wailing cry to his cousin had awakened her.

"It's a long story."

Chandra smiled pleasantly and crossed the room to perch cross-legged on the end of her bed. "I think I deserve to hear it," she pointed out. "Unless it's," she paused significantly, "personal."

Darvish finally managed to force the door upright on its own. "It's not personal," he sighed, getting a better grip on the sunrobe. "It's just long."

Chandra waited patiently, looking as expectant as she knew how.

"Oh, all right." He crossed to the window and squinted out. Chandra obviously planned on staying right where she was until he told all. "King Harith was holding an Open Court. . . ."

The catalog of the previous night's disasters didn't go as badly as Darvish had expected. To his surprise, he found Chandra an attentive and intelligent listener, perhaps the best he'd ever had. She interrupted seldom with questions and when she did they were always to clarify a point he'd missed or skimmed over.

". . . and after I threw them out the window, Aaron. . . ." He paused and took a deep breath. "Aaron," he tried again, but anger rose up and choked off the words.

"It's all right." She reached out and grabbed his elbow, stopping his staccato pacing. "I heard that part." She shrugged, apologetically; Wizards of the Nine did not eavesdrop. "He called out rather loudly."

Darvish met her eyes, nodded once—an unconscious echo of Aaron's minimalist body language—and threw himself beside her on the bed, somehow managing to maintain sunrobe and dignity. "It's a real pity," he ground the words out as if he was grinding an edge onto his blade, "that I'll never have the chance to meet Aaron's father so I can kill the One abandoned son-of-a-bitch."

"I'd thought that myself," Chandra told him, blinking rapidly to clear the tears from her eyes.

"Hey," Darvish reached up a large finger and traced the moist path down her cheek. "I thought Wizards of the Nine didn't cry?"

Chandra jerked her head away and scowled. For the second

time in maybe eight years, for the second time that morning, Darvish felt his face flush. "I'm sorry," he said. "Sometimes I'm a facetious jerk."

"Sometimes," Chandra agreed, throwing her braid behind her shoulder. When she thought she could speak without a betraying quaver in her voice, she asked, "Is Aaron okay?"

"He's still asleep. I thought he should sleep as long as he could."

There were dark shadows under Darvish's eyes, but Chandra didn't mention them. She remembered what she'd last seen as she'd slipped back into the darkness of her own room; Aaron cradled in the protective circle of Darvish's arms and Darvish's mouth pressed against the copper hair. She felt her cheeks growing hot and she stirred uncomfortably.

"No," Darvish told her softly. He had a pretty good idea of what she was thinking.

"Actually," she said, realizing it as she spoke, "I didn't think you would. You wouldn't take advantage of his vulnerability like that. He needed a friend, not a lover."

Darvish stared at the girl in silence for a moment and wondered if she knew the compliment she had just paid him. No one at court, from his most exalted father to the most supercilious noble would have doubted for a moment that he'd taken Aaron to his bed. Tears burned behind his lids and he tossed his head to clear them away. "Thank you," he said at last.

She sensed what it meant to him, smiled self-consciously, and lightly touched his hand. "I'll go see about getting you some clothes." Unfolding her legs, she slipped off the bed and sped out of the room.

A few moments later, she was back.

Darvish, still seated where'd she'd left him, looked up in surprise. "That was fast."

She bit her lip and looked sheepish. "We, uh, we forgot about money."

Darvish looked momentarily blank. "Money?"

One Below, we're going to save Ischia and we don't know how to buy breakfast? "Wizards of the Nine," Chandra managed, before she collapsed against the door, helpless with giggles, "don't . . . worry . . . about money." It wasn't *that* funny, but she couldn't seem to stop laughing.

Darvish grinned and shook his head. "Neither do princes, obviously." He stood, made a last minute save of the sunrobe, and headed for the other room. "Good thing we're traveling with a thief."

"Good thing," Chandra agreed, wiping her eyes and managing to achieve a shaky control.

Wizards of the Nine don't laugh at themselves either, Darvish thought with satisfaction, and he paused on the threshold. "Chandra, why don't you want your cousin to inherit? Is he an evil man?"

"No." Although she had no idea where it came from—she hadn't thought of her cousin in a nineday or more—she tried to answer the question. "He's just a, well, a man." She frowned. Admitting that, the next step was easier. "It's not that he'd do a bad job, exactly, it's just that . . . that. . . ." She clutched at air, searching for the words.

"That he wouldn't do as good a job as you would?"

"Well. . . ." Her chin rose defiantly. "Yes."

Darvish smiled and, leaving the confused wizard to puzzle over their last exchange, went into the other room to look for Aaron's belt pouch.

"A thousand pardons, Gracious Lord."

Lord Balin waved his guards back and studied the pudgy merchant who, racing along the docks, had almost slammed into him. "It's of little importance," he assured the man. "No harm was done."

The merchant stopped bobbing obeisances. "Thank you, Gracious Lord." He wiped a sweating forehead with a handkerchief so heavily scented with lime that even from a distance it overcame the fish and salt and tar smell of Ischia harbor, then shuffled impatiently, waiting for the foreign lord to move on.

The foreign lord stayed right where he was. "Where were you heading in such a hurry?"

"A ship, my lord. I have passage on a ship."

Lord Balin frowned. There were a great many ships in the harbor that seemed to be loading the citizens of Ischia as cargo. "You're leaving the city, then?"

"Only for a time, Gracious Lord." He glanced up at the taller man, saw interest, and almost visibly swelled. "There is a rumor, Gracious Lord," he confided, "that The Stone is missing and Prince Darvish has been sent after it."

"Surely you are too astute a man to listen to rumor," Lord Balin said evenly, neither voice nor face giving any indication of the sudden fear clamped around his heart. *Chandra. If The Stone is missing and Darvish gone after it, where is my daughter?*

"Ah, my lord, but there are facts as well." He began counting them off on heavily ringed fingers. "All platforms to the Lady—the volcano, Gracious Lord, we call her the Lady—are closed, not only the public ones, but I have a nephew, a priest, who tells me that temple platforms are closed as well—and there are wizards on all of them. A great cloud of smoke—you can't see it from here, Gracious Lord—hangs over the palace and the temple and begins to move down over the nobles' townhouses. My nephew is certain that the temple suite Lord Darvish is said to be in is empty. And most telling of all, Gracious Lord, the earth has moved. Not once, but twice."

"Is there panic?"

"Not yet, Gracious Lord, for His Most Exalted Majesty and His Royal Highness Prince Shahin, the Heir, are still in the palace and the people feel if they remain. . . ." He waved his hands, unable to articulate exactly what the people felt. "But if the earth moves again, Gracious Lord. . . . You have not picked a good time to visit Ischia." He flushed as he realized his last words might have been thought to be a criticism. "Begging your pardon, Gracious Lord."

Lord Balin waved a silent dismissal and watched the pudgy man scurry thankfully away. Then he turned and looked thoughtfully up the steep slope of the city to where the white marble of the palace gleamed in the sunlight. He had sent no word that he was coming, nor did he now wear any visible insignia showing his name or rank. He wanted to storm into the throne room and demand his daughter but. . . .

"We walk," he said to the four guards he'd brought from the ship.

Silently, they moved into formation around him.

By the time Lord Balin reached the last set of terraces leading to the palace, he could see the smoke. Half expecting thick black clouds, he was relieved to see it was no more than a thin haze. And he was dismayed to see it at all. The city, if not panicked, certainly seethed on the edge and it would take very little to turn the questions and confusion into riot. Business seemed to go on as usual, despite rumors, but the mood felt brittle and likely to shatter at any moment.

He personally didn't care if the entire country sank into the sea, as long as he found his daughter first.

A small crowd stood in clumps scattered about the square before the palace. Fruit and candy vendors wandered among them, and a juggler, perched on the steps of the central fountain, threw four daggers and a pomegranate in a glittering cascade.

As Lord Balin entered the square, the conversations closest to him stopped and the silence spread out behind him like a banner. His dress, his bearing, his guards, proclaimed him noble; it didn't matter that he wasn't of Cisali. Even the juggler caught his knives and stood quietly watching.

"Gracious Lord!" A woman's voice stopped him at the palace gate. "Is it true? Has The Stone been taken? Are we all going to die?"

Her questions hung in the hot air like the haze of smoke and Lord Balin thought for an instant that the smell of sulfur had grown stronger. These were not his people, but they were people and they deserved an answer. If he could not give them the truth, neither would he add to the tensions.

"Your king," he said, half turning to face the square, "remains. And *I* have just arrived."

"But, Gracious Lord, they say. . . ."

"They say a great many foolish things." He forced a smile. "I try not to believe what *they* say."

As he passed through the gate, he heard the babble of conversation rise again and he wondered how much longer such wordplay would suffice.

An official of the court stood by the gate guard, an ingratiating smile plastered across her broad face. "Gracious Lord," she intoned bowing slightly, "that was very well done. You are . . . ?"

"Lord Atam Balin." He stretched out his left hand with the heavy gold signet. "I wish to see your king."

The bow was repeated, much deeper. "Gracious Lord, if we had but known. Your messenger. . . ."

"I sent no messenger. I am not here for ceremony. I wish to see your king." His tone added, *Don't make me repeat this a third time.*

"Lord Balin."

The official started at the voice and dropped to one knee.

"My most exalted father is unavailable at the moment," Shahin continued, stepping forward. "Perhaps I would do instead?"

Sometime later, behind the closed doors of the crown prince's suite, Shahin shook his head and said quietly, "I don't know where she is, but as far as I know she never made it to the palace. I'm sorry."

Lord Balin felt the blood drain away from his face and the world went dark. *She never made it to the palace.* . . . Strong hands on his shoulders guided him into a chair. *She never made it to the palace.* . . . Unresponsive fingers were wrapped about a metal goblet. *She never made it to the palace.* . . .

"Drink," a voice commanded.

He drank and, slowly, the world came back. With a steady hand, although the knuckles were white, he set the goblet carefully on the small table beside his chair and stood. "You have been most helpful, Your Royal Highness, but as I must now search elsewhere for my daughter, I must leave and begin."

"Wait." Shahin studied the older man for a moment and came to a sudden decision. "You say your daughter is a wizard. Could she have come and gone again unseen?"

He offered hope and Lord Balin grabbed for it. "She could have. She's very powerful."

"The day your daughter would have arrived to speak with my brother, he left to search for The Stone of Ischia."

Lord Balin sat down again. "Then the rumors are true."

Shahin nodded. "They are."

"Where . . . ?"

"To Tivolic, the Ytaili capital."

"Then I must go after. . . ." His voice trailed off.

Shahin remained silent while Lord Balin thought, watching the man's expression as he turned possibilities over in his mind.

"No one must know," he said at last. "If the people of the city discover it, the panic will destroy Ischia as surely as the volcano. The Prince Darvish goes to Ytaili to recover The Stone in secret to prevent war between the two countries, which would again destroy Ischia as surely as the volcano. If I sail in to Tivolic, demanding my daughter, I could, myself, be responsible for destroying Ischia." He passed a shaking hand over his face and looked up at Shahin pleadingly. "Can I at least be sure that she was with him?"

*   *   *

"I remember the day well, Your Royal Highness," Oham's voice was impassive.

"Before your prince went into the temple, did a young woman visit him in his rooms?"

"No, Your Royal Highness."

"The young woman is a wizard," Lord Balin broke in. "She would have been disguised in some way."

"I do not remember any visitors that afternoon, Gracious Lord."

"Your Royal Highness?"

Shahin looked down at the young dresser kneeling trembling by Oham's side. "What is it?"

"I don't remember that afternoon at all."

Oham stiffened. "Please excuse him, Your Royal Highness."

"You don't understand, Your Royal Highness. I remember that morning. And that evening." Fadi's voice cracked under the stress. He blushed and went on. "But I have no memory of the afternoon at all."

Shahin turned to Lord Balin. "Could Chandra do this?"

"Yes." The word was almost lost in the great sigh of relief.

"Thank you both. You may go."

Oham rose fluidly off his knees at the crown prince's dismissal and began backing from the room, but Fadi stayed a moment longer.

"Gracious Lord?"

Lord Balin looked down into the boy's dark eyes and surprisingly found comfort in his expression. "Yes?"

"You needn't worry about your daughter, Gracious Lord. If she's with Prince Darvish, he'll keep her safe. He's . . . I mean. . . ." Suddenly overcome by confusion, Fadi stammered into silence.

Lord Balin lightly touched his hair. "Thank you," he said softly.

As close to scarlet as a young man of his complexion could get, Fadi backed quickly from the room.

"You are, of course, welcome to stay," Shahin told him, "until they return. Of course, if they don't return," he spread his hands helplessly, "you're welcome to die with the rest of us. Your own people, might prefer that you live."

"I don't know your brother, Prince Shahin, but I'll take that boy's opinion over some I've heard. It takes a special kind of man to inspire love like that. And you, Prince Shahin, don't know my daughter." Lord Balin's head went up proudly. "She's a Wizard of the Nine and I choose to believe that between the two of them, you'll get your Stone back. I *will* be here when she returns."

Shahin smiled. It had been so long since he'd done it, it felt strange on his face. "There's more to the story."

Lord Balin nodded. "There always is. You can tell me while we wait for your most exalted father to see me."

"Prince Shahin takes much upon himself."

"I am glad he told me, Most Exalted. His story keeps me from blundering in and destroying your carefully laid plans."

King Jaffar's eyes narrowed, but he couldn't deny the truth of what Lord Balin said. "A hue and cry raised for your missing daughter would certainly attract unwanted attention," he admitted.

"As I understand what is happening, I am willing to wait here, quietly."

"Surely, Gracious Lord," the lord chancellor stepped forward, his brow creased, "you will return home. Your people will need you. You can await your daughter there without the danger of dying with Ischia."

Lord Balin studied the lord chancellor for a long moment. "I know what my daughter is capable of, Lord Chancellor, and I do not think she and your Prince Darvish will fail. Your counsel leads me to believe you fear otherwise. I wonder, given those fears, why *you* stay?"

"I remain by the side of my king." The lord chancellor bowed deeply toward the throne.

"Would it not make more sense for you to escort your king to safety, from which he may continue to rule in health no matter what happens here?"

"My king chooses to remain with his people."

"Enough." King Jaffar leaned forward and both men returned their attention to him. "You are no subject of mine, Lord Balin, and I will not command you as though you were. If you wish to await your daughter's return here in Ischia, my palace is at your disposal. You will, of course, remain silent about The Stone."

"I will, of course, Most Exalted." Lord Balin watched the lord chancellor, hands tucked within the sleeves of his robe, move back to stand behind the rosewood throne. "And I hope my continued presence will help to reassure the people of Ischia that all is well."

King Jaffar almost smiled. "That had occurred to me." Then his face grew hard again. "Prince Shahin is not presently in grace with the throne. It would be best if you spend little time with him."

Lord Balin inclined his head. "I hear your words, Most Exalted."

"Well?" Prince Shahin asked, offering the older man a drink. He'd made it very clear that he expected his servants to be busy elsewhere while he and Lord Balin talked.

Nodding his thanks, Lord Balin accepted the goblet. "If the lord chancellor was a little fatter," he sighed wearily, "you could drop him into the volcano and solve most of your problems with a single stroke."

"You have sent a message to the wizard?"

"Yes, Gracious Majesty. The Most Wise Palaton has been informed that Prince Darvish and the thief are in the city."

"I want those two found, Lord Rahman."

The elderly lord spread his hands. "The patrols continue to search, Gracious Majesty, but Tivolic is a large city and if the young thief has friends amongst his kind. . . ."

King Harith drummed his fingers on the arm of his throne. "His kind," he snorted. "Offer a purse of gold and a full pardon to anyone who gives information leading to their capture and that should take care of *his kind.*"

"I'm sorry. I can't. It hurts."

Darvish reached out and shook Chandra's shoulder gently. "Hey, it's all right. With the beard gone I don't look like Shahin anymore and with the illusion on my eyes I don't look like me. I'll be fine."

Chandra lifted her face up out of her hands and glared at him. "You'll be fine? What if I can never focus power again?"

"Don't worry," Darvish said reassuringly. "We'll come up with another way to get The Stone."

"I'm not talking about The Stone, you overmuscled moron! I'm talking about me!" Her voice cracked on the last word and she buried her face again. *I'm not going to cry. I'm not!* She hadn't

cried when trying to change Darvish's appearance had sent her
writhing to the floor in pain and she wasn't going to cry now.

"You just need time to heal," Aaron said calmly. "Consider the
violence of the attack you survived. Is it any wonder you still have
a few open wounds?"

"It'll get better?" Chandra was heartily embarrassed to hear
the quaver in her voice.

"If you stop picking the scab off it."

"That's disgusting, Aaron." His right shoulder lifted slightly
and fell in a minimal shrug and she managed a weak smile. This
brown-haired, brown-skinned, brown-clothed little man with
Aaron's voice and Aaron's manner would take some getting used
to. Walnut stain; she studied him critically. Aaron managed without power. And Dar . . . well, Dar managed, too, more or less. So
she couldn't focus power for the moment. Her legs and her brain
still worked fine. She pulled a long breath in and out through her
nose and got briskly to her feet. "Well," she said. "Let's go."

On the stairs, when she'd bounded down out of earshot,
Darvish murmured, "You made her feel a lot better. I didn't know
you knew so much about wizards and power."

"I don't."

"You don't? You lied?"

"I made her feel a lot better, remember?"

Darvish couldn't think of anything to say to that, so they descended the remainder of the stairs in silence.

"Well?" Aaron asked as they caught up to Chandra on the
street. "Where to?" Darvish had said he had a plan and Aaron was
glad of it. He wasn't up to planning; he felt as if his life had been
suspended somehow, cut loose and floating. He felt very exposed.
To his relief, Darvish and Chandra had treated him no differently
when he'd finally staggered out of bed, heavy-eyed and tired after
a dream-filled and restless night. He couldn't have borne it if
they'd offered sympathy or comfort. He didn't need either. He
needed them unchanged and he needed time to convince himself
that he didn't have to carry the guilt for Ruth's death any longer.
It wasn't going to be easy to let that go.

"We're going down toward the harbor," Darvish explained,
squinting into the setting sun and flipping up the hood of his sunrobe. "I'm looking for a wineshop."

"Why?" Chandra asked, peering out from under the stiffened brim of her own hood.

For a moment, Darvish heard not, "Why?" but, "Going to drink yourself into a stupor?" which is what the question would have meant in Ischia. Then he realized, if Chandra asked, she wanted to know. If she meant something else, she wouldn't bother with sarcasm.

"I'm going to find myself." He smiled the old self-mocking grin that had put any number of hearts at court in a flutter. Chandra's didn't appear to be fluttering.

"I beg your pardon?"

"Not me, exactly. But someone like me. A younger son with too much time on his hands and nothing to do, no place to belong. But wanting to belong so badly he's willing to play the part they set out for him of drunkard and fool."

Her face softened with sympathy. "Now that you know that," she said, reaching out and briefly squeezing his hand, "you can stop."

The grin grew a little sad but no less self-mocking. "Chandra, I *always* knew it."

They didn't travel all the way to the harbor but to the street just back of the docks and warehouses where the sailors and dock workers went to spend their pay. A thousand exotic things were for sale there, from silks to spices to an hour's pleasure, and buyers and sellers haggled cheerfully at the top of their lungs. Aaron could understand why Darvish went to the Ischia equivalent rather than stay at court. At least here if he were a drunkard and a fool it was because he *was* a drunkard and a fool and not because the people expected him to act as one.

"Any particular wineshop?" Chandra wanted to know, her head swiveling from side to side as she tried to see everything at once.

Darvish shrugged. "It doesn't matter. He'll be in one of them."

"Will he be able to help?" Aaron asked as they plunged into the crowds.

"He may not know where The Stone is, but I guarantee he'll know something that will lead us to it. Gossip and speculation are a favored pastime at court and no one thinks to watch their tongue around his type."

Aaron nodded thoughtfully. He'd seen that himself during the short time he'd been with Darvish in the palace. He opened his mouth to ask another question, then snapped it shut as he closed his hand about a small wrist whose fingers were attempting to dip into his belt pouch. The failed pickpocket, a skinny, sexless child of no more than seven was pale with terror under the dirt but knew better than to attract attention by fighting to get free.

"I didn't mean nothin'," it squeaked.

Aaron stared at the small thief for a number of heartbeats, then said, "You should have waited until the crowd ran interference for you." With his free hand he reached into the pouch and flipped a Ytaili silver wheel into the air. The coin flashed once in the sunlight, then a grubby hand shot out and it disappeared. Aaron released the wrist he still held and the child scrambled away.

"No honor amongst thieves?" Darvish asked.

"None," Aaron snorted and his expression added, *Don't bother me about it.*

"You're too good a thief, Aaron, my lad."

"Not now, Faharra. Please."

"There!" Darvish stopped suddenly, a hand on each of his companions' shoulders. "He's just turned onto the street, short man, slender, in bright green and gold."

"I see him," Chandra said.

Aaron nodded.

Although the sun had not yet set, the young man was weaving as he made his way down the street. He tossed long dark curls back off his face, smiled charmingly, and greeted everyone as if they were friends of his heart he had been too long parted from.

Which, Darvish mused, *was entirely possible.*

They watched as he made his way into one of the less reputable looking wineshops, passing by the tiny patio and its kicked in the corner piles of debris for the dark and secret interior. His pair of guards, not bothering to hide either their boredom or their disapproval, followed.

"He's just a kid," Chandra murmured. "I wonder who he is?"

"We should know," Darvish agreed. "Wait here." It only took him a moment to find out; the whores were well acquainted with the young man. "He's the king's nephew. Too close to the throne to be allowed his own life. Too far to have any sort of official duties."

"And by encouraging this," Chandra's wave took in the whores, the wineshop, "it keeps him unable to build a power base."

Both men turned to look at her in some surprise.

"I *am* my father's heir," she pointed out sharply.

As they moved toward the wineshop, Darvish felt his shoulders begin to tense. They reached the edge of the patio, and the smell of the place hit him, not just the wine but the sweat and the smoke and the close dark comfort of it.

"I can't go in there." The muscles of his shoulders and back were tied in painful knots. His teeth were clenched so tightly his ears ached.

Aaron slipped an arm under Darvish's elbow and got him moving again. To hesitate, to appear weak in this neighborhood invited trouble. He steered the unresponsive prince between two buildings and into a quiet alley, then he let go and stepped back.

Darvish managed a shaky grin and jerked his hands up through his hair. "Sorry." He gulped in great lungfuls of the fetid air, which at least didn't smell like his past. "I—I thought I could do it. I thought it wouldn't bother me. I was wrong."

"We need you, Dar. You can get him talking. We can't."

"He's our only lead to The Stone, Dar," Chandra added.

"You think I don't know that!" He turned suddenly and drove his fist forward, hard enough to split a knuckle and mark the yellow brick with red. When he pulled his arm back for a second blow, Aaron slipped between him and the wall. Gray eyes met brown and held them. Slowly, Darvish's hand unclenched.

"I think I know a way," Chandra said softly. "Use the soul-link."

Grateful for the chance to break an eye contact that had acquired a life of its own, Darvish pivoted back to face her. "What are you talking about?" he snapped. "You can't use a soul-link for anything. It's a leash, nothing more."

"Oh, no," Chandra disagreed, "that's what it's used for, that's not what it is." A sudden noise out on the street, caused her to move forward and lower her voice. "Don't you remember when they first put it in? You were having weird thoughts and feelings that you knew weren't yours?"

"They stopped," Aaron pointed out. His face had fallen into the completely expressionless mask he wore when he was most disturbed. That the soul-link was a physical tie to Darvish he could handle, barely. That it might be an emotional joining as well. . . .

"No, they didn't stop. You just stopped noticing them. Dar, you can draw on Aaron's strength to get through this. You did it before, when you were fighting the wine."

"I drew on Aaron's strength?"

"Yes."

Darvish remembered how Aaron had looked the morning he'd finally come back to himself. *So I was responsible for that as well. One Below, but I have a lot to answer for.*

"You can do it again."

"No."

"Why not? Aaron doesn't mind."

The barb in her voice pulled Darvish up out of the melancholy he had fallen into. He took a step toward the wizard and hissed through his teeth, "Are you crazy? You *heard* what he went through last night."

"Dar. . . ." The last thing Aaron wanted was for Darvish to have access to what he thought, what he felt. At the same time, he had never wanted anything so badly in all his life. "I've strength enough for *this.*" He twisted his lips up into the closest he could come to a smile as Darvish faced him again. "I'm good at self-denial."

"So you're to carry my weight again tonight?" Darvish's words were bitter. He hadn't thought he could despise himself more than he had that morning by the sea. He could. He did.

"So he's willing to help a friend." Chandra met both the gray eyes and the brown with a steady stare of her own. "We don't have time to dance around your ego, Dar." She put her hands on her hips and glared. "Say thank you and let's get going on this."

After a moment, Darvish stopped gaping at her. "Thank you," he said, a little stunned.

"Yeah," Aaron replied, in much the same tone. "No problem."

They glanced at each other, saw identical poleaxed expressions and began to laugh.

Chandra rolled her eyes. Men.

Merchants, sailors, and whores moved sullenly out of the way as the patrol of city guard moved the length of the street.

As far as the patrol leader was concerned, she and her men were wasting their time. This neighborhood held a thousand hidey-holes and few friends of authority, and an evening spent searching vermin infested wineshops would leave them with nothing more than queasy stomachs and flea bites on their ankles. They sure as

the Nine wouldn't find any sign of the two men twisting the
king's tail.

But, she hitched up her sword belt, *orders are orders.* "Stay together, and keep your eyes open. If anyone wants to claim the reward, bring them to me." Choosing a wineshop at random, she
waved the patrol toward the door. She'd lead them into battle but
she'd be damned if she'd lead them into that.

"May we buy you a drink, my lord?"

The young lord looked up and smiled broadly. He had a charming pair of dimples and thick eyelashes that swept coquettishly
against the curve of his cheek. "You certainly may," he told them,
inspecting each with obvious approval. "One big drink, or three
little ones?"

"Your preference," Darvish said cheerfully, sitting down and
matching the smile. Behind it, he held tight to his end of the soul-
link.

"Three big ones, then." He tossed blue-black curls back off his
face. "Why waste time?"

It wasn't difficult to turn the talk to Cisali, to Ischia, to The
Stone.

"I don't know nuthin' 'bout no Stone." He leaned forward and
a delicately embroidered sleeve dragged through a blood-red puddle of wine. "Bud I betcha I know who would. Uncle Gracious
Majesty King gets lots of letters from Ischia." Poking his finger
into the puddle, he quickly sketched a likeness of the king on the
splintered wood of the table, then sat staring down at it proudly.
"It's good, isn't it?"

"Yes," Darvish told him gently, "it's good." And it was, even
considering the media and the shakiness of the artist. He'd captured exactly the king Darvish remembered from Shahin's wedding and captured exactly the look Darvish himself remembered
receiving. "Has King Harith been sent any letters lately?"

"Course he has. Lots."

"In the last nineday?"

"Lots. At least one."

"I bet you don't know where he keeps them."

He poured another nearly full goblet of wine down his throat.
"Bet I do," he coughed out at last. "Keeps them locked in his gracious private ocif . . . office. Saw them when he was yelling at me

yesterday." His brow furrowed. "Maybe today. Uncle Gracious Majesty King yells a lot," he confided sadly.

"I'm sure he does."

"Are you goin'? I thought you could stay and we could, I mean, all of us could, we could. . . ."

"We have something we have to do."

The young lord sighed. "Everyone has something they have to do."

Darvish reached out and tenderly brushed the black curls back. "I know," he said.

He managed to follow Aaron and Chandra outside and got clear of the inn before he had to stop and hug himself hard, waiting for the trembling to run its course. The solid feel of Aaron in his mind helped. The warm, physical touch of his and Chandra's presence helped more.

"Dar." Aaron's voice was soft but insistent. "We have to move on. There's a patrol searching the street."

Darvish nodded. He couldn't trust his voice. With Aaron holding one arm and Chandra the other, he somehow got his legs to move and, one step at a time, they headed back to The Gallows.

"We have to get the letters," he said when he could. "If they were written in the last nineday, they're not likely to be from Yasimina asking for another set of One abandoned peacocks. Ischia will never be safe if we don't find the traitor. Aaron, can you break into the palace? Into the king's private office?"

Aaron smiled strangely at a memory he didn't voice. All he said was, "Yes."

"Milord?"

He looked up from the picture he was drawing in the spilled wine and smiled charmingly. "Yes?"

"We're looking for two men. . . ."

"Two?" He sighed. "I'd settle for one. Or a woman. Or a large dog. Small horse." He giggled. "Most Gracious Uncle hates it when I say that. Thinks I'm a pervert." Suddenly, he reached out and anxiously clutched at the patrol leader's arm. "I'm not, you know. 's just a joke."

The patrol leader pulled sticky fingers off her wrist brace. "I'm sure, milord."

"Should we take him with us?" one of the guards asked her as she turned away in disgust.

She snorted. "He wouldn't thank us. Let's go, people. There's nothing here."

The young man watched them leave, then raised his hand for another drink. On the table, the sketch he'd done of Darvish dried and disappeared.

Chapter Sixteen

"It won't work." Aaron's voice was flat. "You're just too big."

Chandra looked up from the pieces of apple peel she'd been trying to lay out in a single strand. The imported fruit had cost almost as much as the rest of the meal. "You'll have to let me remove the soul-link," she said, not for the first time. "You haven't got a choice."

"And what if it knocks you out?" Darvish snapped, pushing away his low table and slopping coffee out onto the polished wood. "How is Aaron supposed to get over the wall if you can't punch a hole through the wards?"

"Aaron won't be going over the wall if I don't get rid of the soul-link," Chandra pointed out. They'd argued in circles all through the meal and she was tired of it; she preferred having her brain power-burned than having the argument continue. "I can live with a little pain. We *don't* have a choice."

"No." Darvish shot to his feet and stamped over to the window. "It's too dangerous for you. I won't allow it."

"You won't . . ." Chandra began, teeth showing, but Aaron shook his head gently and she bit the rest of the comment off.

"Dar." Aaron moved silently up to stand behind him. Darvish continued to stare out at the lights of Ytaili. "If we have to enter another tavern, I'll—we'll—be there for you. You won't have to face it alone."

"Is that what you think I'm really worried about?" Darvish laughed bitterly and turned. "Well, you're right. As usual. This must be getting awfully tiresome for you; always being right where I'm concerned." He reached out and grabbed Aaron's chin. "Afraid you're going to be my new crutch? That I'll suck you dry just to get through all those bits of life I'm too much of a coward to face on my own?"

Aaron remained perfectly still in Darvish's grip, fighting and winning against the urge to twist free. "You can lean on me without the soul-link," he said softly.

"Lean on you?" Again the bitter laugh. "I don't know if you've noticed this or not, but lately you've been a little unstable yourself."

"I've noticed." There were no walls left to hide behind. "You lean on me. I'll lean on you."

And why can't I think of a single witty thing to say to that? Darvish wondered, searching Aaron's face for hidden meanings or sarcasm he knew he wouldn't find.

"Well?" Chandra asked at last, strongly suspecting that if she didn't do something about it, they'd stand and stare at each other all night.

So slowly that it was almost a caress, Darvish released Aaron's chin. "Do it," he said.

"We've got another problem." Chandra peered over at the wall of the palace, barely visible even though her eyes had grown used to the night, and twirled the wet end of her braid between two fingers. "I'm going to have to go in with Aaron."

Darvish muttered something unintelligible—and, Chandra suspected, uncomplimentary—under his voice. Aaron quite clearly said, "No."

Chandra ground her teeth and squirmed around behind the low parapet until she could see the two men lying beside her on the roof. "I can't open the wards from here," she explained, snapping each word out. They had a lot of nerve refusing before hearing her reasons. "I'd need to use too much power. A lot of good it would do, Aaron sneaking over the wall, if I'm going to be lying here screaming."

"Oh, I don't know," Darvish mused. "It might be a good distraction. I'm kidding," he added hastily, his teeth flashing white in the shadow of his face and one arm raised to fend off Chandra's fist. "Can't you make him a charm to get him through?"

"I suppose I could fake it if I could touch the wards." She shrugged, wasn't certain they saw it in the darkness, and said, "Same result as removing them though."

Darvish slammed his fist lightly against the brick. "Bugger the Nine."

"But I *can* get us both through. With my eyes closed and one hand tied behind my back. It's a different kind of spell, takes almost no power, and the Nine," she waved a hand at the stars in case they were unsure which nine she referred to, "will be in a perfect position in a very few moments."

"You can do it without hurting yourself?"

"Yes."

"That's what you said about removing the soul-link."

"I never did," Chandra told him indignantly. "I said I could stand the pain. And," she pointed out, "I did stand it."

"I know you did, Chandra." Darvish spoke soothingly. He in no way wanted to negate what the young wizard had already gone through, but he needed to make sure she understood that accompanying a thief over the palace wall was not the same thing as sitting safely in their room at The Gallows. "But you screamed."

"Only once."

"Once would alert the guard."

"I *told* you, this is a different kind of magic."

"What will you do inside?" Aaron asked suddenly, leaning across Darvish so that he didn't have to raise his voice.

Chandra rolled her eyes, "I'm a Wizard of the Nine, not a thief. I'll sit quietly at the base of the wall weaving a notice-me-not until you come back."

"You'll destroy yourself," Aaron said bluntly. "You don't know how long I'll take."

"So I'll sit in a shadow!"

"Shh!" Darvish cautioned.

Chandra pointedly ignored him, but lowered her voice again. "You'll have to come back to me. You'll need me to get out."

"How well and how fast can you climb?" Darvish surrendered. It was time to start making the best of a bad situation. He certainly didn't want Aaron to take Chandra over that wall, but even less did he want the traitor in Ischia to go free and that's what would happen if they couldn't steal those letters.

She studied the wall, this time actually seeing the physical structure and not the intertwined lines of power rising from it. It was a little over twice her height and the stones looked smooth and set flush. "Up that? Not very," she admitted grudgingly.

"Dar, could you throw her to the top?"

"We have to go through the wards together," Chandra interjected before Darvish could speak. "Holding hands at the very least."

Darvish sighed and shook his head. "Aaron can climb to my shoulders and take your hand. From there he can get himself through the ward at the same time as I toss you up and when this is all over we can make a living as street acrobats. Come on," he rolled to his feet and, crouching low, started for the stairs, "let's get this over with before my brain convinces me how One abandoned the whole idea is."

"You may have to distract a guard," Aaron pointed out, scuttling along beside him.

"I'll sleep with the One abandoned guard," Darvish grunted. "if that's what it takes to get on with this." For the first time in over a nineday he didn't feel embarrassed at needing a drink. Any sane man would need a drink under these circumstances. *Ischia may be dying under a river of molten rock and I'm throwing a mouthy wizard into the palace of Ytaili. Nine Above and One Below, why me?*

He touched the emptiness where the soul-link had been and a muscle jumped in his jaw. *In a few days,* Chandra had told them, *you'll forget you ever had it.* Glancing over at Aaron moving down the stairs beside him, he doubted that. He doubted that very much.

"Are you all right?"

Chandra wiped at the blood dribbling from her lip and managed a weak nod. Then her legs gave out. She slid down the wall to land knees at her chin and back braced against the cool stone; crumpled but basically upright.

Aaron squatted in front of her, the center tufts of his brows pulled down so tightly they touched. "You said it wouldn't hurt," he accused.

She smiled wanly. "I lied."

He didn't bother asking her why; the answer seemed self-evident. They'd still be on the roof arguing if she'd admitted how much opening the wards would take out of her.

Senses straining for any indication that they'd been heard, Aaron glanced around the small courtyard; it hadn't changed since the last time he'd visited. The statue of an ancient king rose up dark and foreboding in the center of the tiny square and at his feet curved a single stone bench flanked by squat pots of ivy. There were obvious signs the courtyard had been larger once, but internal pressure from the palace had forced expansion almost to the wall. The old king fought a losing battle for space with buildings and bureaucracy.

The pale glow of a lamp shone through one of the upper windows, but the night absorbed its light long before it hit the ground. At the base of the wall, the shadows were impenetrable.

"Wait here," Aaron told her, his lips against her ear. She smelled vaguely like apricots and as a silky strand of thick brown hair brushed against his nose, he forgot for a moment what else he was going to say and asked instead, "Are you going to be all right?"

Chandra rubbed at her temples and wished that Aaron would stop breathing quite so loudly. "I'll be fine," she whispered irritably. "All I have to do is sit here and. . . ."

Aaron's finger stopped the final word.

Chandra stiffened, then froze as the slap of sandals against paving stones and a brusque, "You there! What are you doing here?" sounded clearly from the street side of the wall.

"I'm waiting for you," Darvish's voice had gone low and throaty, holding both an invitation and a promise.

"You're what?" The guard now sounded more surprised than threatening.

"I've been trying to meet you for some time. I bribed one of the other guards to find out what section of wall you'd be walking."

"You what?"

As much as it hurt her head, Chandra had to smile at the new tone in the guard's voice. She wondered what Darvish was doing in order to inspire such ragged breathing.

"Why don't I walk along with you and we'll talk."

"My wife. . . ."

"Doesn't have to know."

The double footsteps faded along the wall and the murmured words were lost to distance.

Aaron's face was unreadable in the darkness. Chandra wished she could call enough power to see if he needed reassurance, but she suspected that for the moment even so small an amount would knock her writhing to the ground. His voice gave nothing away.

"Stay here," he said, and vanished.

She knew he didn't actually vanish—not even she could sustain the focus necessary for that and *she* was a Wizard of the Nine—but one moment he was beside her and the next he was gone. For a heartbeat, an Aaron-shaped shadow became visible against one of the buildings, and then she was alone.

At first, she concentrated on regaining her strength, on soothing the raw channels that felt as though she'd taken ragged-edged nails and clawed at the abraded surface. She watched the dance of the Nine, all but the Sixth visible over the edge of the palace, and used their cool light as a balm.

Then she counted the dark on dark windows that faced the tiny courtyard, beginning with the one still glowing faintly with light.

Then she fidgeted.

She realized suddenly she had no idea how long Aaron should take and thus no idea of how long she should wait before finding Darvish and mounting a rescue. He'd been gone a very long time, but surely she'd hear if a thief were captured within the palace. Maybe not. Aaron had said this courtyard was far away from anything important; which was why he used it. Perhaps he heroically resisted betraying their mission in a Chamber of the Fourth even now.

Carefully, she stood, sliding her back up the wall, remaining in heavy shadow. She took a deep breath.

You're being ridiculous. Look at the Nine. He hasn't been gone that long.

A horse passed by out on the street and she found herself thinking of Ischia, where, because of the terraces almost no one kept horses and litters were the preferred transportation of the wealthy. Which made her think of home and how ridiculous a litter would look at home where almost everyone rode. Which made her think of her cousin inheriting. Which made her angry. She was the heir, not him. He'd never even made an effort to learn about the common people he might one day be ruling.

And how much have you learned about the common people in the last five years, asked a little voice.

Her shin banged into the edge of the bench and she looked up in astonishment at the worn features of the stone king. She hadn't realized she'd moved away from the wall. Eyes darting from side to side, she checked the surrounding buildings. All the windows were dark and shuttered against the night, including the one that had been open and lit a short while before.

Almost trembling with relief, she turned, intending to retreat back to the wall where Aaron expected to find her.

"Ahh!" The man-shaped shadow leapt back with a great fluttering of robes and a lot of white showing around his eyes.

Chandra mirrored his motion almost exactly. The bench caught her behind the knees and she sat down, hard, the jolt stabbing pain up behind the bridge of her nose.

The shadow gathered itself together and stepped aggressively forward. "What are you doing here?" it demanded, the effect a little lessened by a sudden octave change on the last word.

A wizard, Chandra realized. The outline of the robes was unmistakable. He didn't sound dangerous, but he was certainly capable of calling the guard. What was she supposed to answer? *What would Aaron say? Aaron wouldn't get himself into this kind of a situation. All right.* She took a deep breath, *What would Darvish say?*

"I'm, uh, waiting for a man." Darvish would have gotten the delivery smoother, *had* gotten the delivery smoother, but then Darvish practiced.

The young wizard came close enough to acquire a face and his scowl slipped into embarrassment. "Oh. I'm sorry, milady, it's just that I've never seen anyone else in this courtyard."

"That's why we chose it," Chandra told him. It certainly sounded like a logical reason.

"Oh," he said again.

Chandra was fascinated to learn that a blush could be heard.

"I'll just be going then, milady."

"No, wait." This was her chance to learn about the wizard who had The Stone. Even this . . . this young man, should have noticed the power signature hanging over the city. "He's late and I'm a little afraid of the dark." She patted the bench beside her, beginning to enjoy herself. "Please, would you stay?"

He hesitated a moment, feet shuffling against the flagstones, then he sat. He was pleasant looking enough, although he should have shaved and given the mustache another try in a few years.

"Oh, you're a wizard!" she exclaimed as though she'd just noticed. It sounded ridiculously false to her ear, but she had to say something to keep him from asking who she waited for.

He visibly preened. "I," he said, "am a Wizard of the Fifth."

She stretched her mouth into a smile and wondered if batting her eyes would be taking things just a bit too far. "I feel much safer now."

He returned the smile and ducked his head away, suddenly shy, realizing that "milady" was no older than he was.

"You must do lots of important work."

The self-important tone strengthened. "His Most Gracious Majesty depends on me."

Chandra recoiled a little, trying to make her expression fearful. She had no way of telling if the young man had augmented his night sight. It was an easy spell, but he was only a Wizard of the Fifth, after all. "You aren't that new, really powerful wizard the court is buzzing about?"

"No, no," he hastened to reassure her. "That is, I'm . . . I'm powerful, but I'm not new. I came into my powers years ago."

"Oh." Most wizards came into their power at puberty and although Chandra herself as a Wizard of the Nine had been an early developer, she doubted this wizard had had his power for "years."

He took her silence for continued trepidation. "Don't worry about old Palaton," he scoffed. "He almost never comes into the city."

Chandra hoped she looked sufficiently awed. "You know him?"

The young man, himself considerably in awe of a wizard whose power signature had suddenly flared and now hung over the city like a storm cloud, never stopped to consider how a person without talent would find Palaton any more than a peculiar old man. "Of course, I know him. I am a Wizard of the Fifth."

"Oh. Yes, of course." *Pompous little twit.* She looked down at her fingers laced on her lap and wondered how to end the conversation. *His name is Palaton and he lives outside the city. We should be able to find him with that.*

"Um, look, if your, uh, man isn't coming, perhaps I . . ."

"No. I don't think so." She shook her head, thinking furiously. "Sometimes it just takes him longer to get away. And he has to be so careful in case Her Gracious Ma . . . oh." She covered her mouth with both hands and turned away in what she hoped was believable confusion.

His mouth worked wetly, but no sound emerged.

"Uh," he managed at last, and stood. "I'd, uh, better be going then."

"He would so hate to be seen," Chandra agreed.

Seconds later, she was alone in the tiny courtyard once more.

"The king's mistress?" asked a quiet voice behind her.

Heart in her throat, she whirled around. The statue of the ancient king stared down at her, one hand raised as though in benediction. Then a shadow separated itself from a fold in the stone robe and dropped to the bench beside her.

"One Below." It was most definitely a prayer. She tried to remember how to breathe again. "Aaron, if you ever. . . ."

Teeth flashed in the walnut stain. "Sorry."

"No, you aren't," Chandra muttered but relented when he really did look upset. "Did you get it?"

He touched his breast and she heard the faint rustle of parchment.

"Good, let's get out of here." She stood, took two steps forward and stopped. "Aaron, how are we going to get over the wall without Darvish?"

Without Darvish. Aaron touched the empty place where Darvish had been. Except that Darvish had been in more than that one place for some time now. He shied away from the thought, the voices of childhood priests suddenly grown loud in memory.

"If I boost you to the top, can you hold the wards open long enough for me to get through?"

Hold the wards open; not just slip through, but hold them open. Her head began to throb and her nails bit into her palms in memory of the pain. From what she could see of Aaron's expression he realized what he asked her and she trusted him enough to know that meant there was no other way. Hold the wards open. "Be quick," she said, just barely managing to keep the quaver from her voice.

He moved as quickly as he could, but that was almost not quick enough. The fire began to burn and sear again and she couldn't prevent a whimper from escaping. She felt a scream building and knew that in another heartbeat it would be too strong to hold back.

Then she was falling.

Then she was caught in strong arms that held her close and whispered with Darvish's voice, "Hush, little one, you're safe."

It didn't seem worth it to argue with the form of address.

The crowd outside the palace gates surged back and forth like an angry sea. Its numbers had been growing since early evening as the frightened men and women of Ischia gathered to demand answers. The smoke rising from a hundred torches mixed with the smoke from the volcano, thickening it, darkening it, adding to the rumors and the fear. A constant ebb and flow of sound rose with the smoke and beat against the palace walls.

"Show us The Stone!"

"The Stone!"

"The Stone!"

The cry came from a thousand throats, in a thousand voices. It would grow angrier as the night progressed and if there were no answer—and there would not be—it would feed on itself, turning to panic and riot.

The lord chancellor stood in the gatehouse, gazing out over the square, able to see and remain unseen. He had dismissed the guards who normally stood watch in the small airless room, needing to be alone with his thoughts. Plump hands tucked in the loose green sleeves of his robe, he frowned at those thoughts and hoped he hadn't made a crucial mistake.

"My Lord Chancellor."

He turned slowly and bowed, graceful despite his bulk and his age. "My prince. And my Lord Balin." He smiled apologetically. "I am sorry, my lord, that His Most Exalted Majesty has no time to spend with you. He has," fingers waved toward the window slits, "other things on his mind just now."

"I am aware of those other things," Lord Balin said shortly.

"Yes. Of course." The lord chancellor studied the foreign lord. "His Royal Highness told you. I remember now. So awkward to explain the absence of your future son-in-law otherwise."

"Since you bring it up," Lord Balin's lips curved in a smile that more closely resembled a scimitar's edge than a gesture of friendliness, "I was wondering why you suggested Prince Darvish for a mission of such importance, one on which the entire fate of Ischia depends, when he has a reputation as a drunkard and a fool."

"And yet, with that reputation you betrothed your only daughter to him," the lord chancellor pointed out mildly.

Lord Balin·flushed, but his voice remained steady as he replied, "I did not know His Highness's reputation at the time. You did, my Lord Chancellor."

"Ah, but a reputation may not be all there is to a man. Is that not right, my prince?" Shahin's eyes narrowed as the lord chancellor continued placidly, "Did you not place young Fadi, the beloved son of one of your own people in your brother's service, sure that there he would remain unmolested? In spite of your brother's reputation?"

"I did," Shahin growled. "But then I never believed him abusive, only weak, and of late I've been able to see the man Darvish might have been if not for your attempts to destroy him. Or do you deny you guided him toward what he became?"

"Deny it?" For the first time the lord chancellor's voice held passion. "No, my prince, I will not deny it. Do you think *I* could not see the type of man your brother might have been? At fifteen he was well on his way to it when I began to, as you say, destroy him. He was large and strong, almost beautiful yet still masculine. He had the potential to be the best swordsman this part of the world had ever seen and, in spite of my *destruction,* still almost managed it. He was intelligent, kind, gentle by choice, and strong when he had to be. And," the lord chancellor was almost shouting at the astonished crown prince, "he had something your most exalted father does not and had it stronger, my prince, than you. He had the common touch. Even as he has become, even as they have seen him, the people love him still."

Shahin retreated a step before the older man's vehemence.

"Most dangerous of all, he is a third son! You, who stand to inherit a kingdom, have no idea what that means, my prince. He has nothing. Nothing." His voice dropped and the two men listening openmouthed had to strain to hear the next words. "The rest of your siblings had found diversions, but Darvish had potential— was potential, my prince. Had he become the man he should have been, he could have taken it all. Had he tired of his nothing, and what man would not, the people of Cisali would have given him the throne."

"But Darvish would not. . . ."

"Perhaps he wouldn't have. But a powerful man with no power is dangerous." The lord chancellor sighed and for a moment looked old and tired. "My duty is to your most exalted father, to the throne, and I have done my duty. The people may still love him, but they will not follow him. Your inheritance, my prince, is safe. And now," he drew himself up, becoming once again the self-assured statesman, "I must carry out his Most Exalted Majesty's commands concerning this." Once again, fingers waved toward the window slits.

On cue, came the sound of rocks striking the outside wall of the gatehouse.

"What has my most exalted father commanded?" Shahin asked, stepping back out of the chancellor's path.

"The guards are to be doubled before the barricades on the public platforms."

Shahin frowned. "But that will only further convince the people that The Stone is missing."

"Do you question His Most Exalted Majesty's commands?" the lord chancellor asked mildly, pausing in the doorway. "If I may remind you, my prince, you have already been pardoned for treason. I would not suggest you try your father again." Then he was gone.

Shahin sagged against the wall and rubbed his temples. The diatribe on Darvish he had not anticipated.

Lord Balin shook his head. "The lord chancellor seems to have an answer for everything and everything he says makes logical sense."

"It always has," Shahin said bitterly, turning to peer out at the angry mob. "I never questioned him myself until he began attacking Yasimina. And now, for perfectly logical and completely unfounded reasons he is almost the only one with access to the king."

"As you say," Lord Balin mused, "for perfectly logical reasons. And yet, he never did answer why he sent Prince Darvish to retrieve The Stone. . . ."

"You can put me down now," Chandra muttered. "I'm fine."

"I'll put you down on your bed," Darvish told her, starting up the second flight of stairs, "and not before."

Chandra sighed, but as she'd already discovered squirming had absolutely no effect on Darvish's grip she let her head fall back against his shoulder. The play of muscles under her cheek intrigued her. Although she'd been conscious for only the last little bit of the trip, he'd apparently carried her all the way from the palace and still seemed to show no signs of flagging. After a half dozen steps she said, "You're very strong."

He smiled. "Thank you. You're very brave."

Chandra accepted that as her due.

"And very stupid."

"What?" she yelled, twisting up to face him and immediately wishing she hadn't. When the red cleared from her vision she saw he was frowning down at her.

"You could have killed yourself."

"I found out where The Stone is," she protested.

"Dumb luck. You lied about what opening the wards would do to you." He shifted her weight a little. "Okay, that was brave. But if you'd died, or screamed, you'd have trapped Aaron behind warded walls and left him to the mercies of the Fourth. Not considering *that* was stupid. And how do you think we'd have felt if you died?"

"I found out where The Stone is," she repeated sulkily. The big ox was right, but everything had worked out fine so what was he complaining about. "Aaron wasn't trapped and I didn't die."

"Thank the Nine and One for that." It wasn't the first time Darvish had thanked the gods that night. He'd thanked them pretty much continuously from the moment Chandra's limp body had slid off the wall and into his arms. He'd thanked them for Chandra's sake. For Aaron's. For his own. He turned sideways, carried her through the door Aaron held open, and laid her gently on her bed. Then he pushed her back into a horizontal position as she tried to sit up. "Lie down," he commanded squeezing her shoulder gently, "and rest."

As lying down was infinitely preferable to sitting up, Chandra stayed put.

Darvish watched her for a moment and, when he was satisfied she wasn't going to move, held out his hand to Aaron.

The packet of parchment was thick and Darvish spread it out on the end of Chandra's bed in some puzzlement. Government documents made up most of it. "Aaron, why didn't you just bring the letters from Ischia?"

Aaron's brows raised. "They aren't exactly stamped with the royal seal," he pointed out. "I brought everything in the desk."

Darvish shook his head, eyes sweeping over the page in his hand; a list of merchants likely to protest a further tax. "Sorry. I forgot you weren't in a position to read through this garbage."

"Dar." The prince glanced up and Aaron spread his arms. "I can't read."

Chandra tried to look as though she'd known it all along, while Darvish slowly turned a deep red.

Aaron only smiled. "It's not that common a skill. You're a prince, Dar. You've had a better education than most."

"But you can read your own language," Darvish sputtered. "I mean, from the north. . . ."

"It's a priest's skill where I come from." He reached down and pushed a new parchment into Darvish's hand. "And not all of them learn it. *Are* the traitor's letters in there?"

"Uh. . . ." Hurriedly, Darvish shuffled through the pile. His face grew grim as he pulled a letter free. "Yes," he said through clenched teeth, "one of them at least."

"Do you recognize the writing?" Chandra asked. She'd raised herself up on her elbows to see better, to the Nine with the pain in her head. "It's a good thing you wouldn't use a scribe for this kind of thing."

An accurate, although not complimentary, description of Aaron filled the page in a flowing, cursive script. Darvish jammed a hand back through his hair in frustration. "It looks familiar," he admitted, "but I just don't know. I just don't know! Bugger the Nine!" With a sudden vicious movement, he crumpled the parchment and flung it across the room. "Let's thank the One you took that chance," he snapped at Chandra, rising and striding for the door. "It looks like you got the only information we can use. Get some sleep, we go after this Palaton at dawn."

Chandra decided not to protest that they didn't know exactly where Palaton was. From the expression on Darvish's face that wouldn't be the case for long. She lay back against the pillows and concentrated on rehealing her tattered power channels.

Aaron retrieved the letter, smoothed it, slipped it into the front of his shirt, and, picking up the lamp, silently followed Darvish from the room.

He caught up to him at the foot of the stairs. Darvish had taken two steps toward the bar and the wine barrels and stared across the remaining distance, naked longing twisting his face.

"I need a drink," he said softly as Aaron came up beside him.

Aaron thought of a hundred, a thousand things to say. He touched Darvish lightly on the back of one bare wrist and settled for, "I know."

Just for a moment, Darvish had the strangest feeling that the soul-link was back. That Aaron's strength was there for him if he needed it.

The lava was a hand's span below the golden cup. The wizards were failing. It would all be over soon.

"I have your word you will rescue me?"

Palaton had smiled. "You present me with The Stone and I will

*rescue you in such a way that you will be a hero to the people."
He'd looked thoughtful. "Provided any survive."*

"A hero?"

*"That will make your task of rebuilding, and ruling under His
Gracious Majesty much easier, won't it?" Long, thin fingers had
laced together. "I'll make it look like the last thing the wizards
manage to do is fling you to safety."*

"Will you have power to do that?"

"With The Stone I will have power to do anything."

"Then you will have The Stone."

*Palaton had bowed, a slight graceful movement. "And you will
have Cisali. Although you will have it without Ischia."*

It would all be over soon. And then, it would begin.

Chapter Seventeen

"We go through his front gate? That's it?"

"That's it," Darvish agreed, watching the few remaining stars disappear in the spreading gray of dawn. "And we keep going until we get The Stone."

"Not much of a plan." Aaron closed his pouch and then settled the belt around his waist. Although he'd been up for much of the night, he'd found no information at all on the Most Wise Palaton's house or grounds or habits. Sources that made it a point to know who held every item of worth in the city, and how easy those items of worth were to obtain, knew nothing and expressed a distinct lack of interest in knowing more. Nor did they question their lack of interest which to Aaron best indicated the Most Wise Palaton's abilities. "You know, we'll probably die."

"I know Ischia will *definitely* die unless I, we, bring back The Stone." The last star went out and he turned from the window. "I haven't been much of a prince up until now, but if I have to balance my life against Ischia. . . ." He let his voice trail off, took a deep breath, and started again. "I can't ask either of you to come with me. This isn't your fight."

"The One it isn't!" Chandra snapped. "Nine Wizards of the Nine created The Stone to keep Ischia safe and now some other wizard has run off with it, As a Wizard of the Nine I should think that involves me." Her tone dared either of them to suggest it didn't.

"You could die," Darvish reiterated, bluntly.

"I could've died any number of times since I started on this, this . . ." She frowned and searched for the right words. Adventure, sounded as if she weren't taking it seriously enough and only bards could use quest with a straight face. ". . . rescue mission. If

I die attempting to retrieve The Stone, at least my death will have meaning." Drawing herself up, she tossed her braid back over her shoulder. "I'll die like a Wizard of the Nine."

At any other time Darvish would have smiled, or laughed outright at such a bombastic pronouncement, but he knew she meant it so he only inclined his head and said, "Thank you." The prince was glad of the wizard. He stood less than no chance without her along. The man, as much as he wished her to be safely out of it, was glad of her company.

He turned to Aaron. Pale gray eyes regarded him steadily, and Aaron's expression seemed to indicate that the option of not going didn't apply to him. Between one heartbeat and the next Darvish realized it didn't. And why.

Nine Above, he . . . I mean, I . . . We. . . .

"Why not wait until night?" His eyes now hooded and his expression carefully blank, Aaron bent to buckle on a sandal.

"It wouldn't make any difference," Chandra broke in. Any more long, soulful, *silent* looks between those two and she was going to bash their heads together. "Palaton has The Stone. I've felt its power and I know what *I* could do with it." Cautiously, she tested her focus; it was tender but no longer painful although the power of The Stone was a continuous background thrum. "Night, day; it won't matter to him."

"Then we don't wait." Darvish strapped on the small guardsman's buckler. "We go, now."

Aaron nodded. "Then if everyone knows we're coming, this is how I suggest we get through the gate. . . ."

Back in the center of the city, the bell in the temple tower rang twice and it was officially dawn. At each of Tivolic's five gates, guards gave the go-ahead to brawny young men who put their backs to the windlasses that would open the city for another day.

The senior guard at the North Gate yawned, scratched at the place where his leather jerkin bit into his armpit and wondered why they bothered. What with the houses of the rich stretching along the river and the houses of the not-so-rich stretching along the road, not to mention the new temple that had just gone up, there were almost as many buildings outside the city as in it. He squinted east where streaks of pink and gray were giving way to blue and the great golden ball of the sun seemed to be sitting in the middle of the Duce Florintyn's olive groves. Then he squinted up the long empty length of the North Road and sighed. Give him the East Gate any day. At least the steady stream of market traffic kept a man awake.

Yawning, he wandered back in under the wall and propped his shoulders against the cool stone. The first of what would soon become a steady stream of men and women headed out to a day of service amid the estates of the wealthy. A heartbeat later he jerked erect and tried to yank the night's creases out of his tunic.

"M-most Wise." Frantically, he motioned his partner over. Two years seniority or not, he wasn't going to face a Wizard of the Fourth on his own. It was the same wizard who had stood at the gate the day before, he noted. Not that that helped.

She stared at them both with barely concealed disdain, not so much angry at them as at the circumstances that ordered her out to this gate at dawn for a second day when she'd have much rather still been in bed. The circumstances, however, were not available to be angry at and the guards were.

"If there's anything we can do, Most Wise."

"Stay out of my way. Both of you." She twitched her red-brown robes closer around her legs and sneered at three young women as they passed, their chattering silenced by her gaze. "You will continue to watch for the outlander and his companion."

It wasn't exactly a question, but the senior guard figured it would be safer to answer it than ignore it. "Yes, Most Wise. A small man with red hair and pale skin and a large man, dark but with blue eyes."

"I know what they look like, idiot!" she snarled. "Now take up posts and watch. And don't interfere with the servants." Her voice became a dangerous purr that put both men more in alliance with her. This anger was not only directed away from them but toward something they could understand. "One forbid that the merchant-princes should have to wait to have their asses wiped."

The servants hurried by in ones and twos, young and old, men and women, and the Wizard of the Fourth scowled at them all indiscriminately.

"The description is useless. Even an outlander and a drunk will have brains enough to disguise themselves when they know they are discovered." The two other wizards with her in the small office nodded in agreement.

"You will watch for the soul-link," Lord Rahman had replied

mildly. "We know the soul-link is still in effect. You said so yourself; that you sensed it while trailing the ward."

"They could have had it removed since," she snapped.

"You three have assured me that you are the only Wizards of the Fourth in the city at present and as you all are in the service of His Most Gracious Majesty I assume you would inform me if you had been approached by enemies of the throne."

During the answering pause, she glanced sideways at her companions. Neither of them looked guilty. Nor, however, did they look about to speak.

"There was a wizard on the *Gryphon*," she said pointedly.

Lord Rahman tapped the parchment on the table before him. "A Wizard of the Seventh creates storms," he said, "not a wizard of the Fourth. If the wizard from the *Gryphon* survived the sea and if she still travels with the two we search for, she will not be able to remove the soul-link."

"Palaton could remove it." She put all the loathing felt for someone new and powerful into the name. That he had not become involved in the power struggles around the palace somehow made it worse.

"Palaton, as you well know, is a Wizard of the Nine and is not relevant to this discussion." The genial sarcasm left his voice and it grew cold. "I have had enough argument, Most Wise. If you wish to leave His Gracious Majesty's service, tell me now. If not, you will keep watch at the gates to ensure that the king's enemies do not leave the city should they evade the patrols now searching for them."

"There are three of us and five gates." Her voice was equally cold. Wizards of the Fourth feared no man but neither did she wish to find a new patron.

"You will watch at River, North, and Dawn Gates."

"Day and night?"

"No." Lord Rahman smiled tightly. He hated dealing with wizards. "At night you may rest. The gates are locked then, after all."

That had been two nights ago and this was her second morning staring into the stupid common faces scurrying out to their stupid common jobs. Carefully, she rehearsed the words of the binding spell and tied and untied knots in the bit of string that went with it.

"Let them come through this gate," she prayed to her stern god, "and they'll pay for every bit of discomfort I've had to endure."

"This is stupid!"

"Milady, please."

"I will not be quiet. This is stupid! Stupid! Stupid! Stupid!"

The Wizard of the Fourth watched curiously as a young woman of obvious middle-class merchant lineage approached the gate. Beside her scurried a small, harried man in a clerk's robe that almost exactly matched in color the nondescript brown of his hair. Following the required two paces behind was a private guard, listening to the conversation of his betters with every sign of enjoyment. The wizard frowned. A small man and a large one. She reached out with power. No soul-link.

"If Father wants his business blessed, why can't he go to the temple we always go to?"

"The oracle, milady . . ." The small man kept his voice low and soothing. It seemed to have no effect. As they came closer, the wizard saw he had cut himself shaving and a tiny piece of cloth still adhered to his narrow jaw. The shape of his face declared he had outland blood, but in a city that depended heavily on trade, so did a large part of the population.

"Of course, the oracle." Her voice dripped with loudly expressed scorn. "A priest tells Father that all signs point to the new temple and *I* have to get up at the crack of dawn and walk forever out into the country! *I* think it's just to get Father's money out there to pay for having built it!"

The wizard tended to agree with the sentiment. In her experience, money commanded most of the oracles read by priests. The large man, as though aware of her interest, caught her eye and winked. *Well, he certainly has nothing to hide.* The guilty—guilty of anything—did not make themselves known to Wizards of the Fourth. She scanned his tight leathers appreciatively. *And he certainly isn't hiding much either.* His eyes, she noted—large eyes, long-lashed—were brown. A soft inviting brown.

"Milady, please, lower your voice."

"Why?"

"People are sleeping."

"So?"

The wizard's frown deepened. There was something about the girl she didn't like. . . . Not entirely certain why, she reached out again with power.

And slid right into the power signature that had been hovering over the city and on the edge of every wizard's consciousness for a double nineday. Palaton! How dare he interfere with her work! She would have words to say with Lord Rahman about this.

Furious and fuming, she glared at the backs of the girl and her companions as they walked up the North Road toward the gleaming bulk of the new temple. One last, "This is stupid!" drifted back. Come to think of it, it was pretty obvious what she didn't like about the girl.

"I wish you joy of her," she muttered at the two men and began devising suitably scathing epithets about the *Most Wise* Palaton to deliver to Lord Rahman.

"You were right, Aaron."

"Of course, he was right." Chandra tried to convince her heart it could now start beating more slowly and fought the urge to turn and see if the Wizard of the Fourth still watched them. She had no real understanding of what she had done to the wizard's probe; somehow she had slid it through her own channels and into The Stone and done it without the wizard noticing. As it would only demand explanations she couldn't give, she decided not to tell Aaron and Darvish. "My father says that if you're going to hire an expert," she gave her brightly colored cotton sash a tug just to have something to do with her hands, "the least you can do is take his advice. No one would have believed we were servants and even if they did, you'd look ridiculous trying to sneak out with a sword."

"We're through the gate," Darvish told her acerbically, wiping damp palms against his thighs. "You can stop babbling now."

"Babbling? Huh! I was great." She glared up at him. "All you had to do was look big and mean."

"We were lucky," Aaron told them shortly. He realized that their stretched nerves found release in the bickering, but he couldn't listen to it any longer. He'd give his right arm for something, anything, resembling a plan.

They walked in silence for a time, then Chandra spit out the end of her braid and said, "I wonder why he hasn't tried to stop us."

Aaron shrugged. "We haven't been a threat."

"Or he doesn't think we're a threat at all." Chandra frowned. She hated not being taken seriously.

"A point in our favor," Darvish mused, loosening his sword in its sheath as they arrived at their destination. "He's overconfident."

"Or he's right." Aaron squinted up at the property's double gates, the delicate filigree bathed in the pale gold light of the rising sun. It didn't look like a gate designed to keep people out.

The gate was unlocked, not surprising as the thin decorative metal wouldn't have held against a determined assault. To their surprise, it was also unwarded.

As far as Aaron could see, the garden appeared empty. The frenzied barking of a dog sounded down the road and from beyond the wizard's house came the constant mutter of the river. Metallic wind chimes danced in morning breezes and rang an almost tuneful cacophony. Tall lilies rustled along the path. Nothing looked threatening. Nothing sounded threatening. Yet the knowledge of threat hung so precisely over Palaton's estate that Aaron felt he could draw a line across the gateway to define it. He *hated* working without a plan.

"Shouldn't we go over the wall?" Chandra whispered.

Aaron shrugged. "If he knows we're coming, why make it more difficult for ourselves?"

Chandra shuddered as she passed between the carved pillars of pale stone that bracketed the gateway. The signature of The Stone was now so overpowering she could see it, pulsing red-gold, if she closed her eyes. Almost, she could see it with them open. And she wanted it. The desire was so sudden and so strong that for a heartbeat it was all there was in the world.

It took nine Wizards of the Nine nine years to create the artifact. *And, oh, what I could do with it.*

"Chandra? Are you all right?"

Darvish's soft question brought her back to the garden and she turned her head just enough to see his worried frown. Unsure of her voice, she managed a vaguely reassuring smile. She didn't want him getting the wrong idea. *Of course, I'm all right. Why wouldn't I be?* I'm *not the one with the problems.*

The wide drive curved slightly northward from the gate to the door, the crushed limestone already reflecting back the early morning light. As Darvish unbuckled his sword belt, he squinted, marking the distance they'd have to travel. No obstacles. *Not likely.* He took a deep breath and tightened his right hand around the warm leather of the scabbard.

The drive was untrapped. Aaron realized that wasn't unusual, not even the most paranoid of homeowners wanted to risk sending legitimate visitors into a spiked pit, but it made him nervous.

He longed for the night and shadows to wrap him about in obscurity. This reminded him too much of his father's attacks on neighboring keeps which usually began with smashing down any barricades and moved on to mass slaughter by both sides. What was a thief doing here, in the light of day?

"You're too good a thief, Aaron, my lad."

"Good enough for this, Faharra?" He flexed damp fingers. *"I doubt it."*

Chandra fought the urge to say, "It's too quiet," or something else equally inane and reached into her pocket for the handful of rice she'd gotten from the kitchen of The Gallows. Rice was not the usual medium for the spell, but it was the only thing resembling a grain or a seed available. Murmuring under her breath, she began to pour it from one hand to the other.

They'd rounded the curve of the drive when the six fighters stepped out of nothing.

Darvish drew his sword and tossed the scabbard and belt to one side.

"Now then, lad, let's have none of that." A grizzled veteran stepped out of the line of guards and beamed genially, her expression of goodwill lessened somewhat by the angle of her nose and a scar that puckered one cheek. "There's six of us and only three of you. One of you," she amended after a swift examination of Aaron and Chandra. "We'd rather not have to kill you, so why not just throw down your sword?"

"We'd rather not have to kill you either," Darvish told her with his most charming smile. He wondered how much longer Chandra needed for her spell and how long he'd last if she wasn't ready soon. He really *didn't* want to kill anyone but suspected the guards would not be fighting under that handicap. "So why don't you just let us by and we'll forget we ever met."

She shook her head. "Sorry, lad."

As they charged, Chandra threw the rice.

Four guards fell.

"Two to one," Darvish said softly as, moving too quickly to stop, the older woman and a very young man closed with him.

He caught the first strike on his blade, the second on his buckler. His first and second blows were blocked as well. After a moment, the young man stumbled, a long line of red running diagonally across his thigh. He swore and swung around to protect his injured leg.

"Sleep," Chandra told him, and threw the last of the rice in his face.

Like his fellows, he was asleep before he hit the ground.

Teeth clenched against his weight, Chandra pulled him clear.

Aaron watched as a vicious backhanded swipe sliced into the rim of Darvish's buckler. He should help. The curved swords were useless to him, but there were daggers in plenty on the guards. His father preferred the hand ax but had trained him with daggers as well.

"You've the best eye and steadiest hand in the keep, Aaron, my son. I'm proud of you."

"I don't want you to be proud of me, Father."

Daggers belonged to the past.

Darvish, used to exploiting the advantage of being a left-handed swordsman, found everything he threw blocked with a grim intensity and a joyless smile. The woman was good. She was very good.

He grunted in pain and looked down with some surprise as her sword slashed through his leathers and slid along his ribs.

She was better than he was.

He fell with the blow and came up under her guard.

Almost.

The last four inches of his edge took her cleanly across the throat, drawing another joyless smile below the first.

Her eyes had just enough time to register disbelief before she died.

"Darvish! You're hurt!"

"I know." He drew in a long shuddering breath and gingerly touched his side. There was less blood than he expected, but it hurt like all Nine Above. "I don't suppose you can heal it?"

Chandra blushed. "No, I. . . ."

"Never mind." He tried a grin that didn't quite work. "You took out five of them. You've paid your way."

Aaron moved silently to Darvish's side. The wound was long but shallow and angled in such a way that it didn't cut off the use of his arm. He'd seen worse, but not on Darvish and he found that made all the difference. "Take off your sash," he commanded Chandra over his shoulder.

She frowned but obeyed. Aaron was a thief, not a fighter, but she still thought he should have done something to help. After all, he'd helped the *last* time.

Shaking out the long piece of fabric, Aaron wound it quickly around Darvish's ribs, up over his shoulder, and secured the fringed end. "Better?" he asked, forcing his hands not to tremble at the pain he knew he'd caused.

Darvish carefully raised his right arm to block an imaginary opponent. "Not really," he winced, sucking air through his teeth.

Aaron's lips thinned, but he tried to match Darvish's matter-of-fact tone. "At least you won't bleed to death." He slid out of the clerk's robe. "Shall we get on with this?"

Wiping his sword with the offered robe, his movements exaggeratedly precise, Darvish nodded. "Let's."

Chandra decided to allow them the look they then exchanged. They'd kept it short and she figured they both needed it.

The door to the house was locked but whether in response to the fight or because of the hour they had no way of knowing. Aaron loved the complicated mechanical locks of the rich. They gave access to a thief the way a lowly bolt or bar did not. He slipped a long flexible tool from his pouch and bent to work.

In six heartbeats, maybe seven, the door swung open.

The interior was dim and cool, light passing through the thick stone latticework that made up the front wall and lying in broken patterns on the tile floor.

Palaton smiled into the mirror that showed, not his reflection, but the three at his door. "I will call the girl to me," he told his companion, running his hands gently around the gilded edges of the mirror's frame. "And then you will put the other two away where they can be forgotten."

"Where to now?" Darvish whispered.

Touching the red-gold pulse that had wrapped around her like a cloak as she passed through the door, Chandra let her need for The Stone answer. "Up," she sighed. "We have to go up."

"All right." He made his way to the nearest set of folding doors. "Then we look for stairs."

The very proper servant about to open the doors from the other side was as astonished as Darvish, but the prince recovered faster. Throwing his sword to his right hand, he lunged forward, yanked the man against his uninjured side, and clapped a massive palm over a mouth just about to open in a terrified yell.

"Now what do we do with him?" he asked, breathing a little heavily as the motion jerked his wound around.

"Slit his throat."

"Shut up, Father."

Chandra stepped forward, feeling as though she moved through a dream, and touched the man just between his rolling eyes. "Sleep," she told him, and wasn't surprised when he slumped against Darvish's hold, although without a grain or seed to help focus and form the power the spell shouldn't have worked. "The Stone," she said by way of explanation, and, stepping over limp legs, followed the call deeper into the house.

"You'd think a wizard would protect his people against things like this," Darvish muttered as he let the sleeping servant slide the rest of the way down his body and onto the floor.

Chandra paused and looked back at him. "Why? Wizards aren't in the habit of breaking into each other's houses. Do you arm your servants against attacks by other princes?"

Darvish looked a little concerned at the defensive tone in her voice and Aaron's brows were high as he moved to Darvish's side, asking, "Should I scout ahead?"

"No, we stay together. We've enough potential for disaster without dividing it by three."

Aaron nodded, that made sense to him, but Chandra only shrugged, turned, and once again began following the call of The Stone. Exchanging worried looks, the two men followed.

Drawn by the inner call of The Stone, Chandra walked the length of the new room and went through the double latticed doors at its far end, heading deeper into the house. Eyes straight ahead, completely unaware of her surroundings, she crossed another room and came face-to-face with a large mirror in a gilded frame. There had been mirrors in both of the previous rooms she realized suddenly; they were important although she couldn't remember how or why.

The mirror hung in a wide corridor that ran the width of the house. It took her a moment to realize that her expected reflection was not present, just a broad expanse of silvered glass with a red-gold fire burning in the heart of it. She moved closer. The fire grew.

"Chandra, be careful!" Darvish didn't like the way Chandra stared at her reflection nor did he much like the way she advanced on it. His own reflection stared back at him, brows drawn down in worry.

"I know what I'm doing," Chandra said without turning. The red-gold fire had become a jewel that spun just beyond her reach. She moved closer and laid one hand against the cool glass. "I'm a Wizard of the Nine." If she just reached a little, she knew she could get it.

"Chandra!"

As fast as the two men moved, the mirror moved faster. By the time they reached it, only a red-gold glow remained and that too faded, leaving them staring at their aghast reflections.

Darvish raised his sword to strike at the glass, but Aaron grabbed his arm and dragged it down. "Dar, no! If she's in the mirror and you smash it, you may kill her. If she's gone through it, you may trap her where she is." He held his grip until the trembling left Dar's muscles and they began to relax, then he released the sword arm and stepped back.

Breathing heavily, nostrils flaring, Darvish jerked away from the glass that seemed to mock him by being nothing more than it appeared. "She isn't dead." He wouldn't allow her to be dead. "We find Palaton. And if she's been hurt, we make him pay." *But she isn't dead.* He started down the corridor, coldly furious at Palaton, at himself. "I should've warned her. He brought The Stone to Ytaili with a mirror. I knew he used them. I should've warned her."

Aaron fell into step behind him. "I should have warned her, too." And with the words, the walls had slammed up again, fully formed, trapping emotion behind them. They'd been a part of him for so long and he'd been without them for such a short time that he couldn't knock them down. Nor did he try. After all, he'd failed Chandra. "As much my fault as yours."

"No. The responsibility was mine." Too wrapped up in his own anger and guilt he didn't hear the echo of the void in Aaron's voice. His greatest fear was that Palaton had taken Chandra hostage and would offer to trade her life for The Stone. *She knew that she could die but, Nine Above, don't make it my choice.*

Their sandals whispered quietly against the tiles as they hurried along the corridor, deeper into the house. At a cross corridor, they paused, listened, but heard nothing more than their own labored breathing and the soft chink of metal against stone as Darvish rested his sword point against the floor.

"That way," he said, and pointed. "Keep moving away from the door. We'll have to pass another mirror. Don't look in it."

But they both glanced quickly as they sped past. First Darvish, then Aaron. Hoping they'd see Chandra staring out at them. Terrified they'd see Chandra staring out at them.

They saw their own reflection scurrying single file down the hall of a wizard's house, nothing more.

When Aaron's image stepped beyond the mirror's range, its surface grew brightly silver and a single ripple ran top to bottom down the glowing length. The man-shaped creature that stepped through into the corridor should have been too large to fit between the borders of the gilded frame. The floor should have trembled under its weight. Aaron should have felt its fetid breath on the back of his neck.

It fit easily through the borders of the frame.

It made no more noise than the fall of dust in an empty room.

It had no breath to give it away.

Aaron felt the hair on the back of his neck rise and he half turned. His mind had no time to understand what he saw before blackness claimed him.

Darvish heard the sound of heels thudding against wood. He whirled about in time to see Aaron's feet disappearing into the mirror.

"NO!"

Diving forward, sprawling his full height along the floor, he grabbed out desperately as the ripple shimmered up through the glass, bottom to top, and screamed as a quarter inch of his middle finger was sliced cleanly off. Blood sprayed against the mirror as he snatched his hand back and bundled the fringed end of Chandra's sash around it. Then he sat for a moment on the floor and tried to calm his ragged breathing. Panic would help neither his companion nor himself.

He'd screamed more from Aaron's loss than the loss of his fingertip, the latter having happened too quickly and too cleanly to do more than send a jolt up his arm. The pain radiating out from it now, sending every muscle from wrist to shoulder into weak spasms, more than made up for that, but it remained nothing beside Aaron's loss and the feeling that an essential part of him had been ripped away.

Gingerly, he unwrapped the end of the sash. From what he could see through fresh blood welling up, the mirror had cut hrough flesh and nail and bone, crushing nothing, merely vening the middle finger with the two flanking it. *Thank the One, t's not my sword hand.* Bracing his sword against the wall, he wkwardly cut free a piece of cloth. More awkwardly still, he got t around his finger and tied it with a bit of fringe, using his teeth o pull the knot tight and put pressure on the wound. The rough andage was already soaked through, but it was the best he could lo and he wouldn't waste more time on it. Palaton's servants must ave heard the scream and above all else he had to avoid getting nto a fight he couldn't win.

Finding Palaton is still the best idea, he thought, standing and wiping sweat from his forehead with the back of his sword hand. *Find the stairs, I find Palaton.* He started on in the direction he'd een going, deeper into the house.

The corridor ended in a brilliantly executed mosaic and another cross corridor, both of which showed the silver shiver of a mirror centered in their end walls.

Bugger the Nine! He flattened against the tiles. *Perhaps if I keep my reflection out of the glass. . . .*

Hearing voices to his right, he sidled cautiously toward a pair of latticed doors, folded open. The sunlight spilling through them athed a heavy wooden door set in the opposite wall with bright gold. Riding the light came the sharp scent of fresh cut oranges and a quiet conversation.

". . . less tense if you're going to serve in a wizard's kitchen, oy." The voice was a woman's, the tone dry and almost disapproving.

"But I tell you, I *did* hear someone scream." The last word cracked and jumped an octave.

"And I tell you, unless they're screaming about the food, ignore them. Get me a larger bowl."

Silently, Darvish moved out into the sunlight. Surely there would be stairs by the kitchens to take food up to the wizard. He could see ovens and the end of a large table, but the cook and her helper were out of sight and as long as he couldn't see them. . . . He studied the latch of the wooden door and paused. The hinges were metal. Could he risk the noise of the door opening giving him away? Could he risk not opening the door when the stairs he sought might be behind it?

And then the decision became moot as he stepped away from the wall and his reflection touched the closer of the two mirrors.

It shivered.

In one fluid movement, he crossed the hall and flung the door open with his mutilated hand.

The stairs behind it stretched down.

For less than a heartbeat, dust motes danced as the brilliant sunlight spilled into the darkness below. Then the door was closed again with Darvish behind it, forehead resting against the heavy wood, straining with all he had left to hear the wizard's guardian approach.

He heard nothing except his blood pounding a distraction in his ears and began to think that he had moved in time. Then the feel of the of the corridor changed. The fine hair on the back of Darvish's neck rose. Something was out there. Something. . . .

Muscles tensed, he prepared to throw himself forward the instant the door began to move. If the One was with him, he could slam the heavy wood against his opponent and gain a slight advantage.

And then the feeling went away.

But it didn't go far.

"What are you doing in here?" The cook's voice rose to such a volume that it defeated walls, corridor, and door, and Darvish heard her as though she stood beside him. "Go back to your master! Go on! Get!"

Her voice grew louder as she pursued the creature out of the kitchen. "Oh, no, right off of this level! You go back into your nasty mirror before I take a broom to you."

There was a long pause while the heaviness lifted out of the air. "That's better." Although he heard no sound, Darvish imagined her dusting off her hands. "Wizard promised me no magic in my kitchen and I'll hold him to that promise, by the One. There's nothing to be afraid of, boy." Her voice trailed off into reassurances.

Slowly, very slowly, Darvish pushed the door open and squinted into the sunlight. The corridor was empty. No creature of magic stood waiting for him. Weak with reaction, he leaned against the cool wall of the stairwell and breathed a heavy sigh of relief.

Up from the depths came the unmistakable smell of wine.

He swallowed and found himself descending.

So there's wine. That doesn't mean Aaron is not there as well. A wine cellar is a perfectly logical place to hide captives.

Another step, and then another, and then two more. His head remained in sunlight, his feet in shadow. Three more steps and he waited while his eyes grew accustomed to the dark. Enough light followed him down the stairs that he was able to make out a small table holding a squat pitcher and a mug. Against the far wall he could just barely differentiate the rounded shadows of barrels in the darkness.

The last step and the cool stone of the cellar floor pressed up against his sandals. The air didn't so much smell of wine, as it was wine, and Darvish drew in great lungfuls of it. The pain of his wounds receded before a need so strong that his sword lay on the table and the pitcher was in his hand before he was aware of moving.

One drink, to give me strength. I've lost a lot of blood. Nine Above, surely I deserve that much. Perhaps the wine would fill the aching emptiness where Aaron had been.

Working by touch, ignoring the torment that rode up his arm when he knocked his fingers against the wood, he shoved the thumb of his wounded hand through the ring on the cover of the first barrel and yanked it up. The smell of the wine grew thicker, wrapping like a heavy blanket around Darvish's head. He plunged the pitcher into the darkness and brought it up dripping.

To prove he still had control, he carried it untasted back to the table and filled the mug. Then he sat on the bottom step and raised the mug to his lips.

Just one. To give me strength.

Chapter Eighteen

Aaron regained consciousness slowly, aware first of the cool tiles below and the brightly colored mosaic on the ceiling above. Cautiously, he laid his palms flat against the floor and pushed himself up into a sitting position. The room swam in and out of focus. After a moment it settled, and he took a look at where he was.

The room was small and square. Heavy wooden doors were centered in two of the walls and a third wall was made up of the stone patterning that fronted the house. He had no idea what the room was normally used for as the only thing in it besides himself was a tall metal urn filled with long stalks of dried grasses.

He stood, waited again while the room shifted focus, then checked both doors. Bolted. His pouch of tools still hung around his waist, but it would do him no good.

He peered through the opening in the stonework, scanning the garden. The stone was more than a foot thick and he could no more hope to go through it than he could go through the solid stone of the walls. Returning to the center of the room, he sat. He was trapped. There was no way out.

Behind the walls in his mind he could feel grief and guilt and terror battling to get free. Outside the walls, he felt nothing, not even a physical reaction to whatever had rendered him unconscious before bringing him here. He vaguely remembered a huge misshapen man, decided it must have been magical and, with no reason to care, left it at that.

So I've failed one last time and finally get to die. He didn't know how he knew but he was sure, with a terrible certainty, that no one would come to release him, that slowly, hunger and thirst would bring the end he'd waited for for so long.

"The Clan Heir never surrenders, remember that, boy."

"Shut up, Father."

"If you want your cousin's death, Aaron, my lad, you're going at it the wrong way."

"Shut up, Faharra."

He pushed the voices of the past back behind the wall but one rose up loud and strong to take their place.

NO!

It was Darvish's voice, but Aaron couldn't remember ever hearing the prince cry out the word with such desperation, such pain, such incredible loss. It echoed through his head and the walls trembled.

"Leave me alone," Aaron whispered, his hands curling into fists on his lap. "I failed you, too."

NO!

"I left you alone. I was taken when you needed me. Ruth, Faharra, Chandra, you. I fail everyone. Let me die."

NO!

He threw back his head, the white column of his throat exposed and vulnerable, and wailed, "I have nothing to live for!"

NO!

"You don't understand!" he screamed at the voice, leaping to his feet. "It doesn't matter, I can't get out!"

Aaron stood panting in the silence, listening to his breath, listening to his heart pounding in his chest, and staring at the huge metal urn. The doors were solid wood and bolted, but the brackets holding the bolt were secured only in the wood, not bolted in turn themselves or it would show on his side of the door. There was a way out.

His father's way.

Moving with exaggerated care, much the way Chandra had moved when she was following the call of The Stone, Aaron walked across to the urn and tipped out the grasses. It was large and heavy, but he'd always been stronger than he appeared and he lifted it with little trouble. Slowly, he approached one of the doors.

His father's way. The way of mindless violence, of brute force. The way he'd turned from so many years before when Ruth screamed his name.

And now I prove myself my father's son.

The urn slipped from lax fingers and rang against the floor.

I can't.

NO!

"SHUT UP, DAR!"

But Darvish didn't shut up and the voice kept denying, over and over again, its incredible loss.

Aaron remembered arms that had held him when he cried and he picked up the urn by its fluted neck and slammed the solid metal base into the door.

The reverberation of the blow almost flung it from his hands, but he hung on and struck again.

And again.

And again.

He didn't know when he fell into the rhythm he'd last heard being beaten into a young girl's back by a length of leather. He didn't know when the tears started pouring down his cheeks. He didn't know when he began screaming Ruth's name. He didn't know when the blood from the scars on his chest soaked through his thin shirt.

He only knew the door, and that Darvish was on the other side of it, and that he'd do anything he had to to ease the pain in that cry.

When the wood finally surrendered and splintered and released the bracket; when the bolt clattered to the floor and the door flew open; when silence fell again. . . .

Aaron looked down the empty corridor. Arms trembling, he set the battered urn gently on the floor. He felt strangely calm, and empty. For the first time in five years, Ruth had stopped screaming his name. He didn't think he'd ever hear her again. Or his father. Or Faharra.

"I'm my father's son," he said softly. But then, he always had been. He drew a deep shuddering breath and went to find Darvish and Chandra and The Stone and a reason for living.

Darvish licked his lips and stared down into the mug. He had been sitting like that, not drinking, for longer than he cared to think. The wine fumes teased him, wove seductive spells around him and yet somehow, every time he brought the mug to his mouth, he lowered it, contents untasted.

"I deserve this drink," he said to the darkness. "I've fought for it, bled for it, risked my ass for it."

Around him, the wine agreed but then, that was the beauty of wine. It always agreed.

He shifted his mutilated hand in his lap and sucked air through his teeth at the pain. "This," he lifted the cup, "was the one thing that was mine."

Again, the wine agreed.

"I wanted a friend, Aaron." It didn't really matter that Aaron couldn't hear the answer. He'd probably forgotten the question. "Just a friend. That was all." His voice grew rough. "I thought you'd understand and you did and now they've taken that from me, too." The wine would ease the loss, mask the ache, bring forgetfulness. "Nine Above!" The curse bounced off the back wall and echoed through the cellar. "What kind of prince has to rescue a thief from the Chamber of the Fourth to find a friend?"

This kind of prince, said the wine.

"It wasn't my fault! They never gave me anything to do. Nothing meaningful. Nor would they let me live a life of my own. Do you know," he asked the mug he clutched so tightly, "what that does to a man?" His laugh held the old self-mockery and he lifted the battered mug in a gay salute. "Yes, I suppose you do."

By accident, he tilted the liquid at exactly the right angle and could, in spite of the dim light, see himself reflected in its smooth surface.

"They never gave me anything to do," he repeated softly. His hand trembled. The reflection wavered and dissolved. Although he tried frantically, he couldn't find himself again and this frightened him.

As he continued to stare into the wine, the fear changed, his lips twisted into a snarl, and an unexpected anger rose to take its place. The anger lifted him to his feet, throwing the mug as hard as he was able against the far wall.

"Except this once! They shit on me for eight years and then they expect me to do the impossible." The rage burned through him and out. "I never wanted to be a hero! I only wanted to belong!" He snatched his sword up from the table. "So I'm going to save Chandra and Aaron." A vicious backhand swing sent the pitcher slamming into the stone, spraying wine. "And I'm going to get The Stone." He brought his blade down on the table like an ax and wood chips flew. "And my most exalted father can take the One Abandoned chunk of rock and choke on it!"

Still burning, he spun on the ball of one foot and bounded up the stairs.

The cook looked up in some surprise when the tall warrior

strode into the kitchen, but she carefully and immediately schooled her features, ignoring for the moment, young Ahmid, who had dropped her second best mixing bowl and was now opening and closing his mouth like a landed fish. "How may I help you, milord?"

"The stairs, going up—where are they?"

It was not her business to protect the wizard from swordsmen. Her duty was to prepare and serve the food. Besides, he had a weapon drawn and looked likely to use it. "The stairs are at the other end of this hall, milord."

Darvish nodded his thanks and left. As he broke into a trot, he heard the cook snap, "What are you staring at, standing there in a pile of broken crockery? Clean it up."

The stairs were where the cook had said, rising, shadowed and cool, into the upper story of the house. Turning slightly to one side and shifting his grip on the sword, Darvish began to climb. The anger had faded a little although its heat still kept his thinking clear. He felt remarkably calm. This would finish things, one way or another.

". . . functioning as a power storage, it also focuses the power it stores and this enables it to draw in more power as it needs it."

Chandra nodded thoughtfully. "That would make sense if it was created to hold the volcano of Ischia in check permanently."

"Ah, but because of The Stone's ability to focus, once a Wizard of the Nine is in tune with it there is no longer any need for elaborate preparations." Palaton's dark eyes almost glowed with his enthusiasm. "Any spell, of any magnitude, can be instantly performed."

"Without pain?" Chandra asked, frowning up at the older wizard.

"The only pain occurs while tuning yourself to The Stone." He sat down in the wood and leather armchair facing The Stone and rubbed his temples with long fingers. "You actually came through that better than I did. It is possible your power potential is higher. We will have to test it, of course."

"Of course," Chandra agreed absently, peering into the red-gold heart of The Stone. It rested in a cup atop a delicate spire of gold much as it had in Ischia except that this spire rose up from a golden base, not a cauldron of molten rock. *What an opportunity. To work with The Stone, to discover its secrets, what it is capable of. To discover the knowledge of the ancient wizards and to be able to use it again.*

"Chandra!"

She started and whirled. It took her a moment to pierce the red-gold veil and find a memory to match the large, sword-wielding figure by the door, then it took her another moment to reconcile the changes. The memory had never looked so grim, nor had such lines drawn deep by the corners of his mouth. "Dar? You look terrible. Are you all right?"

"Are you?" His heart had given a sudden leap at the sight of her, then had settled back into the angry pounding that had driven him from the wine cellar. She appeared to be physically unharmed but. . . . He moved farther into the room, noting and discarding the huge open windows, the profusion of plants, and the few pieces of heavy old furniture scattered about. The only items of importance were Chandra, The Stone, and the man who had to be Palaton.

Chandra rolled her eyes at Darvish's scowl. "Of course I'm all right."

He frowned; she was obviously enchanted. Hopefully, dealing with Palaton would deal with that as well. "Move away from The Stone," he commanded quietly.

"Dar!" She shifted to better shield The Stone with her body and began to weave a gentling spell just in case. She didn't think he'd attack her, but he had such a grim expression on his face she couldn't be sure. "It isn't like you think. We've been wrong all along."

"And the attack at the inn never happened?"

"It wasn't an attack. I misunderstood. He had to be sure that I was a Wizard of the Nine, so he offered me the power of The Stone."

"And nearly killed you."

Darvish stepped sideways and Chandra moved as well. "He didn't mean to," she told him. "Palaton isn't a bad person, he's a Wizard of the Nine. He's like me."

"He's like you?"

She didn't understand his tone but hoped the question indicated he was willing to be reasonable. "Yes."

"Really." The word dropped into the room like a thrown dagger. Darvish, while continuing to keep part of his attention on the man seated behind the glow of The Stone, locked his eyes on Chandra's. "Then ask the Most Wise what he's done with Aaron."

"Aaron?"

"You do *remember* Aaron?"

"Don't be stupid, Dar," she snapped. "Of course, I remember Aaron. He's fine. He's somewhere safe until Palaton can deal with him."

"Deal with him?" The sword point came up.

"Oh, for the One's sake, not like that!" It was her turn to glare. "I think Palaton's been pretty understanding about the whole thing considering we broke into his house."

Aaron was safe. The iron band around Darvish's chest loosened a little and his voice was less like a weapon as he asked, "Can the Most Wise Palaton not speak for himself?"

"He can." Palaton came to stand by Chandra, resting one thin hand lightly on her shoulder. He towered over the younger wizard but then, he towered over most people and noted with interest that this prince of Ischia could look him right in the eye. "We have work to do, Chandra," he reminded her impatiently.

"Palaton." Chandra twisted to smile up at him as she said his name and Darvish felt his stomach knot. It wasn't the smile of adoration he'd feared but an even more dangerous smile between equals. "This is the Prince Darvish I told you about."

Palaton inclined his head a barely perceptible amount.

Ignoring the introduction, Darvish dove forward and slammed his sword so hard into an unseen barrier that his entire arm went numb and he barely managed to keep his feet.

"DARVISH!" Chandra's eyes blazed. "You haven't been listening to a word I've said! Palaton is not an enemy! He's a Wizard of the Nine. Like me!"

"Then what's he doing with The Stone of Ischia?" Darvish snarled, backing a little away and searching for the parameters of the barrier.

"He's studying it. Look," she continued in a more reasonable tone of voice, "this," a sweep of her hand indicated The Stone, "is an artifact of the Wizards of the Nine. It holds an incredible potential for knowledge."

"So he's studied it. He's also stolen it and now I've come to take it back."

Chandra sighed. "Dar, you don't understand. He hasn't finished. And *I* haven't even started."

"And Ischia will die for your longing for knowledge?"

"Well, no, but. . . ."

His brows drew down. He was no longer entirely certain that Chandra was under an enchantment. "Then you will give me The Stone," he growled. "Now."

"No, we. . . ."

"Then Ischia will die."

"But. . . ."

"Unless you two Wizards of the Nine," the title was as bitterly sarcastic as he could make it, "know another way to stop the volcano."

"No, not yet, but that's my whole point. Working with The Stone, we might find a way."

"And the people of Ischia will pay for that knowledge with their lives."

"No."

"Yes, Chandra! They die! All of them!"

"But. . . ." Confused, she looked up at Palaton. This wasn't the way it was supposed to be. This wasn't the way he had explained things would happen when he'd thrilled her with the reasons he'd taken The Stone and now offered her a place at his side.

"There will always be more people, Chandra," Palaton said quietly. "But there is only one Stone. If you turn your back on a chance to study it, to study your heritage, it will not come again. You are a wizard of the Nine, are you not?"

Her chin came up. "Yes, I am," she declared emphatically. But she wouldn't meet Darvish's eyes. Everything was so much clearer before he showed up.

"Will you turn your back on knowledge? Will you turn your back on what you are?" Palaton demanded.

"Will you turn your back on the people of Ischia?" Darvish asked grimly. "Because if you would, then I'm very glad tradition will make your cousin your father's heir."

"What?" That got her attention as nothing else he had said had, and she whirled to face him, hands clenched into fists. *How dare he judge her.*

"You're trading the certain death of hundreds of people . . . of *my* people, for the chance to play with a new toy. Oh, a very powerful toy," he conceded with a sneer, "but that's all it is to both of you. A toy."

"It isn't like that, Dar," she pleaded with him to understand. The constant pulse, pulse, pulse of The Stone made it difficult, almost impossible to think of anything else.

"Hundreds, thousands of men, women, and children will die. Your fault, Chandra. And you don't care."

Dying? Hundreds, thousands dying? Had she forgotten that? "I *do* care."

"Ha!" She flinched back as though he'd physically struck out at her. His voice remained a low merciless growl as he continued. "If *this* is a Wizard of the Nine, if *this* is what your father saw you growing into, I'm not surprised he chose to live in the past."

"Don't!"

Darvish ignored her pained wail although it added another wound to the ones he carried already for his people's sake. "Is *this* what you are, Chandra?" He pointed with the sword point at Palaton. "A Wizard of the Nine? A murdering, friendless . . ."

"Enough. You are wasting our valuable time." Palaton raised a hand, The Stone grew brighter for a heartbeat, and. . . .

"No!" Tears rolled down Chandra's cheeks, but she caught the power Palaton threw and twisted it aside.

A square section of the parquet floor to Darvish's right flared and the next instant became charcoal and ash. Darvish remained where he was but shifted his weight onto the balls of his feet, his blade pressing against the barrier surrounding both wizards. When it went down, Palaton was his.

"Dar's right." Chandra straightened her shoulders and faced the other wizard squarely. "You made me forget the people."

"I did not make you forget anything." Palaton sounded vaguely amused. "I reminded you of what you are: a Wizard of the Nine."

She sniffed, looking both absurdly young and strangely dignified. "But that's not *all* I am. If it's all you are, then I'm sorry for you. We're taking The Stone back to Ischia."

"No." He shook his head. "You are not."

Again, The Stone grew brighter.

Chandra paled and swayed, then visibly pulled herself together. Her brow furrowed in concentration.

The Stone grew brighter still.

Eyes wide with surprise, Palaton jerked as though stung. "Amazing," he murmured. "The amount of power you can conduct is truly amazing." The furrows in his brow grew deeper. "You may be the stronger, but I think you will find that the knowledge you threw over for *people* is not to be so casually despised."

Sweat glistened on Chandra's skin, rivulets gathering along her collarbone to run down between her breasts.

The barrier disappeared.

The moment Darvish felt his sword tip press on nothing, he threw his weight behind it for the killing blow.

Massive, misshapen hands clamped his arms to his sides, gripping so tightly he cried out. His sword clattered to the floor as his fingers spasmed in pain. Caught fast, Darvish could only watch as the two wizards fought their silent battle and The Stone blazed. He threw back his head and howled in frustration.

The sound echoed through the room. Lost in it was the noise of a slight body sliding over a broad window sill.

Standing silently in the dappled shadow of a broad leafed plant, Aaron knew Palaton would soon deal with him as well. He was too good a thief not to recognize a man with all the angles covered. If it wasn't another monstrosity, like the one that held Darvish, he had no doubt it would be something equally effective. Where, then, to throw his strength? At the creature holding Darvish? At the wizard himself?

He squinted at The Stone.

One chance.

Removing his belt pouch, he stepped out into the room and with all his remaining strength threw it—not at the creature, not at the wizard, not at The Stone—at the thin golden spire below The Stone. The spire snapped off at its base. Impossibly slowly, The Stone began to fall.

"No," Palaton gasped and spun out of the power lock with Chandra.

Chandra gulped air, raised a trembling hand, and destroyed the creature holding Darvish.

Darvish dove forward, caught up the broken spire, slammed the jagged end up and into Palaton's heart.

As the Wizard fell, he stretched out desperate hands for The Stone and together they crashed to the ground. When Chandra reached him, he wasn't quite dead. He gazed at the red-gold glow between his fingers, wearing an expression close to contentment and said quite clearly, "Almost worth dying to touch it at last." His voice grew wistful. "It was what I always wanted to do."

Exhaling very, very slowly, he died.

Darvish got carefully to his feet. Aaron walked slowly forward to stand by his side. The three of them stood looking down at Palaton and The Stone which had grown, perhaps, a little less bright.

The silence that fell seemed to isolate them in that room, push them outside of time. The light appeared sharper, the air cleaner, Like being caught in crystal, Darvish thought. He touched Aaron lightly on the shoulder and said, "Are you all right?"

The crystal shattered. The world returned.

Aaron nodded. Now was not the time to tell just how all right he was—despite the open wound his chest had again become. They'd have time for that later when there'd be a number of other things to be told as well, He noted the new bandage and the darker stains on the old one. "You?"

"Yeah." Slowly he lowered himself to the floor beside Chandra.

Her eyes bright, Chandra lifted her head. "I'm sorry," she whispered. "It was just that he . . . he. . . ." Her lower lip began to tremble and tears ran silently down her cheeks. At first, she resisted the pressure of Darvish's arms; then, with a strangled cry, she threw herself against his chest and sobbed.

"He was the first person to understand what it meant to be a Wizard of the Nine," Darvish finished gently, holding her close. "It's okay. Most people would do worse than you did for understanding."

"What's worse than betraying your friends?" she asked, her voice tight.

Darvish pushed her chin up until she had to meet his eyes. "Not stopping when you realize that's what you're doing."

Chandra looked from Darvish to Aaron and managed a watery smile in return.

The new silence had all the world in it and although there were a thousand more things to say, the silence seemed to say them all.

Aaron squatted by the body and took a closer look at The Stone. "How do we get it back to Ischia?" he asked, lacing his fingers together to prevent them from reaching out and touching it. While he could sympathize with Palaton's desire, he vividly remembered the thief in Herrak's chamber with his hands rotting away and he had no intention of becoming the newest resurrection of that thief.

"And is there an Ischia to get it back to?" Darvish bent carefully and retrieved his sword.

"I can find out."

"What?"

"Palaton. . . ." Taking a deep breath and rubbing her nose against her sleeve, she began again. How could a man she'd known for such a little time have made so much of an impression? "Palaton told me The Stone can be used for scrying. Distance doesn't seem to matter." She knelt across the body from Aaron. Palaton's eyes were open, staring at The Stone. Lower lip between her teeth and a tear trembling on a lower lash, she brushed them closed. "I can find out about Ischia."

"Nine and One, yes!" Darvish got stiffly to his feet and moved to stand at Aaron's back. "Hurry, Chandra. Please."

The Stone grew brighter.

The guards fell back before the howling rush of people without a blow being exchanged. The few that attempted to hold their posts were overwhelmed by numbers and pushed aside, the rest threw down their weapons and joined the citizens of Ischia in tearing down the barricades.

"The Stone! The Stone! THE STONE!" The cry rang hoarsely from a thousand throats as the public platforms were gained at last. The rush forward sent three in the front rank over the edge and their screams still sounded when shouts of "The Stone!" stopped and a wail rose from those near enough to see.

The molten rock seethed and boiled not a finger's span below the golden cup, a cup empty of The Stone of Ischia.

Almost as though the unwilling sacrifices had strengthened it, the volcano surged against the weakening bonds that held it. The wizards began to sway. On the royal platform, the heir spoke impassionedly with a slightly older man who shook his head in emphatic refusal and attempted to pull Prince Shahin back into the palace.

A great cloud of smoke boiled up. The crater twisted.

One corner of the public platforms crumbled and a dozen more people fell screaming to their deaths, the rest scrambling frantically backward in hysterical panic.

On the royal platform Shahin crumpled to his knees and the face of the man with him became clearly visible for the first time.

* * *

"Papa, no!"
The Stone blazed.

Coughing and choking in air suddenly heavy with smoke and sulfur, Darvish rubbed the back of his injured hand across his eyes, attempting to clear away the afterimages of red-gold fire.

"Darvish?"

He blinked furiously and his brother's face swam into focus. "Shahin?" He stared incredulously around. The three of them, plus the body of Palaton still clutching The Stone, were on the Royal Platform although a heartbeat before they had been in Ytaili. "Nine and One," he breathed.

"And then some," Aaron agreed, slowly straightening. He reached down a hand to help Chandra up. "Are you all right?"

"I think so." She shook her head, trying to clear it. While whatever she'd done hadn't exactly hurt, her entire body resonated to the pulsing of The Stone and the enormous amount of power she'd focused had left both radiant trails and an annoying throbbing between her ears. "I think I'm. . . ."

"The wizards," came the wail from the public platforms. "The wizards are falling!"

Barely visible through the smoke, the gaunt and exhausted men and women who had held the volcano at bay for two nine-days, collapsed one by one. The last to fall, for an instant holding the power net alone, buckled slowly to the frighteningly clear sound of her spine shattering.

Chandra whirled to face the volcano, arms wide, fingers spread. Caught in mid swell, the molten rock lapped against the lip of the golden cup, then sullenly receded. Hot winds lifted the smoke up and away and no more rose to take its place.

"Aaron, look at The Stone. She's not drawing on its power!"

Aaron's gaze flicked from Chandra to The Stone to Chandra again. "She's holding the Lady of Ischia on her power alone," he said.

"Chandra, what are you doing?" Darvish could see lines of strain on her face already. "Use The Stone!"

"I can't," she grunted, forcing the words out through clenched teeth. "Too close. It was . . . made for this. If I used it now, it would pull me in. I'd get lost . . . in it. You have to put it back." The corners of her mouth trembled as she tried to smile. "Hurry?"

"Darvish!" Shahin grabbed his brother by the arm. "Where did you come from. What's going on?"

Darvish shook himself free. "We're saving your ass," he snapped. This was not the time for long explanations. They still had to figure out *how* to return The Stone to its place. "Any ideas, Aaron?"

"Just one," Aaron told him and he pointed to the Platform of Execution and the cage. He watched Darvish measure the angle of the support beam and the amount of available chain and knew that he understood, both the plan and the part each of them would have to play.

"Should work. How do we carry The Stone?"

Aaron prodded Palaton's rigid corpse with his foot. The journey from Tivolic, however it had been accomplished, seemed to have fused the body into one solid, inflexible piece. "Palaton can carry it. We've no time to be more creative."

"Granted," Darvish admitted grimly. He swung his sword up over his head and chopped down with all his strength. And then again.

Lips tight with revulsion, Aaron quickly scooped up Palaton's severed hands and with them The Stone. The wrists remained stiff and the fingers curved. If he held them carefully together, they should suffice.

The path between the royal platform and the cage more resembled a decorative ledge than something meant to be traveled. It curved, narrow and treacherous, along the inside of the crater with no room for mistakes—on one side sheer rock, on the other, the Lady waited. Aaron and Darvish ran it at full speed, ignoring the danger, ignoring Shahin and Lord Balin, ignoring the shouts from the crowd as they recognized their missing prince. *What good saving Ischia,* they both thought and each knew the other thought it, too, *if Chandra falls?*

At the platform, Aaron set Palaton's hands down and joined Darvish in wrestling the heavy cage out of its rests. With no one to work the winch, they balanced it on the very edge of the stone itself. It took them a frenzied moment to work the bolts free and then another to drag the front half away from the back.

"You okay?" Darvish asked as Aaron climbed inside.

Aaron nodded. "Let's do it." He wanted to sound unaffected for Darvish's sake, but he couldn't seem to get his teeth unclenched.

Darvish heaved the front of the cage shut and secured the bolts. He didn't look at Aaron while he did it. He couldn't have done it and look at Aaron; not for Chandra, not for Ischia. Palaton's flesh felt heavy and cold and Darvish's skin crawled as he carried the hands and their pulsing burden over to the caged thief.

With his own hands crammed through the bars to just past the wrists, Aaron had almost no maneuverability. His fingers were as white as Palaton's as he gripped the grisly calipers.

"Can you hold them?" Darvish asked.

"Just do it," Aaron snarled. He couldn't hear the scrape of steel on stone over the frenzied pounding of blood in his ears. Then, thankfully, all he had room to think of was keeping hold of The Stone as the cage swung out over the pit. For one heart stopping second, the cage, Aaron, The Stone, fell free. A jerk and a grinding of chain later, all three hung an equal distance between the wall of the crater and the golden cup.

Darvish played out the chain until the top of the cage was level with the platform and Aaron's pale face was out of sight, then he raced for the support beam. The thief would have danced along it. The prince scuttled on hands and knees. At the end, he lay on his belly, locked his legs around the ironbound wood, and reached for the chain. The links were warm and slightly gritty under his hands. The muscles in his arms and back straining, he began to swing the cage, slowly at first, then in ever lengthening arcs.

Pressed as tightly as possible against the heated metal, Aaron narrowed his world to the flash of gold below him at the apex of his swing. His feet and lower legs were burned from the radiant heat of the volcano and he could feel blisters rising where his bare skin touched the metal cage. None of that mattered. On his second pass over the cup he began to count. On his third, he dropped The Stone.

The only sound as it fell was the grinding shriek of the abused chain as every man and woman watching held their breath. It tumbled, growing brighter as it drew closer to the molten rock, then suddenly flared, a miniature red-gold sun. When the after-images died and thousands of pairs of watering eyes strained toward the golden cup, The Stone of Ischia was back where it belonged—the captured fire captive once again.

After a moment of complete and absolute silence, the crowd went wild; screaming, shouting, weeping for joy. The crater echoed with the sound.

"The Stone! The Stone! THE STONE!"

Chapter Nineteen

On the royal platform, Chandra lowered her arms.

"Chandra?" Lord Balin, oblivious to everything except his daughter, touched her lightly on the shoulder.

She half turned and began to speak, then her eyes rolled up and she pitched forward into her father's arms.

She saw his terror when she opened her eyes, felt his love, his pride, his fear; knew it was all for her. For a heartbeat, she felt a sense of power as strong as the power of The Stone. With a word or a motion she could ruin this man who so desperately held her. A heartbeat later, she reached up a trembling hand and tentatively touched his cheek.

"Papa?" she asked.

They cried together for a time.

Moving with frantic haste, Darvish dragged the cage up onto the platform. His blood slicked fingers fought desperately with the bolt while Aaron watched, head lolling slightly to one side. Teeth clenched with the effort, he forced the front and back of the cage apart and pulled the younger man free.

Aaron swayed but managed to stay on his feet.

"How badly are you hurt?" Darvish demanded, wanting to touch him, afraid to touch him.

"I don't know." He was, in fact, strangely disinterested in the whole thing and what pain there was seemed to come from far away. "But I don't think I want to do that again,"

"You won't ever have to," Darvish promised softly, brushing a flake of ash from one high cheekbone. They stood staring at each other until the sound of the crowds chanting Darvish's name reminded them where they were.

"Sounds like you're a hero," Aaron told him, one corner of his mouth twitching up into a smile.

Darvish snorted and jerked his head toward the royal platform where a portly figure in deep green had just appeared. "It won't last. Can you walk back up there? The path isn't wide enough for me to carry you."

"Sure." He'd walked narrower ledges, hadn't he? And nothing hurt too much. Of course, he couldn't really feel his legs and that might prove a bit of a problem, but he'd get by. He waved a hand at the blood that dripped sporadically from the sodden bandage around Darvish's finger. "Can *you?*"

"As long as I don't walk on my hands." Gently he steered Aaron toward the path. "You first." He could catch him even if he couldn't carry him. "What did you do with. . . . ?"

"I dropped them. Why? Did you want me to keep them?"

Darvish winced. "Aaron. . . ."

Shahin met them at the edge of the royal platform. "You should have waited," he chided, helping Aaron through the narrow gap in the railing and holding out a hand to his brother. "I sent guards to open the doors."

"Doors," Darvish repeated. He twisted and looked back at the Platform of Execution.

As they watched, the huge ironbound doors slammed open, the crash of the metal striking the rock audible even above the noise of the crowd. Trumpeters dressed in royal livery emerged, blowing a fanfare as they came.

Darvish cocked an eyebrow at his brother, who shrugged. "I sent a pair of guards," Shahin told him. "This isn't *my* idea."

Then a figure in robes of brilliant white appeared, dazzling in the sunlight. A huge ruby set amid the gleaming gold of the crown blazed on his brow, almost outshining The Stone itself. He raised his arms and the crowd fell silent.

"The Stone has been returned!" King Jaffar's voice filled the crater, echoing faintly between the palace and the temple. "Ischia has been saved!" With a flourish that seemed to encompass both the people and The Stone and still direct the attention to himself, he lowered his arms.

Shahin shook his head. "It looks like he was about to face the crowd when you three appeared and he decided to wait. He's just managed to tie the throne to the recovery of The Stone." The heir's voice held a trace of admiration as he added, "Everything he does, he does for the good of the realm."

The chanting began again but this time, they chanted the king's name.

Darvish sighed and, although he knew His Most Exalted Majesty wouldn't be able to hear, said quietly, "Hello, Father."

Shahin heard and lightly touched his brother's shoulder. Finding he had nothing to say, for there was nothing he could say, he shook off the mood and peered into Darvish's face. "Your eyes are still brown."

"Chandra," Darvish said shortly, turning away from the crater. "Is she all right?"

Lord Balin looked up—his daughter's head resting on his chest, her body curled within the circle of his arms—and nodded. His eyes were bright and his cheeks were damp. "She says she just needs to rest."

"Don't listen to her," Darvish cautioned. "She needs a healer."

Lord Balin smiled at the protective tones in the young prince's voice. "Thank you, Your Highness. Your brother assures me that healers are on the way." He pressed his lips against Chandra's hair.

The hand that rested on his shoulder, clutched his tunic so tightly the knuckles went white. She hadn't forgotten, nor forgiven, the five years when she'd lived as no more than a shadow behind his grief but for now, Chandra had found her father and for now, that was enough.

"If I may presume, Your Highness," the lord chancellor stepped forward and bowed, his face respectfully expressionless, "my congratulations on returning The Stone."

Darvish inclined his head, a muscle in his jaw jumping.

"You didn't expect to see him again, did you?" Shahin asked, carefully watching the lord chancellor's face.

"No, my prince," he admitted, spreading plump hands, "I did not."

"Because of the way you had destroyed him."

"Because, my prince, he would be in opposition to a wizard and a king."

"And yet you supported my suggestion that he go."

"As I said before, my prince, I agreed with you that he was the only man for the task. And time, it seems, has proven us both correct."

Darvish looked from his brother's suspicious scowl to the lord chancellor's bland self-assurance. "Shahin," he said, reaching into the front of his vest with his good hand, "we didn't just return The Stone. We, that is, Aaron found a number of letters. . . ."

From the moment the wizards had begun to fall with him not yet called to safety, the lord chancellor had been walking a thin line. Almost tripping over Palaton's mutilated body when he finally forced himself out onto the royal platform to discover what was happening, pushed him closer to the edge. The mention of letters tipped him over and the veneer cracked.

Afterward, no one could figure out where he thought he was running to. Eyes wide, he darted across the platform, moving with a speed completely inconsistent with his age and size, and tripped over what remained of Palaton's arms, stretched out where Darvish had left them. With a strange, gurgling cry, he slammed into the rail and began to fall.

Aaron threw himself sideways, grabbed for the lord chancellor's disappearing legs, and somehow managed to hang on.

"Too many deaths already," he said, after a frantic Darvish and three guards had dragged both of them back onto the platform. He touched Darvish gently on the cheek and sighed into darkness.

Aaron recognized the ceiling. Stucco. A good thief stayed away from stucco. The angle was wrong though and the breeze blowing in through the open shutters should be striking his other cheek. He stirred restlessly.

"Dar, he's awake."

Chandra's voice. She was all right, then. The volcano hadn't destroyed her. The edge of the bed sagged under someone's weight. He struggled to sit up. Large hands slipped behind his shoulders and gently lifted him, then just as gently eased him back on the piled pillows.

"Thank you, Oham." Darvish smiled up at his dresser. The big man nodded and moved away from the bed.

Aaron spent a moment just drinking in the sight of the prince. Bathed in sunlight, he had a bandage glowing a brilliant white wrapped about his chest and another around one of the fingers of his right hand. His damp hair shone with blue-black highlights and the plain gold earring he'd worn for so long had been replaced by a sapphire drop the same color as his. . . . "Your eyes are blue again."

"Yes." The long thick lashes swept down to cover them for a moment.

Aaron suddenly realized where he was and felt his face grow hot. "I'm in your bed." The words tumbled out of his mouth in an embarrassed cascade.

"Yes," Darvish said again, his smile broadening.

Feeling his breath catch in his throat, Aaron searched desperately for something to say. His mind felt vaguely disconnected, as though it were going to float off at any moment. "Uh, I heard Chandra."

"I'm right here, Aaron." She moved up to stand behind Darvish. Her eyes were rimmed with shadow and finely etched lines bracketed the corners of her mouth. "You've been asleep for two days," she blurted out. "How are you feeling?"

"Two days!" How could he have slept for two days?

"Shhh." Darvish laid a hand gently on his chest, resting it there until he calmed. "The healers gave you something to keep you asleep. But, now you're awake, how *are* you feeling?"

He hadn't actually thought about it, but now that it had been brought to mind he found he hurt all over. Given Darvish's sudden look of worry, he wasn't going to mention it. He raised a shoulder a hair's breadth and dropped it again. "I've been worse."

Darvish gave a shout of relieved laughter. "Not according to Karida, who was, by the way, rather angry about the mess you made of her earlier healing. She made me promise to keep you in bed for the next nineday at least." His eyes twinkled. "It wasn't a hard promise to make."

Which brought them right back to the subject Aaron had been trying to change. He tried again, fighting through the fuzziness that threatened to envelope him. "The Stone?"

"Still back where it belongs," Chandra told him. "None the worse for ever having been gone." A shadow slid across her face and she looked out at something the two men couldn't see. "We gave Palaton to the volcano," she added softly.

Darvish reached up and lightly gripped the hand that rested on his shoulder. Aaron's heart lurched as he remembered what had brought Chandra to Ischia in the first place and how things had changed. Quickly, he schooled his face to show nothing of what he felt.

"The lord chancellor confessed everything," Darvish said, completely unaware of the near panic his sympathetic touch had caused. "Ischia, and, if possible, Father and Shahin were to be destroyed. Ytaili would step in—Ramdan has no interest in politics or power and wouldn't stand a chance—and the lord chancellor would be given what was left of Cisali to govern. He'd grown tired of being a powerful man with no power and approached King Harith at Shahin's wedding. You," he released Chandra and caught up Aaron's hand instead, "ruined their plan right at the start. Without you and your specialized knowledge, we'd have never discovered where The Stone was taken and then where it was sent. He tried to make up for that by sending me after it, sure I'd fail, but just to make certain, he let the king of Ytaili know we were coming. You and Chandra took care of that. And me. You'll never know how much I. . . ." His voice broke and he had to stop speaking to regain control.

Chandra cuffed him lightly on the back of the head. "Skip it," she suggested, her own voice a little hoarse. "We know."

Darvish smiled gratefully up at her and cleared his throat. "Anyway," he continued, including Aaron in the smile, "when we showed up with The Stone, he decided to bluff it out. After all, he was no worse off than he had been. He never supposed we'd bring that letter back with us as well." He took a deep breath and shook his head as though to clear it of an unpleasant memory. "There wasn't a lot of him left when the twins got through."

Out in the garden, a peacock screamed and all three of them jumped.

"Bugger the Nine!" Darvish swore. "I really wish they wouldn't do that. Oh, yes," he grinned, "speaking of the Most Blessed Yasimina, Shahin found out this morning she's expecting a most blessed event. He's beside himself and even Father seemed pleased, although," the grin broadened, "he never showed much interest in Ramdan's frequent additions to the family. Shahin and Father apparently had a bit of a falling out while we were gone but seem to have pretty much reconciled." Darvish shook his head. "Suddenly forced to recognize certain, uh, failings in our family upbringing, Shahin's even talking of reclaiming the twins from the Fourth."

Aaron had to ask. Not knowing was worse than knowing. He hoped. "And you?"

"Well, Shahin seems to think that Father will now clasp me to his breast and make a place for me at court." Darvish's mouth twisted and he gave a short, humorless laugh. "Less than three

ninedays ago that was all I wanted. Now. . . ." He spread his
hands. "Now I realize that you can't be given a place, you have to
make one for yourself." His expression grew a little sheepish. He
cleared his throat and fixed his gaze on the wall above Aaron's
head. "Chandra and I have decided to go through with this marriage after all."

All other pain receded before the pain of that and suddenly
Aaron knew what it meant to truly want to die. The walls that had
protected him for so long lay in ruins and it hurt too much to put
up new ones; all he could do was lie there and listen and hope it
would be over soon.

"We're friends and that's more than most treaty marriages
have going for them," Darvish continued, beginning to look a little less embarrassed. "It'll give me a place to start over—it'd be
too easy to slip back into the old ways around here—and it'll get
the traditionalists off Chandra's back. Married, she can continue
as both her father's heir and a Wizard of the Nine. Maybe some
day she'll realize she's so strong I don't have a hope without the
Nine of fogging her focus." He grinned and winced as Chandra
cuffed him again. "But if that never happens, we'll either take a
hand in raising her cousin's children or if we want one of our own,
you can steal it for us. . . . Aaron, what is it?" He leaned forward,
startled by the sudden welling of tears in Aaron's eyes.

Aaron tried to gain control, tried to say something wry and
witty but the tears rolling down his cheeks betrayed him. To his
horror he heard a voice, barely recognizable as his own, say, "I
didn't think you wanted. . . ." His throat closed on the rest and he
turned his head away, eyes squeezed shut unable to stop the
wracking sobs that shook his entire body. Warm hands cupped his
face and gently forced his head back around.

"Aaron, look at me."

The sobs died to long shuddering breaths and Aaron opened
his eyes, sure he'd see disgust, or worse, pity.

"You thought I didn't want you." Darvish's voice held hurt and
anger about equally mixed. "You One abandoned idiot. I like
Chandra well enough, but I love you."

The words fell into what remained of the void and filled it.

A moment later he was weeping into the curve of Darvish's
shoulder. He couldn't stop. But strong arms wrapped around him
and Darvish didn't seem to mind.

Chandra shook her head and laid one hand lightly on the black hair, the other on the copper. "If you think I was willing to take *him* without *you*," she said softly, "think again." Then, doubting very much that they'd even heard her, she slipped quietly out onto the balcony and smiled up into the warmth of the morning sun. Life was working out just fine.

She could feel the pull of The Stone, a faint pulsing along the channels now attuned to it, a teasing touch of its vast power and potential. *I may be a Wizard of the Nine,* she thought acerbically at it, *but that's no more all I am than this is all you are.*

From back in the room, she could hear quiet sounds of comfort and, chewing contentedly on the end of her braid, she eavesdropped shamelessly.

Down below, in the garden, a peacock arched his iridescent neck and spread the magnificent fan of his tail.

The palace blazed with light and rang with sound as the court celebrated a royal wedding. It spilled into the square outside the gate where the people seemed determined to show the nobility how to really party. Darvish was *their* prince after all.

Oblivious to the merriment below, a shadow slipped across the small room outside the king's bedchamber, footfalls making less sound than a heartbeat on the thick carpets. The lack of illumination didn't seem to matter for the shadow moved unerringly to the ornate brackets that held the royal staff.

At the ceremony a few hours before, the emerald crowning the staff had blazed, a beacon of brilliant green that almost seemed to have an inner light of its own.

With one hand steadying the wooden shaft, long fingers reached out and gripped the stone.

". . . and he told me he loved me, Faharra." Aaron leaned back against the wall of the mausoleum, the brass urn on his lap. Even in the cool of the night, he could feel his face flush. "I couldn't tell him how I felt, how I feel, not yet, but he understands." He'd been sitting there since moonrise, telling Faharra everything that had happened.

"He's taking all three dressers with him. Even the lord chancellor's man. Chandra insists he doesn't need all three, but Oham's been with him for years, it would break Fadi's heart to be left behind, and the lord chancellor's man has nowhere else to go."

He paused while the temple bells pealed, filling the necropolis with joyous sound. Throughout the night, as each of the Nine rose to the apex of their starry dance, the priests rang the Nine's blessing on the marriage.

Tugging a long green ribbon from inside his dark vest, he ran the silken length of it around and through his fingers. "This is off Chandra's wedding gown." The demon wings rose and he grinned. "She told me the green is fertility symbolism. Not particularly subtle when you think of it. I offered to steal them a chicken if they need to stain the sheets, but Chandra says she'll manage." A gold thread gleamed in the moonlight as he turned the ribbon in his hands. "The gold thread is for Dar. They've fought every day for the last week. Prince Shahin says that's normal, then he laughs and wishes me luck. He'll make a good king, Faharra, I wish you could be here to see." Running beside the gold, twined around it in places, burned a copper thread. "That copper thread's for me." He swallowed to clear a sudden tightness from his throat. "Chandra insisted they weave one into every ribbon." Remembering the looks on the seamstresses' faces, he shook his head. "And there were a lot of ribbons." Of course, Chandra could've asked them to make the additions in the dark, standing on their heads and they'd have done it. Nothing was too good for the three who'd saved Ischia.

He stopped for a moment, unsure of how to go on.

"I didn't forget my vow, Faharra. I had the emerald in my hand." It seemed that the entire necropolis waited for him to continue And behind him, in the dark of the mausoleum, he could feel the weight of Faharra's kin. He stroked the embossed curve of the urn.

"I couldn't do it." He draped the ribbon around the neck and knotted it. "I thought, maybe, you'd rather have this instead."

A heartbeat's worry that he'd feel like a fool disappeared. It felt right. He sat for a little longer, then he sighed, stood, and carried the urn back into the mausoleum.

At the edge of the boundary between light and dark he paused, then stepped over into shadow and settled Faharra back into the arms of the One Below. He ran his finger down the ribbon for the last time and raised one foot to turn and leave. As he had before, he put it down again.

"Take care of her," he told the goddess, his voice diamond

bright in the realm of the dead. "She was the best gem cutter Ischia has ever known."

On the way out, he stole a small brass incense burner from its
niche by the door; just to keep his hand in. While slipping it into
the deep pocket of his trousers, he could almost hear Faharra's ap-
proving cackle.

As the door swung closed, a chance ray of moonlight swept
across the altar. Caught by the metallic thread in the ribbon, it
lightened the green, burnished the gold, and turned the copper to
a red-gold flame.

TANYA HUFF

VALOR'S CHOICE

"Readers who enjoy military SF will love Tanya Huff's
VALOR'S CHOICE. Howlingly funny and very
suspenseful. I enjoyed every word."
—*scifi.com*

Staff Sergeant Torin Kerr was a battle-hardened professional.
So when she and those in her platoon who'd survived the last
deadly encounter with the Others were yanked from a well-
deserved leave for what was supposed to be "easy" duty as
the honor guard for a diplomatic mission to the non-Confedera-
tion world of the Silsviss, she was ready for anything. Sure,
there'd been rumors of the Others being spotted in this sector
of space. But there were always rumors. Everything seemed
to be going perfectly. Maybe too perfectly. . . .

0-88677-896-4 $6.99

Tanya Huff

☐ **NO QUARTER**	UE2698—$5.99
☐ **FIFTH QUARTER**	UE2651—$5.99
☐ **SING THE FOUR QUARTERS**	UE2628—$5.99
☐ **THE QUARTERED SEA**	UE2839—$6.99

He Sang water more powerfully than any other bard—but could even
Benedikt Sing a ship beyond the known world?

☐ **GATE OF DARKNESS, CIRCLE OF LIGHT**	UE2386—$4.50
☐ **THE FIRE'S STONE**	UE2445—$5.99
☐ **SUMMON THE KEEPER**	UE2784—$5.99

VICTORY NELSON, INVESTIGATOR:
Otherworldly Crimes A Specialty

☐ **BLOOD PRICE: Book 1**	UE2471—$5.99
☐ **BLOOD TRAIL: Book 2**	UE2502—$5.99
☐ **BLOOD LINES: Book 3**	UE2530—$5.99
☐ **BLOOD PACT: Book 4**	UE2582—$5.99
☐ **BLOOD DEBT: Book 5**	UE2739—$5.99

Prices slightly higher in Canada **DAW: 150**

Payable in U.S. funds only. No cash/COD accepted. Postage & handling: U.S./CAN. $2.75 for one
book, $1.00 for each additional, not to exceed $6.75; Int'l $5.00 for one book, $1.00 each additional.
We accept Visa, Amex, MC ($10.00 min.), checks ($15.00 fee for returned checks) and money
orders. Call 800-788-6262 or 201-933-9292, fax 201-896-8569; refer to ad #150.

Penguin Putnam Inc.
P.O. Box 12289, Dept. B
Newark, NJ 07101-5289

Bill my: ☐Visa ☐MasterCard ☐Amex_____(expires)
Card#_____

Please allow 4-6 weeks for delivery.
Foreign and Canadian delivery 6-8 weeks.

Signature_____

Bill to:

Name_____

Address_____City_____

State/ZIP_____

Daytime Phone #_____

Ship to:

Name_____	Book Total	$_____
Address_____	Applicable Sales Tax	$_____
City_____	Postage & Handling	$_____
State/Zip_____	Total Amount Due	$_____

This offer subject to change without notice.

FIONA PATTON

"Rousing adventure, full of color and spectacular magic"—*Locus*

In the kingdom of Branion, the hereditary royal line is blessed—or cursed—with the power of the Flame, a magic against which no one can stand. But when used by one not strong enough to control it, the power of the Flame can just as easily consume its human vessel, as destroy whatever foe it had been unleased against. . . .

Michelle West

The Sun Sword:

☐ **THE BROKEN CROWN**   UE2740—$6.99

☐ **THE UNCROWNED KING**   UE2801—$6.99

The uneasy peace within the Dominion's borders was shattered when treacherous forces seized the crown by slaughtering all members of the ruling Clan Leonne. Now in a neighboring empire, the sole surviving heir to the throne, a young man never destined to rule, must prove his worthiness to claim the crown, even as his family's murderers and their sinister demonic allies plot his doom.

The Sacred Hunt:

☐ **HUNTER'S OATH**   UE2681—$5.50

☐ **HUNTER'S DEATH**   UE2706—$5.99

Prices slightly higher in Canada.   **DAW 203X**

Eluki bes Shahar

THE HELLFLOWER SERIES

☐ **HELLFLOWER (Book 1)**   UE2475—$3.99

Butterfly St. Cyr had a well-deserved reputation as an honest and dependable smuggler. But when she and her partner, a highly illegal artificial intelligence, rescued Tiggy, the son and heir to one of the most powerful of the hellflower mercenary leaders, it looked like they'd finally taken on more than they could handle. For his father's enemies had sworn to see that Tiggy and Butterfly never reached his home planet alive. . . .

☐ **DARKTRADERS (Book 2)**   UE2507—$4.50

With her former partner Paladin—the death-to-possess Old Federation artificial intelligence—gone off on a private mission, Butterfly didn't have anybody to back her up when Tiggy's enemies decided to give the word "ambush" a whole new and all-too-final meaning.

☐ **ARCHANGEL BLUES (Book 3)**   UE2543—$4.50

Darktrader Butterfly St. Cyr and her partner Tiggy seek to complete the mission they started in DARKTRADERS, to find and destroy the real Archangel, Governor-General of the Empire, the being who is determined to wield A.I. powers to become the master of the entire universe.